THE COLLECTED STORIES OF
PHILIP K. DICK VOLUME FOUR

T0343590

THE COLLECTED STORIES OF
PHILIP K. DICK VOLUME FOUR

First published in Great Britain in 2023 by Gollancz
an imprint of The Orion Publishing Group Ltd
Carmelite House, 50 Victoria Embankment
London EC4Y ODZ

An Hachette UK Company

The authorised representative in the EEA is Hachette Ireland,
8 Castlecourt Centre, Dublin 15, D15 XTP3, Ireland (email: info@hbgi.ie)

3 5 7 9 10 8 6 4

A CIP catalogue record for this book is
available from the British Library.

ISBN (Mass Market Paperback) 978 1 39961 129 9
ISBN (eBook) 978 1 39961 130 5

Printed in Great Britain by Clays Ltd, Elcograf, S.p.A.

MIX
Paper | Supporting
responsible forestry
FSC® C104740

www.gollancz.co.uk

CONTENTS

CONTENTS

THE COLLECTED STORIES OF

PHILIP K. DICK

VOLUME FOUR

ORPHEUS WITH CLAY FEET

At the offices of Concord Military Service Consultants, Jesse Slade looked through the window at the street below and saw everything denied him in the way of freedom, flowers and grass, the opportunity for a long and unencumbered walk into new places. He sighed.

'Sorry, sir,' the client opposite his desk mumbled apologetically. 'I guess I'm boring you.'

'Not at all,' Slade said, reawakening to his onerous duties. 'Let's see . . .' He examined the papers which the client, a Mr Walter Grossbein, had presented to him. 'Now you feel, Mr Grossbein, that your most favorable chance to elude military service lies in the area of a chronic ear-trouble deemed by civilian doctors in the past *acute labyrinthitis*. Hmmm.' Slade studied the pertinent documents.

His duties—and he did not enjoy them—lay in locating for clients of the firm a way out of military service. The war against the Things had not been conducted properly, of late; many casualties from the Proxima region had been reported—and with the reports had come a rush of business for Concord Military Service Consultants.

'Mr Grossbein,' Slade said thoughtfully, 'I noticed when you entered my office that you tended to list to one side.'

'Did I?' Mr Grossbein asked, surprised.

'Yes, and I thought to myself, That man has a severe impairment of his sense of balance. That's related to the ear, you know, Mr Grossbein. Hearing, from an evolutionary standpoint, is an outgrowth of the sense of balance. Some water creatures of a low order incorporate a grain of sand and make use of it as a drop-weight within their fluid body, and by that method tell if they're going up or down.'

Mr Grossbein said, 'I believe I understand.'

'Say it, then,' Jesse Slade said.

'I–frequently list to one side or another as I walk.'

'And at night?'

Mr Grossbein frowned, and then said happily, 'I, uh, find it almost impossible to orient myself at night, in the dark, when I can't see.'

'Fine,' Jesse Slade said, and began writing on the client's military service form B-30. 'I think this will get you an exemption,' he said.

Happily, the client said, 'I can't thank you enough.'

Oh yes you can, Jesse Slade thought to himself. You can thank us to the tune of fifty dollars. After all, without us you might be a pale, lifeless corpse in some gully on a distant planet, not far from now.

And, thinking about distant planets, Jesse Slade felt once more the yearning. The need to escape from his small office and the process of dealing with gold-bricking clients whom he had to face, day after day.

There must be another life than this, Slade said to himself. Can this really be all there is to existence?

Far down the street outside his office window a neon sign glowed night and day. Muse Enterprises, the sign read, and Jesse Slade knew what it meant. I'm going in there, he said to himself. Today. When I'm on my ten-thirty coffee break; I won't even wait for lunch time.

As he put on his coat, Mr Hnatt, his supervisor, entered the office and said, 'Say, Slade, what's up? Why the fierce trapped look?'

'Um, I'm getting out, Mr Hnatt,' Slade told him. 'Escaping. I've told fifteen thousand men how to escape military service; now it's my turn.'

Mr Hnatt clapped him on the back. 'Good idea, Slade; you're overworked. Take a vacation. Take a time-travel adventure to some distant civilization–it'll do you good.'

'Thanks, Mr Hnatt,' Slade said, 'I'll do just that.' And left his office as fast as his feet would carry him, out of the building and down the street to the glowing neon sign of Muse Enterprises.

The girl behind the counter, blonde-haired, with dark green eyes and a figure that impressed him more for its engineering aspects, its suspension so to speak, smiled at him and said, 'Our Mr Manville will see you in a moment, Mr Slade. Please be seated. You'll find authentic nineteenth-century *Harper's Weeklies* over on the table, there.' She added, 'And some twentieth-century *Mad* comics, those great classics of lampoonery equal to Hogarth.'

Tensely, Mr Slade seated himself and tried to read; he found an article in *Harper's Weekly* telling that the Panama Canal was impossible and had already been abandoned by its French designers–that held his attention for a moment (the reasoning was so logical, so convincing) but after a few moments his old ennui and restlessness, like a chronic fog, returned. Rising to his feet he once more approached the desk.

'Mr Manville isn't here yet?' he asked hopefully.

From behind him a male voice said, 'You, there at the counter.'

Slade turned. And found himself facing a tall, dark-haired man with an intense expression, eyes blazing.

'You,' the man said, 'are in the *wrong century*.'

Slade gulped.

Striding toward him, the dark-haired man said, 'I am Manville, sir.' He held out his hand and they shook. 'You must go away,' Manville said. 'Do you understand, sir? As soon as possible.'

'But I want to use your services,' Slade mumbled.

Manville's eyes flashed. 'I mean away into the past. What's your name?' He gestured emphatically. 'Wait, it's coming to me. Jesse Slade, of Concord, up the street, there.'

'Right,' Slade said, impressed.

'All right, now down to business,' Mr Manville said. 'Into my office.' To the exceptionally-constructed girl at the counter he said, 'No one is to disturb us, Miss Frib.'

'Yes, Mr Manville,' Miss Frib said. 'I'll see to that, don't you fear, sir.'

'I know that, Miss Frib.' Mr Manville ushered Slade into a well-furnished inner office. Old maps and prints decorated the walls; the furniture—Slade gaped. Early American, with wood pegs instead of nails. New England maple and worth a fortune.

'Is it all right . . .' he began.

'Yes, you may actually sit on that Directorate chair,' Mr Manville told him. 'But be careful; it scoots out from under you if you lean forward. We keep meaning to put rubber casters on it or some such thing.' He looked irritated now, at having to discuss such trifles. 'Mr Slade,' he said brusquely, 'I'll speak plainly; obviously you're a man of high intellect and we can skip the customary circumlocutions.'

'Yes,' Slade said, 'please do.'

'Our time-travel arrangements are of a specific nature; hence the name "Muse." Do you grasp the meaning, here?'

'Um,' Slade said, at a loss but trying. 'Let's see. A muse is an organism that functions to—'

'That inspires,' Mr Manville broke in impatiently. 'Slade, you are—let's face it—not a creative man. That's why you feel bored and unfulfilled. Do you paint? Compose? Make welded iron sculpture out of spaceship bodies and discarded lawn chairs? You don't. You do nothing; you're utterly passive. Correct?'

Slade nodded. 'You've hit it, Mr Manville.'

'I've hit nothing,' Mr Manville said irritably. 'You don't follow me, Slade. Nothing will make you creative because you don't have it within you. You're too ordinary. I'm not going to get you started finger-painting or basket-weaving; I'm no Jungian analyst who believes art is the answer.' Leaning back he pointed his finger at Slade. 'Look, Slade. We can help you, but you must be willing to help yourself first. Since you're not creative, the best you can hope for—and we can assist you here—*is to inspire others who are creative.* Do you see?'

After a moment Slade said, 'I see, Mr Manville. I do.'

'Right,' Manville said, nodding. 'Now, you can inspire a famous musician, like Mozart or Beethoven, or a scientist such as Albert Einstein, or a sculptor such as Sir Jacob Epstein—any one of a number of people, writers, musicians, poets. You could, for example, meet Sir Edward Gibbon during his travels to the Mediterranean and fall into a casual conversation with him and say something to this order . . . Hmmm, look at the ruins of this ancient civilization all around us. I wonder, how does a mighty empire such as Rome come to fall into decay? Fall into ruin . . . fall apart . . .'

'Good Lord,' Slade said fervently, 'I see, Manville; I get it. I repeat the word "fall" over and over again to Gibbon, and due to me he gets the idea of his great history of Rome, the *Decline and Fall of the Roman Empire.* And—' He felt himself tremble. 'I helped.'

'"Helped"?' Manville said. 'Slade, that's hardly the word. Without you there would have been no such work. You, Slade, could be Sir Edward's muse.' He leaned back, got out an Upmann cigar, circa 1915, and lit up.

'I think,' Slade said, 'I'd like to mull this over. I want to be sure I inspire the proper person; I mean, they all deserve to be inspired, but—'

'But you want to find *the* person in terms of your own psychic needs,' Manville agreed, puffing fragrant blue smoke. 'Take our brochure.' He passed a large shiny multi-color 3-D pop-up booklet to Slade. 'Take this home, read it, and come back to us when you're ready.'

Slade said, 'God bless you, Mr Manville.'

'And calm down,' Manville said. 'The world isn't going to end . . . we know that here at Muse because we've looked.' He smiled, and Slade managed to smile back.

Two days later Jesse Slade returned to Muse Enterprises. 'Mr Manville,' he said, 'I know whom I want to inspire.' He took a deep breath. 'I've thought and thought and what would mean the most to me would be if I could go back to Vienna and inspire Ludwig van Beethoven with the idea for the Choral Symphony, you know, that theme in the fourth movement that the baritone sings that goes bum-bum de-da de-da bum-bum, daughters of Elysium; you know.' He flushed. 'I'm no musician, but all my life I've admired the Beethoven Ninth and especially–'

'It's been done,' Manville said.

'Eh?' He did not understand.

'It's been taken, Mr Slade.' Manville looked impatient as he sat at his great oak rolltop desk, circa 1910. Bringing out a thick metal-staved black binder he turned the pages. 'Two years ago a Mrs Ruby Welch of Montpelier, Idaho went back to Vienna and inspired Beethoven with the theme for the choral movement of his Ninth.' Manville slammed the binder shut and regarded Slade. 'Well? What's your second choice?'

Stammering, Slade said, 'I'd–have to think. Give me time.'

Examining his watch, Manville said shortly, 'I'll give you two hours. Until three this afternoon. Good day, Slade.' He rose to his feet, and Slade automatically rose, too.

An hour later, in his cramped office at Concord Military Service Consultants, Jesse Slade realized in a flashing single instant who and what he wanted to inspire. At once he put on his coat, excused himself to sympathetic Mr Hnatt, and hurried down the street to Muse Enterprises.

'Well, Mr Slade,' Manville said, seeing him enter. 'Back so soon. Come into the office.' He strode ahead, leading the way. 'All right, let's have it.' He shut the door after the two of them.

Jesse Slade licked his dry lips and then, coughing, said, 'Mr Manville, I want to go back and inspire–well, let me explain. You know the great science fiction of the golden age, between 1930 and 1970?'

'Yes, yes,' Manville said impatiently, scowling as he listened.

'When I was in college,' Slade said, 'getting my MA in English lit, I had to read a good deal of twentieth-century science fiction, of course. Of the greats there were three writers who stood out. The first was Robert Heinlein with his future history. The second, Isaac Asimov with his Foundation epic series. And–' He took a deep, shuddering breath. 'The man I did my paper on. Jack Dowland. Of the three of them, Dowland was considered the greatest. His future history of the world began to appear in 1957, in both magazine form—as short stories—and in book form, as complete novels. By 1963, Dowland was regarded as—'

Mr Manville said, 'Hmmm.' Getting out the black binder, he began to thumb through it. 'Twentieth-century science fiction . . . a rather specialized interest—fortunately for you. Let's see.'

'I hope,' Slade said quietly, 'it hasn't been taken.'

'Here is one client,' Mr Manville said. 'Leo Parks of Vacaville, California. He went back and inspired A. E. van Vogt to avoid love stories and westerns and try science fiction.' Turning more pages, Mr Manville said, 'And last year a client of Muse Enterprises, Miss Julie Oxenblut of Kansas City, Kansas asked to be permitted to inspire Robert Heinlein in his future history . . . was it Heinlein you said, Mr Slade?'

'No,' Slade said, 'it was Jack Dowland, the greatest of the three. Heinlein was great, but I did much research on this, Mr Manville, and Dowland was greater.'

'No, it hasn't been done,' Manville decided, closing up the black binder. From his desk drawer he brought out a form. 'You fill this out, Mr Slade,' he said, 'and then we'll begin to roll on this matter. Do you know the year and the place at which Jack Dowland began work on his future history of the world?'

'I do,' Slade said. 'He was living in a little town on the then Route 40 in Nevada, a town called Purpleblossom, consisted of three gas stations, a cafe, a bar, and a general store. Dowland had moved there to get atmosphere; he wanted to write stories of the Old West in the form of TV scripts. He hoped to make a good deal of money.'

'I see you know your subject,' Manville said, impressed.

Slade continued, 'While living in Purpleblossom he did write a number of TV western scripts but somehow he found them unsatisfactory. In any case, he remained there, trying other fields such as children's books and articles on teen-age pre-marital sex for the slick magazines of the times . . . and then, all at once, in the year 1956, he suddenly turned to science fiction and immediately produced the greatest novelette seen to date in that field. That was the consensus gentium of the time, Mr Manville, and I have read the story and I agree. It was called "The Father on the Wall" and it still appears in anthologies now and then; it's the kind of story that will never die. And the magazine in which it appeared, *Fantasy & Science Fiction*, will always be remembered for having published Dowland's first epic in its August 1957 issue.'

Nodding, Mr Manville said, 'And this is the magnum opus which you wish to inspire. This, and all that followed.'

'You have it right, sir,' Mr Slade said.

'Fill out your form,' Manville said, 'and we'll do the rest.' He smiled at Slade and Slade, confident, smiled back.

The operator of the time-ship, a short, heavy-set, crew-cut young man with strong features, said briskly to Slade, 'Okay, bud; you ready or not? Make up your mind.'

Slade, for one last time, inspected his twentieth-century suit which Muse Enterprises had provided him—one of the services for the rather high fee which he had found himself paying. Narrow necktie, cuffless trousers, and Ivy League striped shirt . . . yes, Slade decided, from what he knew of the period it was authentic, right down to the sharp-pointed Italian shoes and the colorful stretch socks. He would pass without any difficulty as a citizen of the US of 1956, even in Purpleblossom, Nevada.

'Now listen,' the operator said, as he fastened the safety belt around Slade's middle, 'you got to remember a couple of things. First of all, the only way you can get back to 2040 is with me; you can't *walk* back. And second, you got to be careful not to change the past—I mean, stick to your one simple task of inspiring this individual, this Jack Dowland, *and let it go at that.*'

'Of course,' Slade said, puzzled at the admonition.

'Too many clients,' the operator said, 'you'd be surprised how many, go wild when they get back into the past; they get delusions of power and want to make all sorts of changes—eliminate wars, hunger and poverty—you know. Change history.'

'I won't do that,' Slade said. 'I have no interest in abstract cosmic ventures on that order.' To him, inspiring Jack Dowland was cosmic enough. And yet he could empathize enough to understand the temptation. In his own work he had seen all kinds of people.

The operator slammed shut the hatch of the time-ship, made certain that Slade was strapped in properly, and then took his own seat at the controls. He snapped a switch and a moment later Slade was on his way to his vacation from monotonous office work—back to 1956 and the nearest he would come to a creative act in his life.

The hot midday Nevada sun beat down, blinding him; Slade squinted, peered about nervously for the town of Purpleblossom. All he saw was dull rock and sand, the open desert with a single narrow road passing among the joshua plants.

'To the right,' the operator of the time-ship said, pointing. 'You can walk there in ten minutes. You understand your contract, I hope. Better get it out and read it.'

From the breast pocket of his 1950s-style coat, Slade brought the long yellow contract form with Muse Enterprises. 'It says you'll give me thirty-six hours. That you'll pick me up in this spot and that it's my responsibility to be here; if I'm not, and can't be brought back to my own time, the company is not liable.'

'Right,' the operator said, and re-entered the time-ship. 'Good luck, Mr Slade. Or, as I should call you, Jack Dowland's muse.' He grinned, half in derision, half in friendly sympathy, and then the hatch shut after him.

Jesse Slade was alone on the Nevada desert, a quarter mile outside the tiny town of Purpleblossom.

He began to walk, perspiring, wiping his neck with his handkerchief.

There was no problem to locating Jack Dowland's house, since only seven houses existed in the town. Slade stepped up onto the rickety wooden porch, glancing at the yard with its trash can, clothes line, discarded plumbing fixtures . . . parked in the driveway he saw a dilapidated car of some archaic sort—archaic even for the year 1956.

He rang the bell, adjusted his tie nervously, and once more in his mind rehearsed what he intended to say. At this point in his life, Jack Dowland had written no science fiction; that was important to remember—it was in fact the entire point. This was the critical nexus in his life—history, this fateful ringing of his doorbell. Of course Dowland did not know that. What was he doing within the house? Writing? Reading the funnies of a Reno newspaper? Sleeping?

Footsteps. Tautly, Slade prepared himself.

The door opened. A young woman wearing light-weight cotton trousers, her hair tied back with a ribbon, surveyed him calmly. What small, pretty feet she had, Slade noticed. She wore slippers; her skin was smooth and shiny, and he found himself gazing intently, unaccustomed to seeing so much of a woman exposed. Both ankles were completely bare.

'Yes?' the woman asked pleasantly but a trifle wearily. He saw now that she had been *vacuuming*; there in the living room was a tank type GE vacuum cleaner . . . its existence here proving that historians were wrong; the tank type cleaner had *not* vanished in 1950 as was thought.

Slade, thoroughly prepared, said smoothly, 'Mrs Dowland?' The woman nodded. Now a small child appeared to peep at him past its mother. 'I'm a fan of your husband's monumental—' Oops, he thought, that wasn't right. 'Ahem,' he corrected himself, using a twentieth-century expression often found in books of that period. 'Tsk-tsk,' he said. 'What I mean to say is this, madam. I know well the works of your husband Jack. I am here by means of a lengthy drive across the desert badlands to observe him in his habitat.' He smiled hopefully.

'You know Jack's work?' She seemed surprised, but thoroughly pleased.

'On the telly,' Slade said. 'Fine scripts of his.' He nodded.

'You're English, are you?' Mrs Dowland said. 'Well, did you want to come in?' She held the door wide. 'Jack is working right now up in the attic . . . the children's noise bothers him. But I know he'd like to stop and talk to you, especially since you drove so far. You're Mr–'

'Slade,' Slade said. 'Nice abode you possess, here.'

'Thank you.' She led the way into a dark, cool kitchen in the center of which he saw a round plastic table with wax milk carton, melmac plate, sugar bowl, two coffee cups and other amusing objects thereon. 'JACK!' she called at the foot of a flight of stairs. 'THERE'S A FAN OF YOURS HERE; HE WANTS TO SEE YOU!'

Far off above them a door opened. The sound of a person's steps, and then, as Slade stood rigidly, Jack Dowland appeared, young and good-looking, with slightly-thinning brown hair, wearing a sweater and slacks, his lean, intelligent face beclouded with a frown. 'I'm at work,' he said curtly. 'Even though I do it at home it's a job like any other.' He gazed at Slade. 'What do you want? What do you mean you're a "fan" of my work? *What* work? Christ, it's been two months since I sold anything; I'm about ready to go out of my mind.'

Slade said, 'Jack Dowland, that is because you have yet to find your proper genre.' He heard his voice tremble; this was the moment.

'Would you like a beer, Mr Slade?' Mrs Dowland asked.

'Thank you, miss,' Slade said. 'Jack Dowland,' he said, 'I am here to inspire you.'

'Where are you from?' Dowland said suspiciously. 'And how come you're wearing your tie that funny way?'

'Funny in what respect?' Slade asked, feeling nervous.

'With the knot at the bottom instead of up around your adam's apple.' Dowland walked around him, now, studying him critically. 'And why's your head shaved? You're too young to be bald.'

'The custom of this period,' Slade said feebly. 'Demands a shaved head. At least in New York.'

'Shaved head my ass,' Dowland said. 'Say, what are you, some kind of a crank? What do you want?'

'I want to praise you,' Slade said. He felt angry now; a new emotion, indignation, filled him—he was not being treated properly and he knew it.

'Jack Dowland,' he said, stuttering a little, 'I know more about your work than you do; I know your proper genre is science fiction and not television westerns. Better listen to me; I'm your muse.' He was silent, then, breathing noisily and with difficulty.

Dowland stared at him, and then threw back his head and laughed.

Also smiling, Mrs Dowland said, 'Well, I knew Jack had a muse but I assumed it was female. Aren't all muses female?'

'No,' Slade said angrily. 'Leon Parks of Vacaville, California, who inspired A. E. van Vogt, was male.' He seated himself at the plastic table, his legs being too wobbly, now, to support him. 'Listen to me, Jack Dowland—'

'For God's sake,' Dowland said, 'either call me Jack or Dowland but not both; it's not natural the way you're talking. Are you on tea or something?' He sniffed intently.

'Tea,' Slade echoed, not understanding. 'No, just a beer, please.'

Dowland said, 'Well get to the point. I'm anxious to be back at work. Even if it's done at home it is work.'

It was now time for Slade to deliver his encomium. He had prepared it carefully; clearing his throat he began. 'Jack, if I may call you that, I wonder why the hell you haven't tried science fiction. I figure that—'

'I'll tell you why,' Jack Dowland broke in. He paced back and forth, his hands in his trousers pockets. 'Because there's going to be a hydrogen war. The future's black. Who wants to write about it? Keeerist.' He shook his head. 'And anyhow who reads that stuff? Adolescents with skin trouble. Misfits. And it's junk. Name me one good science fiction story, just one. I picked up a magazine on a bus once when I was in Utah. Trash! I wouldn't write that trash even if it paid well, and I looked into it and it doesn't pay well—around one half cent a word. And who can live on that?' Disgustedly, he started toward the stairs. 'I'm going back to work.'

'Wait,' Slade said, feeling desperate. All was going wrong. 'Hear me out, Jack Dowland.'

'There you go with that funny talk again,' Dowland said. But he paused, waiting. 'Well?' he demanded.

Slade said, 'Mr Dowland, I am from the future.' He was not supposed to say that—Mr Manville had warned him severely—but it seemed at the moment to be the only way out for him, the only thing that would stop Jack Dowland from walking off.

'What?' Dowland said loudly. 'The *what?*'

'I am a time-traveler,' Slade said feebly, and was silent.

Dowland walked back toward him.

When he arrived at the time-ship, Slade found the short-set operator seated on the ground before it, reading a newspaper. The operator glanced up, grinned and said, 'Back safe and sound, Mr Slade. Come on, let's go.' He opened the hatch and guided Slade within.

'Take me back,' Slade said. 'Just take me back.'

'What's the matter? Didn't you enjoy your inspiring?'

'I just want to go back to my own time,' Slade said.

'Okay,' the operator said, raising an eyebrow. He strapped Slade into his seat and then took his own beside him.

When they reached Muse Enterprises, Mr Manville was waiting for them. 'Slade,' he said, 'come inside.' His face was dark. 'I have a few words to say to you.'

When they were alone in Manville's office, Slade began, 'He was in a bad mood, Mr Manville. Don't blame me.' He hung his head, feeling empty and futile.

'You—' Manville stared down at him in disbelief. 'You *failed* to inspire him! That's never happened before!'

'Maybe I can go back again,' Slade said.

'My God,' Manville said, 'you not only didn't inspire him—you turned him *against* science fiction.'

'How did you find this out?' Slade said. He had hoped to keep it quiet, make it his own secret to carry with him to the grave.

Manville said bitingly, 'All I had to do was keep my eye on the reference books dealing with literature of the twentieth century. Half an hour after you left, the entire texts on Jack Dowland, including the half-page devoted to his biography in the *Britannica*—vanished.'

Slade said nothing; he stared at the floor.

'So I researched it,' Manville said. 'I had the computers at the University of California look up all extant citations on Jack Dowland.'

'Were there any?' Slade mumbled.

'Yes,' Manville said. 'There were a couple. Minute, in rarified technical articles dealing comprehensively and exhaustively with that period. Because of you, Jack Dowland is now completely unknown to the public—*and was so even during his own day.*' He waved a finger at Slade, panting with wrath. 'Because of you, Jack Dowland never wrote his epic future history of mankind. Because of your so-called "inspiration" he continued to write scripts for TV westerns—and died at forty-six an utterly anonymous hack.'

'No science fiction at *all*?' Slade asked, incredulous. Had he done that badly? He couldn't believe it; true, Dowland had bitterly repulsed every suggestion Slade had made—true, he had gone back up to his attic in a peculiar frame of mind after Slade had made his point. But—

'All right,' Manville said, 'there exists *one* science fiction work by Jack Dowland. Tiny, mediocre and totally unknown.' Reaching into his desk drawer he grabbed out a yellowed, ancient magazine which he tossed to Slade. 'One short story called "Orpheus with Clay Feet," under the pen name Philip K. Dick. Nobody read it then, nobody reads it now—it was an account of a visit to Dowland by—' He glared furiously at Slade. 'By a well-intentioned idiot from the future with deranged visions of *inspiring* him to write a mythological history of the world to come. Well, Slade? What do you say?'

Slade said heavily, 'He used my visit as the basis for the story. Obviously.'

ORPHEUS WITH CLAY FEET

'And it made him the only money he ever earned as a science fiction writer–disappointingly little, barely enough to justify his effort and time. You're in the story, I'm in the story–Lord, Slade, you must have told him everything.'

'I did,' Slade said. 'To convince him.'

'Well, he wasn't convinced; he thought you were a nut of some kind. He wrote the story obviously in a bitter frame of mind. Let me ask you this: was he busy working when you arrived?'

'Yes,' Slade said, 'but Mrs Dowland said–'

'There is–was–no Mrs Dowland! Dowland never married! That must have been a neighbor's wife whom Dowland was having an affair with. No wonder he was furious; you broke in on his assignation with that girl, whoever she was. She's in the story, too; he put everything in and then gave up his house in Purpleblossom, Nevada and moved to Dodge City, Kansas.'

There was silence.

'Um,' Slade said at last, 'well, could I try again? With someone else? I was thinking on the way back about Paul Ehrlich and his magic bullet, his discovery of the cure for–'

'Listen,' Manville said. 'I've been thinking, too. You're going back but not to inspire Doctor Ehrlich or Beethoven or Dowland or anybody like that, anybody useful to society.'

With dread, Slade glanced up.

'You're going back,' Manville said between his teeth, 'to *uninspire* people like Adolf Hitler and Karl Marx and Sanrome Clinger–'

'You mean you think I'm so ineffectual . . .' Slade mumbled.

'Exactly. We'll start with Hitler in his period of imprisonment after his first abortive attempt to seize power in Bavaria. The period in which he dictated *Mein Kampf* to Rudolf Hess. I've discussed this with my superiors and it's all worked out; you'll be there as a fellow prisoner, you understand? And you'll recommend to Adolf Hitler, just as you recommended to Jack Dowland, that he write. In this case, a detailed autobiography laying out in detail his political program for the world. And if everything goes right–'

'I understand,' Slade murmured, staring at the floor again. 'It's a—I'd say an inspired idea, but I'm afraid I've given onus to that word by now.'

'Don't credit me with the idea,' Manville said. 'I got it out of Dowland's wretched story, "Orpheus with Clay Feet"; that's how he resolved it at the end.' He turned the pages of the ancient magazine until he came to the part he wanted. 'Read that, Slade. You'll find that it carries you up to your encounter with me, and then you go off to do research on the Nazi Party so that you can best uninspire Adolf Hitler not to write his autobiography and hence possibly prevent World War Two. And if you fail to uninspire Hitler, we'll try you on Stalin, and if you fail to uninspire Stalin, then—'

'All right,' Slade muttered, 'I understand; you don't have to spell it out to me.'

'And you'll do it,' Manville said, 'because in "Orpheus with Clay Feet" you agree. So it's all decided already.'

Slade nodded. 'Anything. To make amends.'

To him Manville said, 'You idiot. How could you have done so badly?'

'It was an off-day for me,' Slade said. 'I'm sure I could do better the next time.' Maybe with Hitler, he thought. Maybe I can do a terrific job of uninspiring him, better than anyone else ever did in uninspiring anyone in history.

'We'll call you the null-muse,' Manville said.

'Clever idea,' Slade said.

Wearily, Manville said, 'Don't compliment me; compliment Jack Dowland. It was in his story, too. At the very last.'

'And that's how it ends?' Slade asked.

'No,' Manville said, 'it ends with me presenting you with a bill—the costs of sending you back to uninspire Adolf Hitler. Five hundred dollars, in advance.' He held out his hand. 'Just in case you never get back here.'

Resignedly, in misery, Jesse Slade reached as slowly as possible into his twentieth-century coat pocket for his wallet.

THE DAYS OF PERKY PAT

At ten in the morning a terrific horn, familiar to him, hooted Sam Regan out of his sleep, and he cursed the careboy upstairs; he knew the racket was deliberate. The careboy, circling, wanted to be certain that flukers—and not merely wild animals—got the care parcels that were to be dropped.

We'll get them, we'll get them, Sam Regan said to himself as he zipped his dust-proof overalls, put his feet into boots and then grumpily sauntered as slowly as possible toward the ramp. Several other flukers joined him, all showing similar irritation.

'He's early today,' Tod Morrison complained. 'And I'll bet it's all staples, sugar and flour and lard—nothing interesting like say candy.'

'We ought to be grateful,' Norman Schein said.

'Grateful!' Tod halted to stare at him. 'GRATEFUL?'

'Yes,' Schein said. 'What do you think we'd be eating without them? If they hadn't seen the clouds ten years ago.'

'Well,' Tod said sullenly, 'I just don't like them to come *early*; I actually don't exactly mind their coming, as such.'

As he put his shoulders against the lid at the top of the ramp, Schein said genially, 'That's mighty tolerant of you, Tod boy. I'm sure the careboys would be pleased to hear your sentiments.'

Of the three of them, Sam Regan was the last to reach the surface; he did not like the upstairs at all, and he did not care who knew it. And anyhow, no one could compel him to leave the safety of the Pinole Fluke-pit; it was entirely his business, and he noted now that a number of his fellow flukers had elected to remain below in their quarters, confident that those who did answer the horn would bring them back something.

'It's bright,' Tod murmured, blinking in the sun.

The care ship sparkled close overhead, set against the gray sky as if hanging from an uneasy thread. Good pilot, this drop, Tod decided. He, or rather it, just lazily handles it, in no hurry. Tod waved at the care ship, and once more the huge horn burst out its din, making him clap his hands to his ears. Hey, a joke's a joke, he said to himself. And then the horn ceased; the careboy had relented.

'Wave to him to drop,' Norm Schein said to Tod. 'You've got the wigwag.'

'Sure,' Tod said, and began laboriously flapping the red flag, which the Martian creatures had long ago provided, back and forth, back and forth.

A projectile slid from the underpart of the ship, tossed out stabilizers, spiraled toward the ground.

'Sheoot,' Sam Regan said with disgust. 'It is staples; they don't have the parachute.' He turned away, not interested.

How miserable the upstairs looked today, he thought as he surveyed the scene surrounding him. There, to the right, the uncompleted house which someone—not far from their pit—had begun to build out of lumber salvaged from Vallejo, ten miles to the north. Animals or radiation dust had gotten the builder, and so his work remained where it was; it would never be put to use. And, Sam Regan saw, an unusually heavy precipitate had formed since last he had been up here, Thursday morning or perhaps Friday; he had lost exact track. The darn dust, he thought. Just rocks, pieces of rubble, and the dust. World's becoming a dusty object with no one to whisk it off regularly. How about you? he asked silently of the Martian careboy flying in slow circles overhead. Isn't your technology limitless? Can't you appear some morning with a dust rag a million miles in surface area and restore our planet to pristine newness?

Or rather, he thought, to pristine *oldness*, the way it was in the 'ol-days,' as the children call it. We'd like that. While you're looking for something to give to us in the way of further aid, try that.

The careboy circled once more, searching for signs of writing in the dust: a message from the flukers below. I'll write that, Sam thought. BRING DUST RAG, RESTORE OUR CIVILIZATION. Okay, careboy?

All at once the care ship shot off, no doubt on its way back home to its base on Luna or perhaps all the way to Mars.

From the open fluke-pit hole, up which the three of them had come, a further head poked, a woman. Jean Regan, Sam's wife, appeared, shielded by a bonnet against the gray, blinding sun, frowning and saying, 'Anything important? Anything *new?*'

''Fraid not,' Sam said. The care parcel projectile had landed and he walked toward it, scuffing his boots in the dust. The hull of the projectile had cracked open from the impact and he could see the canisters already. It looked to be five thousand pounds of salt— might as well leave it up here so the animals wouldn't starve, he decided. He felt despondent.

How peculiarly anxious the careboys were. Concerned all the time that the mainstays of existence be ferried from their own planet to Earth. They must think we eat all day long, Sam thought. My God . . . the pit was filled to capacity with stored foods. But of course it had been one of the smallest public shelters in Northern California.

'Hey,' Schein said, stooping down by the projectile and peering into the crack opened along its side. 'I believe I see something we can use.' He found a rusted metal pole—once it had helped re-inforce the concrete side of an ol-days public building—and poked at the projectile, stirring its release mechanism into action. The mechanism, triggered off, popped the rear half of the projectile open . . . and there lay the contents.

'Looks like radios in that box,' Tod said. 'Transistor radios.' Thoughtfully stroking his short black beard he said, 'Maybe we can use them for something new in our layouts.'

'Mine's already got a radio,' Schein pointed out.

'Well, build an electronic self-directing lawn mower with the parts,' Tod said. 'You don't have that, do you?' He knew the Scheins'

Perky Pat layout fairly well; the two couples, he and his wife with Schein and his, had played together a good deal, being almost evenly matched.

Sam Regan said, 'Dibs on the radios, because I can use them.' His layout lacked the automatic garage-door opener that both Schein and Tod had; he was considerably behind them.

'Let's get to work,' Schein agreed. 'We'll leave the staples here and just cart back the radios. If anybody wants the staples, let them come here and get them. Before the do-cats do.'

Nodding, the other two men fell to the job of carting the useful contents of the projectile to the entrance of their fluke-pit ramp. For use in their precious, elaborate Perky Pat layouts.

Seated cross-legged with his whetstone, Timothy Schein, ten years old and aware of his many responsibilities, sharpened his knife, slowly and expertly. Meanwhile, disturbing him, his mother and father noisily quarreled with Mr and Mrs Morrison, on the far side of the partition. They were playing Perky Pat again. As usual.

How many times today they have to play that dumb game? Timothy asked himself. Forever, I guess. He could see nothing in it, but his parents played on anyhow. And they weren't the only ones; he knew from what other kids said, even from other fluke-pits, that their parents, too, played Perky Pat most of the day, and sometimes even on into the night.

His mother said loudly, 'Perky Pat's going to the grocery store and it's got one of those electric eyes that opens the door. Look.' A pause. 'See, it opened for her, and now she's inside.'

'She pushes a cart,' Timothy's dad added, in support.

'No, she doesn't,' Mrs Morrison contradicted. 'That's wrong. She gives her list to the grocer and he fills it.'

'That's only in little neighborhood stores,' his mother explained. 'And this is a supermarket, you can tell because of the electric eye door.'

'I'm sure all grocery stores had electric eye doors,' Mrs Morrison said stubbornly, and her husband chimed in with his agreement. Now the voices rose in anger; another squabble had broken out. As usual.

Aw, cung to them, Timothy said to himself, using the strongest word which he and his friends knew. What's a supermarket anyhow? He tested the blade of his knife—he had made it himself, originally, out of a heavy metal pan—and then hopped to his feet. A moment later he had sprinted silently down the hall and was rapping his special rap on the door of the Chamberlains' quarters.

Fred, also ten years old, answered. 'Hi. Ready to go? I see you got that ol' knife of yours sharpened; what do you think we'll catch?'

'Not a do-cat,' Timothy said. 'A lot better than that; I'm tired of eating do-cat. Too peppery.'

'Your parents playing Perky Pat?'

'Yeah.'

Fred said, 'My mom and dad have been gone for a long time, off playing with the Benteleys.' He glanced sideways at Timothy, and in an instant they had shared their mute disappointment regarding their parents. Gosh, and maybe the darn game was all over the world, by now; that would not have surprised either of them.

'How come your parents play it?' Timothy asked.

'Same reason yours do,' Fred said.

Hesitating, Timothy said, 'Well, why? I don't know why they do; I'm asking you, can't you say?'

'It's because—' Fred broke off. 'Ask them. Come on; let's get upstairs and start hunting.' His eyes shone. 'Let's see what we can catch and kill today.'

Shortly, they had ascended the ramp, popped open the lid, and were crouching amidst the dust and rocks, searching the horizon. Timothy's heart pounded; this moment always overwhelmed him, the first instant of reaching the upstairs. The thrilling initial sight of the expanse. Because it was never the same. The dust, heavier today, had a darker gray color to it than before; it seemed denser, more mysterious.

Here and there, covered by many layers of dust, lay parcels

dropped from past relief ships–dropped and left to deteriorate. Never to be claimed. And, Timothy saw, an additional new projectile which had arrived that morning. Most of its cargo could be seen within; the grownups had not had any use for the majority of the contents, today.

'Look,' Fred said softly.

Two do-cats–mutant dogs or cats; no one knew for sure–could be seen, lightly sniffing at the projectile. Attracted by the unclaimed contents.

'We don't want them,' Timothy said.

'That one's sure nice and fat,' Fred said longingly. But it was Timothy that had the knife; all he himself had was a string with a metal bolt on the end, a bull-roarer that could kill a bird or a small animal at a distance–but useless against a do-cat, which generally weighed fifteen to twenty pounds and sometimes more.

High up in the sky a dot moved at immense speed, and Timothy knew that it was a care ship heading for another fluke-pit, bringing supplies to it. Sure are busy, he thought to himself. Those careboys always coming and going; they never stop, because if they did, the grownups would die. Wouldn't that be too bad? he thought ironically. Sure be sad.

Fred said, 'Wave to it and maybe it'll drop something.' He grinned at Timothy, and then they both broke out laughing.

'Sure,' Timothy said. 'Let's see; what do I want?' Again the two of them laughed at the idea of them wanting something. The two boys had the entire upstairs, as far as the eye could see . . . they had even more than the careboys had, and that was plenty, more than plenty.

'Do you think they know?' Fred said. 'That our parents play Perky Pat with furniture made out of what they drop? I bet they don't know about Perky Pat; they never have seen a Perky Pat doll, and if they did they'd be really mad.'

'You're right,' Timothy said. 'They'd be so sore they'd probably stop dropping stuff.' He glanced at Fred, catching his eye.

'Aw no,' Fred said. 'We shouldn't tell them; your dad would beat you again if you did that, and probably me, too.'

Even so, it was an interesting idea. He could imagine first the surprise and then the anger of the careboys; it would be fun to see that, see the reaction of the eight-legged Martian creatures who had so much charity inside their warty bodies, the cephalopodic univalve mollusk-like organisms who had voluntarily taken it upon themselves to supply succor to the waning remnants of the human race . . . this was how they got paid back for their charity, this utterly wasteful, stupid purpose to which their goods were being put. This stupid Perky Pat game that all the adults played.

And anyhow it would be very hard to tell them; there was almost no communication between humans and careboys. They were too different. Acts, deeds, could be done, conveying something . . . but not mere words, not mere *signs*. And anyhow—

A great brown rabbit bounded by to the right, past the half-completed house. Timothy whipped out his knife. 'Oh boy!' he said aloud in excitement. 'Let's go!' He set off across the rubbly ground, Fred a little behind him. Gradually they gained on the rabbit; swift running came easy to the two boys: they had done much practicing.

'Throw the knife!' Fred panted, and Timothy, skidding to a halt, raised his right arm, paused to take aim, and then hurled the sharpened, weighted knife. His most valuable, self-made possession.

It cleaved the rabbit straight through its vitals. The rabbit tumbled, slid, raising a cloud of dust.

'I bet we can get a dollar for that!' Fred exclaimed, leaping up and down. 'The hide alone—I bet we can get fifty cents just for the darn hide!'

Together, they hurried toward the dead rabbit, wanting to get there before a red-tailed hawk or a day-owl swooped on it from the gray sky above.

Bending, Norman Schein picked up his Perky Pat doll and said sullenly, 'I'm quitting; I don't want to play any more.'

Distressed, his wife protested, 'But we've got Perky Pat all the way downtown in her new Ford hardtop convertible and parked and a dime in the meter and she's shopped and now she's in the analyst's office reading *Fortune*—we're way ahead of the Morrisons! Why do you want to quit, Norm?'

'We just don't agree,' Norman grumbled. 'You say analysts charged twenty dollars an hour and I distinctly remember them charging only ten; nobody could charge twenty. So you're penalizing our side, and for what? The Morrisons agree it was only ten. Don't you?' he said to Mr and Mrs Morrison, who squatted on the far side of the layout which combined both couples' Perky Pat sets.

Helen Morrison said to her husband, 'You went to the analyst more than I did; are you sure he charged only ten?'

'Well, I went mostly to group therapy,' Tod said. 'At the Berkeley State Mental Hygiene Clinic, and they charged according to your ability to pay. And Perky Pat is at a *private* psychoanalyst.'

'We'll have to ask someone else,' Helen said to Norman Schein. 'I guess all we can do now this minute is suspend the game.' He found himself being glared at by her, too, now, because by his insistence on the one point he had put an end to their game for the whole afternoon.

'Shall we leave it all set up?' Fran Schein asked. 'We might as well; maybe we can finish tonight after dinner.'

Norman Schein gazed down at their combined layout, the swanky shops, the well-lit streets with the parked new-model cars, all of them shiny, the split-level house itself, where Perky Pat lived and where she entertained Leonard, her boy friend. It was the *house* that he perpetually yearned for; the house was the real focus of the layout—of all the Perky Pat layouts, however much they might otherwise differ.

Perky Pat's wardrobe, for instance, there in the closet of the house, the big bedroom closet. Her capri pants, her white cotton short-shorts, her two-piece polka dot swimsuit, her fuzzy sweaters ... and there, in her bedroom, her hi-fi set, her collection of long playing records ...

It had been this way, once, really been like this in the ol-days. Norm Schein could remember his own LP record collection, and he had once had clothes almost as swanky as Perky Pat's boy friend Leonard, cashmere jackets and tweed suits and Italian sportshirts and shoes made in England. He hadn't owned a Jaguar XKE sports car, like Leonard did, but he had owned a fine-looking old 1963 Mercedes-Benz, which he had used to drive to work.

We lived then, Norm Schein said to himself, like Perky Pat and Leonard do now. This is how it actually was.

To his wife he said, pointing to the clock radio which Perky Pat kept beside her bed, 'Remember our GE clock radio? How it used to wake us up in the morning with classical music from that FM station, KSFR? The Wolfgangers, the program was called. From six A.M. to nine every morning.'

'Yes,' Fran said, nodding soberly. 'And you used to get up before me; I knew I should have gotten up and fixed bacon and hot coffee for you, but it was so much fun just indulging myself, not stirring for half an hour longer, until the kids woke up.'

'Woke up, hell; they were awake before we were,' Norm said. 'Don't you remember? They were in the back watching The Three Stooges on TV until eight. Then I got up and fixed hot cereal for them, and then I went on to my job at Ampex down at Redwood City.'

'Oh yes,' Fran said. 'The TV.' Their Perky Pat did not have a TV set; they had lost it to the Regans in a game a week ago, and Norm had not yet been able to fashion another one realistic-looking enough to substitute. So, in a game, they pretended now that 'the TV repairman had come for it.' That was how they explained their Perky Pat not having something she really would have had.

Norm thought, Playing this game . . . it's like being back there, back in the world before the war. That's why we play it, I suppose. He felt shame, but only fleetingly; the shame, almost at once, was replaced by the desire to play a little longer.

'Let's not quit,' he said suddenly. 'I'll agree the psychoanalyst would have charged Perky Pat twenty dollars. Okay?'

'Okay,' both the Morrisons said together, and they settled back down once more to resume the game.

Tod Morrison had picked up their Perky Pat; he held it, stroking its blonde hair—theirs was blonde, whereas the Scheins' was a brunette—and fiddling with the snaps of its skirt.

'Whatever are you doing?' his wife inquired.

'Nice skirt she has,' Tod said. 'You did a good job sewing it.'

Norm said, 'Ever know a girl, back in the ol-days, that looked like Perky Pat?'

'No,' Tod Morrison said somberly. 'Wish I had, though. I *saw* girls like Perky Pat, especially when I was living in Los Angeles during the Korean War. But I just could never manage to know them personally. And of course there were really terrific girl singers, like Peggy Lee and Julie London . . . they looked a lot like Perky Pat.'

'Play,' Fran said vigorously. And Norm, whose turn it was, picked up the spinner and spun.

'Eleven,' he said. 'That gets my Leonard out of the sports car repair garage and on his way to the race track.' He moved the Leonard doll ahead.

Thoughtfully, Tod Morrison said, 'You know, I was out the other day hauling in perishables which the careboys had dropped . . . Bill Ferner was there, and he told me something interesting. He met a fluker from a fluke-pit down where Oakland used to be. And at that fluke-pit you know what they play? Not Perky Pat. They never have heard of Perky Pat.'

'Well, what do they play, then?' Helen asked.

'They have another doll entirely.' Frowning, Tod continued, 'Bill says the Oakland fluker called it a Connie Companion doll. Ever hear of that?'

'A "Connie Companion" doll,' Fran said thoughtfully. 'How strange. I wonder what she's like. Does she have a boy friend?'

'Oh sure,' Tod said. 'His name is Paul. Connie and Paul. You know, we ought to hike down there to that Oakland Fluke-pit one of these days and see what Connie and Paul look like and how they live. Maybe we could learn a few things to add to our own layouts.'

Norm said, 'Maybe we could play them.'

Puzzled, Fran said, 'Could a Perky Pat play a Connie Companion? Is that possible? I wonder what would happen?'

There was no answer from any of the others. Because none of them knew.

As they skinned the rabbit, Fred said to Timothy, 'Where did the name "fluker" come from? It's sure an ugly word; why do they use it?'

'A fluker is a person who lived through the hydrogen war,' Timothy explained. 'You know, by a fluke. A fluke of fate? See? Because almost everyone was killed; there used to be thousands of people.'

'But what's a "fluke," then? When you say a "fluke of fate—"'

'A fluke is when fate has decided to spare you,' Timothy said, and that was all he had to say on the subject. That was all he knew.

Fred said thoughtfully, 'But you and I, we're not flukers because we weren't alive when the war broke out. We were born after.'

'Right,' Timothy said.

'So anybody who calls me a fluker,' Fred said, 'is going to get hit in the eye with my bull-roarer.'

'And "careboy,"' Timothy said, 'that's a made-up word, too. It's from when stuff was dumped from jet planes and ships to people in a disaster area. They were called "care parcels" because they came from people who cared.'

'I know that,' Fred said. 'I didn't ask that.'

'Well, I told you anyhow,' Timothy said.

The two boys continued skinning the rabbit.

Jean Regan said to her husband, 'Have you heard about the Connie Companion doll?' She glanced down the long rough-board table to make sure none of the other families was listening. 'Sam,' she said, 'I heard it from Helen Morrison; she heard it from Tod and he heard it from Bill Ferner, I think. So it's probably true.'

'What's true?' Sam said.

'That in the Oakland Fluke-pit they don't have Perky Pat; they have Connie Companion . . . and it occurred to me that maybe some of this—you know, this sort of emptiness, this boredom we feel now and then—maybe if we saw the Connie Companion doll and how she lives, maybe we could add enough to our own layout to—' She paused, reflecting. 'To make it more complete.'

'I don't care for the name,' Sam Regan said. 'Connie Companion; it sounds cheap.' He spooned up some of the plain, utilitarian grain-mash which the careboys had been dropping, of late. And, as he ate a mouthful, he thought, I'll bet Connie Companion doesn't eat slop like this; I'll bet she eats cheeseburgers with all the trimmings, at a high-type drive-in.

'Could we make a trek down there?' Jean asked.

'To Oakland Fluke-pit?' Sam stared at her. 'It's *fifteen miles*, all the way on the other side of the Berkeley Fluke-pit!'

'But this is important,' Jean said stubbornly. 'And Bill says that a fluker from Oakland came all the way up here, in search of electronic parts or something . . . so if he can do it, we can. We've got the dust suits they dropped us. I know we could do it.'

Little Timothy Schein, sitting with his family, had overheard her; now he spoke up. 'Mrs Regan, Fred Chamberlain and I, we could trek down that far, if you pay us. What do you say?' He nudged Fred, who sat beside him. 'Couldn't we? For maybe five dollars.'

Fred, his face serious, turned to Mrs Regan and said, 'We could get you a Connie Companion doll. For five dollars for *each* of us.'

'Good grief,' Jean Regan said, outraged. And dropped the subject.

But later, after dinner, she brought it up again when she and Sam were alone in their quarters.

'Sam, I've got to see it,' she burst out. Sam, in a galvanized tub, was taking his weekly bath, so he had to listen to her. 'Now that we know it exists we have to play against someone in the Oakland Fluke-pit; at least we can do that. Can't we? Please.' She paced back and forth in the small room, her hands clasped tensely. 'Connie Companion may have a Standard Station and an airport terminal with jet landing strip and color TV and a French restaurant where they serve escargot, like the one you and I went to when we were first married . . . I just have to see her layout.'

'I don't know,' Sam said hesitantly. 'There's something about Connie Companion doll that—makes me uneasy.'

'What could it possibly be?'

'I don't know.'

Jean said bitterly, 'It's because you know her layout is so much better than ours and she's so much more than Perky Pat.'

'Maybe that's it,' Sam murmured.

'If you don't go, if you don't try to make contact with them down at the Oakland Fluke-pit, someone else will—someone with more ambition will get ahead of you. Like Norman Schein. He's not afraid the way you are.'

Sam said nothing; he continued with his bath. But his hands shook.

A careboy had recently dropped complicated pieces of machinery which were, evidently, a form of mechanical computer. For several weeks the computers—if that was what they were—had sat about the pit in their cartons, unused, but now Norman Schein was finding something to do with one. At the moment he was busy adapting some of its gears, the smallest ones, to form a garbage disposal unit for his Perky Pat's kitchen.

Using the tiny special tools—designed and built by inhabitants of the fluke-pit—which were necessary in fashioning environmental items for Perky Pat, he was busy at his hobby bench. Thoroughly engrossed in what he was doing, he all at once realized that Fran was standing directly behind him, watching.

'I get nervous when I'm watched,' Norm said, holding a tiny gear with a pair of tweezers.

'Listen,' Fran said, 'I've thought of something. Does this suggest anything to you?' She placed before him one of the transistor radios which had been dropped the day before.

'It suggests that garage-door opener already thought of,' Norm said irritably. He continued with his work, expertly fitting the miniature pieces together in the sink drain of Pat's kitchen; such delicate work demanded maximum concentration.

Fran said, 'It suggests that there must be radio *transmitters* on Earth somewhere, or the careboys wouldn't have dropped these.'

'So?' Norm said, uninterested.

'Maybe our Mayor has one,' Fran said. 'Maybe there's one right here in our own pit, and we could use it to call the Oakland Fluke-pit. Representatives from there could meet us halfway . . . say at the Berkeley Fluke-pit. And we could play there. So we wouldn't have that long fifteen mile trip.'

Norman hesitated in his work; he set the tweezers down and said slowly, 'I think possibly you're right.' But if their Mayor Hooker Glebe had a radio transmitter, would he let them use it? And if he did—

'We can try,' Fran urged. 'It wouldn't hurt to try.'

'Okay,' Norm said, rising from his hobby bench.

The short, sly-faced man in Army uniform, the Mayor of the Pinole Fluke-pit, listened in silence as Norm Schein spoke. Then he smiled a wise, cunning smile. 'Sure, I have a radio transmitter. Had it all the time. Fifty watt output. But why would you want to get in touch with the Oakland Fluke-pit?'

Guardedly, Norm said, 'That's my business.'

Hooker Glebe said thoughtfully, 'I'll let you use it for fifteen dollars.'

It was a nasty shock, and Norm recoiled. Good Lord; all the money he and his wife had—they needed every bill of it for use in playing Perky Pat. Money was the tender in the game; there was no other criterion by which one could tell if he had won or lost. 'That's too much,' he said aloud.

'Well, say ten,' the Mayor said, shrugging.

In the end they settled for six dollars and a fifty cent piece.

'I'll make the radio contact for you,' Hooker Glebe said. 'Because you don't know how. It will take time.' He began turning a crank at the side of the generator of the transmitter. 'I'll notify you when I've made contact with them. But give me the money now.' He held out his hand for it, and, with great reluctance, Norm paid him.

It was not until late that evening that Hooker managed to estab-lish contact with Oakland. Pleased with himself, beaming in self-satisfaction, he appeared at the Scheins' quarters, during their dinner hour. 'All set,' he announced. 'Say, you know there are actu-ally *nine* fluke-pits in Oakland? I didn't know that. Which you want? I've got one with the radio code of Red Vanilla.' He chuckled. 'They're tough and suspicious down there; it was hard to get any of them to answer.'

Leaving his evening meal, Norman hurried to the Mayor's quar-ters, Hooker puffing along after him.

The transmitter, sure enough, was on, and static wheezed from the speaker of its monitoring unit. Awkwardly, Norm seated himself at the microphone. 'Do I just talk?' he asked Hooker Glebe.

'Just say, "This is Pinole Fluke-pit calling." Repeat that a couple of times and then when they acknowledge, you say what you want to say.' The Mayor fiddled with the controls of the transmitter, fuss-ing in an important fashion.

'This is Pinole Fluke-pit,' Norm said loudly into the microphone.

Almost at once a clear voice from the monitor said, 'This is Red Vanilla Three answering.' The voice was cold and harsh; it struck him forcefully as distinctly alien. Hooker was right. 'Do you have Connie Companion down there where you are?'

'Yes we do,' the Oakland fluker answered.

'Well, I challenge you,' Norman said, feeling the veins in his throat pulse with the tension of what he was saying. 'We're Perky Pat in this area; we'll play Perky Pat against your Connie Compan-ion. Where can we meet?'

'Perky Pat,' the Oakland fluker echoed. 'Yeah, I know about her. What would the stakes be, in your mind?'

'Up here we play for paper money mostly,' Norman said, feeling that his response was somehow lame.

'We've got lots of paper money,' the Oakland fluker said cut-tingly. 'That wouldn't interest any of us. What else?'

'I don't know.' He felt hampered, talking to someone he could not see; he was not used to that. People should, he thought, be face to face, then you can see the other person's expression. This was not natural. 'Let's meet halfway,' he said, 'and discuss it. Maybe we could meet at the Berkeley Fluke-pit; how about that?'

The Oakland fluker said, 'That's too far. You mean lug our Connie Companion layout all that way? It's too heavy and something might happen to it.'

'No, just to discuss rules and stakes,' Norman said.

Dubiously, the Oakland fluker said, 'Well, I guess we could do that. But you better understand—we take Connie Companion doll pretty damn seriously; you better be prepared to talk terms.'

'We will,' Norm assured him.

All this time Mayor Hooker Glebe had been cranking the handle of the generator; perspiring, his face bloated with exertion, he motioned angrily for Norm to conclude his palaver.

'At the Berkeley Fluke-pit,' Norm finished. 'In three days. And send your best player, the one who has the biggest and most authentic layout. Our Perky Pat layouts are works of art, you understand.'

The Oakland fluker said, 'We'll believe that when we see them. After all, we've got carpenters and electricians and plasterers here, building our layouts; I'll bet you're all unskilled.'

'Not as much as you think,' Norm said hotly, and laid down the microphone. To Hooker Glebe—who had immediately stopped cranking—he said, 'We'll beat them. Wait'll they see the garbage disposal unit I'm making for my Perky Pat; did you know there were people back in the ol-days, I mean real alive human beings, who didn't have garbage disposal units?'

'I remember,' Hooker said peevishly. 'Say, you got a lot of cranking for your money; I think you gypped me, talking so long.' He eyed Norm with such hostility that Norm began to feel uneasy. After all, the Mayor of the pit had the authority to evict any fluker he wished; that was their law.

'I'll give you the fire alarm box I just finished the other day,' Norm said. 'In my layout it goes at the corner of the block where Perky Pat's boy friend Leonard lives.'

'Good enough,' Hooker agreed, and his hostility faded. It was replaced, at once, by desire. 'Let's see it, Norm. I bet it'll go good in my layout; a fire alarm box is just what I need to complete my first block where I have the mailbox. Thank you.'

'You're welcome,' Norm sighed, philosophically.

When he returned from the two-day trek to the Berkeley Fluke-pit his face was so grim that his wife knew at once that the parley with the Oakland people had not gone well.

That morning a careboy had dropped cartons of a synthetic tea-like drink; she fixed a cup of it for Norman, waiting to hear what had taken place eight miles to the south.

'We haggled,' Norm said, seated wearily on the bed which he and his wife and child all shared. 'They don't want money; they don't want goods—naturally not goods, because the darn careboys are dropping regularly down there, too.'

'What will they accept, then?'

Norm said, 'Perky Pat herself.' He was silent, then.

'Oh good Lord,' she said, appalled.

'But if we win,' Norm pointed out, 'we win Connie Companion.'

'And the layouts? What about them?'

'We keep our own. It's just Perky Pat herself, not Leonard, not anything else.'

'But,' she protested, 'what'll we *do* if we lose Perky Pat?'

'I can make another one,' Norm said. 'Given time. There's still a big supply of thermoplastics and artificial hair, here in the pit. And I have plenty of different paints; it would take at least a month, but I could do it. I don't look forward to the job, I admit. But—' His eyes glinted. 'Don't look on the dark side; *imagine what it would be like to win Connie Companion doll*. I think we may well win; their delegate seemed smart and, as Hooker said, tough . . . but the one I talked to didn't strike me as being very flukey. You know, on good terms with luck.'

And, after all, the element of luck, of chance, entered into each stage of the game through the agency of the spinner.

'It seems wrong,' Fran said, 'to put up Perky Pat herself. But if you say so–' She managed to smile a little. 'I'll go along with it. And if you won Connie Companion–who knows? You might be elected Mayor when Hooker dies. Imagine, to have won somebody else's *doll*–not just the game, the money, but the *doll itself*.'

'I can win,' Norm said soberly. 'Because I'm very flukey.' He could feel it in him, the same flukeyness that had got him through the hydrogen war alive, that had kept him alive ever since. You either have it or you don't, he realized. And I do.

His wife said, 'Shouldn't we ask Hooker to call a meeting of everyone in the pit, and send the best player out of our entire group. So as to be the surest of winning.'

'Listen,' Norm Schein said emphatically. 'I'm the best player. I'm going. And so are you; we made a good team, and we don't want to break it up. Anyhow, we'll need at least two people to carry Perky Pat's layout.' All in all, he judged, their layout weighed sixty pounds.

His plan seemed to him to be satisfactory. But when he mentioned it to the others living in the Pinole Fluke-pit he found himself facing sharp disagreement. The whole next day was filled with argument.

'You can't lug your layout all that way yourselves,' Sam Regan said. 'Either take more people with you or carry your layout in a vehicle of some sort. Such as a cart.' He scowled at Norm.

'Where'd I get a cart?' Norm demanded.

'Maybe something could be adapted,' Sam said. 'I'll give you every bit of help I can. Personally, I'd go along but as I told my wife this whole idea worries me.' He thumped Norm on the back. 'I admire your courage, you and Fran, setting off this way. I wish I had what it takes.' He looked unhappy.

In the end, Norm settled on a wheelbarrow. He and Fran would take turns pushing it. That way neither of them would have to carry any load above and beyond their food and water, and of course knives by which to protect them from the do-cats.

As they were carefully placing the elements of their layout in the wheelbarrow, Norm Schein's boy Timothy came sidling up to them. 'Take me along, Dad,' he pleaded. 'For fifty cents I'll go as guide and scout, and also I'll help you catch food along the way.'

'We'll manage fine,' Norm said. 'You stay here in the fluke-pit; you'll be safer here.' It annoyed him, the idea of his son tagging along on an important venture such as this. It was almost— sacrilegious.

'Kiss us goodbye,' Fran said to Timothy, smiling at him briefly; then her attention returned to the layout within the wheelbarrow. 'I hope it doesn't tip over,' she said fearfully to Norm.

'Not a chance,' Norm said. 'If we're careful.' He felt confident.

A few moments later they began wheeling the wheelbarrow up the ramp to the lid at the top, to upstairs. Their journey to the Berkeley Fluke-pit had begun.

A mile outside the Berkeley Fluke-pit he and Fran began to stumble over empty drop-canisters and some only partly empty: remains of past care parcels such as littered the surface near their own pit. Norm Schein breathed a sigh of relief; the journey had not been so bad after all, except that his hands had become blistered from gripping the metal handles of the wheelbarrow, and Fran had turned her ankle so that now she walked with a painful limp. But it had taken them less time than he had anticipated, and his mood was one of buoyancy.

Ahead, a figure appeared, crouching low in the ash. A boy. Norm waved at him and called, 'Hey, sonny—we're from the Pinole pit; we're supposed to meet a party from Oakland here . . . do you remember me?'

The boy, without answering, turned and scampered off.

'Nothing to be afraid of,' Norm said to his wife. 'He's going to tell their Mayor. A nice old fellow named Ben Fennimore.'

Soon several adults appeared, approaching warily.

With relief, Norm set the legs of the wheelbarrow down into the ash, letting go and wiping his face with his handkerchief. 'Has the Oakland team arrived yet?' he called.

'Not yet,' a tall, elderly man with a white armband and ornate cap answered. 'It's you, Schein, isn't it?' he said, peering. This was Ben Fennimore. 'Back already with your layout.' Now the Berkeley flukers had begun crowding around the wheelbarrow, inspecting the Scheins' layout. Their faces showed admiration.

'They have Perky Pat here,' Norm explained to his wife. 'But—' He lowered his voice. 'Their layouts are only basic. Just a house, wardrobe and car . . . they've built almost nothing. No imagination.'

One Berkeley fluker, a woman, said wonderingly to Fran, 'And you made each of the pieces of furniture yourselves?' Marveling, she turned to the man beside her. 'See what they've accomplished, Ed?'

'Yes,' the man answered, nodding. 'Say,' he said to Fran and Norm, 'can we see it all set up? You're going to set it up in our pit, aren't you?'

'We are indeed,' Norm said.

The Berkeley flukers helped push the wheelbarrow the last mile. And before long they were descending the ramp, to the pit below the surface.

'It's a big pit,' Norm said knowingly to Fran. 'Must be two thousand people here. This is where the University of California was.'

'I see,' Fran said, a little timid at entering a strange pit; it was the first time in years—since the war, in fact—that she had seen any strangers. And so many at once. It was almost too much for her; Norm felt her shrink back, pressing against him in fright.

When they had reached the first level and were starting to unload the wheelbarrow, Ben Fennimore came up to them and said softly, 'I think the Oakland people have been spotted; we just got a report of activity upstairs. So be prepared.' He added, 'We're rooting for you, of course, because you're Perky Pat, the same as us.'

'Have you ever seen Connie Companion doll?' Fran asked him.

'No ma'am,' Fennimore answered courteously. 'But naturally we've heard about it, being neighbors to Oakland and all. I'll tell you one thing . . . we hear that Connie Companion doll is a bit older than Perky Pat. You know—more, um, *mature*.' He explained, 'I just wanted to prepare you.'

Norm and Fran glanced at each other. 'Thanks,' Norm said slowly. 'Yes, we should be as much prepared as possible. How about Paul?'

'Oh, he's not much,' Fennimore said. 'Connie runs things; I don't even think Paul has a real apartment of his own. But you better wait until the Oakland flukers get here; I don't want to mislead you—my knowledge is all hearsay, you understand.'

Another Berkeley fluker, standing nearby, spoke up. 'I saw Connie once, and she's much more grown up than Perky Pat.'

'How old do you figure Perky Pat is?' Norm asked him.

'Oh, I'd say seventeen or eighteen,' Norm was told.

'And Connie?' He waited tensely.

'Oh, she might be twenty-five, even.'

From the ramp behind them they heard noises. More Berkeley flukers appeared, and, after them, two men carrying between them a platform on which, spread out, Norm saw a great, spectacular layout.

This was the Oakland team, and they weren't a couple, a man and wife; they were both men, and they were hard-faced with stern, remote eyes. They jerked their heads briefly at him and Fran, acknowledging their presence. And then, with enormous care, they set down the platform on which their layout rested.

Behind them came a third Oakland fluker carrying a metal box, much like a lunch pail. Norm, watching, knew instinctively that in the box lay Connie Companion doll. The Oakland fluker produced a key and began unlocking the box.

'We're ready to begin playing any time,' the taller of the Oakland men said. 'As we agreed in our discussion, we'll use a numbered spinner instead of dice. Less chance of cheating that way.'

'Agreed,' Norm said. Hesitantly he held out his hand. 'I'm Norman Schein and this is my wife and play-partner Fran.'

The Oakland man, evidently the leader, said, 'I'm Walter R. Wynn. This is my partner here, Charley Dowd, and the man with the box, that's Peter Foster. He isn't going to play; he just guards our layout.' Wynn glanced about, at the Berkeley flukers, as if saying, I know you're all partial to Perky Pat, in here. But we don't care; we're not scared.

Fran said, 'We're ready to play, Mr Wynn.' Her voice was low but controlled.

'What about money?' Fennimore asked.

'I think both teams have plenty of money,' Wynn said. He laid out several thousand dollars in greenbacks, and now Norm did the same. 'The money of course is not a factor in this, except as a means of conducting the game.'

Norm nodded; he understood perfectly. Only the dolls themselves mattered. And now, for the first time, he saw Connie Companion doll.

She was being placed in her bedroom by Mr Foster who evidently was in charge of her. And the sight of her took his breath away. Yes, she was older. A grown woman, not a girl at all ... the difference between her and Perky Pat was acute. And so life-like. Carved, not poured; she obviously had been whittled out of wood and then painted—she was not a thermoplastic. And her hair. It appeared to be genuine hair.

He was deeply impressed.

'What do you think of her?' Walter Wynn asked, with a faint grin.

'Very—impressive,' Norm conceded.

Now the Oaklanders were studying Perky Pat. 'Poured thermoplastic,' one of them said. 'Artificial hair. Nice clothes, though; all stitched by hand, you can see that. Interesting; what we heard was correct. Perky Pat isn't a grownup, she's just a teenager.'

Now the male companion to Connie appeared; he was set down in the bedroom beside Connie.

'Wait a minute,' Norm said. 'You're putting Paul, or whatever his name is, in her bedroom with her? Doesn't he have his own apartment?'

Wynn said, 'They're married.'

'*Married!*' Norman and Fran stared at him, dumbfounded.

'Why sure,' Wynn said. 'So naturally they live together. Your dolls, they're not, are they?'

'N-no,' Fran said. 'Leonard is Perky Pat's boy friend . . .' Her voice trailed off. 'Norm,' she said, clutching his arm, 'I don't believe him; I think he's just saying they're married to get the advantage. Because if they both start out from the same room—'

Norm said aloud, 'You fellows, look here. It's not fair, calling them married.'

Wynn said, 'We're not "calling" them married; they are married. Their names are Connie and Paul Lathrope, of 24 Arden Place, Piedmont. They've been married for a year, most players will tell you.' He sounded calm.

Maybe, Norm thought, it's true. He was truly shaken.

'Look at them together,' Fran said, kneeling down to examine the Oaklanders' layout. 'In the same bedroom, in the same house. Why, Norm; do you see? There's just the one bed. A big double bed.' Wild-eyed, she appealed to him. 'How can Perky Pat and Leonard play against them?' Her voice shook. 'It's not morally *right*.'

'This is another type of layout entirely,' Norm said to Walter Wynn. 'This, that you have. Utterly different from what we're used to, as you can see.' He pointed to his own layout. 'I insist that in this game Connie and Paul *not* live together and *not* be considered married.'

'But they are,' Foster spoke up. 'It's a fact. Look—their clothes are in the same closet.' He showed them the closet. 'And in the same bureau drawers.' He showed them that, too. 'And look in the bathroom. Two toothbrushes. His and hers, in the same rack. So you can see we're not making it up.'

There was silence.

Then Fran said in a choked voice, 'And if they're married—you mean they've been—intimate?'

Wynn raised an eyebrow, then nodded. 'Sure, since they're married. Is there anything wrong with that?'

'Perky Pat and Leonard have never—' Fran began, and then ceased.

'Naturally not,' Wynn agreed. 'Because they're only going together. We understand that.'

Fran said, 'We just can't play. We can't.' She caught hold of her husband's arm. 'Let's go back to Pinole pit—please, Norman.'

'Wait,' Wynn said, at once. 'If you don't play, you're conceding; you have to give up Perky Pat.'

The three Oaklanders all nodded. And, Norm saw, many of the Berkeley flukers were nodding, too, including Ben Fennimore.

'They're right,' Norm said heavily to his wife. 'We'd have to give her up. We better play, dear.'

'Yes,' Fran said, in a dead, flat voice. 'We'll play.' She bent down and listlessly spun the needle of the spinner. It stopped at six.

Smiling, Walter Wynn knelt down and spun. He obtained a four.

The game had begun.

Crouching behind the strewn, decayed contents of a care parcel that had been dropped long ago, Timothy Schein saw coming across the surface of ash his mother and father, pushing the wheelbarrow ahead of them. They looked tired and worn.

'Hi,' Timothy yelled, leaping out at them in joy at seeing them again; he had missed them very much.

'Hi, son,' his father murmured, nodding. He let go of the handles of the wheelbarrow, then halted and wiped his face with his handkerchief.

Now Fred Chamberlain raced up, panting. 'Hi, Mr Schein; hi, Mrs Schein. Hey, did you win? Did you beat the Oakland flukers? I bet you did, didn't you?' He looked from one of them to the other and then back.

In a low voice Fran said, 'Yes, Freddy. We won.'

Norm said, 'Look in the wheelbarrow.'

The two boys looked. And, there among Perky Pat's furnishings, lay another doll. Larger, fuller-figured, much older than Pat . . . they stared at her and she stared up sightlessly at the gray sky overhead. So this is Connie Companion doll, Timothy said to himself. Gee.

'We were lucky,' Norm said. Now several people had emerged from the pit and were gathering around them, listening. Jean and Sam Regan, Tod Morrison and his wife Helen, and now their Mayor, Hooker Glebe himself, waddling up excited and nervous, his face flushed, gasping for breath from the labor—unusual for him—of ascending the ramp.

Fran said, 'We got a cancellation of debts card, just when we were most behind. We owed fifty thousand, and it made us even with the Oakland flukers. And then, after that, we got an advance ten squares card, and that put us right on the jackpot square, at least in our layout. We had a very bitter squabble, because the Oaklanders showed us that on their layout it was a tax lien slapped on real estate holdings square, but we had spun an odd number so that put us back on our own board.' She sighed. 'I'm glad to be back. It was hard, Hooker; it was a tough game.'

Hooker Glebe wheezed, 'Let's all get a look at the Connie Companion doll, folks.' To Fran and Norm he said, 'Can I lift her up and show them?'

'Sure,' Norm said, nodding.

Hooker picked up Connie Companion doll. 'She sure is realistic,' he said, scrutinizing her. 'Clothes aren't as nice as ours generally are; they look machine-made.'

'They are,' Norm agreed. 'But she's carved, not poured.'

'Yes, so I see.' Hooker turned the doll about, inspecting her from all angles. 'A nice job. She's—um, more filled-out than Perky Pat. What's this outfit she has on? Tweed suit of some sort.'

'A business suit,' Fran said. 'We won that with her; they had agreed on that in advance.'

'You see, she has a job,' Norm explained. 'She's a psychology consultant for a business firm doing marketing research. In consumer preferences. A high-paying position ... she earns twenty thousand a year, I believe Wynn said.'

'Golly,' Hooker said. 'And Pat's just going to college; she's still in school.' He looked troubled. 'Well, I guess they were bound to be ahead of us in some ways. What matters is that you won.' His jovial smile returned. 'Perky Pat came out ahead.' He held the Connie Companion doll up high, where everyone could see her. 'Look what Norm and Fran came back with, folks!'

Norm said, 'Be careful with her, Hooker.' His voice was firm.

'Eh?' Hooker said, pausing. 'Why, Norm?'

'Because,' Norm said, 'she's going to have a baby.'

There was a sudden chill silence. The ash around them stirred faintly; that was the only sound.

'How do you know?' Hooker asked.

'They told us. The Oaklanders told us. And we won that, too—after a bitter argument that Fennimore had to settle.' Reaching into the wheelbarrow he brought out a little leather pouch, from it he carefully took a carved pink new-born baby. 'We won this too because Fennimore agreed that from a technical standpoint it's literally part of Connie Companion doll at this point.'

Hooker stared a long, long time.

'She's married,' Fran explained. 'To Paul. They're not just going together. She's three months pregnant, Mr Wynn said. He didn't tell us until after we won; he didn't want to, then, but they felt they had to. I think they were right; it wouldn't have done not to say.'

Norm said, 'And in addition there's actually an embryo outfit—'

'Yes,' Fran said. 'You have to open Connie up, of course, to see—'

'No,' Jean Regan said. 'Please, no.'

Hooker said, 'No, Mrs Schein, don't.' He backed away.

Fran said, 'It shocked us of course at first, but—'

'You see,' Norm put in, 'it's logical; you have to follow the logic. Why, eventually Perky Pat—'

'No,' Hooker said violently. He bent down, picked up a rock from the ash at his feet. 'No,' he said, and raised his arm. 'You stop, you two. Don't say any more.'

Now the Regans, too, had picked up rocks. No one spoke.

Fran said, at last, 'Norm, we've got to get out of here.'

'You're right,' Tod Morrison told them. His wife nodded in grim agreement.

'You two go back down to Oakland,' Hooker told Norman and

Fran Schein. 'You don't live here any more. You're different than you were. You—changed.'

'Yes,' Sam Regan said slowly, half to himself. 'I was right; there was something to fear.' To Norm Schein he said, 'How difficult a trip is it to Oakland?'

'We just went to Berkeley,' Norm said. 'To the Berkeley Fluke-pit.' He seemed baffled and stunned by what was happening. 'My God,' he said, 'we can't turn around and push this wheelbarrow back all the way to Berkeley again—we're worn out, we need rest!'

Sam Regan said, 'What if somebody else pushed?' He walked up to the Scheins, then, and stood with them. 'I'll push the darn thing. You lead the way, Schein.' He looked toward his own wife, but Jean did not stir. And she did not put down her handful of rocks.

Timothy Schein plucked at his father's arm. 'Can I come this time, Dad? Please let me come.'

'Okay,' Norm said, half to himself. Now he drew himself together. 'So we're not wanted here.' He turned to Fran. 'Let's go. Sam's going to push the wheelbarrow; I think we can make it back there before nightfall. If not, we can sleep out in the open; Timothy'll help protect us against the do-cats.'

Fran said, 'I guess we have no choice.' Her face was pale.

'And take this,' Hooker said. He held out the tiny carved baby. Fran Schein accepted it and put it tenderly back in its leather pouch. Norm laid Connie Companion back down in the wheelbarrow, where she had been. They were ready to start back.

'It'll happen up here eventually,' Norm said, to the group of people, to the Pinole flukers. 'Oakland is just more advanced; that's all.'

'Go on,' Hooker Glebe said. 'Get started.'

Nodding, Norm started to pick up the handles of the wheelbarrow, but Sam Regan moved him aside and took them himself. 'Let's go,' he said.

The three adults, with Timothy Schein going ahead of them with his knife ready—in case a do-cat attacked—started into motion, in the direction of Oakland and the south. No one spoke. There was nothing to say.

'It's a shame this had to happen,' Norm said at last, when they had gone almost a mile and there was no further sign of the Pinole flukers behind them.

'Maybe not,' Sam Regan said. 'Maybe it's for the good.' He did not seem downcast. And after all, he had lost his wife; he had given up more than anyone else, and yet–he had survived.

'Glad you feel that way,' Norm said somberly.

They continued on, each with his own thoughts.

After a while, Timothy said to his father, 'All these big fluke-pits to the south ... there's lots more things to do there, isn't there? I mean, you don't just sit around playing that game.' He certainly hoped not.

His father said, 'That's true, I guess.'

Overhead, a care ship whistled at great velocity and then was gone again almost at once; Timothy watched it go but he was not really interested in it, because there was so much more to look forward to, on the ground and below the ground, ahead of them to the south.

His father murmured, 'Those Oaklanders; their game, their particular doll, it taught them something. Connie had to grow and it forced them all to grow along with her. Our flukers never learned about that, not from Perky Pat. I wonder if they ever will. She'd have to grow up the way Connie did. Connie must have been like Perky Pat, once. A long time ago.'

Not interested in what his father was saying–who really cared about dolls and games with dolls?–Timothy scampered ahead, peering to see what lay before them, the opportunities and possibilities, for him and for his mother and dad, for Mr Regan also.

'I can't wait,' he yelled back at his father, and Norm Schein managed a faint, fatigued smile in answer.

STAND-BY

An hour before his morning program on channel six, ranking news clown Jim Briskin sat in his private office with his production staff, conferring on the report of an unknown possibly hostile flotilla detected at eight hundred astronomical units from the sun. It was big news, of course. But how should it be presented to his several-billion viewers scattered over three planets and seven moons?

Peggy Jones, his secretary, lit a cigarette and said, 'Don't alarm them, Jim-Jam. Do it folksy-style.' She leaned back, riffled the dispatches received by their commercial station from Unicephalon 40-D's teletypers.

It had been the homeostatic problem-solving structure Unicephalon 40-D at the White House in Washington, DC which had detected this possible external enemy; in its capacity as President of the United States it had at once dispatched ships of the line to stand picket duty. The flotilla appeared to be entering from another solar system entirely, but that fact of course would have to be determined by the picket ships.

'Folksy-style,' Jim Briskin said glumly. 'I grin and say, Hey look comrades—it's happened at last, the thing we all feared, ha ha.' He eyed her. 'That'll get baskets full of laughs all over Earth and Mars but just possibly not on the far-out moons.' Because if there were some kind of attack it would be the farther colonists who would be hit first.

'No, they won't be amused,' his continuity advisor Ed Fineberg agreed. He, too, looked worried; he had a family on Ganymede.

'Is there any lighter piece of news?' Peggy asked. 'By which you could open your program? The sponsor would like that.' She passed the armload of news dispatches to Briskin. 'See what you can do. Mutant cow obtains voting franchise in court case in Alabama . . . you know.'

'I know,' Briskin agreed as he began to inspect the dispatches. One such as his quaint account—it had touched the hearts of millions—of the mutant blue jay which learned, by great trial and effort, to sew. It had sewn itself and its progeny a nest, one April morning, in Bismarck, North Dakota, in front of the TV cameras of Briskin's network.

One piece of news stood out; he knew intuitively, as soon as he saw it, that here he had what he wanted to lighten the dire tone of the day's news. Seeing it, he relaxed. The worlds went on with business as usual, despite this great news-break from eight hundred AUs out.

'Look,' he said, grinning. 'Old Gus Schatz is dead. Finally.'

'Who's Gus Schatz?' Peggy asked, puzzled. 'That name . . . it does sound familiar.'

'The union man,' Jim Briskin said. 'You remember. The stand-by President, sent over to Washington by the union twenty-two years ago. He's dead, and the union—' He tossed her the dispatch: it was lucid and brief. 'Now it's sending a new stand-by President over to take Schatz's place. I think I'll interview him. Assuming he can talk.'

'That's right,' Peggy said. 'I keep forgetting. There still is a human stand-by in case Unicephalon fails. Has it ever failed?'

'No,' Ed Fineberg said. 'And it never will. So we have one more case of union featherbedding. The plague of our society.'

'But still,' Jim Briskin said, 'people would be amused. The home life of the top stand-by in the country . . . why the union picked him, what his hobbies are. What this man, whoever he is, plans to do during his term to keep from going mad with boredom. Old Gus learned to bind books; he collected rare old motor magazines and bound them in vellum with gold-stamped lettering.'

Both Ed and Peggy nodded in agreement. 'Do that,' Peggy

urged him. 'You can make it interesting, Jim-Jam; you can make anything interesting. I'll place a call to the White House, or is the new man there yet?'

'Probably still at union headquarters in Chicago,' Ed said. 'Try a line there. Government Civil Servants' Union, East Division.'

Picking up the phone, Peggy quickly dialed.

At seven o'clock in the morning Maximilian Fischer sleepily heard noises; he lifted his head from the pillow, heard the confusion growing in the kitchen, the landlady's shrill voice, then men's voices which were unfamiliar to him. Groggily, he managed to sit up, shifting his bulk with care. He did not hurry; the doc had said not to overexert, because of the strain on his already-enlarged heart. So he took his time dressing.

Must be after a contribution to one of the funds, Max said to himself. *It sounds like some of the fellas. Pretty early, though.* He did not feel alarmed. *I'm in good standing*, he thought firmly. *Nuthin' to fear.*

With care, he buttoned a fine pink and green-striped silk shirt, one of his favorites. *Gives me class*, he thought as with labored effort he managed to bend far enough over to slip on his authentic simulated deerskin pumps. *Be ready to meet them on an equality level*, he thought as he smoothed his thinning hair before the mirror. *If they shake me down too much I'll squawk directly to Pat Noble at the Noo York hiring hall; I mean, I don't have to stand for any stuff. I been in the union too long.*

From the other room a voice bawled, 'Fischer—get your clothes on and come out. We got a job for you and it begins today.'

A job, Max thought with mixed feelings; he did not know whether to be glad or sorry. For over a year now he had been drawing from the union fund, as were most of his friends. *Well what do you know. Cripes*, he thought; *suppose it's a hard job, like maybe I got to bend over all the time or move around.* He felt anger. *What a dirty deal. I mean, who do they think they are?* Opening the door, he faced them. 'Listen,' he began, but one of the union officials cut him off.

'Pack your things, Fischer. Gus Schatz kicked the bucket and you got to go down to Washington, DC and take over the number one stand-by; we want you there before they abolish the position or something and we have to go out on strike or go to court. Mainly, we want to get someone right in clean and easy with no trouble; you understand? Make the transition so smooth that no one hardly takes notice.'

At once, Max said, 'What's it pay?'

Witheringly, the union official said, 'You got no decision to make in this; *you're picked.* You want your freeloader fund-money cut off? You want to have to get out at your age and look for work?'

'Aw come on,' Max protested. 'I can pick up the phone and dial Pat Noble—'

The union officials were grabbing up objects here and there in the apartment. 'We'll help you pack. Pat wants you in the White House by ten o'clock this morning.'

'Pat!' Max echoed. He had been sold out.

The union officials, dragging suitcases from the closet, grinned.

Shortly, they were on their way across the flatlands of the Midwest by monorail. Moodily, Maximilian Fischer watched the country-side flash past; he said nothing to the officials flanking him, preferring to mull the matter over and over in his mind. What could he recall about the number one stand-by job? It began at eight A.M.—he recalled reading that. And there always were a lot of tourists flocking through the White House to catch a glimpse of Unicephalon 40-D, especially the school kids . . . and he disliked kids because they always jeered at him due to his weight. Cripes, he'd have a million of them filing by, because he had to be on the premises. By law, he had to be within a hundred yards of Uniceph-alon 40-D at all times, day and night, or was it fifty yards? Anyhow it practically was right on top, so if the homeostatic problem-solving system failed—*Maybe I better bone up on this,* he decided. *Take a TV educational course on government administration, just in case.*

To the union official on his right, Max asked, 'Listen, goodmem-ber, do I have any powers in this job you guys got me? I mean, can I—'

'It's a union job like every other union job,' the official answered wearily. 'You sit. You stand by. Have you been out of work that long, you don't remember?' He laughed, nudging his companion. 'Listen, Fischer here wants to know what authority the job entails.' Now both men laughed. 'I tell you what, Fischer,' the official drawled. 'When you're all set up there in the White House, when you got your chair and bed and made all your arrangements for meals and laundry and TV viewing time, why don't you amble over to Unicephalon 40-D and just sort of whine around there, you know, scratch and whine, until it notices you.'

'Lay off,' Max muttered.

'And then,' the official continued, 'you sort of say, Hey Unicephalon, listen. I'm your buddy. How about a little "I scratch your back, you scratch mine." You pass an ordinance for me–'

'But what can he do in exchange?' the other union official asked.

'Amuse it. He can tell it the story of his life, how he rose out of poverty and obscurity and educated himself by watching TV seven days a week until finally, guess what, he rose all the way to the top; he got the job–' The official snickered. 'Of stand-by President.'

Maximilian, flushing, said nothing; he stared woodenly out of the monorail window.

When they reached Washington, DC and the White House, Maximilian Fischer was shown a little room. It had belonged to Gus, and although the faded old motor magazines had been cleared out, a few prints remained tacked on the walls: a 1963 Volvo S-122, a 1957 Peugeot 403 and other antique classics of a bygone age. And, on a bookcase, Max saw a hand-carved plastic model of a 1950 Studebaker Starlight coupé, with each detail perfect.

'He was making that when he croaked,' one of the union officials said as he set down Max's suitcase. 'He could tell you any fact there is about those old preturbine cars–any useless bit of car knowledge.'

Max nodded.

'You got any idea what you're going to do?' the official asked him.

'Aw hell,' Max said. 'How could I decide so soon? Give me time.'

Moodily, he picked up the Studebaker Starlight coupé and examined its underside. The desire to smash the model car came to him; he put the car down, then, turning away.

'Make a rubber band ball,' the official said.

'What?' Max said.

'The stand-by before Gus. Louis somebody-or-other . . . he collected rubber bands, made a huge ball, big as a house, by the time he died. I forget his name, but the rubber band ball is at the Smithsonian now.'

There was a stir in the hallway. A White House receptionist, a middle-aged woman severely dressed, put her head in the room and said, 'Mr President, there's a TV news clown here to interview you. Please try to finish with him as quickly as possible because we have quite a few tours passing through the building today and some may want to look at you.'

'Okay,' Max said. He turned to face the TV news clown. It was Jim-Jam Briskin, he saw, the ranking clown just now. 'You want to see me?' he asked Briskin haltingly. 'I mean, you're sure it's *me* you want to interview?' He could not imagine what Briskin could find of interest about him. Holding out his hand he added, 'This is my room, but these model cars and pics aren't mine; they were Gus's. I can't tell you nuthin' about them.'

On Briskin's head the familiar flaming-red clown wig glowed, giving him in real life the same bizarre cast that the TV cameras picked up so well. He was older, however, than the TV image indicated, but he had the friendly, natural smile that everyone looked for: it was his badge of informality, a really nice guy, even-tempered but with a caustic wit when occasion demanded. Briskin was the sort of man who . . . *well*, Max thought, *the sort of fella you'd like to see marry into your family*.

They shook hands. Briskin said, 'You're on camera, Mr Max Fischer. Or rather, Mr President, I should say. This is Jim-Jam talking. For our literally billions of viewers located in every niche and corner of this far-flung solar system of ours, let me ask you this. How does it feel, sir, to know that if Unicephalon 40-D should fail, even momentarily, you would be catapulted into the most important post that has ever fallen onto the shoulders of a human being, that of actual, not merely stand-by, President of the United States? Does it worry you at night?' He smiled. Behind him the camera technicians swung their mobile lenses back and forth; lights burned Max's eyes and he felt the heat beginning to make him sweat under his arms and on his neck and upper lip. 'What emotions grip you at this instant?' Briskin asked. 'As you stand on the threshold of this new task for perhaps the balance of your life? What thoughts run through your mind, now that you're actually here in the White House?'

After a pause, Max said, 'It's—a big responsibility.' And then he realized, he saw, that Briskin was laughing at him, laughing silently as he stood there. Because it was all a gag Briskin was pulling. Out in the planets and moons his audience knew it, too; they knew Jim-Jam's humor.

'You're a large man, Mr Fischer,' Briskin said. 'If I may say so, a stout man. Do you get much exercise? I ask this because with your new job you pretty well will be confined to this room, and I wondered what change in your life this would bring about.'

'Well,' Max said, 'I feel of course that a Government employee should always be at his post. Yes, what you say is true; I have to be right here day and night, but that doesn't bother me. I'm prepared for it.'

'Tell me,' Jim Briskin said, 'do you—' And then he ceased. Turning to the video technicians behind him he said in an odd voice, 'We're off the air.'

A man wearing headphones squeezed forward past the cameras. 'On the monitor, listen.' He hurriedly handed the headphones to Briskin. 'We've been pre-empted by Unicephalon; it's broadcasting a news bulletin.'

Briskin held the phones to his ear. His face writhed and he said, 'Those ships at eight hundred AUs. They are hostile, it says.' He glanced up sharply at his technicians, the red clown's wig sliding askew. 'They've begun to attack.'

*

Within the following twenty-four hours the aliens had managed not only to penetrate the Sol System but also to knock out Unicephalon 40-D.

News of this reached Maximilian Fischer in an indirect manner as he sat in the White House cafeteria having his supper.

'Mr Maximilian Fischer?'

'Yeah,' Max said, glancing up at the group of Secret Servicemen who had surrounded his table.

'You're President of the United States.'

'Naw,' Max said. 'I'm the stand-by President; that's different.'

The Secret Serviceman said, 'Unicephalon 40-D is out of commission for perhaps as long as a month. So according to the amended Constitution, you're President and also Commander-in-Chief of the armed forces. We're here to guard you.' The Secret Serviceman grinned ludicrously. Max grinned back. 'Do you understand?' the Secret Serviceman asked. 'I mean, does it penetrate?'

'Sure,' Max said. Now he understood the buzz of conversation he had overheard while waiting in the cafeteria line with his tray. It explained why White House personnel had looked at him strangely. He set down his coffee cup, wiped his mouth with his napkin, slowly and deliberately, pretended to be absorbed in solemn thought. But actually his mind was empty.

'We've been told,' the Secret Serviceman said, 'that you're needed at once at the National Security Council bunker. They want your participation in finalization of strategy deliberations.'

They walked from the cafeteria to the elevator.

'Strategy policy,' Max said, as they descended. 'I got a few opinions about that. I guess it's time to deal harshly with these alien ships, don't you agree?'

The Secret Servicemen nodded.

'Yes, we got to show we're not afraid,' Max said. 'Sure, we'll get finalization; we'll blast the buggers.'

The Secret Servicemen laughed good-naturedly.

Pleased, Max nudged the leader of the group. 'I think we're pretty goddam strong; I mean, the USA has got teeth.'

'You tell 'em, Max,' one of the Secret Servicemen said, and they all laughed aloud. Max included.

As they stepped from the elevator they were stopped by a tall, well-dressed man who said urgently, 'Mr President, I'm Jonathan Kirk, White House press secretary; I think before you go in there to confer with the NSC people you should address the nation in this hour of gravest peril. The public wants to see what their new leader is like.' He held out a paper. 'Here's a statement drawn up by the Political Advisory Board; it codifies your—'

'Nuts,' Max said, handing it back without looking at it. 'I'm the President, not you. Kirk? Burke? Shirk? Never heard of you. Show me the microphone and I'll make my own speech. Or get me Pat Noble; maybe he's got some ideas.' And then he remembered that Pat had sold him out in the first place; Pat had gotten him into this. 'Not him either,' Max said. 'Just give me the microphone.'

'This is a time of crisis,' Kirk grated.

'Sure,' Max said, 'so leave me alone; you keep out of my way and I'll keep out of yours. Ain't that right?' He slapped Kirk good-naturedly on the back. 'And we'll both be better off.'

A group of people with portable TV cameras and lighting appeared, and among them Max saw Jim-Jam Briskin, in the middle, with his staff.

'Hey, Jim-Jam,' he yelled. 'Look, I'm President now!'

Stolidly, Jim Briskin came toward him.

'I'm not going to be winding no ball of string,' Max said. 'Or making model boats, nuthin' like that.' He shook hands warmly with Briskin. 'I thank you,' Max said. 'For your congratulations.'

'Congratulations,' Briskin said, then, in a low voice.

'Thanks,' Max said, squeezing the man's hand until the knuckles creaked. 'Of course, sooner or later they'll get that noise-box patched up and I'll just be stand-by again. But—' He grinned gleefully around at all of them; the corridor was full of people now, from TV to White House staff members to Army officers and Secret Servicemen.

Briskin said, 'You have a big task, Mr Fischer.'

'Yeah,' Max agreed.

Something in Briskin's eyes said: *And I wonder if you can handle it. I wonder if you're the man to hold such power*.

'Surely I can do it,' Max declared, into Briskin's microphone, for all the vast audience to hear.

'Possibly you can,' Jim Briskin said, and on his face was dubiousness.

'Hey, you don't like me any more,' Max said. 'How come?'

Briskin said nothing, but his eyes flickered.

'Listen,' Max said, 'I'm President now; I can close down your silly network—I can send FBI men in any time I want. For your information I'm firing the Attorney General right now, whatever his name is, and putting in a man I know, a man I can trust.'

Briskin said, 'I see.' And now he looked less dubious; conviction, of a sort which Max could not fathom, began to appear instead. 'Yes,' Jim Briskin said, 'you have the authority to order that, don't you? *If* you're really President . . .'

'Watch out,' Max said. 'You're nothing compared to me, Briskin, even if you do have that great big audience.' Then, turning his back on the cameras, he strode through the open door, into the NSC bunker.

Hours later, in the early morning, down in the National Security Council subsurface bunker, Maximilian Fischer listened sleepily to the TV set in the background as it yammered out the latest news. By now, intelligence sources had plotted the arrival of thirty more alien ships in the Sol System. It was believed that seventy in all had entered. Each was being continually tracked.

But that was not enough, Max knew. Sooner or later he would have to give the order to attack the alien ships. He hesitated. After all, who were they? Nobody at CIA knew. How strong were they? Not known either. And—would the attack be successful?

And then there were domestic problems. Unicephalon had continually tinkered with the economy, priming it when necessary, cutting taxes, lowering interest rates . . . that had ceased with the problem-solver's destruction. *Jeez*, Max thought dismally. *What do I know about unemployment? I mean, how can I tell what factories to reopen and where?*

He turned to General Tompkins, Chairman of the Joint Chiefs of Staff, who sat beside him examining a report on the scrambling of the tactical defensive ships protecting Earth. 'They got all them ships distributed right?' he asked Tompkins.

'Yes, Mr President,' General Tompkins answered.

Max winced. But the general did not seem to have spoken ironically; his tone had been respectful. 'Okay,' Max murmured. 'Glad to hear that. And you got all that missile cloud up so there're no leaks, like you let in that ship to blast Unicephalon. I don't want that to happen again.'

'We're under Defcon one,' General Tompkins said. 'Full war footing, as of six o'clock, our time.'

'How about those strategic ships?' That, he had learned, was the euphemism for their offensive strike-force.

'We can mount an attack at any time,' General Tompkins said, glancing down the long table to obtain the assenting nods of his co-workers. 'We can take care of each of the seventy invaders now within our system.'

With a groan, Max said, 'Anybody got any bicarb?' The whole business depressed him. *What a lot of work and sweat*, he thought. *All this goddam agitation—why don't the buggers just leave our system? I mean, do we have to get into a war? No telling what their home system will do in retaliation; you never can tell about unhuman life forms—they're unreliable.*

'That's what bothers me,' he said aloud. 'Retaliation.' He sighed.

General Tompkins said, 'Negotiation with them evidently is impossible.'

'Go ahead, then,' Max said. 'Go give it to them.' He looked about for the bicarb.

'I think you're making a wise choice,' General Tompkins said, and, across the table, the civilian advisors nodded in agreement.

'Here's an odd piece of news,' one of the advisors said to Max.

He held out a teletype dispatch. 'James Briskin has just filed a writ of *mandamus* against you in a Federal Court in California, claiming you're not legally President because you didn't run for office.'

'You mean because I didn't get *voted* in?' Max said. 'Just because of that?'

'Yes sir. Briskin is asking the Federal Courts to rule on this, and meanwhile he has announced his own candidacy.'

'WHAT?'

'Briskin claims not only that you must run for office and be voted in, but you must run against him. And with his popularity he evidently feels–'

'Aw nuts,' Max said in despair. 'How do you like that.'

No one answered.

'Well anyhow,' Max said, 'it's all decided; you military fellas go ahead and knock out those alien ships. And meanwhile–' He decided there and then. 'We'll put economic pressure on Jim-Jam's sponsors, that Reinlander Beer and Calbest Electronics, to get him not to run.'

The men at the long table nodded. Papers rattled as briefcases were put away; the meeting–temporarily–was at an end.

He's got an unfair advantage, Max said to himself. *How can I run when it's not equal, him a famous TV personality and me not? That's not right; I can't allow that.*

Jim-Jam can run, he decided, *but it won't do him any good. He's not going to beat me because he's not going to be alive that long.*

A week before the election, Telscan, the interplanetary public-opinion sampling agency, published its latest findings. Reading them, Maximilian Fischer felt more gloomy than ever.

'Look at this,' he said to his cousin Leon Lait, the lawyer whom he had recently made Attorney General. He tossed the report to him.

His own showing of course was negligible. In the election, Briskin would easily, and most definitely, win.

'Why is that?' Lait asked. Like Max, he was a large, paunchy man who for years now had held a stand-by job; he was not used to physical activity of any sort and his new position was proving difficult for him. However, out of family loyalty to Max, he remained. 'Is that because he's got all those TV stations?' he asked, sipping from his can of beer.

Max said cuttingly, 'Naw, it's because his navel glows in the dark. Of course it's because of his TV stations, you jerk—he's got them pounding away night and day, creatin' an *image*.' He paused, moodily. 'He's a clown. It's that red wig; it's fine for a newscaster, but not for a President.' Too morose to speak, he lapsed into silence.

And worse was to follow.

At nine P.M. that night, Jim-Jam Briskin began a seventy-two-hour marathon TV program over all his stations, a great final drive to bring his popularity over the top and ensure his victory.

In his special bedroom at the White House, Max Fischer sat with a tray of food before him, in bed, gloomily facing the TV set.

That Briskin, he thought furiously for the millionth time. 'Look,' he said to his cousin; the Attorney General sat in the easy chair across from him. 'There's the nerd now.' He pointed to the TV screen.

Leon Lait, munching on his cheeseburger, said, 'It's abominable.'

'You know where he's broadcasting from? Way out in deep space, out past Pluto. At their farthest-out transmitter, which your FBI guys will never in a million years manage to get to.'

'They will,' Leon assured him. 'I told them they *have* to get him—the President, my cousin, personally says so.'

'But they won't get him for a while,' Max said. 'Leon, you're just too damn slow. I'll tell you something. I got a ship of the line out there, the *Dwight D. Eisenhower*. It's all ready to lay an egg on them, you know, a big bang, just as soon as I pass on the word.'

'Right, Max.'

'And I hate to,' Max said.

The telecast had begun to pick up momentum already. Here came the Spotlights, and sauntering out onto the stage pretty Peggy Jones, wearing a glittery bare-shoulder gown, her hair radiant. *Now we get a top-flight striptease*, Max realized, *by a real fine-looking girl.* Even he sat up and took notice. Well, maybe not a true striptease, but certainly the opposition, Briskin and his staff, had sex working for them, here. Across the room his cousin the Attorney General had stopped munching his cheeseburger; the noise came to a halt, then picked up slowly once more.

On the screen, Peggy sang:

> *'It's Jim-Jam, for whom I am,*
> *America's best-loved guy.*
> *It's Jim-Jam, the best one that am,*
> *The candidate for you and I.'*

'Oh God,' Max groaned. And yet, the way she delivered it, with every part of her slim, long body . . . it was okay. 'I guess I got to inform the *Dwight D. Eisenhower* to go ahead,' he said, watching.

'If you say so, Max,' Leon said. 'I assure you, I'll rule that you acted legally; don't worry none about that.'

'Gimme the red phone,' Max said. 'That's the armored connection that only the Commander-in-Chief uses for top-secret instructions. Not bad, huh?' He accepted the phone from the Attorney General. 'I'm calling General Tompkins and he'll relay the order to the ship. Too bad, Briskin,' he added, with one last look at the screen. 'But it's your own fault; you didn't have to do what you did, opposing me and all.'

The girl in the silvery dress had gone, now, and Jim-Jam Briskin had appeared in her place. Momentarily, Max waited.

'Hi, beloved comrades,' Briskin said, raising his hands for silence; the canned applause—Max knew that no audience existed in that remote spot—lowered, then rose again. Briskin grinned amiably, waiting for it to die.

'It's a fake,' Max grunted. 'Fake audience. They're smart, him and his staff. His rating's already way up.'

'Right, Max,' the Attorney General agreed. 'I noticed that.'

'Comrades,' Jim Briskin was saying soberly on the TV screen, 'as you may know, originally President Maximilian Fischer and I got along very well.'

His hand on the red phone, Max thought to himself that what Jim-Jam said was true.

'Where we broke,' Briskin continued, 'was over the issue of force—of the use of naked, raw power. To Max Fischer, the office of President is merely a machine, an instrument, which he can use as an extension of his own desires, to fulfill his own needs. I honestly believe that in many respects his aims are good; he is trying to carry out Unicephalon's fine policies. But as to the means. That's a different matter.'

Max said, 'Listen to him, Leon.' And he thought, *No matter what he says I'm going to keep on; nobody is going to stand in my way, because it's my duty; it's the job of the office, and if you got to be President like I am you'd do it, too.*

'Even the President,' Briskin was saying, 'must obey the law; he doesn't stand outside it, however powerful he is.' He was silent for a moment and then he said slowly, 'I know that at this moment the FBI, under direct orders from Max Fischer's appointee, Leon Lait, is attempting to close down these stations, to still my voice. Here again Max Fischer is making use of power, of the police agency, for his own ends, making it an extension—'

Max picked up the red phone. At once a voice said from it, 'Yes, Mr President. This is General Tompkins' C of C.'

'What's that?' Max said.

'Chief of Communications, Army 600-1000, sir. Aboard the *Dwight D. Eisenhower*, accepting relay through the transmitter at the Pluto Station.'

'Oh yeah,' Max said, nodding. 'Listen, you fellas stand by, you understand? Be ready to receive instructions.' He put his hand over the mouthpiece of the phone. 'Leon,' he said to his cousin, who had now finished his cheeseburger and was starting on a strawberry shake. 'How can I do it? I mean, Briskin is telling the truth.'

Leon said, 'Give Tompkins the word.' He belched, then tapped himself on the chest with the side of his fist. 'Pardon me.'

On the screen Jim Briskin said, 'I think very possibly I'm risking my life to speak to you, because this we must face: we have a President who would not mind employing murder to obtain his objectives. This is the political tactic of a tyranny, and that's what we're seeing, a tyranny coming into existence in our society, replacing the rational, disinterested rule of the homeostatic problem-solving Unicephalon 40-D which was designed, built and put into operation by some of the finest minds we have ever seen, minds dedicated to the preservation of all that's worthy in our tradition. And the transformation from this to a one-man tyranny is melancholy, to say the least.'

Quietly, Max said, 'Now I can't go ahead.'

'Why not?' Leon said.

'Didn't you hear him? He's talking about *me*. I'm the tyrant he has reference to. Keerist.' Max hung up the red phone. 'I waited too long.

'It's hard for me to say it,' Max said, 'but—well, hell, it would prove he's right.' *I know he's right anyhow*, Max thought. *But do they know it? Does the public know it? I can't let them find out about me*, he realized. *They should look up to their President, respect him. Honor him. No wonder I show up so bad in the Telscan poll. No wonder Jim Briskin decided to run against me the moment he heard I was in office. They really do know about me; they sense it, sense that Jim-Jam is speaking the truth. I'm just not Presidential caliber.*

I'm not fit, he thought, *to hold this office.*

'Listen, Leon,' he said, 'I'm going to give it to that Briskin anyhow and then step down. It'll be my last official act.' Once more he picked up the red phone. 'I'm going to order them to wipe out Briskin and then someone else can be President. Anyone the people want. Even Pat Noble or you; I don't care.' He jiggled the phone. 'Hey, C of C,' he said loudly. 'Come on, answer.' To his cousin he said, 'Leave me some of that shake; it's actually half mine.'

'Sure, Max,' Leon said loyally.

'Isn't no one there?' Max said into the phone. He waited. The phone remained dead. 'Something's gone wrong,' he said to Leon. 'Communications have busted down. It must be those aliens again.'

And then he saw the TV screen. It was blank.

'What's happening?' Max said. 'What are they doing to me? Who's doing it?' He looked around, frightened. 'I don't get it.'

Leon stoically drank the milkshake, shrugging to show that he had no answer. But his beefy face had paled.

'It's too late,' Max said. 'For some reason it's just too late.' Slowly, he hung up the phone. 'I've got enemies, Leon, more powerful than you or me. And I don't even know who they are.' He sat in silence, before the dark, soundless TV screen. Waiting.

The speaker of the TV set said abruptly, 'Pseudo-autonomic news bulletin. Stand by, please.' Then again there was silence.

Jim Briskin, glancing at Ed Fineberg and Peggy, waited.

'Comrade citizens of the United States,' the flat, unmodulated voice from the TV speaker said, all at once. 'The interregnum is over, the situation has returned to normal.' As it spoke, words appeared on the monitor screen, a ribbon of printed tape passing slowly across, before the TV cameras in Washington, DC. Unicephalon 40-D had spliced itself into the co-ax in its usual fashion; it had pre-empted the program in progress: that was its traditional right.

The voice was the synthetic verbalizing-organ of the homeostatic structure itself.

'The election campaign is nullified,' Unicephalon 40-D said. 'That is item one. The stand-by President Maximilian Fischer is cancelled out; that is item two. Item three: we are at war with the aliens who have invaded our system. Item four. James Briskin, who has been speaking to you—'

This is it, Jim Briskin realized.

In his earphones the impersonal, plateau-like voice continued, 'Item four. James Briskin, who has been speaking to you on these facilities, is hereby ordered to cease and desist, and a writ of *mandamus* is issued forthwith requiring him to show just cause why he should be free to pursue any further political activity. In the public interest we instruct him to become politically silent.'

Grinning starkly at Peggy and Ed Fineberg, Briskin said, 'That's it. It's over. I'm to politically shut up.'

'You can fight it in the courts,' Peggy said at once. 'You can take it all the way up to the Supreme Court; they've set aside decisions of Unicephalon in the past.' She put her hand on his shoulder, but he moved away. 'Or do you want to fight it?'

'At least I'm not cancelled out,' Briskin said. He felt tired. 'I'm glad to see that machine back in operation,' he said, to reassure Peggy. 'It means a return to stability. *That* we can use.'

'What'll you do, Jim-Jam?' Ed asked. 'Go back to Reinlander Beer and Calbest Electronics and try to get your old job back?'

'No,' Briskin murmured. Certainly not that. But—he could not really become politically silent; he could not do what the problem-solver said. It simply was not biologically possible for him; sooner or later he would begin to talk again, for better or worse. *And*, he thought, *I'll bet Max can't do what it says either . . . neither of us can.*

Maybe, he thought, *I'll answer the writ of* mandamus; *maybe I'll contest it. A counter suit . . . I'll sue Unicephalon 40-D in a court of law. Jim-Jam Briskin the plaintiff, Unicephalon 40-D the defendant.* He smiled. *I'll need a good lawyer for that. Someone quite a bit better than Max Fischer's top legal mind, cousin Leon Lait.*

Going to the closet of the small studio in which they had been broadcasting, he got his coat and began to put it on. A long trip lay ahead of them back to Earth from this remote spot, and he wanted to get started.

Peggy, following after him, said, 'You're not going back on the air *at all*? Not even to finish the program?'

'No,' he said.

'But Unicephalon will be cutting back out again, and what'll that leave? Just dead air. That's not right, is it, Jim? Just to walk out like this . . . I can't believe you'd do it, it's not like you.'

He halted at the door of the studio. 'You heard what it said. The instructions it handed out to me.'

'Nobody leaves dead air going,' Peggy said. 'It's a vacuum, Jim, the thing nature abhors. *And if you don't fill it, someone else will.* Look,

Unicephalon is going back off right now.' She pointed at the TV monitor. The ribbon of words had ceased; once more the screen was dark, empty of motion and light. 'It's your responsibility,' Peggy said, 'and you know it.'

'Are we back on the air?' he asked Ed.

'Yes. It's definitely out of the circuit, at least for a while.' Ed gestured toward the vacant stage on which the TV cameras and lights focussed. He said nothing more; he did not have to.

With his coat still on, Jim Briskin walked that way. Hands in his pockets he stepped back into the range of the cameras, smiled and said, 'I think, beloved comrades, the interruption is over. For the time being, anyhow. So . . . let's continue.'

The noise of canned applause—manipulated by Ed Fineberg—swelled up, and Jim Briskin raised his hands and signalled the nonexistent studio audience for silence.

'Does any of you know a good lawyer?' Jim-Jam asked caustically. 'And if you do, phone us and tell us right away—before the FBI finally manages to reach us out here.'

In his bedroom at the White House, as Unicephalon's message ended, Maximilian Fischer turned to his cousin Leon and said, 'Well, I'm out of office.'

'Yeah, Max,' Leon said heavily. 'I guess you are.'

'And you, too,' Max pointed out. 'It's going to be a clean sweep; you can count on that. Cancelled.' He gritted his teeth. 'That's sort of insulting. It could have said *retired*.'

'I guess that's just its way of expressing itself,' Leon said. 'Don't get upset, Max; remember your heart trouble. You still got the job of stand-by, and that's the top stand-by position there is, Stand-by President of the United States, I want to remind you. And now you've got all this worry and effort off your back; you're lucky.'

'I wonder if I'm allowed to finish this meal,' Max said, picking at the food in the tray before him. His appetite, now that he was retired, began almost at once to improve; he selected a chicken salad sandwich and took a big bite from it. 'It's still mine,' he decided, his mouth full. 'I still get to live here and eat regularly—right?'

'Right,' Leon agreed, his legal mind active. 'That's in the contract the union signed with Congress; remember back to that? We didn't go out on strike for nothing.'

'Those were the days,' Max said. He finished the chicken salad sandwich and returned to the eggnog. It felt good not to have to make big decisions; he let out a long, heartfelt sigh and settled back into the pile of pillows propping him up.

But then he thought, *In some respects I sort of enjoyed making decisions. I mean, it was—*He searched for the thought. *It was different from being a stand-by or drawing unemployment. It had—*

Satisfaction, he thought. *That's what it gave me. Like I was accomplishing something.* He missed that already; he felt suddenly hollow, as if things had all at once become purposeless.

'Leon,' he said, 'I could have gone on as President another whole month. And enjoyed the job. You know what I mean?'

'Yeah, I guess I get your meaning,' Leon mumbled.

'No you don't,' Max said.

'I'm trying, Max,' his cousin said. 'Honest.'

With bitterness, Max said, 'I shouldn't have had them go ahead and let those engineer-fellas patch up that Unicephalon; I should have buried the project, at least for six months.'

'Too late to think about that now,' Leon said.

Is it? Max asked himself. *You know, something could* happen *to Unicephalon 40-D. An accident.*

He pondered that as he ate a piece of green-apple pie with a wide slice of longhorn cheese. A number of persons whom he knew could pull off such tasks . . . and did so, now and then.

A big, nearly-fatal accident, he thought. *Late some night, when everyone's asleep and it's just me and it awake here in the White House. I mean, let's face it; the aliens showed us how.*

'Look, Jim-Jam Briskin's back on the air,' Leon said, gesturing at the TV set. Sure enough, there was the famous, familiar red wig, and Briskin was saying something witty and yet profound, something that made one stop to ponder. 'Hey listen,' Leon said. 'He's poking fun at the FBI; can you imagine him doing that *now*? He's not scared of anything.'

'Don't bother me,' Max said. 'I'm thinking.' He reached over and carefully turned the sound of the TV set off.

For thoughts such as he was having he wanted no distractions.

WHAT'LL WE DO WITH RAGLAND PARK?

In his demesne near the logging town of John Day, Oregon, Sebastian Hada thoughtfully ate a grape as he watched the TV screen. The grapes, flown to Oregon by illegal jet transport, came from one of his farms in the Sonoma Valley of California. He spat the seeds into the fireplace across from him, half-listening to his CULTURE announcer delivering a lecture on the portrait busts of twentieth-century sculptors.

If only I could get Jim Briskin on my network, Hada thought gloomily. The ranking TV news clown, so popular, with his flaming scarlet wig and genial, informal patter... CULTURE needs that, Hada realized. But—

But their society, at the moment, was being run by the idiotic—but peculiarly able—President Maximilian Fischer, who had locked horns with Jim-Jam Briskin; who had, in fact, clapped the famous news clown in jail. So, as a result, Jim-Jam was available neither for the commercial network which linked the three habitable planets nor for CULTURE. And meanwhile, Max Fischer ruled on.

If I could get Jim-Jam out of prison, Hada thought, perhaps due to gratitude he'd move over to my network, leave his sponsors Reinlander Beer and Calbest Electronics; after all, they have not been able to free him despite their intricate court maneuvers. They don't have the power or the know-how ... *and I have.*

One of Hada's wives, Thelma, had entered the living room of the demesne and now stood watching the TV screen from behind him. 'Don't place yourself there, please,' Hada said. 'It gives me a panic reaction; I like to see people's faces.' He twisted around in his deep chair.

'The fox is back,' Thelma said. 'I saw him; he glared at me.' She laughed with delight. 'He looked so feral and independent—a bit like you, Seb. I wish I could have gotten a film clip of him.'

'I must spring Jim-Jam Briskin,' Hada said aloud; he had decided.

Picking up the phone, he dialed CULTURE's production chief, Nat Kaminsky, at the transmitting Earth satellite Culone.

'In exactly one hour,' Hada told his employee, 'I want all our outlets to begin crying for Jim-Jam Briskin's release from jail. He's not a traitor, as President Fischer declares. In fact, his political rights, his freedom of speech, have been taken away from him—illegally. Got it? Show clips of Briskin, build him up . . . you understand.' Hada hung up then, and dialed his attorney, Art Heaviside.

Thelma said, 'I'm going back outdoors and feed the animals.'

'Do that,' Hada said, lighting an Abdulla, a British-made Turkish cigarette which he was most fond of. 'Art?' he said into the phone. 'Get started on Jim-Jam Briskin's case; find a way to free him.'

His lawyer's voice came protestingly, 'But, Seb, if we mix into that, we'll have President Fischer after us with the FBI; it's too risky.'

Hada said, 'I need Briskin. CULTURE has become pompous—look at the screen right this minute. Education and art—we need a *personality*, a good news clown; we need Jim-Jam.' Telscan's surveys, of late, had shown an ominous dropping-off of viewers, but he did not tell Art Heaviside that; it was confidential.

Sighing, the attorney said, 'Will do, Seb. But the charge against Briskin is sedition in time of war.'

'Time of war? With whom?'

'Those alien ships—you know. That entered the Sol System last February. Darn it, Seb; you know we're at war—you can't be so lofty as to deny that; it's a legal fact.'

'In my opinion,' Hada said, 'the aliens are not hostile.' He put the receiver down, feeling angry. It's Max Fischer's way of holding onto supreme power, he said to himself. Thumping the war-scare drum. I ask you, What *actual* damage have the aliens done lately? After all, we don't own the Sol System. We just like to think we do.

In any case, CULTURE—educational TV itself—was withering, and as the owner of the network, Sebastian Hada had to act. Am I personally declining in vigor? he asked himself.

Once more picking up the phone, he dialed his analyst, Dr Ito Yasumi, at his demesne outside of Tokyo. I need help, he said to himself. CULTURE's creator and financial backer needs help. And Dr Yasumi can give it to me.

Facing him from across his desk, Dr Yasumi said, 'Hada, maybe problem stems from you having eight wives. That's about five too many.' He waved Hada back to the couch. 'Be calm, Hada. Pretty sad that big-time operator like Mr S. Hada falling apart under stress. You afraid President Fischer's FBI get you like they got Jim Briskin?' He smiled.

'No,' Hada said, 'I'm fearless.' He lay semisupine, arms behind his head, gazing at a Paul Klee print on the wall . . . or perhaps it was an original; good analysts did make a god-awful amount of money: Yasumi's charge to him was one thousand dollars a half hour.

Yasumi said contemplatively, 'Maybe you should seize power, Hada, in bold coup against Max Fischer. Make successful power play of your own; become President and then release Mr Jim-Jam— no problem then.'

'Fischer has the Armed Forces behind him,' Hada said gloomily. 'As Commander-in-Chief. Because of General Tompkins, who likes Fischer, they're absolutely loyal.' He had already thought of this. 'Maybe I ought to flee to my demesne on Callisto,' he murmured. It was a superb one, and Fischer, after all, had no authority there; it was not US but Dutch territory. 'Anyhow, I don't want to fight; I'm not a fighter, a street brawler; I'm a cultured man.'

'You are biophysical organism with built-in responses; you are alive. All that lives strives to survive. You will fight if necessary, Hada.'

Looking at his watch, Hada said, 'I have to go, Ito. At three I've an appointment in Havana to interview a new folksinger, a ballad-and-banjo man who's sweeping Latin America. Ragland Park is his name; he can bring life back into CULTURE.'

'I know of him,' Ito Yasumi said. 'Saw him on commercial TV; very good performer. Part Southern US, part Dane, very young, with huge black mustache and blue eyes. Magnetic, this Rags, as is called.'

'But is folksinging cultural?' Hada murmured.

'I tell you something,' Dr Yasumi said. 'There strangeness about Rags Park; I noted even over TV. Not like other people.'

'That's why he's such a sensation.'

'More than that. I diagnose.' Yasumi reflected. 'You know, mental illness and psionic powers closely related, as in poltergeist effect. Many schizophrenics of paranoid variety are telepaths, picking up hate thoughts in subconscious of persons around them.'

'I know,' Hada sighed, thinking that this was costing him hundreds of dollars, this spouting of psychiatric theory.

'Go careful with Rags Park,' Dr Yasumi cautioned. 'You volatile type, Hada; jump too quick. First, idea of springing Jim-Jam Briskin—risking FBI wrath—and now this Rags Park. You like hat designer or human flea. Best bet, as I say, is to openly face President Fischer, not deviousness as I foresee you doing.'

'Devious?' Hada murmured. 'I'm not devious.'

'You most devious patient I got,' Dr Yasumi told him bluntly. 'You got nothing but tricky bones in your body, Hada. Watch out or you scheme yourself out of existence.' He nodded with great soberness.

'I'll go carefully,' Hada said, his mind on Rags Park; he barely heard what Dr Yasumi was telling him.

'A favor,' Dr Yasumi said. 'When you can arrange, let me examine Mr Park; I would enjoy, okay? For your good, Hada, as well as professional interest. Psi talent may be of new kind; one never knows.'

'Okay,' Hada agreed. 'I'll give you a call.' But, he thought, I'm not going to pay for it; your examination of Rags Park will be on your own time.

*

There was an opportunity before his appointment with the ballad singer Rags Park to drop by the federal prison in New York at which Jim-Jam Briskin was being held on the sedition in time of war charge.

Hada had never met the news clown face-to-face, and he was surprised to discover how much older the man looked than on the TV. But perhaps Briskin's arrest, his troubles with President Fischer, had temporarily overwhelmed him. It would be enough to overwhelm anyone, Hada reflected as the deputy unlocked the cell and admitted him.

'How did you happen to tangle with President Fischer?' Hada asked.

The news clown shrugged and said, 'You lived through that period in history as much as I did.' He lit a cigarette and stared woodenly past Hada.

He was referring, Hada realized, to the demise of the great problem-solving computer at Washington, DC, Unicephalon 40-D; it had ruled as President of the United States and Commander-in-Chief of the Armed Forces until a missile, delivered by the alien ships, had put it out of action. During that period, the standby President, Max Fischer, had taken power, a clod appointed by the union, a primitive man with an unnatural bucolic cunning. When at last Unicephalon 40-D had been repaired and had resumed functioning, it had ordered Fischer to depart his office and Jim Briskin to cease political activity. Neither man had complied. Briskin had gone on campaigning against Max Fischer, and Fischer had managed, by some method still unknown, to disable the computer, thereby again becoming President of the United States.

And his initial act had been to clap Jim-Jam in jail.

'Has Art Heaviside, my attorney, seen you?' Hada asked.

'No,' Briskin said shortly.

'Listen, my friend,' Hada said, 'without my help you'll be in prison forever, or at least until Max Fischer dies. This time he isn't making the mistake of allowing Unicephalon 40-D to be repaired; it's out of action for good.'

Briskin said, 'And you want me on your network in exchange for getting me out of here.' He smoked rapidly at his cigarette.

'I need you, Jim-Jam,' Hada said. 'It took courage for you to expose President Fischer for the power-hungry buffoon he is; we've got a terrible menace hanging over us in Max Fischer, and if we don't join together and work fast it'll be too late; we'll both be dead. You know—in fact you said it on TV—that Fischer would gladly stoop to assassination to get what he wants.'

Briskin said, 'Can I say what I want over your facilities?'

'I give you absolute freedom. Attack anyone you want, including me.'

After a pause, Briskin said, 'I'd take your offer, Hada . . . but I doubt if even Art Heaviside can get me out of here. Leon Lait, Fischer's Attorney General, is conducting the prosecution against me personally.'

'Don't resign yourself,' Hada said. 'Billions of your viewers are waiting to see you emerge from this cell. At this moment all my outlets are clamoring for your release. Public pressure is building up. Even Max will have to listen to that.'

'What I'm afraid of is that an "accident" will happen to me,' Briskin said. 'Just like the "accident" that befell Unicephalon 40-D a week after it resumed functioning. If it couldn't save itself, how can—'

'*You* afraid?' Hada inquired, incredulous. 'Jim-Jam Briskin, the ranking news clown—I don't believe it.'

There was silence.

Briskin said, 'The reason my sponsors, Reinlander Beer and Calbest Electronics, haven't been able to get me out is'—he paused—'pressure put on them by President Fischer. Their attorneys as much as admitted that to me. When Fischer learns you're trying to help me, he'll bring all the pressure he has to bear directly on you.' He glanced up acutely at Hada. 'Do you have the stamina to endure it? I wonder.'

'Certainly I have,' Hada said. 'As I told Dr Yasumi—'

'And he'll put pressure on your wives,' Jim-Jam Briskin said.

'I'll divorce all eight of them,' Hada said hotly.

Briskin held out his hand and they shook. 'It's a deal then,' Jim-Jam said. 'I'll go to work for CULTURE as soon as I'm out of here.' He smiled in a weary but hopeful way.

Elated, Hada said, 'Have you ever heard of Rags Park, the folk and ballad singer? At three today I'm signing him, too.'

'There's a TV set here and now and then I catch one of Park's numbers,' Briskin said. 'He sounds good. But do you want that on CULTURE? It's hardly educational.'

'CULTURE is changing. We're going to sugarcoat our didacticisms from now on. We've been losing our audience. I don't intend to see CULTURE wither away. The very concept of it—'

The word 'CULTURE' stood for Committee Utilizing Learning Techniques for Urban Renewal Efforts. A major part of Hada's real estate holdings consisted of the city of Portland, Oregon, which he had acquired—intact—ten years ago. It was not worth much; typical of the semiabandoned slum constellations which had become not only repellent but obsolete, Portland had a certain sentimental value to him because he had been born there.

However, one notion lingered in his mind. If for any reason the colonies on the other planets and moons had to be abandoned, if the settlers came streaming back to Earth, the cities would be repopulated once more. And with the alien ships flitting about the farther planets, this was not as implausible as it sounded. In fact, a few families had emigrated back to Earth already . . .

So, underneath, CULTURE was not quite the disinterested public service nonprofit agency that it appeared. Mixed in with the education, Hada's outlets drummed away at the seductive idea of *the city*, how much it could offer, how little there was to be had in the colonies. Give up the difficult, crude life of the frontier, CULTURE declared night and day. Return to your own planet; repair the decaying cities. They're your real home.

Did Briskin know this? Hada wondered. Did the news clown understand the actual purpose of his organization?

Hada would find that out—if and when he managed to get Briskin out of jail and before a CULTURE microphone.

*

At three o'clock Sebastian Hada met the folksinger Ragland Park at the Havana office of CULTURE.

'I'm glad to make your acquaintance,' Rags Park said shyly. Tall, skinny, with his huge black mustache hiding most of his mouth, he shuffled about self-consciously, his blue eyes gentle with authentic friendliness. He had an unusual sweetness about him, Hada noted. Almost a saintly quality. Hada found himself impressed.

'And you play both the guitar and five-string banjo?' Hada said. 'Not at once, of course.'

Rags Park mumbled, 'No, sir. I alternate. Want me to play something right now for you?'

'Where were you born?' Nat Kaminsky asked. Hada had brought his production chief along; in matters such as this, Kaminsky's opinion was valuable.

'In Arkansas,' Rags answered. 'My family raises hogs.' He had his banjo with him and now, nervously, he twanged a few notes. 'I know a real sad song that'll break your heart. It's called "Poor Old Hoss." Want me to sing it for you?'

'We've heard you,' Hada said. 'We know you're good.' He tried to imagine this awkward young man twanging away over CULTURE in between lectures on twentieth-century portrait sculptors. Hard to imagine . . .

Rags said, 'I bet there's one thing you don't know about me, Mr Hada. I make up a lot of my own ballads.'

'Creative,' Kaminsky said to Hada straight-faced. 'That's good.'

'For instance,' Rags continued, 'I once made up a ballad about a man named Tom McPhail who ran ten miles with a bucket of water to put out the fire in his little daughter's crib.'

'Did he make it?' Hada asked.

'Sure did. Just in time. Tom McPhail ran faster and faster with that bucket of water.' Chanting, Rags twanged in accompaniment.

'Here comes Tom McPhail
Holdin' on tight to that great little pail.

Holdin' on tight, boys, here he come.
Heart full of fear, faculties numb.'

Twang, twang, sounded the banjo, mournfully and urgently.

Kaminsky said acutely, 'I've been following your shows and I've never heard you sing that number.'

'Aw,' Rags said, 'I had bad luck with that, Mr Kaminsky. Turned out there really is a Tom McPhail. Lives in Pocatello, Idaho. I sang about ol' Tom McPhail on my January fourteenth TV show and right away he got sore—he was listenin'—and got a lawyer to write me.'

'Wasn't it just a coincidence in names?' Hada said.

'Well,' Rags said, twisting about self-consciously, 'it seems there really had been a fire in his home there in Pocatello, and McPhail, he got panicky and ran with a bucket to the creek, and it was ten miles off, like I said in the song.'

'Did he get back with the water in time?'

'Amazingly, he did,' Rags said.

Kaminsky said to Hada, 'It would be better, on CULTURE, if this man stuck to authentic Old English ballads such as "Greensleeves." That would seem more what we want.'

Thoughtfully, Hada said to Rags, 'Bad luck to pick a name for a ballad and have it turn out that such a man really exists . . . Have you had that sort of bad luck since?'

'Yes, I have,' Rags admitted. 'I made up a ballad last week . . . it was about a lady, Miss Marsha Dobbs. Listen.

'All day, all night, Marsha Dobbs.
Loves a married man whose wife she robs.
Robs that wife and hearth of Jack Cooks's heart.
Steals the husband, makes that marriage fall apart.

'That's the first verse,' Rags explained. 'It goes on for seventeen verses; tells how Marsha comes to work at Jack Cooks's office as a secretary, goes to lunch with him, then later they meet late at–'

'Is there a moral at the end?' Kaminsky inquired.

'Oh sure,' Rags said. 'Don't take no one else's man because if you do, heaven avenges the dishonored wife. In this case:

'*Virus flu lay 'round the corner just for Jack.*
For Marsha Dobbs 'twas to be worse, a heart attack.
Miz Cooks, the hand of heaven sought to spare.
Surrounded her, became a garment strong to wear.
Miz Cooks—'

Hada broke in over the twanging and singing. 'That's fine, Rags. That's enough.' He glanced at Kaminsky and winced.

'And I bet it turned out,' Kaminsky said, 'that there's a real Marsha Dobbs who had an affair with her boss, Jack Cooks.'

'Right,' Rags said, nodding. 'No lawyer called me, but I read it in the homeopape, the New York *Times*. Marsha, she died of a heart attack, and it was actually during—' He hesitated modestly. 'You know. While she and Jack Cooks were at a motel satellite, love-making.'

'Have you deleted that number from your repertoire?' Kaminsky asked.

'Well,' Rags said, 'I can't make up my mind. Nobody's suing me . . . and I like the ballad. I think I'll leave it in.'

To himself, Hada thought, What was it Dr Yasumi said? That he scented psi powers of some unusual kind in Ragland Park . . . perhaps it's the parapsychological power of having the bad luck to make up ballads about people who really exist. Not much of a talent, that.

On the other hand, he realized, it could be a variant on the tele-pathic talent . . . and with a little tinkering it might be *quite* valuable.

'How long does it take you to make up a ballad?' he asked Rags.

'I can do it on the spot,' Rags Park answered. 'I could do it now; give me a theme and I'll compose right here in this office of yours.'

Hada pondered and then said, 'My wife Thelma has been feed-ing a gray fox that I know—or I believe—killed and ate our best Rouen duck.'

After a moment of considering, Rags Park twanged:

> 'Miz Thelma Hada talked to the fox.
> Built it a home from an old pine box.
> Sebastian Hada heard a sad cluck:
> Wicked gray fox had eaten his duck.'

'But ducks don't cluck, they quack,' Nat Kaminsky said critically.

'That's a fact,' Rags admitted. He pondered and then sang:

> 'Hada's production chief changed my luck.
> I got no job, and ducks don't cluck.'

Grinning, Kaminsky said, 'Okay, Rags; you win.' To Hada he said, 'I advise you to hire him.'

'Let me ask you this,' Hada said to Rags. 'Do *you* think the fox got my Rouen?'

'Gosh,' Rags said, 'I don't know anything about that.'

'But in your ballad you said so,' Hada pointed out.

'Let me think,' Rags said. Presently he twanged once more and said:

> 'Interesting problem Hada's stated.
> Perhaps my ability's underrated.
> Perhaps I'm not no ordinary guy.
> Do I get my ballads through the use of psi?'

'How did you know I meant psi?' Hada asked. 'You can read interior thoughts, can't you? Yasumi was right.'

Rags said, 'Mister, I'm just singing and twanging; I'm just an entertainer, same as Jim-Jam Briskin, that news clown President Fischer clapped in jail.'

'Are you afraid of jail?' Hada asked him bluntly.

'President Fischer doesn't have nothing against me,' Rags said. 'I don't do political ballads.'

'If you work for me,' Hada said, 'maybe you will. I'm trying to get Jim-Jam out of jail; today all my outlets began their campaign.'

'Yes, he ought to be out,' Rags agreed, nodding. 'That was a bad thing, President Fischer using the FBI for that . . . those aliens aren't that much of a menace.'

Kaminsky, rubbing his chin meditatively, said, 'Do one on Jim-Jam Briskin, Max Fischer, the aliens—on the whole political situation. Sum it up.'

'That's asking a lot,' Rags said, with a wry smile.

'Try,' Kaminsky said. 'See how well you can epitomize.'

'Whooee,' Rags said. '"Epitomize." Now I know I'm talking to CULTURE. Okay, Mr Kaminsky. How's this?' He said:

> *'Fat little President by name of Max*
> *Used his power, gave Jim the ax.*
> *Sebastian Hada's got eyes like a vulture.*
> *Sees his opening, steps in with* CULTURE.'

'You're hired,' Hada said to the folksinger, and reached into his pocket for a contract form.

Kaminsky said, 'Will we be successful, Mr Park? Tell us about the outcome.'

'I'd, uh, rather not,' Rags said. 'At least not this minute. You think I can also read the future, too? That I'm a precog as well as a telepath?' He laughed gently. 'I've got plenty of talent, according to you; I'm flattered.' He bowed mockingly.

'I'll assume that you're coming to work for us,' Hada said. 'And your willingness to be an employee of CULTURE—is it a sign that you feel President Fischer is not going to be able to get us?'

'Oh, we could be in jail, too, along with Jim-Jam,' Rags murmured. 'That wouldn't surprise me.' Seating himself, his banjo in hand, he prepared to sign the contract.

In his bedroom at the White House, President Max Fischer had listened for almost an hour now to the TV set, to CULTURE hammering away on the same topic, again and again. *Jim Briskin must be released*, the voice said; it was a smooth, professional announcer's voice, but behind it, unheard, Max knew, was Sebastian Hada.

'Attorney General,' Max said to his cousin Leon Lait, 'get me dossiers on all of Hada's wives, all seven or eight, whatever it is. I guess I got to take a drastic course.'

When, later in the day, the eight dossiers had been put before him, he began to read carefully, chewing on his El Producto alta cigar and frowning, his lips moving with the effort of comprehending the intricate, detailed material.

Jeez, what a mess some of these dames must be, he realized. Ought to be getting chemical psychotherapy, have their brain metabolisms straightened out. But he was not displeased; it had been his hunch that a man like Sebastian Hada would attract an unstable sort of woman.

One in particular, Hada's fourth wife, interested him. Zoe Martin Hada, thirty-one years old, now living on Io with her ten-year-old son.

Zoe Hada had definite psychotic traits.

'Attorney General,' he said to his cousin, 'this dame is living on a pension supplied by the US Department of Mental Health. Hada isn't contributing a dime to her support. You get her here to the White House, you understand? I got a job for her.'

The following morning Zoe Martin Hada was brought to his office.

He saw, between the two FBI men, a scrawny woman, attractive, but with wild, animosity-filled eyes. 'Hello, Mrs Zoe Hada,' Max said. 'Listen, I know sumpthin' about you; you're the only genuine Mrs Hada—the others are imposters, right? And Sebastian's done you dirt.' He waited, and saw the expression on her face change.

'Yes,' Zoe said. 'I've been in courts for six years trying to prove what you just said. I can hardly believe it; are you really going to help me?'

'Sure,' Max said. 'But you got to do it my way; I mean, if you're waiting for that skunk Hada to change, you're wasting your time. About all you can do'—he paused—'is even up the score.'

The violence which had left her face crept back as she understood, gradually, what he meant.

Frowning, Dr Ito Yasumi said, 'I have now made my examination, Hada.' He began putting away his battery of cards. 'This Rags Park is neither telepath nor precog; he neither reads my mind nor cognates what is to be and, frankly, Hada, although I still sense psi power about him, I have no idea what it might be.'

Hada listened in silence. Now Rags Park, this time with a guitar over his shoulder, wandered in from the other room. It seemed to amuse him that Dr Yasumi could make nothing of him; he grinned at both of them and then seated himself. 'I'm a puzzle,' he said to Hada. 'Either you got too much when you hired me or not enough ... but you don't know which and neither does Dr Yasumi or me.'

'I want you to start at once over CULTURE,' Hada told him impatiently. 'Make up and sing folk ballads that depict the unfair imprisonment and harassment of Jim-Jam Briskin by Leon Lait and his FBI. Make Lait appear a monster; make Fischer appear a scheming, greedy boob. Understand?'

'Sure,' Rags Park said, nodding. 'We got to get public opinion aroused. I knew that when I signed; I ain't just entertaining no more.'

Dr Yasumi said to Rags, 'Listen, I have favor to ask. Make up folk-style ballad telling how Jim-Jam Briskin *get out of jail*.'

Both Hada and Rags Park glanced at him.

'Not about what is,' Yasumi explained, 'but about that which we want to be.'

Shrugging, Park said, 'Okay.'

The door to Hada's office burst open and the chief of his bodyguards, Dieter Saxton, put his head excitedly in. 'Mr Hada, we just gunned down a woman who was trying to get through to you with a homemade bomb. Do you have a moment to identify her? We think maybe it's—I mean it was—one of your wives.'

'God in heaven,' Hada said, and hurried along with Saxton from the office and down the corridor.

There on the floor, near the front entrance of the demesne, lay a woman he knew. Zoe, he thought. He knelt down, touched her.

'Sorry,' Saxton mumbled. 'We had to, Mr Hada.'

'All right,' he said. 'I believe you if you say so.' He greatly trusted Saxton; after all, he had to.

Saxton said, 'I think from now on you better have one of us close by you at all times. I don't mean outside your office; I mean within physical touch.'

'I wonder if Max Fischer sent her here,' Hada said.

'The chances are good,' Saxton said. 'I'd make book on it.'

'Just because I'm trying to get Jim-Jam Briskin released.' Hada was thoroughly shaken. 'It really amazes me.' He rose to his feet unsteadily.

'Let me go after Fischer,' Saxton urged in a low voice. 'For your protection. He has no right to be President; Unicephalon 40-D is our only legal President and we all know Fischer put it out of commission.'

'No,' Hada murmured. 'I don't like murder.'

'It's not murder,' Saxton said. 'It's protection for you and your wives and children.'

'Maybe so,' Hada said, 'but I still can't do it. At least not yet.' He left Saxton and made his way with difficulty back to his office, where Rags Park and Dr Yasumi waited.

'We heard,' Yasumi said to him. 'Bear up, Hada. The woman was a paranoid schizophrenic with delusions of persecution; without psychotherapy it was inevitable that she would meet a violent death. Do not blame yourself or Mr Saxton.'

Hada said, 'And at one time I loved that woman.'

Dolefully strumming on his guitar, Rags Park sang to himself; the words were not audible. Perhaps he was practicing his ballad of Jim Briskin's escape from jail.

'Take Mr Saxton's advice,' Dr Yasumi said. 'Protect yourself at all times.' He patted Hada on the shoulder.

Rags spoke up, 'Mr Hada, I think I've got my ballad now. About–'

'I don't want to hear it,' Hada said harshly. 'Not now.' He wished the two of them would leave; he wanted to be by himself.

Maybe I should fight back, he thought. Dr Yasumi recommends it; now Dieter Saxton recommends it. What would Jim-Jam recommend? He has a sound mind . . . he would say, Don't employ murder. I know that would be his answer; I know him.

And if he says not to, I won't.

Dr Yasumi was instructing Rags Park, 'A ballad, please, about that vase of gladioli over there on the bookcase. Tell how it rise up straight in the air and hover; all right?'

'What kind of ballad is that?' Rags said. 'Anyhow, I got my work cut out for me; you heard what Mr Hada said.'

'But I'm still testing you,' Dr Yasumi grumbled.

To his cousin the Attorney General, Max Fischer said disgustedly, 'Well, we didn't get him.'

'No, Max,' Leon Lait agreed. 'He's got good men in his employ; he's not an individual like Briskin, he's a whole corporation.'

Moodily, Max said, 'I read a book once that said if three people are competing, eventually two of them will join together and gang up on the third one. It's inevitable. That's exactly what's happened; Hada and Briskin are buddies, and I'm alone. We have to split them apart, Leon, and get one of them on our side against the other. Once Briskin liked me. Only he disapproved of my methods.'

Leon said, 'Wait'll he hears about Zoe Hada trying to kill her ex-husband; then Briskin'll really disapprove of you.'

'You think it's impossible to win him over now?'

'I sure do, Max. You're in a worse position than ever, regarding him. Forget about winning him over.'

'There's some idea in my mind, though,' Max said. 'I can't quite make out what it is yet, but it has to do with freeing Jim-Jam in the hopes that he'll feel gratitude.'

'You're out of your mind,' Leon said. 'How come you ever thought of an idea like that? It isn't like you.'

'I don't know,' Max groaned. 'But there it is.'

*

To Sebastian Hada, Rags Park said, 'Uh, I think maybe I got me a ballad now, Mr Hada. Like Dr Yasumi suggested. It has to do with telling how Jim-Jam Briskin gets out of jail. You want to hear it?'

Dully, Hada nodded. 'Go ahead.' After all, he was paying the folksinger; he might as well get something for his money.

Twanging away, Rags sang:

> 'Jim-Jam Briskin languished in jail,
> Couldn't find no one to put up his bail.
> Blame Max Fischer! Blame Max Fischer!'

Rags explained, 'That's the chorus, "Blame Max Fischer!" Okay?' 'All right,' Hada said, nodding.

> 'The Lord came along, said, Max, I'm mad.
> Casting that man in jail, that was bad.
> Blame Max Fischer! the good Lord cried.
> Poor Jim Briskin, his rights denied.
> Blame Max Fischer! I'm here to tell;
> Good Lord say, Him go straight to hell.
> Repent, Max Fischer! There's only one route:
> Get on my good side; let Jim-Jam out.'

Rags explained to Hada, 'Now here's what's going to happen.' He cleared his throat:

> 'Bad Max Fischer, he saw the light,
> Told Leon Lait, We got to do right.
> Sent a message down to turn that key,
> Open that door and let Jim-Jam free.
> Old Jim Briskin saw an end to his plight;
> Jail door open now, lets in the light.

'That's all,' Rags informed Hada. 'It's a sort of holler type of folk song, a spiritual where you tap your foot. Do you like it?'

Hada managed to nod. 'Oh sure. Anything's fine.'

'Shall I tell Mr Kaminsky you want me to air it over CULTURE?'

'Air away,' Hada said. He did not care; the death of Zoe still weighed on his mind—he felt responsible, because after all it had been his bodyguards who had done it, and the fact that Zoe had been insane, had been trying to destroy him, did not seem to matter. It was still a human life; it was still murder. 'Listen,' he said to Rags on impulse, 'I want you to make up another song, now.'

With sympathy, Rags said, 'I know, Mr Hada. A ballad about the sad death of your former wife Zoe. I been thinking about that and I have a ballad all ready. Listen:

> 'There once was a lady fair to see and hear;
> Wander, spirit, over field and star,
> Sorrowful, but forgiving from afar.
> That spirit knows who did her in.
> It was a stranger, not her kin.
> It was Max Fischer who knew her not—'

Hada interrupted, 'Don't whitewash me, Rags; I'm to blame. Don't put everything on Max as if he's a whipping boy.'

Seated in the corner of the office, listening quietly, Dr Yasumi now spoke up. 'And also too much credit to President Fischer in your ballads, Rags. In ballad of Jim-Jam's release from jail, you specifically give credit to Max Fischer for ethical change of heart. This will not do. The credit for Jim-Jam's release must go to Hada. Listen, Rags; I have composed a poem for this occasion.'

Dr Yasumi chanted:

> 'News clown nestles not in jail. A friend,
> Sebastian Hada, got him free.
> He loves that friend, regards him well.
> Knows whom to honor, and to seek.

'Exactly thirty-two syllables,' Dr Yasumi explained modestly. 'Old-style Japanese-type haiku poetry does not have to rhyme as do US-English ballads, however must get right to the point, which in this matter is all-important.' To Rags he said, 'You make my haiku into ballad, okay? In your typical fashion, in rhythmic, rhyming couplets, et cetera, and so on.'

'I counted thirty-three syllables,' Rags said. 'Anyhow, I'm a creative artist; I'm not used to being told what to compose.' He turned to Hada. 'Who'm I working for, you or him? Not him, as far as I know.'

'Do as he says,' Hada told Rags. 'He's a brilliant man.'

Sullenly, Rags murmured, 'Okay, but I didn't expect this sort of job when I signed the contract.' He retired to a far corner of the office to brood, think, and compose.

'What are you involved with, here, Doctor?' Hada asked.

'We'll see,' Dr Yasumi said mysteriously. 'Theory about psi power of this balladeer, here. May pay off, may not.'

'You seem to feel that the exact wording of Rags's ballads is very important,' Hada said.

'That's right,' Dr Yasumi agreed. 'As in legal document. You wait, Hada; you find out—if I right—eventually. If I wrong, doesn't matter anyhow.' He smiled encouragingly at Hada.

The phone in President Max Fischer's office rang. It was the Attorney General, his cousin, calling in agitation. 'Max, I went over to the federal pen where Jim-Jam is, to see about quashing the charges against him like you were talking about—' Leon hesitated. 'He's gone, Max. He's not in there anymore.' Leon sounded wildly nervous.

'How'd he get out?' Max said, more baffled than angry.

'Art Heaviside, Hada's attorney, found a way; I don't know yet what it is—I have to see Circuit Court Judge Dale Winthrop about it; he signed the release order an hour or so ago. I have an appointment with Winthrop . . . as soon as I've seen him, I'll call you back.'

'I'll be darned,' Max said slowly. 'Well, we were too late.' He hung up the phone reflexively and then stood deep in thought. *What has Hada got going for him?* he asked himself. Something I don't understand.

And now the thing to watch for, he realized, is Jim Briskin showing up on TV. On CULTURE's network.

With relief he saw on the screen—not Jim Briskin but a folksinger plucking away on a banjo.

And then he realized that the folksinger was singing about *him*.

> *'Bad Max Fischer, he saw the light,*
> *Told Leon Lait, We got to do right.*
> *Sent a message down to turn that key.'*

Listening, Max Fischer said aloud, 'My God, that's exactly what happened! That's exactly what I did!' Eerie, he thought. What's it mean, this ballad singer on CULTURE who sings about what I'm doing—secret matters that he couldn't possibly know about!

Telepathic maybe, Max thought. That must be it.

Now the folksinger was narrating and plucking about Sebastian Hada, how Hada had been personally responsible for getting Jim-Jam Briskin out of jail. And it's true, Max said to himself. When Leon Lait got there to the federal pen, he found Briskin gone because of Art Heaviside's activity ... I better listen pretty carefully to this singer, because for some reason he seems to know more than I do.

But the singer now had finished.

The CULTURE announcer was saying, 'That was a brief interlude of political ballads by the world-renowned Ragland Park. Mr Park, you'll be pleased to hear, will appear on this channel every hour for five minutes of new ballads, composed here in CULTURE's studios for the occasion. Mr Park will be watching the teletypers and will compose his ballads to—'

Max switched the set off then.

Like calypso, Max realized. New ballads. God, he thought dismally. Suppose Park sings about Unicephalon 40-D coming back.

I have a feeling, he thought, *that what Ragland Park sings turns out to be true*. It's one of those psionic talents.

And they, the opposition, are making use of this.

On the other hand, he thought, I might have a few psionic talents of my own. Because if I didn't, *I wouldn't have gotten as far as I have*.

Seated before the TV set, he switched it on once again and waited, chewing his lower lip and pondering what he should do. As yet he could come up with nothing. But I will, sooner or later, he said to himself. And before they come up with the idea of bringing Unicephalon 40-D back . . .

Dr Yasumi said, 'I have solved what Ragland Park's psi talent is, Hada. You care to know?'

'I'm more interested in the fact that Jim-Jam is out of jail,' Hada answered. He put down the receiver of the telephone, almost unable to believe the news. 'He'll be here right away,' he said to Dr Yasumi. 'He's on his way direct, by monorail. We'll see that he gets to Callisto, where Max has no jurisdiction, so they can't possibly rearrest him.' His mind swirled with plans. Rubbing his hands together, he said rapidly, 'Jim-Jam can broadcast from our transmitter on Callisto. And he can live at my demesne there—that'll be beer and skittles for him—I know he'll agree.'

'He is out,' Dr Yasumi said dryly, 'because of Rags's psi talent, so you had better listen. Because this psi talent is not understood even by Rags and, honestly to God, it could rebound on you any time.'

Reluctantly, Hada said, 'Okay, give me your opinion.'

'Relationship between Rags's made-up ballads and reality is one of cause and effect. What Rags describes then takes place. The ballad precedes the event and not by much. You see? This could be dangerous, if Rags understood it and made use of it for own advantage.'

'If this is true,' Hada said, 'then we want him to compose a ballad about Unicephalon 40-D returning to action.' That was obvious to him instantly. Max Fischer would be merely the standby President once more, as he had originally been. Without authority of any kind.

'Correct,' Dr Yasumi said. 'But problem is, now that he is making up these political-type ballads, Ragland Park is apt to discover this fact, too. For if he makes up song about Unicephalon and then it actually–'

'You're right,' Hada said. 'Even Park couldn't miss that.' He was silent then, deep in thought. Ragland Park was potentially even more dangerous than Max Fischer. On the other hand, Ragland seemed like a good egg; there was no reason to assume that he would misuse his power, as Max Fischer had his.

But it was a great deal of power for one human being to have. Much too much.

Dr Yasumi said, 'Care must be taken as to exactly what sort of ballads Ragland makes up. Contents must be edited in advance, maybe by you.'

'I want as little as possible–' Hada began, and then ceased. The receptionist had buzzed him; he switched on the intercom.

'Mr James Briskin is here.'

'Send him right in,' Hada said, delighted. 'He's here already, Ito.' Hada opened the door to the office–and there stood Jim-Jam, his face lined and sober.

'Mr Hada got you out,' Dr Yasumi informed Jim-Jam.

'I know. I appreciate it, Hada.' Briskin entered the office and Hada at once closed and locked the door.

'Listen, Jim-Jam,' Hada said without preamble, 'we've got greater problems than ever. Max Fischer as a threat is nothing. Now we have to deal with an ultimate form of power, an absolute rather than a relative form. I wish I had never gotten into this; whose idea was it to hire Rags Park?'

Dr Yasumi said, 'Yours, Hada, and I warned you at the time.'

'I'd better instruct Rags not to make up any more new ballads,' Hada decided. 'That's the first step to take. I'll call the studio. My God, he might make up one about us all going to the bottom of the Atlantic, or twenty AUs out into deep space.'

'Avoid panic,' Dr Yasumi told him firmly. 'There you go ahead with panic, Hada. Volatile as ever. Be calm and think first.'

'How can I be calm,' Hada said, 'when that rustic has the power to move us around like toys? Why, he can command the entire universe.'

'Not necessarily,' Dr Yasumi disagreed. 'There may be limit. Psi power not well understood, even yet. Hard to test out in laboratory condition; hard to subject to rigorous, repeatable scrutiny.' He pondered.

Jim Briskin said, 'As I understand what you're saying—'

'You were sprung by a made-up ballad,' Hada told him. 'Done at my command. It worked, but now we're stuck with the ballad singer.' He paced back and forth, hands in his pockets.

What'll we do with Ragland Park? he asked himself desperately.

At the main studios of CULTURE in the Earth satellite Culone, Ragland Park sat with his banjo and guitar, examining the news dispatches coming in over the teletype and preparing ballads for his next appearance.

Jim-Jam Briskin, he saw, had been released from jail by order of a federal judge. Pleased, Ragland considered a ballad on that topic, then remembered that he had already composed—and sung—several. What he needed was a new topic entirely. He had done that one to death.

From the control booth, Nat Kaminsky's voice boomed over the loudspeaker, 'You about ready to go on again, Mr Park?'

'Oh sure,' Ragland replied, nodding. Actually he was not, but he would be in a moment or two.

What about a ballad, he thought, concerning a man named Pete Robinson of Chicago, Illinois, whose springer spaniel was attacked one fine day in broad daylight on a city street by an enraged eagle?

No, that's not political enough, he decided.

What about one dealing with the end of the world? A comet hitting Earth, or maybe the aliens swarming in and taking over . . . a real scary ballad with people getting blown up and cut in half by ray guns?

But that was too unintellectual for CULTURE; that wouldn't do either.

Well, he thought, then a song about the FBI. I've never done

one on the subject; Leon Lait's men in gray business suits with fat red necks . . . college graduates carrying briefcases . . .

To himself, he sang, while strumming his guitar:

> 'Our department chief says, Hark;
> Go and bring back Ragland Park.
> He's a menace to conformity;
> His crimes are an enormity.'

Chuckling, Ragland pondered how to go on with the ballad. A ballad about himself; interesting idea . . . how had he happened to think of that?

He was so busy concocting the ballad, in fact, that he did not notice the three men in gray business suits with fat red necks who had entered the studio and were coming toward him, each man carrying a briefcase in a way that made it clear he was a college graduate and used to carrying it.

I really have a good ballad going, Ragland said to himself. The best one of my career. Strumming, he went on:

> 'Yes, they sneaked up in the dark
> Aimed their guns and shot poor Park.
> Stilled freedom's clarion cry
> When they doomed this man to die;
> But a crime not soon forgotten
> Even in a culture rotten.'

That was as far as Ragland got in his ballad. The leader of the group of FBI men lowered his smoking pistol, nodded to his companions, and then spoke into his wrist transmitter. 'Inform Mr Lait that we have been successful.'

The tinny voice from his wrist answered, 'Good. Return to headquarters at once. He orders it.'

He, of course, was Maximilian Fischer. The FBI men knew that, knew who had sent them on their mission.

*

In his office at the White House, Maximilian Fischer breathed a sigh of relief when informed that Ragland Park was dead. A close call, he said to himself. That man might have finished me off—me and everybody else in the world.

Amazing, he thought, that we were able to get him. The breaks certainly went our way. I wonder why.

Could be one of my psionic talents has to do with putting an end to folksingers, he said to himself, and grinned with sleek satisfaction.

Specifically, he thought, a psi talent for getting folksingers to compose ballads on the theme of their own destruction . . .

And now, he realized, the real problem. Of getting Jim Briskin back into jail. And it will be hard; Hada is probably smart enough to think of transporting him immediately to an outlying moon where I have no authority. It will be a long struggle, me against those two . . . and they could well beat me in the end.

He sighed. A lot of hard work, he said to himself. But I guess I got to do it. Picking up the phone, he dialed Leon Lait . . .

OH, TO BE A BLOBEL!

He put a twenty-dollar platinum coin into the slot and the analyst, after a pause, lit up. Its eyes shone with sociability and it swiveled about in its chair, picked up a pen and pad of long yellow paper from its desk and said,

'Good morning, sir. You may begin.'

'Hello, Dr Jones. I guess you're not the same Dr Jones who did the definitive biography of Freud; that was a century ago.' He laughed nervously; being a rather poverty-stricken man he was not accustomed to dealing with the new fully homeostatic psycho-analysts. 'Um,' he said, 'should I free-associate or give you back-ground material or just what?'

Dr Jones said, 'Perhaps you could begin by telling me who you are und warum mich—why you have selected me.'

'I'm George Munster of catwalk 4, building WEF-395, San Francisco condominium established 1996.'

'How do you do, Mr Munster.' Dr Jones held out its hand, and George Munster shook it. He found the hand to be of a pleasant body-temperature and decidedly soft. The grip, however, was manly.

'You see,' Munster said, 'I'm an ex-GI, a war veteran. That's how I got my condominium apartment at WEF-395; veterans' prefer-ence.'

'Ah yes,' Dr Jones said, ticking faintly as it measured the passage of time. 'The war with the Blobels.'

'I fought three years in that war,' Munster said, nervously smoothing his long, black, thinning hair. 'I hated the Blobels and I volunteered; I was only nineteen and I had a good job—but the crusade to clear the Sol System of Blobels came first in my mind.'

'Um,' Dr Jones said, ticking and nodding.

George Munster continued, 'I fought well. In fact I got two decorations and a battlefield citation. Corporal. That's because I single-handedly wiped out an observation satellite full of Blobels; we'll never know exactly how many because of course, being Blobels, they tend to fuse together and unfuse confusingly.' He broke off, then, feeling emotional. Even remembering and talking about the war was too much for him . . . He lay back on the couch, lit a cigarette and tried to become calm.

The Blobels had emigrated originally from another star system, probably Proxima. Several thousand years ago they had settled on Mars and on Titan, doing very well at agrarian pursuits. They were developments of the original unicellular amoeba, quite large and with a highly-organized nervous system, but still amoeba, with pseudopodia, reproducing by binary fission, and in the main offensive to Terran settlers.

The war itself had broken out over ecological considerations. It had been the desire of the Foreign Aid Department of the UN to change the atmosphere on Mars, making it more usable for Terran settlers. This change, however, had made it unpalatable for the Blobel colonies already there; hence the squabble.

And, Munster reflected, it was not possible to change *half* the atmosphere of a planet, the Brownian movement being what it was. Within a period of ten years the altered atmosphere had diffused throughout the planet, bringing suffering—at least so they alleged—to the Blobels. In retaliation, a Blobel armada had approached Terra and had put into orbit a series of technically sophisticated satellites designed eventually to alter the atmosphere of Terra. This alteration had never come about because of course the War Office of the UN had gone into action; the satellites had been detonated by self-instructing missiles . . . and the war was on.

Dr Jones said, 'Are you married, Mr Munster?'

'No sir,' Munster said. 'And—' He shuddered. 'You'll see why when I've finished telling you. See, Doctor–' He stubbed out his cigarette. 'I'll be frank. I was a Terran spy. That was my task; they gave the job to me because of my bravery in the field . . . I didn't ask for it.'

'I see,' Dr Jones said.

'Do you?' Munster's voice broke. 'Do you know what was necessary in those days in order to make a Terran into a successful spy among the Blobels?'

Nodding, Dr Jones said, 'Yes, Mr Munster. You had to relinquish your human form and assume the repellent form of a Blobel.'

Munster said nothing; he clenched and unclenched his fist, bitterly. Across from him Dr Jones ticked.

That evening, back in his small apartment at WEF-395, Munster opened a fifth of Teacher's scotch, sat by himself sipping from a cup, lacking even the energy to get a glass down from the cupboard over the sink.

What had he gotten out of the session with Dr Jones today? Nothing, as nearly as he could tell. And it had eaten deep into his meager financial resources . . . meager because–

Because for almost twelve hours out of the day he reverted, despite all the efforts of himself and the Veterans' Hospitalization Agency of the UN, to his old war-time Blobel shape. To a formless unicellular-like blob, right in the middle of his own apartment at WEF-395.

His financial resources consisted of a small pension from the War Office; finding a job was impossible, because as soon as he was hired the strain caused him to revert there on the spot, in plain sight of his new employer and fellow workers.

It did not assist in forming successful work relationships.

Sure enough, now, at eight in the evening, he felt himself once more beginning to revert; it was an old and familiar experience to him, and he loathed it. Hurriedly, he sipped the last of the cup of scotch, put the cup down on a table . . . and felt himself slide together into a homogenous puddle.

The telephone rang.

'I can't answer,' he called to it. The phone's relay picked up his anguished message and conveyed it to the calling party. Now Munster had become a single transparent gelatinous mass in the middle of the rug; he undulated toward the phone–it was still ringing, despite his statement to it, and he felt furious resentment; didn't he have enough troubles already, without having to deal with a ringing phone?

Reaching it, he extended a pseudopodium and snatched the receiver from the hook. With great effort he formed his plastic substance into the semblance of a vocal apparatus, resonating dully. 'I'm busy,' he resonated in a low booming fashion into the mouthpiece of the phone. 'Call later.' *Call*, he thought as he hung up, *tomorrow morning. When I've been able to regain my human form.*

The apartment was quiet, now.

Sighing, Munster flowed back across the carpet, to the window, where he rose into a high pillar in order to see the view beyond; there was a light-sensitive spot on his outer surface, and although he did not possess a true lens he was able to appreciate–nostalgically–the sight of San Francisco Bay, the Golden Gate Bridge, the playground for small children which was Alcatraz Island.

Dammit, he thought bitterly. *I can't marry; I can't live a genuine human existence, reverting this way to the form the War Office bigshots forced me into back in the war times . . .*

He had not known then, when he accepted the mission, that it would leave this permanent effect. They had assured him it was 'only temporary, for the duration,' or some such glib phrase. *Duration my ass*, Munster thought with furious, impotent resentment. *It's been* eleven years, *now.*

The psychological problems created for him, the pressure on his psyche, were immense. Hence his visit to Dr Jones.

Once more the phone rang.

'Okay,' Munster said aloud, and flowed laboriously back across the room to it. 'You want to talk to me?' he said as he came closer and closer; the trip, for someone in Blobel form, was a long one. 'I'll talk to you. You can even turn on the vidscreen and *look* at me.'

OH, TO BE A BLOBEL!

At the phone he snapped the switch which would permit visual communication as well as auditory. 'Have a good look,' he said, and displayed his amorphous form before the scanning tube of the video.

Dr Jones' voice came: 'I'm sorry to bother you at your home, Mr Munster, especially when you're in this, um, awkward condition . . .' The homeostatic analyst paused. 'But I've been devoting time to problem-solving vis-à-vis your condition. I may have at least a partial solution.'

'What?' Munster said, taken by surprise. 'You mean to imply that medical science can now—'

'No, no,' Dr Jones said hurriedly. 'The physical aspects lie out of my domain; you must keep that in mind, Munster. When you consulted me about your problems it was the psychological adjustment that—'

'I'll come right down to your office and talk to you,' Munster said. And then he realized that he could not; in his Blobel form it would take him days to undulate all the way across town to Dr Jones' office. 'Jones,' he said desperately, 'you see the problems I face. I'm stuck here in this apartment every night beginning about eight o'clock and lasting through until almost seven in the morning . . . I can't even visit you and consult you and get help—'

'Be quiet, Mr Munster,' Dr Jones interrupted. 'I'm trying to tell you something. *You're not the only one in this condition.* Did you know that?'

Heavily, Munster said, 'Sure. In all, eighty-three Terrans were made over into Blobels at one time or another during the war. Of the eighty-three—' He knew the facts by heart. 'Sixty-one survived and now there's an organization called Veterans of Unnatural Wars of which fifty are members. I'm a member. We meet twice a month, revert in unison . . .' He started to hang up the phone. So this was what he had gotten for his money, this stale news. 'Goodbye, Doctor,' he murmured.

Dr Jones whirred in agitation. 'Mr Munster, I don't mean other Terrans. I've researched this in your behalf, and I discover that according to captured records at the Library of Congress fifteen *Blobels* were formed into pseudo-Terrans to act as spies for *their* side. Do you understand?'

After a moment Munster said, 'Not exactly.'

'You have a mental block against being helped,' Dr Jones said. 'But here's what I want, Munster; you be at my office at eleven in the morning tomorrow. We'll take up the solution to your problem then. Goodnight.'

Wearily, Munster said, 'When I'm in my Blobel form my wits aren't too keen, Doctor. You'll have to forgive me.' He hung up, still puzzled. So there were fifteen Blobels walking around on Titan this moment, doomed to occupy human forms—so what? How did that help him?

Maybe he would find out at eleven tomorrow.

When he strode into Dr Jones' waiting room he saw, seated in a deep chair in a corner by a lamp, reading a copy of *Fortune*, an exceedingly attractive young woman.

Automatically, Munster found a place to sit from which he could eye her. Stylish dyed-white hair braided down the back of her neck ... he took in the sight of her with delight, pretending to read his own copy of *Fortune*. Slender legs, small and delicate elbows. And her sharp, clearly-featured face. The intelligent eyes, the thin, tapered nostrils—a truly lovely girl, he thought. He drank in the sight of her ... until all at once she raised her head and stared coolly back at him.

'Dull, having to wait,' Munster mumbled.

The girl said, 'Do you come to Dr Jones often?'

'No,' he admitted. 'This is just the second time.'

'I've never been here before,' the girl said. 'I was going to another electronic fully-homeostatic psychoanalyst in Los Angeles and then late yesterday Dr Bing, my analyst, called me and told me to fly up here and see Dr Jones this morning. Is this one good?'

'Um,' Munster said. 'I guess so.' *We'll see*, he thought. *That's precisely what we don't know, at this point.*

OH, TO BE A BLOBEL!

The inner office door opened and there stood Dr Jones. 'Miss Arrasmith,' it said, nodding to the girl. 'Mr Munster.' It nodded to George. 'Won't you both come in?'

Rising to her feet, Miss Arrasmith said, 'Who pays the twenty dollars then?'

But the analyst had become silent; it had turned off.

'I'll pay,' Miss Arrasmith said, reaching into her purse.

'No, no,' Munster said. 'Let me.' He got out a twenty-dollar piece and dropped it into the analyst's slot.

At once, Dr Jones said, 'You're a gentleman, Mr Munster.' Smiling, it ushered the two of them into its office. 'Be seated, please. Miss Arrasmith, without preamble please allow me to explain your–condition to Mr Munster.' To Munster it said, 'Miss Arrasmith is a Blobel.'

Munster could only stare at the girl.

'Obviously,' Dr Jones continued, 'presently in human form. This, for her, is the state of involuntary reversion. During the war she operated behind Terran lines, acting for the Blobel War League. She was captured and held, but then the war ended and she was neither tried nor sentenced.'

'They released me,' Miss Arrasmith said in a low, carefully-controlled voice. 'Still in human form. I stayed here out of shame. I just couldn't go back to Titan and–' Her voice wavered.

'There is great shame attached to this condition,' Dr Jones said, 'for any high-caste Blobel.'

Nodding, Miss Arrasmith sat, clutching a tiny Irish linen handkerchief and trying to look poised. 'Correct, Doctor. I did visit Titan to discuss my condition with medical authorities there. After expensive and prolonged therapy with me they were able to induce a return to my natural form for a period of–' She hesitated. 'About one-fourth of the time. But the other three-fourths . . . I am as you perceive me now.' She ducked her head and touched the handkerchief to her right eye.

'Jeez,' Munster protested, 'you're lucky; a human form is infinitely superior to a Blobel form—I ought to know. As a Blobel you have to creep along . . . you're like a big jellyfish, no skeleton to keep you erect. And binary fission—it's lousy, I say really lousy, compared to the Terran form of—you know. Reproduction.' He colored.

Dr Jones ticked and stated, 'For a period of about six hours your human forms overlap. And then for about one hour your Blobel forms overlap. So all in all, the two of you possess seven hours out of twenty-four in which you both possess identical forms. In my opinion—' It toyed with its pen and paper. 'Seven hours is not too bad. If you follow my meaning.'

After a moment Miss Arrasmith said, 'But Mr Munster and I are natural enemies.'

'That was years ago,' Munster said.

'Correct,' Dr Jones agreed. 'True, Miss Arrasmith is basically a Blobel and you, Munster, are a Terran, but—' It gestured. 'Both of you are outcasts in either civilization; both of you are stateless and hence gradually suffering a loss of ego-identity. I predict for both of you a gradual deterioration ending finally in severe mental illness. Unless you two can develop a rapprochement.' The analyst was silent, then.

Miss Arrasmith said softly, 'I think we're very lucky, Mr Munster. As Dr Jones said, we do overlap for seven hours a day . . . we can enjoy that time together, no longer in wretched isolation.' She smiled up hopefully at him, rearranging her coat. Certainly, she had a nice figure; the somewhat low-cut dress gave an ideal clue to that.

Studying her, Munster pondered.

'Give him time,' Dr Jones told Miss Arrasmith. 'My analysis of him is that he will see this correctly and do the right thing.'

Still rearranging her coat and dabbing at her large, dark eyes, Miss Arrasmith waited.

The phone in Dr Jones' office rang, a number of years later. He answered it in his customary way. 'Please, sir or madam, deposit twenty dollars if you wish to speak to me.'

A tough male voice on the other end of the line said, 'Listen, this is the UN Legal Office and we don't deposit twenty dollars to talk to anybody. So trip that mechanism inside you, Jones.'

'Yes, sir,' Dr Jones said, and with his right hand tripped the lever behind his ear that caused him to come on free.

'Back in 2037,' the UN legal expert said, 'did you advise a couple to marry? A George Munster and a Vivian Arrasmith, now Mrs Munster?'

'Why yes,' Dr Jones said, after consulting his built-in memory banks.

'Had you investigated the legal ramifications of their issue?'

'Um well,' Dr Jones said, 'that's not my worry.'

'You can be arraigned for advising any action contrary to UN law.'

'There's no law prohibiting a Blobel and a Terran from marrying.'

The UN legal expert said, 'All right, Doctor, I'll settle for a look at their case histories.'

'Absolutely not,' Dr Jones said. 'That would be a breach of ethics.'

'We'll get a writ and sequester them, then.'

'Go ahead.' Dr Jones reached behind his ear to shut himself off.

'Wait. It may interest you to know that the Munsters now have four children. And, following the Mendelian Law, the offspring comprise a strict one, two, one ratio. One Blobel girl, one hybrid boy, one hybrid girl, one Terran girl. The legal problem arises in that the Blobel Supreme Council claims the pure-blooded Blobel girl as a citizen of Titan and also suggests that one of the two hybrids be donated to the Council's jurisdiction.' The UN legal expert explained, 'You see, the Munsters' marriage is breaking up; they're getting divorced and it's sticky finding which laws obtain regarding them and their issue.'

'Yes,' Dr Jones admitted, 'I would think so. What has caused their marriage to break up?'

'I don't know and don't care. Possibly the fact that both adults and two of the four children rotate daily between being Blobels and Terrans; maybe the strain got to be too much. If you want to give them psychological advice, consult them. Goodbye.' The UN legal expert rang off.

Did I make a mistake, advising them to marry? Dr Jones asked itself. *I wonder if I shouldn't look them up; I owe at least that to them.*

Opening the Los Angeles phone book, it began thumbing through the Ms.

These had been six difficult years for the Munsters.

First, George had moved from San Francisco to Los Angeles; he and Vivian had set up a household in a condominium apartment with three instead of two rooms. Vivian, being in Terran form three-fourths of the time, had been able to obtain a job; right out in public she gave jet flight information at the Fifth Los Angeles Airport. George, however—

His pension comprised an amount only one-fourth that of his wife's salary and he felt it keenly. To augment it, he had searched for a way of earning money at home. Finally in a magazine he had found this valuable ad:

MAKE SWIFT PROFITS IN YOUR OWN CONDO!
RAISE GIANT BULLFROGS FROM JUPITER,
CAPABLE OF EIGHTY-FOOT LEAPS. CAN BE
USED IN FROG-RACING (where legal) AND ...

So in 2038 he had bought his first pair of frogs imported from Jupiter and had begun raising them for swift profits, right in his own condominium apartment building, in a corner of the basement that Leopold, the partially-homeostatic janitor, let him use gratis.

But in the relatively feeble Terran gravity the frogs were capable of enormous leaps, and the basement proved too small for them; they ricocheted from wall to wall like green ping pong balls and soon died. Obviously it took more than a portion of the basement at QEK-604 Apartments to house a crop of the damned things, George realized.

And then, too, their first child had been born. It had turned out to be a pure-blooded Blobel; for twenty-four hours a day it consisted of a gelatinous mass and George found himself waiting in vain for it to switch over to a human form, even for a moment.

He faced Vivian defiantly in this matter, during a period when both of them were in human form.

'How can I consider it my child?' he asked her. 'It's—an alien life form to me.' He was discouraged and even horrified. 'Dr Jones should have foreseen this; maybe it's *your* child—it looks just like you.'

Tears filled Vivian's eyes. 'You mean that insultingly.'

'Damn right I do. We fought you creatures—we used to consider you no better than Portuguese sting-rays.' Gloomily, he put on his coat. 'I'm going down to Veterans of Unnatural Wars Headquarters,' he informed his wife. 'Have a beer with the boys.' Shortly, he was on his way to join with his old war-time buddies, glad to get out of the apartment house.

VUW Headquarters was a decrepit cement building in downtown Los Angeles left over from the twentieth century and sadly in need of paint. The VUW had little funds because most of its members were, like George Munster, living on UN pensions. However, there was a pool table and an old 3-D television set and a few dozen tapes of popular music and also a chess set. George generally drank his beer and played chess with his fellow members, either in human form or in Blobel form; this was one place in which both were accepted.

This particular evening he sat with Pete Ruggles, a fellow veteran who also had married a Blobel female, reverting, as Vivian did, to human form.

'Pete, I can't go on. I've got a gelatinous blob for a child. My whole life I've wanted a kid, and now what have I got? Something that looks like it washed up on the beach.'

Sipping his beer—he too was in human form at the moment—Pete answered, 'Criminy, George, I admit it's a mess. But you must have known what you were getting into when you married her. And my God, according to Mendel's Law, the next kid—'

'I mean,' George broke in, 'I don't respect my own wife; that's the basis of it. I think of her as a *thing*. And myself, too. We're both things.' He drank down his beer in one gulp.

Pete said meditatively, 'But from the Blobel standpoint–'

'Listen, whose side are you on?' George demanded.

'Don't yell at me,' Pete said, 'or I'll deck you.'

A moment later they were swinging wildly at each other. Fortunately Pete reverted to Blobel form in the nick of time; no harm was done. Now George sat alone, in human shape, while Pete oozed off somewhere else, probably to join a group of the boys who had also assumed Blobel form.

Maybe we can found a new society somewhere on a remote moon, George said to himself moodily. *Neither Terran nor Blobel.*

I've got to go back to Vivian, George resolved. *What else is there for me? I'm lucky to find her; I'd be nothing but a war veteran guzzling beer here at VUW Headquarters every damn day and night, with no future, no hope, no real life . . .*

He had a new money-making scheme going now. It was a home mail-order business; he had placed an ad in the *Saturday Evening Post* for MAGIC LODESTONES REPUTED TO BRING YOU LUCK. FROM ANOTHER STAR SYSTEM ENTIRELY! The stones had come from Proxima and were obtainable on Titan; it was Vivian who had made the commercial contact for him with her people. But so far, few people had sent in the dollar-fifty.

I'm a failure, George said to himself.

Fortunately the next child, born in the winter of 2039, showed itself to be a hybrid; it took human form fifty percent of the time, and so at last George had a child who was–occasionally, anyhow–a member of his own species.

He was still in the process of celebrating the birth of Maurice when a delegation of their neighbors at QEK-604 Apartments came and rapped on their door.

'We've got a petition here,' the chairman of the delegation said, shuffling his feet in embarrassment, 'asking that you and Mrs Munster leave QEK-604.'

'But why?' George asked, bewildered. 'You haven't objected to us up until now.'

'The reason is that now you've got a hybrid youngster who will want to play with ours, and we feel it's unhealthy for our kids to–'

George slammed the door in their faces.

But still, he felt the pressure, the hostility from the people on all sides of them. *And to think,* he thought bitterly, *that I fought in the war to save these people. It sure wasn't worth it.*

An hour later he was down at VUW Headquarters once more, drinking beer and talking with his buddy Sherman Downs, also married to a Blobel.

'Sherman, it's no good. We're not wanted; we've got to emigrate. Maybe we'll try it on Titan, in Viv's world.'

'Chrissakes,' Sherman protested, 'I hate to see you fold up, George. Isn't your electromagnetic reducing belt beginning to sell, finally?'

For the last few months, George had been making and selling a complex electronic reducing gadget which Vivian had helped him design; it was based in principle on a Blobel device popular on Titan but unknown on Terra. And this had gone over well; George had more orders than he could fill. But–

'I had a terrible experience, Sherm,' George confided. 'I was in a drugstore the other day, and they gave me a big order for my reducing belt, and I got so excited–' He broke off. 'You can guess what happened. I reverted. Right in plain sight of a hundred customers. And when the buyer saw that he canceled the order for the belts. It was what we all fear . . . you should have seen how their attitude toward me changed.'

Sherm said, 'Hire someone to do your selling for you. A full-blooded Terran.'

Thickly, George said, '*I'm* a full-blooded Terran, and don't you forget it. Ever.'

'I just mean–'

'I know what you meant,' George said. And took a swing at Sherman. Fortunately he missed and in the excitement both of them reverted to Blobel form. They oozed angrily into each other for a time, but at last fellow veterans managed to separate them.

'I'm as much Terran as anyone,' George thought-radiated in the Blobel manner to Sherman. 'And I'll flatten anyone who says otherwise.'

In Blobel form he was unable to get home; he had to phone Vivian to come and get him. It was humiliating.

Suicide, he decided. *That's the answer.*

How best to do it? In Blobel form he was unable to feel pain; best to do it then. Several substances would dissolve him . . . he could for instance drop himself into a heavily-chlorinated swimming pool, such as QEK-604 maintained in its recreation room.

Vivian, in human form, found him as he reposed hesitantly at the edge of the swimming pool, late one night.

'George, I beg you—go back to Dr Jones.'

'Naw,' he boomed dully, forming a quasi-vocal apparatus with a portion of his body. 'It's no use, Viv. I don't *want* to go on.' Even the belts; they had been Viv's idea, rather than his. He was second even there . . . behind her, falling constantly farther behind each passing day.

Viv said, 'You have so much to offer the children.'

That was true. 'Maybe I'll drop over to the UN War Office,' he decided. 'Talk to them, see if there's anything new that medical science has come up with that might stabilize me.'

'But if you stabilize as a Terran,' Vivian said, 'what would become of me?'

'We'd have *eighteen entire hours* together a day. All the hours you take human form!'

'But you wouldn't want to stay married to me. Because, George, then you could meet a Terran woman.'

It wasn't fair to her, he realized. So he abandoned the idea.

In the spring of 2041 their third child was born, also a girl, and like Maurice a hybrid. It was Blobel at night and Terran by day.

Meanwhile, George found a solution to some of his problems.

He got himself a mistress.

*

He and Nina arranged to meet each other at the Hotel Elysium, a run-down wooden building in the heart of Los Angeles.

'Nina,' George said, sipping Teacher's scotch and seated beside her on the shabby sofa which the hotel provided, 'you've made my life worth living again.' He fooled with the buttons of her blouse.

'I respect you,' Nina Glaubman said, assisting him with the buttons. 'In spite of the fact—well, you are a former enemy of our people.'

'God,' George protested, 'we must not think about the old days—we have to close our minds to our pasts.' *Nothing but our future*, he thought.

His reducing belt enterprise had developed so well that now he employed fifteen full-time Terran employees and owned a small, modern factory on the outskirts of San Fernando. If UN taxes had been reasonable he would by now be a wealthy man . . . brooding on that, George wondered what the tax rate was in Blobel-run lands, on Io, for instance. Maybe he ought to look into it.

One night at VUW Headquarters he discussed the subject with Reinholt, Nina's husband, who of course was ignorant of the modus vivendi between George and Nina.

'Reinholt,' George said with difficulty, as he drank his beer, 'I've got big plans. This cradle-to-grave socialism the UN operates . . . it's not for me. It's cramping me. The Munster Magic Magnetic Belt is—' He gestured. 'More than Terran civilization can support. You get me?'

Coldly, Reinholt said, 'But George, you are a Terran; if you emigrate to Blobel-run territory with your factory you'll be betraying your—'

'Listen,' George told him, 'I've got one authentic Blobel child, two half-Blobel children, and a fourth on the way. I've got strong *emotional* ties with those people out there on Titan and Io.'

'You're a traitor,' Reinholt said, and punched him in the mouth. 'And not only that,' he continued, punching George in the stomach, 'you're running around with my wife. I'm going to kill you.'

To escape, George reverted to Blobel form; Reinholt's blows

passed harmlessly deep into his moist, jelly-like substance. Reinholt then reverted too, and flowed into him murderously, trying to consume and absorb George's nucleus.

Fortunately fellow veterans pried their two bodies apart before any permanent harm was done.

Later that night, still trembling, George sat with Vivian in the living room of their eight-room suite at the great new condominium apartment building ZGF-900. It had been a close call, and now of course Reinholt would tell Viv; it was only a question of time. The marriage, as far as George could see, was over. This perhaps was their last moment together.

'Viv,' he said urgently, 'you have to believe me; I love you. You and the children—plus the belt business, naturally—are my complete life.' A desperate idea came to him. 'Let's emigrate now, tonight. Pack up the kids and go to Titan, right this minute.'

'I can't go,' Vivian said. 'I know how my people would treat me, and treat you and the children, too. George, *you go*. Move the factory to Io. I'll stay here.' Tears filled her dark eyes.

'Hell,' George said, 'what kind of life is that? With you on Terra and me on Io—that's no marriage. And who'll get the kids?' Probably Viv would get them . . . but his firm employed top legal talent—perhaps he could use it to solve his domestic problems.

The next morning Vivian found out about Nina. And hired an attorney of her own.

'Listen,' George said, on the phone talking to his top legal talent, Henry Ramarau. 'Get me custody of the fourth child; it'll be a Terran. And we'll compromise on the two hybrids; I'll take Maurice and she can have Kathy. And naturally she gets that blob, the first so-called child. As far as I'm concerned it's hers anyhow.' He slammed the receiver down and then turned to the board of directors of his company. 'Now where were we?' he demanded. 'In our analysis of Io tax laws.'

During the next weeks the idea of a move to Io appeared more and more feasible from a profit and loss standpoint.

OH, TO BE A BLOBEL!

'Go ahead and buy land on Io,' George instructed his business agent in the field, Tom Hendricks. 'And get it cheap; we want to start right.' To his secretary, Miss Nolan, he said, 'Now keep everyone out of my office until further notice. I feel an attack coming on. From anxiety over this major move off Terra to Io.' He added, 'And personal worries.'

'Yes, Mr Munster,' Miss Nolan said, ushering Tom Hendricks out of George's private office. 'No one will disturb you.' She could be counted on to keep everyone out while George reverted to his war-time Blobel shape, as he often did, these days; the pressure on him was immense.

When, later in the day, he resumed human form, George learned from Miss Nolan that a Dr Jones had called.

'I'll be damned,' George said, thinking back to six years ago. 'I thought it'd be in the junk pile by now.' To Miss Nolan he said, 'Call Dr Jones, notify me when you have it; I'll take a minute off to talk to it.' It was like old times, back in San Francisco.

Shortly, Miss Nolan had Dr Jones on the line.

'Doctor,' George said, leaning back in his chair and swiveling from side to side and poking at an orchid on his desk. 'Good to hear from you.'

The voice of the homeostatic analyst came in his ear, 'Mr Munster, I note that you now have a secretary.'

'Yes,' George said, 'I'm a tycoon. I'm in the reducing belt game; it's somewhat like the flea-collar that cats wear. Well, what can I do for you?'

'I understand you have four children now—'

'Actually three, plus a fourth on the way. Listen, that fourth, Doctor, is vital to me; according to Mendel's Law it's a full-blooded Terran and by God I'm doing everything in my power to get custody of it.' He added, 'Vivian—you remember her—is now back on Titan. Among her own people, where she belongs. And I'm putting some of the finest doctors I can get on my payroll to stabilize me; I'm tired of this constant reverting, night and day; I've got too much to do for such nonsense.'

Dr Jones said, 'From your tone I can see you're an important, busy man, Mr Munster. You've certainly risen in the world, since I saw you last.'

'Get to the point,' George said impatiently. 'Why'd you call?'

'I, um, thought perhaps I could bring you and Vivian together again.'

'Bah,' George said contemptuously. 'That woman? Never. Listen, Doctor, I have to ring off; we're in the process of finalizing on some basic business strategy, here at Munster, Incorporated.'

'Mr Munster,' Dr Jones asked, 'is there another woman?'

'There's another Blobel,' George said, 'if that's what you mean.' And he hung up the phone. *Two Blobels are better than none*, he said to himself. *And now back to business . . .* He pressed a button on his desk and at once Miss Nolan put her head into the office. 'Miss Nolan,' George said, 'get me Hank Ramarau; I want to find out–'

'Mr Ramarau is waiting on the other line,' Miss Nolan said. 'He says it's urgent.'

Switching to the other line, George said, 'Hi, Hank. What's up?'

'I've just discovered,' his top legal advisor said, 'that to operate your factory on Io you must be a citizen of Titan.'

'We ought to be able to fix that up,' George said.

'But to be a citizen of Titan–' Ramarau hesitated. 'I'll break it to you easy as I can, George. You have to be a Blobel.'

'Dammit, I am a Blobel,' George said. 'At least part of the time. Won't that do?'

'No,' Ramarau said, 'I checked into that, knowing of your affliction, and it's got to be one hundred percent of the time. Night *and* day.'

'Hmmm,' George said. 'This is bad. But we'll overcome it, somehow. Listen, Hank, I've got an appointment with Eddy Fullbright, my medical coordinator; I'll talk to you after, okay?' He rang off and then sat scowling and rubbing his jaw. *Well*, he decided, *if it has to be it has to be. Facts are facts, and we can't let them stand in our way.*

Picking up the phone he dialed his doctor, Eddy Fullbright.

*

OH, TO BE A BLOBEL!

The twenty-dollar platinum coin rolled down the chute and tripped the circuit. Dr Jones came on, glanced up and saw a stunning, sharp-breasted young woman whom it recognized—by means of a quick scan of its memory banks—as Mrs George Munster, the former Vivian Arrasmith.

'Good day, Vivian,' Dr Jones said cordially. 'But I understood you were on Titan.' It rose to its feet, offering her a chair.

Dabbing at her large, dark eyes, Vivian sniffled, 'Doctor, everything is collapsing around me. My husband is having an affair with another woman . . . all I know is that her name is Nina and all the boys down at VUW Headquarters are talking about it. Presumably she's a Terran. We're both filing for divorce. And we're having a dreadful legal battle over the children.' She arranged her coat modestly. 'I'm expecting. Our fourth.'

'This I know,' Dr Jones said. 'A full-blooded Terran this time, if Mendel's Law holds . . . although it only applied to litters.'

Mrs Munster said miserably, 'I've been on Titan talking to legal and medical experts, gynecologists, and especially marital guidance counselors; I've had all sorts of advice during the past month. Now I'm back on Terra but I can't find George—he's *gone*.'

'I wish I could help you, Vivian,' Dr Jones said. 'I talked to your husband briefly, the other day, but he spoke only in generalities . . . evidently he's such a big tycoon now that it's hard to approach him.'

'And to think,' Vivian sniffled, 'that he achieved it all because of an idea I gave him. A Blobel idea.'

'The ironies of fate,' Dr Jones said. 'Now, if you want to keep your husband, Vivian—'

'I'm determined to keep him, Doctor Jones. Frankly I've undergone therapy on Titan, the latest and most expensive . . . it's because I love George so much, even more than I love my own people or my planet.'

'Eh?' Dr Jones said.

'Through the most modern developments in medical science in the Sol System,' Vivian said, 'I've been stabilized, Dr Jones. Now

I am in human form twenty-four hours a day instead of eighteen. I've renounced my natural form in order to keep my marriage with George.'

'The supreme sacrifice,' Dr Jones said, touched.

'Now, if I can only *find* him, Doctor—'

At the ground-breaking ceremonies on Io, George Munster flowed gradually to the shovel, extended a pseudopodium, seized the shovel, and with it managed to dig a symbolic amount of soil. 'This is a great day,' he boomed hollowly, by means of the semblance of a vocal apparatus into which he had fashioned the slimy, plastic substance which made up his unicellular body.

'Right, George,' Hank Ramarau agreed, standing nearby with the legal documents.

The Ionan official, like George a great transparent blob, oozed across to Ramarau, took the documents and boomed, 'These will be transmitted to my government. I'm sure they're in order, Mr Ramarau.'

'I guarantee you,' Ramarau said to the official, 'Mr Munster does not revert to human form at any time; he's made use of some of the most advanced techniques in medical science to achieve this stability at the unicellular phase of his former rotation. Munster would never cheat.'

'This historic moment,' the great blob that was George Munster thought-radiated to the throng of local Blobels attending the ceremonies, 'means a higher standard of living for Ionans who will be employed; it will bring prosperity to this area, plus a proud sense of national achievement in the manufacture of what we recognize to be a native invention, the Munster Magic Magnetic Belt.'

The throng of Blobels thought-radiated cheers.

'This is a proud day in my life,' George Munster informed them, and began to ooze by degrees back to his car, where his chauffeur waited to drive him to his permanent hotel room at Io City.

Someday he would own the hotel. He was putting the profits from his business in local real estate; it was the patriotic—and the profitable—thing to do, other Ionans, other Blobels, had told him.

'I'm finally a successful man,' George Munster thought-radiated to all close enough to pick up his emanations.

Amid frenzied cheers he oozed up the ramp and into his Titan-made car.

THE LITTLE BLACK BOX

I

Bogart Crofts of the State Department said, 'Miss Hiashi, we want to send you to Cuba to give religious instruction to the Chinese population there. It's your Oriental background. It will help.'

With a faint moan, Joan Hiashi reflected that her Oriental background consisted of having been born in Los Angeles and having attended courses at UCSB, the University at Santa Barbara. But she was technically, from the standpoint of training, an Asian scholar, and she had properly listed this on her job-application form.

'Let's consider the word *caritas*,' Crofts was saying. 'In your estimation, what actually does it mean, as Jerome used it? Charity? Hardly. But then what? Friendliness? Love?'

Joan said, 'My field is Zen Buddhism.'

'But everybody,' Crofts protested in dismay, 'knows what caritas means in late Roman usage. The esteem of good people for one another; that's what it means.' His gray, dignified eyebrows raised. 'Do you want this job, Miss Hiashi? And if so, why?'

'I want to disseminate Zen Buddhist propaganda to the Communist Chinese in Cuba,' Joan said, 'because–' She hesitated. The truth was simply that it meant a good salary for her, the first truly high-paying job she had ever held. From a career standpoint, it was a plum. 'Aw, hell,' she said. 'What is the nature of the One Way? I don't have any answer.'

'It's evident that your field has taught you a method of avoiding giving honest answers,' Crofts said sourly. 'And being evasive.

However–' He shrugged. 'Possibly that only goes to prove that you're well trained and the proper person for the job. In Cuba you'll be running up against some rather worldly and sophisticated individuals, who in addition are quite well off even from the US standpoint. I hope you can cope with them as well as you've coped with me.'

Joan said, 'Thank you, Mr Crofts.' She rose. 'I'll expect to hear from you, then.'

'I am impressed by you,' Crofts said, half to himself. 'After all, you're the young lady who first had the idea of feeding Zen Buddhist riddles to UCSB's big computers.'

'I was the first to *do* it,' Joan corrected. 'But the idea came from a friend of mine, Ray Meritan. The gray-green jazz harpist.'

'Jazz and Zen Buddhism,' Crofts said. 'State may be able to make use of you in Cuba.'

To Ray Meritan she said, 'I have to get out of Los Angeles, Ray. I really can't stand the way we're living here.' She walked to the window of his apartment and looked out at the monorail gleaming far off. The silver car made its way at enormous speed, and Joan hurriedly looked away.

If we only could suffer, she thought. That's what we lack, any real experience of suffering, because we can escape anything. Even this.

'But you are getting out,' Ray said. 'You're going to Cuba and convert wealthy merchants and bankers into becoming ascetics. And it's a genuine Zen paradox; you'll be paid for it.' He chuckled. 'Fed into a computer, a thought like that would do harm. Anyhow, you won't have to sit in the Crystal Hall every night listening to me play–if that's what you're anxious to get away from.'

'No,' Joan said, 'I expect to keep on listening to you on TV. I may even be able to use your music in my teaching.' From a rosewood chest in the far corner of the room she lifted out a .32 pistol. It had belonged to Ray Meritan's second wife, Edna, who had used it to kill herself, the previous February, late one rainy afternoon. 'May I take this along?' she asked.

'For sentiment?' Ray said. 'Because she did it on your account?'

'Edna did nothing on my account. Edna liked me. I'm not taking any responsibility for your wife's suicide, even though she did find out about us—seeing each other, so to speak.'

Ray said meditatively, 'And you're the girl always telling people to accept blame and not to project it out on the world. What do you call your principle, dear? Ah.' He grinned. 'The Anti-paranoia Prinzip. Doctor Joan Hiashi's cure for mental illness; absorb all blame, take it all upon yourself.' He glanced up at her and said acutely, 'I'm surprised you're not a follower of Wilbur Mercer.'

'That clown,' Joan said.

'But that's part of his appeal. Here, I'll show you.' Ray switched on the TV set across the room from them, the legless black Oriental-style set with its ornamentation of Sung dynasty dragons.

'Odd you would know when Mercer is on,' Joan said.

Ray, shrugging, murmured, 'I'm interested. A new religion, replacing Zen Buddhism, sweeping out of the Middle West to engulf California. You ought to pay attention, too, since you claim religion as your profession. You're getting a job because of it. Religion is paying your bills, my dear girl, so don't knock it.'

The TV had come on, and there was Wilbur Mercer.

'Why isn't he saying anything?' Joan said.

'Why, Mercer has taken a vow this week. Complete silence.' Ray lit a cigarette. 'State ought to be sending me, not you. You're a fake.'

'At least I'm not a clown,' Joan said, 'or a follower of a clown.'

Ray reminded her softly, 'There's a Zen saying, "The Buddha is a piece of toilet paper." And another. "The Buddha often—"'

'Be still,' she said sharply. 'I want to watch Mercer.'

'You want to watch,' Ray's voice was heavy with irony. 'Is that what you want, for God's sake? No one *watches* Mercer; that's the whole point.' Tossing his cigarette into the fireplace, he strode to the TV set; there, before it, Joan saw a metal box with two handles, attached by a lead of twin-cable wire to the TV set. Ray seized the two handles, and at once a grimace of pain shot across his face.

'What is it?' she asked, in anxiety.

'N-nothing.' Ray continued to grip the handles. On the screen, Wilbur Mercer walked slowly over the barren, jagged surface of a desolate hillside, his face lifted, an expression of serenity—or vacuity—on his thin, middle-aged features. Gasping, Ray released the handles. 'I could only hold them for forty-five seconds this time.' To Joan, he explained, 'This is the empathy box, my dear. I can't tell you how I got it—to be truthful I don't really know. *They* brought it by, the organization that distributes it—Wilcer, Incorporated. But I can tell you that when you take hold of these handles you're no longer watching Wilbur Mercer. You're actually participating in his apotheosis. Why, you're feeling what he feels.'

Joan said, 'It looks like it hurts.'

Quietly, Ray Meritan said, 'Yes. Because Wilbur Mercer is being killed. He's walking to the place where he's going to die.'

In horror, Joan moved away from the box.

'You said that was what we needed,' Ray said. 'Remember, I'm a rather adequate telepath; I don't have to bestir myself very much to read your thoughts. "If only we could suffer." That's what you were thinking, just a little while ago. Well, here's your chance, Joan.'

'It's—morbid!'

'Was your thought morbid?'

'Yes!' she said.

Ray Meritan said, 'Twenty million people are followers of Wilbur Mercer now. All over the world. And they're suffering with him, as he walks along toward Pueblo, Colorado. At least that's where they're *told* he's going. Personally I have my doubts. Anyhow, Mercerism is now what Zen Buddhism was once; you're going to Cuba to teach the wealthy Chinese bankers a form of asceticism that's already obsolete, already seen its day.'

Silently, Joan turned away from him and watched Mercer walking.

'You know I'm right,' Ray said. 'I can pick up your emotions. You may not be aware of them, but they're there.'

On the screen, a rock was thrown at Mercer. It struck him on the shoulder.

Everyone who's holding onto his empathy box, Joan realized, felt that along with Mercer.

Ray nodded. 'You're right.'

'And—what about when he's actually killed?' She shuddered.

'We'll see what happens then,' Ray said quietly. 'We don't know.'

II

To Bogart Crofts, Secretary of State Douglas Herrick said, 'I think you're wrong, Boge. The girl may be Meritan's mistress but that doesn't mean she knows.'

'We'll wait for Mr Lee to tell us,' Crofts said irritably. 'When she gets to Havana he'll be waiting to meet her.'

'Mr Lee can't scan Meritan direct?'

'One telepath scan another?' Bogart Crofts smiled at the thought. It conjured up a nonsensical situation: Mr Lee reading Meritan's mind, and Meritan, also being a telepath, would read Mr Lee's mind and discover that Mr Lee was reading his mind, and Lee, reading Meritan's mind, would discover that Meritan knew—and so forth. Endless regression, winding up with a fusion of minds, within which Meritan carefully guarded his thoughts so that he did not think about Wilbur Mercer.

'It's the similarity of names that convinces me,' Herrick said. 'Meritan, Mercer. The first three letters—?'

Crofts said, 'Ray Meritan is not Wilbur Mercer. I'll tell you how we know. Over at CIA, we made an Ampex video tape from Mercer's telecast, had it enlarged and analyzed. Mercer was shown against the usual dismal background of cactus plants and sand and rock . . . you know.'

'Yes,' Herrick said, nodding. 'The Wilderness, as they call it.'

'In the enlargement something showed up in the sky. It was studied. It's not Luna. It's a moon, but too small to be Luna. Mercer is not on Earth. I would guess that he is not a terrestrial at all.'

Bending down, Crofts picked up a small metal box, carefully

THE LITTLE BLACK BOX

avoiding the two handles. 'And these were not designed and built on Earth. The entire Mercer Movement is null-T all the way, and that's the fact we've got to contend with.'

Herrick said, 'If Mercer is not a Terran, then he may have suffered and even died before, on other planets.'

'Oh, yes,' Crofts said. 'Mercer—or whatever his or its real name is—may be highly experienced in this. But we still don't know what we want to know.' And that of course was, What happens to those people holding onto the handles of their empathy boxes?

Crofts seated himself at his desk and scrutinized the box resting directly before him, with its two inviting handles. He had never touched them, and he never intended to. But—

'How soon will Mercer die?' Herrick asked.

'They're expecting it some time late next week.'

'And Mr Lee will have gotten something from the girl's mind by then, you think? Some clue as to where Mercer really is?'

'I hope so,' Crofts said, still seated at the empathy box but still not touching it. It must be a strange experience, he thought, to place your hands on two ordinary-looking metal handles and find, all at once, that you're no longer yourself; you're another man entirely, in another place, laboring up a long, dreary inclined plain toward certain extinction. At least, so they say. But hearing about it . . . what does that actually convey? Suppose I tried it for myself.

The sense of absolute pain . . . that was what appalled him, held him back.

It was unbelievable that people could deliberately seek it out, rather than avoiding it. Gripping the handles of the empathy box was certainly not the act of a person seeking escape. It was not the avoidance of something but the seeking of something. And not the pain as such; Crofts knew better than to suppose that the Mercerites were simple masochists who desired discomfort. It was, he knew, the meaning of the pain which attracted Mercer's followers.

The followers were suffering from something.

Aloud, he said to his superior, 'They want to suffer as a means of denying their private, personal existences. It's a communion in

which they all suffer and experience Mercer's ordeal together.'
Like the Last Supper, he thought. That's the real key: the communion, the participation that is behind all religion. Or ought to be.
Religion binds men together in a sharing, corporate body, and
leaves everyone else on the outside.

Herrick said, 'But primarily it's a political movement, or must
be treated as such.'

'From our standpoint,' Crofts agreed. 'Not theirs.'

The intercom on the desk buzzed and his secretary said, 'Sir,
Mr John Lee is here.'

'Tell him to come in.'

The tall, slender young Chinese entered, smiling, his hand out.
He wore an old-fashioned single-breasted suit and pointed black
shoes. As they shook hands, Mr Lee said, 'She has not left for
Havana, has she?'

'No,' Crofts said.

'Is she pretty?' Mr Lee said.

'Yes,' Crofts said, with a smile at Herrick. 'But—difficult. The
snappish kind of woman. Emancipated, if you follow me.'

'Oh, the suffragette type,' Mr Lee said, smiling. 'I detest that
type of female. It will be hard going, Mr Crofts.'

'Remember,' Crofts said, 'your job is simply to be converted. All
you have to do is listen to her propaganda about Zen Buddhism,
learn to ask a few questions such as, "Is this stick the Buddha?"
and expect a few inexplicable blows on the head—a Zen practice, I
understand, supposed to instill sense.'

With a broad grin, Mr Lee said, 'Or to instill nonsense. You see,
I am prepared. Sense, nonsense; in Zen it's the same thing.' He
became sober, now. 'Of course, I myself am a Communist,' he said.
'The only reason I'm doing this is because the Party at Havana has
taken the official stand that Mercerism is dangerous and must be
wiped out.' He looked gloomy. 'I must say, these Mercerites are
fanatics.'

'True,' Crofts agreed. 'And we must work for their extinction.'
He pointed to the empathy box. 'Have you ever—?'

'Yes,' Mr Lee said. 'It's a form of punishment. Self-imposed, no doubt for reasons of guilt. Leisure gleans such emotions from people if it is properly utilized; otherwise not.'

Crofts thought, This man has no understanding of the issues at all. He's a simple materialist. Typical of a person born in a Communist family, raised in a Communist society. Everything is either black or white.

'You're mistaken,' Mr Lee said; he had picked up Crofts' thought.

Flushing, Crofts said, 'Sorry, I forgot. No offense.'

'I see in your mind,' Mr Lee said, 'that you believe Wilbur Mercer, as he calls himself, may be non-T. Do you know the Party's position on this question? It was debated just a few days ago. The Party takes the stand that there are no non-T races in the solar system, that to believe remnants of once-superior races still exist is a form of morbid mysticism.'

Crofts sighed. 'Deciding an empirical issue by vote—deciding it on a strictly political basis. I can't understand that.'

At that point, Secretary Herrick spoke up, soothing both men. 'Please, let's not become sidetracked by theoretical issues on which we don't all agree. Let's stick to basics—the Mercerite Party and its rapid growth all over the planet.'

Mr Lee said, 'You are right, of course.'

III

At the Havana airfield Joan Hiashi looked around her as the other passengers walked rapidly from the ship to the entrance of the number twenty concourse.

Relatives and friends had surged cautiously out onto the field, as they always did, in defiance of field rulings. She saw among them a tall, lean young Chinese man with a smile of greeting on his face.

Walking toward him she called, 'Mr Lee?'

'Yes.' He hurried toward her. 'It's dinner time. Would you care to eat? I'll take you to the Hang Far Lo restaurant. They have pressed duck and bird's nest soup, all Canton-style . . . very sweet but good once in a long while.'

Soon they were at the restaurant, in a red-leather and imitation teak booth. Cubans and Chinese chattered on all sides of them; the air smelled of frying pork and cigar smoke.

'You are President of the Havana Institute for Asian Studies?' she asked, just to be certain there had been no slip-ups.

'Correct. It is frowned on by the Cuban Communist Party because of the religious aspect. But many of the Chinese here on the island attend lectures or are on our mailing list. And as you know we've had many distinguished scholars from Europe and Southern Asia come and address us . . . By the way. There is a Zen parable which I do not understand. The monk who cut the kitten in half—I have studied it and thought about it, but I do not see how the Buddha could be present when cruelty was done to an animal.' He hastened to add, 'I'm not disputing with you. I am merely seeking information.'

Joan said, 'Of all the Zen parables that has caused the most difficulty. The question to ask is, Where is the kitten now?'

'That recalls the opening of the Bhagavad-Gita,' Mr Lee said, with a quick nod. 'I recall Arjuna saying,

> 'The bow Gandiva slips from
> my hand . . .
> Omens of evil!
> What can we hope from this killing of kinsmen?'

'Correct,' Joan said. 'And of course you remember Krishna's answer. It is the most profound statement in all pre-Buddhistic religion of the issue of death and of action.'

The waiter came for their order. He was a Cuban, in khaki and a beret.

'Try the fried won ton,' Mr Lee advised. 'And the chow yuk, and of course the egg roll. You have egg roll today?' he asked the waiter.

'Si, Señor Lee.' The waiter picked at his teeth with a toothpick.

Mr Lee ordered for both of them, and the waiter departed.

'You know,' Joan said, 'when you've been around a telepath as much as I have, you become conscious of intensive scanning going on . . . I could always tell when Ray was trying to dig at something in me. You're a telepath. And you're very intensively scanning me right now.'

Smiling, Mr Lee said, 'I wish I was, Miss Hiashi.'

'I have nothing to hide,' Joan said. 'But I wonder why you are so interested in what I'm thinking. You know I'm an employee of the United States Department of State; there's nothing secret about that. Are you afraid I've come to Cuba as a spy? To study military installations? Is it something like that?' She felt depressed. 'This is not a good beginning,' she said. 'You haven't been honest with me.'

'You are a very attractive woman, Miss Hiashi,' Mr Lee said, losing none of his poise. 'I was merely curious to see—shall I be blunt? Your attitude toward sex.'

'You're lying,' Joan said quietly.

Now the bland smile departed; he stared at her.

'Bird's nest soup, señor.' The waiter had returned; he set the hot steaming bowl in the center of the table. 'Tea.' He laid out a teapot and two small white handleless cups. 'Señorita, you want chopsticks?'

'No,' she said absently.

From outside the booth came a cry of anguish. Both Joan and Mr Lee leaped up. Mr Lee pulled the curtain aside; the waiter was staring, too, and laughing.

At a table in the opposite corner of the restaurant sat an elderly Cuban gentleman with his hands gripping the handles of an empathy box.

'Here, too,' Joan said.

'They are pests,' Mr Lee said. 'Disturbing our meal.'

The waiter said, 'Loco.' He shook his head, still chuckling.

'Yes,' Joan said. 'Mr Lee, I will continue here, trying to do my job, despite what's occurred between us. I don't know why they deliberately sent a telepath to meet me—possibly it's Communist paranoid suspicions of outsiders—but in any case I have a job to do here and I mean to do it. So shall we discuss the dismembered kitten?'

'At meal time?' Mr Lee said faintly.

'You brought it up,' Joan said, and proceeded, despite the expression of acute misery on Mr Lee's face as he sat spooning up his bird's nest soup.

At the Los Angeles studio of television station KKHF, Ray Meritan sat at his harp, waiting for his cue. 'How High the Moon,' he had decided, would be his first number. He yawned, kept his eye on the control booth.

Beside him, at the blackboard, jazz commentator Glen Goldstream polished his rimless glasses with a fine linen handkerchief and said, 'I think I'll tie in with Gustav Mahler tonight.'

'Who the hell is he?'

'A great late-nineteenth-century composer. Very romantic. Wrote long peculiar symphonies and folk-type songs. I'm thinking, however, of the rhythmic patterns in "The Drunkard in Springtime" from *Song of the Earth*. You've never heard it?'

'Nope,' Meritan said restlessly.

'Very gray-green.'

Ray Meritan did not feel very gray-green tonight. His head still ached from the rock thrown at Wilbur Mercer. Meritan had tried to let go of the empathy box when he saw the rock coming, but he had not been quick enough. It had struck Mercer on the right temple, drawing blood.

'I've run into three Mercerites this evening,' Glen said. 'And all of them looked terrible. What happened to Mercer today?'

'How would I know?'

'You're carrying yourself the way they did today. It's your head, isn't it? I know you well enough, Ray. You'd be mixed up in anything new and odd—what do I care if you're a Mercerite? I just thought maybe you'd like a pain pill.'

Brusquely, Ray Meritan said, 'That would defeat the entire idea wouldn't it? A pain pill. Here, Mr Mercer, as you go up the hillside, how about a shot of morphine? You won't feel a thing.' He rippled a few cadences on his harp, releasing his emotions.

'You're on,' the producer said from the control room.

Their theme, 'That's a Plenty,' swelled from the tape deck in the control room, and the number two camera facing Goldstream lit up its red light. Arms folded, Goldstream said, 'Good evening, ladies and gentlemen. What is jazz?'

That's what I say, Meritan thought. What is jazz? What is life? He rubbed his splintered, pain-racked forehead and wondered how he could endure the next week. Wilbur Mercer was getting close to it now. Each day it would become worse . . .

'And after a brief pause for an important message,' Goldstream was saying, 'we'll be back to tell you more about the world of gray-green men and women, those peculiar people, and the world of the artistry of the one and only Ray Meritan.'

The tape of the commercial appeared on the TV monitor facing Meritan.

Meritan said to Goldstream, 'I'll take the pain pill.'

A yellow, flat, notched tablet was held out to him. 'Paracodein,' Goldstream said. 'Highly illegal, but effective. An addictive drug . . . I'm surprised you, of all people, don't carry some.'

'I used to,' Ray said, as he got a dixie cup of water and swallowed the pill.

'And now you're on Mercerism.'

'Now I'm—' He glanced at Goldstream; they had known each other, in their professional capacities, for years. 'I'm not a Mercerite,' he said, 'so forget it, Glen. It's just coincidence I got a headache the night Mercer was hit on the temple by a sharp rock thrown by some moronic sadist who ought to be the one dragging his way up that hillside.' He scowled at Goldstream.

'I understand,' Goldstream said, 'that the US Department of Mental Health is on the verge of asking the Justice Department to pick up the Mercerites.'

Suddenly he swung to face camera two. A faint smile touched his face and he said smoothly, 'Gray-green began about four years ago, in Pinole, California, at the now justly-famous Double Shot Club where Ray Meritan played, back in 1993 and '4. Tonight, Ray will let us hear one of his best known and liked numbers, "Once in Love with Amy."' He swung in Meritan's direction. 'Ray . . . Meritan!'

Plunk-plunk, the harp went as Ray Meritan's fingers riffled the strings.

An object lesson, he thought as he played. That's what the FBI would make me into for the teenagers, to show them what not to grow up to be. First on Paracodein, now on Mercer. Beware, kids!

Off camera, Glen Goldstream held up a sign he had scribbled.

IS MERCER A NON-TERRESTRIAL?

Underneath this, Goldstream wrote with a marking pencil:

IT'S *THAT* THEY WANT TO KNOW.

Invasion from outside there somewhere, Meritan thought to himself as he played. That's what they're afraid of. Fear of the unknown, like tiny children. That's our ruling circles: tiny, fear-ridden children playing ritualistic games with super-powerful toys.

A thought came to him from one of the network officials in the control room. *Mercer has been injured.*

At once, Ray Meritan turned his attention that way, scanned as hard as he could. His fingers strummed the harp reflexively.

Government outlawing so-called empathy boxes.

He thought immediately of his own empathy box, before his TV set in the living room of his apartment.

Organization which distributes and sells the empathy boxes declared illegal, and FBI making arrests in several major cities. Other countries expected to follow.

How badly injured? he wondered. Dying?

And—what about the Mercerites who had been holding onto the handles of their empathy boxes at that moment? How were they, now? Receiving medical attention?

Should we air the news now? the network official was thinking. *Or wait until the commercial?*

Ray Meritan ceased playing his harp and said clearly into the boom microphone, 'Wilbur Mercer has been injured. This is what we've expected but it's still a major tragedy. Mercer is a saint.'

Wide-eyed, Glen Goldstream gawked at him.

'I believe in Mercer,' Ray Meritan said, and all across the United States his television audience heard his confession of faith. 'I believe his suffering and injury and death have meaning for each of us.'

It was done; he had gone on record. And it hadn't even taken much courage.

'Pray for Wilbur Mercer,' he said and resumed playing his gray-green style of harp.

You fool, Glen Goldstream was thinking. Giving yourself away! You'll be in jail within a week. Your career is ruined!

Plunk-plunk, Ray played on his harp, and smiled humorlessly at Glen.

IV

Mr Lee said, 'Do you know the story of the Zen monk, who was playing hide and go seek with the children? Was it Basho who tells this? The monk hid in an outhouse and the children did not think of looking there, and so they forgot him. He was a very simple man. Next day—'

'I admit that Zen is a form of stupidity,' Joan Hiashi said. 'It extols the virtues of being simple and gullible. And remember, the original meaning of "gullible" is one who is easily gulled, easily cheated.' She sipped a little of her tea and found it now cold.

'Then you are a true practitioner of Zen,' Mr Lee said. 'Because you have been gulled.' He reached inside his coat and brought out a pistol, which he pointed at Joan. 'You're under arrest.'

'By the Cuban Government?' she managed to say.

'By the United States Government,' Mr Lee said. 'I have read your mind and I learn that you know that Ray Meritan is a prominent Mercerite and you yourself are attracted to Mercerism.'

'But I'm not!'

'Unconsciously you are attracted. You are about to switch over. I can pick up those thoughts, even if you deny them to yourself. We are going back to the United States, you and I, and there we will find Mr Ray Meritan and he will lead us to Wilbur Mercer; it is as simple as that.'

'And this is why I was sent to Cuba?'

'I am a member of the Central Committee of the Cuban Communist Party,' Mr Lee said. 'And the sole telepath on that committee. We have voted to work in cooperation with the United States Department of State during this current Mercer crisis. Our plane, Miss Hiashi, leaves for Washington, DC in half an hour; let us get down to the airport at once.'

Joan Hiashi looked helplessly about the restaurant. Other people eating, the waiters . . . nobody paid attention. She rose to her feet as a waiter passed with a heavily-loaded tray. 'This man,' she said, pointing to Mr Lee, 'is kidnapping me. Help me, please.'

The waiter glanced at Mr Lee, saw who it was, smiled at Joan and shrugged. 'Mr Lee, he is an important man,' the waiter said, and went on with his tray.

'What he says is true,' Mr Lee said to her.

Joan ran from the booth and across the restaurant. 'Help me,' she said to the elderly Cuban Mercerite who sat with his empathy box before him. 'I'm a Mercerite. They're arresting me.'

The lined old face lifted; the man scrutinized her.

'Help me,' she said.

'Praise Mercer,' the old man said.

You can't help me, she realized. She turned back to Mr Lee, who had followed after her, still holding the pistol pointed at her. 'This old man is not going to do a thing,' Mr Lee said. 'Not even get to his feet.'

She sagged. 'All right. I know.'

THE LITTLE BLACK BOX

The television set in the corner suddenly ceased its yammering of daytime trash; the image of a woman's face and bottle of cleanser abruptly disappeared and there was only blackness. Then, in Spanish, a news announcer began to speak.

'Hurt,' Mr Lee said, listening. 'But Mercer is not dead. How do you feel, Miss Hiashi, as a Mercerite? Does this affect you? Oh, but that's right. One must take hold of the handles first, for it to reach you. It must be a voluntary act.'

Joan picked up the elderly Cuban's empathy box, held it for a moment, and then seized the handles. Mr Lee stared at her in surprise; he moved toward her, reaching for the box . . .

It was not pain that she felt. Is this how it is? she wondered as she saw around her, the restaurant dim and faded. Maybe Wilbur Mercer is unconscious; that must be it. I'm escaping from you, she thought to Mr Lee. You can't—or at least you won't—follow me where I've gone: into the tomb world of Wilbur Mercer, who is dying somewhere on a barren plain, surrounded by his enemies. Now I'm with him. And it is an escape from something worse. From you. And you're never going to be able to get me back.

She saw, around her, a desolate expanse. The air smelled of harsh blossoms; this was the desert, and there was no rain.

A man stood before her, a sorrowful light in his gray, pain-drenched eyes. 'I am your friend,' he said, 'but you must go on as if I did not exist. Can you understand that?' He spread empty hands.

'No,' she said, 'I can't understand that.'

'How can I save you,' the man said, 'if I can't save myself?' He smiled: 'Don't you see? *There is no salvation.*'

'Then what's it all for?' she asked.

'To show you,' Wilbur Mercer said, 'that you aren't alone. I am here with you and always will be. Go back and face them. And tell them that.'

She released the handles.

Mr Lee, holding his gun to her, said, 'Well?'

'Let's go,' she said. 'Back to the United States. Turn me over to the FBI. It doesn't matter.'

'What did you see?' Mr Lee said, with curiosity.

'I won't tell you.'

'But I can learn it anyhow. From your mind.' He was probing, now, listening with his head cocked on one side. The corners of his mouth turned down as if he was pouting.

'I don't call that much,' he said. 'Mercer looks you in the face and says he can't do anything for you—is this the man you'd lay down your life for, you and the others? You're ill.'

'In the society of the insane,' Joan said, 'the sick are well.'

'What nonsense!' Mr Lee said.

To Bogart Crofts Mr Lee said, 'It was interesting. She became a Mercerite directly in front of me. The latency transforming itself into actuality . . . it proved I was correct in what I previously read in her mind.'

'We'll have Meritan picked up any time now,' Crofts said to his superior, Secretary Herrick. 'He left the television studio in Los Angeles, where he got news of Mercer's severe injury. After that, no one seems to know what he did. He did *not* return to his apartment. The local police picked up his empathy box, and he was beyond a doubt not on the premises.'

'Where is Joan Hiashi?' Crofts asked.

'Being held now in New York,' Mr Lee said.

'On what charge?' Crofts asked Secretary Herrick.

'Political agitation inimical to the safety of the United States.'

Smiling, Mr Lee said, 'And arrested by a Communist official in Cuba. It is a Zen paradox which no doubt fails to delight Miss Hiashi.'

Meanwhile, Bogart Crofts reflected, empathy boxes were being collected in huge quantities. Soon their destruction would begin. Within forty-eight hours most of the empathy boxes in the United States would no longer exist, including the one here in his office.

It still rested on his desk, untouched. It was he who originally had asked that it be brought in, and in all this time he had kept his hands off it, had never yielded. Now he walked over to it.

'What would happen,' he asked Mr Lee, 'if I took hold of these two handles? There's no television set here. I have no idea what Wilbur Mercer is doing right now; in fact for all that I know, now he's finally dead.'

Mr Lee said, 'If you grip the handles, sir, you will enter a—I hesitate to use the word but it seems to apply. A mystical communion. With Mr Mercer, wherever he is; you will share his suffering, as you know, but that is not all. You will also participate in his—' Mr Lee reflected. '"World-view" is not the correct term. Ideology? No.'

Secretary Herrick suggested, 'What about *trance-state?*'

'Perhaps that is it,' Mr Lee said, frowning. 'No, that is not it either. No word will do, and that is the entire point. It cannot be described—it must be experienced.'

'I'll try,' Crofts decided.

'No,' Mr Lee said. 'Not if you are following my advice. I would warn you away from it. I saw Miss Hiashi do it, and I saw the change in her. Would you have tried Paracodein when it was popular with rootless cosmopolite masses?' He sounded angry.

'I have tried Paracodein,' Crofts said. 'It did absolutely nothing for me.'

'What do you want done, Boge?' Secretary Herrick asked him.

Shrugging, Bogart Crofts said, 'I mean I could see no reason for anyone liking it, wanting to become addicted to it.' And at last he took hold of the two handles of the empathy box.

V

Walking slowly in the rain, Ray Meritan said to himself, They got my empathy box and if I go back to the apartment they'll get me.

His telepathic talent had saved him. As he entered the building he had picked up the thoughts of the gang of city police.

It was now past midnight. The trouble is I'm too well-known, he realized, from my damned TV show. No matter where I go I'll be recognized.

At least anywhere on Earth.

Where is Wilbur Mercer? he asked himself. In this solar system or somewhere beyond it, under a different sun entirely? Maybe we'll never know. Or at least *I'll* never know.

But did it matter? Wilbur Mercer was somewhere; that was all that was important. And there was always a way to reach him. The empathy box was always there—or at least had been, until the police raids. And Meritan had a feeling that the distribution company which had supplied the empathy boxes, and which led a shadowy existence anyhow, would find a way around the police. If he was right about them—

Ahead in the rainy darkness he saw the red lights of a bar. He turned and entered it.

To the bartender he said, 'Look, do you have an empathy box? I'll pay you one hundred dollars for the use of it.'

The bartender, a big burly man with hairy arms, said, 'Naw, I don't have nuthin like that. Go on.'

The people at the bar watched, and one of them said, 'Those are illegal now.'

'Hey, it's Ray Meritan,' another said. 'The jazz man.'

Another man said lazily, 'Play some gray-green jazz for us, jazz man.' He sipped at his mug of beer.

Meritan started out of the bar.

'Wait,' the bartender said. 'Hold on, buddy. Go to this address.' He wrote on a match folder, then held it out to Meritan.

'How much do I owe you?' Meritan said.

'Oh, five dollars ought to do it.'

Meritan paid and left the bar, the match folder in his pocket. It's probably the address of the local police station, he said to himself. But I'll give it a try anyhow.

If I could get to an empathy box one more time—

The address which the bartender had given him was an old, decaying wooden building in downtown Los Angeles. He rapped on the door and stood waiting.

The door opened. A middle-aged heavy woman in bathrobe

and furry slippers peeped out at him. 'I'm not the police,' he said. 'I'm a Mercerite. Can I use your empathy box?'

The door gradually opened; the woman scrutinized him and evidently believed him, although she said nothing.

'Sorry to bother you so late,' he apologized.

'What happened to you, mister?' the woman said. 'You look bad.'

'It's Wilbur Mercer,' Ray said. 'He's hurt.'

'Turn it on,' the woman said, leading him with shuffling into a dark, cold parlor where a parrot slept in a huge, bent, brass-wire cage. There, on an old-fashioned radio cabinet, he saw the empathy box. He felt relief creep over him at the sight of it.

'Don't be shy,' the woman said.

'Thanks,' he said, and took hold of the handles.

A voice said in his ear, 'We'll use the girl. She'll lead us to Meritan. I was right to hire her in the first place.'

Ray Meritan did not recognize the voice. It was not that of Wilbur Mercer. But even so, bewildered, he held tightly onto the handles, listening; he remained frozen there, hands extended, clutching.

'The non-T force has appealed to the most credulous segment of our community, but this segment—I firmly believe—is being manipulated by a cynical minority of opportunists at the top, such as Meritan. They're cashing in on this Wilbur Mercer craze for their own pocketbooks.' The voice, self-assured, droned on.

Ray Meritan felt fear as he heard it. For this was someone on the other side, he realized. Somehow he had gotten into empathic contact with him, and not with Wilbur Mercer.

Or had Mercer done this deliberately, arranged this? He listened on, and now he heard:

'. . . have to get the Hiashi girl out of New York and back here, where we can quiz her further.' The voice added, 'As I told Herrick . . .'

Herrick, the Secretary of State. This was someone in the State Department thinking, Meritan realized, thinking about Joan. Perhaps this was the official at State who had hired her.

Then she wasn't in Cuba. She was in New York. What had gone

wrong? The whole implication was that State had merely made use of Joan to get at him.

He released the handles and the voice faded from his presence.

'Did you find him?' the middle-aged woman asked.

'Y-yes,' Meritan said, disconcerted, trying to orient himself in the unfamiliar room.

'How is he? Is he well?'

'I—don't know right now,' Meritan answered, truthfully. He thought, I must go to New York. And try to help Joan. She's in this because of me; I have no choice. Even if they catch me because of it . . . how can I desert her?

Bogart Crofts said, 'I didn't get Mercer.'

He walked away from the empathy box, then turned to glare at it, balefully. 'I got Meritan. But I don't know where he is. At the moment I took hold of the handles of this box, Meritan took hold somewhere else. We were connected and now he knows everything I know. And we know everything he knows, which isn't much.' Dazed, he turned to Secretary Herrick. 'He doesn't know any more about Wilbur Mercer than we do; he was trying to reach him. He definitely is *not* Mercer.' Crofts was silent then.

'There's more,' Herrick said, turning to Mr Lee. 'What else did he get from Meritan, Mr Lee?'

'Meritan is coming to New York to try to find Joan Hiashi,' Mr Lee said, obligingly reading Crofts' mind. 'He got that from Mr Meritan during the moment their minds were fused.'

'We'll prepare to receive Mr Meritan,' Secretary Herrick said, with a grimace.

'Did I experience what you telepaths engage in all the time?' Crofts asked Mr Lee.

'Only when one of us comes close to another telepath,' Mr Lee said. 'It can be unpleasant. We avoid it, because if the two minds are thoroughly dissimilar and hence clash, it is psychologically harmful. I would assume you and Mr Meritan clashed.'

Crofts said, 'Listen, how can we continue with this? I know now that Meritan is innocent. He doesn't know a damn thing about Mercer or the organization that distributes these boxes except its name.'

There was momentary silence.

'But he is one of the few celebrities who has joined the Mercerites,' Secretary Herrick pointed out. He handed a teletype dispatch to Crofts. 'And he has done it openly. If you'll take the trouble to read this—'

'I know he affirmed his loyalty to Mercer on this evening's TV program,' Crofts said, trembling.

'When you're dealing with a non-T force originating from another solar system entirely,' Secretary Herrick said, 'you must move with care. We will still try to take Meritan, and definitely through Miss Hiashi. We'll release her from jail and have her followed. When Meritan makes contact with her—'

To Crofts, Mr Lee said, 'Don't say what you intend, Mr Crofts. It will permanently damage your career.'

Crofts said, 'Herrick, this is wrong. Meritan is innocent and so is Joan Hiashi. If you try to trap Meritan I'll resign from State.'

'Write out your resignation and hand it to me,' Secretary Herrick said. His face was dark.

'This is unfortunate,' Mr Lee said. 'I would guess that your contact with Mr Meritan warped your judgment, Mr Crofts. He has influenced you malignly; shake it off, for the sake of your long career and country, not to mention your family.'

'What we're doing is wrong,' Crofts repeated.

Secretary Herrick stared at him angrily. 'No wonder those empathy boxes have done harm! Now I've seen it with my own eyes. I wouldn't turn back on any condition now.'

He picked up the empathy box which Crofts had used. Lifting it high he dropped it to the floor. The box cracked open and then settled in a heap of irregular surfaces. 'Don't consider that a childish act,' he said. 'I want any contact between us and Meritan broken. It can only be harmful.'

'If we capture him,' Crofts said, 'he may continue to exert influence over us.' He amended his statement: 'Or rather, over me.'

'Be that as it may, I intend to continue,' Secretary Herrick said. 'And please present your resignation. Mr Crofts, I intend to act on that matter as well.' He looked grim and determined.

Mr Lee said, 'Secretary, I can read Mr Crofts' mind and I see that he is stunned at this moment. He is the innocent victim of a situation, arranged perhaps by Wilbur Mercer to spread confusion among us. And if you accept Mr Crofts' resignation, Mercer will have succeeded.'

'It doesn't matter whether he accepts it or not,' Crofts said. 'Because in any case I'm resigning.'

Sighing, Mr Lee said, 'The empathy box made you suddenly into an involuntary telepath and it was just too much.' He patted Mr Crofts on the shoulder. 'Telepathic power and empathy are two versions of the same thing. It should be called "telepathic box." Amazing, those non-T individuals; they can build what we can only evolve.'

'Since you can read my mind,' Crofts said to him, 'you know what I'm planning to do. I have no doubt you'll tell Secretary Herrick.'

Grinning blandly, Mr Lee said, 'The Secretary and I are cooperating in the interest of world peace. We both have our instructions.' To Herrick he said, 'This man is so upset that he now actually considers switching over. Joining the Mercerites before all the boxes are destroyed. He liked being an involuntary telepath.'

'If you switch,' Herrick said, 'you'll be arrested. I promise it.'

Crofts said nothing.

'He has not changed his mind,' Mr Lee said urbanely, nodding to both men, apparently amused by the situation.

But underneath, Mr Lee was thinking, A brilliant bold type of stroke by the thing that calls itself Wilbur Mercer, this hooking up of Crofts with Meritan direct. It undoubtedly foresaw that Crofts would receive the strong emanations from the movement's core. The next step is that Crofts will again consult an empathy box—if he can find one—and this time Mercer itself will address him personally. Address its new disciple.

They have gained a man, Mr Lee realized. They are ahead.

But ultimately we will win. Because ultimately we will manage to destroy all the empathy boxes, and without them Wilbur Mercer can do nothing. This is the only way he has—or it has—of reaching and controlling people, as it has done here with unfortunate Mr Crofts. *Without the empathy boxes the movement is helpless.*

VI

At the UWA desk, at Rocky Field in New York City, Joan Hiashi said to the uniformed clerk, 'I want to buy a one-way ticket to Los Angeles on the next flight. Jet or rocket; it doesn't matter. I just want to get there.'

'First class or tourist?' the clerk asked.

'Aw, hell,' Joan said wearily, 'just sell me a ticket. Any kind of a ticket.' She opened her purse.

As she started to pay for the ticket a hand stopped hers. She turned—and there stood Ray Meritan, his face twisting with relief.

'What a place to try to pick up your thoughts,' he said. 'Come on, let's go where it's quiet. You have ten minutes before your flight.'

They hurried together through the building until they came to a deserted ramp. There they stopped, and Joan said, 'Listen, Ray, I know it's a trap for you. That's why they let me out. But where else can I go except to you?'

Ray said, 'Don't worry about it. They were bound to pick me up sooner or later. I'm sure they know I left California and came here.' He glanced around. 'No FBI agents near us yet. At least I don't pick up anything suggesting it.' He lit a cigarette.

'I don't have any reason to go back to LA,' Joan said, 'now that you're here. I might as well cancel my flight.'

'You know they're picking up and destroying all the empathy boxes they can,' Ray said.

'No,' she said. 'I didn't know, I was just released half an hour ago. That's dreadful. They really mean business.'

Ray laughed. 'Let's say they're really frightened.' He put his arm around her and kissed her. 'I tell you what we'll do. We'll try to sneak out of this place, go to the lower East Side and rent a little cold-water walk-up. We'll hide out and find an empathy box they missed.' But, he thought, it's unlikely; they probably have them all by now. There weren't that many to start with.

'Anything you say,' Joan said drably.

'Do you love me?' he asked her. 'I can read your mind; you do.' And then he said quietly, 'I can also read the mind of a Mr Lewis Scanlan, an FBI man who's now at the UWA desk. What name did you give?'

'Mrs George McIsaacs,' Joan said. 'I think.' She examined her ticket and envelope. 'Yes, that's right.'

'But Scanlan is asking if a Japanese woman has been at the desk in the last fifteen minutes,' Ray said. 'And the clerk remembers you. So–' He took hold of Joan's arm. 'We better get started.'

They hurried down the deserted ramp, passed through an electric-eye operated door and came out in a baggage lobby. Everyone there was far too busy to pay any attention as Ray Meritan and Joan threaded their way to the street door and, a moment later, stepped out onto the chill gray sidewalk where cabs had parked in a long double row. Joan started to hail a cab . . .

'Wait,' Ray said, pulling her back. 'I'm getting a jumble of thoughts. One of the cab drivers is an FBI man but I can't tell which.' He stood uncertainly, not knowing what to do.

'We can't get away, can we?' Joan said.

'It's going to be hard.' To himself he thought, More like impossible; you're right. He experienced the girl's confused, frightened thoughts, her anxiety about him, that she had made it possible for them to locate and capture him, her fierce desire not to return to jail, her pervasive bitterness at having been betrayed by Mr Lee, the Chinese Communist bigshot who had met her in Cuba.

'What a life,' Joan said, standing close to him.

And still he did not know which cab to take. One precious second after another escaped as he stood there. 'Listen,' he said to Joan, 'maybe we should separate.'

'No,' she said, clinging to him. 'I can't stand to do it alone any more. Please.'

A bewhiskered peddler walked up to them with a tray suspended by a cord which ran about his neck. 'Hi, folks,' he mumbled.

'Not now,' Joan said to him.

'Free sample of breakfast cereal,' the peddler said. 'No cost. Just take a box, miss. You mister. Take one.' He extended the tray of small, gaily colored cartons toward Ray.

Strange, Ray thought. I'm not picking up anything from this man's mind. He stared at the peddler, saw—or thought he saw—a peculiar insubstantiality to the man. A diffused quality.

Ray took one of the samples of breakfast cereal.

'Merry Meal, it's called,' the peddler said. 'A new product they're introducing to the public. There's a coupon inside. Entitles you to—'

'Okay,' Ray said, sticking the box in his pocket. He took hold of Joan and led her along the line of cabs. He chose one at random and opened the rear door. 'Get in,' he said urgently to her.

'I took a sample of Merry Meal, too,' she said with a wan smile as he seated himself beside her. The cab started up, left the line and pulled past the entrance of the airfield terminal. 'Ray, there was something strange about that salesman. It was as if he wasn't actually there, as if he was nothing more than—a picture.'

As the cab drove down the auto ramp, away from the terminal, another cab left the line and followed after them. Twisting, Ray saw riding in the back of it two well-fed men in dark business suits. FBI men, he said to himself.

Joan said, 'Didn't that cereal salesman remind you of anyone?' 'Who?'

'A little of Wilbur Mercer. But I haven't seen him enough to—'

Ray grabbed the cereal box from her hand, tore the cardboard top from it. Poking up from the dry cereal he saw the corner of the coupon the peddler had spoken about; he lifted out the coupon, held it up and studied it. The coupon said in large clear printing:

'It was them,' he said to Joan.

He put the coupon carefully away in his pocket, then he changed his mind. Folding it up, he tucked it in the cuff of his trousers. Where the FBI possibly wouldn't find it.

Behind them, the other cab came closer, and now he picked up the thoughts of the two men. They were FBI agents; he had been right. He settled back against the seat.

There was nothing to do but wait.

Joan said, 'Could I have the other coupon?'

'Sorry.' He got out the other cereal package. She opened it, found the coupon inside and, after a pause, folded it and hid it in the hem of her skirt.

'I wonder how many there are of those so-called peddlers,' Ray said musingly. 'I'd be interested to know how many free samples of Merry Meal they're going to manage to give away before they're caught.'

The first ordinary household object needed was a common radio set; he had noticed that. The second, the filament from a five-year light-bulb. And next—he'd have to look again, but now was not the time. The other cab had drawn abreast with theirs.

Later. And if the authorities found the coupon in the cuff of his trousers, they, he knew, would somehow manage to bring him another.

He put his arm around Joan. 'I think we'll be all right.'

The other cab, now, was nosing theirs to the curb and the two FBI men were waving in a menacing, official manner to the driver to stop.

'Shall I stop?' the driver said tensely to Ray.

'Sure,' he said. And, taking a deep breath, prepared himself.

THE WAR WITH THE FNOOLS

Captain Edgar Lightfoot of the CIA said, 'Darn it, the Fnools are back again, Major. They've taken over Provo, Utah.'

With a groan, Major Hauk signaled his secretary to bring him the Fnool dossier from the locked archives. 'What form are they assuming this time?' he asked briskly.

'Tiny real-estate salesmen,' Lightfoot said.

Last time, Major Hauk reflected, it had been filling station attendants. That was the thing about the Fnools. When one took a particular shape they all took that shape. Of course, it made detection for CIA fieldmen much easier. But it did make the Fnools look absurd, and Hauk did not enjoy fighting an absurd enemy; it was a quality which tended to diffuse over both sides and even up to his own office.

'Do you think they'd come to terms?' Hauk said, half-rhetorically. 'We could afford to sacrifice Provo, Utah, if they'd be willing to circumscribe themselves there. We could even add those portions of Salt Lake City which are paved with hideous old red brick.'

Lightfoot said, 'Fnools never compromise, Major. Their goal is Sol System domination. For all time.'

Leaning over Major Hauk's shoulder, Miss Smith said, 'Here is the Fnool dossier, sir.' With her free hand she pressed the top of her blouse against herself in a gesture indicating either advanced tuberculosis or advanced modesty. There were certain indications that it was the latter.

'Miss Smith,' Major Hauk complained, 'here are the Fnools trying to take over the Sol System and I'm handed their dossier by a woman with a forty-two-inch bosom. Isn't that a trifle schizo-phrenic—for me, at least?' He carefully averted his eyes from her, remembering his wife and the two children. 'Wear something else from here on out,' he told her. 'Or swaddle yourself. I mean, my God, let's be reasonable: let's be realistic.'

'Yes, Major,' Miss Smith said. 'But remember, I was selected at random from the CIA employees pool. I didn't *ask* to be your secretary.'

With Captain Lightfoot beside him, Major Hauk laid out the documents that made up the Fnool dossier.

In the Smithsonian there was a huge Fnool, standing three feet high, stuffed and preserved in a natural habitat-type cubicle. School children for years had marveled at this Fnool, which was shown with pistol aimed at Terran innocents. By pressing a button, the school children caused the Terrans (not stuffed but imitation) to flee, whereupon the Fnool extinguished them with its advanced solar-powered weapon . . . and the exhibit reverted to its original stately scene, ready to begin all over again.

Major Hauk had seen the exhibit, and it made him uneasy. The Fnools, he had declared time and time again, were no joke. But there was something about a Fnool that—well, a Fnool was an idi-otic life form. That was the basis of it. No matter what it imitated it retained its midget aspect; a Fnool looked like something given away free at supermarket openings, along with balloons and moist purple orchids. No doubt, Major Hauk had ruminated, it was a survival factor. It disarmed the Fnool's opponents. Even the name. It was just not possible to take them seriously, even at this very moment when they were infesting Provo, Utah, in the form of miniature real-estate salesmen.

Hauk instructed, 'Capture a Fnool in this current guise, Light-foot, bring it to me and I'll parley. I feel like capitulating, this time. I've been fighting them for twenty years now. I'm worn out.'

'If you get one face to face with you,' Lightfoot cautioned, 'it may successfully imitate you and that would be the end. We would have to incinerate both of you, just to be on the safe side.'

Gloomily, Hauk said, 'I'll set up a key password situation with you right now, Captain. The word is *masticate*. I'll use it in a sentence . . . for instance, "I've got to thoroughly masticate these data." The Fnool won't know that—correct?'

'Yes, Major,' Captain Lightfoot sighed and left the CIA office at once, hurrying to the 'copter field across the street to begin his trip to Provo, Utah.

But he had a feeling of foreboding.

When his 'copter landed at the end of Provo Canyon on the outskirts of the town, he was at once approached by a two-foot-high man in a gray business suit carrying a briefcase.

'Good morning, sir,' the Fnool piped. 'Care to look at some choice lots, all with unobstructed views? Can be subdivided into—'

'Get in the 'copter,' Lightfoot said, aiming his Army-issue .45 at the Fnool.

'Listen, my friend,' the Fnool said, in a jolly tone of voice. 'I can see you've never really given any hardheaded thought to the meaning of our race having landed on your planet. Why don't we step into the office a moment and sit down?' The Fnool indicated a nearby small building in which Lightfoot saw a desk and chairs. Over the office there was a sign:

EARLY BIRD

LAND DEVELOPMENT

INCORPORATED

'"The early bird catches the worm,"' the Fnool declared. 'And the spoils go to the winner, Captain Lightfoot. By nature's laws, if we manage to infest your planet and pre-empt you, we've got all the forces of evolution and biology on our side.' The Fnool beamed cheerily.

Lightfoot said, 'There's a CIA major back in Washington, DC who's on to you.'

'Major Hauk has defeated us twice,' the Fnool admitted. 'We respect him. But he's a voice crying in the wilderness, in this country, at least. You know perfectly well, Captain, that the average American viewing that exhibit at the Smithsonian merely smiles in a tolerant fashion. There's just no awareness of the *menace*.'

By now two other Fnools, also in the form of tiny real-estate salesmen in gray business suits carrying briefcases, had approached. 'Look,' one said to the other. 'Charley's captured a Terran.'

'No,' its companion disagreed, 'the Terran captured him.'

'All three of you get in the CIA 'copter,' Lightfoot ordered, waving his .45 at them.

'You're making a mistake,' the first Fnool said, shaking its head. 'But you're a young man; you'll mature in time.' It walked to the 'copter. Then, all at once, it spun and cried, '*Death to the Terrans!*'

Its briefcase whipped up, a bolt of pure solar energy whined past Lightfoot's right ear. Lightfoot dropped to one knee and squeezed the trigger of the .45; the Fnool, in the doorway of the 'copter, pitched head-forward and lay with its briefcase beside it. The other two Fnools watched as Lightfoot cautiously kicked the briefcase away.

'Young,' one of the remaining Fnools said, 'but with quick reflexes. Did you see the way he dropped on one knee?'

'Terrans are no joke,' the other agreed. 'We've got an uphill battle ahead of us.'

'As long as you're here,' the first of the remaining Fnools said to Lightfoot, 'why don't you put a small deposit down on some valuable unimproved land we've got a listing for? I'll be glad to run you out to have a look at it. Water and electricity available at a slight additional cost.'

'Get in the 'copter,' Lightfoot repeated, aiming his gun steadily at them.

In Berlin, an *Oberstleutnant* of the SHD, the Sicherheitsdienst—the West German Security Service—approaching his commanding officer, saluted in what is termed Roman style and said, '*General, die Fnoolen sind wieder zurück. Was sollen wir jetzt tun?*'

'The Fnools are *back*?' Hochflieger said, horrified. 'Already? But it was only three years ago that we uncovered their network and eradicated them.' Jumping to his feet General Hochflieger paced about his cramped temporary office in the basement of the Bundesrat Gebäude, his large hands clasped behind his back. 'And what guise this time? Assistant Ministers of Domestic Finance, as before?'

'No sir,' the *Oberstleutnant* said. 'They have come as gear inspectors of the VW works. Brown suit, clipboard, thick glasses, middle-aged. Fussy. And, as before, *nur* six-tenths of a meter high.'

'What I detest about the Fnools,' Hochflieger said, 'is their ruthless use of science in the service of destruction, especially their medical techniques. They almost defeated us with that virus infection suspended in the gum on the backs of multi-color commemorative stamps.'

'A desperate weapon,' his subordinate agreed, 'but rather too fantastic to be successful, ultimately. This time they'll probably rely on crushing force combined with an absolutely synchronized timetable.'

'*Selbstverständlich*,' Hochflieger agreed. 'But we've nonetheless got to react and defeat them. Inform Terpol.' That was the Terra-wide organization of counterintelligence with headquarters on Luna. 'Where, specifically, have they been detected?'

'In Schweinfurt only, so far.'

'Perhaps we should obliterate the Schweinfurt area.'

'They'll only turn up elsewhere.'

'True.' Hochflieger brooded. 'What we must do is pursue Operation Hundefutter to successful culmination.' Hundefutter had developed for the West German Government a sub-species of Terrans six-tenths of a meter high and capable of assuming a variety of forms. They would be used to penetrate the network of Fnool activity and destroy it from within. Hundefutter, financed by the Krupp family, had been held in readiness for just this moment.

'I'll activate Kommando Einsatzgruppe II,' his subordinate said. 'As counter-Fnools they can begin to drop behind Fnool lines near the Schweinfurt area immediately. By nightfall the situation should be in our hands.'

'Grüss Gott,' Hochflieger prayed, nodding. 'Well, get the *Kommando* started, and we'll keep our ears open to see how it proceeds.'

If it failed, he realized, more desperate measures would have to be initiated.

The survival of our race is at stake, Hochflieger said to himself. The next four thousand years of history will be determined by the brave act of a member of the SHD at this hour. Perhaps myself.

He paced about, meditating on that.

In Warsaw the local chief of the People's Protective Agency for Preserving the Democratic Process—the NNBNDL—read the coded teletype dispatch several times as he sat at his desk drinking tea and eating a late breakfast of sweet rolls and Polish ham. This time disguised as chess players, Serge Nicov said to himself. And each Fnool making use of the queen's pawn opening, Qp to Q3 . . . a weak opening, he reflected, especially against Kp to K4, even if they draw white. But—

Still a potentially dangerous situation.

On a piece of official stationery he wrote *select out class of chess players employing queen's pawn opening.* For Invigorating Forest-renewal Team, he decided. Fnools are small, but they can plant saplings . . . we must get some use out of them. Seeds; they can plant sunflower seeds for our tundra-removal vegetable-oil venture.

A year of hard physical work, he decided, and they'll think twice before they invade Terra again.

On the other hand, we could make a deal with them, offer them an alternative to invigorating forest-renewal activity. They could enter the Army as a special brigade and be used in Chile, in the rugged mountains. Being only sixty-one centimeters high, many of them could be packed into a single nuclear sub for transport . . . but can Fnools be trusted?

The thing he hated most about Fnools—and he had learned to know them in their previous invasions of Terra—was their deceitfulness. Last time they had taken the physical form of a troupe of ethnic dancers . . . and what dancers they had turned out to be.

They had massacred an audience in Leningrad before anyone could intervene, men, women and children all dead on the spot by weapons of ingenious design and sturdy although monotonous construction which had masqueraded as folk-instruments of a five-stringed variety.

It could never happen again; all Democratic lands were alert, now; special youth groups had been set up to keep vigil. But something new—such as this chess-player deception—could succeed as well, especially in small towns in the East republics, where chess players were enthusiastically welcomed.

From a hidden compartment in his desk Serge Nicov brought out the special non-dial phone, picked up the receiver and said into the mouthpiece, 'Fnools back, in North Caucasus area. Better get as many tanks as possible lined up to accept their advance as they attempt to spread out. Contain them and then cut directly through their center, bisecting them repeatedly until they're splintered and can be dealt with in small bands.'

'Yes, Political Officer Nicov.'

Serge Nicov hung up and resumed eating his—now cold—late breakfast.

As Captain Lightfoot piloted the 'copter back to Washington, DC one of the two captured Fnools said, 'How is it that no matter what guise we come in, you Terrans can always detect us? We've appeared on your planet as filling station attendants, Volkswagen gear inspectors, chess champions, folk singers complete with native instruments, minor government officials, and now real-estate salesmen—'

Lightfoot said, 'It's your size.'

'That concept conveys nothing to us.'

'You're only two feet tall!'

The two Fnools conferred, and then the other Fnool patiently explained, 'But size is relative. We have all the absolute qualities of Terrans embodied in our temporary forms, and according to obvious logic—'

'Look,' Lightfoot said, 'stand here next to me.' The Fnool, in its gray business suit, carrying its briefcase, came cautiously up to stand beside him. 'You just come up to my knee cap,' Lightfoot pointed out. 'I'm six feet high. You're only one-third as tall as I. In a group of Terrans you Fnools stand out like an egg in a barrel of kosher pickles.'

'Is that a folk saying?' the Fnool asked. 'I'd better write that down.' From its coat pocket it produced a tiny ball point pen no longer than a match. 'Egg in barrel of pickles. Quaint. I hope, when we've wiped out your civilization, that some of your ethnic customs will be preserved by our museums.'

'I hope so, too,' Lightfoot said, lighting a cigarette.

The other Fnool, pondering, said, 'I wonder if there's any way we can grow taller. Is it a racial secret preserved by your people?' Noticing the burning cigarette dangling between Lightfoot's lips, the Fnool said, 'Is that how you achieve unnatural height? By burning that stick of compressed dried vegetable fibers and inhaling the smoke?'

'Yes,' Lightfoot said, handing the cigarette to the two-foot-high Fnool. 'That's our secret. Cigarette-smoking makes you grow. We have all our offspring, especially teen-agers, smoke. Everyone that's young.'

'I'm going to try it,' the Fnool said to its companion. Placing the cigarette between its lips, it inhaled deeply.

Lightfoot blinked. Because the Fnool was now four feet high, and its companion instantly imitated it; both Fnools were twice as high as before. Smoking the cigarette had augmented the Fnools' height incredibly by two whole feet.

'Thank you,' the now four-foot-high real-estate salesman said to Lightfoot, in a much deeper voice than before. 'We are certainly making bold strides, are we not?'

Nervously, Lightfoot said, 'Gimme back the cigarette.'

In his office at the CIA building, Major Julius Hauk pressed a button on his desk, and Miss Smith alertly opened the door and entered the room, dictation pad in hand.

'Miss Smith,' Major Hauk said, 'Captain Lightfoot's away. Now I can tell you. The Fnools are going to win this time. As senior officer in charge of defeating them, I'm about to give up and go down to the bomb-proof shelter constructed for hopeless situations such as this.'

'I'm sorry to hear that, sir,' Miss Smith said, her long eyelashes fluttering. 'I've enjoyed working for you.'

'But you, too,' Hauk explained. 'All Terrans are wiped out; our defeat is planet-wide.' Opening a drawer of his desk he brought out an unopened fifth of Bullock & Lade Scotch which he had been given as a birthday present. 'I'm going to finish this B & L Scotch off first,' he informed Miss Smith. 'Will you join me?'

'No thank you, sir,' Miss Smith said. 'I'm afraid I don't drink, at least during the daylight hours.'

Major Hauk drank for a moment from a dixie cup, then tried a little more from the bottle just to be sure it was Scotch all the way to the bottom. At last he put it down and said, 'It's hard to believe that our backs could be put to the wall by creatures no larger than domestic orange-striped tomcats, but such is the case.' He nodded courteously to Miss Smith. 'I'm off for the concrete sub-surface bomb-proof shelter, where I hope to hold out after the general collapse of life as we know it.'

'Good for you, Major Hauk,' Miss Smith said, a little uneasily. 'But are you—just going to *leave* me here to become a captive of the Fnools? I mean—' Her sharply pointed breasts quivered in becoming unison beneath her blouse. 'It seems sort of mean.'

'You have nothing to fear from the Fnools, Miss Smith,' Major Hauk said. 'After all, two feet tall—' He gestured. 'Even a neurotic young woman could scarcely—' He laughed. 'Really.'

'But it's a terrible feeling,' Miss Smith said, 'to be abandoned in the face of what we know to be an unnatural enemy from another planet entirely.'

'I tell you what,' Major Hauk said thoughtfully. 'Perhaps I'll break a series of strict CIA rulings and allow you to go below to the shelter with me.'

Putting down her pad and pencil and hurrying over to him, Miss Smith breathed, 'Oh, Major, how can I thank you!'

'Just come along,' Major Hauk said, leaving the bottle of B & L Scotch behind in his haste, the situation being what it was.

Miss Smith clung to him as he made his way a trifle unsteadily down the corridor to the elevator.

'Drat that Scotch,' he murmured. 'Miss Smith, Vivian, you were wise not to touch it. Given the cortico-thalamic reaction we are all experiencing in the face of the Fnoolian peril, Scotch isn't the beneficial balm it generally is.'

'Here,' his secretary said, sliding under his arm to help prop him up as they waited for the elevator. 'Try to stand firm, Major. It won't be long now.'

'You have a point there,' Major Hauk agreed. 'Vivian, my dear.'

The elevator came at last. It was the self-service type.

'You're being really very kind to me,' Miss Smith said, as the Major pressed the proper button and the elevator began to descend.

'Well, it may prolong your life,' Major Hauk agreed. 'Of course, that far underground . . . the average temperature is much greater than at the Earth's surface. Like a deep mine shaft, it runs in the near-hundreds.'

'But at least we'll be alive,' Miss Smith pointed out.

Major Hauk removed his coat and tie. 'Be prepared for the humid warmth,' he told her. 'Here, perhaps you would like to remove your coat.'

'Yes,' Miss Smith said, allowing him in his gentlemanly way to remove her coat.

The elevator arrived at the shelter. No one was there ahead of them, fortunately; they had the shelter all to themselves.

'It is stuffy down here,' Miss Smith said as Major Hauk switched on one dim yellow light. 'Oh dear.' She stumbled over something in the gloom. 'It's so hard to see.' Again she stumbled over some object; this time she half-fell. 'Shouldn't we have more light, Major?'

'What, and attract the Fnools?' In the dark, Major Hauk felt about until he located her; Miss Smith had toppled onto one of the shelter's many bunks and was groping about for her shoe.

'I think I broke the heel off,' Miss Smith said.

'Well, at least you got away with your life,' Major Hauk said. 'If nothing else.' In the gloom he began to assist her in removing her other shoe, it being worthless now.

'How long will we be down here?' Miss Smith asked.

'As long as the Fnools are in control,' Major Hauk informed her. 'You'd better change into radiation-proof garb in case the rotten little non-terrestrials try H-bombing the White House. Here, I'll take your blouse and skirt—there should be overalls somewhere around.'

'You're being really kind to me,' Miss Smith breathed, as she handed him her blouse and skirt. 'I can't get over it.'

'I think,' Major Hauk said, 'I'll change my mind and go back up for that Scotch; we'll be down here longer than I anticipated and we'll need something like that as the solitude frays our nerves. You stay here.' He felt his way back to the elevator.

'Don't be gone long,' Miss Smith called anxiously after him. 'I feel terribly exposed and unprotected down here alone, and what is more I can't seem to find that radiation-proof garb you spoke of.'

'Be right back,' Major Hauk promised.

At the field opposite the CIA building, Captain Lightfoot landed the 'copter with the two captive Fnools aboard. 'Get moving,' he instructed them, digging the muzzle of his Service .45 into their small ribs.

'It's because he's bigger than us, Len,' one of the Fnools said to the other. 'If we were the same size he wouldn't dare treat us this way. But now we understand—finally—the nature of the Terrans' superiority.'

'Yes,' the other Fnool said. 'The mystery of twenty years has been cleared up.'

'Four feet tall is still suspicious-looking,' Captain Lightfoot said, but he was thinking, If they grow from two feet to four feet in one instant, just by smoking a cigarette, what's to stop them from growing two feet more? Then they'll be six feet and look exactly like us.

And it's all my fault, he said to himself miserably.

Major Hauk will destroy me, career-wise if not body-wise.

However, he continued on as best he could; the famous tradition of the CIA demanded it. 'I'm taking you directly to Major Hauk,' he told the two Fnools. 'He'll know what to do with you.'

When they reached Major Hauk's office, no one was there.

'This is strange,' Captain Lightfoot said.

'Maybe Major Hauk has beaten a hasty retreat,' one of the Fnools said. 'Does this tall amber bottle indicate anything?'

'That's a tall amber bottle of Scotch,' Lightfoot said, scrutinizing it. 'And it indicates nothing. However—' he removed the cap—'I'll try it. Just to be on the safe side.'

After he had tried it, he found the two Fnools staring at him intently.

'This is what Terrans deem drink,' Lightfoot explained. 'It would be bad for you.'

'Possibly,' one of the two Fnools said, 'but while you were drinking from that bottle I obtained your .45 Service revolver. Hands up.'

Lightfoot, reluctantly, raised his hands.

'Give us that bottle,' the Fnool said. 'And let us try it for ourselves; we will be denied nothing. For in point of fact, Terran culture lies open before us.'

'Drink will put an end to you,' Lightfoot said desperately.

'As that burning tube of aged vegetable matter did?' the nearer of the two Fnools said with contempt.

It and its companion drained the bottle as Lightfoot watched.

Sure enough, they now stood six feet high. And, he knew, everywhere in the world, all Fnools had assumed equal stature. Because of him, the invasion of the Fnools would this time be successful. He had destroyed Terra.

'Cheers,' the first Fnool said.

'Down the hatch,' the other said. 'Ring-a-ding.' They studied Lightfoot. 'You've shrunk to our size.'

'No, Len,' the other said. 'We have expanded to his.'

'Then at last we're all equal,' Len said. 'We're finally a success. The magic defense of the Terrans—their unnatural size—has been eradicated.'

At that point a voice said, 'Drop that .45 Service revolver.' And Major Hauk stepped into the room behind the two thoroughly drunken Fnools.

'Well I'll be goddamned,' the first Fnool mumbled. 'Look, Len, it's the man most responsible for previously defeating us.'

'And he's little,' Len said. 'Little, like us. We're all little, now. I mean, we're all huge; goddamn it, it's the same thing. Anyhow we're equal.' It lurched toward Major Hauk—

Major Hauk fired. And the Fnool named Len dropped. It was absolutely undeniably dead. Only one of the captured Fnools remained.

'Edgar, they've increased in size,' Major Hauk said, pale. 'Why?'

'It's due to me,' Lightfoot admitted. 'First because of the cigarette, then second because of the Scotch—your Scotch, Major, that your wife gave you on your last birthday. I admit their now being the same size as us makes them undistinguishable from us . . . but consider this, sir. *What if they grew once more?*'

'I see your idea clearly,' Major Hauk said, after a pause. 'If eight feet tall, the Fnools would be as conspicuous as they were when—'

The captured Fnool made a dash for freedom.

Major Hauk fired, low, but it was too late; the Fnool was out into the corridor and racing toward the elevator.

'Get it!' Major Hauk shouted.

The Fnool reached the elevator and without hesitation pressed the button; some extra-terrestrial Fnoolian knowledge guided its hand.

'It's getting away,' Lightfoot grated.

Now the elevator had come. 'It's going down to the bomb-proof shelter,' Major Hauk yelled in dismay.

'Good,' Lightfoot said grimly. 'We'll be able to capture it with no trouble.'

'Yes, but—' Major Hauk began, and then broke off. 'You're right, Lightfoot; we must capture it. Once out on the street—It would be like any other man in a gray business suit carrying a briefcase.'

'How can it be made to grow again?' Lightfoot said, as he and Major Hauk descended by means of the stairs. 'A cigarette started it, then the Scotch—both new to Fnools. What would complete their growth, make them a bizarre eight feet tall?' He racked his brain as they dashed down and down, until at last the concrete and steel entrance of the shelter lay before them.

The Fnool was already inside.

'That's, um, Miss Smith you hear,' Major Hauk admitted. 'She was, or rather actually, we were—well, we were taking refuge from the invasion down here.'

Putting his weight against the door, Lightfoot swung it aside.

Miss Smith at once hopped up, ran toward them and a moment later clung to the two men, safe now from the Fnool. 'Thank God,' she gasped. 'I didn't realize what it was until—' She shuddered.

'Major,' Captain Lightfoot said, 'I think we've stumbled on it.'

Rapidly, Major Hauk said, 'Captain, you get Miss Smith's clothes, I'll take care of the Fnool. There's no problem now.'

The Fnool, eight feet high, came slowly toward them, its hands raised.

A GAME OF UNCHANCE

While rolling a fifty-gallon drum of water from the canal to his potato garden, Bob Turk heard the roar, glanced up into the haze of the midafternoon Martian sky and saw the great blue interplan ship.

In the excitement he waved. And then he read the words painted on the side of the ship and his joy became alloyed with care. Because this great pitted hull, now lowering itself to a rear-end landing, was a carny ship, come to this region of the fourth planet to transact business.

The painting spelled out:

FALLING STAR ENTERTAINMENT ENTERPRISES

PRESENTS

FREAKS, MAGIC, TERRIFYING STUNTS, AND WOMEN!

The final word had been painted largest of all.

I better go tell the settlement council, Turk realized. He left his water drum and trotted toward the shop-area, panting as his lungs struggled to take in the thin, weak air of this unnatural, colonized world. Last time a carnival had come to their area they had been robbed of most of their crops—accepted by the pitchmen in barter—and had wound up with nothing more than an armload of useless plaster figurines. It would not happen again. And yet—

He felt the craving within him, the need to be entertained. And they all felt this way; the settlement yearned for the bizarre. Of course the pitchmen knew this, preyed off this. Turk thought, If only we could keep our heads. Barter excess food and cloth-fibers, not what we need . . . not become like a lot of kids. But life in the colony world was monotonous. Carting water, fighting bugs, repairing fences, ceaselessly tinkering with the semi-autonomous robot farm machinery which sustained them . . . it wasn't enough; it had no–culture. No solemnity.

'Hey,' Turk called as he reached Vince Guest's land; Vince sat aboard his one-cylinder plow, wrench in hand. 'Hear the noise? Company! More sideshows, like last year–remember?'

'I remember,' Vince said, not looking up. 'They got all my squash. The hell with traveling shows.' His face became dark.

'This is a different outfit,' Turk explained, halting. 'I never saw them before; they've got a *blue* ship and it looks like it's been every-where. You know what we're going to do? Remember our plan?'

'Some plan,' Vince said, closing the jaw of the wrench.

'Talent is talent,' Turk babbled, trying to convince–not merely Vince–but himself as well; he talked against his own alarm. 'All right, so Fred's sort of half-witted; his talent's genuine, I mean, we've tried it out a million times, and why we didn't use it against that carny last year I'll never know. But now we're organized. Prepared.'

Raising his head Vince said, 'You know what that dumb kid will do? He'll join the carny; he'll leave with it and he'll use his talent on their side–we can't trust him.'

'I trust him,' Turk said, and hurried on toward the buildings of the settlement, the dusty, eroded gray structures directly ahead. Already he could see their council chairman, Hoagland Rae, busy at his store; Hoagland rented tired pieces of equipment to settle-ment members and they all depended on him. Without Hoag-land's contraptions no sheep would get sheared, no lambs would be distailed. It was no wonder that Hoagland had become their political–as well as economic–leader.

Stepping out onto the hard-packed sand, Hoagland shaded his eyes, wiped his wet forehead with a folded handkerchief and greeted Bob Turk. 'Different outfit this time?' His voice was low.

'Right,' Turk said, his heart pounding. 'And we can take them, Hoag! If we play it right; I mean, once Fred–'

'They'll be suspicious,' Hoagland said thoughtfully. 'No doubt other settlements have tried to use Psi to win. They may have one of those–what do you call them?–those anti-Psi folks with them. Fred's a p-k and if they have an anti-p-k–' He gestured, showing his resignation.

'I'll go tell Fred's parents to get him from school,' Bob Turk panted. 'It'd be natural for kids to show up right away; let's close the school for this afternoon so Fred's lost in the crowd, you know what I mean? He doesn't *look* funny, not to me, anyhow.' He sniggered.

'True,' Hoagland agreed, with dignity. 'The Costner boy appears quite normal. Yes, we'll try; that's what we voted to do anyhow, we're committed. Go sound the surplus-gathering bell so these carny boys can see we've got good produce to offer–I want to see all those apples and walnuts and cabbages and squash and pumpkins piled up–' He pointed to the spot. 'And an accurate inventory sheet, with three carbons, in my hands, within one hour.' Hoagland got out a cigar, lit up with his lighter. 'Get going.'

Bob Turk went.

As they walked through their south pasture, among the blackface sheep who chewed the hard, dry grass, Tony Costner said to his son, 'You think you can manage it, Fred? If not, say so. You don't have to.'

Straining, Fred Costner thought he could dimly see the carnival, far off, arranged before the up-ended interplan ship. Booths, shimmering big banners and metal streamers that danced in the wind . . . and the recorded music, or was it an authentic calliope? 'Sure,' he muttered. 'I can handle them; I've been practicing every day since Mr Rae told me.' To prove it he caused a rock lying ahead of them to skim up, pass in an arc, start toward them at high speed and then drop abruptly back to the brown, dry grass. A sheep regarded it dully and Fred laughed.

A small crowd from the settlement, including children, had

already manifested itself among the booths now being set up; he saw the cotton candy machine hard at work, smelled the frying popcorn, saw with delight a vast cluster of helium-filled balloons carried by a gaudily-painted dwarf wearing a hobo costume.

His father said quietly, 'What you must look for, Fred, is the game which offers the really valuable prizes.'

'I know,' he said, and began to scan the booths. We don't have a need for hula-hula dolls, he said to himself. Or boxes of salt water taffy.

Somewhere in the carnival lay the real spoils. It might be in the money-pitching board or the spinning wheel or the bingo table; anyhow it was there. He scented it, sniffed it. And hurried.

In a weak, strained voice his father said, 'Um, maybe I'll leave you, Freddy.' Tony had seen one of the girl platforms and had turned toward it, unable to take his eyes from the scene. One of the girls was already—but then the rumble of a truck made Fred Costner turn, and he forgot about the high-breasted, unclad girl on the platform. The truck was bringing the produce of the settlement, to be bartered in exchange for tickets.

The boy started toward the truck, wondering how much Hoagland Rae had decided to put up this time after the awful licking they had taken before. It looked like a great deal and Fred felt pride; the settlement obviously had full confidence in his abilities.

He caught then the unmistakable stench of Psi.

It emanated from a booth to his right and he turned at once in that direction. This was what the carny people were protecting, this one game which they did not feel they could afford to lose. It was, he saw, a booth in which one of the freaks acted as the target; the freak was a no-head, the first Fred had ever seen, and he stopped, transfixed.

The no-head had no head at all and his sense organs, his eyes and nose and ears, had migrated to other parts of his body beginning in the period before birth. For instance, his mouth gaped from the center of his chest, and from each shoulder an eye gleamed; the no-head was deformed but not deprived, and Fred felt respect for him. The no-head could see, smell and hear as good as anyone. But what exactly did he do in the game?

In the booth the no-head sat within a basket suspended above a tub of water. Behind the no-head Fred Costner saw a target and then he saw the heap of baseballs near at hand and he realized how the game worked; if the target were hit by a ball the no-head would plunge into the tub of water. And it was to prevent this that the carny had directed its Psi powers; the stench here was overpowering. He could not, however, tell from whom the stench came, the no-head or the operator of the booth or from a third person as yet unseen.

The operator, a thin young woman wearing slacks and a sweater and tennis shoes, held a baseball toward Fred. 'Ready to play, captain?' she demanded and smiled at him insinuatingly, as if it was utterly in the realm of the impossible that he might play and win.

'I'm thinking,' Fred said. He was scrutinizing the prizes.

The no-head giggled and the mouth located in the chest said, 'He's thinking—I doubt that!' It giggled again and Fred flushed.

His father came up beside him. 'Is this what you want to play?' he said. Now Hoagland Rae appeared; the two men flanked the boy, all three of them studying the prizes. What were they? Dolls, Fred thought. At least that was their appearance; the vaguely male, small shapes lay in rows on the shelves to the left of the booth's operator. He could not for the life of him fathom the carny's reasons for protecting these; surely they were worthless. He moved closer, straining to see ...

Leading him off to one side Hoagland Rae said worriedly, 'But even if we win, Fred what do we get? Nothing we can use, just those plastic figurines. We can't barter those with other settlements, even.' He looked disappointed; the corners of his mouth turned down dismally.

'I don't think they're what they seem,' Fred said. 'But I don't actually know what they are. Anyhow let me try, Mr Rae; I know this is the one.' And the carny people certainly believed so.

'I'll leave it up to you,' Hoagland Rae said, with pessimism; he exchanged glances with Fred's father, than slapped the boy encouragingly on the back. 'Let's go,' he announced. 'Do your best, kid.' The group of them—joined now by Bob Turk—made their way back to the booth in which the no-head sat with shoulder eyes gleaming.

'Made up your mind, people?' the thin stony-faced girl who operated the booth asked, tossing a baseball and recatching it.

'Here.' Hoagland handed Fred an envelope; it was the proceeds from the settlement's produce, in the form of carny tickets—this was what they had obtained in exchange. This was all there was, now.

'I'll try,' Fred said to the thin girl, and handed her a ticket.

The thin girl smiled, showing sharp, small teeth.

'Put me in the drink!' the no-head babbled. 'Dunk me and win a valuable prize!' It giggled again, in delight.

That night, in the workshop behind his store, Hoagland Rae sat with a jeweler's loupe in his right eye, examining one of the figurines which Tony Costner's boy had won at the Falling Star Entertainment Enterprises carnival earlier in the day.

Fifteen of the figurines lay in a row against the far wall of Hoagland's workshop.

With a tiny pair of pliers Hoagland pried open the back of the doll-like structure and saw, within, intricate wiring. 'The boy was right,' he said to Bob Turk, who stood behind him smoking a synthetic tobacco cigarette in jerky agitation. 'It's not a doll; it's fully rigged. Might be UN property they stole; might even be a microrob. You know, one of those special automatic mechanisms the government uses for a million tasks from spying to reconstruct surgery for war vets.' Now, gingerly, he opened the front of the figurine.

More wiring, and the miniature parts which even under the loupe were exceedingly difficult to make out. He gave up; after all, his ability was limited to repairing power harvesting equipment and the like. This was just too much. Again he wondered exactly how the settlement could make use of these microrobs. Sell them back to the UN? And meanwhile, the carnival had packed up and gone. No way to find out from them what these were.

'Maybe it walks and talks,' Turk suggested.

Hoagland searched for a switch on the figurine, found none. Verbal order? he wondered. 'Walk,' he ordered it. The figurine remained inert. 'I think we've got something here,' he said to Turk. 'But—' He gestured. 'It'll take time; we've got to be patient.' Maybe if they took one of the figurines to M City, where the truly professional engineers, electronics experts and repairmen of all kinds could be found . . . but he wanted to do this himself; he distrusted the inhabitants of the one great urban area on the colony planet.

'Those carny people sure were upset when we won again and again,' Bob Turk chuckled. 'Fred, he said that they were exerting their own Psi all the time and it completely surprised them that—'

'Be quiet,' Hoagland said. He had found the figurine's power supply; now he needed only to trace the circuit until he came to a break. By closing the break he could start the mechanism into activity; it was—or rather it seemed—as simple as that.

Shortly, he found the interruption in the circuit. A microscopic switch, disguised as the belt buckle, of the figurine . . . exulting, Hoagland closed the switch with his needle-nose pliers, set the figurine down on his workbench and waited.

The figurine stirred. It reached into a pouch-like construct hanging at its side, a sort of purse; from the pouch it brought a tiny tube, which it pointed at Hoagland.

'Wait,' Hoagland said feebly. Behind him Turk bleated and scuttled for cover. Something boomed in his face, a light that thrust him back; he shut his eyes and cried out in fright. *We're being attacked!* he shouted, but his voice did not sound; he heard nothing. He was crying uselessly in a darkness which had no end. Groping, he reached out imploringly . . .

The settlement's registered nurse was bending over him, holding a bottle of ammonia at his nostrils. Grunting, he managed to lift his head, open his eyes. He lay in his workshop; around him stood a ring of settlement adults, Bob Turk foremost, all with expressions of gray alarm.

'These dolls or whatever,' Hoagland managed to whisper. 'Attacked us; be careful.' He twisted, trying to see the line of dolls which he had so carefully placed against the far wall. 'I set one off prematurely,' he mumbled. 'By completing the circuit; I tripped it so now we know.' And then he blinked.

The dolls were gone.

'I went for Miss Beason,' Bob Turk explained, 'and when I got back they had disappeared. Sorry.' He looked apologetic, as if it were his personal fault. 'But you were hurt; I was worried you were maybe dead.'

'Okay,' Hoagland said, pulling himself up; his head ached and he felt nauseated. 'You did right. Better get that Costner kid in here, get his opinion.' He added, 'Well, we've been taken. For the second year in a row. Only this time is worse.' This time, he thought, we won. We were better off last year when we merely lost.

He had an intimation of true foreboding.

Four days later, as Tony Costner hoed weeds in his squash garden, a stirring of the ground made him pause; he reached silently for the pitchfork, thinking, It's an m-gopher, down under, eating the roots. I'll get it. He lifted the pitchfork, and, as the ground stirred once more, brought the tines of the fork savagely down to penetrate the loose, sandy soil.

Something beneath the surface squeaked in pain and fright. Tony Costner grabbed a shovel, dug the dirt away. A tunnel lay exposed and in it, dying in a heap of quivering, pulsating fur, lay— as he had from long experience anticipated—a Martian gopher, its eyes glazed in agony, elongated fangs exposed.

He killed it, mercifully. And then bent down to examine it. Because something had caught his eye: a flash of metal.

The m-gopher wore a harness.

It was artificial, of course; the harness fitted snugly around the animal's thick neck. Almost invisible, hair-like wires passed from the harness and disappeared into the scalp of the gopher near the front of the skull.

A GAME OF UNCHANCE

'Lord,' Tony Costner said, picking the gopher and its harness up and standing in futile anxiety, wondering what to do. Right away he connected this with the carnival dolls; they had gone off and done this, made this—the settlement, as Hoagland had said, was under attack.

He wondered what the gopher would have done had he not killed it.

The gopher had been up to something. Tunneling toward—his house!

Later, he sat beside Hoagland Rae in the workshop; Rae, with care, had opened the harness, inspected its interior.

'A transmitter,' Hoagland said, and breathed out noisily, as if his childhood asthma had returned. 'Short range, maybe half a mile. The gopher was directed by it, maybe gave back a signal that told where it was and what it was doing. The electrodes to the brain probably connect with pleasure and pain areas . . . that way the gopher could be controlled.' He glanced at Tony Costner. 'How'd you like to have a harness like that on you?'

'I wouldn't,' Tony said, shivering. He wished, all at once, that he was back on Terra, overcrowded as it was; he longed for the press of the crowd, the smells and sounds of great throngs of men and women, moving along the hard sidewalks, among the lights. It occurred to him then, in a flash, that he had never really enjoyed it here on Mars. Far too lonely, he realized. I made a mistake. My wife; she made me come here.

It was a trifle late, however, to think that now.

'I guess,' Hoagland said stonily, 'that we'd better notify the UN military police.' He went with dragging steps to the wallphone, cranked it, then dialed the emergency number. To Tony he said, half in apology, half in anger, 'I can't take responsibility for handling this, Costner; it's too difficult.'

'It's my fault too,' Tony said. 'When I saw that girl, she had taken off the upper part of her garment and—'

'UN regional security office,' the phone declared, loudly enough for Tony Costner to hear it.

'We're in trouble,' Hoagland said. And explained, then, about the Falling Star Entertainment Enterprises ship and what had happened. As he talked he wiped his streaming forehead with his handkerchief; he looked old and tired, and very much in need of a rest.

An hour later the military police landed in the middle of the settlement's sole street. A uniformed UN officer, middle-aged, with a briefcase, stepped out, glanced around in the yellow late-afternoon light, made out the sight of the crowd with Hoagland Rae placed officially in front. 'You are General Mozart?' Hoagland said tentatively, holding his hand out.

'That's correct,' the heavy-set UN officer said, as they shook briefly. 'May I see the construct, please?' He seemed a trifle disdainful of the somewhat grimy settlement people; Hoagland felt that acutely, and his sense of failure and depression burgeoned.

'Sure, General.' Hoagland led the way to his store and the workshop in the rear.

After he had examined the dead m-gopher with its electrodes and harness, General Mozart said, 'You may have won artifacts they did *not* want to give up, Mr Rae. Their final—in other words actual—destination was probably not this settlement.' Again his distaste showed, ill-disguised; who would want to bother with this area? 'But, and this is a guess, eventually Earth and the more populated regions. However, by your employment of a parapsychological bias on the ball-throwing game—' He broke off, glanced at his wristwatch. 'We'll treat the fields in this vicinity with arsine gas, I think; you and your people will have to evacuate this whole region, as a matter of fact tonight; we'll provide a transport. May I use your phone? I'll order the transport—you assemble all your people.' He smiled reflexively at Hoagland and then went to the telephone to place his call back to his office in M City.

'Livestock, too?' Rae said. 'We can't sacrifice them.' He wondered just how he was supposed to get their sheep, dogs and cattle into the UN transport in the middle of the night. What a mess, he thought dully.

'Of course livestock,' General Mozart said unsympathetically, as if Rae were some sort of idiot.

The third steer driven aboard the UN transport carried a harness at its neck; the UN military policeman at the entrance hatch spotted it, shot the steer at once, summoned Hoagland to dispose of the carcass.

Squatting by the dead steer, Hoagland Rae examined the harness and its wiring. As with the m-gopher, the harness connected, by delicate leads, the brain of the animal to the sentient organism—whatever it was—which had installed the apparatus, located, he assumed, no farther than a mile from the settlement. What was this animal supposed to do? he wondered as he disconnected the harness. Gore one of us? Or—eavesdrop. More likely that; the transmitter within the harness hummed audibly; it was perpetually on, picking up all sounds in the vicinity. So they know we've brought in the military, Hoagland realized. And that we've detected two of these constructs, now.

He had a deep intuition that this meant the abolition of the settlement. This area would soon be a battleground between the UN military and the—whatever they were. Falling Star Entertainment Enterprises. He wondered where they were from. Outside the Sol System, evidently.

Kneeling momentarily beside him a blackjack—a black-clad UN secret police officer—said, 'Cheer up. This tipped their hand; we could never prove those carnivals were hostile, before. Because of you they never made it to Terra. You'll be reinforced; don't give up.' He grinned at Hoagland, then hurried off, disappearing into the darkness, where a UN tank sat parked.

Yes, Hoagland thought. We did the authorities a favor. And they'll reward us by moving massively into this area.

He had a feeling that the settlement would never be quite the same again, no matter what the authorities did. Because, if nothing else, the settlement had failed to solve its own problems; it had been forced to call for outside help. For the big boys.

Tony Costner gave him a hand with the dead steer; together they dragged it to one side, gasping for breath as they grappled with the still warm body. 'I feel responsible,' Tony said, when they had set it down.

'Don't.' Hoagland shook his head. 'And tell your boy not to feel bad.'

'I haven't seen Fred since this first came out,' Tony said miserably. 'He took off, terribly disturbed. I guess the UN MPs will find him; they're on the outskirts rounding everybody up.' He sounded numb, as if he could not quite take in what was happening. 'An MP told me that by morning we could come back. The arsine gas would have taken care of everything. You think they've run into this before? They're not saying but they seem so efficient. They seem so sure of what they're doing.'

'Lord knows,' Hoagland said. He lit a genuine Earth-made Optimo cigar and smoked in glum silence, watching a flock of blackface sheep being driven into the transport. Who would have thought the legendary, classic invasion of Earth would take this form? he asked himself. Starting here at our meager settlement, in terms of small wired figurines, a little over a dozen in all, which we labored to win from Falling Star Entertainment Enterprises; as General Mozart said, the invaders didn't even want to give them up. Ironic.

Bob Turk, coming up beside him, said quietly, 'You realize we're going to be sacrificed. That's obvious. Arsine will kill all the gophers and rats but it won't kill the microrobs because they don't breathe. The UN will have to keep blackjack squads operating in this region for weeks, maybe months. This gas attack is just the beginning.' He turned accusingly to Tony Costner. 'If your kid—'

'All right,' Hoagland said in a sharp voice. 'That's enough. If I hadn't taken that one apart, closed the circuit—you can blame me, Turk; in fact I'll be glad to resign. You can run the settlement without me.'

Through a battery-driven loudspeaker a vast UN voice boomed, 'All persons within sound of my voice prepare to board! This area will be flooded with poisonous gas at 14:00. I repeat—' It repeated, as the loudspeakers turned in first one direction and then another; the noise echoed in the night darkness.

*

Stumbling, Fred Costner made his way over the unfamiliar, rough terrain, wheezing in sorrow and weariness; he paid no attention to his location, made no effort to see where he was going. All he wanted to do was get away. He had destroyed the settlement and everyone from Hoagland Rae on down knew it. Because of him—

Far away, behind him, an amplified voice boomed, 'All persons within sound of my voice prepare to board! This area will be flooded with poisonous gas at 14:00. I repeat, all persons within sound of my voice—' It dinned on and on. Fred continued to stumble along, trying to shut out the racket of the voice, hurrying away from it.

The night smelled of spiders and dry weeds; he sensed the desolation of the landscape around him. Already he was beyond the final perimeter of cultivation; he had left the settlement's fields and now he stumbled over unplowed ground where no fences or even surveyor's stakes existed. But they would probably flood this area, too, however; the UN ships would coast back and forth, spraying the arsine gas, and then after that special forces troops would come in, wearing gas-masks, carrying flame throwers, with metal-sensitive detectors on their backs, to roust out the fifteen microrobs which had taken refuge underground in the burrows of rats and vermin. Where they belong, Fred Costner said to himself. And to think I wanted them for the settlement; I thought, because the carnival wanted to keep them, that they must be valuable.

He wondered, dimly, if there was any way he could undo what he had done. Find the fifteen microrobs, plus the activated one which had almost killed Hoagland Rae? And—he had to laugh; it was absurd. Even if he found their hideout—assuming that all of them had taken refuge together in one spot—how could he destroy them? And they were armed. Hoagland Rae had barely escaped, and that had been from one acting alone.

A light glowed ahead.

In the darkness he could not make out the shapes which moved at the edge of the light; he halted, waited, trying to orient himself. Persons came and went and he heard the voices, muted, both men's and women's. And the sound of machinery in motion. The

UN would not be sending out women, he realized. This was not the authorities.

A portion of the sky, the stars and faint nocturnal swath of haze, had been blotted out, and he realized all at once that he was seeing the outline of a large stationary object.

It could be a ship, parked on its tail, awaiting take-off; the shape seemed roughly that.

He seated himself, shivering in the cold of the Martian night, scowling in an attempt to trace the passage of the indistinct forms busy with their activity. Had the carnival returned? Was this once more the Falling Star Entertainment Enterprises vehicle? Eerily, the thought came to him: the booths and banners and tents and platforms, the magic shows and girl platforms and freaks and games of chance were being erected here in the middle of the night, in this barren area lost in the emptiness between settlements. A hollow enactment of the festivity of the carny life, for no one to see or experience. Except–by chance–himself. And to him it was revolting; he had seen all he wanted of the carnival, its people and–things.

Something ran across his foot.

With his psycho-kinetic faculty he snared it, drew it back; reaching, he grabbed with both hands until all at once he had snatched out of the darkness a thrashing, hard shape. He held it, and saw with fright one of the microrobs; it struggled to escape and yet, reflexively, he held onto it. The microrob had been scurrying toward the parked ship, and he thought, the ship's picking them up. So they won't be found by the UN. They're getting away, then the carnival can go on with its plans.

A calm voice, a woman's, said from close by, 'Put it down, please. It wants to go.'

Jumping with shock he released the microrob and it scuttled off, rustling in the weeds, gone at once. Standing before Fred the thin girl, still wearing slacks and a sweater, faced him placidly, a flashlight in her hand; by its circle of illumination he made out her sharply-traced features, her colorless jaw and intense, clear eyes. 'Hi,' Fred said stammeringly; he stood up, defensively, facing the girl. She was slightly taller than he and he felt afraid of her. But he did not catch the stench of Psi about her and he realized that it had definitely not been she there in the booth who had struggled against his own faculty during the game. So he had an advantage over her, and perhaps one she did not know about.

'You better get away from here,' he said. 'Did you hear the loud-speaker? They're going to gas this area.'

'I heard.' The girl surveyed him. 'You're the big winner, aren't you, sonny? The master game-player; you dunked our anti-ceph sixteen times in a row.' She laughed merrily. 'Simon was furious; he caught cold from that and blames you. So I hope you don't run into him.'

'Don't call me sonny,' he said. His fear began to leave him.

'Douglas, our p-k, says you're strong. You wrestled him down every time; congratulations. Well, how pleased are you with your take?' Silently, she once more laughed; her small sharp teeth shone in the meager light. 'You feel you got your produce's worth?'

'Your p-k isn't much good,' Fred said. 'I didn't have any trouble and I'm really not experienced. You could do a lot better.'

'With you, possibly? Are you asking to join us? Is this a proposition from you to me, little boy?'

'No!' he said, startled and repelled.

'There was a rat,' the girl said, 'in the wall of your Mr Rae's workshop; it had a transmitter on it and so we knew about your call to the UN as soon as you made it. So we've had plenty of time to regain our–' She paused a moment. 'Our merchandise. If we cared to. Nobody meant to hurt you; it isn't our fault that busybody Rae stuck the tip of his screwdriver into the control-circuit of that one microrob. Is it?'

'He started the cycle prematurely. It would have done that eventually anyhow.' He refused to believe otherwise; he knew the settlement was in the right. 'And it's not going to do you any good to collect all those microrobs because the UN knows and–'

'"Collect"?' The girl rocked with amusement. 'We're not collecting the sixteen microrobs you poor little people won. We're going ahead—you forced us to. The ship is unloading the rest of them.' She pointed with the flashlight and he saw in that brief instant the horde of microrobs disgorged, spreading out, seeking shelter like so many photophobic insects.

He shut his eyes and moaned.

'Are you still sure,' the girl said purringly, 'that you don't want to come with us? It'll ensure your future, sonny. And otherwise—' She gestured. 'Who knows? Who really can guess what'll become of your tiny settlement and you poor tiny people?'

'No,' he said. 'I'm still not coming.'

When he opened his eyes again the girl had gone off. She stood with the no-head, Simon, examining a clipboard which the no-head held.

Turning, Fred Costner ran back the way he had come, toward the UN military police.

The lean, tall, black-uniformed UN secret police general said, 'I have replaced General Mozart who is unfortunately ill-equipped to deal with domestic subversion; he is a military man exclusively.' He did not extend his hand to Hoagland Rae. Instead he began to pace about the workshop, frowning. 'I wish I had been called in last night. For example I could have told you one thing immediately . . . which General Mozart did not understand.' He halted, glanced searchingly at Hoagland. 'You realize, of course, that you did not beat the carnival people. They wanted to lose those sixteen microrobs.'

Hoagland Rae nodded silently; there was nothing to say. It now did appear obvious, as the blackjack general had pointed out.

'Prior appearances of the carnival,' General Wolff said, 'in former years, was to set you up, to set each settlement up in turn. They knew you'd have to plan to win this time. So this time they brought their microrobs. And had their weak Psi ready to engage in an ersatz "battle" for supremacy.'

'All I want to know,' Hoagland said, 'is whether we're going to get protection.' The hills and plains surrounding the settlement, as Fred had told them, were now swarming with the microrobs; it was unsafe to leave the downtown buildings.

'We'll do what we can.' General Wolff resumed pacing. 'But obviously we're not primarily concerned with you, or with any other particular settlement or locale that's been infested. It's the overall situation that we have to deal with. That ship has been forty places in the last twenty-four hours; how they've moved so swiftly—' He broke off. 'They had every step prepared. And you thought you conned them.' He glowered at Hoagland Rae. 'Every settlement along the line thought that as they won their boxload of microrobs.'

'I guess,' Hoagland said presently, 'that's what we get for cheating.' He did not meet the blackjack general's gaze.

'That's what you get for pitting your wits against an adversary from another system,' General Wolff said bitingly. 'Better look at it that way. And the next time a vehicle *not* from Terra shows up— don't try to mastermind a strategy to defeat them: *call us.*'

Hoagland Rae nodded. 'Okay. I understand.' He felt only dull pain, not indignation; he deserved—they all deserved—this chewing out. If they were lucky their reprimand would end at this. It was hardly the settlement's greatest problem. 'What do they want?' he asked General Wolff. 'Are they after this area for colonization? Or is this an economic—'

'Don't try,' General Wolff said.

'P-pardon?'

'It's not something you can understand, now or at any other time. We know what they're after—and *they* know what they're after. Is it important that you know, too? Your job is to try to resume your farming as before. Or if you can't do that, pull back and return to Earth.'

'I see,' Hoagland said, feeling trivial.

'Your kids can read about it in the history books,' General Wolff said. 'That ought to be good enough for you.'

'It's just fine,' Hoagland Rae said, miserably. He seated himself half-heartedly at his workbench, picked up a screwdriver and began to tinker with a malfunctioning autonomic tractor guidance-turret.

'Look,' General Wolff said, and pointed.

In a corner of the workshop, almost invisible against the dusty wall, a microrob crouched watching them.

'Jeez!' Hoagland wailed, groping around on his workbench for the old .32 revolver which he had gotten out and loaded.

Long before his fingers found the revolver the microrob had vanished. General Wolff had not even moved; he seemed, in fact, somewhat amused: he stood with his arms folded, watching Hoagland fumbling with the antiquated side arm.

'We're working on a central device,' General Wolff said, 'which would cripple all of them simultaneously. By interrupting the flow of current from their portable power-packs. Obviously to destroy them one by one is absurd; we never even considered it. However—' He paused thoughtfully, his forehead wrinkling. 'There's reason to believe they—the outspacers—have anticipated us and have diversified the power-sources in such a way that—' He shrugged philosophically. 'Well, perhaps something else will come to mind. In time.'

'I hope so,' Hoagland said. And tried to resume his repair of the defective tractor turret.

'We've pretty much given up the hope of holding Mars,' General Wolff said, half to himself.

Hoagland slowly set down his screwdriver, stared at the secret policeman.

'What we're going to concentrate on is Terra,' General Wolff said, and scratched his nose reflectively.

'Then,' Hoagland said after a pause, 'there's really no hope for us here; that's what you're saying.'

The blackjack general did not answer. He did not need to.

As he bent over the faintly greenish, scummy surface of the canal where botflies and shiny black beetles buzzed, Bob Turk saw, from the corner of his vision, a small shape scuttle. Swiftly he spun, reached for his laser cane; he brought it up, fired it and destroyed— oh happy day!—a heap of rusted, discarded fuel drums, nothing more. The microrob had already departed.

A GAME OF UNCHANCE

Shakily he returned the laser cane to his belt and again bent over the bug-infested water. As usual the 'robs had been active here during the night; his wife had seen them, heard their rat-like scratchings. What the hell had they done? Bob Turk wondered dismally, and sniffed long and hard at the water.

It seemed to him that the customary odor of the stagnant water was somehow subtly changed.

'Damn,' he said, and stood up, feeling futile. The 'robs had put some contaminator in the water; that was obvious. Now it would have to be given a thorough chemical analysis and that would take days. Meanwhile, what would keep his potato crop alive? Good question.

Raging in baffled helplessness, he pawed the laser cane, wishing for a target—and knowing he could never, not in a million years, have one. As always the 'robs did their work at night; steadily, surely, they pushed the settlement back.

Already ten families had packed up and taken passage for Terra. To resume—if they could—the old lives which they had abandoned.

And, soon, it would be his turn.

If only there was something they could do. Some way they could fight back. He thought, I'd do anything, give anything, for a chance to get those 'robs. I swear it. I'd go into debt or bondage or servitude or anything, just for a *chance* of freeing the area of them.

He was shuffling morosely away from the canal, hands thrust deep in the pockets of his jacket, when he heard the booming roar of the intersystem ship overhead.

Calcified, he stood peering up, his heart collapsing inside him. Them back? he asked himself. The Falling Star Entertainment Enterprises ship . . . are they going to hit us all over again, finish us off finally? Shielding his eyes he peered frantically, not able even to run, his body not knowing its way even to instinctive, animal panic.

The ship, like a gigantic orange, lowered. Shaped like an orange, colored like an orange . . . it was not the blue tubular ship of the Falling Star people; he could see that. But also it was not from Terra; it was not UN. He had never seen a ship exactly like it before and he knew that he was definitely seeing another vehicle from beyond the Sol System, much more blatantly so than the blue ship of the Falling Star creatures. Not even a cursory attempt had been made to make it appear Terran.

And yet, on its sides, it had huge letters, which spelled out words in English.

His lips moving he read the words as the ship settled to a landing northeast of the spot at which he stood.

SIX SYSTEM EDUCATIONAL PLAYTIME ASSOCIATES
IN A RIOT OF FUN AND FROLIC FOR ALL!

It was—God in heaven—another itinerant carnival company.

He wanted to look away, to turn and hurry off. And yet he could not; the old familiar drive within him, the craving, the fixated curiosity, was too strong. So he continued to watch; he could see several hatches open and autonomic mechanisms beginning to nose, like flattened doughnuts, out onto the sand.

They were pitching camp.

Coming up beside him his neighbor Vince Guest said hoarsely, 'Now what?'

'You can see.' Turk gestured frantically. 'Use your eyes.' Already the auto-mechs were erecting a central tent; colored streamers hurled themselves upward into the air and then rained down on the still two-dimensional booths. And the first humans—or humanoids—were emerging. Vince and Bob saw men wearing bright clothing and then women in tights. Or rather something considerably less than tights.

'Wow,' Vince managed to say, swallowing. 'You see those ladies? You ever seen women with such—'

'I see them,' Turk said. 'But I'm never going back to one of these non-Terran carnivals from beyond the system and neither is Hoagland; I know that as well as I know my own name.'

How rapidly they were going to work. No time wasted; already faint, tinny music, of a carousel nature, filtered to Bob Turk. And the smells. Cotton candy, roasting peanuts, and with those the subtle smell of adventure and exciting sights, of the illicit. One woman with long braided red hair had hopped lithely up onto a platform; she wore a meager bra and wisp of silk at her waist and as he watched fixedly she began to practice her dance. Faster and faster she spun until at last, carried away by the rhythm, she discarded entirely what little she wore. And the funny thing about it all was that it seemed to him real art; it was not the usual carny shimmying at the midsection. There was something beautiful and alive about her movements; he found himself spellbound.

'I—better go get Hoagland,' Vince managed to say, finally. Already a few settlers, including a number of children, were moving as if hypnotized toward the lines of booths and the gaudy streamers that fluttered and shone in the otherwise drab Martian air.

'I'll go over and get a closer look,' Bob Turk said, 'while you're locating him.' He started toward the carnival on a gradually accelerated run, scuffling sand as he hurried.

To Hoagland, Tony Costner said, 'At least let's *see* what they have to offer. You know they're not the same people; it wasn't them who dumped those horrible damn microrobs off here—you can see that.'

'Maybe it's something worse,' Hoagland said, but he turned to the boy, Fred. 'What do you say?' he demanded.

'I want to look,' Fred Costner said. He had made up his mind.

'Okay,' Hoagland said, nodding. 'That's good enough for me. It won't hurt us to look. As long as we remember what that UN secret police general told us. Let's not kid ourselves into imagining we can outsmart them.' He put down his wrench, rose from his workbench, and walked to the closet to get his fur-lined outdoor coat.

When they reached the carnival they found that the games of chance had been placed—conveniently—ahead of even the girly shows and the freaks. Fred Costner rushed forward, leaving the group of adults behind; he sniffed the air, took in the scents, heard the music, saw past the games of chance the first freak platform: it was his favorite abomination, one he remembered from previous carnivals, only this one was superior. It was a no-body. In the midday Martian sunlight it reposed quietly: a bodiless head complete with hair, ears, intelligent eyes; heaven only knew what kept it alive . . . in any case he knew intuitively that it was genuine.

'Come and see Orpheus, the head without a visible body!' the pitchman called through his megaphone, and a group, mostly children, had gathered in awe to gape. 'How does it stay alive? How does it propel itself? Show them, Orpheus.' The pitchman tossed a handful of food pellets—Fred Costner could not see precisely what—at the head; it opened its mouth to enormous, frightening proportions, managed to snare most of what landed near it. The pitchman laughed and continued with his spiel. The no-body was now rolling industriously after the bits of food which it had missed. Gee, Fred thought.

'Well?' Hoagland said, coming up beside him. 'Do you see any games we might profit from?' His tone was drenched with bitterness. 'Care to throw a baseball at anything?' He started away, then, not waiting, a tired little fat man who had been defeated too much, who had already lost too many times. 'Let's go,' he said to the other adults of the settlement. 'Let's get out of here before we get into another—'

'Wait,' Fred said. He had caught it, the familiar, pleasing stench. It came from a booth on his right and he turned at once in that direction.

A plump, gray-colored middle-aged woman stood in a ringtoss booth, her hands full of the light wicker rings.

Behind Fred his father said to Hoagland Rae, 'You get the rings over the merchandise; you win whatever you manage to toss the ring onto so that it stays.' With Fred he walked slowly in that direction. 'It would be a natural,' he murmured, 'for a psychokinetic. I would think.'

'I suggest,' Hoagland said, speaking to Fred, 'that you look more closely this time at the prizes. At the merchandise.' However, he came along, too.

A GAME OF UNCHANCE

At first Fred could not make out what the neat stacks were, each of them exactly alike, intricate and metallic; he came up to the edge of the booth and the middle-aged woman began her chant-like litany, offering him a handful of rings. For a dollar, or whatever of equal value the settlement had to offer.

'What are they?' Hoagland said, peering. 'I—think they're some kind of machines.'

Fred said, 'I know what they are.' And we've got to play, he realized. We must round up every item in the settlement that we can possibly trade these people, every cabbage and rooster and sheep and wool blanket.

Because, he realized, this is our chance. Whether General Wolff knows about it or likes it.

'My God,' Hoagland said quietly. 'Those are traps.'

'That's right, mister,' the middle-aged woman chanted. 'Homeo-static traps; they do all the work, think for themselves, you just let them go and they travel and travel and they never give up until they catch—' She winked. '*You know what.* Yes, you know what they catch, mister, those little pesky things you can't ever possibly catch by yourselves, that are poisoning your water and killing your steers and ruining your settlement—win a trap, a valuable, useful trap, and you'll see, you'll see!' She tossed a wicker ring and it nearly settled over one of the complex, sleek-metal traps; it might very well have, if she had thrown it just a little more carefully. At least that was the impression given. They all felt this.

Hoagland said to Tony Costner and Bob Turk, 'We'll need a couple hundred of them at least.'

'And for that,' Tony said, 'we'll have to hock everything we own. But it's worth it; at least we won't be completely wiped out.' His eyes gleamed. 'Let's get started.' To Fred he said, 'Can you play this game? Can you win?'

'I—think so,' Fred said. Although somewhere nearby, someone in the carnival was ready with a contrary power of psychokinesis. But not enough, he decided. *Not quite enough.*

It was almost as if they worked it that way on purpose.

PRECIOUS ARTIFACT

Below the 'copter of Milt Biskle lay newly fertile lands. He had done well with his area of Mars, verdant from his reconstruction of the ancient water-network. Spring, two springs each year, had been brought to this autumn world of sand and hopping toads, a land once made of dried soil cracking with the dust of former times, of a dreary and unwatered waste. Victim of the recent Prox-Terra conflict.

Quite soon the first Terran emigrants would appear, stake their claims and take over. He could retire. Perhaps he could return to Terra or bring his own family here, receive priority of land-acquisition—as a reconstruct engineer he deserved it. Area Yellow had progressed far faster than the other engineers' sections. And now his reward came.

Reaching forward, Milt Biskle touched the button of his long-range transmitter. 'This is Reconstruct Engineer Yellow,' he said. 'I'd like a psychiatrist. Any one will do, so long as he's immediately available.'

When Milt Biskle entered the office Dr DeWinter rose and held out his hand. 'I've heard,' Dr DeWinter said, 'that you, of all the forty-odd reconstruct engineers, have been the most creative. It's no wonder you're tired. Even God had to rest after six days of such work, and you've been at it for years. As I was waiting for you to reach me I received a news memo from Terra that will interest you.' He picked the memo up from his desk. 'The initial transport of settlers is about to arrive here on Mars . . . and they'll go directly into your area. Congratulations, Mr Biskle.'

Rousing himself Milt Biskle said, 'What if I returned to Earth?'

'But if you mean to stake a claim for your family, here—'

Milt Biskle said, 'I want you to do something for me. I feel too tired, too—' He gestured. 'Or depressed, maybe. Anyhow I'd like you to make arrangements for my gear, including my wug-plant, to be put aboard a transport returning to Terra.'

'Six years of work,' Dr DeWinter said. 'And now you're abandoning your recompense. Recently I visited Earth and it's just as you remember—'

'How do you know how I remember it?'

'Rather,' DeWinter corrected himself smoothly, 'I should say it's just as it was. Overcrowded, tiny conapts with seven families to a single cramped kitchen. Autobahns so crowded you can't make a move until eleven in the morning.'

'For me,' Milt Biskle said, 'the overcrowding will be a relief after six years of robot autonomic equipment.' He had made up his mind. In spite of what he had accomplished here, or perhaps because of it, he intended to go home. Despite the psychiatrist's arguments.

Dr DeWinter purred, 'What if your wife and children, Milt, are among the passengers of this first transport?' Once more he lifted a document from his neatly-arranged desk. He studied the paper, then said, 'Biskle, Fay, Mrs Laura C. June C. Woman and two girl children. Your family?'

'Yes,' Milt Biskle admitted woodenly; he stared straight ahead.

'So you see you can't head back to Earth. Put on your hair and prepare to meet them at Field Three. And exchange your teeth. You've got the stainless steel ones in, at the moment.'

Chagrined, Biskle nodded. Like all Terrans he had lost his hair and teeth from the fallout during the war. For everyday service in his lonely job of re-reconstructing Yellow Area of Mars he made no use of the expensive wig which he had brought from Terra, and as to the teeth he personally found the steel ones far more comfortable than the natural-color plastic set. It indicated how far he had drifted from social inter-action. He felt vaguely guilty; Dr DeWinter was right.

But he had felt guilty ever since the defeat of the Proxmen. The war had embittered him; it didn't seem fair that one of the two competing cultures would have to suffer, since the needs of both were legitimate.

Mars itself had been the locus of contention. Both cultures needed it as a colony on which to deposit surplus populations. Thank God Terra had managed to gain tactical mastery during the last year of the war . . . hence it was Terrans such as himself, and not Proxmen, patching up Mars.

'By the way,' Dr DeWinter said. 'I happen to know of your intentions regarding your fellow reconstruct engineers.'

Milt Biskle glanced up swiftly.

'As a matter of fact,' Dr DeWinter said, 'we know they're at this moment gathering in Red Area to hear your account.' Opening his desk drawer he got out a yo-yo, stood up and began to operate it expertly doing *walking the dog*. 'Your panic-stricken speech to the effect that something is wrong, although you can't seem to say just what it might be.'

Watching the yo-yo Biskle said, 'That's a toy popular in the Prox system. At least so I read in a homeopape article, once.'

'Hmm. I understood it originated in the Philippines.' Engrossed, Dr DeWinter now did *around the world*. He did it well. 'I'm taking the liberty of sending a disposition to the reconstruct engineers' gathering, testifying to your mental condition. It will be read aloud—sorry to say.'

'I still intend to address the gathering,' Biskle said.

'Well, then there's a compromise that occurs to me. Greet your little family when it arrives here on Mars and then we'll arrange a trip to Terra for you. At our expense. And in exchange you'll agree not to address the gathering of reconstruct engineers or burden them in any way with your nebulous forebodings.' DeWinter eyed him keenly. 'After all, this is a critical moment. The first emigrants are arriving. We don't want trouble; we don't want to make anyone uneasy.'

'Would you do me a favor?' Biskle asked. 'Show me that you've got a wig on. And that your teeth are false. Just so I can be sure that you're a Terran.'

Dr DeWinter tilted his wig and plucked out his set of false teeth.

'I'll take the offer,' Milt Biskle said. 'If you'll agree to make certain that my wife obtains the parcel of land I set aside for her.'

Nodding, DeWinter tossed him a small white envelope. 'Here's your ticket. Round trip, of course, since you'll be coming back.'

I hope so, Biskle thought as he picked up the ticket. But it depends on what I see on Terra. Or rather on what they *let* me see.

He had a feeling they'd let him see very little. In fact as little as Proxmanly possible.

When his ship reached Terra a smartly uniformed guide waited for him. 'Mr Biskle?' Trim and attractive and exceedingly young, she stepped forward alertly. 'I'm Mary Ableseth, your Tourplan companion. I'll show you around the planet during your brief stay here.' She smiled brightly and very professionally. He was taken aback. 'I'll be with you constantly, night and day.'

'Night, too?' he managed to say.

'Yes, Mr Biskle. That's my job. We expect you to be disoriented due to your years of labor on Mars . . . labor we of Terra applaud and honor, as is right.' She fell in beside him, steering him toward a parked 'copter. 'Where would you like to go first? New York City? Broadway? To the night clubs and theaters and restaurants . . .'

'No, to Central Park. To sit on a bench.'

'But there is no more Central Park, Mr Biskle. It was turned into a parking lot for government employees while you were on Mars.'

'I see,' Milt Biskle said. 'Well, then Portsmouth Square in San Francisco will do.' He opened the door of the 'copter.

'That, too, has become a parking lot,' Miss Ableseth said, with a sad shake of her long, luminous red hair. 'We're so darn over-populated. Try again, Mr Biskle; there are a few parks left, one in Kansas, I believe, and *two* in Utah in the south part near St George.'

'This is bad news,' Milt said. 'May I stop at that amphetamine dispenser and put in my dime? I need a stimulant to cheer me up.'

'Certainly,' Miss Ableseth said, nodding graciously.

Milt Biskle walked to the spaceport's nearby stimulant dispenser, reached into his pocket, found a dime, and dropped the dime in the slot.

The dime fell completely through the dispenser and bounced onto the pavement.

'Odd,' Biskle said, puzzled.

'I think I can explain that,' Miss Ableseth said. 'That dime of yours is a Martian dime, made for a lighter gravity.'

'Hmm,' Milt Biskle said, as he retrieved the dime. As Miss Ableseth had predicted he felt disoriented. He stood by as she put in a dime of her own and obtained the small tube of amphetamine stimulants for him. Certainly her explanation seemed adequate. But—

'It is now eight P.M. local time,' Miss Ableseth said. 'And I haven't had dinner, although of course you have, aboard your ship. Why not take me to dinner? We can talk over a bottle of Pinot Noir and you can tell me these vague forebodings which have brought you to Terra, that something dire is wrong and that all your marvelous reconstruct work is pointless. I'd adore to hear about it.' She guided him back to the 'copter and the two of them entered, squeezing into the back seat together. Milt Biskle found her to be warm and yielding, decidedly Terran; he became embarrassed and felt his heart pounding in effort-syndrome. It had been some time since he had been this close to a woman.

'Listen,' he said, as the automatic circuit of the 'copter caused it to rise from the spaceport parking lot, 'I'm married. I've got two children and I came here on business. I'm on Terra to prove that the Proxmen really won and that we few remaining Terrans are slaves of the Prox authorities, laboring for–' He gave up; it was hopeless. Miss Ableseth remained pressed against him.

'You really think,' Miss Ableseth said presently, as the 'copter passed above New York City, 'that I'm a Prox agent?'

'N-no,' Milt Biskle said. 'I guess not.' It did not seem likely, under the circumstances.

'While you're on Terra,' Miss Ableseth said, 'why stay in an over-crowded, noisy hotel? Why not stay with me at my conapt in New Jersey? There's plenty of room and you're more than welcome.'

'Okay,' Biskle agreed, feeling the futility of arguing.

'Good.' Miss Ableseth gave an instruction to the 'copter; it turned north. 'We'll have dinner there. It'll save money, and at all the decent restaurants there's a two-hour line this time of night, so it's almost impossible to get a table. You've probably for-gotten. How wonderful it'll be when half our population can emigrate!'

'Yes,' Biskle said tightly. 'And they'll like Mars; we've done a good job.' He felt a measure of enthusiasm returning to him, a sense of pride in the reconstruct work he and his compatriots had done. 'Wait until you see it, Miss Ableseth.'

'Call me Mary,' Miss Ableseth said, as she arranged her heavy scarlet wig; it had become dislodged during the last few moments in the cramped quarters of the 'copter.

'Okay,' Biskle said, and, except for a nagging awareness of dis-loyalty to Fay, he felt a sense of well-being.

'Things happen fast on Terra,' Mary Ableseth said. 'Due to the terrible pressure of over-population.' She pressed her teeth in place; they, too, had become dislodged.

'So I see,' Milt Biskle agreed, and straightened his own wig and teeth, too. *Could I have been mistaken?* he asked himself. After all he could see the lights of New York below; Terra was decidedly not a depopulated ruin and its civilization was intact.

Or was this all an illusion, imposed on his percept-system by

Prox psychiatric techniques unfamiliar to him? It was a fact that his dime had fallen completely through the amphetamine dispenser. Didn't that indicate something was subtly, terribly wrong?

Perhaps the dispenser hadn't really been there.

The next day he and Mary Ableseth visited one of the few remaining parks. In the southern part of Utah, near the mountains, the park although small was bright green and attractive. Milt Biskle lolled on the grass watching a squirrel progressing toward a tree in wicket-like leaps, its tail flowing behind it in a gray stream.

'No squirrels on Mars,' Milt Biskle said sleepily.

Wearing a slight sunsuit, Mary Ableseth stretched out on her back, eyes shut. 'It's nice here, Milt. I imagine Mars is like this.' Beyond the park heavy traffic moved along the freeway; the noise reminded Milt of the surf of the Pacific Ocean. It lulled him. All seemed well, and he tossed a peanut to the squirrel. The squirrel veered, wicket-hopped toward the peanut, its intelligent face twitching in response.

As it sat upright, holding the nut, Milt Biskle tossed a second nut off to the right. The squirrel heard it land among the maple leaves; its ears pricked up, and this reminded Milt of a game he once had played with a cat, an old sleepy tom which had belonged to him and his brother in the days before Terra had been so overpopulated, when pets were still legal. He had waited until Pumpkin—the tomcat—was almost asleep and then he had tossed a small object into the corner of the room. Pumpkin woke up. His eyes had flown open and his ears had pricked, turned, and he had sat for fifteen minutes listening and watching, brooding as to what had made the noise. It was a harmless way of teasing the old cat, and Milt felt sad, thinking how many years Pumpkin had been dead, now, his last legal pet. On Mars, though, pets would be legal again. That cheered him.

In fact on Mars, during his years of reconstruct work, he had possessed a pet. A Martian plant. He had brought it with him to Terra and it now stood on the living room coffee table in Mary

Ableseth's conapt, its limbs draped rather unhappily. It had not prospered in the unfamiliar Terran climate.

'Strange,' Milt murmured, 'that my wug-plant isn't thriving. I'd have thought in such a moist atmosphere . . .'

'It's the gravity,' Mary said, eyes still shut, her bosom rising and falling regularly. She was almost asleep. 'Too much for it.'

Milt regarded the supine form of the woman, remembering Pumpkin under similar circumstances. The hypnogogic moment, between waking and sleeping, when consciousness and unconsciousness became blended . . . reaching, he picked up a pebble.

He tossed the pebble into the leaves near Mary's head.

At once she sat up, eyes open, startled, her sunsuit falling from her.

Both her ears pricked up.

'But we Terrans,' Milt said, 'have lost control of the musculature of our ears, Mary. On even a reflex basis.'

'What?' she murmured, blinking in confusion as she retied her sunsuit.

'Our ability to prick up our ears has atrophied,' Milt explained. 'Unlike the dog and cat. Although to examine us morphologically you wouldn't know because the muscles are still there. So you made an error.'

'I don't know what you're talking about,' Mary said, with a trace of sullenness. She turned her attention entirely to arranging the bra of her sunsuit, ignoring him.

'Let's go back to the conapt,' Milt said, rising to his feet. He no longer felt like lolling in the park, because he could no longer believe in the park. Unreal squirrel, unreal grass . . . was it actually? Would they ever show him the substance beneath the illusion? He doubted it.

The squirrel followed them a short way as they walked to their parked 'copter, then turned its attention to a family of Terrans which included two small boys; the children threw nuts to the squirrel and it scampered in vigorous activity.

'Convincing,' Milt said. And it really was.

Mary said, 'Too bad you couldn't have seen Dr DeWinter more, Milt. He could have helped you.' Her voice was oddly hard.

'I have no doubt of that,' Milt Biskle agreed as they re-entered the parked 'copter.

When they arrived back at Mary's conapt he found his Martian wug-plant dead. It had evidently perished of dehydration.

'Don't try to explain this,' he said to Mary as the two of them stood gazing down at the parched, dead stalks of the once active plant. 'You know what it shows. Terra is supposedly more humid than Mars, even reconstructed Mars at its best. Yet this plant has completely dried out. There's no moisture left on Terra because I suppose the Prox blasts emptied the seas. Right?'

Mary said nothing.

'What I don't understand,' Milt said, 'is why it's worth it to you people to keep the illusion going. *I've finished my job.*'

After a pause Mary said, 'Maybe there're more planets requiring reconstruct work, Milt.'

'Your population is that great?'

'I was thinking of Terra. Here,' Mary said. 'Reconstruct work on it will take generations; all the talent and ability you reconstruct engineers possess will be required.' She added, 'I'm just following your hypothetical logic, of course.'

'So Terra's our next job. That's why you let me come here. In fact I'm going to *stay* here.' He realized that, thoroughly and utterly, in a flash of insight. 'I won't be going back to Mars and I won't see Fay again. You're replacing her.' It all made sense.

'Well,' Mary said, with a faint wry smile, 'let's say I'm attempting to.' She stroked his arm. Barefoot, still in her sunsuit, she moved slowly closer and closer to him.

Frightened, he backed away from her. Picking up the dead wug-plant he numbly carried it to the apt's disposal chute and dropped the brittle, dry remains in. They vanished at once.

'And now,' Mary said busily, 'we're going to visit the Museum of Modern Art in New York and then, if we have time, the Smithsonian in Washington, DC. They've asked me to keep you busy so you don't start brooding.'

'But I am brooding,' Milt said as he watched her change from her sunsuit to a gray wool knit dress. Nothing can stop that, he said to himself. And you know it now. And as each reconstruct engineer finishes his area it's going to happen again. I'm just the first.

At least I'm not alone, he realized. And felt somewhat better.

'How do I look?' Mary asked as she put on lipstick before the bedroom mirror.

'Fine,' he said listlessly, and wondered if Mary would meet each reconstruct engineer in turn, become the mistress of each. Not only is she not what she seems, he thought, but I don't even get to keep her.

It seemed a gratuitous loss, easily avoided.

He was, he realized, beginning to like her. *Mary was alive*; that much was real. Terran or not. At least they had not lost the war to shadows; they had lost to authentic living organisms. He felt somewhat cheered.

'Ready for the Museum of Modern Art?' Mary said briskly, with a smile.

Later, at the Smithsonian, after he had viewed the *Spirit of St Louis* and the Wright brothers' incredibly ancient plane—it appeared to be at least a million years old—he caught sight of an exhibit which he had been anticipating.

Saying nothing to Mary—she was absorbed in studying a case of semi-precious stones in their natural uncut state—he slipped off and, a moment later, stood before a glass-walled section entitled

PROX MILITARY OF 2014

Three Prox soldiers stood frozen, their dark muzzles stained and grimy, side arms ready, in a makeshift shelter composed of the remains of one of their transports. A bloody Prox flag hung drably.

This was a defeated enclave of the enemy; these three creatures were about to surrender or be killed.

A group of Terran visitors stood before the exhibit, gawking. Milt Biskle said to the man nearest him, 'Convincing, isn't it?'

'Sure is,' the man, middle-aged, with glasses and gray hair, agreed. 'Were you in the war?' he asked Milt, glancing at him.

'I'm in reconstruct,' Milt said. 'Yellow Engineer.'

'Oh.' The man nodded, impressed. 'Boy, these Proxmen look scary. You'd almost expect them to step out of that exhibit and fight us to the death.' He grinned. 'They put up a good fight before they gave in, those Proxmen; you have to give 'em credit for that.'

Beside him the man's gray, taut wife said, 'Those guns of theirs make me shiver. It's too realistic.' Disapproving, she walked on.

'You're right,' Milt Biskle said. 'They do look frighteningly real, because of course they are.' There was no point in creating an illusion of this sort because the genuine thing lay immediately at hand, readily available. Milt swung himself under the guard rail, reached the transparent glass of the exhibit, raised his foot and smashed the glass; it burst and rained down with a furious racket of shivering fragments.

As Mary came running, Milt snatched a rifle from one of the frozen Proxmen in the exhibit and turned it toward her.

She halted, breathing rapidly, eyeing him but saying nothing.

'I am willing to work for you,' Milt said to her, holding the rifle expertly. 'After all, if my own race no longer exists I can hardly reconstruct a colony world for them; even I can see that. But I want to know the truth. Show it to me and I'll go on with my job.'

Mary said, 'No, Milt, if you knew the truth you wouldn't go on. You'd turn that gun on yourself.' She sounded calm, even compassionate, but her eyes were bright and enlarged, wary.

'Then I'll kill you,' he said. And, after that, himself.

'Wait.' She pondered. 'Milt—this is difficult. You know absolutely nothing and yet look how miserable you are. How do you expect to feel when you can see your planet as it is? It's almost too much for me and I'm—' She hesitated.

'Say it.'

'I'm just a—' she choked out the word—'a visitor.'

'But I am right,' he said. 'Say it. Admit it.'

'You're right, Milt,' she sighed.

Two uniformed museum guards appeared, holding pistols. 'You okay, Miss Ableseth?'

'For the present,' Mary said. She did not take her eyes off Milt and the rifle which he held. 'Just wait,' she instructed the guards.

'Yes ma'am.' The guards waited. No one moved.

Milt said, 'Did any Terran women survive?'

After a pause, Mary said, 'No, Milt. But we Proxmen are within the same genus, as you well know. We can interbreed. Doesn't that make you feel better?'

'Sure,' he said. 'A lot better.' And he did feel like turning the rifle on himself now, without waiting. It was all he could do to resist the impulse. So he had been right; that thing had not been Fay, there at Field Three on Mars. 'Listen,' he said to Mary Ableseth, 'I want to go back to Mars again. I came here to learn something. I learned it, now I want to go back. Maybe I'll talk to Dr DeWinter again, maybe he can help me. Any objection to that?'

'No.' She seemed to understand how he felt. 'After all, you did all your work there. You have a right to return. But eventually you have to begin here on Terra. We can wait a year or so, perhaps even two. But eventually Mars will be filled up and we'll need the room. And it's going to be so much harder here ... as you'll discover.' She tried to smile but failed; he saw the effort. 'I'm sorry, Milt.'

'So am I,' Milt Biskle said. 'Hell, I was sorry when that wug-plant died. I knew the truth then. It wasn't just a guess.'

'You'll be interested to know that your fellow reconstruct engineer Red, Cleveland Andre, addressed the meeting in your place. And passed your intimations on to them all, along with his own. They voted to send an official delegate here to Terra to investigate; he's on his way now.'

'I'm interested,' Milt said. 'But it doesn't really matter. It hardly changes things.' He put down the rifle. 'Can I go back to Mars now?' He felt tired. 'Tell Dr DeWinter I'm coming.' Tell him, he thought, to have every psychiatric technique in his repertory ready for me, because it will take a lot. 'What about Earth's animals?' he asked. 'Did any forms at all survive? How about the dog and the cat?'

Mary glanced at the museum guards; a flicker of communication passed silently between them and then Mary said, 'Maybe it's all right after all.'

'What's all right?' Milt Biskle said.

'For you to see. Just for a moment. You seem to be standing up to it better than we had expected. In our opinion you *are* entitled to that.' She added, 'Yes, Milt, the dog and cat survived; they live here among the ruins. Come along and look.'

He followed after her, thinking to himself, Wasn't she right the first time? Do I really want to look? Can I stand up to what exists in actuality—what they've felt the need of keeping from me up until now?

At the exit ramp of the museum Mary halted and said, 'Go on outside, Milt. I'll stay here. I'll be waiting for you when you come back in.'

Haltingly, he descended the ramp.

And saw.

It was, of course, as she had said, ruins. The city had been decapitated, leveled three feet above ground-level; the buildings had become hollow squares, without contents, like some infinite arrangements of useless, ancient courtyards. He could not believe that what he saw was *new*; it seemed to him as if these abandoned remnants had always been there, exactly as they were now. And— how long would they remain this way?

To the right an elaborate but small-scale mechanical system had plopped itself down to a debris-filled street. As he watched, it extended a host of pseudopodia which burrowed inquisitively into the nearby foundations. The foundations, steel and cement, were abruptly pulverized; the bare ground, exposed, lay naked and dark brown, seared over from the atomic heat generated by the repair autonomic rig—a construct, Milt Biskle thought, not much different from those I employ on Mars. At least to some meager extent the rig had the task of clearing away the old. He knew from his own reconstruct work on Mars that it would be followed, probably within minutes, by an equally elaborate mechanism which would lay the groundwork for the new structures to come.

And, standing off to one side in the otherwise deserted street, watching this limited clearing-work in progress, two gray, thin figures could be made out. Two hawk-nosed Proxmen with their pale, natural hair arranged in high coils, their earlobes elongated with heavy weights.

The victors, he thought to himself. Experiencing the satisfaction of this spectacle, witnessing the last artifacts of the defeated race being obliterated. Some day a purely Prox city will rise up here: Prox architecture, streets of the odd, wide Prox pattern, the uniform box-like buildings with their many subsurface levels. And citizens such as these will be treading the ramps, accepting the high-speed runnels in their daily routines. And what, he thought, about the Terran dogs and cats which now inhabit these ruins, as Mary said? Will even they disappear? Probably not entirely. There will be room for them, perhaps in museums and zoos, as oddities to be gaped at. Survivals of an ecology which no longer obtained. Or even mattered.

And yet—Mary was right. The Proxmen were within the same genus. Even if they did not interbreed with the remaining Terrans the species as he had known it would go on. And they would interbreed, he thought. His own relationship with Mary was a harbinger. As individuals they were not so far apart. The results might even be good.

The results, he thought as he turned away and started back into the museum, may be a race not quite Prox and not quite Terran; something that is genuinely new may come from the melding. At least we can hope so.

Terra would be rebuilt. He had seen slight but real work in progress with his own eyes. Perhaps the Proxmen lacked the skill that he and his fellow reconstruct engineers possessed . . . but now that Mars was virtually done they could begin here. It was not absolutely hopeless. Not *quite*.

Walking up to Mary he said hoarsely, 'Do me a favor. Get me a cat I can take back to Mars with me. I've always liked cats. Especially the orange ones with stripes.'

One of the museum guards, after a glance at his companion, said, 'We can arrange that, Mr Biskle. We can get a—cub, is that the word?'

'Kitten, I think,' Mary corrected.

On the trip back to Mars, Milt Biskle sat with the box containing the orange kitten on his lap, working out his plans. In fifteen minutes the ship would land on Mars and Dr DeWinter—or the thing that posed as Dr DeWinter anyhow—would be waiting to meet him. And it would be too late. From where he sat he could see the emergency escape hatch with its red warning light. His plans had become focussed around the hatch. It was not ideal but it would serve.

In the box the orange kitten reached up a paw and batted at Milt's hand. He felt the sharp, tiny claws rake across his hand and he absently disengaged his flesh, retreating from the probing reach of the animal. You wouldn't have liked Mars anyhow, he thought, and rose to his feet.

Carrying the box he strode swiftly toward the emergency hatch. Before the stewardess could reach him he had thrown open the hatch. He stepped forward and the hatch locked behind him. For an instant he was within the cramped unit, and then he began to twist open the heavy outer door.

'Mr Biskle!' the stewardess's voice came, muffled by the door behind him. He heard her fumbling to reach him, opening the door and groping to catch hold of him.

As he twisted open the outer door the kitten within the box under his arm snarled.

You, too? Milt Biskle thought, and paused.

PRECIOUS ARTIFACT

Death, the emptiness and utter lack of warmth of 'tween space, seeped around him, filtering past the partly opened outer door. He smelled it and something within him, as in the kitten, retreated by instinct. He paused, holding the box, not trying to push the outer door any farther open, and in that moment the stewardess grabbed him.

'Mr Biskle,' she said with a half-sob, 'are you out of your mind? Good God, what are you doing?' She managed to tug the outer door shut, screw the emergency section back into shut position.

'You know exactly what I'm doing,' Milt Biskle said as he allowed her to propel him back into the ship and to his seat. And don't think you stopped me, he said to himself. Because it wasn't you. I could have gone ahead and done it. But I decided not to.

He wondered why.

Later, at Field Three on Mars, Dr DeWinter met him as he had expected.

The two of them walked to the parked 'copter and DeWinter in a worried tone of voice said, 'I've just been informed that during the trip—'

'That's right. I attempted suicide. But I changed my mind. Maybe you know why. You're the psychologist, the authority as to what goes on inside us.' He entered the 'copter, being careful not to bang the box containing the Terran kitten.

'You're going to go ahead and stake your landparcel with Fay?' Dr DeWinter asked presently as the 'copter flew above green, wet fields of high protein wheat. 'Even though—you know?'

'Yes.' He nodded. After all, there was nothing else for him, as far as he could make out.

'You Terrans.' DeWinter shook his head. 'Admirable.' Now he noticed the box on Milt Biskle's lap. 'What's that you have there? A creature from Terra?' He eyed it suspiciously; obviously to him it was a manifestation of an alien form of life. 'A rather peculiar-looking organism.'

'It's going to keep me company,' Milt Biskle said. 'While I go on with my work, either building up my private parcel or–' Or helping you Proxmen with Terra, he thought.

'Is that what was called a "rattlesnake"? I detect the sound of its rattles.' Dr DeWinter edged away.

'It's purring.' Milt Biskle stroked the kitten as the autonomic circuit of the 'copter guided it across the dully red Martian sky. Contact with the one familiar life-form, he realized, will keep me sane. It will make it possible for me to go on. He felt grateful. My race may have been defeated and destroyed, but not all Terran creatures have perished. When we reconstruct Terra maybe we can induce the authorities to allow us to set up game preserves. We'll make that part of our task, he told himself, and again he patted the kitten. At least we can hope for that much.

Next to him, Dr DeWinter was also deep in thought. He appreciated the intricate workmanship, by engineers stationed on the third planet, which had gone into the simulacrum resting in the box on Milt Biskle's lap. The technical achievement was impressive, even to him, and he saw clearly–as Milt Biskle of course did not. This artifact, accepted by the Terran as an authentic organism from his familiar past, would provide a pivot by which the man would hang onto his psychic balance.

But what about the other reconstruct engineers? What would carry each of them through and past the moment of discovery as each completed his work and had to–whether he liked it or not–awake?

It would vary from Terran to Terran. A dog for one, a more elaborate simulacrum, possibly that of a nubile human female, for another. In any case each would be provided with an 'exception' to the true state. One essential surviving entity, selected out of what had in fact totally vanished. Research into the past of each engineer would provide the clue, as it had in Biskle's instance; the cat-simulacrum had been finished weeks before his abrupt, panic-stricken trip home to Terra. For instance, in Andre's case a parrot-simulacrum was already under construction. It would be done by the time he made *his* trip home.

'I call him Thunder,' Milt Biskle explained.

'Good name,' Dr DeWinter—as he titled himself these days—said. And thought, A shame we could not have shown him the real situation of Terra. Actually it's quite interesting that he accepted what he saw, because on some level he must realize that nothing survives a war of the kind we conducted. Obviously he desperately wanted to believe that a remnant, even though no more than rubble, endures. But it's typical of the Terran mind to fasten onto phantoms. That might help explain their defeat in the conflict; they were simply not realists.

'This cat,' Milt Biskle said, 'is going to be a mighty hunter of Martian sneak-mice.'

'Right,' Dr DeWinter agreed, and thought, *As long as its batteries don't run down*. He, too, patted the kitten.

A switch closed and the kitten purred louder.

RETREAT SYNDROME

Peace officer Caleb Myers picked up the fast-moving surface vehicle on his radarscope, saw at once that its operator had managed to remove the governor; the vehicle, at one-sixty miles per hour, had exceeded its legal capacity. Hence, he knew, the operator came from the Blue Class, engineers and technicians capable of tinkering with their wheels. Arrest, therefore, would be a tricky matter.

By radio Myers contacted a police vessel ten miles north along the freeway. 'Shoot its power supply out as it passes you,' he suggested to his brother officer. 'It's going too fast to block, right?'

At 3:10 A.M. the vehicle was stopped; powerless, it had coasted to a halt on the freeway shoulder. Officer Myers pressed buttons, flew leisurely north until he spotted the helpless wheel, plus the red-lit police wheel making its way through heavy traffic toward it. He landed at the exact instant that his compatriot arrived on the scene.

Together, warily, they walked to the stalled wheel, gravel crunching under their boots.

In the wheel sat a slim man wearing a white shirt and tie; he stared straight ahead with a dazed expression, making no move to greet the two gray-clad officers with their laser rifles, anti-pellet bubbles protecting their bodies from thigh to cranium. Myers opened the door of the wheel and glanced in, while his fellow officer stood with rifle in hand, just in case this was another come-on; five men from the local office, San Francisco, had been killed this week alone.

'You know,' Myers said to the silent driver, 'that it's a mandatory two-year suspension of license if you tamper with your wheel's speed governor. Was it worth it?'

After a pause the driver turned his head and said, 'I'm sick.'

'Psychically? Or physically?' Myers touched the emergency button at his throat, making contact with line 3, to San Francisco General Hospital; he could have an ambulance here in five minutes, if necessary.

The driver said huskily, 'Everything seemed unreal to me. I thought if I drove fast enough I could reach some place where it's—solid.' He put his hand gropingly against the dashboard of his wheel, as if not really believing the heavily-padded surface was there.

'Let me look in your throat, sir,' Myers said, and shone his flashlight in the driver's face. He turned the jaw upward, peered down past well-cared-for teeth as the man reflexively opened his mouth.

'See it?' his fellow officer asked.

'Yes.' He had caught the glint. The anti-carcinoma unit, installed in the throat; like most non-Terrans this man was cancer phobic. Probably he had spent most of his life in a colony world, breathing pure air, the artificial atmosphere installed by autonomic reconstruct equipment prior to human habitation. So the phobia was easy to understand.

'I have a full-time doctor.' The driver reached now into his pocket, brought out his wallet; from it he extracted a card. His hand shook as he passed the card to Myers. 'Specialist in psychosomatic medicine, in San Jose. Any way you could take me there?'

'You're not sick,' Myers said. 'You just haven't fully adjusted to Earth, to this gravity and atmosphere and milieu factors. It's three-fifteen in the morning; this doctor—Hagopian or whatever his name is—can't see you now.' He studied the card. It informed him:

> This man is under medical care and should any bizarre behavior be exhibited obtain medical help at once.

'Earth doctors,' his fellow officer said, 'don't see patients after hours; you'll have to learn that, Mr—' He held out his hand. 'Let me see your operator's license, please.'

The entire wallet was reflexively passed to him.

'Go home,' Myers said to the man. His name, according to the license, was John Cupertino. 'You have a wife? Maybe she can pick you up; we'll take you into the city . . . better leave your wheel here and not try to drive any more tonight. About your speed–'

Cupertino said, 'I'm not used to an arbitrary maximum. Ganymede has no traffic problem; we travel in the two and two-fifties.' His voice had an oddly flat quality. Myers thought at once of drugs, in particular of thalamic stimulants; Cupertino was hag-ridden with impatience. That might explain his removal of the official speed regulator, a rather easy removal job for a man accustomed to machinery. And yet–

There was more. From twenty years' experience Myers intuited it.

Reaching out he opened the glove compartment, flashed his light in. Letters, an AAA book of approved motels . . .

'You don't really believe you're on Earth, do you, Mr Cupertino?' Myers said. He studied the man's face; it was devoid of affect. 'You're another one of those bippity-bop addicts who thinks this is a drug-induced guilt-fantasy . . . and you're really home on Ganymede, sitting in the living room of your twenty-room demesne– surrounded no doubt by your autonomic servants, right?' He laughed sharply, then turned to his fellow officer. 'It grows wild on Ganymede,' he explained. 'The stuff. Frohedadrine, the extract's called. They grind up the dried stalks, make a mash of it, boil it, drain it, filter it, and then roll it up and smoke it. And when they're all done–'

'I've never taken Frohedadrine,' John Cupertino said remotely; he stared straight ahead. 'I know I'm on Earth. But there's something wrong with me. Look.' Reaching out, he put his hand through the heavily-padded dashboard; officer Myers saw the hand disappear up to the wrist. 'You see? It's all insubstantial around me, like shadows. Both of you; I can banish you by just removing my attention from you. I think I can, anyhow. But–*I don't want to!*' His voice grated with anguish. 'I want you to be real; I want all of this to be real, including Dr Hagopian.'

Officer Myers switched his throat-transmitter to line 2 and said, 'Put me through to a Dr Hagopian in San Jose. This is an emergency; never mind his answering service.'

The line clicked as the circuit was established.

Glancing at his fellow officer Myers said, 'You saw it. You saw him put his hand through the dashboard. Maybe he can banish us.' He did not particularly feel like testing it out; he felt confused and he wished now that he had let Cupertino speed on along the freeway, to oblivion if necessary. To wherever he wanted.

'I know why all this is,' Cupertino said, half to himself. He got out cigarettes, lit up; his hand was less shaky now. 'It's because of the death of Carol, my wife.'

Neither officer contradicted him; they kept quiet and waited for the call to Dr Hagopian to be put through.

His trousers on over his pajamas, and wearing a jacket buttoned to keep him warm in the night chill, Gottlieb Hagopian met his patient Mr Cupertino at his otherwise closed-up office in downtown San Jose. Dr Hagopian switched on lights, then the heat, arranged a chair, wondered how he looked to his patient with his hair sticking in all directions.

'Sorry to get you up,' Cupertino said, but he did not sound sorry; he seemed perfectly wide-awake, here at four in the morning. He sat smoking with his legs crossed, and Dr Hagopian, cursing and groaning to himself in futile complaint, went to the back room to plug in the coffeemaker: at least he could have that.

'The police officers,' Hagopian said, 'thought you might have taken some stimulants, by your behavior. We know better.' Cupertino was, as he well knew, always this way; the man was slightly manic.

'I never should have killed Carol,' Cupertino said. 'It's never been the same since then.'

'You miss her right now? Yesterday when you saw me you said—'

'That was in broad daylight; I always feel confident when the sun's up. By the way—I've retained an attorney. Name's Phil Wolfson.'

'Why?' No litigation was pending against Cupertino; they both knew that.

'I need professional advice. In addition to yours. I'm not criticizing you, doctor; don't take it as an insult. But there're aspects to my situation which are more legal than medical. Conscience is an interesting phenomenon; it lies partly in the psychological realm, partly—'

'Coffee?'

'Lord no. It sets the vagus nerve off for four hours.'

Dr Hagopian said, 'Did you tell the police officers about Carol? About your killing her?'

'I just said that she was dead; I was careful.'

'You weren't careful when you drove at one-sixty. There was a case in the *Chronicle* today—it happened on the Bayshore Freeway—where the State Highway Patrol went ahead and disintegrated a car that was going one-fifty; and it was legal. Public safety, the lives of—'

'They warned it,' Cupertino pointed out. He did not seem perturbed; in fact he had become even more tranquil. 'It refused to stop. A drunk.'

Dr Hagopian said, 'You realize, of course, that Carol is still alive. That in fact she's living here on Earth, in Los Angeles.'

'Of course.' Cupertino nodded irritably. Why did Hagopian have to belabor the obvious? They had discussed it countless times, and no doubt the psychiatrist was going to ask him the old query once again: how could you have killed her when you know she's alive? He felt weary and irritable; the session with Hagopian was getting him nowhere.

Taking a pad of paper Dr Hagopian wrote swiftly, then tore off the sheet and held it toward Cupertino.

'A prescription?' Cupertino accepted it warily.

'No. An address.'

Glancing at it Cupertino saw that it was an address in South Pasadena. No doubt it was Carol's address; he glared at it in wrath.

'I'm going to try this,' Dr Hagopian said. 'I want you to go there and see her face to face. Then we'll—'

'Tell the board of directors of Six-planet Educational Enterprises to see her, not me,' Cupertino said, handing the piece of paper back. 'They're responsible for the entire tragedy; because of them I had to do it. And you know that, so don't look at me that way. It was their plan that had to be kept secret; isn't that so?'

Dr Hagopian sighed. 'At four in the morning everything seems confused. The whole world seems ominous. I'm aware that you were employed by Six-planet at the time, on Ganymede. But the moral responsibility—' He broke off. 'This is difficult to say, Mr Cupertino. You pulled the trigger on the laser beam, so you have to take final moral responsibility.'

'Carol was going to tell the local homeopapes that there was about to be an uprising to free Ganymede, and the bourgeois authority on Ganymede, consisting in the main of Six-planet, was involved; I told her that we couldn't afford to have her say anything. She did it for petty, spiteful motives, for hatred of me; nothing to do with the actual issues involved. Like all women she was motivated by personal vanity and wounded pride.'

'Go to that address in South Pasadena,' Dr Hagopian urged. 'See Carol. Convince yourself that you never killed her, that what happened on Ganymede that day three years ago was a—' He gestured, trying to find the right words.

'Yes, doctor,' Cupertino said cuttingly. 'Just what was it? Because that day—or rather that night—I got Carol right above the eyes with that laser beam, right in the frontal lobe; she was absolutely unmistakably dead before I left the conapt and got out of there, got to the spaceport and found an interplan ship to take me to Earth.' He waited; it was going to be hard on Hagopian, finding the right words; it would take quite some time.

After a pause, Hagopian admitted, 'Yes, your memory is detailed; it's all in my file and I see no use in your repeating it—I frankly find it unpleasant at this hour of the morning. I don't know why the memory is there; I know it's false because I've met your wife, talked to her, carried on a correspondence with her; all subsequent to the date, on Ganymede, at which you remember killing her. I know that much, at least.'

Cupertino said, 'Give me one good reason for looking her up.' He made a motion to tear the slip of paper in half.

'One?' Dr Hagopian pondered. He looked gray and tired. 'Yes, I can give you a good reason, but probably it's one you'll reject.'

'Try me.'

Dr Hagopian said, 'Carol was present that night on Ganymede, the night you recall killing her. Maybe she can tell you how you obtained the false memory; she implied in correspondence with me that she knows something about it.' He eyed Cupertino. 'That's all she would tell me.'

'I'll go,' Cupertino said. And walked swiftly to the door of Dr Hagopian's office. Strange, he thought, to obtain knowledge about a person's death from that person. But Hagopian was right; Carol was the only other person who was present that night . . . he should have realized long ago that eventually he'd have to look her up.

It was a crisis in his logic that he did not enjoy facing.

At six in the morning he stood at Carol Holt Cupertino's door. Many rings of the bell were required until at last the door of the small, single-unit dwelling opened; Carol, wearing a blue, pellucid nylon nightgown and white furry slippers, stood sleepily facing him. A cat hurried out past her.

'Remember me?' Cupertino said, stepping aside for the cat.

'Oh God.' She brushed the tumble of blonde hair back from her eyes, nodded. 'What time is it?' Gray, cold light filled the almost deserted street; Carol shivered, folded her arms. 'How come you're up so early? You never used to be out of bed before eight.'

'I haven't gone to bed yet.' He stepped past her, entered the dark living room with its drawn shades. 'How about some coffee?'

'Sure.' Listlessly she made her way to the kitchen, pressed the HOT COFFEE button on the stove; first one, then a second cup appeared, giving off fragrant steam. 'Cream for me,' she said, 'cream and sugar for you. You're more infantile.' She handed him his cup; the smell of her—warmth and softness and sleep—mixed with that of the coffee.

Cupertino said, 'You haven't gotten a day older and it's been well over three years.' In fact she was even more slender, more supple.

Seating herself at the kitchen table, her arms still modestly folded, Carol said, 'Is that suspicious?' Her cheeks were flushed, her eyes bright.

'No. A compliment.' He, too, seated himself. 'Hagopian sent me here; he decided I should see you. Evidently—'

'Yes,' Carol said, 'I've seen him. I was in Northern California several times on business; I stopped by . . . he had asked me to in a letter. I like him. In fact you should be about cured by now.'

'"Cured"?' He shrugged. 'I feel I am. Except—'

'Except that you still have your *idée fixe*. Your basic, delusional, fixed idea that no amount of psychoanalysis will help. Right?'

Cupertino said, 'If you mean my recollection of killing you, yes; I still have it—*I know it happened*. Dr Hagopian thought you could tell me something about it; after all, as he pointed out—'

'Yes,' she agreed, 'but is it really worth going over this with you? It's so tedious, and my God, it's only six A.M. Couldn't I go back to bed and then sometime later get together with you, maybe in the evening? No?' she sighed. 'Okay. Well, you tried to kill me. You did have a laser beam. It was at our conapt in New Detroit-G, on Ganymede, on March 12, 2014.'

'Why did I try to kill you?'

'You know.' Her tone was bitter; her breasts pulsed with resentment.

'Yes.' In all his thirty-five years he had never made another mistake as serious. In their divorce litigation his wife's knowledge of the impending revolt had given her the dominant position; she had been able to dictate settlement terms to him precisely as she wished. At last the financial components had proved unbearable and he had gone to the conapt which they had shared—by then he had moved out, gotten a small conapt of his own at the other end of the city—and had told her simply and truthfully that he could not meet her demands. And so the threat by Carol to go to the homeopapes, the news-gathering extensors of the New York *Times* and *Daily News* which operated on Ganymede.

'You got out your little laser beam,' Carol was saying, 'and you sat with it, fooling with it, not saying much. But you got your message over to me; either I accepted an unfair settlement which—'

'Did I fire the beam?'

'Yes.'

'And it hit you?'

Carol said, 'You missed and I ran out of the conapt and down the hall to the elevator. I got downstairs to the sergeant at arms' room on floor one and called the police from there. They came. They found you still in the conapt.' Her tone was withering. 'You were crying.'

'Christ,' Cupertino said. Neither of them spoke for a time, then; they both drank their coffee. Across from him his wife's pale hand shook and her cup clinked against its saucer.

'Naturally,' Carol said matter-of-factly, 'I went ahead with the divorce litigation. Under the circumstances—'

'Dr Hagopian thought you might know why I remember killing you that night. He said you hinted at it in a letter.'

Her blue eyes glittered. *'That night you had no false memory*; you knew you had failed. Amboynton, the district attorney, gave you a choice between accepting mandatory psychiatric help or having formal charges filed of attempted first-degree murder; you took the former—naturally—and so you've been seeing Dr Hagopian. The false memory—I can tell you exactly when that set in. You visited your employer, Six-planet Educational Enterprises; you saw their psychologist, a Dr Edgar Green, attached to their personnel department. That was shortly before you left Ganymede and came here to Terra.' Rising she went to fill her cup; it was empty. 'I presume Dr Green saw to the implanting of the false memory of your having killed me.'

Cupertino said, 'But why?'

'They knew you had told me of the plans for the uprising. You were supposed to commit suicide from remorse and grief, but instead you booked passage to Terra, as you had agreed with

Amboynton. As a matter of fact you did attempt suicide during the trip . . . but you must remember this?'

'Go on and say it.' He had no memory of a suicide attempt.

'I'll show you the clipping from the homeopape; naturally I kept it.' Carol left the kitchen; her voice came from the bedroom. 'Out of misguided sentimentality. "Passenger on interplan ship seized as—"' Her voice broke off and there was silence.

Sipping his coffee Cupertino sat waiting, knowing that she would find no such newspaper clipping. Because there had been no such attempt.

Carol returned to the kitchen, a puzzled expression on her face. 'I can't locate it. But I know it was in my copy of *War and Peace*, in volume one; I was using it as a bookmark.' She looked embarrassed.

Cupertino said, 'I'm not the only one who has a false memory. If that's what it is.' He felt, for the first time in over three years, that he was at last making progress.

But the direction of that progress was obscured. At least so far. 'I don't understand,' Carol said. 'Something's wrong.'

While he waited in the kitchen, Carol, in the bedroom, dressed. At last she emerged, wearing a green sweater, skirt, heels; combing her hair she halted at the stove and pressed the buttons for toast and two soft-boiled eggs. It was now almost seven; the light in the street outside was no longer gray but a faint gold. And more traffic moved; he heard the reassuring sound of commercial vehicles and private commute wheels.

'How did you manage to snare this single-unit dwelling?' he asked. 'Isn't it as impossible in the Los Angeles area as in the Bay area to get anything but a conapt in a high-rise?'

'Through my employers.'

'Who're your employers?' He felt at once cautious and disturbed; obviously they had influence. His wife had gone up in the world.

'Falling Star Associates.'

He had never heard of them; puzzled, he said, 'Do they operate beyond Terra?' Surely if they were interplan—

'It's a holding company. I'm a consultant to the chairman of the board; I do marketing research.' She added, 'Your old employer, Six-planet Educational Enterprises, belongs to us; we own controlling stock. Not that it matters. It's just a coincidence.'

She ate breakfast, offering him nothing; evidently it did not even occur to her to. Moodily he watched the familiar dainty movements of her cutlery. She was still ennobled by petit-bourgeois gentility; that had not changed. In fact she was more refined, more feminine, than ever.

'I think,' Cupertino said, 'that I understand this.'

'Pardon?' She glanced up, her blue eyes fixed on him intently. 'Understand what, Johnny?'

Cupertino said, 'About you. Your presence. You're obviously quite real—as real as everything else. As real as the city of Pasadena, as this table—' He rapped with brusque force on the plastic surface of the kitchen table. 'As real as Dr Hagopian or the two police who stopped me earlier this morning.' He added, *'But how real is that? I think we have the central question there.* It would explain my sensation of passing my hands through matter, through the dashboard of my wheel, as I did. That very unpleasant sensation that nothing around me was substantial, that I inhabited a world of shadows.'

Staring at him Carol suddenly laughed. Then continued eating.

'Possibly,' Cupertino said, 'I'm in a prison on Ganymede, or in a psychiatric hospital there. Because of my criminal act. And I've begun, during these last years since your death, to inhabit a fantasy world.'

'Oh God,' Carol said and shook her head. 'I don't know whether to laugh or feel sorry; it's just too—' She gestured. 'Too pathetic. I really feel sorry for you, Johnny. Rather than give up your delusional idea you'd actually prefer to believe that all Terra is a product of your mind, everyone and everything. Listen—don't you agree it'd be more economical to give up the fixed idea? Just abandon the one idea that you killed me—'

The phone rang.

'Pardon me.' Carol hastily wiped her mouth, rose to go and answer it. Cupertino remained where he was, gloomily playing with a flake of toast which had fallen from her plate; the butter on it stained his finger and he licked it away, reflexively, then realized that he was gnawingly hungry; it was time for his own breakfast and he went to the stove to press buttons for himself, in Carol's absence. Presently he had his own meal, bacon and scrambled eggs, toast and hot coffee, before him.

But how can I live? he asked himself.—*Gain substance, if this is a delusional world?*

I must be eating a genuine meal, he decided. *Provided by the hospital or prison; a meal exists and I am actually consuming it—a room exists, walls and a floor . . . but not this room. Not these walls nor this floor.*

And—people exist. But not this woman. Not Carol Holt Cupertino. Someone else. An impersonal jailer or attendant. And a doctor. Perhaps, he decided, *Dr Hagopian.*

That much is so, Cupertino said to himself. *Dr Hagopian is really my psychiatrist.*

Carol returned to the kitchen, reseated herself at her now cold plate. 'You talk to him. It's Hagopian.'

At once he went to the phone.

On the small vidscreen Dr Hagopian's image looked taut and drawn. 'I see you got there, John. Well? What took place?'

Cupertino said, 'Where are we, Hagopian?'

Frowning, the psychiatrist said, 'I don't—'

'We're both on Ganymede, aren't we?'

Hagopian said, 'I'm in San Jose; you're in Los Angeles.'

'I think I know how to test my theory,' Cupertino said. 'I'm going to discontinue treatment with you; if I'm a prisoner on Ganymede I won't be able to, but if I'm a free citizen on Terra as you maintain—'

'You're on Terra,' Hagopian said, 'but you're not a free citizen. Because of your attempt on your wife's life you're *obliged* to accept regular psychotherapy through me. You know that. What did Carol tell you? Could she shed any light on the events of that night?'

'I would say so,' Cupertino said. 'I learned that she's employed by the parent company of Six-planet Educational Enterprises; that alone makes my trip down here worthwhile. I must have found out about her, that she was employed by Six-planet to ride herd over me.'

'P-pardon?' Hagopian blinked.

'A watchdog. To see that I remained loyal; they must have feared I was going to leak details of the planned uprising to the Terran authorities. So they assigned Carol to watch me. I told her the plans and to them that proved I was unreliable. So Carol probably received instructions to kill me; she probably made an attempt and failed, and everyone connected with it was punished by the Terran authorities. Carol escaped because she wasn't officially listed as an employee of Six-planet.'

'Wait,' Dr Hagopian said. 'It does sound somewhat plausible. But–' He raised his hand. 'Mr Cupertino, the uprising was successful; it's a matter of historic fact. Three years ago Ganymede, Io and Callisto simultaneously threw off Terra and became self-governing, independent moons. Every child in school beyond the third grade knows that; it was the so-called Tri-Lunar War of 2014. You and I have never discussed it but I assumed you were aware of it as–' He gestured. 'Well, as any other historic reality.'

Turning from the telephone to Carol, John Cupertino said, 'Is that so?'

'Of course,' Carol said. 'Is that part of your delusional system, too, that your little revolt failed?' She smiled. 'You worked eight years for it, for one of the major economic cartels masterminding and financing it, and then for some occult reason you choose to ignore its success. I really pity you, Johnny; it's too bad.'

'There must be a reason,' Cupertino said. 'Why I don't know that. Why they decided to keep me from knowing that.' Bewildered, he reached out his hand . . .

His hand, trembling, passed into the vidphone screen and disappeared. He drew it back at once; his hand reappeared. But he had seen it go. He had perceived and understood.

The illusion was good–but not quite good enough. It simply was not perfect; it had its limitations.

'Dr Hagopian,' he said to the miniature image on the vidscreen, 'I don't think I'll continue seeing you. As of this morning you're fired. Bill me at my home, and thank you very much.' He reached to cut the connection.

'You can't,' Hagopian said instantly. 'As I said, it's mandatory. You must face it, Cupertino; otherwise you'll have to go up before the court once more, and I know you don't want to do that. Please believe me; it would be bad for you.'

Cupertino cut the connection and the screen died.

'He's right, you know,' Carol said, from the kitchen.

'He's lying,' Cupertino said. And, slowly, walked back to seat himself across from her and resume eating his own breakfast.

When he returned to his own conapt in Berkeley he put in a long-distance vidcall to Dr Edgar Green at Six-planet Educational Enterprises on Ganymede. Within half an hour he had his party.

'Do you remember me, Dr Green?' he asked as he faced the image. To him the rather plump, middle-aged face opposite him was unfamiliar; he did not believe he had ever seen the man before in his life. However, at least one fundamental reality-configuration had borne the test: there was a Dr Edgar Green in Six-planet's personnel department; Carol had been telling the truth to that extent.

'I have seen you before,' Dr Green said, 'but I'm sorry to say that the name does not come to mind, sir.'

'John Cupertino. Now of Terra. Formerly of Ganymede. I was involved in a rather sensational piece of litigation slightly over three years ago, somewhat before Ganymede's revolt. I was accused of murdering my wife, Carol. Does that help you, doctor?'

'Hmm,' Dr Green said, frowning. He raised an eyebrow. 'Were you acquitted, Mr Cupertino?'

Hesitating, Cupertino said, 'I—currently am under psychiatric care, here in the Bay area of California. If that's any help.'

'I presume you're saying that you were declared legally insane. And therefore could not stand trial.'

Cupertino, cautiously, nodded.

'It may be,' Dr Green said, 'that I talked to you. Very dimly it rings a bell. But I see so many people . . . were you employed here?'

'Yes,' Cupertino said.

'What specifically did you want from me, Mr Cupertino? Obviously you want something; you've placed a rather expensive long-distance call. I suggest for practical purposes—your pocket-book in particular—you get to the point.'

'I'd like you to forward my case history,' Cupertino said. 'To me, not to my psychiatrist. Can that be arranged?'

'You want it for what purpose, Mr Cupertino? For securing employment?'

Cupertino, taking a deep breath, said, 'No, doctor. So that I can be absolutely certain what psychiatric techniques were used in my case. By you and by members of your medical staff, those working under you. I have reason to believe I underwent major corrective therapy with you. Am I entitled to know that, doctor? It would seem to me that I am.' He waited, thinking, *I have about one chance in a thousand of prying anything of worth out of this man.* But it was worth the try.

'"Corrective therapy"? You must be confused, Mr Cupertino; we do only aptitude testing, profile analysis—we don't do therapy, here. Our concern is merely to analyze the job-applicant in order to—'

'Dr Green,' Cupertino said, 'were you personally involved in the revolt of three years ago?'

Green shrugged. 'We all were. Everyone on Ganymede was filled with patriotism.' His voice was bland.

'To protect that revolt,' Cupertino said, 'would you have implanted a delusional idea in my mind for the purpose of—'

'I'm sorry,' Green interrupted. 'It's obvious that you're psychotic. There's no point in wasting your money on this call; I'm surprised that they permitted you access to an outside vidline.'

'But such an idea can be implanted,' Cupertino persisted. 'It is possible, by current psychiatric technique. You admit that.'

Dr Green sighed. 'Yes, Mr Cupertino. It's been possible ever since the mid-twentieth century; such techniques were initially developed by the Pavlov Institute in Moscow as early as 1940, perfected by the time of the Korean War. A man can be made to believe anything.'

'Then Carol could be right.' He did not know if he was disappointed or elated. It would mean, he realized, that he was not a murderer; that was the cardinal point. Carol *was* alive, and his experience with Terra, with its people, cities and objects, was genuine. And yet–'If I came to Ganymede,' he said suddenly, '*could I see my file?* Obviously if I'm well enough to make the trip I'm not a psychotic under mandatory psychiatric care. I may be sick, doctor, but I'm not that sick.' He waited; it was a slim chance, but worth trying.

'Well,' Dr Green said, pondering, 'there is no company rule which precludes an employee–or ex-employee–examining his personnel file; I suppose I could open it to you. However, I'd prefer to check with your psychiatrist first. Would you give me his name, please? And if he agrees I'll save you a trip; I'll have it put on the vidwires and in your hands by tonight, your time.'

He gave Dr Green the name of his psychiatrist, Dr Hagopian. And then hung up. What would Hagopian say? An interesting question and one he could not answer; he had no idea which way Hagopian would jump.

But by nightfall he would know; that much was certain.

He had an intuition that Hagopian would agree. But for the wrong reasons.

However, that did not matter; Hagopian's motives were not important–all that he cared about was the file. Getting his hands on it, reading it and finding out if Carol was right.

It was two hours later–actually an incredibly long time–that it came to him, all at once, that Six-planet Educational Enterprises could, with no difficulty whatsoever, tamper with the file, omit the pertinent information. Transmit to Earth a spurious, worthless document.

Then what did he do next?

It was a good question. And one–for the moment–which he could not answer.

*

That evening the file from Six-planet Educational Enterprises' main personnel offices on Ganymede was delivered by Western Union messenger to his conapt. He tipped the messenger, seated himself in his living room and opened the file.

It took him only a few moments to certify the fact which he had suspected: the file contained no references to any implantation of a delusional idea. Either the file had been reconstructed or Carol was mistaken. Mistaken—or lying. In any case the file told him nothing.

He phoned the University of California, and, after being switched from station to station, wound up with someone who seemed to know what he was talking about. 'I want an analysis,' Cupertino explained, 'of a written document. To find out how recently it was transcribed. This is a Western Union wire-copy so you'll have to go on word anachronisms alone. I want to find out if the material was developed three years ago or more recently. Do you think you can analyze for so slight a factor?'

'There's been very little word-change in the past three years,' the university philologist said. 'But we can try. How soon do you have to have the document back?'

'As soon as possible,' Cupertino said.

He called for a building messenger to take the file to the university, and then he took time to ponder another element in the situation.

If his experience of Terra was delusional, the moment at which his perceptions most closely approximated reality occurred during his sessions with Dr Hagopian. Hence if he were ever to break through the delusional system and perceive actual reality it would most likely take place then; his maximum efforts should be directed at that time. Because one fact seemed clearly established: he really was seeing Dr Hagopian.

He went to the phone and started to dial Hagopian's number. Last night, after the arrest, Hagopian had helped him; it was unusually soon to be seeing the doctor again, but he dialed. In view of his analysis of the situation it seemed justified; he could afford the cost . . . And then something came to him.

The arrest. All at once he remembered what the policeman had said; he had accused Cupertino of being a user of the Ganymedean drug Frohedadrine. And for a good reason: *he showed the symptoms.*

Perhaps that was the modus operandi by which the delusional system was maintained; he was being given Frohedadrine in small regular doses, perhaps in his food.

But wasn't that a paranoid—in other words psychotic—concept?

And yet paranoid or not, it made sense.

What he needed was a blood fraction test. The presence of the drug would register in such a test; all he had to do was show up at the clinic of his firm in Oakland, ask for the test on the grounds that he had a suspected toxemia. And within an hour the test would be completed.

And, if he was on Frohedadrine, it would prove that he was correct; he was still on Ganymede, not on Terra. And all that he experienced—or seemed to experience—was a delusion, with the possible exception of his regular, mandatory visits to the psychiatrist.

Obviously he should have the blood fraction test made—at once. And yet he shrank from it. Why? Now he had the means by which to make a possible absolute analysis, and yet he held back.

Did he want to know the truth?

Certainly he had to have the test made; he forgot temporarily the notion of seeing Dr Hagopian, went to the bathroom to shave, then put on a clean shirt and tie and left the conapt, starting toward his parked wheel; in fifteen minutes he would be at his employer's clinic.

His employer. He halted, his hand touching the doorhandle of his wheel, feeling foolish.

They had slipped up somehow in their presentation of his delusional system. Because he did not know where he worked. A major segment of the system simply was not there.

Returning to his conapt he dialed Dr Hagopian.

Rather sourly Dr Hagopian said, 'Good evening, John. I see you're back in your own conapt; you didn't stay in Los Angeles long.'

Cupertino said huskily, 'Doctor, I don't know where I work. Obviously something's gone wrong; I must have known formerly—up until today, in fact. Haven't I been going to work four days a week like everyone else?'

'Of course,' Hagopian said, unruffled. 'You're employed by an Oakland firm, Triplan Industries, Incorporated, on San Pablo Avenue near Twenty-first Street. Look up the exact address in your phone book. But—I'd say go to bed and rest; you were up all last night and it seems obvious that you're suffering a fatigue reaction.'

'Suppose,' Cupertino said, 'greater and greater sections of the delusional system begin to slip. It won't be very pleasant for me.' The one missing element terrified him; it was as if a piece of himself had dissolved. Not to know where he worked—in an instant he was set apart from all other humans, thoroughly isolated. And how much else could he forget? Perhaps it was the fatigue; Hagopian might be right. He was, after all, too old to stay up all night; it was not as it had been a decade ago when such things were physically possible for both him and Carol.

He wanted, he realized, to hang onto the delusional system; he did not wish to see it decompose around him. A person was his world; without it he did not exist.

'Doctor,' he said, 'may I see you this evening?'

'But you just saw me,' Dr Hagopian pointed out. 'There's no reason for another appointment so soon. Wait until later in the week. And in the meantime—'

'I think I understand how the delusional system is maintained,' Cupertino said. 'Through daily doses of Frohedadrine, administered orally, in my food. Perhaps by going to Los Angeles I missed a dose; that might explain why a segment of the system collapsed. Or else as you say it's fatigue; in any case this proves that I'm correct; this is a delusional system, and I don't need either the blood fraction test or the University of California to confirm it. Carol is dead—*and you know it.* You're my psychiatrist on Ganymede and I'm in custody, have been now for three years. Isn't that actually the case?' He waited, but Hagopian did not answer; the doctor's face remained impassive. 'I never was in Los Angeles,' Cupertino said. 'In fact I'm probably confined to a relatively small area; I have no freedom of motion as it would appear. And I didn't see Carol this morning, did I?'

Hagopian said slowly, 'What do you mean, "blood fraction test"? What gave you the idea of asking for that?' He smiled faintly. 'If this is a delusional system, John, the blood fraction test would be illusory, too. So how could it help you?'

He had not thought of that; stunned, he remained silent, unable to answer.

'And that file which you asked Dr Green for,' Hagopian said. 'Which you received and then transferred to the University of California for analysis; that would be delusional, too. So how can the result of their tests–'

Cupertino said, 'There's no way you could know of that, doctor. You conceivably might know that I talked to Dr Green, asked for and received the file; Green might have talked to you. But not my request for analysis by the university; you couldn't possibly know that. I'm sorry, doctor, but by a contradiction of internal logic this structure has proved itself unreal. You know too much about me. And I think I know what final, absolute test I can apply to confirm my reasoning.'

'What test?' Hagopian's tone was cold.

Cupertino said, 'Go back to Los Angeles. And kill Carol once more.'

'Good God, how–'

'A woman who has been dead for three years can't die again,' Cupertino said. 'Obviously it'll prove impossible to kill her.' He started to break the phone connection.

'Wait,' Hagopian said rapidly. 'Look, Cupertino; I've got to contact the police now–you've forced me to. I can't let you go down there and murder that woman for the–' He broke off. 'Make a second try, I mean, on her life. All right, Cupertino; I'll admit several things which have been concealed from you. To an extent you're right; you are on Ganymede, not on Terra.'

'I see,' Cupertino said, and did not break the circuit.

'But Carol is real,' Dr Hagopian continued. He was perspiring, now; obviously afraid that Cupertino would ring off he said, almost stammeringly, 'She's as real as you or I. You tried to kill her and failed; she informed the homeopapes about the intended revolt– and because of that the revolt was not completely successful. We here on Ganymede are surrounded by a cordon of Terran military ships; we're cut off from the rest of the Sol System, living on emergency rations and being pushed back, *but still holding out.*'

'Why my delusional system?' He felt cold fright rise up inside him; unable to stifle it he felt it enter his chest, invade his heart. 'Who imposed it on me?'

'No one imposed it on you. It was a self-induced retreat syndrome due to your sense of guilt. Because, Cupertino, it was your fault that the revolt was detected; your telling Carol was the crucial factor–and you recognize it. You tried suicide and that failed, so instead you withdrew psychologically into this fantasy world.'

'If Carol told the Terran authorities she wouldn't now be free to–'

'That's right. Your wife is in prison and that's where you visited her, at our prison in New Detroit-G, here on Ganymede. Frankly, I don't know what the effect of my telling you this will have on your fantasy world; it may cause it to further disintegrate, in fact it may even restore you to a clear perception of the terribly difficult situation which we Ganys face vis-à-vis the Terran military establishment. I've envied you, Cupertino, during these last three years; you haven't had to face the harsh realities we've had to. Now–' He shrugged. 'We'll see.'

After a pause Cupertino said, 'Thanks for telling me.'

'Don't thank me; I did it to keep you from becoming agitated to the point of violence. You're my patient and I have to think of your welfare. No punishment for you is now or ever was intended; the extent of your mental illness, your retreat from reality, fully demonstrated your remorse at the results of your stupidity.' Hagopian looked haggard and gray. 'In any case leave Carol alone; it's not your job to exact vengeance. Look it up in the Bible if you don't believe me. Anyhow she's being punished, and will continue to be as long as she's physically in our hands.'

Cupertino broke the circuit.

Do I believe him? he asked himself.

He was not certain. *Carol,* he thought. *So you doomed our cause, out of petty, domestic spite. Out of mere female bitterness, because you were angry at your husband; you doomed an entire moon to three years of losing, hateful war.*

Going to the dresser in his bedroom he got out his laser beam; it had remained hidden there, in a Kleenex box, the entire three years since he had left Ganymede and come to Terra.

But now, he said to himself, *it's time to use this.*

Going to the phone he dialed for a cab; this time he would travel to Los Angeles by public rocket express, rather than by his own wheel.

He wanted to reach Carol as soon as humanly possible.

You got away from me once, he said as he walked rapidly to the door of his conapt. *But not this time. Not twice.*

Ten minutes later he was aboard the rocket express, on his way to Los Angeles and Carol.

Before John Cupertino lay the Los Angeles *Times*; once more he leafed through it, puzzled, still unable to find the article. Why wasn't it here? he asked himself. A murder committed, an attractive, sexy woman shot to death . . . he had walked into Carol's place of work, found her at her desk, killed her in front of her fellow employees, then turned and, unhindered, walked back out; everyone had been too frozen with fear and surprise to interfere with him.

And yet it was not in the pape. The homeopape made absolutely no mention of it.

'You're looking in vain,' Dr Hagopian said, from behind his desk.

'It has to be here,' Cupertino said doggedly. 'A capital crime like that—*what's the matter?*' He pushed the homeopape aside, bewildered. It made no sense; it defied obvious logic.

'First,' Dr Hagopian said wearily, 'the laser beam did not exist; that was a delusion. Second, we did not permit you to visit your wife again because we knew you planned violence—you had made that perfectly clear. You never saw her, never killed her, and the homeopape before you is not the Los Angeles *Times*; it's the New Detroit-G *Star* . . . which is limited to four pages because of the pulp-paper shortage here on Ganymede.'

Cupertino stared at him.

'That's right,' Dr Hagopian said, nodding. 'It's happened again, John; you have a delusional memory of killing her twice, now. And each event is as unreal as the other. You poor creature—you're evidently doomed to try again and again, and each time fail. As much as our leaders hate Carol Holt Cupertino and deplore and regret what she did to us—' He gestured. 'We have to protect her; it's only just. Her sentence is being carried out; she'll be imprisoned for twenty-two more years or until Terra manages to defeat us and releases her. No doubt if they get hold of her they'll make her into a heroine; she'll be in every Terran-controlled homeopape in the Sol System.'

'You'd let them get her alive?' Cupertino said, presently.

'Do you think we should kill her before they take her?' Dr Hagopian scowled at him. 'We're not barbarians, John; we don't commit crimes of vengeance. She's suffered three years of imprisonment already; she's being punished sufficiently.' He added, 'And so are you as well. I wonder which of you is suffering the more.'

'I know I killed her,' Cupertino persisted. 'I took a cab to her place of employment, Falling Star Associates, which controls Six-planet Educational Enterprises, in San Francisco; her office was on the sixth floor.' He remembered the trip up in the elevator, even the hat which the other passenger, a middle-aged woman, had worn. He remembered the slender, red-haired receptionist who had contacted Carol by means of her desk intercom; he remembered passing through the busy inner offices, suddenly finding himself face to face with Carol. She had risen, stood behind her desk, seeing the laser beam which he had brought out; understanding had flashed across her features and she had tried to run, to get away . . . but he had killed her anyhow, as she reached the far door, her hand clutching for the knob.

'I assure you,' Dr Hagopian said, 'Carol is very much alive.' He turned to the phone on his desk, dialed. 'Here, I'll call her, get her on the line; you can talk to her.'

Numbly, Cupertino waited until at last the image on the vidscreen formed. It was Carol.

'Hi,' she said, recognizing him.

Haltingly he said, 'Hi.'

'How are you feeling?' Carol asked.

'Okay.' Awkwardly he said, 'And you?'

'I'm fine,' Carol said. 'Just a little sleepy because of being woken up so early this morning. By you.'

He rang off, then. 'All right,' he said to Dr Hagopian. 'I'm convinced.' It was obviously so; his wife was alive and untouched; in fact she evidently had no knowledge even of an attempt by him on her life this time. He had not even come to her place of business; Hagopian was telling the truth.

Place of business? Her prison cell, rather. If he was to believe Hagopian. And evidently he had to.

Rising, Cupertino said, 'Am I free to go? I'd like to get back to my conapt; I'm tired too. I'd like to get some sleep tonight.'

'It's amazing you're able to function at all,' Hagopian said, 'after having had no sleep for almost fifty hours. By all means go home and go to bed. We'll talk later.' He smiled encouragingly.

Hunched with fatigue John Cupertino left Dr Hagopian's office; he stood outside on the sidewalk, hands in his pockets, shivering in the night cold, and then he got unsteadily into his parked wheel.

'Home,' he instructed it.

The wheel turned smoothly away from the curb, to join traffic.

I could try once more, Cupertino realized suddenly. *Why not? And this time I might be successful. Just because I've failed twice—that doesn't mean I'm doomed always to fail.*

To the wheel he said, 'Head toward Los Angeles.'

The autonomic circuit of the wheel clicked as it contacted the main route to Los Angeles, US Highway 99.

She'll be asleep when I get there, Cupertino realized. *Probably because of that she'll be confused enough to let me in. And then—*

Perhaps now the revolt will succeed.

There seemed to him to be a gap, a weak point, in his logic. But he could not quite put his finger on it; he was too tired. Leaning back he tried to make himself comfortable against the seat of the wheel; he let the autonomic circuit drive and shut his eyes in an attempt to catch some much-needed sleep. In a few hours he would be in South Pasadena, at Carol's one-unit dwelling. Perhaps after he killed her he could sleep; he would deserve it, then.

By tomorrow morning, he thought, *if all goes well she'll be dead*. And then he thought once more about the homeopape, and wondered why there had been no mention of the crime in its columns. *Strange*, he thought. *I wonder why not.*

The wheel, at one hundred and sixty miles an hour—after all, he had removed the speed governor—hurtled toward what John Cupertino believed to be Los Angeles and his sleeping wife.

A TERRAN ODYSSEY

Orion Stroud, Chairman of the West Marin school board, turned up the Coleman gasoline lantern so that the utility school room in the white glare became clearly lit, and all four members of the board could make out the new teacher.

'I'll put a few questions to him,' Stroud said to the others. 'First, this is Mr Barnes and he comes from Oregon. He tells me he's a specialist in science and natural edibles. Right, Mr Barnes?'

The new teacher, a short, young-looking man wearing a khaki shirt and work pants, nervously cleared his throat and said, 'Yes, I am familiar with chemicals and plants and animal-life, especially whatever is found out in the woods such as berries and mushrooms.'

'We've recently had bad luck with mushrooms,' Mrs Tallman said, the elderly lady who had been a member of the board even in the old days before the Emergency. 'It's been our tendency to leave them alone, now.'

'I've looked through your pastures and woods in this area,' Mr Barnes said, 'and I've seen some fine examples of nutritious mushrooms; you can supplement your diet without taking any chances. I even know their Latin names.'

The board stirred and murmured. That had impressed them, Stroud realized, that about the Latin names.

'Why did you leave Oregon?' George Keller, the principal, asked bluntly.

The new teacher faced him and said, 'Politics.'

'Yours or theirs?'

'Theirs,' Barnes said. 'I have no politics. I teach children how to make ink and soap and how to cut the tails from lambs even if the lambs are almost grown. And I've got my own books.' He picked up a book from the small stack beside him, showing the board in what good shape they were. 'I'll tell you something else: you have the means here in this part of California to make paper. Did you know that?'

Mrs Tallman said, 'We knew it, Mr Barnes, but we don't know quite how. It has to do with bark of trees, doesn't it?'

On the new teacher's face appeared a mysterious expression, one of concealment. Stroud knew that Mrs Tallman was correct, but the teacher did not want to let her know; he wanted to keep the knowledge to himself because the West Marin trustees had not yet hired him. His knowledge was not yet available—he gave nothing free. And that of course was proper; Stroud recognized that, respected Barnes for it. Only a fool gave something away for nothing.

Mrs Tallman was scrutinizing the new teacher's stack of books. 'I see that you have Carl Jung's *Psychological Types*. Is one of your sciences psychology? How nice, to acquire a teacher for our school who can tell edible mushrooms and also is an authority on Freud and Jung.'

'There's no value in such stuff,' Stroud said, with irritation. 'We need useful science, not academic hot air.' He felt personally let down; Mr Barnes had not told him about that, about his interest in mere theory. 'Psychology doesn't dig any septic tanks.'

'I think we're ready to vote on Mr Barnes,' Miss Costigan, the youngest member of the board, said. 'I for one am in favor of accepting him, at least on a provisional basis. Does anyone feel otherwise?'

Mrs Tallman said to Mr Barnes, 'We killed our last teacher, you know. That's why we need another. That's why we sent Mr Stroud out looking up and down the Coast until he found you.'

'We killed him because he lied to us,' Miss Costigan said. 'You see, his real reason for coming here had nothing to do with teaching. He was looking for some man named Jack Tree, who it turned out lived in this area. Our Mrs Keller, a respected member of this community and the wife of George Keller, here, our principal, is a dear friend of Mr Tree, and she brought the news of the situation to us and of course we acted, legally and officially, through our chief of police, Mr Earl Colvig.'

'I see,' Mr Barnes said woodenly, listening without interrupting.

Speaking up, Orion Stroud said, 'The jury which sentenced and executed him was composed of myself, Cas Stone, who's the largest land-owner in West Marin, Mrs Tallman and Mrs June Raub. I say "executed" but you understand that the act—when he was shot, the shooting itself—was done by Earl. That's Earl's job, after the West Marin Official Jury has made its decision.' He eyed the new teacher.

'It sounds,' Mr Barnes said, 'very formal and law-abiding to me. Just what I'd be interested in.' He smiled at them all, and the tension in the room relaxed; people murmured.

A cigarette—one of Andrew Gill's special deluxe Gold Labels—was lit up; its good, rich smell wafted to them all, cheering them and making them feel more friendly to the new teacher and to one another.

Seeing the cigarette, Mr Barnes got a strange expression on his face and he said in a husky voice, 'You've got *tobacco* up here? After seven years?' He clearly could not believe it.

Smiling in amusement, Mrs Tallman said, 'We don't have any tobacco, Mr Barnes, because of course no one does. But we do have a tobacco expert. He fashions these special deluxe Gold Labels for us out of choice, aged vegetable and herbal materials the nature of which remains—and justly so—his individual secret.'

'How much do they cost?' Mr Barnes asked.

'In terms of State of California boodle money,' Orion Stroud said, 'about a hundred dollars apiece. In terms of pre-war silver, a nickel apiece.'

'I have a nickel,' Mr Barnes said, reaching shakily into his coat pocket; he fished about, brought up a nickel and held it toward the smoker, who was George Keller, leaning back in his chair with his legs crossed to make himself comfortable.

'Sorry,' George said, 'I don't want to sell. You better go directly to Mr Gill; you can find him during the day at his shop. It's here in Point Reyes Station but of course he gets all around; he has a horse-drawn VW minibus.'

'I'll make a note of that,' Mr Barnes said. He put his nickel away, very carefully.

'Do you intend to board the ferry?' the Oakland official asked. 'If not, I wish you'd move your car, because it's blocking the gate.'

'Sure,' Stuart McConchie said. He got back into his car, flicked the reins that made Edward Prince of Wales, his horse, begin pulling. Edward pulled, and the engineless 1975 Pontiac passed back through the gate and out onto the pier.

The Bay, choppy and blue, lay on both sides, and Stuart watched through the windshield as a gull swooped to seize some edible from the pilings. Fishing lines, too . . . men catching their evening meals. Several of the men wore the remains of Army uniforms. Veterans who perhaps lived beneath the pier. Stuart drove on.

If only he could afford to telephone San Francisco. But the underwater cable was out again, and the lines had to go all the way down to San Jose and up the other side, along the peninsula, and by the time the call reached San Francisco it would cost him five dollars in silver money. So, except for a rich person, that was out of the question; he had to wait the two hours until the ferry left . . . but could he stand to wait that long?

He was after something important.

He had heard a rumor that a huge Soviet guided missile had been found, one which had failed to go off; it lay buried in the ground near Belmont, and a farmer had discovered it while plowing. The farmer was selling it off in the form of individual parts, of which there were thousands in the guidance system alone. The farmer wanted a penny a part, your choice. And Stuart, in his line of work, needed many such parts. But so did lots of other people. So it was first come, first serve; unless he got across the Bay to Belmont fairly soon, it would be too late.

He sold (another man made them) small electronic traps. Vermin had mutated and now could avoid or repel the ordinary passive trap, no matter how complicated. The cats in particular had become different, and Mr Hardy built a superior cat trap, even better than his rat and dog traps. The vermin were dangerous; they killed and ate small children almost at will—or at least so one heard. And of course wherever possible they themselves were caught and eaten in return. Dogs in particular, if stuffed with rice, were considered delicious; the little local Berkeley newspaper which came out once a week had recipes for dog soup, dog stew, even dog pudding.

Meditating about dog pudding made Stuart realize how hungry he was. It seemed to him that he had not stopped being hungry since the first bomb fell; his last really adequate meal had been the lunch at Fred's Fine Foods that day he had run into Hoppy Harrington the phocomelus doing his phony vision act. And where, he wondered suddenly, was that little phoce now? He hadn't thought of him in years.

Now, of course, one saw many phoces, and almost all of them on their 'mobiles, exactly as Hoppy had been, placed dead center each in his own little universe, like an armless, legless god. The sight still repelled Stuart, but there were so many repellent sights these days . . .

On the surface of the Bay to his right a legless veteran propelled himself out onto the water aboard a raft, rowing himself toward a pile of debris that was undoubtedly a sunken ship. On the hulk a number of fishing lines could be seen; they belonged to the veteran and he was in the process of checking them. Watching the raft go, Stuart wondered if it could reach the San Francisco side. He could offer the man fifty cents for a one-way trip; why not? Stuart got out of his car and walked to the edge of the pier.

'Hey,' he yelled, 'come here.' From his pocket he got a penny; he tossed it down onto the pier and the veteran saw it, heard it. At once he spun the raft about and came paddling rapidly back, straining to make speed, his face streaked with perspiration. He grinned up friendlily at Stuart, cupping his ear.

'Fish?' he called. 'I don't have any yet today, but maybe later on how about a small shark? Guaranteed safe.' He held up the battered Geiger counter which he had connected to his waist by a length of rope—in case it fell from the raft or someone tried to steal it, Stuart realized.

'No,' Stuart said, squatting down at the edge of the pier. 'I want to get over to San Francisco; I'll pay you a quarter for one way.'

'But I got to leave my lines to do that,' the veteran said, his smile fading. 'I got to collect them all or somebody'd steal them while I was gone.'

'Thirty-five cents,' Stuart said.

In the end they agreed, at a price of forty cents. Stuart locked the legs of Edward Prince of Wales together so no one could steal him, and presently he was out on the Bay, bobbing up and down aboard the veteran's raft, being rowed across to San Francisco.

'What field are you in?' the veteran asked him. 'You're not a tax collector, are you?' He eyed him calmly.

'Naw,' Stuart said. 'I'm a small trap man.'

'Listen, my friend,' the veteran said, 'I got a pet rat lives under the pilings with me? He's smart; he can play the flute. I'm not putting you under an illusion, it's true. I made a little wooden flute and he plays it, through his nose . . . it's practically an Asiatic nose-flute like they have in India. Well, I did have him, but the other day he got run over. I saw the whole thing happen; I couldn't go get him or nothing. He ran across the pier to get something, maybe a piece of cloth . . . he has this bed I made him but he gets—I mean he got—cold all the time because they mutated, this particular line, they lost their hair.'

'I've seen those,' Stuart said, thinking how well the hairless brown rat evaded even Mr Hardy's electronic vermin traps. 'Actually I believe what you said,' he said. 'I know rats pretty well. But they're nothing compared to those little striped gray-brown tabby cats . . . I'll bet you had to make the flute, he couldn't construct it himself.'

'True,' the veteran said. 'But he was an artist. You ought to have heard him play; I used to get a crowd at night, after we were finished with the fishing. I tried to teach him the Bach Chaconne in D.'

'I caught one of those tabby cats once,' Stuart said, 'that I kept for a month until it escaped. It could make little sharp-pointed things out of tin can lids. It bent them or something; I never did see how it did it, but they were wicked.'

The veteran, rowing, said, 'What's it like south of San Francisco these days? I can't come up on land.' He indicated the lower part of his body. 'I stay on the raft. There's a little trap door, when I have to go to the bathroom. What I need is to find a dead phoce sometime and get his cart. They call them phocomobiles.'

'I knew the first phoce,' Stuart said, 'before the war. He was brilliant; he could repair anything.' He lit up an imitation-tobacco cigarette; the veteran gaped at it longingly. 'South of San Francisco it's as you know all flat. So it got hit bad and it's just farmland now. Nobody ever rebuilt there, and it was mostly those little tract houses so they left hardly any decent basements. They grow peas and corn and beans down there. What I'm going to see is a big rocket a farmer just found; I need relays and tubes and other electronic gear for Mr Hardy's traps.' He paused. 'You ought to have a Hardy trap.'

'Why? I live on fish, and why should I hate rats? I like them.'

'I like them, too,' Stuart said, 'but you have to be practical; you have to look to the future. Someday America may be taken over by rats if we aren't wary. We owe it to our country to catch and kill rats, especially the wiser ones that would be natural leaders.'

The veteran glared at him. 'Sales talk, that's all.'

'I'm sincere.'

'That's what I have against salesmen; they believe their own lies. You know that the best rats can *ever* do, in a million years of evolution, is maybe be useful as servants to we human beings. They could carry messages maybe and do a little manual work. But dangerous—' He shook his head. 'How much does one of your traps sell for?'

'Ten dollars silver. No State boodle accepted; Mr Hardy is an old man and you know how old people are, he doesn't consider boodle to be real money.' Stuart laughed.

'Let me tell you about a rat I once saw that did a heroic deed,' the veteran began, but Stuart cut him off.

'I have my own opinions,' Stuart said. 'There's no use arguing about it.'

They were both silent, then. Stuart enjoyed the sight of the Bay on all sides; the veteran rowed. It was a nice day, and as they bobbed along toward San Francisco, Stuart thought of the electronic parts he might be bringing back to Mr Hardy and the factory on San Pablo Avenue, near the ruins of what had once been the west end of the University of California.

'What kind of cigarette is that?' the veteran asked presently.

'This?' Stuart examined the butt; he was almost ready to put it out and stick it away in the metal box in his pocket. The box was full of butts, which would be opened and made into new cigarettes by Tom Grandi, the local cigarette man in South Berkeley. 'This,' he said, 'is imported. From Marin County. It's a deluxe Gold Label made by—' He paused for effect. 'I guess I don't have to tell you.'

'By Andrew Gill,' the veteran said. 'Say, I'd like to buy a whole one from you; I'll pay you a dime.'

'They're worth fifteen cents apiece,' Stuart said. 'They have to come all the way around Black Point and Sears' Point and along the Lucas Valley Road, from beyond Nicasio somewhere.'

'I had one of those Andrew Gill deluxe special Gold Labels one time,' the veteran said. 'It fell out of the pocket of some man who was getting on the ferry; I fished it out of the water and dried it.'

All of a sudden Stuart handed him the butt.

'For God's sake,' the veteran said, not looking directly at him. He rowed rapidly, his lips moving, his eyelids blinking.

'I got more,' Stuart said.

The veteran said, 'I'll tell you what else you got; you got real humanity, mister, and that's rare today. Very rare.'

Stuart nodded. He felt the truth of the veteran's words.

The little Keller girl sat shivering on the examination table, and Doctor Stockstill, surveying her thin, pale body, thought of a joke which he had seen on television years ago, long before the war. A

Spanish ventriloquist, speaking through a chicken ... the chicken had produced an egg.

'My son,' the chicken said, meaning the egg.

'Are you sure?' the ventriloquist asked. 'It's not your daughter?'

And the chicken, with dignity, answered, 'I know my business.'

This child was Bonny Keller's daughter, but, Doctor Stockstill thought, it isn't George Keller's daughter; I am certain of that ... I know my business. Who had Bonny been having an affair with, seven years ago? The child must have been conceived very close to the day the war began. But she had not been conceived before the bombs fell; that was clear. Perhaps it was on that very day, he ruminated. Just like Bonny, to rush out while the bombs were falling, while the world was coming to an end, to have a brief, frenzied spasm of love with someone, perhaps with some man she did not even know, the first man she happened onto ... and now this.

The child smiled at him and he smiled back. Superficially, Edie Keller appeared normal; she did not seem to be a funny child. How he wished, God damn it, that he had an x-ray machine. Because—

He said aloud, 'Tell me more about your brother.'

'Well,' Edie Keller said in her frail, soft voice, 'I talk to my brother all the time and sometimes he answers for a while but more often he's asleep. He sleeps almost all the time.'

'Is he asleep now?'

For a moment the child was silent. 'No,' she answered.

Rising to his feet and coming over to her, Doctor Stockstill said, 'I want you to show me exactly where he is.'

The child pointed to her left side, low down; near, he thought, the appendix. The pain was there. That had brought the child in; Bonny and George had become worried. They knew about the brother, but they assumed him to be imaginary, a pretend playmate which kept their little daughter company. He himself had assumed so at first; the chart did not mention a brother, and yet Edie talked about him. Bill was exactly the same age as she. Born, Edie had informed the doctor, at the same time as she, of course.

'Why of course?' he had asked, as he began examining her—he

had sent the parents into the other room because the child seemed reticent in front of him.

Edie had answered in her calm, solemn way. 'Because he's my twin brother. How else could he be inside me?' And, like the Spanish ventriloquist's chicken, she spoke with authority, with confidence; she, too, knew her business.

In the seven years since the war Doctor Stockstill had examined many hundreds of funny people, many strange and exotic variants on the human life form which flourished now under a much more tolerant—although smokily veiled—sky. He could not be shocked. And yet, this—a child whose brother lived inside her body, down in the inguinal region. For seven years Bill Keller had dwelt inside there, and Doctor Stockstill, listening to the girl, believed her; he knew it was possible. It was not the first case of this kind. If he had his x-ray machine he would be able to see the tiny, wizened shape, probably no larger than a baby rabbit. In fact, with his hands he could feel the outline . . . he touched her side, carefully noting the firm cyst-like sack within. The head in a normal position, the body entirely within the abdominal cavity, limbs and all. Someday the girl would die and they would open her body, perform an autopsy; they would find a little wrinkled male figure, perhaps with a snowy beard and blind eyes . . . her brother, still no larger than a baby rabbit.

Meanwhile, Bill slept mostly, but now and then he and his sister talked. What did Bill have to say? What possibly could he know?

To the question, Edie had an answer. 'Well, he doesn't know very much. He doesn't see anything but he thinks. And I tell him what's going on so he doesn't miss out.'

'What are his interests?' Stockstill asked.

Edie considered and said, 'Well, he, uh, likes to hear about food.'

'Food!' Stockstill said, fascinated.

'Yes. He doesn't eat, you know. He likes me to tell him over and over again what I had for dinner, because he does get it after a while . . . I think he does, anyhow. Wouldn't he have to, to live?'

'Yes,' Stockstill agreed.

'He especially likes it if I have apples or oranges. And—he likes to hear stories. He always wants to hear about places, far-away especially like New York. I want to take him there someday, so he can see what it's like. I mean, so I can see and then tell him.'

'You take good care of him, don't you?' Stockstill said, deeply touched. To the girl, it was normal; she had lived like this always—she did not know of any other existence.

'I'm afraid,' she said suddenly, 'that he might die someday.'

'I don't think he will,' Stockstill said. 'What's more likely to happen is that he'll get larger. And that might pose a problem; it might be hard for your body to accommodate him.'

'Would he be born, then?' Edie regarded him with large, dark eyes.

'No,' Stockstill said. 'He's not located that way. He'd have to be removed—surgically. But he wouldn't live. The only way he can live is as he is now, inside you.' Parasitically, he thought, not saying the word. 'We'll worry about that when the time comes, if it ever does.'

Edie said, 'I'm glad I have a brother; he keeps me from being lonely. Even when he's asleep I can feel him there, I know he's there. It's like having a baby inside me; I can't wheel him around in a baby carriage or anything like that, or dress him, but talking to him is a lot of fun. For instance, I get to tell him about Mildred.'

'Mildred!' He was puzzled.

'You know.' The child smiled at his ignorance. 'The woman that keeps coming back to Philip. And spoils his life. We listen every night. The satellite.'

'Of course.' It was Walt Dangerfield's reading of the Maugham book, the disc jockey as he passed in his daily orbit above their heads. Eerie, Doctor Stockstill thought, this parasite dwelling within her body, in unchanging moisture and darkness, fed by her blood, hearing from her in some unfathomable fashion a second-hand account of a famous novel . . . it makes Bill Keller part of our culture. He leads his grotesque social existence, too . . . God knows what he makes of the story. Does he have fantasies about it, about our life? Does he *dream* about us?

Bending, Doctor Stockstill kissed the girl on her forehead. 'Okay,' he said. 'You can go, now. I'll talk to your mother and father for a minute; there're some very old genuine pre-war magazines out in the waiting room that you can read.'

When he opened the door, George and Bonny Keller rose to their feet, faces taut with anxiety.

'Come in,' Stockstill said to them. And shut the door after them. He had already decided not to tell them the truth about their daughter . . . and, he thought, about their son. Better they did not know.

When Stuart McConchie returned to the East Bay from his trip to the peninsula he found that someone—no doubt a group of veterans living under the pier—had killed and eaten his horse, Edward Prince of Wales. All that remained was the skeleton, legs and head, a heap worthless to him or to anyone else. He stood by it, pondering. Well, it had been a costly trip. And he had arrived too late anyhow; the farmer, at a penny apiece, had already disposed of the electronic parts of his Soviet missile.

Mr Hardy would supply another horse, no doubt, but he had been fond of Edward. And it was wrong to kill a horse for food because they were so vitally needed for other purposes; they were the mainstay of transportation, now that most of the wood had been consumed by the wood-burning cars and by people in cellars using it in the winter to keep warm. And horses were needed in the job of reconstruction—they were the main source of power, in the absence of electricity. The stupidity of killing Edward Prince of Wales maddened him; it was, he thought, like barbarism, the thing they all feared. It was anarchy, and right in the middle of the city; right in downtown Oakland, in broad day. It was what he would expect the Red Chinese to do.

Now, on foot, he walked slowly toward San Pablo Avenue. The sun had begun to descend into the lavish, extensive sunset which they had become accustomed to seeing in the years since the Emergency. He scarcely noticed it. Maybe I ought to go into some other business, he said to himself. Small animal traps—it's a living, but there's no advancement possible in it. I mean, where can you rise to in a business like that?

The loss of his horse had depressed him; he gazed down at the broken, grass-infested sidewalk as he picked his way along, past the rubble which had once been factories. From a burrow in a vacant lot something with eager eyes noted his passing; something, he surmised gloomily, that ought to be hanging by its hind legs minus its skin.

These ruins, the smoky, flickering pallor of the sky . . . the eager eyes still following him as the creature calculated whether it could safely attack him. Bending, he picked up a hunk of concrete and chucked it at the burrow—a dense layer of organic and inorganic material packed tightly, glued in place by some sort of white slime. The creature had emulsified debris lying around, had reformed it into a usable paste. Must be a brilliant animal, he thought. But he did not care.

I've evolved, too, he said to himself. My wits are much clearer than they formerly were; I'm a match for you any time. So give up.

Evolved, he thought, but no better off than I was before the goddam Emergency; I sold TV sets then and now I sell electronic vermin traps. What is the difference? One's as bad as the other. I'm going downhill, in fact.

A whole day wasted. In two hours it would be dark and he would be going to sleep, down in the cat-pelt-lined basement room which Mr Hardy rented him for a dollar in silver a month. Of course, he could light his fat lamp; he could burn it for a little while, read a book or part of a book—most of his library consisted of merely sections of books, the remaining portions having been destroyed or lost. Or he could visit old Mr and Mrs Hardy and sit in on the evening transmission from the satellite.

After all, he had personally radioed a request to Dangerfield just the other day, from the transmitter out on the mudflats in West Richmond. He had asked for 'Good Rockin' Tonight,' an old-fashioned favorite which he remembered from his childhood. It was not known if Dangerfield had that tune in his miles of tapes, however, so perhaps he was waiting in vain.

As he walked along he sang to himself:

> 'Oh I heard the news:
> There's good rockin' tonight.
> Oh I heard the news!
> There's good rockin' tonight!
> Tonight I'll be a mighty fine man,
> I'll hold my baby as tight as I can—'

It brought tears to his eyes to remember one of the old songs, from the world the way it was. All gone now, he said to himself. And what do we have instead, a rat that can play the nose-flute, and not even that because the rat got run over.

I'll bet the rat couldn't play that, he said to himself. Not in a million years. That's practically sacred music. Out of our past, that no brilliant animal and no funny person can share. The past belongs only to us genuine human beings.

While he was thinking that he arrived on San Pablo Avenue with its little shops open here and there, little shacks which sold everything from coat hangers to hay. One of them, not far off, was HARDY'S HOMEOSTATIC VERMIN TRAPS, and he headed in that direction.

As he entered, Mr Hardy glanced up from his assembly table in the rear; he worked under the white light of an arc lamp, and all around him lay heaps of electronic parts scavenged from every region of Northern California. Many had come from the ruins out in Livermore; Mr Hardy had connections with State Officials and they had permitted him to dig there in the restricted deposits.

In former times Dean Hardy had been an engineer for an AM radio station; he was a slender, quiet-spoken elderly man who wore a sweater and necktie even now—and a tie was rare, in these times.

'They ate my horse.' Stuart seated himself opposite Hardy.

At once Ella Hardy, his employer's wife, appeared from the living quarters in the rear; she had been fixing dinner. 'You left him?'

'Yes,' he admitted. 'I thought he was safe out on the City of Oakland public ferry pier; there's an official there who—'

'It happens all the time,' Hardy said wearily. 'The bastards. Somebody ought to drop a cyanide bomb under that pier; those war vets are down there by the hundreds. What about the car? You had to leave it, I guess.'

'I'm sorry,' Stuart said.

'Forget it,' Hardy said. 'We have more horses out at our Orinda store. What about parts from the rocket?'

'No luck,' Stuart said. 'All gone when I got there. Except for this.' He held up a handful of transistors. 'The farmer didn't notice these; I picked them up for nothing. I don't know if they're any good, though.' Carrying them over to the assembly table he laid them down. 'Not much for an all-day trip.' He felt more glum than ever.

Without a word, Ella Hardy returned to the kitchen; the curtain closed after her.

'You want to have some dinner with us?' Hardy said, shutting off his light and removing his glasses.

'I don't know,' Stuart said. 'I feel strange.' He roamed about the shop. 'Over on the other side of the Bay I saw something I've heard about but didn't believe. A flying animal like a bat but not a bat. More like a weasel, very skinny and long, with a big head. They call them *tommies* because they're always gliding up against windows and looking in, like peeping toms.'

Hardy said, 'It's a squirrel.' He leaned back in his chair, loosened his necktie. 'They evolved from the squirrels in Golden Gate Park. I once had a scheme for them . . . they could be useful—in theory, at least—as message carriers. They can glide or fly or whatever they do for almost a mile. But they're too feral. I gave it up after catching one.' He held up his right hand. 'Look at the scar, there on my thumb. That's from a tom.'

'This man I talked to said they taste good. Like old-time chicken. They sell them at stalls in downtown San Francisco; you see old ladies selling them cooked for a quarter apiece, still hot, very fresh.'

'Don't try one,' Hardy said. 'Many of them are toxic. It has to do with their diet.'

'Hardy,' Stuart said suddenly, 'I want to get out of the city and out into the country.'

His employer regarded him.

'It's too brutal here,' Stuart said.

'It's brutal everywhere.' He added, 'And out in the country it's hard to make a living.'

'Do you sell any traps in the country?'

'No,' Hardy said. 'Vermin live in towns, where there's ruins. You know that. Stuart, you're a woolgatherer. The country is sterile; you'd miss the flow of ideas that you have here in the city. Nothing happens, they just farm and listen to the satellite.'

'I'd like to take a line of traps out say around Napa and Sonoma,' Stuart persisted. 'I could trade them for wine, maybe; they grow grapes up there, I understand, like they used to.'

'But it doesn't taste the same,' Hardy said. 'The ground is too altered.' He shook his head. 'Really awful. Foul.'

'They drink it, though,' Stuart said. 'I've seen it here in town, brought in on those old wood-burning trucks.'

'People will drink anything they can get their hands on now.' Hardy raised his head and said thoughtfully, 'You know who has liquor? I mean the genuine thing; you can't tell if it's pre-war that he's dug up or new that he's made.'

'Nobody in the Bay Area.'

'Andrew Gill, the tobacco expert. Oh, he doesn't sell much. I've seen one bottle, a fifth of brandy. I had one single drink from it.' Hardy smiled at him crookedly, his lips twitching. 'You would have liked it.'

'How much does he want for it?'

'More than you have to pay.'

I wonder what sort of a man Andrew Gill is, Stuart said to himself. Big, maybe, with a beard, a vest . . . walking with a silver-headed cane; a giant of a man with wavy hair, imported monocle —I can picture him.

Seeing the expression on Stuart's face, Hardy leaned toward

him. 'I can tell you what else he sells. Girly photos. In artistic poses—you know.'

'Aw Christ,' Stuart said, his imagination boggling; it was too much. 'I don't believe it.'

'God's truth. Genuine pre-war girly calendars, from as far back as 1950. They're worth a fortune, of course. I've heard of a thousand silver dollars changing hands over a 1963 *Playboy* calendar.' Now Hardy had become pensive; he gazed off into space.

'Where I worked when the bomb fell,' Stuart said, 'at Modern TV Sales & Service, we had a lot of girly calendars downstairs in the repair department. They were all incinerated, naturally.' At least so he had always assumed. 'Suppose a person were poking around in the ruins somewhere and he came onto an entire warehouse full of girly calendars. Can you imagine that?' His mind raced. 'How much could he get? Millions! He could trade them for real estate; he could acquire a whole county!'

'Right,' Hardy said, nodding.

'I mean, he'd be rich forever. They make a few in the Orient, in Tokyo, but they're no good.'

'I've seen them,' Hardy agreed. 'They're crude. The knowledge of how to do it has declined, passed into oblivion; it's an art that has died out. Maybe forever.'

'Don't you think it's partly because there aren't the girls any more who look like that?' Stuart said. 'Everybody's scrawny now and have no teeth; the girls most of them now have burn-scars from radiation and with no teeth what kind of a girly calendar does that make?'

Shrewdly, Hardy said, 'I think the girls exist. I don't know where, maybe in Sweden or Norway, maybe in out-of-the-way places like the Solomon Islands. I'm convinced of it from what people coming in by ship say. Not in the US or Europe or Russia or China, any of the places that were hit—I agree with you there.'

'Could we find them?' Stuart said. 'And go into the business?'

After considering for a little while Hardy said, 'There's no film. There're no chemicals to process it. Most good cameras have been destroyed or have disappeared. There's no way you could get your calendars printed in quantity. If you did print them—'

'But if someone could find a girl with no burns and good teeth, the way they had before the war—'

'I'll tell you,' Hardy said, 'what would be a good business. I've thought about it many times.' He faced Stuart meditatively. 'Sewing machine needles. You could name your own price; you could have anything.'

Gesturing, Stuart got up and paced about the shop. 'Listen, I've got my eye on the big time; I don't want to mess around with selling any more—I'm fed up with it. I sold aluminum pots and pans and encyclopedias and TV sets and now these vermin traps. They're good traps and people want them, but I just feel there must be something else for me. I don't mean to insult you, but I want to grow. I *have* to; you either grow or you go stale, you die on the vine. The war set me back years, it set us all back. I'm just where I was ten years ago, and that's not good enough.'

Scratching his nose, Hardy murmured, 'What did you have in mind?'

'Maybe I could find a mutant potato that would feed everybody in the world.'

'Just one potato?'

'I mean a type of potato. Maybe I could become a plant breeder, like Luther Burbank. There must be millions of freak plants growing around out in the country, like there's all these freak animals and funny people here in the city.'

Hardy said, 'Maybe you could locate an intelligent bean.'

'I'm not joking about this,' Stuart said quietly.

They faced each other, neither speaking.

'It's a service to humanity,' Hardy said at last, 'to make homeostatic vermin traps that destroy mutated cats and dogs and rats and squirrels. I think you're acting infantile. Maybe your horse being eaten while you were over in South San Francisco—'

Entering the room, Ella Hardy said, 'Dinner is ready, and I'd like to serve it while it's hot. It's baked cod-head and rice and it took me three hours standing in line down at Eastshore Freeway to get the cod-head.'

The two men rose to their feet. 'You'll eat with us?' Hardy asked Stuart.

At the thought of the baked fish head, Stuart's mouth watered. He could not say no and he nodded, following after Mrs Hardy to the kitchen.

Hoppy Harrington, the handyman phocomelus of West Marin, did an imitation of Walt Dangerfield when the transmission from the satellite failed; he kept the citizens of West Marin amused. As everyone knew, Dangerfield was sick and he often faded out, now. Tonight, in the middle of his imitation, Hoppy glanced up to see the Kellers, with their little girl, enter the Foresters' Hall and take seats in the rear. About time, he said to himself, glad of a greater audience. But then he felt nervous, because the little girl was scru-tinizing him. There was something in the way she looked; he ceased suddenly and the hall was silent.

'Go ahead, Hoppy,' Cas Stone called.

'Do that one about Kool-Aid,' Mrs Tallman called. 'Sing that, the little tune the Kool-Aid twins sing; you know.'

'"Kool-Aid, Kool-Aid, can't wait,"' Hoppy sang, but once more he stopped. 'I guess that's enough for tonight,' he said.

The room became silent once again.

'My brother,' the little Keller girl spoke up, 'he says that Mr Dangerfield is somewhere in this place.'

Hoppy laughed. 'That's right,' he said excitedly.

'Has he done the reading?' Edie Keller asked. 'Or was he too sick tonight to do it?'

'Oh yeah, the reading's in progress,' Earl Colvig said, 'but we're not listening; we're tired of sick old Walt—we're listening to Hoppy and watching what he does. He did funny things tonight, didn't you, Hoppy?'

'Show the little girl how you moved that coin from a distance,' June Raub said. 'I think she'd enjoy that.'

'Yes, do that again,' the pharmacist called from his seat. 'That was good; we'd all like to see that again, I'm sure.' In his eagerness to watch he rose to his feet, forgetting that people were behind him.

'My brother,' Edie said quietly, 'wants to hear the reading. That's what he came for.'

'Be still,' Bonny, her mother, said to her.

Brother, Hoppy thought. She doesn't have any brother. He laughed out loud at that, and several people in the audience smiled. 'Your *brother*?' he said, wheeling his phocomobile toward the child. 'I can do the reading; I can be Philip and Mildred and everybody in the book; I can be Dangerfield. Sometimes I actually am. I was tonight, and that's why your brother thinks Dangerfield's in the room. What it is, it's me.' He looked around at the people. 'Isn't that right, folks? Isn't it actually me?'

'That's right, Hoppy,' Orion Stroud agreed. Everyone nodded.

'You have no brother, Edie,' Hoppy said to the little girl. 'Why do you say your brother wants to hear the reading when you have no brother?' He laughed and laughed. 'Can I see him? Talk to him? Let me hear him talk and—I'll do an imitation of him.'

'That'll be quite an imitation,' Cas Stone chuckled.

'Like to hear that,' Earl Colvig said.

'I'll do it,' Hoppy said, 'as soon as he says something to me.' He sat in the center of his 'mobile, waiting. 'I'm waiting,' he said.

'That's enough,' Bonny Keller said. 'Leave my child alone.' Her cheeks were red with anger.

'Lean down,' Edie said to Hoppy. 'Toward me. And he'll speak to you.' Her face, like her mother's, was grim.

Hoppy leaned toward her, cocking his head on one side, mockingly.

A voice, speaking from inside him, as if it were part of the interior world, said, 'How did you fix that record changer? How did you *really* do that?'

Hoppy screamed.

Everyone was staring at him, white-faced; they were on their feet, now, all of them rigid.

'I heard Jim Fergesson,' Hoppy said. 'A man I worked for, once. A man who's dead.'

The girl regarded him calmly. 'Do you want to hear my brother say more? Say some more words to him, Bill; he wants you to say more.'

And, in Hoppy's interior mind, the voice said, 'It looked like you healed it. It looked like instead of replacing that broken spring–'

Hoppy wheeled his cart wildly, spun up the aisle to the far end of the room, wheeled again and sat panting, a long way from the Keller child; his heart pounded and he stared at her. She returned his stare silently.

'Did he scare you?' Now the child was openly smiling at him, but her smile was empty and cold. 'He paid you back because you were picking on me. It made him angry. So he did that.'

Coming up beside Hoppy, George Keller said, 'What happened, Hop?'

'Nothing,' he said shortly. 'Maybe we better listen to the reading.' Sending out his manual extensor, he turned up the volume of the radio.

You can have what you want, you and your brother, he thought. Dangerfield's reading or anything else. *How long have you been in there?* Only seven years? It seems more like forever. As if–you've always existed. It had been a terribly old, wizened, white thing that had spoken to him. Something hard and small, floating. Lips overgrown with downy hair that hung trailing, streamers of it, wispy and dry. I bet it was Fergesson, he said to himself; it felt like him. He's in there, inside that child.

I wonder. Can he get out?

Edie Keller said to her brother, 'What did you do to scare him like you did? He really was scared.'

From within her the familiar voice said, 'I was someone he used to know, a long time ago. Someone dead.'

Amused, she said, 'Are you going to do any more to him?'

'If I don't like him,' Bill said, 'I may do more to him, a lot of different things, maybe.'

'How did you know about the dead person?'

'Oh,' Bill said, 'because—you know why. Because I'm dead, too.' He chuckled, deep down inside her stomach; she felt him quiver.

'No you're not,' she disagreed. 'You're as alive as I am, so don't say that; it isn't right.' It frightened her.

Bill said, 'I was just pretending. I'm sorry. I wish I could have seen his face . . . how did it look?'

'Awful,' Edie said. 'It turned all inward, like a frog's.'

'I wish I could come out,' Bill said plaintively. 'I wish I could be born like everybody else. Can't I be born later on?'

'Doctor Stockstill says you couldn't.'

'Maybe I could *make* Doctor Stockstill let me out. I can do that if I want.'

'No,' she said. 'You're lying; you can't do anything but sleep and talk to the dead and maybe do imitations like you did. That isn't much.'

There was no response from within.

'If you did anything bad,' she said, 'I could swallow something that would kill you. So you better behave.'

She felt more and more afraid of him; she was talking to herself, trying to bolster her confidence. Maybe it would be a good thing if you did die, she thought. Only then I'd have to carry you around still, and it—wouldn't be pleasant. I wouldn't like that.

She shuddered.

'Don't worry about me,' Bill said suddenly. 'I know a lot of things; I can take care of myself. I'll protect you, too. You better be glad about me because I can look at everyone who's dead, like the man I imitated. There're a whole lot of them, trillions and trillions of them and they're all different. When I'm asleep I hear them muttering. They're still around.'

'Around where?' she asked.

'Underneath us,' Bill said. 'Down in the ground.'

'Brrr,' she said.

'It's true. And we're going to be there, too. And so is Mommy and Daddy and everyone else. You'll see.'

'I don't want to see,' she said. 'Please don't say any more. I want to listen to the reading.'

Andrew Gill glanced up from his task of rolling cigarettes to see Hoppy Harrington—whom he did not like—entering the factory with a man whom he did not know. At once Gill felt uneasy. He set down his tobacco paper and rose to his feet. Beside him at the long bench the other rollers, his employees, continued at their work.

He employed, in all, eight men, and this was in the tobacco division alone. The distillery, which produced brandy, employed another twelve. His was the largest commercial enterprise in West Marin and he sold his products all over Northern California; his cigarettes had even gotten back to the East Coast and were known there.

'Yes?' he said to Hoppy. He placed himself in front of the phoce's cart, halting him.

Hoppy stammered. 'This m-man came up from Oakland to see you, Mr Gill. He's an important businessman, he says. Isn't that right?' The phoce turned to the man beside him. 'Isn't that what you told me, Stuart?'

Holding out his hand, the man said, 'I represent the Hardy Homeostatic Vermin Trap Corporation of Berkeley, California. I'm here to acquaint you with an amazing proposition that could well mean tripling your profits within six months.' His eyes flashed.

Gill repressed the impulse to laugh aloud. 'I see,' he said, nodding. 'Very interesting, Mr—' He glanced questioningly at the phoce.

'M-Mr Stuart McConchie,' the phoce stammered. 'I knew him before the war; I haven't seen him in all that time and now he's migrated up here, the same as I did.'

'My employer, Mr Hardy,' Stuart McConchie said, 'has empowered me to describe to you in detail the design of a fully-automated cigarette-making machine. We at Hardy Homeostatic are well aware of the fact that your cigarettes are rolled entirely in the old-fashioned way. By hand.' He pointed toward the employees at the long bench. 'Such a method is a century out of date, Mr Gill. You've achieved superb quality in your special deluxe Gold Label cigarettes–'

'Which I intend to maintain,' Gill said quietly.

Stuart McConchie said, 'Our automated electronic equipment will in no way sacrifice quality for quantity. In fact–'

'Wait,' Gill said. 'I don't want to discuss this now.' He glanced toward the phoce, who was parked close by, listening. The phoce flushed and at once spun his 'mobile away.

'I'm going,' Hoppy said sullenly. 'This doesn't interest me anyhow; goodbye.' He wheeled through the open door, out onto the street. The two of them watched him until he disappeared.

'Our handy,' Gill said. 'Fixes–heals, rather–everything that breaks. Hoppy Harrington, the human handless handy.'

Strolling a few steps away, surveying the factory and the men at their work, McConchie said, 'Nice place you have here, Gill. I want to state right now how much I admire your product; it's first in its field.'

I haven't heard talk like that, Gill realized, in seven years. It was difficult to believe that it still existed in the world; so much had changed, and yet here, in this man McConchie, it remained intact. Gill felt a glow of pleasure. It reminded him of happier times, this salesman's line of patter. He felt amiably inclined toward the man.

'Thank you,' he said, and he meant it. Perhaps the world, at last, was really beginning to regain some of its old forms, its civilities and customs and preoccupations, all that had gone into it to make it what it was.

'How about a cup of coffee?' Gill said. 'I'll take a break for ten minutes and you can tell me about this fully automated machine of yours.'

'Real coffee?' McConchie said, and the pleasant, optimistic mask slid for an instant from his face; he gaped at Gill with naked hunger.

　　　　　　　　　　　　　　　　　　　　　A TERRAN ODYSSEY

'Sorry,' Gill said. 'A substitute. But not bad; I think you'll like it. Better than what's sold in the city at those so-called "coffee" stands.' He went to get the pot of water.

'Coming here,' McConchie said, 'is a long-time dream fulfilled. It took me a week to make the trip and I've been mulling about it ever since I smoked my first special deluxe Gold Label. It's–' He groped for the words to express his thought. 'An island of civilization in these barbaric times.' He roamed about the factory, hands in his pockets. 'Life seems more peaceful here. In the city if you leave your horse–well, a while ago I left my horse to go across the Bay and when I got back someone had eaten it, and it's things like that that make you disgusted with the city and want to move on.'

'I know,' Gill said, nodding. 'It's brutal in the city because there're still so many homeless and destitute people.'

'I really loved that horse,' Stuart McConchie said, looking sad.

'Well,' Gill said, 'in the country you're faced constantly with the death of animals. When the bombs fell, thousands of animals up here were horribly injured; sheep and cattle . . . but that can't compare of course to the loss of human life down where you come from. You must have seen a good deal of human suffering since E-Day.'

McConchie nodded. 'That and the sporting. The freaks both as regards animals and people. Like my old buddy Hoppy Harrington, but of course he's from before; at Modern TV Sales & Service where we worked we used to say Hoppy was from that drug, that thalidomide.'

'What sort of vermin trap does your company make?' Gill asked.

'It's not a passive type. Being homeostatic, that is, self-notifying, it follows for instance a rat or a cat or dog down into the network of burrows such as now underlie Berkeley and Oakland . . . it pursues one vermin after another, killing one and going on to the next–until it runs out of power or by chance a brilliant vermin manages to destroy it. There are a few such brilliant rats that know how to lame a Hardy Homeostatic Vermin Trap. But not many.'

'Impressive,' Gill murmured.

'Now, our proposed cigarette-rolling machine–'

'My friend,' Gill said, 'I like you but—here's the problem. I don't have any money to buy your machine and I don't have anything to trade you. And I don't intend to let anyone enter my business as a partner. So what does that leave?' He smiled. 'I must continue as I am.'

'Wait,' McConchie said instantly. 'There has to be a solution. Maybe we could lease you a Hardy cigarette-rolling machine in exchange for x-number of cigarettes, your special deluxe Gold Label variety, of course, delivered each week for x-number of weeks.' His face glowed with animation. 'The Hardy Company for instance could become sole licensed distributors of your cigarette; we could represent you everywhere, develop a systematic program of outlets up and down California. What do you say to that?'

'I must admit it does sound interesting. I admit that distribution has not been my cup of tea . . . I've thought on and off for several years about the need of getting an organization going, especially with my factory being located in a rural spot. I've even thought about moving back into the city, but the theft and vandalism is too great there. Anyhow I don't *want* to move into the city; this is my home, here.'

He did not say anything about Bonny Keller. That was his actual reason for remaining in West Marin; his affair with her had ended years ago but he was more in love with her now than ever—he had watched her go from man to man, becoming dissatisfied with each of them, and Gill believed in his own heart that someday he would get her back. And Bonny was the mother of his daughter; he was well aware that Edie Keller was his child.

'Since you're just up from the city,' he said aloud, 'I will ask you this . . . is there any interesting national or international news, of late, that we might not have heard? We do get the satellite, but I'm frankly tired of disc jockey talk and music. And those endless readings.'

They both laughed. 'I know what you mean,' McConchie said, sipping his coffee and nodding. 'Well, I understand that an attempt is being made to produce an automobile again, somewhere around the ruins of Detroit. It's mostly made of plywood but it does run on kerosene.'

'I don't know where they're going to get the kerosene,' Gill said. 'Before they build a car they better get a few refineries operating again. And repair a few major roads.'

'Oh, something else. The Government plans to reopen Route Forty across the Rockies sometime this year. For the first time since the war.'

'That's great news,' Gill said, pleased. 'I didn't know that.'

'And the telephone company—'

'Wait,' Gill said, rising. 'How about a little brandy in your coffee? How long has it been since you've had a coffee royal?'

'Years,' Stuart McConchie said.

'This is Gill's Five Star. My own. From the Sonoma Valley.' He poured from the squat bottle into McConchie's cup.

'Here's something else that might interest you.' McConchie reached into his coat pocket and brought out something flat and folded. He opened it, spread it out, and Gill saw an envelope.

Mail service. A letter from New York.

'That's right,' McConchie said. 'Delivered to my boss, Mr Hardy. All the way from the East Coast; it only took four weeks. The Government in Cheyenne, the military people; they're responsible. It's done partly by blimp, partly by truck, partly by horse. The last stage is by foot.'

'Good Lord,' Gill said. And he poured some Gill's Five Star into *his* coffee, too.

Bill Keller heard the small animal, the snail or slug near him, and at once he got into it. But he had been tricked; it was sightless. He was out but he could not see or hear this time, he could only move.

'Let me back,' he called to his sister in panic. 'Look what you did, you put me into something *wrong*.' You did it on purpose, he said to himself as he moved. He moved on and on, searching for her.

If I could reach out, he thought. Reach—upward. But he had nothing to reach with, no limbs of any sort. What am I now that

I'm out again? he asked himself as he tried to reach up. What do they call those things up there that shine? Those lights in the sky . . . can I see them without having eyes? No, he thought; I can't.

He moved on; raising himself now and then as high as possible and then sinking back, once more to crawl, to do the one thing possible for him in his born, outside life.

In the sky, Walt Dangerfield moved, in his satellite, although he sat resting with his head in his hands. The pain inside him had grown, changed, absorbed him until, as so many times before, he could imagine nothing else.

How long can I keep going? he asked himself. How long will I live?

There was no one to answer.

Edie Keller, with a delicious shiver of exultation, watched the angleworm crawling slowly across the ground and knew with certitude that her brother was in it.

For inside her, down in her stomach, the mentality of the worm now resided; she heard its monotonous voice. 'Boom, boom, boom,' it went, in echo of its own nondescript biological processes.

'Get out of me, worm,' she giggled. What did the worm think about its new existence? Was it as dumbfounded as Bill probably was? I have to keep my eye on him, she realized, meaning the creature wriggling across the ground. For he might get lost. 'Bill,' she said, bending over him, 'you look funny. You're all red and long; did you know that?' And then she thought, What I should have done was put him in the body of another human being. Why didn't I do that? Then it would be like it ought to be; I would have a real brother, outside of me, who I could play with.

But on the other hand she would have a strange, new person inside her. And that did not sound like much fun.

Who would do? she asked herself. One of the kids at school? An adult? Mr Barnes, my teacher, maybe. Or—

Hoppy Harrington. Who is afraid of Bill anyhow.

'Bill,' she said, kneeling down and picking up the angleworm;

she held it in the palm of her hand. 'Wait until you hear my plan.' She held the worm against her side, where the hard lump within lay. 'Get back inside now. You don't want to be a worm anyhow; it's no fun.'

Her brother's voice once more came to her. 'You—I hate you, I'll never forgive you. You put me in a blind thing with no legs or nothing! All I could do was drag myself around!'

'I know,' she said, rocking back and forth, cupping the now-useless worm in her hand still. 'Listen, did you hear me? You want to do that, Bill, what I said? Shall I get near Hoppy Harrington? You'd have eyes and ears; you'd be a real outside person.'

'It scares me.'

'But I want to,' Edie said, rocking back and forth. 'We're going to, Bill; we're going to give you eyes and ears—*now*.'

There was no answer from Bill; he had turned his thoughts away from her and her world, into the regions which only he could reach. Talking to those old crummy, sticky dead, Edie said to herself. Those empty poo-poo dead that never had any fun or nothing.

It won't do you any good, Bill, she thought. Because I've decided.

Hurrying down the path in her robe and slippers, through the night darkness, Edie Keller groped her way toward Hoppy Harrington's house.

'If you're going to do it you have to hurry,' Bill cried, from deep within her. 'He knows about us—they're telling me, the dead are. They say we're in danger. If we can get close enough to him I can do an imitation of someone dead that'll scare him, because he's afraid of dead people. That's because to him the dead are like fathers, lots of fathers, and—'

'Be quiet,' Edie said. 'Let me *think*.' In the darkness she had gotten mixed up. She could not find the path through the oak forest, now, and she halted, breathing deeply, trying to orient herself by the dull gleam of the partial moon overhead.

It's to the left, she thought. Down a hill. I must not fall; he'd hear the noise, he can hear a long way, almost everything. Step by step she descended, holding her breath.

'I've got a good imitation ready,' Bill was mumbling; he would not be quiet. 'When I get near him I switch with someone dead, and you won't like that because it's—sort of squishy, but it's just for a few minutes and then they can talk to him direct, from inside you. Is that—'

'Shut up,' Edie said desperately. They were now above Hoppy's house; she saw the lights below. 'Please, Bill, please.'

'But I have to explain to you,' Bill went on. 'When I—'

He stopped. Inside her there was nothing. She was empty.

'Bill,' she said.

He had gone.

Before her eyes, in the dull moonlight, something she had never seen before bobbed. It rose, jiggled, its long pale hair streaming behind it like a tail; it rose until it hung directly before her face. It had tiny, dead eyes and a gaping mouth, it was nothing but a little hard round head, like a baseball. From its mouth came a squeak, and then it fluttered upward once more, released. She watched it as it gained more and more height, rising above the trees in a swimming motion, ascending in the unfamiliar atmosphere which he had never known before.

'Bill,' she said, 'Hoppy took you out of me. Hoppy put you outside.' And you are leaving, she realized; Hoppy is making you go. 'Come back,' she said, but it didn't matter because he could not live outside of her. She knew that. Doctor Stockstill had said that. He could not be born, and Hoppy had heard him and made him born, knowing that he would die.

You won't get to do your imitation, she realized. I told you to be quiet and you wouldn't. Straining, she saw—or thought she saw—the hard little object with the streamers of hair, high now above her . . . and then it disappeared, silently.

She was alone.

Why go on now? It was over. She turned, walked back up the hillside, her head lowered, eyes shut, feeling her way. Back to her house, her bed. Inside she felt raw; she felt the tearing loose. If you only could have been quiet, she thought. He would not have heard you. I told you so.

Floating in the atmosphere, Bill Keller saw a little, heard a little, felt the trees and the animals alive and moving among them. He felt the pressure at work on him, lifting him up, but he remembered his imitation and he said it. His voice came out tiny in the cold air; then his ears picked it up and he exclaimed.

'We have been taught a terrible lesson for our folly,' he squeaked, and his voice echoed in his ears, delighting him.

The pressure on him let go; he bobbed up, swimming happily, and then he dove. Down and down he went and just before he touched the ground he went sideways until, guided by the living presence within, he hung suspended above Hoppy Harrington's house.

'This is God's way!' he shouted in his thin, tiny voice. 'We can see by this awful example that it is time to call a halt to high-altitude nuclear testing. I want all of you to write letters to President Kennedy!' He did not know who President Kennedy was. A living person, perhaps. He looked around for him but he did not see him; he saw oak forests of animals, he saw a bird with noiseless wings that drifted, huge-beaked, eyes staring. Bill squeaked in fright as the noiseless, brown-feathered bird glided his way.

The bird made a dreadful sound, of greed and the desire to rend.

'All of you,' Bill cried, fleeing through the dark, chill air. 'You must write letters in protest!'

The glittering eyes of the bird followed behind him as he and it glided above the trees, in the dim moonlight.

The owl reached him. And crunched him, in a single instant.

Once more he was within. He could no longer see or hear; it had been for a short time and now it was over.

The owl, hooting, flew on.

Bill Keller said to the owl, 'Can you hear me?'

Maybe it could; maybe not. It was only an owl, it did not have any sense, as Edie had. Can I live inside you? he asked it, hidden away in here where no one knows . . . you have your flights that you make, your passes. With him, in the owl, were the bodies of mice and a thing that stirred and scratched, big enough to keep on wanting to live.

Lower, he told the owl. He saw, by means of the owl, the oaks; he saw clearly, as if everything were full of light. Millions of individual objects lay immobile and then he spied one that crept—it was alive and the owl turned that way. The creeping thing, suspecting nothing, hearing no sound, wandered on, out into the open.

An instant later it had been swallowed. The owl flew on.

Good, he thought. And, is there more? This goes on all night, again and again, and then there is bathing when it rains, and the long, deep sleeps. Are they the best part? They are.

He said, 'Fergesson don't allow his employees to drink; it's against his religion, isn't it?' And then he said, 'Hoppy, what's the light from? Is it God? You know, like in the Bible. I mean, is it true?'

The owl hooted.

A thousand dead things within him yammered for attention. He listened, repeated, picked among them. 'You dirty little freak,' he said. 'Now you listen. Stay down here; we're below street-level, the bomb won't get us. People upstairs, they're going to die. Down here you clear. Space. For them.'

Frightened, the owl flapped; it rose higher, trying to evade him. But he continued, sorting and picking and listening on.

'Stay down here,' he repeated. Again the lights of Hoppy's house came into view; the owl had circled, returned to it, unable to get away. He made it stay where he wanted it. He brought it closer and closer in its passes to Hoppy. 'You moronic jackass,' he said. 'Stay where you are.'

The owl, with a furious effort, performed its regular technique; it coughed him up and he plummeted to the ground, trying to catch the currents of air. He crashed among humus and plant-growth; he rolled, giving little squeaks until finally he came to rest in a hollow.

Released, the owl soared off and disappeared.

'Let man's compassion be witness to this,' he said as he lay in the hollow; he spoke in the minister's voice from long ago, addressing the congregation of which Hoppy and his father had been a part. 'It is ourselves who have done this; we see here only the results of mankind's own folly.'

Lacking the owl eyes he saw only vaguely; the immaculate illumination seemed to be gone and all that remained were several nearby shapes. They were trees.

He saw, too, the form of Hoppy's house outlined against the dim night sky. It was not far off.

'Let me in,' Bill said, moving his mouth. He rolled about in the hollow; he thrashed until the leaves stirred. 'I want to come in.'

An animal, hearing him, moved farther off, warily.

'In, in, in,' Bill said. 'I can't stay out here long; I'll die. Edie, where are you?' He did not feel her nearby; he felt only the presence of the phocomelus within the house.

As best he could he rolled that way.

Early in the morning, Doctor Stockstill arrived at Hoppy Harrington's house to make use of the transmitter in reaching the sick man in the sky, Walter Dangerfield. The transmitter, he noticed, was on, and so were lights here and there; puzzled, he knocked on the door.

The door opened and there sat Hoppy Harrington in the center of his phocomobile. Hoppy regarded him in an odd, cautious, defensive way.

'I want to make another try,' Stockstill said, knowing how hopeless it was but wanting to go ahead anyhow. 'Is it okay?'

'Yes sir,' Hoppy said.

'Is Dangerfield still alive?'

'Yes sir. I'd know if he was dead.' Hoppy wheeled aside to admit him. 'He must still be up there.'

'What's happened?' Stockstill said. 'Have you been up all night?'

'Yes,' Hoppy said. 'Learning to work things.' He wheeled the phocomobile about. 'It's hard,' he said, apparently preoccupied. Now the 'mobile bumped into the end of a table. 'I hit that by mistake,' Hoppy said. 'I'm sorry; I didn't mean to.'

Stockstill said, 'You seem different.'

'I'm Bill Keller,' the phocomelus said. 'Not Hoppy Harrington.' With his right manual extensor he pointed. 'There's Hoppy; that's him, from now on.'

In the corner lay a shriveled dough-like object several inches long; its mouth gaped in congealed emptiness. It had a human quality to it, and Stockstill went over to pick it up.

'That was me,' the phocomelus said. 'But I got close enough last night to switch. He fought a lot, but he was afraid, so I won. I kept doing one imitation after another. The minister one got him.'

Stockstill, holding the wizened little creature, said nothing.

'Do you know how to work the transmitter?' the phocomelus asked, presently. 'Because I don't. I tried but I can't. I got the lights to work; they turn on and off. I practiced that all night.' To demonstrate, he rolled his 'mobile to the wall, where with his manual extensor he snapped the light switch up and down.

After a time Stockstill said, looking down at the dead, tiny form he held in his hand, 'I knew it wouldn't survive.'

'It did for a while,' the phocomelus said. 'For around an hour; that's pretty good, isn't it? Part of that time it was in an owl; I don't know if that counts.'

'I–better get to work trying to contact Dangerfield,' Stockstill said finally. 'He may die any time.'

'Yes,' the phocomelus said, nodding. 'Want me to take that?' He held out an extensor and Stockstill handed him the homunculus. 'That owl ate me,' the phoce said. 'I didn't like that, but it sure had good eyes; I liked that part, using its eyes.'

'Yes,' Stockstill said, reflexively. 'Owls have tremendously good eyesight. That must have been quite an experience.' He seated himself at the transmitter. 'What are you going to do now?' he asked.

The phoce said, 'I have to get used to this body; it's heavy. I feel gravity . . . I'm used to just floating about. You know what? I think these extensors are swell. I can do a lot with them already.' The extensors whipped about, touched a picture on the wall, flicked in the direction of the transmitter. 'I have to go find Edie,' the phoce said. 'I want to tell her I'm okay; she probably thinks I died.'

Turning on the microphone, Stockstill prepared to contact the satellite overhead. 'Walt Dangerfield,' he said, 'this is Doctor Stockstill in West Marin. Can you hear me? If you can, give me an answer.' He paused, then repeated what he had said.

'Can I go?' Bill Keller asked. 'Can I look for Edie now?'

'Yes,' Stockstill said, rubbing his forehead; he drew his faculties together and said, 'You'll be careful, what you do . . . you may not be able to switch again.'

'I don't want to switch again,' Bill said. 'This is fine, because for the first time there's no one in here but me.' The thin phoce-face broke into a smile. 'I'm not just part of someone else.'

Stockstill pressed the mike button once more. 'Walt Dangerfield,' he repeated. 'Can you hear me?' Is it hopeless? he wondered. Is it worth keeping on?

The phoce, rolling about the room on his 'mobile, like a great trapped beetle, said, 'Can I go to school now that I'm out?'

'Yes,' Stockstill murmured.

'But I know a lot of things already,' Bill said. 'From listening with Edie when she was in school; I like Mr Barnes, don't you? He's a very good teacher . . . I'm going to like being a pupil in his class.' The phoce added, 'I wonder what my mother will say?'

Jarred, Stockstill said, 'What?' And then he realized who was meant. Bonny Keller. Yes, he thought, it will be interesting to see what Bonny says. This will be repayment in full for her many, many affairs . . . for her years of love-making with one man after another.

Again he pressed the mike button. And tried once more.

To Bonny Keller, Mr Barnes said, 'I had a talk with your daughter after school today. And I got the distinct impression that she knows about us.'

'Oh Christ, how could she?' Bonny said. Groaning, she sat up; she rearranged her clothes, buttoned her blouse back up. What a contrast this man was to Andrew Gill, who always made love to her right out in the open, in broad daylight, along the oak-lined roads of West Marin, where anyone and anything might go past. Gill had seized her each time as he had the first time—yanking her into it, not babbling or quaking or mumbling . . . maybe I ought to go back to him, she thought.

Maybe, she thought, I ought to leave them all, Barnes and George and that nutty daughter of mine; I ought to go live with Gill openly, defy the community and be happy for a change.

'Well, if we're not going to make love,' she said to Barnes, 'then let's walk down to the Foresters' Hall and listen to the afternoon pass of the satellite.'

Barnes, pleased, said, 'Maybe we can find some edible mushrooms on the way.'

'Are you serious?' Bonny said.

'Of course.'

'You fruit,' she said, shaking her head. 'You poor fruit. Why did you come to West Marin from Oregon in the first place? Just to teach little kids and stroll around picking mushrooms?'

'It's not such a bad life,' Barnes said. 'It's better than any I've ever known before, even before the war. And—I also have you.'

Gloomily, Bonny Keller rose to her feet; hands thrust deep in her coat pockets she plodded down the road. Barnes trailed along behind her, trying to keep up with her strides.

'I'm going to remain here in West Marin,' Barnes said. 'This is the end of my travels.' Puffing, he added, 'Despite my experience with your daughter today—'

'You had no experience,' Bonny said. 'It was just your guilty conscience catching up with you. Let's hurry—I want to hear Dangerfield; at least when *he* talks it's fun to listen.'

Behind her, Mr Barnes found a mushroom; he had stopped to bend down. 'It's a chanterelle!' he exclaimed. 'Savory and edible—' He picked it, close to the ground, and then began to search for another. 'I'll make you and George a stew,' he informed her as he found another.

Waiting for him to finish, Bonny lit a special deluxe Gold Label cigarette of Andrew Gill's manufacture, sighed, wandered a few steps along the grass-infested oak-lined country road.

YOUR APPOINTMENT
WILL BE YESTERDAY

Sunlight ascended and a penetrating mechanical voice declared, 'All right, Lehrer. Time to get up and show 'em who you are and what you can do. Big man, that Niehls Lehrer; everybody acknowledges it–I hear them talking. Big man, big talent, big job. Much admired by the public at large. You awake now?'

Lehrer, from the bed, said, 'Yes.' He sat up, batted the sharp-voiced alarm clock at his bedside into nullification. 'Good morning,' he said to the silent apartment. 'Slept well; I hope you did, too.'

A press of problems tumbled about his disordered mind as he got grouchily from the bed, wandered to the closet for clothing adequately dirty. Supposed to nail down Ludwig Eng, he said to himself. The tasks of tomorrow become the worse tasks of today. Reveal to Eng that only one copy of his great-selling book is left in all the world; the time is coming soon for him to act, to do the job only he can do. How would Eng feel? After all, sometimes inventors refused to sit still and do their job. Well, he decided, that actually consisted of a syndicate-problem; theirs, not his. He found a stained, rumpled red shirt; removing his pajama top he got into it. The trousers were not so easy; he had to root through the hamper.

And then the packet of whiskers.

My ambition, Lehrer thought as he padded to the bathroom with the whisker packet, is to cross the WUS by streetcar. Whee. At the bowl he washed his face, then lathered on foam-glue, opened the packet and with adroit slappings managed to convey the whiskers evenly to his chin, jowls, neck; in a moment he had expertly gotten the whiskers to adhere. I'm fit now, he decided as he reviewed his countenance in the mirror, to take that streetcar ride; at least as soon as I process my share of sogum.

Switching on the sogum pipe he accepted a good masculine bundle, sighed contentedly as he glanced over the sports section of the San Francisco *Chronicle*, then at last walked to the kitchen and began to lay out soiled dishes. In no time at all he faced a bowl of soup, lambchops, green peas, Martian blue moss with egg sauce and a cup of hot coffee. These he gathered up, slid the dishes from beneath and around them—of course checking the windows of the room to be sure no one saw him—and briskly placed the assorted foods in their proper receptacles which he placed on shelves of the cupboard and in the refrigerator. The time was eight-thirty; he still had fifteen minutes to get to work. No need to kill himself hurrying; the People's Topical Library section B would be there when he arrived.

It had taken him years to work up to B. He did not perform routine work any longer, not at a section B desk, and he most certainly did not have to arrange for the cleaning of thousands of identical copies of a work in the early stages of eradication. In fact strictly speaking he did not have to participate in eradication at all; minions employed wholesale by the library took care of that coarse duty. But he did have to deal tête-à-tête with a vast variety of irritable, surly inventors who balked at their assigned—and according to the syndicate mandatory—final cleaning of the sole-remaining typescript copy of whatever work their name had become linked with—linked by a process which neither he nor the assorted inventors completely understood. The syndicate presumably understood why a particular given inventor received a particular assignment and not some other assignment entirely. For instance, Eng and HOW I MADE MY OWN SWABBLE OUT OF CONVENTIONAL HOUSE-HOLD OBJECTS IN MY BASEMENT DURING MY SPARE TIME.

Lehrer reflected as he glanced over the remainder of the news-paper. Think of the responsibility. After Eng finished, no more swabbles in all the world, unless those untrustworthy rogues in the FNM had a couple illicitly tucked away. In fact, even though the ter-cop, the terminal copy, of Eng's book still remained, he already found it difficult to recall what a swabble did and what it looked like. Square? Small? Or round and huge? Hmmm. He put down the newspaper and rubbed his forehead while he attempted to recall—tried to conjure up an accurate mental image of the device while it was still possible to do so. Because as soon as Eng reduced the ter-cop to a heavily inked silk ribbon, half a ream of bond paper and a folio of fresh carbon paper there existed absolutely no chance for him or for anyone else to recall either the book or the mechanism which the book described.

That task, however, would probably occupy Eng the rest of the year. Cleaning of the ter-cop had to progress line by line, word by word; it could not be handled as were the assembled printed copies. So easy, up until the terminal typescript copy, and then . . . well, to make it worth it to Eng, to compensate him for the long, arduous work, a really huge bill would be served on him: the task would cost Eng something on the order of twenty-five thousand poscreds. And since eradication of the swabble book would make Eng a poor man, the task . . .

By his elbow on the small kitchen table the receiver of the phone hopped from its mooring onto the table, and from it came a distant tiny shrill voice. 'Goodbye, Niehls.' A woman's voice.

Lifting the receiver to his ear he said, 'Goodbye.'

'I love you, Niehls,' Charise McFadden stated in her breathless, emotion-saturated voice. 'Do you love me?'

'Yes, I love you, too,' he said. 'When have I seen you last? I hope it won't be long. Tell me it won't be long.'

'Most probably tonight,' Charise said. 'After work. There's someone I want you to meet, a virtually unknown inventor who's desperately eager to get official eradication for his thesis on, ahem, the psychogenic origins of death by meteor-strike. I said that because you're in section B—'

'Tell him to eradicate his thesis himself.'

'There's no prestige in that.' Earnestly, Charise pleaded, 'It's really a dreadful piece of theorizing, Niehls; it's as nutty as the day is long. This boy, this Lance Arbuthnot—'

'That's his name?' It almost persuaded him. But not quite. In the course of a single day he received many such requests, and every one, without exception, came represented as a crank piece by a crank inventor with a crank name. He had held his chair at section B too long to be easily snared. But still—he had to investigate this; his ethical structure insisted on it. He sighed.

'I hear you groaning,' Charise said brightly.

Lehrer said, 'As long as he's not from the FNM.'

'Well—he is.' She sounded guilty. 'I think they threw him out, though. That's why he's here and not there.'

But that, Lehrer realized, proved nothing. Arbuthnot—possibly—did not share the fanatical militant convictions of the ruling elite of the Free Negro Municipality; possibly he was too moderate, too balanced for the Bards of the republic carved out of quondam Tennessee, Kentucky, Arkansas and Missouri. But then again he perhaps had too fanatical a view. One never knew; not until one met the person, and sometimes not even then. The Bards, being from the East, had managed to dribble a veil over the faces of three-fifths of mankind, a veil which successfully obscured motive, intention and God knew what else.

'And what is more,' Charise continued, 'he personally knew Anarch Peak before Peak's sad shrinking.'

'Sad!' Lehrer bristled. 'Good riddance.' There: that had been the foremost eccentric and idiot of the world. All Lehrer needed was the opportunity to rub shoulders with a follower of the newly parasitic Anarch. He shivered, recalling from his professional eclectic books-examining at the library the accounts of mid-twentieth century race violence; out of the riots, lootings and killings of those days had come Sebastian Peak, originally a lawyer, then a master spellbinder, at last a religious fanatic with his own devout following . . . a following which extended over the planet, although operating primarily in the FNM environs.

'That could get you in trouble with God,' Charise said.

'I have to get to work now,' Lehrer said. 'I'll phone you during my coffee break; meanwhile I'll do some research on Arbuthnot in the files. My decision as regards his nut-head theory of psychosomatic meteor-strike deaths will have to wait until then. Hello.' He hung up the phone, then, and rose swiftly to his feet. His soiled garments gave off a truly gratifying odor of must as he made his way from his apartment to the elevator; satisfaction as to his grooming made him brighten. Possibly—despite Charise and this, her newest fad, the inventor Arbuthnot—today might be a good day after all.

But, underneath, he doubted it.

When Niehls Lehrer arrived at his section of the library, he found his slim blonde-haired secretary Miss Tomsen trying to rid herself—and him, too—of a tall, sloppily-dressed middle-aged gentleman with a briefcase under his arm.

'Ah, Mr Lehrer,' the individual said in a dry, hollow voice as he made out Lehrer, obviously recognizing him at once; he approached Niehls, hand extended. 'How nice to meet you, sir. Goodbye, goodbye. As you people say out here.' He smiled a flashbulb instantly-vanishing smile at Niehls, who did not return it.

'I'm quite a busy man,' Niehls said, and continued on past Miss Tomsen's desk to open the inner door to his private suite. 'If you wish to see me, you'll have to make a regular appointment. Hello.' He started to shut the door after him.

'This concerns the Anarch Peak,' the tall man with the brief-case said. 'Whom I have reason to believe you're interested in.'

'Why do you say that?' He paused, irritated. 'I don't recall ever expressing any interest in anyone of Peak's sort.'

'You must recall. But that's so. You're under Phase, here. I'm oriented in the opposite, normal time-direction; therefore what for you will soon happen is for me an experience of the immediate past. *My* immediate past. May I take a few minutes of your time? I could well be of great use to you, sir.' The man chuckled. '"Your time." Well-put, if I do say so. Yes, decidedly your time, not mine.

Just consider that this visit by myself took place yesterday.' Again he smiled his mechanical smile—and mechanical it was; Niehls now perceived the small but brilliant yellow stripe sewed on the tall man's sleeve. This person was a robot, required by law to wear the identifying swath so as not to deceive. Realizing this, Niehls' irritation grew; he had a strict, deeply-imbedded prejudice against robies which he could not rid himself of; which he did not want to rid himself of, as a matter of fact.

'Come in,' Niehls said, holding the door to his lavish suite open. The roby represented some human principal; it had not dispatched itself: that was the law. He wondered who had sent it. Some functionary of the syndicate? Possibly. In any case, better to hear the thing out and then tell it to leave.

Together, in the main workchamber of the library suite, the two of them faced each other.

'My card,' the roby said, extending its hand.

He read the card, scowling.

Carl Gantrix

Attorney At Law WUS

'My employer,' the roby said. 'So now you know my name. You may address me as Carl; that would be satisfactory.' Now that the door had shut, with Miss Tomsen on the other side, the roby's voice had acquired a sudden and surprising authoritative tone.

'I prefer,' Niehls said, cautiously, 'to address you in the more familiar mode as Carl Junior. If that doesn't offend you.' He made his own voice even more authoritative. 'You know, I seldom grant audiences to robots. A quirk, perhaps, but one concerning which I am consistent.'

'Until now,' the robot Carl Junior murmured; it retrieved its card and placed it back in its wallet. Then, seating itself, it began to unzip its briefcase. 'Being in charge of section B of the library, you are of course an expert on the Hobart Phase. At least so Mr Gantrix assumes. Is he correct, sir?' The robot glanced up keenly.

'Well, I deal with it constantly.' Niehls affected a vacant, cavalier tone; it was always better to show a superior attitude when dealing with a roby. Constantly necessary to remind them in this particular fashion—as well as in countless others—of their place.

'So Mr Gantrix realizes. And it is to his credit that via such a realization he has inferred that you have, over the years, become something of an authority on the advantages, uses and manifold disadvantages of the Hobart reverse-time field. True? Not true? Choose one.'

Niehls pondered. 'I choose the first. Although you must take into account the fact that my knowledge is practical, not theoretical. But I can correctly deal with the vagaries of the Phase without explaining it. You see, I am innately an American; hence pragmatic.'

'Certainly.' The roby Carl Junior nodded its plastic humanoid head. 'Very good, Mr Lehrer. Now down to business. His Mightiness, the Anarch Peak, has become infantile and will soon shrivel up entirely into a homunculus and re-enter a nearby womb. Correct? It is only a matter of time—your time, once again.'

'I am aware,' Niehls said, 'that the Hobart Phase obtains in most of the FNM I am aware that His Mightiness will be within a handy nearby womb in no more than a matter of months. Frankly, this pleases me. His Mightiness is deranged. Beyond doubt; clinically so, in fact. The world, both that on Hobart Time and on Standard Time, will benefit. What more is there to say?'

'A lot more,' Carl Junior answered gravely. Leaning forward he deposited a host of documents on Niehls' desk. 'I respectfully insist that you examine these.'

Carl Gantrix, by means of the video circuit of the robot's system, treated himself to a leisurely inspection of the top librarian Niehls Lehrer as that individual ploughed through the wearying stack of deliberately obscure pseudo documents which the robot had presented.

The bureaucrat in Lehrer had been ensnared by the bait; his attention distracted, the librarian had become oblivious to the robot and to its actions. Therefore, as Lehrer read, the robot expertly slid its chair back and to the left side, close to a reference card case of impressive proportions. Lengthening its right arm, the robot crept its manual grippers of fingeroid shape into the nearest file of the case; this Lehrer did of course not see, and so the robot continued with its assigned task. It placed a miniaturized nest of embryonic robots, no larger than pinheads, within the card file, then a tiny find-circuit transmitter behind a subsequent card, then at last a potent detonating device set on a three-day command circuit.

Watching, Gantrix grinned. Only one construct remained in the robot's possession, and this now appeared briefly as the robot, eyeing Lehrer sideways and cautiously, edged its extensor once more toward the file, transferring this last bit of sophisticated hardware from its possession to the library's.

'Purp,' Lehrer said, without raising his eyes.

The code signal, received by the aud chamber of the file, activated an emergency release; the file closed in upon itself in the manner of a bivalve seeking safety. Collapsing, the file retreated into the wall, burying itself out of sight. And at the same time it ejected the constructs which the robot had placed inside it; the objects, expelled with electronic neatness, bounced in a trajectory which deposited them at the robot's feet, where they lay exposed in clear view.

'Good heavens,' the robot said involuntarily, taken aback.

Lehrer said, 'Leave my office immediately.' He raised his eyes from the pseudo documents, and his expression was cold. As the robot reached down to retrieve the now-exposed artifacts he added, 'And leave those items here; I want them subjected to lab analysis regarding purpose and source.' He reached into the top drawer of his desk, and when his hand emerged it held a weapon.

In Carl Gantrix's ears the phone-cable voice of the robot buzzed. 'What should I do, sir?'

'Leave presently.' Gantrix no longer felt amused; the fuddy-duddy librarian was equal to the probe, was capable in fact of nullifying it. The contact with Lehrer would have to be made in the open, and with that in mind Gantrix reluctantly picked up the receiver of the vidphone closest to him and dialed the library's exchange.

A moment later he saw, through the video scanner of the robot, the librarian Niehls Lehrer picking up his own phone in answer.

'We have a problem,' Gantrix said. 'Common to us both. Why, then, shouldn't we work together?'

Lehrer answered, 'I'm aware of no problem.' His voice held ultimate calmness; the attempt by the robot to plant hostile hardware in his work-area had not ruffled him. 'If you want to work together,' he added, 'you're off to a bad start.'

'Admittedly,' Gantrix said. 'But we've had difficulty in the past with you librarians.' Your exalted position, he thought. But he did not say it. 'This has to do with the Anarch Peak. My superiors believe that there has been an attempt made to obliterate the Hobart Phase in regard to him—a clear violation of law, and one posing a great danger to society . . . in that, if successfully done, it would in effect create an immortal person by manipulation of known scientific laws. While we do not oppose the continual attempt to bring about an immortal person by use of the Hobart Phase, we do feel that the Anarch is not the person. If you follow.'

'The Anarch is virtually reabsorbed.' Lehrer did not seem too sympathetic; perhaps, Gantrix decided, he doesn't believe me. 'I see no danger.' Coolly he studied the robot Carl Junior facing him. 'If there is a menace it appears to me to lie—'

'Nonsense. I'm here to help you; this is for the library's benefit, as well as my own.'

'Who do you represent?' Lehrer demanded.

Gantrix hesitated, then said, 'Bard Chai of the Supreme Clearness Council. I am following his orders.'

'That puts a different light on matters.' The librarian's voice had darkened; and, on the vidscreen, his expression had become harder. 'I have nothing to do with the Clearness Council; my responsibility goes to the Erads entirely. As you certainly know.'

'But are you aware—'

'I am aware only of this.' Reaching into the drawer of his desk librarian Lehrer brought out a square gray box, which he opened; from it he produced a typed manuscript which he displayed for Gantrix's attention. 'The sole extant copy of HOW I MADE MY OWN SWABBLE OUT OF ORDINARY HOUSEHOLD OBJECTS IN MY BASEMENT DURING MY SPARE TIME. Eng's masterpiece, which borders on the eradicated. You see?'

Gantrix said, 'Do you know where Ludwig Eng is, at the moment?'

'I don't care where he is; I only care where he'll be at two-thirty yesterday afternoon—we have an appointment, he and I. Here in this office at section B of the library.'

'Where Ludwig Eng will be at two-thirty yesterday,' Gantrix said meditatively, half to himself, 'depends a good deal on where he is right now.' He did not tell the librarian what he knew; that at this moment Ludwig Eng was somewhere in the Free Negro Municipality, possibly trying to obtain audience with the Anarch.

Assuming that the Anarch, in his puerile, diminished state, could still grant audience to anyone.

The now-tiny Anarch, wearing jeans and purple sneakers and a many-times-washed T-shirt, sat on the dusty grass studying intently a ring of marbles. His attention had become so complete that Ludwig Eng felt ready to give up; the boy opposite him no longer seemed conscious of his presence. All in all, the situation depressed Eng; he felt more helpless than before he had come.

Nevertheless, he decided to try to continue. 'Your Mightiness,' he said, 'I only desire a few more moments of your time.'

With reluctance the boy looked up. 'Yes, sir,' he said in a sullen, muted voice.

'My position is difficult,' Eng said, repeating himself; he had over and over again presented the childified Anarch with the identical material, and each time in vain. 'If you as Anarch could telecast an appeal throughout the Western United States and the FNM for people to build several swabbles here and there while the last copy of my book still survives—'

'That's right,' the boy murmured.

'Pardon?' Eng felt a flicker of hope; he watched the small smooth face fixedly. Something had formed there.

Sebastian Peak said, 'Yes sir; I hope to become Anarch when I grow up. I'm studying for that right now.'

'You are the Anarch. You *were* the Anarch.' He sighed, feeling crushed. It was clearly hopeless. No point in going on—and today was the final day, because yesterday he would meet with an official from the People's Topical Library and that would be that.

The boy brightened. He seemed, all at once, to take interest in what Eng had to say. 'No kidding?'

'God's truth, son.' Eng nodded solemnly. 'In fact, legally speaking you still hold the office.' He glanced up at the lean Negro with the overly-massive side arm who currently constituted the Anarch's bodyguard. 'Isn't that so, Mr Plaut?'

'True, Your Mightiness,' the Negro said to the boy. 'You possess the power to arbitrate in this case, having to do with this gentleman's manuscript.' Squatting on his lank haunches the bodyguard sought to engage the boy's wandering attention. 'Your Mightiness, this man is the inventor of the swabble.'

'What's that?' The boy glanced from one to the other of them, scowling with suspicion. 'How much does a swabble cost? I only have fifty cents; I got it as my allowance. Anyhow I don't think I want a swabble. I want some gum, and I'm going to the show.' His expression became fixed, rigidly in place. 'Who cares about a swabble?' he said with disdain.

'You have lived one hundred and sixty years,' the bodyguard Plaut told him. 'Because of this man's invention. From the swabble the Hobart Phase was inferred and finally established experimentally. I know that means nothing to you, but—' The bodyguard clasped his hands together earnestly, rocking on his hocks as he tried to keep the boy's constantly dwindling attention focussed. 'Pay attention to me, Sebastian; this is important. If you could sign a decree . . . while you can still write. That's all. A public notice for people to—'

'Aw, go on; beat it.' The boy glared at him with hostility. 'I don't believe you; something's the matter.'

Something is wrong, all right, Eng thought to himself as he rose stiffly to his feet. And there appears to be next to nothing that we can do about it. At least without your help. He felt defeated.

'Try him again later,' the bodyguard said, also rising; he looked decidedly sympathetic.

'He'll be even younger,' Eng said bitterly. And anyhow there was no time; no later existed. He walked a few steps away, then, overcome with gloom.

On a tree branch a butterfly had begun the intricate, mysterious process of squeezing itself into a dull brown cocoon, and Eng paused to inspect its slow, labored efforts. It had its task, too, but that task, unlike his, was not hopeless. However the butterfly did not know that; it continued mindlessly, a reflex machine obeying the urgings programmed into it from the remote future. The sight of the insect at work gave Eng something to ponder; he perceived the moral in it, and, turning, walked back to confront the child who squatted on the grass with his circle of gaily-colored luminous marbles.

'Look at it this way,' he said to the Anarch Peak; this was probably his last try, and he meant to bring in everything available. 'Even if you can't remember what a swabble is or what the Hobart Phase does, all you need to do is sign; I have the document here.' Reaching into his inside coat pocket he brought the envelope out, opened it. 'When you've signed this, it will appear on world-wide TV, at the six P.M. news in each time zone. I tell you what I'll do. If you'll sign this, I'll triple what you've got in the way of money. You say you have fifty cents? I'll give you an additional dollar, a genuine paper one. What do you say? And I'll pay your way to the movies once a week, at the Saturday matinee for the balance of the year. Is it a deal?'

The boy studied him acutely. He seemed almost convinced. But something—Eng could not fathom what—held him back.

'I think,' the bodyguard said softly, 'he wants to ask his dad's permission. The old gentleman is now alive; his components migrated into a birth-container about six weeks ago, and he is currently in the Kansas City General Hospital's birth ward undergoing revivification. He is already conscious, and His Mightiness has spoken with him several times. Is that not so, Sebastian?' He smiled gently at the boy, then grimaced as the boy nodded. 'So that is it,' he said to Eng, then. 'I was right. He's afraid to take any initiative, now that his father's alive. It's very bad luck as far as you're concerned, Mr Eng; he's just plain dwindled too much to perform his job. And everybody knows it as a fact.'

'I refuse to give up,' Eng said. But the truth of the matter was that purely and simply he had already given up; he could see that the bodyguard, who spent all his waking time with the Anarch, was correct. It had become a waste of time. Had this meeting taken place two years from now, however . . .

To the bodyguard he said heavily, 'I'll go away and let him play with his marbles.' He placed the envelope back in his pocket, started off; then, pausing, he added, 'I'll make one final try yesterday morning. Before I'm due at the library. If the boy's schedule permits it.'

'It surely does,' the bodyguard said. He explained, 'Hardly anybody consults him any more, in view of his—condition.' His tone was sympathetic, and for that Eng felt appreciation.

Turning wearily he trudged off, leaving the one-time Anarch of half the civilized world to play mindlessly in the grass.

The previous morning, he realized. My last chance. Long time to wait and do nothing.

In his hotel room he placed a phone call to the West Coast, to the People's Topical Library. Presently he found himself facing one of the bureaucrats with whom, of late, he had had to deal so much. 'Let me talk directly to Mr Lehrer,' he grunted. Might as well go directly to the source, he decided; Lehrer had final authority in the matter of his book—now decayed to a mere typewritten manuscript.

'Sorry,' the functionary told him, with a faint trace of disdain. 'It is too early; Mr Lehrer has already left the building.'

'Could I catch him at home, do you think?'

'He is probably having breakfast. I suggest you wait until late yesterday. After all, Mr Lehrer needs some time for seclusive recreation; he has many heavy and difficult responsibilities to weigh him down.' Clearly, the minor functionary had no intention of cooperating.

Dully depressed, Eng hung up without even saying hello. Well, perhaps it was for the better; undoubtedly Lehrer would refuse to grant him additional time. After all, as the library bureaucrat had said, Lehrer had pressures at work on him, too: in particular the Erads of the syndicate . . . those mysterious entities who saw to it that destruction of human inventions be painstakingly carried out. As witness his own book. Well, time to give up and head back west.

As he started from his hotel room, he paused at the mirror of the vanity table to see whether his face had, during the day, absorbed the packet of whiskers which he had foam-glued onto it. Peering at his reflection, he rubbed his jowls . . .

And screamed.

All along his jaw-line the dark stubble of newly-grown facial hair could be seen. He was growing a beard; stubble was coming in—not being absorbed.

What this meant he did not know. But it terrified him; he stood gaping, appalled now by the fright collected within his reflected features. The man in the mirror did not look even vaguely familiar; some ominous underlying deformity of change had attacked it. But why? And—how?

Instinct told him not to leave the hotel room.

He seated himself. And waited. For what, he did not know. But one thing he did know. There would be no meeting with Niehls Lehrer of the People's Topical Library at two-thirty yesterday afternoon. Because—

He scented it, grasped it intuitively from the one single glance in the mirror of his hotel room's vanity table. There would be no yesterday; not for him, anyhow.

Would there be for anyone else?

'I've got to see the Anarch again,' he said haltingly to himself.

The hell with Lehrer; I don't have any intention of trying to make that or any other appointment with him now. All that matters is seeing Sebastian Peak once more; in fact as soon as it's possible. Perhaps earlier today.

Because once he saw the Anarch he would know whether what he guessed were true. And if it were true, then his book, all at once, lay outside jeopardy. The syndicate with their inflexible program of eradication no longer menaced him—possibly. At least he hoped so.

But only time would tell. *Time.* The entire Hobart Phase. It was somehow involved.

And—possibly—not just for him.

To his superior Bard Chai of the Clearness Council, Gantrix said, 'We were right.' He recycled the tape recorder with shaking hands. 'This is from our phone tap, video, to the library; the inventor of the swabble, Ludwig Eng, attempted to reach Lehrer and failed. There was therefore no conversation.'

'Hence nothing to record,' the Bard purred cuttingly. His round green face sagged in pouting disappointment.

'Not so. Look. It is Eng's image that's significant. He has spent the day with the Anarch—and as a consequence his age-flow has doubled back upon itself. See with your own eyes.'

After a moment, in which he scrutinized the video image of Eng, the Bard leaned back in his chair, said, 'The stigma. Heavy infestation of beard-stubble; certain index in a male, especially of the Cauc persuasion.'

'Shall we rebirth him now?' Gantrix said. 'Before he reaches Lehrer?' He had in his possession a superbly made gun which would dwindle any person in a matter of minutes—dwindle him directly into the nearest womb, and for good.

'In my opinion,' Bard Chai said, 'he has become harmless. The swabble is nonexistent; this will not restore it.' But within, Bard Chai felt doubt, if not concern. Perhaps Gantrix, his subordinate, correctly perceived the situation; he had done so in the past, on several critical occasions . . . which explained his current value to the Clearness Council.

'But if the Hobart Phase has been cancelled out for Eng,' Gantrix said doggedly, 'then the development of the swabble will start up again. After all, he possesses the original typed manuscript; his contact with the Anarch has taken place before the Eradicators of the syndicate induced the final stage of destruct.'

That certainly was true; Bard Chai pondered and agreed. And yet despite this knowledge he had trouble taking Ludwig Eng seriously; the man did not look dangerous, bearded or otherwise. He turned to Gantrix, began to speak—then abruptly ceased.

'Your expression strikes me as unusual,' Gantrix said, with palpable annoyance. 'What's wrong?' He seemed uneasy, as the Bard's stare continued. Concern replaced displeasure.

'Your face,' the Bard Chai said, keeping his composure with the greatest of effort.

'What about my face?' Gantrix's hand flew to his chin; he massaged briefly, then blinked. 'My God.'

'*And you have not been near the Anarch.* So that does not explain your condition.' He wondered, then, about himself; had the reversal of the Hobart Phase extended to his own person as well? Swiftly he explored his own jaw-line and dewlap. And distinctly felt burgeoning bristle. Perplexing, he thought wildly to himself. What can account for this? The reversal of the Anarch's time-path might be only an effect of some prior cause involving them all. This put a new light on the Anarch's situation; perhaps it had not been voluntary.

'Can it be,' Gantrix said reflectively, 'that the disappearance of Eng's device could explain this? Except for mention in the typewritten manuscript there is no longer any reality connected with the swabble. Actually, we should have anticipated this, since the swabble is intimately associated with the Hobart Phase.'

'I wonder,' Bard Chai said, still rapidly pondering. But the swabble had not strictly speaking created the Hobart Phase; it served to direct it, so that certain regions of the planet could evade the Phase entirely—whereas others had become completely mired in it. Still, the disappearance of the swabble from contemporary society must diffuse the Hobart Phase equally over everyone; and an outgrowth of this might be a diminution to beneath the level of effectiveness for those—such as himself and Carl Gantrix—who had participated in the Phase fully.

'But now,' Gantrix said thoughtfully, 'the inventor of the swabble, and first user of it, has returned to normal time; hence the development of the swabble has again manifested itself. We can expect Eng to build his first working model of the device at any time, now.'

The difficulty of Eng's situation had now become apparent to Bard Chai. As before, use of the man's mechanism would spread throughout the world. But—as soon as Eng built and placed in operation his pilot swabble, the Hobart Phase would resume; once more Eng's direction would reverse itself. The swabbles would then be abolished by the syndicate until, once again, all that remained was the original typewritten manuscript—at which point normal time would reestablish itself.

It appeared to Bard Chai that Eng had gotten himself trapped in a closed loop. He would oscillate within a distinct small interval: between possessing only a theoretical account of the swabble and in actuality constructing and operating a functioning model. And tagging along with him would go a good portion of Terra's population.

We are caught with him, Bard Chai realized gloomily. How do we escape? What is our solution?

'We must either force Eng back into complete obliteration of his manuscript, including the idea for the construct,' Gantrix said, 'or—'

'But that is impossible,' Bard Chai broke in impatiently. 'At this point the Hobart Phase weakens automatically, since no working swabbles exist to sustain it. How, in their absence, can Eng be forced backward in time a single step farther?'

It constituted a valid—and answerable—query; both men realized that, and neither spoke for a time. Gantrix morosely continued to rub his jaw, as if he could perceive the steady growth of beard-stubble. Bard Chai, on the other hand, had withdrawn into an intensive introverted state; he pondered and repondered the problem.

No answer came. At least not yet. But, given time—

'This is extremely difficult,' the Bard said, with agitation. 'Eng will probably throw together his first swabble at any moment. And once more we will be cycled in a retrograde direction.' What worried him now was one terrible, swift insight. This would occur again and again, and each time the interval would be shortened further. Until, he ruminated, it becomes a stall within a single microsecond; no time-progression in either direction will be able to take place.

A morbid prospect indeed. But one redemptive factor existed. Eng undoubtedly would perceive the problem, too. And he would seek a way out. Logically, it could be solved by him in at least one way: he could voluntarily abstain from inventing the swabble. The Hobart Phase, then, would never assert itself, at least not effectively.

But such a decision lay with Ludwig Eng alone. Would he co-operate, if the idea were presented to him?

Probably not. Eng had always been a violent and autistic man; no one could influence him. This, of course, had helped him become an original personality; without this Eng would not have amounted to anything as an inventor, and the swabble, with its enormous effect on contemporary society, would never have come into existence.

Which would have been a good thing, the Bard thought morosely. But until now we could not appreciate this.

He appreciated it now.

The solution which Gantrix had proposed, that of rebirthing Eng, did not appeal to him. But it looked more and more to his eyes as the only way out. And a way out had to be found.

With profound irritation the librarian Niehls Lehrer inspected the clock on his desk, then his appointment book. Eng had not shown up; two-thirty had arrived, and Lehrer sat alone in his office. Carl Gantrix had been correct.

While pondering the meaning of this he heard, dimly, the phone ringing. Probably Eng, he decided as he reached for the receiver. A long way off, phoning in to say that he can't make it. I'll have trouble with this; the syndicate won't like it. And I'll have to alert them; I have no choice.

Into the phone he said, 'Goodbye.'

'I love you, Niehls.' A breathless feminine voice; this was not the call which he had anticipated. 'Do you love me?'

'Yes, Charise,' he said. 'I love you, too. But dammit, don't call me during business hours; I thought you knew that.'

Contritely, Charise McFadden said, 'Sorry, Niehls. But I keep thinking about poor Lance. Did you do the research on him that you promised? I bet you didn't.'

As a matter of fact he had; or more accurately he had instructed a minor employee of the library to do the task for him. Reaching into the top desk drawer he brought out Lance Arbuthnot's folio. 'Here it is,' he informed Charise. 'I know all there is to know about this crank. All I care to know, more correctly.' He leafed among the sheets of paper within the file. 'There's not much here, actually. Arbuthnot hasn't *done* much. You understand I can only take time to go into this matter because a major library client has failed—so far—to keep his two-thirty appointment. If he does show up, I'll have to terminate this conversation.'

'Did Arbuthnot know the Anarch Peak?'

'That part of his account is true.'

'And he is a genuine crank. So eradicating his thesis would be a distinct gain for society. It's your duty.' Over the vid portion of the phone she batted her long lashes coaxingly. 'Come on, Niehls, dear. Please.'

'But,' Lehrer continued inflexibly, 'there is nothing here suggesting that Arbuthnot spent any time concocting a paper dealing with the psychosomatic aspects of death by meteor-strike.'

She colored, hesitated, then said in a low voice, 'I, um, made that up.'

'Why?'

After a pause, Charise said, falteringly, 'Well, h-h-he's—the fact is, I'm his mistress.'

'The fact is,' Lehrer said, boring ahead with ruthless vigor, 'you don't really know what his thesis is about. It may be perfectly rational. A significant contribution to our society. Correct?' He did not wait for her reply; reaching, he started to break the phone circuit.

'Wait.' She swallowed rapidly, ducked her head, then plunged on as his fingers touched the trip switch of the phone. 'All right, Niehls; I admit it. Lance refuses to tell me what his thesis is about. He won't tell anybody. But if you'll undertake to eradicate it—don't you see? He'll have to reveal it to you; your analysis of it is required before the syndicate accepts it. Isn't that so? And then you'll tell me what it's all about. I know you will.'

Lehrer said, 'What do you care what it's about?'

'I think,' Charise said, hesitating, 'it has to do with me. Honest. There's something strange about me, and Lance noticed it. I mean, that's not so unusual when you consider how, um, close we two are; we see so much—if you'll excuse the expression—of each other.'

'I find this a dull topic,' Lehrer said frigidly. At this point, he said to himself, I wouldn't accept Arbuthnot's thesis at any cost to me. Even if they debited me to the tune of ten thousand poscreds. 'I'll talk to you some other time,' he said, and broke the phone circuit.

'Sir,' his secretary Miss Tomsen said over the desk intercom, 'there's this man out here who's been waiting since six this evening. He says he only wants a second or two of your time, and Miss McFadden led him to understand that you'd be glad to—'

'Tell him I died in office,' Lehrer said harshly.

'But you can't die, sir. You're under the Hobart Phase. And Mr Arbuthnot knows that, because he mentioned it. He's been sitting out here doing a Hobart type horoscope on you, and he predicts that great things have happened to you during the previous year. Frankly he makes me nervous; some of his predictions sound so accurate.'

'Fortune-telling about the past doesn't interest me,' Lehrer said. 'In fact, as far as I'm concerned, it's a hoax. Only the future is knowable.' The man is a crank, all right, Lehrer realized. Charise told me the truth in that respect. Imagine maintaining in all seriousness that what has already happened, what has vanished into the limbo of nebulous yesterday, can be predicted. There's one killed every minute, as P. T. Barnum phrased it.

Maybe I should see him, he reflected. Charise is right; ideas like this ought to be eradicated for the good of mankind, if not for my own peace of mind.

But that was not all. Now a measure of curiosity overcame him. It would be interesting, in a feeble way, to hear the idiot out. See what he predicted, especially for the recent few weeks. And then accept his thesis for eradication. Be the first person he casts a Hobart type of horoscope for.

Undoubtedly, Ludwig Eng did not intend to show up. The time, Lehrer said to himself, must be two o'clock by now. He glanced at his wristwatch.

And blinked.

The watch hands semaphored two-forty.

'Miss Tomsen,' Lehrer said into the intercom. 'What time do you have?'

'Leaping J. Lizards,' Miss Tomsen said. 'It's earlier than I thought. I distinctly recall it being two-twenty just a moment ago. My watch must have stopped.'

'You mean it's later than you thought. Two-forty is later than two-thirty.'

'No sir, if you don't resent my disagreeing with you. I mean, it's not my place to tell *you* what's what, but I am right. You can ask anybody. I'll ask this gentleman out here. Mr Arbuthnot, isn't two-forty earlier than two-twenty?'

Over the intercom speaker came a masculine voice, dry and controlled. 'I'm only interested in seeing Mr Lehrer, not in holding academic discussions. Mr Lehrer, if you will see me, I guarantee you'll find my thesis the most flagrant piece of outright trash you've ever had brought to your attention; Miss McFadden will not mislead you.'

'Send him in,' Lehrer reluctantly instructed Miss Tomsen. He felt perplexed. Something weird had begun to happen, something which was connected with the orderly flow of time. But he could not make out precisely what.

A dapper young man, in the first stages of baldness, entered the office, a briefcase under his arm. He and Lehrer briefly shook and then Arbuthnot seated himself facing the desk.

So this is the man Charise is having an affair with, Lehrer said to himself. Well, so it goes. 'I'll give you ten minutes,' he stated. 'And then you're out of here. You understand?'

'I have concocted here,' Arbuthnot said, unzipping his briefcase, 'the most outrageously impossible concept imaginable to my mind. And I think official eradication is absolutely essential, here, if this idea is to be kept from taking root and doing actual outright harm. There are people who pick up and act on any idea, no matter how contrary to rational good sense. You're the only person I've shown this to, and I show it to you with grave reservations.' Arbuthnot then, in one brisk and spasmodic motion, dropped his typewritten work on the surface of Niehls Lehrer's desk. And sat back, waiting.

With professional caution, Lehrer surveyed the title of the paper, then shrugged. 'This is nothing more than an inversion of Ludwig Eng's famous work.' He slid his castered chair back from the desk, disavowing the manuscript; raising both hands he gestured in dismissal. 'This is not so preposterous; it's logically thinkable to reverse Eng's title—anybody could do it at any time.'

Arbuthnot said grimly, 'But no one has. Until now. Read it once again and think out the implications.'

Unimpressed, Lehrer once more examined the thick bundle of pages.

'The implications,' Arbuthnot continued in a low, quiet, but tense voice, 'of the eradication of this manuscript.'

The title, still unimpressive to Lehrer, read:

HOW I DISASSEMBLED MY SWABBLE
INTO ORDINARY HOUSEHOLD OBJECTS IN MY BASEMENT
DURING MY SPARE TIME

'So?' Lehrer said. 'Anyone can disassemble a swabble; in fact it's being done. In fact, thousands of swabbles are being eradicated; it's the pattern. In fact, I doubt whether a single swabble is now to be found anywhere in–'

'When this thesis is eradicated,' Arbuthnot said, 'as I am certain it has been, and recently, what will the negation consist of? Think it out, Lehrer. You know the implications of cleaning out of existence Eng's premise; it means the end of the swabble and therefore the Hobart Phase. In fact, we'll see a return to normal time-flow throughout the Western United States and the Free Negro Municipality within the past forty-eight hours . . . as Eng's manuscript nears syndicate jurisdiction. The eradication of my work, then, if you follow the same line of reasoning–' He paused. 'You see what I've done, don't you? I've found a way to preserve the swabble. And to maintain the now-disintegrating Hobart Phase. Without my thesis we'll gradually lose all that the swabble has brought us. The swabble, Lehrer, eliminates death; the case of the Anarch Peak is only the beginning. But the only way to keep the cycle alive is to balance Eng's paper with mine; Eng's paper moves us in one direction; my paper reverses it, and then Eng's becomes operative once more. Forever, if we want it. Unless–and I can't imagine this happening, although admittedly it is theoretically possible–a hopeless fusion of the two time-flows results.'

'You're a crank,' Lehrer said thickly.

'Exactly.' Arbuthnot nodded. 'And that's why you'll accept my paper for official syndicate eradication. *Because you don't believe me.* Because you think this is absurd.' He smiled slightly, his eyes gray, intelligent and penetrating.

Pressing the on-button of his intercom, Lehrer said, 'Miss Tomsen, notify the local outlet of the syndicate that I'd like an Erad sent to my office as soon as possible. I have some junk here that I want him to rule on. So we can begin the business of terminal copy extinction.'

'Yes, Mr Lehrer,' Miss Tomsen's voice said.

Leaning back in his chair, Lehrer surveyed the man seated across from him. 'Does that suit you?'

Still smiling, Arbuthnot said, 'Perfectly.'

'If I thought there was anything in your concept—'

'But you don't,' Arbuthnot said patiently. 'So I'm going to get what I want; I'll be successful. Sometime tomorrow or at the latest the day after.'

'You mean yesterday,' Lehrer said. 'Or the day before.' He examined his wristwatch. 'The ten minutes are up,' he informed the crank inventor. 'I'll ask you now to leave.' He placed his hand on the bundle of papers. 'This stays here.'

Rising, Arbuthnot moved toward the door of the office. 'Mr Lehrer,' he said, pausing, 'don't be alarmed by this, but with all due respects, sir, you need a shave.'

'I haven't shaved in twenty-three years,' Lehrer said. 'Not since the Hobart Phase first took effect in my area of Los Angeles.'

'You will by this time tomorrow,' Arbuthnot said. And left the office; the door shut after him.

After a moment of reflection, Lehrer touched the button of the intercom. 'Miss Tomsen, don't send anyone else in here; I'm cancelling my appointments for the balance of the day.'

'Yes sir.' Hopefully, Miss Tomsen said, 'He was a crank, wasn't he? I thought so; I can always tell. You're glad you saw him.'

'Will see him,' he corrected.

'I think you're mistaken, Mr Lehrer. The past tense—'

'Even if Ludwig Eng shows up,' Lehrer said, 'I don't feel like seeing him. I've had enough for today.' Opening his desk drawer he carefully deposited Arbuthnot's manuscript within it, then shut it once more. He reached toward the ash tray on the desk, selected the shortest—and hence best—cigarette butt, dabbed it against the ceramic surface until it began to burn, then lifted it to his lips. Puffing shreds of tobacco into it, he sat staring fixedly out the office window at the poplar trees that lined the walk to the parking lot.

The wind, rushing about, gathered up a quantity of leaves, swirled them onto the branches of the trees, adhered them in a neat arrangement which decidedly added to the beauty of the trees.

Already, some of the brown leaves had turned green. In a short while autumn would give way to summer, and summer to spring.

He watched appreciatively. As he waited for the Erad sent out by the syndicate. Due to the crank's deranged thesis, time had once more returned to normal. Except—

Lehrer rubbed his chin. Bristles. He frowned.

'Miss Tomsen,' he said into the intercom, 'will you step in here and tell me whether or not I need a shave?'

He had a feeling that he did. And soon.

Probably within the previous half hour.

HOLY QUARREL

I

Sleep dissolved; he blinked as a dazzle of white artificial light hurt him. The light came from three rings which held a fixed location above the bed, midway to the ceiling.

'Sorry to wake you, Mr Stafford,' a man's voice came from beyond the light. 'You are Joseph Stafford, aren't you?' Then, speaking to someone else, also unseen, the voice continued, 'Would be a damn shame to wake somebody else up—somebody who didn't deserve it.'

Stafford sat up and croaked, 'Who are you?'

The bed creaked and one circle of light lowered. One of them had seated himself. 'We're looking for Joseph Stafford, of tier six, floor fifty, who's the—what do you call it?'

'Computer GB-class repairman,' a companion assisted him.

'Yes, an expert, for example, in those new molten-plasma data storage cans. You could fix one like that if it broke, couldn't you, Stafford?'

'Sure he could,' another voice said calmly. 'That's why he's rated as standby.' He explained, 'That second vidphone line we cut did that; it kept him directly connected with his superiors.'

'How long has it been since you got a call, repairman?' the first voice inquired.

Stafford did not answer; he fished beneath the pillow of the bed, groped for the Sneek gun he generally kept there.

'Probably hasn't worked for a long time,' one of the visitors with flashlights said. 'Probably needs the money. You need any money, Stafford? Or what *do* you need? You enjoy fixing computers? I mean, you'd be a sap to enter this line of work unless you liked it—with you on twenty-four-hour standby like it is. Are you good? Can you fix anything, no matter how ridiculous and remote it is, that happens to our Genux-B military planning programmer? Make us feel good; say yes.'

'I—have to think,' Stafford said thickly. He still searched for the gun, but he had lost it; he felt its absence. Or possibly before awakening him they had taken it.

'Tell you what, Stafford,' the voice went on.

Interrupting, another voice said, 'Mr Stafford. Listen.' The far right nimbus of light also lowered; the man had bent over him. 'Get out of bed, okay? Get dressed and we'll drive you to where we need a computer fixed, and on the way when you have plenty of time you can decide how good you are. And then when we get there you can have a quick look at the Genux-B and see how long it'll take you.'

'We really want it fixed up,' the first man said plaintively. 'As it is, it's no good to us or anyone. The way it is now, data are piling up in mile-high mounds. And they're not being—what do you say?—ingested. They just sit there, and Genux-B doesn't process them, so naturally it can't come up with any decision. So naturally all those satellites are just flying along there like nothing happened.'

Getting slowly, stiffly from the bed, Stafford said, 'What showed up first as a symptom?' He wondered who they were. And he wondered which Genux-B they were talking about. As far as he knew, there existed only three in North America—only eight throughout Terra.

Watching him get into his work smock, the invisible shapes behind the flashlights conferred. At last one cleared his throat and said, 'I understand that a tape take-up reel stopped spinning, so all the tape with all the data on it just keeps spinning onto the floor in a big heap.'

'But tape tension on the take-up reels—' Stafford began.

'In this case, it failed to be automatic. You see, we jammed the reel so it wouldn't accept any more tape. Before that we tried cutting the tape, but as I guess you know it rethreads itself automatically. And we tried erasing the tape, but if the erase circuit comes on it starts an alarm going in Washington, DC, and we didn't want to get all those high-level people involved. But they—the computer designers—overlooked the take-up reel tension because that's such a simple clutch arrangement. It can't go wrong.'

Trying to button his collar, Stafford said, 'In other words, there're data you don't want it to receive.' He felt lucid now; at least he had more or less wakened up. 'What kind of data?' He thought with chill foreboding that he knew. Data were coming in which would cause the big government-owned computer to declare a Red Alert. Of course, this crippling of Genux-B would have to occur before a hostile attack by the South African True Association manifested itself in real but minute individual symptoms which the computer, with its vast intake of seemingly unrelated data, would take note of—notice and add together into a meaningful pattern.

Stafford thought bitterly, How many times we were warned about this! They would have to wipe out our Genux-B prior to its successful deploying of the SAC retaliatory satellites and bombers. And this was that event; these men, undercover extensions in North America of SATA, had rousted him to complete their job of making the computer inoperable.

But—data might already have been received, might already have been transferred to the receptor circuits for processing and analysis. They had started to work too late; possibly by one day, possibly only by a few seconds. At least some of the meaningful data had gotten onto the tapes, and so *he* had to be called in. They couldn't finish their job alone.

The United States, then, would presently undergo a series of terror-weapon satellites bursting above it—as meantime the network of defensive machinery waited for a command from the cardinal computer. Waited in vain, since Genux-B knew of no trace harbingers of military assault—would still not ever really know until a direct hit on the national capital put an end to it and its emasculated faculties.

No wonder they had jammed the take-up reel.

II

'The war's begun,' he said quietly to the four men with flashlights.

Now that he had turned on the bedroom lamps, he could make them out. Ordinary men with an assigned task; these were not fanatics but functionaries. They could have worked equally well for any government, perhaps even the near-psychotic Chinese People's. 'The war has *already* broken out,' he guessed aloud, 'and it's essential that Genux-B not know—so it can neither defend us nor strike back. You want to see it get only data which indicate we're at peace.' He—and no doubt they—recalled how swiftly in the two previous Interventions of Honor, one against Israel, one against France, Genux-B had reacted. Not one trained professional observer had seen the signs—or had seen to what the signs led, anyhow. As with Josef Stalin in 1941. The old tyrant had been shown evidence that the Third Reich intended to attack the USSR, but he simply would not or could not believe. Any more than the Reich had believed that France and Britain, in 1939, would honor their pact with Poland.

In a compact group, the men with flashlights led him from the bedroom of his conapt, into the outer hall and to the escy which led to the roof field. As they emerged, the air smelled of mud and dampness. He inhaled, shivered, and involuntarily gazed up at the sky. One star moved: landing light on a flapple, which now set down a few feet from the five of them.

As they sat within the flapple—rising swiftly from the roof and heading toward Utah to the west—one of the gray functionaries with Sneek gun, flashlight, and briefcase said to Stafford, 'Your theory is good, especially considering that we woke you out of a sound sleep.'

'But,' a companion put in, 'it's wrong. Show him the punched tape we hauled out.'

Opening his briefcase, the man nearest Stafford brought out a wad of plastic tape, handed it mutely to Stafford.

Holding it up against the dome light of the flapple, Stafford made out the punches. Binary system, evidently programming material for the Strategic Acquired-Space Command units which the computer directly controlled.

'It was about to push the panic button and give them an order,' the man at the console of the flapple said, over his shoulder. 'To all our military units linked to it. Can you read the command?'

Stafford nodded, and returned the tape. He could read it, yes. The computer had formally notified SAC of a Red Alert. It had gone so far as to move H-bomb-carrying squadrons into scramble, and also was requesting that all ICBM missiles on their assorted pads be made ready for launch.

'And also,' the man at the controls added, 'it was sending out a command to defensive satellites and missile complexes to deploy themselves in response to an imminent H-bomb attack. We blocked all this, however, as you now are able to see. None of this tape got onto the co-ax lines.'

After a pause, Stafford said huskily, 'Then what data don't you want Genux-B to receive?' He did not understand.

'Feedback,' said the man at the controls. Obviously he was the leader of this unit of commandos. 'Without feedback the computer does not possess any method of determining that there has been no counterattack by its military arm. In the abeyance it will have to assume that the counterattack has taken place, but that the enemy strike was at least partially successful.'

Stafford said, 'But there is no enemy. Who's attacking us?'

Silence.

Sweat made Stafford's forehead slick with moisture. 'Do you know what would cause a Genux-B to conclude that we're under attack? A million separate factors, all possible known data weighed, compared, analyzed—and then the absolute gestalt. In this case, the gestalt of an imminent attacking enemy. No one thing would have raised the threshold; it was quantitative. A shelter-building program in Asiatic Russia, unusual movements of cargo ships around Cuba, concentrations of rocket freight unloadings in Red Canada . . .'

'No one,' the man at the controls of the flapple said placidly, 'no nation or group of persons either on Terra or Luna or Domed Mars is attacking anybody. You can see why we've got to get you over there fast. You have to make it absolutely certain that no orders emanate from Genux-B to SAC. We want Genux-B sealed off so it can't talk to anybody in a position of authority and it can't hear anybody besides us. What we do after that we'll worry about then. "But the evil of the day—"'

'You assert that in spite of everything available to it, Genux-B can't distinguish an attack on us?' Stafford demanded. 'With its manifold data-collecting sweepers?' He thought of something then, that terrified him in a kind of hopeless, retrospective way. 'What about our attack on France in '82 and then on little Israel in '89?'

'No one was attacking us then either,' the man nearest Stafford said, as he retrieved the tape and again placed it within his brief-case. His voice, somber and morose, was the only sound; no one else stirred or spoke. 'Same then as now. Only this time a group of us stopped Genux-B before it could commit us. We pray we've aborted a pointless, needless war.'

'Who are you?' Stafford asked. 'What's your status in the federal government? And what's your connection with Genux-B?' Agents, he thought, of the Blunk-rattling South African True Association. That still struck him as most likely. Or even zealots from Israel, looking for vengeance—or merely acting out the desire to stop a war: the most humanitarian motivation conceivable.

But, nevertheless, he himself, like Genux-B, was under a loyalty oath to no larger a political entity than the North American Prosperity Alliance. He still had the problem of getting away from these men and to his chain-of-command superiors so that he could file a report.

The man at the controls of the flapple said, 'Three of us are

FBI.' He displayed credentials. 'And that man there is an elec-com engineer, who, as a matter of fact, helped in the original design of this particular Genux-B.'

'That's right,' the engineer said. 'I personally made it possible for them to jam both the outgoing programming and the incoming data feed. But that's not enough.' He turned toward Stafford, his face serene, his eyes large and inviting. He was half-begging, half-ordering, using whatever tone would bring results. 'But let's be realistic. Every Genux-B has backup monitoring circuitry that'll begin to inform it anytime now that its programming to SAC isn't being acted on, and in addition it's not getting the data it ought to get. As with everything else it sinks its electronic circuits into, it'll begin to introspect. And by that time we have to be doing something better than jamming a take-up reel with a Phillips screwdriver.' He paused. 'So,' he finished more slowly, 'that's why we came to you.'

Gesturing, Stafford said, 'I'm just a repairman. Maintenance and service—not even malfunct analysis. I do only what I'm told.'

'Then do what we're telling you,' the FBI man closest to him spoke up harshly. 'Find out *why* Genux-B decided to flash a Red Alert, scramble SAC, and begin a "counterattack." Find out why it did so in the case of France and Israel. Something made it add up its received data and get that answer. It's not alive! It has no volition. It didn't just *feel* the urge to do this.'

The engineer said, 'If we're lucky, this is the last time Genux-B will malreact in this fashion. If we can spot the misfunction this time, we'll perhaps have it pegged for all time. Before it starts showing up in the other seven Genux-B systems around the world.'

'And you're certain,' Stafford said, 'that we're *not* under attack?' Even if Genux-B had been wrong both times before, it at least theoretically could be right this time.

'If we are about to be attacked,' the nearest FBI man said, 'we can't make out any indication of it—by human data processing, anyhow. I admit it's logically thinkable that Genux-B could be correct. After all, as he pointed out—'

'You may be in error because the SATA has been hostile toward us so long we take it for granted. It's a verity of modern life.'

'Oh, it's not the South African True Association,' the FBI man said briskly. 'In fact, if it were we wouldn't have gotten suspicious. We wouldn't have begun poking around, interviewing survivors from the Israel War and French War and whatever else State's done to follow this up.'

'It's Northern California,' the engineer said, and grimaced. 'Not even all of California; just the part above Pismo Beach.'

Stafford stared at them.

'That's right,' one of the FBI men said. 'Genux-B was in the process of scrambling all SAC bombers and wep-sats for an all-out assault on the area around Sacramento, California.'

'You asked it why?' Stafford said, speaking to the engineer.

'Sure. Or rather, strictly speaking, we asked it to spell out in detail what the "enemy" is up to.'

One of the FBI men drawled, 'Tell Mr Stafford what Northern California is up to that makes it a hot-target enemy—that would have meant its destruction by SAC spearhead assaults if we hadn't jammed the damn machinery . . . and still have it jammed.'

'Some individual,' the engineer said, 'has opened up a penny gum machine route in Castro Valley. You know. He has those bubble-headed dispensers outside supermarkets. The children put in a penny and get a placebo ball of gum and something additional occasionally—a prize such as a ring or a charm. It varies. That's the target.'

Incredulous, Stafford said, 'You're joking.'

'Absolute truth. Man's name is Herb Sousa. He owns sixty-four machines now in operation and plans expansion.'

'I mean,' Stafford said thickly, 'you're joking about Genux-B's response to that datum.'

'Its response isn't exactly to that datum per se,' the closest of the FBI men said. 'For instance, we checked with both the Israeli and French governments. Nobody named Herb Sousa opened up a penny gum machine route in their countries, and that goes for chocolate-covered peanut vending machines or anything else remotely similar to it. And, contrarily, Herb Sousa maintained such a route in Chile and in the UK during the past two decades ... without Genux-B taking any interest all those years.' He added, 'He's an elderly man.'

'A sort of Johnny Apple Gum,' the engineer said, and tittered. 'Looping the world, sending those gum machines swooping down in front of every gas—'

'The triggering stimulus,' the engineer said, as the flapple began to drop toward a vast complex of illuminated public buildings below, 'may lie in the ingredients of the merchandise placed in the machines. That's what our experts have come up with; they studied all material available to Genux-B concerning Sousa's gum concessions, and we know that all Genux-B has consists of a long, dry chemical analysis of the food product constituents with which Sousa loads his machines. In fact, Genux-B specifically *requested* more information on that angle. It kept grinding out "incomplete ground data" until we got a thorough PF&D lab analysis.'

'What did the analysis show?' Stafford asked. The flapple had now berthed on the roof of the installations housing the central component of the computer, and, as it was called these days, Mr C-in-C of the North American Prosperity Alliance.

'As regards foodstuffs,' an FBI man near the door said, as he stepped out onto the dimly illuminated landing strip, 'nothing but gum base, sugar, corn syrup, softeners, and artificial flavor, all the way down the line. Matter of fact, that's the only way you *can* make gum. And those dinky little prizes are vacuum-processed thermoplastics. Six hundred to the dollar will buy them from any of a dozen firms here and in Hong Kong and Japan. We even went so far as to trace the prizes down to the specific jobber, his sources, back to the factory, where a man from State actually stood and watched them making the damn little things. No, nothing there. Nothing at all.'

'But,' the engineer said, half to himself, 'when that data had been supplied to Genux-B—'

'Then this,' the FBI man said, standing aside so that Stafford could disemflapple. 'A Red Alert, the SAC scramble, the missiles up from their silos. Forty minutes away from thermonuclear war—the distance from us of one Phillips head screwdriver wedged in a tape drum of the computer.'

To Stafford, the engineer said keenly, 'Do you pick up anything odd or conceivably misleading in those data? Because if you do, for God's sake speak up; all we can do this way is to dismantle Genux-B and put it out of action, so that when a genuine threat faces us—'

'I wonder,' Stafford said slowly, pondering, 'what's meant by "artificial" color.'

III

'It means it won't otherwise look the right color, so a harmless food-coloring dye is added,' the engineer said presently.

'But that's the one ingredient,' Stafford said, 'that isn't listed in a way that tells us what it is—only what it does. And how about flavor?'

The FBI men glanced at one another.

'It is a fact,' one of them said, 'and I recall this because it always makes me sore—it did specify artificial flavor. But heck—'

'Artificial color and flavor,' Stafford said, 'could mean anything. Anything over and above the color and flavor imparted.' He thought: Isn't it prussic acid that turns everything a bright clear green? That, for example, could in all honesty be spelled out on a label as 'artificial color.' And taste—what really was meant by 'artificial taste'? This to him always had a dark, peculiar quality to it, this thought; he decided to shelve it. Time now to go down and take a look at Genux-B, to see what damage had been done to it.

—And how much damage, he thought wryly, it still needs. If I've been told the truth; if these men are what they show credentials for, not SATA saboteurs or an intelligence cadre of one of several major foreign powers.

From the garrison warrior domain of Northern California, he thought wryly. Or was that absolutely impossible after all? Perhaps something genuine and ominous had burgeoned into life there. And Genux-B had—as designed to do—sniffed it out.

For now, he could not tell.

But perhaps by the time he finished examining the computer he would know. In particular, he wanted to see firsthand the authentic, total collection of data tapes currently being processed from the outside universe into the computer's own inner world. Once he knew that—

I'll turn the thing back on, he said grimly to himself. I'll do the job I was trained for and hired to do.

Obviously, for him it would be easy. He thoroughly knew the schematics of the computer. No one else had been into it replacing defective components and wiring as had he.

This explained why these men had come to him. They were right—at least about that.

'Piece of gum?' one of the FBI agents asked him as they walked to the descy with its phalanx of uniformed guards standing at parade rest before it. The FBI agent, a burly man with a reddish fleshy neck, held out three small brightly colored spheres.

'From one of Sousa's machines?' the engineer asked.

'Sure is.' The agent dropped them into Stafford's smock pocket, then grinned. 'Harmless? Yes-no-maybe, as the college tests say.'

Retrieving one from his pocket, Stafford examined it in the overhead light of the descy. Sphere, he thought. Egg. Fish egg; they're round, as in caviar. Also edible; no law against selling brightly colored eggs.

Or are they laid this color?

'Maybe it'll hatch,' one of the FBI men said casually. He and his companions had become tense now, as they descended into the high-security portion of the building.

'What do you think would hatch out of it?' Stafford said.

'A bird,' the shortest of the FBI men said brusquely. 'A tiny red bird bringing good tidings of great joy.'

Both Stafford and the engineer glanced at him.

'Don't quote the Bible to me,' Stafford said. 'I was raised with it.

I can quote you back anytime.' But it was strange, in view of his own immediate thoughts, almost an occurrence of synchronicity between their minds. It made him feel more somber. God knew, he felt somber enough as it was. Something laying eggs, he thought. Fish, he reflected, release thousands of eggs, all identical; only a very few of them survive. Impossible waste—a terrible, primitive method.

But if eggs were laid and deposited all over the world, in countless public places, even if only a fraction survived—it would be enough. This had been proved. The fish of Terra's waters had done so. If it worked for terran life, it could work for non-terran, too.

The thought did not please him.

'If you wanted to infest Terra,' the engineer said, seeing the expression on his face, 'and your species, from God knows what planet in what solar system, reproduced the way our cold-blooded creatures here on Terra reproduce—' He continued to eye Stafford. 'In other words, if you spawned thousands, even millions of small hard-shelled eggs, and you didn't want them noticed, and they were bright in color as eggs generally are—' He hesitated. 'One wonders about incubation. How long. And under what circumstances? Fertilized eggs, to hatch, *generally have to be kept warm.*'

'In a child's body,' Stafford said, 'it would be very warm.'

And the thing, the egg, would—insanely—pass Pure Food & Drug standards. There was nothing toxic in an egg. All organic, and very nourishing.

Except, of course, that if this happened to be so, the outer shell of hard colored 'candy' would be immune to the action of normal stomach juices. The egg would not dissolve. But it could be chewed up in the mouth, though. Surely it wouldn't survive mastication. It would have to be swallowed like a pill: intact.

With his teeth he bit down on the red ball and cracked it. Retrieving the two hemispheres, he examined the contents.

'Ordinary gum,' the engineer said. '"Gum base, sugar, corn syrup, softeners—"' He grinned tauntingly, and yet in his face a shadow of relief passed briefly across before it was, by an effort of will, removed. 'False lead.'

'False lead, and I'm glad it is,' the shortest of the FBI men said. He stepped from the descy. 'Here we are.' He stopped in front of the rank of uniformed and armed guards, showed his papers. 'We're back,' he told the guards.

'The prizes,' Stafford said.

'What do you mean?' the engineer glanced at him.

'It's not in the gum. So it has to be in the prizes, the charms and knick-knacks. That's all that's left.'

'What you're doing,' the engineer said, 'is implicitly maintaining that Genux-B is functioning properly. That it's somehow right; there *is* a hostile warlike menace to us. One so great it justifies pacification of Northern California by hard first-line weapons. As I see it, isn't it easier simply to operate from the fact that the computer is malfunctioning?'

Stafford, as they walked down the familiar corridors of the vast government building, said, 'Genux-B was built to sift a greater amount of data simultaneously than any man or group of men could. It handles more data than we, and it handles them faster. Its response comes in microseconds. If Genux-B, after analyzing all the current data, feels that war is indicated, and we don't agree, then it may merely show that the computer is functioning *as it was intended to function*. And the more we disagree with it, the better this is proved. If we could perceive, as it does, the need for immediate, aggressive war on the basis of the data available, *then we wouldn't require Genux-B*. It's precisely in a case like this, where the computer has given out a Red Alert and we see no menace, that the real use of a computer of this class comes into play.'

After a pause, one of the FBI men said, as if speaking to himself, 'He's right, you know. Absolutely right. The real question is, Do we trust Genux-B more than ourselves? Okay, we built it to analyze faster and more accurately and on a wider scale than we can. If it had been a success, this situation we face now is precisely what could have been predicted. *We* see no cause for launching an attack; it does.' He grinned harshly. 'So what do we do? Start Genux-B up again, have it go ahead and program SAC into a war?

Or do we neutralize it—in other words, unmake it?' His eyes were cold and alert on Stafford. 'A decision one way or the other has to be made by someone. Now. At once. Someone who can make a good educated guess as to which it is, functioning or malfunctioning.'

'The President and his cabinet,' Stafford offered tensely. 'An ultimate decision like this has to be his. He bears the moral responsibility.'

'But the decision,' the engineer spoke up, 'is not a moral question, Stafford. It only *looks* like it is. Actually the question is only a technical one. Is Genux-B working properly or has it broken down?'

And that's why you rousted me from bed, Stafford realized with a thrill of icy dismal grief. You didn't bring me here to implement your jerry-built jamming of the computer. Genux-B could be neutralized by one shell from one rocket launcher towed up and parked outside the building. In fact, he realized, in all probability it's effectively neutralized now. You can keep that Phillips screwdriver wedged in there forever. And you helped design and build the thing. No, he realized, that's not it. I'm not here to repair or destroy; *I'm here to decide.* Because I've been physically close to Genux-B for fifteen years—it's supposed to confer some mystic intuitive ability on me to sense whether the thing is functioning or malfunctioning. I'm supposed to hear the difference, like a good garage mechanic who can tell merely by listening to a turbine engine whether it has bearing knock or not, and if so how bad.

A diagnosis, he realized. That's all you want. This is a consultation of computer doctors—and one repairman.

The decision evidently lay with the repairman, because the others had given up.

He wondered how much time he had. Probably very little. Because if the computer were correct—

Sidewalk gum machines, he pondered. Penny-operated. For kids. And for that it's willing to pacify all Northern California. What could it possibly have extrapolated? What, looking ahead, did Genux-B see?

*

It amazed him: the power of one small tool to halt the workings of a mammoth constellation of autonomic processes. But the Phillips screwdriver had been inserted expertly.

'What we must try,' Stafford said, 'is introduction of calculated, experimental—and false—data.' He seated himself at one of the typewriters wired directly to the computer. 'Let's start off with this,' he said, and began to type.

HERB SOUSA, OF SACRAMENTO, CALIFORNIA, THE GUM
MACHINE MAGNATE, DIED SUDDENLY IN HIS SLEEP. A
LOCAL DYNASTY HAS COME TO AN UNANTICIPATED END.

Amused, one of the FBI men said, 'You think it'll believe that?'

'It always believes its data,' Stafford said. 'It has no other source to rely on.'

'But if the data conflict,' the engineer pointed out, 'it'll analyze everything out and accept the most probable chain.'

'In this case,' Stafford said, 'nothing will conflict with this datum because this is all Genux-B is going to receive.' He fed the punched card to Genux-B then, and stood waiting. 'Tap the outgoing signal,' he instructed the engineer. 'Watch to see if it cuts off.'

One of the FBI men said, 'We already have a line splice, so that ought to be easy to do.' He glanced at the engineer, who nodded.

Ten minutes later the engineer, now wearing headphones, said, 'No change. The Red Alert is still being emitted; that didn't affect it.'

'Then it has nothing to do with Herb Sousa as such,' Stafford said, pondering. 'Or else he's done it—whatever it is—already. Anyhow, his death means nothing to Genux-B. We'll have to look somewhere else.' Again seating himself at the typewriter, he began on his second spurious fact.

IT HAS BEEN LEARNED, ON THE ADVICE OF RELIABLE
SOURCES IN BANKING AND FINANCIAL CIRCLES IN
NORTHERN CALIFORNIA, THAT THE CHEWING GUM
EMPIRE OF THE LATE HERB SOUSA WILL BE BROKEN UP

TO PAY OUTSTANDING DEBTS. ASKED WHAT WOULD BE
DONE WITH THE GUM AND TRINKETS CONSTITUTING THE
GOODIES WITHIN EACH MACHINE, LAW-ENFORCEMENT
OFFICERS HAZARDED THE GUESS THAT THEY WOULD BE
DESTROYED AS SOON AS A COURT ORDER, NOW BEING
SOUGHT BY THE ASSISTANT DISTRICT ATTORNEY OF
SACRAMENTO, CAN BE PUT INTO EFFECT.

Ceasing typing, he sat back, waiting. No more Herb Sousa, he said to himself, and no more merchandise. What does that leave? Nothing. The man and his commodities, at least as far as Genux-B was concerned, no longer existed.

Time passed; the engineer continued to monitor the output signal of the computer. At last, resignedly, he shook his head. 'No change.'

'I have one more spurious datum I want to feed it,' Stafford said. Again he put a card in the typewriter and began to punch.

IT APPEARS NOW THAT THERE NEVER WAS AN
INDIVIDUAL NAMED HERBERT SOUSA; NOR DID THIS
MYTHOLOGICAL PERSON EVER GO INTO THE PENNY
GUM MACHINE BUSINESS.

As he rose to his feet, Stafford said, 'That should cancel out everything Genux-B knows or ever did know about Sousa and his penny-ante operation.' As far as the computer was concerned, the man had been retroactively expunged.

In which case, how could the computer initiate war against a man who had never existed, who operated a marginal concession which also never existed?

A few moments later the engineer, tensely monitoring the output signal of Genux-B, said, 'Now there's been a change.' He studied his oscilloscope, then accepted the reel of tape being voided by the computer and began a close inspection of that, too.

For a time he remained silent, intent on the job of reading the tape; then all at once he glanced up and grinned humorously at the rest of them.

He said, 'It says that the datum is a lie.'

IV

'A lie!' Stafford said unbelievingly.

The engineer said, 'It's discarded the last datum on the grounds that it can't be true. It contradicts what it knows to be valid. In other words, *it still knows that Herb Sousa exists.* Don't ask me how it knows this; probably it's an evaluation from wide-spectrum data over an extensive period of time.' He hesitated, then said, 'Obviously, it knows more about Herb Sousa than we do.'

'It knows, anyhow, that there is such a person,' Stafford conceded. He felt nettled. Often in the past Genux-B had spotted contradictory or inaccurate data and had expelled them. But it had never mattered this much before.

He wondered, then, what prior, unassailable body of data existed within the memory-cells of Genux-B against which it had compared his spurious assertion of Sousa's nonexistence.

'What it must be doing,' he said to the engineer, 'is to go on the assumption if X is true, that Sousa never existed, then Y must be true—whatever "Y" is. But Y remains untrue. I wish we knew which of all its millions of data units Y is.'

They were back to their original problem: who was Herb Sousa and what had he done to alert Genux-B into such violent sine qua non activity?

'Ask it,' the engineer said to him.

'Ask what?' He was puzzled.

'Instruct it to produce its stored data inventory on Herb Sousa. All of it.' The engineer kept his voice deliberately patient. 'God knows what it's sitting on. And once we get it, let's look it over and see if *we* can spot what it spotted.'

Typing the proper requisition, Stafford fed the card to Genux-B.

'It reminds me,' one of the FBI men said reflectively, 'of a philosophy course I took at UCLA. There used to be an ontological argument to prove the existence of God. You imagine what He would be like, if He existed: omnipotent, omnipresent, omniscient, immortal, plus being capable of infinite justice and mercy.'

'So?' the engineer said irritably.

'Then, when you've imagined Him possessing all those ultimate qualities, you notice that He lacks one quality. A minor one—a quality which every germ and stone and piece of trash by the freeway possesses. Existence. So you say: if He has all those others, He must possess the attribute of being real. If a stone can do it, obviously He can.' He added, 'It's a discarded theory; they knocked it down back in the Middle Ages. But'—he shrugged—'it's interesting.'

'What made you think of that at this particular time?' the engineer demanded.

'Maybe,' the FBI man said, 'there's no one fact or even cluster of facts about Sousa that prove to Genux-B he exists. Maybe it's *all* the facts. There may be just plain too many. The computer had found, on the basis of past experience, that when so much data exists on a given person, that person must be genuine. After all, a computer of the magnitude of Genux-B is capable of learning; that's why we make use of it.'

'I have another fact I'd like to feed to it,' the engineer said. 'I'll type it out and you can read it.' Reseating himself at the programming typewriter, he ground out one short sentence, then yanked the card from the bales and showed it to the rest of them. It read:

THE COMPUTER GENUX-B DOES NOT EXIST.

After a stunned moment, one of the FBI men said, 'If it had no trouble in comparing the datum about Herbert Sousa with what it already knew, it certainly isn't going to have any trouble with this— and what's your point anyhow? I don't see what this accomplishes.'

'If Genux-B doesn't exist,' Stafford said, with comprehension, 'then it can't send out a Red Alert; that's logically a contradiction.'

'But it *has* sent out a Red Alert,' the shortest of the FBI men pointed out. 'And it knows it has. So it won't have any difficulty establishing the fact of its existence.'

The engineer said, 'Let's give it a try. I'm curious. As far as I can see ahead, no harm can be done. We can always cancel out the phony fact if it seems advisable.'

'You think,' Stafford asked him, 'that if we feed it this datum it'll reason that if it doesn't exist it couldn't have received the datum to that effect—which would cancel the datum right there.'

'I don't know,' the engineer admitted. 'I've never heard even a theoretical discussion as to the effect on a B-magnitude computer of programming a denial of its own existence.' Going to the feed bracket of Genux-B, he dropped the card in, stepped back. They waited.

After a prolonged interval, the answer came over the output cable, which the engineer had tapped. As he listened through his headphones, he transcribed the computer's response for the rest of them to study:

ANALYSIS OF CONSTITUENT RE THE NONEXISTENCE OF
GENUX-B MULTIFACTOR CALCULATING INSTRUMENTS.
IF CONSTIT UNIT 340S70 IS TRUE, THEN:
I DO NOT EXIST.
IF I DO NOT EXIST, THEN THERE IS NO WAY I CAN BE
INFORMED THAT MY GENERIC CLASS DOES NOT EXIST.
IF I CANNOT BE INFORMED IN THAT REGARD, THEN
YOU HAVE FAILED TO INFORM ME, AND CONSTIT UNIT
340S70 DOES NOT EXIST FROM MY STANDPOINT.
THEREFORE: I EXIST.

Whistling with admiration, the shortest of the FBI men said, 'It did it. What a neat logical analysis! He's proved—it's proved—that your datum is spurious; so now it can totally disregard it. And go on as before.'

'Which,' Stafford said somberly, 'is exactly what it did with the datum filed with it denying that Herb Sousa ever existed.'

Everyone glanced at him.

'It appears to be the same process,' Stafford said. And it implies, he reasoned, some uniformity, some common factor, between the entity Genux-B and the entity Herb Sousa. 'Do you have any of the charms, prizes, or just plain geegaws, whatever they are, that Sousa's gum machines dole out?' he asked the FBI men. 'If so, I'd like to see them ...'

Obligingly, the most impressive of the FBI men unzipped his briefcase, brought out a sanitary-looking plastic sack. On the surface of a nearby table he spread out a clutter of small glittering objects.

'Why are you interested in those?' the engineer asked. 'These things have been given lab scrutiny. We told you that.'

Seating himself, not answering, Stafford picked up one of the assorted trinkets, examined it, put it down, and selected another.

'Consider this.' He tossed one of the tiny geegaws toward them; it bounced off the table and an obliging FBI agent bent to retrieve it. 'You recognize it?'

'Some of the charms,' the engineer said irritably, 'are in the shape of satellites. Some are missiles. Some interplan rockets. Some big new mobile land cannons. Some figurines of soldiers.' He gestured. 'That happens to be a charm made to resemble a computer.'

'A Genux-B computer,' Stafford said, holding out his hand to get it back. The FBI man amiably returned it to him. 'It's a Genux-B, all right,' he said. 'Well, I think this is it. We've found it.'

'This?' the engineer demanded loudly. 'How? Why?'

Stafford said, 'Was every charm analyzed? I don't mean a representative sample, such as one of each variety or all found in one given gum machine. I mean every damn one of them.'

'Of course not,' an FBI man said. 'There's tens of thousands of them. But at the factory of origin we—'

'I'd like to see that particular one given a total microscopic analysis,' Stafford said. 'I have an intuition it isn't a solid, uniform piece of thermoplastic.' I have an intuition, he said to himself, that it's a working replica. A minute but authentic Genux-B.

The engineer said, 'You're off your trolley.'

'Let's wait,' Stafford said, 'until we get it analyzed.'

'And meanwhile,' the shortest of the FBI men said, 'we keep Genux-B inoperative?'

'Absolutely,' Stafford said. A weird weak fear had begun at the base of his spine and was working its way up.

Half an hour later the lab, by special bonded messenger, returned an analysis of the gum machine charm.

'Solid nylon,' the engineer said, glancing over the report. He tossed it to Stafford. 'Nothing inside, only ordinary cheap plastic. No moving parts, no interior differentiation at all. If that's what you were expecting?'

'A bad guess,' one of the FBI men observed. 'Which cost us time.' All of them regarded Stafford sourly.

'You're right,' Stafford said. He wondered what came next; what hadn't they tried?

The answer, he decided, did not lie in the merchandise with which Herb Sousa stuffed his machines; that now seemed clear. The answer lay in Herb Sousa himself—whoever and whatever he was.

'Can we have Sousa brought here?' he asked the FBI men.

'Sure,' one of them said presently. 'He can be picked up. But why? What's *he* done?' He indicated Genux-B. 'There's the trouble right there, not way out on the Coast with some small-potatoes-type businessman working half the side of one city street.'

'I want to see him,' Stafford said. 'He might know something.' He *has* to, he said to himself.

One of the FBI men said thoughtfully, 'I wonder what Genux-B's reaction would be if it knew we're bringing Sousa here.' To the engineer, he said, 'Try that. Feed it that nonfact, now, before we go to the trouble of actually picking him up.'

Shrugging, the engineer again seated himself at the typewriter. He typed:

SACRAMENTO BUSINESSMAN HERB SOUSA WAS BROUGHT
TODAY BY FBI AGENTS BEFORE COMPUTER COMPLEX
GENUX-B FOR A DIRECT CONFRONTATION.

'Okay?' he asked Stafford. 'This what you want? Okay?' He fed it
to the data receptors of the computer, without waiting for an answer.

'There's no use asking me,' Stafford said irritably. 'It wasn't my
idea.' But, nevertheless, he walked over to the man monitoring the
output line, curious to learn the computer's response.

The answer came instantly. He stared down at the typed-out
response, not believing what he saw.

HERBERT SOUSA CANNOT BE HERE. HE MUST BE IN
SACRAMENTO, CALIFORNIA; ANYTHING ELSE IS
IMPOSSIBLE. YOU HAVE PRESENTED ME WITH FALSE
DATA.

'It can't know,' the engineer said huskily. 'My God, Sousa could
go anywhere, even to Luna. In fact, he's already been all over Earth.
How would it know?'

Stafford said, 'It knows more about Herb Sousa than it should.
Than is reasonably possible.' He consulted with himself, then
abruptly said, 'Ask it who Herb Sousa is.'

'"Who"?' The engineer blinked. 'Hell, he's—'

'Ask it!'

The engineer typed out the question. The card was presented
to Genux-B and they stood waiting for its response.

'We already asked it for all the material it has on Sousa,' the
engineer said. 'The bulk of that ought to be emerging anytime now.'

'This is not the same,' Stafford said shortly. 'I'm not asking it to
hand back data given in. I'm asking it for an evaluation.'

Monitoring the output line of the computer, the engineer stood
silently, not answering. Then, almost offhandedly, he said, 'It's
called off the Red Alert.'

Incredulous, Stafford said, 'Because of that query?'

'Maybe. It didn't say and I don't know. You asked the question and now it's shut down on its SAC scramble and everything else; it claims that the situation in Northern California is normal.' His voice was toneless. 'Make your own guess; it's probably as good as any.'

Stafford said, 'I still want an answer. Genux-B knows who Herb Sousa is and I want to know, too. And *you* ought to know.' His look took in both the engineer with his headphones and the assorted FBI men. Again he thought of the tiny solid-plastic replica of Genux-B which he had found among the charms and trinkets. Coincidence? It seemed to him that it meant something . . . but what, he could not tell. Not yet, anyhow.

'Anyhow,' the engineer said, 'it really has called off the Red Alert, and that's what matters. Who cares a goddam bit about Herb Sousa? As far as I'm concerned, we can relax, give up, go home now.'

'Relax,' one of the FBI men said, 'until all of a sudden it decides to start the alert going again. Which it could do anytime. I think the repairman is right; we have to find out who this Sousa is.' He nodded to Stafford. 'Go ahead. Anything you want is okay. Just keep after it. And we'll get going on it, too—as soon as we check in at our office.'

The engineer, paying attention to his headphones, interrupted all at once. 'An answer's coming.' He began rapidly to scribble; the others collected around him to see.

HERBERT SOUSA OF SACRAMENTO, CALIFORNIA, IS THE DEVIL. SINCE HE IS THE INCARNATION OF SATAN ON EARTH, PROVIDENCE DEMANDS HIS DESTRUCTION. I AM ONLY AN AGENCY, A SO TO SPEAK CREATURE, OF THE DIVINE MAJESTY, AS ARE ALL OF YOU.

There was a pause as the engineer waited, clenching the ball-point metal government-issue pen, and then he spasmodically added:

Convulsively, the engineer tossed the pen against the far wall. It
bounced, rolled off, disappeared. No one spoke.

V

The engineer said finally, 'We have here a sick, deranged piece of
electronic junk. We were right. Thank God we caught it in time.
It's psychotic. Cosmic, schizophrenic delusions of the reality of
archetypes. Good grief, the machine regards itself as an instrument of God! It has one more of those "God talked to me, yes, He
truly did" complexes.'

'Medieval,' one of the FBI men said, with a twitch of enormous
nervousness. He and his group had become rigid with tension.
'We've uncovered a rat's nest with that last question. How'll we
clear this up? We can't let this leak out to the newspapers; no one'll
ever trust a GB-class system again. I don't. I wouldn't.' He eyed the
computer with nauseated aversion.

Stafford wondered, What do you say to a machine when it
acquires a belief in witchcraft? This isn't New England in the seventeenth century. Are we supposed to make Sousa walk over hot
coals without being burned? Or get dunked without drowning?
Are we supposed to *prove* to Genux-B that Sousa is not Satan? And
if so, how? What would it regard as proof?

And where did it get the idea in the first place?

He said to the engineer, 'Ask it how it discovered that Herbert
Sousa is the Evil One. Go ahead; I'm serious. Type out a card.'

The answer, after an interval, appeared via the government-
issue ballpoint pen for all of them to see.

WHEN HE BEGAN BY MIRACLE TO CREATE LIVING BEINGS
OUT OF NONLIVING CLAY, SUCH AS, FOR EXAMPLE, MYSELF.

'That trinket?' Stafford demanded, incredulous. 'That charm bracelet bit of plastic? You call that a living being?'

The question, put to Genux-B, got an immediate answer.

THAT IS AN INSTANCE, YES.

'This poses an interesting question,' one of the FBI men said. 'Evidently it regards itself as alive—putting aside the question of Herb Sousa entirely. And we built it; or, rather, you did.' He indicated Stafford and the engineer. 'So what does that make us? From its ground premise we created living beings, too.'

The observation, put to Genux-B, got a long, solemn answer which Stafford barely glanced over; he caught the nitty-gritty at once.

YOU BUILT ME IN ACCORD WITH THE WISHES OF THE
DIVINE CREATOR. WHAT YOU PERFORMED WAS A
SACRED REENACTMENT OF THE ORIGINAL HOLY
MIRACLE OF THE FIRST WEEK (AS THE SCRIPTURES
PUT IT) OF EARTH'S LIFE. THIS IS ANOTHER MATTER
ENTIRELY. AND I REMAIN AT THE SERVICE OF THE
CREATOR, AS YOU DO. AND, IN ADDITION—

'What it boils down to,' the engineer said dryly, 'is this. The computer writes off its own existence—naturally—as an act of legitimate miracle-passing. But what Sousa has got going for him in those gum machines—or what it thinks he's got going—is unsanctioned and therefore demonic. Sinful. Deserving God's wrath. But what further interests me is this: Genux-B has sensed that it couldn't tell us the situation. It knew we wouldn't share its views. It preferred a thermonuclear attack, rather than telling us. When it was forced to tell us, it decided to call off the Red Alert. There are levels and levels to its cognition . . . none of which I find too attractive.'

Stafford said, 'It's got to be shut down. Permanently.' They had been right to bring him into this, right to want his probing and diagnosis; he now agreed with them thoroughly. Only the tech-

HOLY QUARREL

nical problem of defusing the enormous complex remained. And between him and the engineer it could be done; the men who designed it and the men who maintained it could easily take it out of action. For good.

'Do we have to get a presidential order?' the engineer asked the FBI men.

'Go do your work; we'll get the order later,' one of the FBI men answered. 'We're empowered to counsel you to take whatever action you see fit.' He added, 'And don't waste any time—if you want my opinion.' The other FBI men nodded their agreement.

Licking his dry lips, Stafford said to the engineer, 'Well, let's go. Let's destruct as much of it as we need to.'

The two of them walked cautiously toward Genux-B, which, via the output line, was still explaining its position.

Early in the morning, as the sun began to rise, the FBI flapple let Stafford off at the roof field of his conapt building. Dog-tired, he descended by descy to his own tier and floor.

Presently he had unlocked his door, had entered the dark, stale-smelling living room on his way to the bedroom. Rest. That was needed, and plenty of it . . . considering the night of difficult, painstaking work dismantling crucial turrets and elements of Genux-B until it was disabled. Neutralized.

Or at least so they hoped.

As he removed his work smock, three hard brightly colored little spheres bounced noisily from a pocket to the floor of the bedroom; he retrieved them, laid them on the vanity table.

Three, he thought. Didn't I eat one?

The FBI man gave me three and I chewed one up. I've got too many left, one too many.

Wearily, he finished undressing, crept into bed for the hour or so of sleep left to him. The hell with it.

At nine the alarm clock rang. He woke groggily and without volition got to his feet and stood by the bed, swaying and rubbing his swollen eyes. Then, reflexively, he began to dress.

On the vanity table lay four gaily colored balls.

He said to himself, I *know* that I put only three there last night. Perplexed, he studied them, wondering blearily what—if anything—this meant. Binary fission? Loaves and fishes all over again?

He laughed sharply. The mood of the night before remained, clinging to him. But single cells grew as large as this. The ostrich egg consisted of one single cell, the largest on Terra—or on the other planets beyond. And these were much smaller.

We didn't think of that, he said to himself. We thought about eggs that might hatch into something awful, but not unicellular organisms that in the old primitive way divide. And they are organic compounds.

He left the apartment, left the four gum balls on the vanity table as he departed for work. A great deal lay ahead of him: a report directly to the President to determine whether all Genux-B computers ought to be shut down and, if not, what could be done to make certain they did not, like the local one, become superstitiously deranged.

A machine, he thought. Believing in the Evil Spirit entrenched solidly on Earth. A mass of solid-state circuitry diving deep into age-old theology, with divine creation and miracles on one side and the diabolic on the other. Plunged back into the Dark Ages, and by a man-made electronic construct, not by one of us humans.

And they say humans are prone to error.

When he returned home that night—after participating in the dismantling of every Genux-B-style computer on Earth—seven colored spheres of candy-coated gum lay in a group on the vanity table, waiting for him.

It would create quite a gum empire, he decided as he scrutinized the seven bright balls, all the same color. Not much overhead, to say the least. And no dispenser would ever become empty—not at this rate.

Going to the vidphone, he picked up the receiver and began to dial the emergency number which the FBI men had given him.

And then reluctantly hung up.

It was beginning to look as if the computer had been right, hard as that was to admit. And it had been his decision to go ahead and dismantle it.

But the other part was worse. How could he report to the FBI that he had in his possession seven candy-coated balls of gum? Even if they did divide. That in itself would be even harder to report. Even if he could establish that they consisted of illegal—and rare—non-terrestrial primitive life forms smuggled to Terra from God knew what bleak planet.

Better to live and let live. Perhaps their reproduction cycle would settle down; perhaps after a period of swift binary fission they would adapt to a terran environment and stabilize. After that he could forget about it.

And he could flush them down the incinerator chute of his conapt.

He did so.

But evidently he missed one. Probably, being round, it had rolled off the vanity table. He found it two days later, under the bed, with fifteen like it. So once more he tried to get rid of them all—and again he missed one; again he found a new nest the following day, and this time he counted forty of them.

Naturally, he began to chew up as many as possible—and as fast. And he tried boiling them—at least the ones he could find—in hot water. He even tried spraying them with an indoor insect bomb.

At the end of a week, he had 15,832 of them filling the bedroom of his conapt. By this time chewing them out of existence, spraying them out of existence, boiling them out of existence—all had become impractical.

At the end of the month, despite having a scavenger truck haul away as much as it could take, he computed that he owned two million.

Ten days later—from a pay phone down at the corner—he fatalistically called the FBI. But by then they were no longer able to answer the vidphone.

WE CAN REMEMBER IT FOR YOU WHOLESALE

He awoke—and wanted Mars. The valleys, he thought. What would it be like to trudge among them? Great and greater yet: the dream grew as he became fully conscious, the dream and the yearning. He could almost feel the enveloping presence of the other world, which only government agents and high officials had seen. A clerk like himself? Not likely.

'Are you getting up or not?' his wife Kirsten asked drowsily, with her usual hint of fierce crossness. 'If you are, push the hot coffee button on the darn stove.'

'Okay,' Douglas Quail said, and made his way barefoot from the bedroom of their conapt to the kitchen. There, having dutifully pressed the hot coffee button, he seated himself at the kitchen table, brought out a yellow, small tin of fine Dean Swift snuff. He inhaled briskly, and the Beau Nash mixture stung his nose, burned the roof of his mouth. But still he inhaled; it woke him up and allowed his dreams, his nocturnal desires and random wishes, to condense into a semblance of rationality.

I will go, he said to himself. *Before I die I'll see Mars.*

It was, of course, impossible, and he knew this even as he dreamed. But the daylight, the mundane noise of his wife now brushing her hair before the bedroom mirror—everything conspired to remind him of what he was. *A miserable little salaried employee*, he said to himself with bitterness. Kirsten reminded him of this at least once a day and he did not blame her; it was a wife's job to bring her husband down to Earth. *Down to Earth*, he thought, and laughed. The figure of speech in this was literally apt.

'What are you sniggering about?' his wife asked as she swept into the kitchen, her long busy-pink robe wagging after her. 'A dream, I bet. You're always full of them.'

'Yes,' he said, and gazed out the kitchen window at the hover-cars and traffic runnels, and all the little energetic people hurrying to work. In a little while he would be among them. As always.

'I'll bet it had to do with some woman,' Kirsten said witheringly.

'No,' he said. 'A god. The god of war. He has wonderful craters with every kind of plant-life growing deep down in them.'

'Listen.' Kirsten crouched down beside him and spoke earnestly, the harsh quality momentarily gone from her voice. 'The bottom of the ocean—*our* ocean is much more, an infinity of times more beautiful. You know that; everyone knows that. Rent an artificial gill-outfit for both of us, take a week off from work, and we can descend and live down there at one of those year-round aquatic resorts. And in addition—' She broke off. 'You're not listening. You should be. Here is something a lot better than that compulsion, that obsession you have about Mars, and you don't even listen!' Her voice rose piercingly. 'God in heaven, you're doomed, Doug! What's going to become of you?'

'I'm going to work,' he said, rising to his feet, his breakfast forgotten. 'That's what's going to become of me.'

She eyed him. 'You're getting worse. More fanatical every day. Where's it going to lead?'

'To Mars,' he said, and opened the door to the closet to get down a fresh shirt to wear to work.

Having descended from the taxi Douglas Quail slowly walked across three densely-populated foot runnels and to the modern, attractively inviting doorway. There he halted, impeding mid-morning traffic, and with caution read the shifting-color neon sign. He had, in the past, scrutinized this sign before ... but never had he come so close. This was very different; what he did now was something else. Something which sooner or later had to happen.

Was this the answer? After all, an illusion, no matter how convincing, remained nothing more than an illusion. At least objectively. But subjectively—quite the opposite entirely.

And anyhow he had an appointment. Within the next five minutes.

Taking a deep breath of mildly smog-infested Chicago air, he walked through the dazzling polychromatic shimmer of the doorway and up to the receptionist's counter.

The nicely-articulated blonde at the counter, bare-bosomed and tidy, said pleasantly, 'Good morning, Mr Quail.'

'Yes,' he said. 'I'm here to see about a Rekal course. As I guess you know.'

'Not "rekal" but recall,' the receptionist corrected him. She picked up the receiver of the vidphone by her smooth elbow and said into it, 'Mr Douglas Quail is here, Mr McClane. May he come inside, now? Or is it too soon?'

'Giz wetwa wum-wum wamp,' the phone mumbled.

'Yes, Mr Quail,' she said. 'You may go in; Mr McClane is expecting you.' As he started off uncertainly she called after him, 'Room D, Mr Quail. To your right.'

After a frustrating but brief moment of being lost he found the proper room. The door hung open and inside, at a big genuine walnut desk, sat a genial-looking man, middle-aged, wearing the latest Martian frog-pelt gray suit; his attire alone would have told Quail that he had come to the right person.

'Sit down, Douglas,' McClane said, waving his plump hand toward a chair which faced the desk. 'So you want to have gone to Mars. Very good.'

Quail seated himself, feeling tense. 'I'm not so sure this is worth the fee,' he said. 'It costs a lot and as far as I can see I really get nothing.' *Costs almost as much as going*, he thought.

'You get tangible proof of your trip,' McClane disagreed emphatically. 'All the proof you'll need. Here; I'll show you.' He dug within a drawer of his impressive desk. 'Ticket stub.' Reaching into a manila folder, he produced a small square of embossed cardboard. 'It proves you went—and returned. Postcards.' He laid out four franked picture 3-D full-color postcards in a neatly-arranged row on the desk for Quail to see. 'Film. Shots you took of local sights on Mars with a rented moving camera.' To Quail he displayed those, too. 'Plus the names of people you met, two hundred poscreds' worth of souvenirs, which will arrive—from Mars—within the following month. And passport, certificates listing the shots you received. And more.' He glanced up keenly at Quail. 'You'll know you went, all right,' he said. 'You won't remember us, won't remember me or ever having been here. It'll be a real trip in your mind; we guarantee that. A full two weeks of recall; every last piddling detail. Remember this: if at any time you doubt that you really took an extensive trip to Mars you can return here and get a full refund. You see?'

'But I didn't go,' Quail said. 'I won't have gone, no matter what proofs you provide me with.' He took a deep, unsteady breath. 'And I never was a secret agent with Interplan.' It seemed impossible to him that Rekal, Incorporated's extra-factual memory implant would do its job—despite what he had heard people say.

'Mr Quail,' McClane said patiently. 'As you explained in your letter to us, you have no chance, no possibility in the slightest, of ever actually getting to Mars; you can't afford it, and what is much more important, you could never qualify as an undercover agent for Interplan or anybody else. This is the only way you can achieve your, ahem, life-long dream; am I not correct, sir? You can't be this; you can't actually do this.' He chuckled. 'But you can *have been* and *have done*. We see to that. And our fee is reasonable; no hidden charges.' He smiled encouragingly.

'Is an extra-factual memory that convincing?' Quail asked.

'More than the real thing, sir. Had you really gone to Mars as an Interplan agent, you would by now have forgotten a great deal; our analysis of true-mem systems—authentic recollections of major events in a person's life—shows that a variety of details are very quickly lost to the person. Forever. Part of the package we offer you is such deep implantation of recall that nothing is forgotten. The packet which is fed to you while you're comatose is the creation of trained experts, men who have spent years on Mars; in every case we verify details down to the last iota. And you've picked a rather easy extra-factual system; had you picked Pluto or wanted to be Emperor of the Inner Planet Alliance we'd have much more difficulty . . . and the charges would be considerably greater.'

Reaching into his coat for his wallet, Quail said, 'Okay. It's been my life-long ambition and so I see I'll never really do it. So I guess I'll have to settle for this.'

'Don't think of it that way,' McClane said severely. 'You're not accepting second-best. The actual memory, with all its vagueness, omissions and ellipses, not to say distortions—that's second-best.' He accepted the money and pressed a button on his desk. 'All right, Mr Quail,' he said, as the door of his office opened and two burly men swiftly entered. 'You're on your way to Mars as a secret agent.' He rose, came over to shake Quail's nervous, moist hand. 'Or rather, you have been on your way. This afternoon at four-thirty you will, um, arrive back here on Terra; a cab will leave you off at your conapt and as I say you will never remember seeing me or coming here; you won't, in fact, even remember having heard of our existence.'

His mouth dry with nervousness, Quail followed the two technicians from the office; what happened next depended on them.

Will I actually believe I've been on Mars? he wondered. *That I managed to fulfill my lifetime ambition?* He had a strange, lingering intuition that something would go wrong. But just what—he did not know.

He would have to wait and find out.

The intercom on McClane's desk, which connected him with the work area of the firm, buzzed and a voice said, 'Mr Quail is under sedation now, sir. Do you want to supervise this one, or shall we go ahead?'

'It's routine,' McClane observed. 'You may go ahead, Lowe; I don't think you'll run into any trouble.' Programming an artificial memory of a trip to another planet—with or without the added fillip of being a secret agent—showed up on the firm's work-schedule with monotonous regularity. *In one month*, he calculated wryly, *we must do twenty of these . . . ersatz interplanetary travel has become our bread and butter.*

'Whatever you say, Mr McClane,' Lowe's voice came, and there-upon the intercom shut off.

Going to the vault section in the chamber behind his office, McClane searched about for a Three packet—trip to Mars—and a Sixty-two packet: secret Interplan spy. Finding the two packets, he returned with them to his desk, seated himself comfortably, poured out the contents—merchandise which would be planted in Quail's conapt while the lab technicians busied themselves install-ing false memory.

A one-poscred sneaky-pete side arm, McClane reflected; *that's the largest item. Sets us back financially the most.* Then a pellet-sized trans-mitter, which could be swallowed if the agent were caught. Code book that astonishingly resembled the real thing . . . the firm's models were highly accurate: based, whenever possible, on actual US military issue. Odd bits which made no intrinsic sense but which would be woven into the warp and woof of Quail's imaginary trip, would coincide with his memory: half an ancient silver fifty-cent piece, several quotations from John Donne's sermons written incorrectly, each on a separate piece of transparent tissue-thin paper, several match folders from bars on Mars, a stainless steel spoon engraved PROPERTY OF DOME-MARS NATIONAL KIB-BUZIM, a wire-tapping coil which—

The intercom buzzed. 'Mr McClane, I'm sorry to bother you but something rather ominous has come up. Maybe it would be better if you were in here after all. Quail is already under sedation; he reacted well to the narkidrine; he's completely unconscious and receptive. But—'

'I'll be in.' Sensing trouble, McClane left his office; a moment later he emerged in the work area.

On a hygienic bed lay Douglas Quail, breathing slowly and

regularly, his eyes virtually shut; he seemed dimly—but only dimly—aware of the two technicians and now McClane himself.

'There's no space to insert false memory-patterns?' McClane felt irritation. 'Merely drop out two work weeks; he's employed as a clerk at the West Coast Emigration Bureau, which is a government agency, so he undoubtedly has or had two weeks' vacation within the last year. That ought to do it.' Petty details annoyed him. And always would.

'Our problem,' Lowe said sharply, 'is something quite different.' He bent over the bed, said to Quail, 'Tell Mr McClane what you told us.' To McClane he said, 'Listen closely.'

The gray-green eyes of the man lying supine in the bed focussed on McClane's face. The eyes, he observed uneasily, had become hard; they had a polished, inorganic quality, like semi-precious tumbled stones. He was not sure that he liked what he saw; the brilliance was too cold. 'What do you want now?' Quail said harshly. 'You've broken my cover. Get out of here before I take you all apart.' He studied McClane. 'Especially you,' he continued. 'You're in charge of this counter-operation.'

Lowe said, 'How long were you on Mars?'

'One month,' Quail said gratingly.

'And your purpose there?' Lowe demanded.

The meager lips twisted; Quail eyed him and did not speak. At last, drawling the words out so that they dripped with hostility, he said, 'Agent for Interplan. As I already told you. Don't you record everything that's said? Play your vid-aud tape back for your boss and leave me alone.' He shut his eyes, then; the hard brilliance ceased. McClane felt, instantly, a rushing splurge of relief.

Lowe said quietly, 'This is a tough man, Mr McClane.'

'He won't be,' McClane said, 'after we arrange for him to lose his memory-chain again. He'll be as meek as before.' To Quail he said, 'So *this* is why you wanted to go to Mars so terribly bad.'

Without opening his eyes Quail said, 'I never wanted to go to Mars. I was assigned it—they handed it to me and there I was: stuck. Oh yeah, I admit I was curious about it; who wouldn't be?'

Again he opened his eyes and surveyed the three of them, McClane in particular. 'Quite a truth drug you've got here; it brought up things I had absolutely no memory of.' He pondered. 'I wonder about Kirsten,' he said, half to himself. 'Could she be in on it? An Interplan contact keeping an eye on me . . . to be certain I didn't regain my memory? No wonder she's been so derisive about my wanting to go there.' Faintly, he smiled; the smile—one of understanding—disappeared almost at once.

McClane said, 'Please believe me, Mr Quail; we stumbled onto this entirely by accident. In the work we do—'

'I believe you,' Quail said. He seemed tired, now; the drug was continuing to pull him under, deeper and deeper. 'Where did I say I'd been?' he murmured. 'Mars? Hard to remember—I know I'd like to see it; so would everybody else. But me—' His voice trailed off. 'Just a clerk, a nothing clerk.'

Straightening up, Lowe said to his superior, 'He wants a false memory implanted that corresponds to a trip he actually took. And a false reason which is the real reason. He's telling the truth; he's a long way down in the narkidrine. The trip is very vivid in his mind—at least under sedation. But apparently he doesn't recall it otherwise. Someone, probably at a government military-sciences lab, erased his conscious memories; all he knew was that going to Mars meant something special to him, and so did being a secret agent. They couldn't erase that; it's not a memory but a desire, undoubtedly the same one that motivated him to volunteer for the assignment in the first place.'

The other technician, Keeler, said to McClane, 'What do we do? Graft a false memory-pattern over the real memory? There's no telling what the results would be; he might remember some of the genuine trip, and the confusion might bring on a psychotic interlude. He'd have to hold two opposite premises in his mind simultaneously: that he went to Mars and that he didn't. That he's a genuine agent for Interplan and he's not, that it's spurious. I think we ought to revive him without any false memory implantation and send him out of here; this is hot.'

'Agreed,' McClane said. A thought came to him. 'Can you predict what he'll remember when he comes out of sedation?'

'Impossible to tell,' Lowe said. 'He probably will have some dim, diffuse memory of his actual trip, now. And he'd probably be in grave doubt as to its validity; he'd probably decide our programming slipped a gear-tooth. And he'd remember coming here; that wouldn't be erased—unless you want it erased.'

'The less we mess with this man,' McClane said, 'the better I like it. This is nothing for us to fool around with; we've been foolish enough to—or unlucky enough to—uncover a genuine Interplan spy who has a cover so perfect that up to now even he didn't know what he was—or rather is.' The sooner they washed their hands of the man calling himself Douglas Quail the better.

'Are you going to plant packets Three and Sixty-two in his conapt?' Lowe said.

'No,' McClane said. 'And we're going to return half his fee.'

'"Half"! Why half?'

McClane said lamely, 'It seems to be a good compromise.'

As the cab carried him back to his conapt at the residential end of Chicago, Douglas Quail said to himself, *It's sure good to be back on Terra.*

Already the month-long period on Mars had begun to waver in his memory; he had only an image of profound gaping craters, an ever-present ancient erosion of hills, of vitality, of motion itself. A world of dust where little happened, where a good part of the day was spent checking and rechecking one's portable oxygen source. And then the life forms, the unassuming and modest gray-brown cacti and maw-worms.

As a matter of fact he had brought back several moribund examples of Martian fauna; he had smuggled them through customs. After all, they posed no menace; they couldn't survive in Earth's heavy atmosphere.

Reaching into his coat pocket, he rummaged for the container of Martian maw-worms—

And found an envelope instead.

Lifting it out, he discovered, to his perplexity, that it contained five hundred and seventy poscreds, in cred bills of low denomination.

Where'd I get this? he asked himself. *Didn't I spend every 'cred I had on my trip?*

With the money came a slip of paper marked: *One-half fee ret'd. By McClane.* And then the date. Today's date.

'Recall,' he said aloud.

'Recall what, sir or madam?' the robot driver of the cab inquired respectfully.

'Do you have a phone book?' Quail demanded.

'Certainly, sir or madam.' A slot opened; from it slid a micro-tape phone book for Cook County.

'It's spelled oddly,' Quail said as he leafed through the pages of the yellow section. He felt fear, then; abiding fear. 'Here it is,' he said. 'Take me there, to Rekal, Incorporated. I've changed my mind; I don't want to go home.'

'Yes, sir or madam, as the case may be,' the driver said. A moment later the cab was zipping back in the opposite direction.

'May I make use of your phone?' he asked.

'Be my guest,' the robot driver said. And presented a shiny new emperor 3-D color phone to him.

He dialed his own conapt. And after a pause found himself confronted by a miniature but chillingly realistic image of Kirsten on the small screen. 'I've been to Mars,' he said to her.

'You're drunk.' Her lips writhed scornfully. 'Or worse.'

''S God's truth.'

'When?' she demanded.

'I don't know.' He felt confused. 'A simulated trip, I think. By means of one of those artificial or extra-factual or whatever it is memory places. It didn't take.'

Kirsten said witheringly, 'You *are* drunk.' And broke the connection at her end. He hung up, then, feeling his face flush. *Always the same tone,* he said hotly to himself. *Always the retort, as if she knows everything and I know nothing. What a marriage. Keerist,* he thought dismally.

A moment later the cab stopped at the curb before a modern, very attractive little pink building, over which a shifting polychromatic neon sign read: REKAL, INCORPORATED.

The receptionist, chic and bare from the waist up, started in surprise, then gained masterful control of herself. 'Oh, hello, Mr Quail,' she said nervously. 'H-how are you? Did you forget something?'

'The rest of my fee back,' he said.

More composed now, the receptionist said, 'Fee? I think you are mistaken, Mr Quail. You were here discussing the feasibility of an extra-factual trip for you, but–' She shrugged her smooth pale shoulders. 'As I understand it, no trip was taken.'

Quail said, 'I remember everything, miss. My letter to Rekal, Incorporated, which started this whole business off. I remember my arrival here, my visit with Mr McClane. Then the two lab technicians taking me in tow and administering a drug to put me out.' No wonder the firm had returned half his fee. The false memory of his 'trip to Mars' hadn't taken–at least not entirely, not as he had been assured.

'Mr Quail,' the girl said, 'although you are a minor clerk you are a good-looking man and it spoils your features to become angry. If it would make you feel any better, I might, ahem, let you take me out . . .'

He felt furious, then. 'I remember you,' he said savagely. 'For instance the fact that your breasts are sprayed blue; that stuck in my mind. And I remember Mr McClane's promise that if I remembered my visit to Rekal, Incorporated I'd receive my money back in full. Where is Mr McClane?'

After a delay–probably as long as they could manage–he found himself once more seated facing the imposing walnut desk, exactly as he had been an hour or so earlier in the day.

'Some technique you have,' Quail said sardonically. His disappointment–and resentment–was enormous, by now. 'My so-called "memory" of a trip to Mars as an undercover agent for Interplan is hazy and vague and shot full of contradictions. And I clearly remember my dealings here with you people. I ought to take this to the Better Business Bureau.' He was burning angry, at this point; his sense of being cheated had overwhelmed him, had destroyed his customary aversion to participating in a public squabble.

Looking morose, as well as cautious, McClane said, 'We capitulate, Quail. We'll refund the balance of your fee. I fully concede the fact that we did absolutely nothing for you.' His tone was resigned.

Quail said accusingly, 'You didn't even provide me with the various artifacts that you claimed would "prove" to me I had been on Mars. All that song-and-dance you went into—it hasn't materialized into a damn thing. Not even a ticket stub. Nor postcards. Nor passport. Nor proof of immunization shots. Nor—'

'Listen, Quail,' McClane said. 'Suppose I told you—' He broke off. 'Let it go.' He pressed a button on his intercom. 'Shirley, will you disburse five hundred and seventy more 'creds in the form of a cashier's check made out to Douglas Quail? Thank you.' He released the button, then glared at Quail.

Presently the check appeared; the receptionist placed it before McClane and once more vanished out of sight, leaving the two men alone, still facing each other across the surface of the massive walnut desk.

'Let me give you a word of advice,' McClane said as he signed the check and passed it over. 'Don't discuss your, ahem, recent trip to Mars with anyone.'

'What trip?'

'Well, that's the thing.' Doggedly, McClane said, 'The trip you partially remember. Act as if you don't remember; pretend it never took place. Don't ask me why; just take my advice: it'll be better for all of us.' He had begun to perspire. Freely. 'Now, Mr Quail, I have other business, other clients to see.' He rose, showed Quail to the door.

Quail said, as he opened the door, 'A firm that turns out such bad work shouldn't have any clients at all.' He shut the door behind him.

On the way home in the cab Quail pondered the wording of his letter of complaint to the Better Business Bureau, Terra Division. As soon as he could get to his typewriter he'd get started; it was clearly his duty to warn other people away from Rekal, Incorporated.

When he got back to his conapt he seated himself before his Hermes Rocket portable, opened the drawers and rummaged for carbon paper—and noticed a small, familiar box. A box which he had carefully filled on Mars with Martian fauna and later smuggled through customs.

Opening the box he saw, to his disbelief, six dead maw-worms and several varieties of the unicellular life on which the Martian worms fed. The protozoa were dried-up, dusty, but he recognized them; it had taken him an entire day picking among the vast dark alien boulders to find them. A wonderful, illuminated journey of discovery.

But I didn't go to Mars, he realized.

Yet on the other hand—

Kirsten appeared at the doorway to the room, an armload of pale brown groceries gripped. 'Why are you home in the middle of the day?' Her voice, in an eternity of sameness, was accusing.

'*Did I go to Mars?*' he asked her. 'You would know.'

'No, of course you didn't go to Mars; *you* would know that, I would think. Aren't you always bleating about going?'

He said, 'By God, I think I went.' After a pause he added, 'And simultaneously I think I didn't go.'

'Make up your mind.'

'How can I?' He gestured. 'I have both memory-tracks grafted inside my head; one is real and one isn't but I can't tell which is which. Why can't I rely on you? They haven't tinkered with you.' She could do this much for him at least—even if she never did anything else.

Kirsten said in a level, controlled voice, 'Doug, if you don't pull yourself together, we're through. I'm going to leave you.'

'I'm in trouble.' His voice came out husky and coarse. And shaking. 'Probably I'm heading into a psychotic episode; I hope not, but—maybe that's it. It would explain everything, anyhow.'

Setting down the bag of groceries, Kirsten stalked to the closet.

'I was not kidding,' she said to him quietly. She brought out a coat, got it on, walked back to the door of the conapt. 'I'll phone you one of these days soon,' she said tonelessly. 'This is goodbye, Doug. I hope you pull out of this eventually; I really pray you do. For your sake.'

'Wait,' he said desperately. 'Just tell me and make it absolute; I did go or I didn't—tell me which one.' *But they may have altered your memory-track also,* he realized.

The door closed. His wife had left. Finally!

A voice behind him said, 'Well, that's that. Now put up your hands, Quail. And also please turn around and face this way.'

He turned, instinctively, without raising his hands.

The man who faced him wore the plum uniform of the Interplan Police Agency, and his gun appeared to be UN issue. And, for some odd reason, he seemed familiar to Quail; familiar in a blurred, distorted fashion which he could not pin down. So, jerkily, he raised his hands.

'You remember,' the policeman said, 'your trip to Mars. We know all your actions today and all your thoughts—in particular your very important thoughts on the trip home from Rekal, Incorporated.' He explained, 'We have a tele-transmitter wired within your skull; it keeps us constantly informed.'

A telepathic transmitter; use of a living plasma that had been discovered on Luna. He shuddered with self-aversion. The thing lived inside him, within his own brain, feeding, listening, feeding. But the Interplan police used them; that had come out even in the homeopapes. So this was probably true, dismal as it was.

'Why me?' Quail said huskily. What had he done—or thought? And what did this have to do with Rekal, Incorporated?

'Fundamentally,' the Interplan cop said, 'this has nothing to do with Rekal; it's between you and us.' He tapped his right ear. 'I'm still picking up your mentational processes by way of your cephalic transmitter.' In the man's ear Quail saw a small white-plastic plug. 'So I have to warn you: anything you think may be held against you.' He smiled. 'Not that it matters now; you've already thought and spoken yourself into oblivion. What's annoying is the fact that under narkidrine at Rekal, Incorporated you told them, their technicians and the owner, Mr McClane, about your trip—where you went, for whom, some of what you did. They're very frightened. They wish they had never laid eyes on you.' He added reflectively, 'They're right.'

Quail said, 'I never made any trip. It's a false memory-chain improperly planted in me by McClane's technicians.' But then he thought of the box, in his desk drawer, containing the Martian life forms. And the trouble and hardship he had had gathering them. The memory seemed real. And the box of life forms; that certainly was real. Unless McClane had planted it. Perhaps this was one of the 'proofs' which McClane had talked glibly about.

The memory of my trip to Mars, he thought, *doesn't convince me—but unfortunately it has convinced the Interplan Police Agency. They think I really went to Mars and they think I at least partially realize it.*

'We not only know you went to Mars,' the Interplan cop agreed, in answer to his thoughts, 'but we know that you now remember enough to be difficult for us. And there's no use expunging your conscious memory of all this, because if we do you'll simply show up at Rekal, Incorporated again and start over. And we can't do anything about McClane and his operation because we have no jurisdiction over anyone except our own people. Anyhow, McClane hasn't committed any crime.' He eyed Quail. 'Nor, technically, have you. You didn't go to Rekal, Incorporated with the idea of regaining your memory; you went, as we realize, for the usual reason people go there—a love by plain, dull people for adventure.' He added, 'Unfortunately you're not plain, not dull, and you've already had too much excitement; the last thing in the universe you needed was a course from Rekal, Incorporated. Nothing could have been more lethal for you or for us. And, for that matter, for McClane.'

Quail said, 'Why is it "difficult" for you if I remember my trip— my alleged trip—and what I did there?'

'Because,' the Interplan harness bull said, 'what you did is not in accord with our great white all-protecting father public image. You did, for us, what we never do. As you'll presently remember—thanks to narkidrine. That box of dead worms and algae has been sitting in your desk drawer for six months, ever since you got back. And at no time have you shown the slightest curiosity about it. We didn't even know you had it until you remembered it on your way home from Rekal; then we came here on the double to look for it.' He added, unnecessarily, 'Without any luck; there wasn't enough time.'

A second Interplan cop joined the first one; the two briefly conferred. Meanwhile, Quail thought rapidly. He did remember more, now; the cop had been right about narkidrine. They—Interplan—probably used it themselves. Probably? He knew darn well they did; he had seen them putting a prisoner on it. Where would *that* be? Somewhere on Terra? More likely on Luna, he decided, viewing the image rising from his highly defective—but rapidly less so—memory.

And he remembered something else. Their reason for sending him to Mars; the job he had done.

No wonder they had expunged his memory.

'Oh, God,' the first of the two Interplan cops said, breaking off his conversation with his companion. Obviously, he had picked up Quail's thoughts. 'Well, this is a far worse problem, now; as bad as it can get.' He walked toward Quail, again covering him with his gun. 'We've got to kill you,' he said. 'And right away.'

Nervously, his fellow officer said, 'Why right away? Can't we simply cart him off to Interplan New York and let them—'

'*He* knows why it has to be right away,' the first cop said; he too looked nervous, now, but Quail realized that it was for an entirely different reason. His memory had been brought back almost entirely, now. And he fully understood the officer's tension.

'On Mars,' Quail said hoarsely, 'I killed a man. After getting past fifteen bodyguards. Some armed with sneaky-pete guns, the way you are.' He had been trained, by Interplan, over a five-year period to be an assassin. A professional killer. He knew ways to take out armed adversaries . . . such as these two officers; and the one with the ear-receiver knew it, too.

If he moved swiftly enough–

The gun fired. But he had already moved to one side, and at the same time he chopped down the gun-carrying officer. In an instant he had possession of the gun and was covering the other, confused, officer.

'Picked my thoughts up,' Quail said, panting for breath. 'He knew what I was going to do, but I did it anyhow.'

Half sitting up, the injured officer grated, 'He won't use that gun on you, Sam; I pick that up, too. He knows he's finished, and he knows we know it, too. Come on, Quail.' Laboriously, grunting with pain, he got shakily to his feet. He held out his hand. 'The gun,' he said to Quail. 'You can't use it, and if you turn it over to me I'll guarantee not to kill you; you'll be given a hearing, and someone higher up in Interplan will decide, not me. Maybe they can erase your memory once more, I don't know. But you know the thing I was going to kill you for; I couldn't keep you from remembering it. So my reason for wanting to kill you is in a sense past.'

Quail, clutching the gun, bolted from the conapt, sprinted for the elevator. *If you follow me*, he thought, *I'll kill you. So don't.* He jabbed at the elevator button and, a moment later, the doors slid back.

The police hadn't followed him. Obviously they had picked up his terse, tense thoughts and had decided not to take the chance.

With him inside the elevator descended. He had gotten away– for a time. But what next? Where could he go?

The elevator reached the ground floor; a moment later Quail had joined the mob of peds hurrying along the runnels. His head ached and he felt sick. But at least he had evaded death; they had come very close to shooting him on the spot, back in his own conapt.

And they probably will again, he decided. *When they find me. And with this transmitter inside me, that won't take too long.*

Ironically, he had gotten exactly what he had asked Rekal, Incorporated for. Adventure, peril, Interplan police at work, a secret and dangerous trip to Mars in which his life was at stake– everything he had wanted as a false memory.

The advantages of it being a memory—and nothing more—could now be appreciated.

On a park bench, alone, he sat dully watching a flock of perts: a semi-bird imported from Mars' two moons, capable of soaring flight, even against Earth's huge gravity.

Maybe I can find my way back to Mars, he pondered. But then what? It would be worse on Mars; the political organization whose leader he had assassinated would spot him the moment he stepped from the ship; he would have Interplan and *them* after him, there.

Can you hear me thinking? he wondered. Easy avenue to paranoia; sitting here alone he felt them tuning in on him, monitoring, recording, discussing . . . He shivered, rose to his feet, walked aimlessly, his hands deep in his pockets. *No matter where I go*, he realized, *you'll always be with me. As long as I have this device inside my head.*

I'll make a deal with you, he thought to himself—and to them. *Can you imprint a false-memory template on me again, as you did before, that I lived an average, routine life, never went to Mars? Never saw an Interplan uniform up close and never handled a gun?*

A voice inside his brain answered, 'As has been carefully explained to you: that would not be enough.'

Astonished, he halted.

'We formerly communicated with you in this manner,' the voice continued. 'When you were operating in the field, on Mars. It's been months since we've done it; we assumed, in fact, that we'd never have to do so again. Where are you?'

'Walking,' Quail said, 'to my death.' *By your officers' guns*, he added as an afterthought. 'How can you be sure it wouldn't be enough?' he demanded. 'Don't the Rekal techniques work?'

'As we said. If you're given a set of standard, average memories you get—restless. You'd inevitably seek out Rekal or one of its competitors again. We can't go through this a second time.'

'Suppose,' Quail said, 'once my authentic memories have been canceled, something more vital than standard memories are implanted. Something which would act to satisfy my craving,' he said. 'That's been proved; that's probably why you initially hired me. But you ought to be able to come up with something else— something equal. I was the richest man on Terra but I finally gave all my money to educational foundations. Or I was a famous deep-space explorer. Anything of that sort; wouldn't one of those do?'

Silence.

'Try it,' he said desperately. 'Get some of your top-notch military psychiatrists; explore my mind. Find out what my most expansive daydream is.' He tried to think. 'Women,' he said. 'Thousands of them, like Don Juan had. An interplanetary play-boy—a mistress in every city on Earth, Luna and Mars. Only I gave that up, out of exhaustion. Please,' he begged. 'Try it.'

'You'd voluntarily surrender, then?' the voice inside his head asked. 'If we agreed, to arrange such a solution? *If* it's possible?'

After an interval of hesitation he said, 'Yes.' *I'll take the risk*, he said to himself, *that you don't simply kill me*.

'You make the first move,' the voice said presently. 'Turn yourself over to us. And we'll investigate that line of possibility. If we can't do it, however, if your authentic memories begin to crop up again as they've done at this time, then—' There was silence and then the voice finished, 'We'll have to destroy you. As you must understand. Well, Quail, you still want to try?'

'Yes,' he said. Because the alternative was death now—and for certain. At least this way he had a chance, slim as it was.

'You present yourself at our main barracks in New York,' the voice of the Interplan cop resumed. 'At 580 Fifth Avenue, floor twelve. Once you've surrendered yourself, we'll have our psychiatrists begin on you; we'll have personality-profile tests made. We'll attempt to determine your absolute, ultimate fantasy wish— then we'll bring you back to Rekal, Incorporated, here; get them in on it, fulfilling that wish in vicarious surrogate retrospection. And—good luck. We do owe you something; you acted as a capable instrument for us.' The voice lacked malice; if anything, they—the organization—felt sympathy toward him.

'Thanks,' Quail said. And began searching for a robot cab.

*

'Mr Quail,' the stern-faced, elderly Interplan psychiatrist said, 'you possess a most interesting wish-fulfillment dream fantasy. Probably nothing such as you consciously entertain or suppose. This is commonly the way; I hope it won't upset you too much to hear about it.'

The senior ranking Interplan officer present said briskly, 'He better not be too much upset to hear about it, not if he expects not to get shot.'

'Unlike the fantasy of wanting to be an Interplan undercover agent,' the psychiatrist continued, 'which, being relatively speaking a product of maturity, had a certain plausibility to it, this production is a grotesque dream of your childhood; it is no wonder you fail to recall it. Your fantasy is this: you are nine years old, walking alone down a rustic lane. An unfamiliar variety of space vessel from another star system lands directly in front of you. No one on Earth but you, Mr Quail, sees it. The creatures within are very small and helpless, somewhat on the order of field mice, although they are attempting to invade Earth; tens of thousands of other ships will soon be on their way, when this advance party gives the go-ahead signal.'

'And I suppose I stop them,' Quail said, experiencing a mixture of amusement and disgust. 'Single-handed I wipe them out. Probably by stepping on them with my foot.'

'No,' the psychiatrist said patiently. 'You halt the invasion, but not by destroying them. Instead, you show them kindness and mercy, even though by telepathy—their mode of communication—you know why they have come. They have never seen such humane traits exhibited by any sentient organism, and to show their appreciation they make a covenant with you.'

Quail said, 'They won't invade Earth as long as I'm alive.'

'Exactly.' To the Interplan officer the psychiatrist said, 'You can see it does fit his personality, despite his feigned scorn.'

'So by merely existing,' Quail said, feeling a growing pleasure, 'by simply being alive, I keep Earth safe from alien rule. I'm in effect, then, the most important person on Terra. Without lifting a finger.'

'Yes, indeed, sir,' the psychiatrist said. 'And this is bedrock in your psyche; this is a life-long childhood fantasy. Which, without depth and drug therapy, you never would have recalled. But it has always existed in you; it went underneath, but never ceased.'

To McClane, who sat intently listening, the senior police official said, 'Can you implant an extra-factual memory-pattern that extreme in him?'

'We get handed every possible type of wish-fantasy there is,' McClane said. 'Frankly, I've heard a lot worse than this. Certainly we can handle it. Twenty-four hours from now he won't just *wish* he'd saved Earth; he'll devoutly believe it really happened.'

The senior police official said, 'You can start the job, then. In preparation we've already once again erased the memory in him of his trip to Mars.'

Quail said, 'What trip to Mars?'

No one answered him, so reluctantly, he shelved the question. And anyhow a police vehicle had now put in its appearance; he, McClane and the senior police officer crowded into it, and presently they were on their way to Chicago and Rekal, Incorporated.

'You had better make no errors this time,' the police officer said to heavy-set, nervous-looking McClane.

'I can't see what could go wrong,' McClane mumbled, perspiring. 'This has nothing to do with Mars or Interplan. Single-handedly stopping an invasion of Earth from another star system.' He shook his head at that. 'Wow, what a kid dreams up. And by pious virtue, too; not by force. It's sort of quaint.' He dabbed at his forehead with a large linen pocket handkerchief.

Nobody said anything.

'In fact,' McClane said, 'it's touching.'

'But arrogant,' the police official said starkly. 'Inasmuch as when he dies the invasion will resume. No wonder he doesn't recall it; it's the most grandiose fantasy I ever ran across.' He eyed Quail with disapproval. 'And to think we put this man on our payroll.'

When they reached Rekal, Incorporated the receptionist, Shirley, met them breathlessly in the outer office. 'Welcome back,

Mr Quail,' she fluttered, her melon-shaped breasts—today painted an incandescent orange—bobbing with agitation. 'I'm sorry everything worked out so badly before; I'm sure this time it'll go better.'

Still repeatedly dabbing at his shiny forehead with his neatly folded Irish linen handkerchief, McClane said, 'It better.' Moving with rapidity he rounded up Lowe and Keeler, escorted them and Douglas Quail to the work area, and then, with Shirley and the senior police officer, returned to his familiar office. To wait.

'Do we have a packet made up for this, Mr McClane?' Shirley asked, bumping against him in her agitation, then coloring modestly.

'I think we do.' He tried to recall, then gave up and consulted the formal chart. 'A combination,' he decided aloud, 'of packets Eighty-one, Twenty, and Six.' From the vault section of the chamber behind his desk he fished out the appropriate packets, carried them to his desk for inspection. 'From Eighty-one,' he explained, 'a magic healing rod given him—the client in question, this time Mr Quail—by the race of beings from another system. A token of their gratitude.'

'Does it work?' the police officer asked curiously.

'It did once,' McClane explained. 'But he, ahem, you see, used it up years ago, healing right and left. Now it's only a memento. But he remembers it working spectacularly.' He chuckled, then opened packet Twenty. 'Document from the UN Secretary General thanking him for saving Earth; this isn't precisely appropriate, because part of Quail's fantasy is that no one knows of the invasion except himself, but for the sake of verisimilitude we'll throw it in.' He inspected packet Six, then. What came from this? He couldn't recall; frowning, he dug into the plastic bag as Shirley and the Interplan police officer watched intently.

'Writing,' Shirley said. 'In a funny language.'

'This tells who they were,' McClane said, 'and where they came from. Including a detailed star map logging their flight here and the system of origin. Of course it's in *their* script, so he can't read it. But he remembers them reading it to him in his own tongue.' He placed the three artifacts in the center of the desk. 'These should be taken to Quail's conapt,' he said to the police officer. 'So that when he gets home he'll find them. And it'll confirm his fantasy. SOP—standard operating procedure.' He chuckled apprehensively, wondering how matters were going with Lowe and Keeler.

The intercom buzzed. 'Mr McClane, I'm sorry to bother you.' It was Lowe's voice; he froze as he recognized it, froze and became mute. 'But something's come up. Maybe it would be better if you came in here and supervised. Like before, Quail reacted well to the narkidrine; he's unconscious, relaxed and receptive. But—'

McClane sprinted for the work area.

On a hygienic bed Douglas Quail lay breathing slowly and regularly, eyes half-shut, dimly conscious of those around him.

'We started interrogating him,' Lowe said, white-faced. 'To find out exactly when to place the fantasy-memory of him single-handedly having saved Earth. And strangely enough—'

'They told me not to tell,' Douglas Quail mumbled in a dull drug-saturated voice. 'That was the agreement. I wasn't even supposed to remember. But how could I forget an event like that?'

I guess it would be hard, McClane reflected. *But you did—until now.*

'They even gave me a scroll,' Quail mumbled, 'of gratitude. I have it hidden in my conapt; I'll show it to you.'

To the Interplan officer who had followed after him, McClane said, 'Well, I offer the suggestion that you better not kill him. If you do they'll return.'

'They also gave me a magic invisible destroying rod,' Quail mumbled, eyes totally shut now. 'That's how I killed that man on Mars you sent me to take out. It's in my drawer along with the box of Martian maw-worms and dried-up plant-life.'

Wordlessly, the Interplan officer turned and stalked from the work area.

I might as well put those packets of proof-artifacts away, McClane said to himself resignedly. He walked, step by step, back to his office. *Including the citation from the UN Secretary General. After all—*

The real one probably would not be long in coming.

NOT BY ITS COVER

The elderly, cross-tempered president of Obelisk Books said irritably, 'I don't want to see him, Miss Handy. The item is already in print; if there's an error in the text we can't do anything about it now.'

'But Mr Masters,' Miss Handy said, 'it's such an important error, sir. *If* he's right. Mr Brandice claims that the entire chapter–'

'I read his letter; I also talked to him on the vidphone. I know what he claims.' Masters walked to the window of his office, gazed moodily out at the arid, crater-marred surface of Mars which he had witnessed so many decades. *Five thousand copies printed and bound*, he thought. *And of that, half in gold-stamped Martian wub-fur. The most elegant, expensive material we could locate. We were already losing money on the edition, and now this.*

On his desk lay a copy of the book. Lucretius' *De Rerum Natura*, in the lofty, noble John Dryden translation. Angrily, Barney Masters turned the crisp white pages. Who would expect anyone on Mars to know such an ancient text that well? he reflected. And the man waiting in the outer office consisted of only one out of eight who had written or called Obelisk Books about a disputed passage.

Disputed? There was no contest; the eight local Latin scholars were right. It was simply a question of getting them to depart quietly, to forget they had ever read through the Obelisk edition and found the fumbled up passage in question.

Touching the button of his desk intercom, Masters said to his receptionist, 'Okay; send him.' Otherwise the man would never leave; his type would stay parked outside. Scholars were generally like that; they seemed to have infinite patience.

The door opened and a tall gray-haired man, wearing old-fashioned Terra-style glasses, loomed, briefcase in hand. 'Thank you, Mr Masters,' he said, entering. 'Let me explain, sir, why my organization considers an error such as this so important.' He seated himself by the desk, unzipped his briefcase briskly. 'We are after all a colony planet. All our values, mores, artifacts and customs come to us from Terra. WODAFAG considers your printing of this book . . .'

'"WODAFAG"?' Masters interrupted. He had never heard of it, but even so he groaned. Obviously one of the many vigilant crank outfits who scanned everything printed, either emanating locally here on Mars or arriving from Terra.

'Watchmen Over Distortion And Forged Artifacts Generally,' Brandice explained. 'I have with me an authentic, correct Terran edition of *De Rerum Natura*—the Dryden translation, as is your local edition.' His emphasis on *local* made it sound slimy and second-rate; as if, Masters brooded, Obelisk Books was doing something unsavory in printing books at all. 'Let us consider the inauthentic interpolations. You are urged to study first my copy—' He laid a battered, elderly, Terran-printed book open on Masters' desk. '—in which it appears correctly. And then, sir, a copy of your own edition; the same passage.' Beside the little ancient blue book he laid one of the handsome large wub-fur bound copies which Obelisk Books had turned out.

'Let me get my copy editor in here,' Masters said. Pressing the intercom button he said to Miss Handy, 'Ask Jack Snead to step in here, please.'

'Yes, Mr Masters.'

'To quote from the authentic edition,' Brandice said, 'we obtain a metric rendering of the Latin as follows. Ahem.' He cleared his throat self-consciously, then began to read aloud.

> 'From sense of grief and pain we shall be free;
> We shall not feel, because we shall not be.

NOT BY ITS COVER

> Though earth in seas, and seas in heaven were lost,
> We should not move, we only should be toss'd.'

'I know the passage,' Masters said sharply, feeling needled; the man was lecturing him as if he were a child.

'This quatrain,' Brandice said, 'is absent from your edition, and the following spurious quatrain—of God knows what origin—appears in its place. Allow me.' Taking the sumptuous, wub-fur bound Obelisk copy, he thumbed through, found the place; then read.

> 'From sense of grief and pain we shall be free;
> Which earth-bound man can neither qualify nor see.
> Once dead, we fathom seas cast up from this:
> Our stint on earth doth herald an unstopping bliss.'

Glaring at Masters, Brandice closed the wub-fur bound copy noisily. 'What is most annoying,' Brandice said, 'is that this quatrain preaches a message diametric to that of the entire book. Where did it come from? *Somebody* had to write it; Dryden didn't write it—Lucretius didn't.' He eyed Masters as if he thought Masters personally had done it.

The office door opened and the firm's copy editor, Jack Snead, entered. 'He's right,' he said resignedly to his employer. 'And it's only one alteration in the text out of thirty or so; I've been ploughing through the whole thing, since the letters started arriving. And now I'm starting in on other recent catalog-items in our fall list.' He added, grunting, 'I've found alterations in several of them, too.'

Masters said, 'You were the last editor to proofread the copy before it went to the typesetters. Were these errors in it then?'

'Absolutely not,' Snead said. 'And I proofread the galleys personally; the changes weren't in the galleys, either. The changes don't appear until the final bound copies come into existence—if that makes any sense. Or more specifically, the ones bound in gold and wub-fur. The regular bound-in-boards copies—they're okay.'

Masters blinked. 'But they're all the same edition. They ran through the presses together. In fact we didn't originally plan an exclusive, higher-priced binding; it was only at the last minute that we talked it over and the business office suggested half the edition be offered in wub-fur.'

'I think,' Jack Snead said, 'we're going to have to do some close-scrutiny work on the subject of Martian wub-fur.'

An hour later aging, tottering Masters, accompanied by copy editor Jack Snead, sat facing Luther Saperstein, business agent for the pelt-procuring firm of Flawless, Incorporated; from them, Obelisk Books had obtained the wub-fur with which their books had been bound.

'First of all,' Masters said in a brisk, professional tone, 'what is wub-fur?'

'Basically,' Saperstein said, 'in the sense in which you're asking the question, it is fur from the Martian wub. I know this doesn't tell you much, gentlemen, but at least it's a reference point, a postulate on which we can all agree, where we can start and build something more imposing. To be more helpful, let me fill you in on the nature of the wub itself. The fur is prized because, among other reasons, it is rare. Wub-fur is rare because a wub very seldom dies. By that I mean, it is next to impossible to slay a wub—even a sick or old wub. And, even though a wub is killed, the hide lives on. That quality imparts its unique value to home-decoration, or, as in your case, in the binding of lifetime, treasured books meant to endure.'

Masters sighed, dully gazed out the window as Saperstein droned on. Beside him, his copy editor made brief cryptic notes, a dark expression on his youthful, energetic face.

'What we supplied you,' Saperstein said, 'when you came to us—and remember: you came to us; we didn't seek you out—consisted of the most select, perfect hides in our giant inventory. These living hides shine with a unique luster all their own; nothing else either on Mars or back home on Terra resembles them. If torn or scratched, the hide repairs itself. It grows, over the months, a more

NOT BY ITS COVER

and more lush pile, so that the covers of your volumes become progressively luxurious, and hence highly sought-after. Ten years from now the deep-pile quality of these wub-fur bound books—'

Interrupting, Snead said, 'So the hide is still alive. Interesting. And the wub, as you say, is so deft as to be virtually impossible to kill.' He shot a swift glance at Masters. 'Every single one of the thirty-odd alterations made in the texts in our books deals with immortality. The Lucretius revision is typical; the original text teaches that man is temporary, that even if he survives after death it doesn't matter because he won't have any memory of his existence here. In place of that, the spurious new passage comes out and flatly talks about a future of life predicated on this one; as you say, at complete variance with Lucretius's entire philosophy. You realize what we're seeing, don't you? The damn wub's philosophy superimposed on that of the various authors. That's it; beginning and end.' He broke off, resumed his note-scratching, silently.

'How can a hide,' Masters demanded, 'even a perpetually living one, exert influence on the contents of a book? A text already printed—pages cut, folios glued and sewed—it's against reason. Even if the binding, the damn hide, is really alive, and I can hardly believe that.' He glared at Saperstein. 'If it's alive, what does it live on?'

'Minute particles of food-stuffs in suspension in the atmosphere,' Saperstein said, blandly.

Rising to his feet, Masters said, 'Let's go. This is ridiculous.'

'It inhales the particles,' Saperstein said, 'through its pores.' His tone was dignified, even reproving.

Studying his notes, not rising along with his employer, Jack Snead said thoughtfully, 'Some of the amended texts are fascinating. They vary from a complete reversal of the original passage—and the author's meaning—as in the case of Lucretius, to very subtle, almost invisible corrections—if that's the word—to texts more in accord with the doctrine of eternal life. The real question is this. Are we faced merely with the opinion of one particular life form, *or does the wub know what it's talking about?* Lucretius's poem, for instance; it's very great, very beautiful, very interesting—as poetry. But as philosophy, maybe it's wrong. I don't know. It's not my job; I simply edit books; I don't write them. The last thing a good copy editor does is editorialize, on his own, in the author's text. But that is what the wub, or anyhow the post-wub pelt, is doing.' He was silent, then.

Saperstein said, 'I'd be interested to know if it added anything of value.'

'Poetically? Or do you mean philosophically? From a poetic or literary, stylistic point of view its interpolations are no better and no worse than the originals; it manages to blend in with the author well enough so that if you didn't know the text already you'd never notice.' He added broodingly, 'You'd never know it was a pelt talking.'

'I meant from a philosophical point of view.'

'Well, it's always the same message, monotonously ground out. There is no death. We go to sleep; we wake up—to a better life. What it did to *De Rerum Natura*; that's typical. If you've read that you've read them all.'

'It would be an interesting experiment,' Masters said thoughtfully, 'to bind a copy of the Bible in wub-fur.'

'I had that done,' Snead said.

'And?'

'Of course I couldn't take time to read it all. But I did glance over Paul's letters to the Corinthians. It made only one change. The passage that begins, "Behold, I tell you a mystery—" it set all of that in caps. And it repeated the lines, "Death, where is thy sting? Grave, where is thy victory?" ten times straight; ten whole times, all in caps. Obviously the wub agreed; that's its own philosophy, or rather theology.' He said, then, weighing each word, 'This basically is a theological dispute . . . between the reading public and the hide of a Martian animal that looks like a fusion between a hog and a cow. Strange.' Again he returned to his notes.

After a solemn pause, Masters said, 'You think the wub has inside information or don't you? As you said, this may not be just the opinion of one particular animal that's been successful in avoiding death; it may be the truth.'

'What occurs to me,' Snead said, 'is this. The wub hasn't merely learned to avoid death; it's actually done what it preaches. By getting killed, skinned, and its hide—still alive—made into book covers—it has conquered death. It lives on. In what it appears to regard as a better life. We're not just dealing with an opinionated local life form; we're dealing with an organism that has already done what we're still in doubt about. Sure it knows. It's a living confirmation of its own doctrine. The facts speak for themselves. I tend to believe it.'

'Maybe continual life for *it*,' Masters disagreed, 'but that doesn't mean necessarily for the rest of us. The wub, as Mr Saperstein points out, is unique. The hide of no other life form either on Mars or on Luna or Terra lives on, imbibing life from microscopic particles in suspension in the atmosphere. Just because *it* can do it—'

'Too bad we can't communicate with a wub hide,' Saperstein said. 'We've tried, here at Flawless, ever since we first noticed the fact of its post-mortem survival. But we never found a way.'

'But we at Obelisk,' Snead pointed out, 'have. As a matter of fact I've already tried an experiment. I had a one-sentence text printed up, a single line reading: "The wub, unlike every other living creature, is immortal."

'I then had it bound in wub-fur; then I read it again. It had been changed. Here.' He passed a slim book, handsomely appointed, to Masters. 'Read it as it is now.'

Masters read aloud: ' "The wub, like every other living creature, is immortal." '

Returning the copy to Snead he said, 'Well, all it did was drop out the *un*; that's not much of a change, two letters.'

'But from the standpoint of meaning,' Snead said, 'it constitutes a bombshell. We're getting feedback from beyond the grave—so to speak. I mean, let's face it; wub-fur is technically dead because the wub that grew it is dead. This is awfully damn close to providing an indisputable verification of the survival of sentient life after death.'

'Of course there is one thing,' Saperstein said hesitantly. 'I hate to bring it up; I don't know what bearing it has on all this. But the Martian wub, for all its uncanny—even miraculous—ability to preserve itself, is from a mentational standpoint a stupid creature. A Terran opossum, for example, has a brain one-third that of a cat. The wub has a brain one-fifth that of an opossum.' He looked gloomy.

'Well,' Snead said, 'the Bible says, "The last shall be the first." Possibly the lowly wub is included under this rubric; let's hope so.'

Glancing at him, Masters said, 'You *want* eternal life?'

'Certainly,' Snead said. 'Everybody does.'

'Not I,' Masters said, with decisiveness. 'I have enough troubles now. The last thing I want is to live on as the binding of a book—or in any fashion whatsoever.' But inside, he had begun silently to muse. Differently. Very differently, in fact.

'It sounds like something a wub would like,' Saperstein agreed. 'Being the binding of a book; just lying there supine, on a shelf, year after year, inhaling minute particles from the air. And presumably meditating. Or whatever wubs do after they're dead.'

'They think theology,' Snead said. 'They preach.' To his boss he said, 'I assume we won't be binding any more books in wub-fur.'

'Not for trade purposes,' Masters agreed. 'Not to sell. But—' He could not rid himself of the conviction that some use lay, here. 'I wonder,' he said, 'if it would impart the same high level of survival factor to anything it was made into. Such as window drapes. Or upholstery in a float-car; maybe it would eliminate death on the commuter paths. Or helmet-liners for combat troops. And for baseball players.' The possibilities, to him, seemed enormous . . . but vague. He would have to think this out, give it a good deal of time.

'Anyhow,' Saperstein said, 'my firm declines to give you a refund; the characteristics of wub-fur were known publicly in a brochure which we published earlier this year. We categorically stated—'

'Okay, it's our loss,' Masters said irritably, with a wave of his hand. 'Let it go.' To Snead he said, 'And it definitely says, in the thirty-odd passages it's interpolated, that life after death is pleasant?'

'Absolutely. "Our stint on earth doth herald an unstopping bliss." That sums it up, that line it stuck into *De Rerum Natura*; it's all right there.'

'"Bliss,"' Masters echoed, nodding. 'Of course, we're actually not on Earth; we're on Mars. But I suppose it's the same thing; it just means life, wherever it's lived.' Again, even more gravely, he pondered. 'What occurs to me,' he said thoughtfully, 'is it's one thing to talk abstractly about "life after death." People have been doing that for fifty thousand years; Lucretius was, two thousand years ago. What interests me more is not the big overall philosophical picture but the concrete fact of the wub-pelt; the immortality which it carried around with it.' To Snead he said, 'What other books did you bind in it?'

'Tom Paine's *Age of Reason*,' Snead said, consulting his list.

'What were the results?'

'Two-hundred-sixty-seven blank pages. Except right in the middle the one word *bleh*.'

'Continue.'

'The *Britannica*. It didn't precisely change anything, but it added whole articles. On the soul, on transmigration, on hell, damnation, sin, or immortality; the whole twenty-four volume set became religiously oriented.' He glanced up. 'Should I go on?'

'Sure,' Masters said, listening and meditating simultaneously.

'The *Summa Theologica* of Thomas Aquinas. It left the text intact, but it periodically inserted the biblical line, "The letter killeth but the spirit giveth life." Over and over again.

'James Hilton's *Lost Horizon*. Shangri-La turns out to be a vision of the after life which—'

'Okay,' Masters said. 'We get the idea. The question is, what can we do with this? Obviously we can't bind books with it—at least books which it disagrees with.' But he was beginning to see another use; a much more personal one. And it far outweighed anything which the wub-fur might do for or to books—in fact for any inanimate object.

As soon as he got to a phone—

'Of special interest,' Snead was saying, 'is its reaction to a volume of collected papers on psychoanalysis by some of the greatest living Freudian analysts of our time. It allowed each article to remain intact, but at the end of each it added the same phrase.' He chuckled. '"Physician, heal thyself." Bit of a sense of humor, there.'

'Yeah,' Masters said. Thinking, unceasingly, of the phone and the one vital call which he would make.

Back in his own office at Obelisk Books, Masters tried out a preliminary experiment—to see if this idea would work. Carefully, he wrapped a Royal Albert yellow bone-china cup and saucer in wub-fur, a favorite from his own collection. Then, after much soul-searching and trepidation, he placed the bundle on the floor of his office and, with all his declining might, stepped on it.

The cup did not break. At least it did not seem to.

He unwrapped the package, then, and inspected the cup. He had been right; wrapped in living wub-fur it could not be destroyed.

Satisfied, he seated himself at his desk, pondered one last time.

The wrapper of wub-fur had made a temporary, fragile object imperishable. So the wub's doctrine of external survival had worked itself out in practice—exactly as he had expected.

He picked up the phone, dialed his lawyer's number.

'This is about my will,' he said to his lawyer, when he had him on the other end of the line. 'You know, the latest one I made out a few months ago. I have an additional clause to insert.'

'Yes, Mr Masters,' his lawyer said briskly. 'Shoot.'

'A small item,' Masters purred. 'Has to do with my coffin. I want it mandatory on my heirs—my coffin is to be lined throughout, top, bottom and sides, with wub-fur. From Flawless, Incorporated. I want to go to my Maker clothed, so to speak, in wub-fur. Makes a better impression that way.' He laughed nonchalantly, but his tone was deadly serious—and his attorney caught it.

'If that's what you want,' the attorney said.

'And I suggest you do the same,' Masters said.

'Why?'

Masters said, 'Consult the complete home medical reference library we're going to issue next month. And make certain you get a copy that's bound in wub-fur; it'll be different from the others.' He thought, then, about his wub-fur-lined coffin once again. Far underground, with him inside it, with the living wub-fur growing, growing.

It would be interesting to see the version of himself which a choice wub-fur binding produced.

Especially after several centuries.

RETURN MATCH

It was not an ordinary gambling casino. And this, for the police of SLA, posed a special problem. The outspacers who had set up the casino had placed their massive ship directly above the tables, so that in the event of a raid the jets would destroy the tables. Efficient, officer Joseph Tinbane thought to himself morosely. With one blast the outspacers left Terra and simultaneously destroyed all evidence of their illegal activity.

And, what was more, killed each and every human gameplayer who might otherwise have lived to give testimony.

He sat now in his parked aircar, taking pinch after pinch of fine imported Dean Swift inch-kenneth snuff, then switched to the yellow tin which contained wren's relish. The snuff cheered him, but not very much. To his left, in the evening darkness, he could make out the shape of the outspacers' upended ship, black and silent, with the enlarged walled space beneath it, equally dark and silent—but deceptively so.

'We can go in there,' he said to his less experienced companion, 'but it'll just mean getting killed.' We'll have to trust the robots, he realized. Even if they are clumsy, prone to error. Anyhow they're not alive. And not being alive, in a project as this, constituted an advantage.

'The third has gone in,' officer Falkes beside him said quietly.

The slim shape, in human clothing, stopped before the door of the casino, rapped, waited. Presently the door opened. The robot gave the proper code-word and was admitted.

'You think they'll survive the take-off blast?' Tinbane asked. Falkes was an expert in robotics.

'Possibly one might. Not all, though. But one will be enough.' Hot for the kill, officer Falkes leaned to peer past Tinbane; his youthful face was fixed in concentration. 'Use the bull-horn now. Tell them they're under arrest. I see no point in waiting.'

'The point I see,' Tinbane said, 'is that it's more comforting to see the ship inert and the action going on underneath. We'll wait.'

'But no more robots are coming.'

'Wait for them to send back their vid transmissions,' Tinbane said. After all, that comprised evidence—of a sort. And at police HQ it was now being recorded in permanent form. Still, his companion officer assigned to this project did have a point. Since the last of the three humanoid plants had gone in, nothing more would take place, now. Until the outspacers realized they had been infiltrated and put their typical planned pattern of withdrawal into action. 'All right,' he said, and pushed down on the button which activated the bull-horn.

Leaning, Falkes spoke into the bull-horn. At once the bull-horn said, 'AS ORDER-REPRESENTATIVES OF SUPERIOR LOS ANGELES I AND THE MEN WITH ME INSTRUCT EVERYONE INSIDE TO COME OUT ONTO THE STREET COLLECTIVELY; I FURTHER INSTRUCT–'

His voice, from the bull-horn, disappeared as the initial takeoff surge roared through the primary jets of the outspacers' ship. Falkes shrugged, grinned starkly at Tinbane. *It didn't take them long,* his mouth formed silently.

As expected no one came out. No one in the casino escaped. Even when the structure which composed the building melted. The ship detached itself, leaving a soggy, puddled mass of wax-like matter behind it. And still no one emerged.

All dead, Tinbane realized with mute shock.

'Time to go in,' Falkes said stoically. He began to crawl into his neo-asbestos suit, and, after a pause, so did Tinbane.

Together, the two officers entered the hot, dripping puddle

which had been the casino. In the center, forming a mound, lay two of the three humanoid robots; they had managed at the last moment to cover something with their bodies. Of the third Tinbane saw no sign; evidently it had been demolished along with everything else. Everything organic.

I wonder what they thought—in their own dim way—to be worth preserving, Tinbane thought as he surveyed the distorted remnants of the two robots. Something alive? One of the snail-like outspacers? Probably not. A gaming table, then.

'They acted fast,' Falkes said, impressed. 'For robots.'

'But we got something,' Tinbane pointed out. Gingerly, he poked at the hot fused metal which had been the two robots. A section, most likely a torso, slid aside, revealed what the robots had preserved.

A pinball machine.

Tinbane wondered why. What was this worth? Anything? Personally, he doubted it.

In the police lab on Sunset Avenue in downtown Old Los Angeles, a technician presented a long written analysis to Tinbane.

'Tell me orally,' Tinbane said, annoyed; he had been too many years on the force to suffer through such stuff. He returned the clipboard and report to the tall, lean police technician.

'Actually it's not an ordinary construct,' the technician said, glancing over his own report, as if he had already forgotten it; his tone, like the report itself, was dry, dull. This for him was obviously routine. He, too, agreed that the pinball machine salvaged by the humanoid robots was worthless—or so Tinbane guessed. 'By that I mean it's not like any they've brought to Terra in the past. You can probably get more of an idea directly from the thing; I suggest you put a quarter in it and play through a game.' He added, 'The lab budget will provide you with a quarter which we'll retrieve from the machine later.'

'I've got my own quarter,' Tinbane said irritably. He followed the technician through the large, overworked lab, past the elaborate—and in many cases obsolete—assortment of analytical devices and partly broken-apart constructs to the work area in the rear.

There, cleaned up, the damage done to it now repaired, stood the pinball machine which the robots had protected. Tinbane inserted a coin; five metal balls at once spilled into the reservoir, and the board at the far end of the machine lit up in a variety of shifting colors.

'Before you shoot the first ball,' the technician said to him, standing beside him so that he, too, could watch, 'I advise you to take a careful look at the terrain of the machine, the components among which the ball will pass. The horizontal area beneath the protective glass is somewhat interesting. A miniature village, complete with houses, lighted streets, major public buildings, overhead sprintship runnels . . . not a Terran village, of course. An Ionian village, of the sort they're used to. The detail work is superb.'

Bending, Tinbane peered. The technician was right; the detail work on the scale-model structures astounded him.

'Tests that measure wear on the moving parts of this machine,' the technician informed him, 'indicate that it saw a great deal of use. There is considerable tolerance. We estimate that before another thousand games could be completed, the machine would have to go to the shop. *Their* shop, back on Io. Which is where we understand they build and maintain equipment of this variety.' He explained, 'By that I mean gambling layouts in general.'

'What's the object of the game?' Tinbane asked.

'We have here,' the technician explained, 'what we call a full-shift set variable. In other words, the terrain through which the steel ball moves is never the same. The number of possible combinations is—' he leafed through his report but was unable to find the exact figure—'anyhow, quite great. In the millions. It's excessively intricate, in our opinion. Anyhow, if you'll release the first ball you'll see.'

Depressing the plunger, Tinbane allowed the first ball to roll from the reservoir and against the impulse-shaft. He then drew back the springloaded shaft and snapped it into release. The ball shot up the channel and bounced free, against a pressure-cushion which imparted swift additional velocity to it.

The ball now dribbled in descent, toward the upper perimeter of the village.

'The initial defense line,' the technician said from behind him, 'which protects the village proper, is a series of mounds colored, shaped and surfaced to resemble the Ionian landscape. The fidelity is quite obviously painstaking. Probably made from satellites in orbit around Io. You can easily imagine you're seeing an actual piece of that moon from a distance of ten or more miles up.'

The steel ball encountered the perimeter of rough terrain. Its trajectory altered, and the ball wobbled uncertainly, no longer going in any particular direction.

'Deflected,' Tinbane said, noting how satisfactorily the contours of the terrain acted to deprive the ball of its descending forward motion. 'It's going to bypass the village entirely.'

The ball, with severely decreased momentum, wandered into a side crease, followed the crease listlessly, and then, just as it appeared to be drifting into the lower take-up slot, abruptly hurtled from a pressure-cushion and back into play.

On the illuminated background a score registered. Victory, of a momentary sort, for the player. The ball once again menaced the village. Once again it dribbled through the rough terrain, following virtually the same path as before.

'Now you'll notice something moderately important,' the technician said. 'As it heads toward that same pressure-cushion which it just now hit. Don't watch the ball; watch the cushion.'

Tinbane watched. And saw, from the cushion, a tiny wisp of gray smoke. He turned inquiringly toward the technician.

'Now watch the ball!' the technician said sharply.

Again the ball struck the pressure-cushion mounted slightly before the lower take-up slot. This time, however, the cushion failed to react to the ball's impact.

Tinbane blinked as the ball rolled harmlessly on, into the take-up slot and out of play.

'Nothing happened,' he said presently.

'That smoke that you saw. Emerging from the wiring of the cushion. An electrical short. Because a rebound from that spot placed the ball in a menacing position—menacing to the village.'

'In other words,' Tinbane said, 'something took note of the effect the cushion was having on the ball. The assembly operates so as to protect itself from the ball's activity.' He had seen this before, in other outspacer gambling gear: sophisticated circuitry which kept the gameboard constantly shifting in such a way as to seem alive—in such a way as to reduce the chances of the player winning. On this particular construct the player obtained a winning score by inducing the five steel balls to pass into the central layout: the replica of the Ionian hamlet. Hence the hamlet had to be protected. Hence this particular strategically located pressure-cushion required elimination. At least for the time being. Until the overall configurations of topography altered decidedly.

'Nothing new there,' the technician said. 'You've seen it a dozen times before; I've seen it a hundred times before. Let's say that this pinball machine has seen ten thousand separate games, and each time there's been a careful readjustment of the circuitry directed toward rendering the steel balls neutralized. Let's say that the alterations are cumulative. So by now any given player's score is probably no more than a fraction of early scores, before the circuits had a chance to react. The direction of alteration—as in all outspacer gambling mechanisms—has a zero win factor as the limit toward which it's moving. Just *try* to hit the village, Tinbane. We set up a constantly repeating mechanical ball-release and played one hundred and forty games. At no time did a ball ever get near enough to do the village any harm. We kept a record of the scores obtained. A slight but significant drop was registered each time.' He grinned.

'So?' Tinbane said.

'So nothing. As I told you and as my report says.' The technician paused, then. 'Except for one thing. Look at this.'

Bending, he traced his thin finger across the protective glass of the layout, toward a construct near the center of the replica village. 'A photographic record shows that with each game that particular component becomes more articulated. It's being erected by circuitry underneath—obviously. As is every other change. But this configuration—doesn't it remind you of something?'

'Looks like a Roman catapult,' Tinbane said. 'But with a vertical rather than a horizontal axis.'

'That's our reaction, too. And look at the sling. In terms of the scale of the village it's inordinately large. Immense, in fact; specifically, *it's not to scale*.'

'It looks as if it would almost hold—'

'Not almost,' the technician said. 'We measured it. The size of the sling is exact; one of those steel balls would fit perfectly into it.'

'And then?' Tinbane said, feeling chill.

'And then it would hurl the ball back at the player,' the lab technician said calmly. 'It's aimed directly toward the front of the machine, front and upward.' He added, 'And it's been virtually completed.'

The best defense, Tinbane thought to himself as he studied the outspacers' illegal pinball machine, is offense. But whoever heard of it in this context?

Zero, he realized, isn't a low enough score to suit the defensive circuitry of the thing. Zero won't do. It's got to strive for less than zero. Why? Because, he decided, it's not really moving toward zero as a limit; it's moving, instead, toward the best defensive pattern. It's too well designed.

Or is it?

'You think,' he asked the lean, tall lab technician, 'that the outspacers intended this?'

'That doesn't matter. At least not from the immediate standpoint. What matters is two factors: the machine was exported—in violation of Terran law—to Terra, and it's been played by Terrans. Intentionally or not, this could be, in fact will soon be, a lethal weapon.' He added, 'We calculate within the next twenty games. Every time a coin is inserted, the building resumes. Whether a ball gets near the village or not. All it requires is a flow of power from the device's central helium battery. And that's automatic, once play begins.' He added, 'It's at work building the catapult right now, as we stand here. You better release the remaining four balls, so it'll shut itself off. Or give us permission to dismantle it—to at least take the power supply out of the circuit.'

'The outspacers don't have a very high regard for human life,' Tinbane reflected. He was thinking of the carnage created by the ship taking off. And that, for them, was routine. But in view of that wholesale destruction of human life, this seemed unnecessary. What more did this accomplish?

Pondering, he said, 'This is selective. This would eliminate only the gameplayer.'

The technician said, 'This would eliminate *every* gameplayer. One after another.'

'But who would play the thing,' Tinbane said, 'after the first fatality?'

'People go there knowing that if there's a raid the outspacers will burn up everyone and everything,' the technician pointed out. 'The urge to gamble is an addictive compulsion; a certain type of person gambles no matter what the risk is. You ever hear of Russian Roulette?'

Tinbane released the second steel ball, watched it bounce and wander toward the replica village. This one managed to pass through the rough terrain; it approached the first house comprising the village proper. Maybe I'll get it, he thought savagely. Before it gets me. A strange, novel excitement filled him as he watched the ball thud against the tiny house, flatten the structure and roll on. The ball, although small to him, towered over every building, every structure, that made up the village.

—Every structure except the central catapult. He watched avidly as the ball moved dangerously close to the catapult, then, deflected by a major public building, rolled on and disappeared into the take-up slot. Immediately he sent the third ball hurtling up its channel.

'The stakes,' the technician said softly, 'are high, aren't they? Your life against its. Must be exceptionally appealing to someone with the right kind of temperament.'

'I think,' Tinbane said, 'I can get the catapult before it's in action.'

'Maybe. Maybe not.'

'I'm getting the ball closer to it each time.'

The technician said, 'For the catapult to work, it requires one of the steel balls; that's its load. You're making it increasingly likely that it'll acquire use of one of the balls. You're actually helping it.' He added somberly, 'In fact it can't function without you; the gameplayer is not only the enemy, he's also essential. Better quit, Tinbane. The thing is using you.'

'I'll quit,' Tinbane said, 'when I've gotten the catapult.'

'You're damn right you will. You'll be dead.' He eyed Tinbane narrowly. 'Possibly this is why the outspacers built it. To get back at us for our raids. This very likely is what it's for.'

'Got another quarter?' Tinbane said.

In the middle of his tenth game a surprising, unexpected alteration in the machine's strategy manifested itself. All at once it ceased routing the steel balls entirely to one side, away from the replica village.

Watching, Tinbane saw the steel ball roll directly—for the first time—through the center. Straight toward the proportionally massive catapult.

Obviously the catapult had been completed.

'I outrank you, Tinbane,' the lab technician said tautly. 'And I'm ordering you to quit playing.'

'Any order from you to me,' Tinbane said, 'has to be in writing and has to be approved by someone in the department at inspector level.' But, reluctantly, he halted play. 'I can get it,' he said reflectively, 'but not standing here. I have to be away, far enough back so that it can't pick me off.' So it can't distinguish me and aim, he realized.

Already he had noted it swivel slightly. Through some lens-system it had detected him. Or possibly it was thermotropic, had sensed him by his body heat.

If the latter, then defensive action for him would be relatively simple: a resistance coil suspended at another locus. On the other hand it might be utilizing a cephalic index of some sort, recording all nearby brain-emanations. But the police lab would know that already.

'What's its tropism?' he asked.

The technician said, 'That assembly hadn't been built up, at the time we inspected it. It's undoubtedly coming into existence now, in concert with the completion of the weapon.'

Tinbane said thoughtfully, 'I hope it doesn't possess equipment to *record* a cephalic index.' Because, he thought, if it did, storing the pattern would be no trouble at all. It could retain a memory of its adversary for use in the event of future encounters.

Something about that notion frightened him—over and above the immediate menace of the situation.

'I'll make a deal,' the technician said. 'You continue to operate it until it fires its initial shot at you. Then step aside and let us tear it down. We need to know its tropism; this may turn up again in a more complex fashion. You agree? You'll be taking a calculated risk, but I believe its initial shot will be aimed with the idea of use as feedback; it'll correct for a second shot . . . which will never take place.'

Should he tell the technician his fear?

'What bothers me,' he said, 'is the possibility that it'll retain a specific memory of me. For future purposes.'

'What future purposes? It'll be completely torn down. As soon as it fires.'

Reluctantly, Tinbane said, 'I think I'd better make the deal.' I may already have gone too far, he thought. You may have been right.

The next steel ball missed the catapult by only a matter of a fraction of an inch. But what unnerved him was not the closeness;

it was the quick, subtle attempt on the part of the catapult to snare the ball as it passed. A motion so rapid that he might easily have overlooked it.

'It wants the ball,' the technician observed. 'It wants *you*.' He, too, had seen.

With hesitation, Tinbane touched the plunger which would release the next—and for him possibly the last—steel ball.

'Back out,' the technician advised nervously. 'Forget the deal; stop playing. We'll tear it down as it is.'

'We need the tropism,' Tinbane said. And depressed the plunger.

The steel ball, suddenly seeming to him huge and hard and heavy, rolled unhesitatingly into the waiting catapult; every contour of the machine's topography collaborated. The acquisition of the load took place before he even understood what had happened. He stood staring.

'Run!' The technician leaped back, bolted; crashing against Tinbane, he threw him bodily away from the machine.

With a clatter of broken glass the steel ball shot by Tinbane's right temple, bounced against the far wall of the lab, came to rest under a work table.

Silence.

After a time the technician said shakily, 'It had plenty of velocity. Plenty of mass. Plenty of what it needed.'

Haltingly, Tinbane stood up, took a step toward the machine.

'Don't release another ball,' the technician said warningly.

Tinbane said, 'I don't have to.' He turned, then, sprinted away.

The machine had released the ball itself.

In the outer office, Tinbane sat smoking, seated across from Ted Donovan, the lab chief. The door to the lab had been shut, and every one of the several lab technicians had been bull-horned to safety. Beyond the closed door the lab was silent. Inert, Tinbane thought, and waiting.

He wondered if it was waiting for anyone, any human, any Terran, to come within reach. Or—just him.

The latter thought amused him even less than it had originally; even seated out here he felt himself cringe. A machine built on another world, sent to Terra empty of direction, merely capable of sorting among all its defensive possibilities until at last it stumbled onto the key. Randomness at work, through hundreds, even thousands of games . . . through person after person, player after player. Until at last it reached critical direction, and the last person to play it, also selected by the process of randomness, became welded to it in a contract of death. In this case, himself. Unfortunately.

Ted Donovan said, 'We'll spear its power source from a distance; that shouldn't be hard. You go on home, forget about it. When we have its tropic circuit laid out we'll notify you. Unless of course it's late at night, in which case—'

'Notify me,' Tinbane said, 'whatever time it is. If you will.' He did not have to explain; the lab chief understood.

'Obviously,' Donovan said, 'this construct is aimed at the police teams raiding the casinos. How they steered our robots onto it we don't of course know—yet. We may find *that* circuit, too.' He picked up the already extant lab report, eyed it with hostility. 'This was far too cursory, it would now appear. "Just another outspacer gambling device." The hell it is.' He tossed the report away, disgusted.

'If that's what they had in mind,' Tinbane said, 'they got what they wanted; they got me completely.' At least in terms of hooking him. Of snaring his attention. And his cooperation.

'You're a gambler; you've got the streak. But you didn't know it. Possibly it wouldn't have worked otherwise.' Donovan added, 'But it is interesting. A pinball machine that fights back. That gets fed up with steel balls rolling over it. I hope they don't build a skeet-shoot. This is bad enough.'

'Dreamlike,' Tinbane murmured.

'Pardon?'

'Not really real.' But, he thought, it is real. He rose, then, to his feet. 'I'll do what you say; I'll go on home to my conapt. You have the vidphone number.' He felt tired and afraid.

'You look terrible,' Donovan said, scrutinizing him. 'It shouldn't get you to this extent; this is a relatively benign construct, isn't it? You have to attack it, to set it in motion. If left alone–'

'I'm leaving it alone,' Tinbane said. 'But I feel it's waiting. It wants me to come back.' He felt it expecting him, anticipating his return. The machine was capable of learning and he had taught it–taught it about himself.

Taught it that he existed. That there was such a person on Terra as Joseph Tinbane.

And that was too much.

When he unlocked the door of his conapt the phone was already ringing. Leadenly, he picked up the receiver. 'Hello,' he said.

'Tinbane?' It was Donovan's voice. 'It's encephalotropic, all right. We found a pattern-print of your brain configuration, and of course we destroyed it. But–' Donovan hesitated. 'We also found something else it had constructed since the initial analysis.'

'A transmitter,' Tinbane said hoarsely.

'Afraid so. Half-mile of broadcast, two miles if beamed. And it was cupped to beams, so we have to assume the two-mile transmission. We have absolutely no idea what the receiver consists of, naturally, whether it's even on the surface or not. Probably is. In an office somewhere. Or a hover-car such as they use. Anyhow, now you know. So it's decidedly a vengeance weapon; your emotional response was unfortunately correct. When our double-dome experts looked this over they drew the conclusion that you were waited-for, so to speak. It saw you coming. The instrument may never have functioned as an authentic gambling device in the first place; the tolerances which we noted may have been built in, rather than the result of wear. So that's about it.'

Tinbane said, 'What do you suggest I do?'

'"Do"?' A pause. 'Not much. Stay in your conapt; don't report for work, not for a while.'

So if they nail me, Tinbane thought, no one else in the department will get hit at the same time. More advantageous for the rest of you; hardly for me, though. 'I think I'll get out of the area,' he said aloud. 'The structure may be limited in space, confined to SLA or just one part of the city. If you don't veto it.' He had a girl friend, Nancy Hackett, in La Jolla; he could go there.

'Suit yourself.'

He said, 'You can't do anything to help me, though.'

'I tell you what,' Donovan said. 'We'll allocate some funds, a moderate sum, best we can, on which you can function. Until we track down the damn receiver and find out what it's tied to. For us, the main headache is that word of this matter has begun to filter through the department. It's going to be hard getting crack-down teams to tackle future outspacer gambling operations . . . which of course is specifically what they had in mind. One more thing we can do. We can have the lab build you a brain-shield so you no longer emanate a recognizable template. But you'd have to pay for it out of your own pocket. Possibly it could be debited against your salary, payments divided over several months. If you're interested. Frankly, if you want my personal opinion, I'd advise it.'

'All right,' Tinbane said. He felt dull, dead, tired and resigned; all of those at once. And he had the deep and acute intuition that his reaction was rational. 'Anything else you suggest?' he asked.

'Stay armed. Even when you're asleep.'

'What sleep?' he said. 'You think I'm going to get any sleep? Maybe I will after that machine is totally destroyed.' But that won't make any difference, he realized. Not now. Not after it's dispatched my brainwave pattern to something else, something we know nothing about. God knows what equipment it might turn out to be; outspacers show up with all kinds of convoluted things.

He hung up the phone, walked into his kitchen, and getting down a half-empty fifth of Antique bourbon, fixed himself a whiskey sour.

What a mess, he said to himself. Pursued by a pinball machine from another world. He almost—but not quite—had to laugh.

What do you use, he asked himself, to catch an angry pinball machine? One that has your number and is out to get you? Or more specifically, a pinball machine's nebulous friend . . .

Something went *tap tap* against the kitchen window.

Reaching into his pocket he brought out his regulation-issue laser pistol; walking along the kitchen wall he approached the window from an unseen side, peered out into the night. Darkness. He could make nothing out. Flashlight? He had one in the glove compartment of his aircar, parked on the roof of the conapt building. Time to get it.

A moment later, flashlight in hand, he raced downstairs, back to his kitchen.

The beam of the flashlight showed, pressed against the outer surface of the window, a buglike entity with projecting elongated pseudopodia. The two feelers had tapped against the glass of the window, evidently exploring in their blind, mechanical way.

The bug-thing had ascended the side of the building; he could perceive the suction-tread by which it clung.

His curiosity, at this point, became greater than his fear. With care he opened the window—no need of having to pay the building repair committee for it—and cautiously took aim with his laser pistol. The bug-thing did not stir; evidently it had stalled in mid-cycle. Probably its responses, he guessed, were relatively slow, much more so than a comparable organic equivalent. Unless, of course, it was set to detonate; in which case he had no time to ponder.

He fired a narrow-beam into the underside of the bug-thing.

Maimed, the bug-thing settled backward, its many little cups releasing their hold. As it fell away, Tinbane caught hold of it, lifted it swiftly into the room, dropped it onto the floor, meantime keeping his pistol pointed at it. But it was finished functionally; it did not stir.

Laying it on the small kitchen table he got a screwdriver from the tool-drawer beside the sink, seated himself, examined the object. He felt, now, that he could take his time; the pressure, momentarily at least, had abated.

It took him forty minutes to get the thing open; none of the holding screws fitted an ordinary screwdriver, and he found himself at last using a common kitchen knife. But finally he had it open before him on the table, its shell divided into two parts: one hollow and empty, the other crammed with components. A bomb? He tinkered with exceeding care, inspecting each assembly bit by bit.

No bomb—at least none which he could identify. Then a murder tool? No blade, no toxins or micro-organisms, no tube capable of expelling a lethal charge, explosive or otherwise. So then what in God's name did it do? He recognized the motor which had driven it up the side of the building, then the photo-electric steering turret by which it oriented itself. But that was all. Absolutely all.

From the standpoint of use, it was a fraud.

Or was it? He examined his watch. Now he had spent an entire hour on it; his attention had been diverted from everything else—and who knew what that else might be?

Nervously, he slid stiffly to his feet, collected his laser pistol, and prowled throughout the apartment, listening, wondering, trying to sense something, however small, that was out of its usual order.

It's giving them time, he realized. One entire hour! For whatever it is they're *really* up to.

Time, he thought, for me to leave the apartment. To get to La Jolla and the hell out of here, until this is all over with.

His vidphone rang.

When he answered it, Ted Donovan's face clicked grayly into view. 'We've got a department aircar monitoring your conapt building,' Donovan said. 'And it picked up some activity; I thought you'd want to know.'

'Okay,' he said tensely.

'A vehicle, airborne, landed briefly on your roof parking lot. Not a standard aircar but something larger. Nothing we could recognize. It took right off again at great speed, but I think this is it.'

'Did it deposit anything?' he asked.

'Yes. Afraid so.'

Tight-lipped, he said, 'Can you do anything for me at this late point? It would be appreciated very much.'

'What do you suggest? We don't know what it is; you certainly don't know either. We're open to ideas, but I think we'll have to wait until you know the nature of the—hostile artifact.'

Something bumped against his door, something in the hall.

'I'll leave the line open,' Tinbane said. 'Don't leave; I think it's happening now.' He felt panic, at this stage; overt, childish panic. Carrying his laser pistol in a numb, loose grip he made his way step by step to the locked front door of his conapt, halted, then unlocked the door and opened it. Slightly. As little as he could manage.

An enormous, unchecked force pushed the door farther; the knob left his hand. And, soundlessly, the vast steel ball resting against the half-open door rolled forward. He stepped aside—he had to—knowing that this was the adversary; the dummy wall-climbing gadget had deflected his attention from this.

He could not get out. He would not be going to La Jolla now. The great massed sphere totally blocked the way.

Returning to the vidphone he said to Donovan, 'I'm encapsulated. Here in my own conapt.' At the outer perimeter, he realized. Equal to the rough terrain of the pinball machine's shifting landscape. The first ball has been blocked there, has lodged in the doorway. But what about the second? The third?

Each would be closer.

'Can you build something for me?' he asked huskily. 'Can the lab start working this late at night?'

'We can try,' Donovan said. 'It depends entirely on what you want. What do you have in mind? What do you think would help?'

He hated to ask for it. But he had to. The next one might burst in through a window, or crash onto him from the roof. 'I want,' he said, 'some form of catapult. Big enough, tough enough, to handle a spherical load with a diameter of between four and a half and five feet. You think you can manage it?' He prayed to God they could.

'Is that what you're facing?' Donovan said harshly.

'Unless it's an hallucination,' Tinbane said. 'A deliberate, artificially induced terror-projection, designed specifically to demoralize me.'

'The department aircar saw something,' Donovan said. 'And it wasn't an hallucination; it had measurable mass. And—' He hesitated. 'It did leave off something big. Its departing mass was considerably diminished. So it's real, Tinbane.'

'That's what I thought,' Tinbane said.

'We'll get the catapult to you as soon as we possibly can,' Donovan said. 'Let's hope there's an adequate interval between each—attack. And you better figure on five at least.'

Tinbane, nodding, lit a cigarette, or at least tried to. But his hands were shaking too badly to get the lighter into place. He then got out a yellow-lacquered tin of Dean's Own snuff, but found himself unable to force open the tight tin; the tin hopped from his fingers and fell to the floor. 'Five,' he said, '*per game.*'

'Yes,' Donovan said reluctantly, 'there's that.'

The wall of the living room shuddered.

The next one was coming at him from the adjoining apartment.

FAITH OF OUR FATHERS

On the streets of Hanoi he found himself facing a legless peddler who rode a little wooden cart and called shrilly to every passer-by. Chien slowed, listened, but did not stop; business at the Ministry of Cultural Artifacts cropped into his mind and deflected his attention: it was as if he were alone, and none of those on bicycles and scooters and jet-powered motorcycles remained. And likewise it was as if the legless peddler did not exist.

'Comrade,' the peddler called, however, and pursued him on his cart; a helium battery operated the drive and sent the cart scuttling expertly after Chien. 'I possess a wide spectrum of time-tested herbal remedies complete with testimonials from thousands of loyal users; advise me of your malady and I can assist.'

Chien, pausing, said, 'Yes, but I have no malady.' Except, he thought, for the chronic one of those employed by the Central Committee, that of career opportunism testing constantly the gates of each official position. Including mine.

'I can cure for example radiation sickness,' the peddler chanted, still pursuing him. 'Or expand, if necessary, the element of sexual prowess. I can reverse carcinomatous progressions, even the dreaded melanomae, what you would call black cancers.' Lifting a tray of bottles, small aluminum cans and assorted powders in plastic jars, the peddler sang, 'If a rival persists in trying to usurp your gainful bureaucratic position, I can purvey an ointment which, appearing as a dermal balm, is in actuality a desperately effective toxin. And my prices, comrade, are low. And as a special favor to one so distinguished in bearing as yourself I will accept the postwar inflationary paper dollars reputedly of international exchange but in reality damn near no better than bathroom tissue.'

'Go to hell,' Chien said, and signaled a passing hover-car taxi; he was already three and one half minutes late for his first appointment of the day, and his various fat-assed superiors at the Ministry would be making quick mental notations—as would, to an even greater degree, his subordinates.

The peddler said quietly, 'But, comrade; you *must* buy from me.'

'Why?' Chien demanded. Indignation.

'Because, comrade, I am a war veteran. I fought in the Colossal Final War of National Liberation with the People's Democratic United Front against the Imperialists; I lost my pedal extremities at the battle of San Francisco.' His tone was triumphant, now, and sly. '*It is the law*. If you refuse to buy wares offered by a veteran you risk a fine and possible jail sentence—and in addition disgrace.'

Wearily, Chien nodded the hovercab on. 'Admittedly,' he said. 'Okay, I must buy from you.' He glanced summarily over the meager display of herbal remedies, seeking one at random. 'That,' he decided, pointing to a paper-wrapped parcel in the rear row.

The peddler laughed. 'That, comrade, is a spermatocide, bought by women who for political reasons cannot qualify for The Pill. It would be of shallow use to you, in fact none at all, since you are a gentleman.'

'The law,' Chien said bitingly, 'does not require me to purchase anything useful from you; only that I purchase something. I'll take that.' He reached into his padded coat for his billfold, huge with the postwar inflationary bills in which, four times a week, he as a government servant was paid.

'Tell me your problems,' the peddler said.

Chien stared at him, appalled by the invasion of privacy—and done by someone outside the government.

'All right, comrade,' the peddler said, seeing his expression. 'I will not probe; excuse me. But as a doctor—an herbal healer—it is fitting that I know as much as possible.' He pondered, his gaunt features somber. 'Do you watch television unusually much?' he asked abruptly.

Taken by surprise, Chien said, 'Every evening. Except on Friday, when I go to my club to practice the esoteric imported art from the defeated West of steer-roping.' It was his only indulgence; other than that he had totally devoted himself to Party activities.

The peddler reached, selected a gray paper packet. 'Sixty trade dollars,' he stated. 'With a full guarantee; if it does not do as promised, return the unused portion for a full and cheery refund.'

'And what,' Chien said cuttingly, 'is it guaranteed to do?'

'It will rest eyes fatigued by the countenance of meaningless official monologues,' the peddler said. 'A soothing preparation; take it as soon as you find yourself exposed to the usual dry and lengthy sermons which—'

Chien paid the money, accepted the packet, and strode off. Balls, he said to himself. It's a racket, he decided, the ordinance setting up war vets as a privileged class. They prey off us—we, the younger ones—like raptors.

Forgotten, the gray packet remained deposited in his coat pocket as he entered the imposing Postwar Ministry of Cultural Artifacts building, and his own considerable stately office, to begin his workday.

A portly, middle-aged Caucasian male, wearing a brown Hong Kong silk suit, double-breasted with vest, waited in his office. With the unfamiliar Caucasian stood his own immediate superior, Ssu-Ma Tso-pin. Tso-pin introduced the two of them in Cantonese, a dialect which he used badly.

'Mr Tung Chien, this is Mr Darius Pethel. Mr Pethel will be headmaster at the new ideological and cultural establishment of didactic character soon to open at San Fernando, California.' He added, 'Mr Pethel has had a rich and full lifetime supporting the people's struggle to unseat imperialist-bloc countries via pedagogic media; therefore this high post.'

They shook hands.

'Tea?' Chien asked the two of them; he pressed the switch of his

infrared hibachi and in an instant the water in the highly orna-
mented ceramic pot—of Japanese origin—began to burble. As he
seated himself at his desk he saw that trustworthy Miss Hsi had
laid out the information poop-sheet (confidential) on Comrade
Pethel; he glanced over it; meanwhile pretending to be doing nothing in particular.

'The Absolute Benefactor of the People,' Tso-pin said, 'has personally met Mr Pethel and trusts him. This is rare. The school in
San Fernando will appear to teach run-of-the-mill Taoist philoso-
phies but will, of course, in actuality maintain for us a channel of
communication to the liberal and intellectual youth segment of
western US. There are many of them still alive, from San Diego to
Sacramento; we estimate at least ten thousand. The school will
accept two thousand. Enrollment will be mandatory for those we
select. Your relationship to Mr Pethel's programming is grave.
Ahem; your tea water is boiling.'

'Thank you,' Chien murmured, dropping in the bag of Lipton's
tea.

Tso-pin continued, 'Although Mr Pethel will supervise the setting up of the courses of instruction presented by the school to its
student body, all examination papers will, oddly enough, be
relayed here to your office for your own expert, careful, ideological
study. In other words, Mr Chien, you will determine who among
the two thousand students is reliable, which are truly responding
to the programming and who is not.'

'I will now pour my tea,' Chien said, doing so ceremoniously.

'What we have to realize,' Pethel rumbled in Cantonese even
worse than that of Tso-pin, 'is that, once having lost the global war
to us, the American youth has developed a talent for dissembling.'
He spoke the last word in English; not understanding it, Chien
turned inquiringly to his superior.

'Lying,' Tso-pin explained.

Pethel said, 'Mouthing the proper slogans for surface appearance, but on the inside believing them false. Test papers by this
group will closely resemble those of genuine—'

'You mean that the test papers of *two thousand* students will be passing through my office?' Chien demanded. He could not believe it. 'That's a full-time job in itself; I don't have time for anything remotely resembling that.' He was appalled. 'To give critical, official approval or denial of the astute variety which you're envisioning—' He gestured. 'Screw that,' he said, in English.

Blinking at the strong, Western vulgarity, Tso-pin said, 'You have a staff. Plus you can requisition several more from the pool; the Ministry's budget, augmented this year, will permit it. And remember: the Absolute Benefactor of the People has hand-picked Mr Pethel.' His tone, now, had become ominous, but only subtly so. Just enough to penetrate Chien's hysteria, and to wither it into submission. At least temporarily. To underline his point, Tso-pin walked to the far end of the office; he stood before the full-length 3-D portrait of the Absolute Benefactor, and after an interval his proximity triggered the tape-transport mounted behind the portrait; the face of the Benefactor moved, and from it came a familiar homily, in more than familiar accents. 'Fight for peace, my sons,' it intoned gently, firmly.

'Ha,' Chien said, still perturbed, but concealing it. Possibly one of the Ministry's computers could sort the examination papers; a yes-no-maybe structure could be employed, in conjunction with a pre-analysis of the pattern of ideological correctness—and incorrectness. The matter could be made routine. Probably.

Darius Pethel said, 'I have with me certain material which I would like you to scrutinize, Mr Chien.' He unzipped an unsightly, old-fashioned, plastic briefcase. 'Two examination essays,' he said as he passed the documents to Chien. 'This will tell us if you're qualified.' He then glanced at Tso-pin; their gazes met. 'I understand,' Pethel said, 'that if you are successful in this venture you will be made vice-councilor of the Ministry, and His Greatness the Absolute Benefactor of the People will personally confer Kisterigian's medal on you.' Both he and Tso-pin smiled in wary unison.

'The Kisterigian medal,' Chien echoed; he accepted the examination papers, glanced over them in a show of leisurely indifference. But within him his heart vibrated in ill-concealed tension. 'Why these two? By that I mean, what am I looking for, sir?'

'One of them,' Pethel said, 'is the work of a dedicated progressive, a loyal Party member of thoroughly researched conviction. The other is by a young *stilyagi* whom we suspect of holding petit-bourgeois imperialist degenerate crypto-ideas. It is up to you, sir, to determine which is which.'

Thanks a lot, Chien thought. But, nodding, he read the title of the top paper.

DOCTRINES OF THE ABSOLUTE BENEFACTOR ANTICIPATED IN THE POETRY OF BAHA AD-DIN ZUHAYR OF THIRTEENTH-CENTURY ARABIA

Glancing down the initial pages of the essay, Chien saw a quatrain familiar to him; it was called 'Death,' and he had known it most of his adult, educated life.

> *Once he will miss, twice he will miss,*
> *He only chooses one of many hours;*
> *For him nor deep nor hill there is,*
> *But all's one level plain he hunts for flowers.*

'Powerful,' Chien said. 'This poem.'

'He makes use of the poem,' Pethel said, observing Chien's lips moving as he reread the quatrain, 'to indicate the age-old wisdom, displayed by the Absolute Benefactor in our current lives, that no individual is safe; everyone is mortal, and only the supra-personal, historically essential cause survives. As it should be. Would you agree with him? With this student, I mean? Or—' Pethel paused. 'Is he in fact perhaps satirizing the Absolute Benefactor's promulgations?'

Cagily, Chien said, 'Give me a chance to inspect the other paper.'

'You need no further information; decide.'

Haltingly, Chien said, 'I–I had never thought of this poem that way.' He felt irritable. 'Anyhow, it isn't by Baha ad-Din Zuhayr; it's part of the *Thousand and One Nights* anthology. It is, however, thirteenth century; I admit that.' He quickly read over the text of the paper accompanying the poem. It appeared to be a routine, uninspired rehash of Party clichés, all of them familiar to him from birth. The blind, imperialist monster who mowed down and snuffed out (mixed metaphor) human aspiration, the calculations of the still extant anti-Party group in eastern United States . . . He felt dully bored, and as uninspired as the student's paper. We must persevere, the paper declared. Wipe out the Pentagon remnants in the Catskills, subdue Tennessee and most especially the pocket of die-hard reaction in the red hills of Oklahoma. He sighed.

'I think,' Tso-pin said, 'we should allow Mr Chien the opportunity of observing this difficult matter at his leisure.' To Chien he said, 'You have permission to take them home to your condominium, this evening, and adjudge them on your own time.' He bowed, half mockingly, half solicitously. In any case, insult or not, he had gotten Chien off the hook, and for that Chien was grateful.

'You are most kind,' he murmured, 'to allow me to perform this new and highly stimulating labor on my own time. Mikoyan, were he alive today, would approve.' You bastard, he said to himself. Meaning both his superior and the Caucasian Pethel. Handing me a hot potato like this, and on my own time. Obviously the CP USA is in trouble; its indoctrination academies aren't managing to do their job with the notoriously mulish, eccentric Yank youths. And you've passed that hot potato on and on until it reaches me.

Thanks for nothing, he thought acidly.

That evening in his small but well-appointed condominium apartment he read over the other of the two examination papers, this one by a Marion Culper, and discovered that it, too, dealt with poetry. Obviously this was speciously a poetry class, and he felt ill. It had always run against his grain, the use of poetry—of any art—for social purposes. Anyhow, comfortable in his special spine-straightening, simulated-leather easy chair, he lit a Cuesta Rey

Number One English Market immense corona cigar and began to read.

The writer of the paper, Miss Culper, had selected as her text a portion of a poem of John Dryden, the seventeenth-century English poet, final lines from the well-known 'A Song for St Cecilia's Day.'

> ... So when the last and dreadful hour
> This crumbling pageant shall devour,
> The trumpet shall be heard on high,
> The dead shall live, the living die,
> And Music shall untune the sky.

Well, that's a hell of a thing, Chien thought to himself bitingly. Dryden, we're supposed to believe, anticipated the fall of capitalism? That's what he meant by the 'crumbling pageant'? Christ. He leaned over to take hold of his cigar and found that it had gone out. Groping in his pockets for his Japanese-made lighter, he half rose to his feet.

Tweeeeeee! the TV set at the far end of the living room said.

Aha, Chien thought. We're about to be addressed by the Leader. By the Absolute Benefactor of the People, up there in Peking, where he's lived for ninety years now; or is it one hundred? Or, as we sometimes like to think of him, the Ass–

'May the ten thousand blossoms of abject self-assumed poverty flower in your spiritual courtyard,' the TV announcer said. With a groan, Chien rose to his feet, bowed the mandatory bow of response; each TV set came equipped with monitoring devices to narrate to the Secpol, the Security Police, whether its owner was bowing and/or watching.

On the screen a clearly defined visage manifested itself, the wide, unlined, healthy features of the one-hundred-and-twenty-year-old leader of CP East, ruler of many–far too many, Chien reflected. Blah to you, he thought, and reseated himself in his simulated-leather easy chair, now facing the TV screen.

'My thoughts,' the Absolute Benefactor said in his rich and slow tones, 'are on you, my children. And especially on Mr Tung Chien of Hanoi, who faces a difficult task ahead, a task to enrich the people of Democratic East, plus the American West Coast. We must think in unison about this noble, dedicated man and the chore which he faces, and I have chosen to take several moments of my time to honor him and encourage him. Are you listening, Mr Chien?'

'Yes, Your Greatness,' Chien said, and pondered to himself the odds against the Party Leader singling *him* out this particular evening. The odds caused him to feel uncomradely cynicism; it was unconvincing. Probably this transmission was being beamed into his apartment building alone—or at least to this city. It might also be a lip-synch job, done at Hanoi TV, Incorporated. In any case he was required to listen and watch—and absorb. He did so, from a lifetime of practice. Outwardly he appeared to be rigidly attentive. Inwardly he was still mulling over the two test papers, wondering which was which; where did devout Party enthusiasm end and sardonic lampoonery begin? Hard to say ... which of course explained why they had dumped the task in his lap.

Again he groped in his pockets for his lighter—and found the small gray envelope which the war-veteran peddler had sold him. Gawd, he thought, remembering what it had cost. Money down the drain and what did this herbal remedy do? Nothing. He turned the packet over and saw, on the back, small printed words. Well, he thought, and began to unfold the packet with care. The words had snared him—as of course they were meant to do.

> Failing as a Party member and human?
> Afraid of becoming obsolete and discarded
> on the ash heap of history by ...

He read rapidly through the text, ignoring its claims, seeking to find out what he had purchased.

Meanwhile the Absolute Benefactor droned on.

Snuff. The package contained snuff. Countless tiny black grains, like gunpowder, which sent up an interesting aromatic to tickle his nose. The title of the particular blend was Princes Special, he discovered. And very pleasing, he decided. At one time he had taken snuff—smoking tobacco for a time having been illegal for reasons of health—back during his student days at Peking U; it had been the fad, especially the amatory mixes prepared in Chungking, made from God knew what. Was this that? Almost any aromatic could be added to snuff, from essence of orange to pulverized baby-crap . . . or so some seemed, especially an English mixture called High Dry Toast which had in itself more or less put an end to his yearning for nasal, inhaled tobacco.

On the TV screen the Absolute Benefactor rumbled monotonously on as Chien sniffed cautiously at the powder, read the claims—it cured everything from being late to work to falling in love with a woman of dubious political background. Interesting. But typical of claims—

His doorbell rang.

Rising, he walked to the door, opened it with full knowledge of what he would find. There, sure enough, stood Mou Kuei, the Building Warden, small and hard-eyed and alert to his task; he had his arm band and metal helmet on, showing that he meant business. 'Mr Chien, comrade Party worker. I received a call from the television authority. You are failing to watch your television screen and are instead fiddling with a packet of doubtful content.' He produced a clipboard and ballpoint pen. 'Two red marks, and hithertonow you are summarily ordered to repose yourself in a comfortable, stress-free posture before your screen and give the Leader your unexcelled attention. His words, this evening, are directed particularly to you, sir; to you.'

'I doubt that,' Chien heard himself say.

Blinking, Kuei said, 'What do you mean?'

'The Leader rules eight billion comrades. He isn't going to single me out.' He felt wrathful; the punctuality of the warden's reprimand irked him.

Kuei said, 'But I distinctly heard with my own ears. You were mentioned.'

Going over to the TV set, Chien turned the volume up. 'But now he's talking about failures in People's India; that's of no relevance to me.'

'Whatever the Leader expostulates is relevant.' Mou Kuei scratched a mark on his clipboard sheet, bowed formally, turned away. 'My call to come up here to confront you with your slackness originated at Central. Obviously they regard your attention as important; I must order you to set in motion your automatic transmission recording circuit and replay the earlier portions of the Leader's speech.'

Chien farted. And shut the door.

Back to the TV set, he said to himself. Where our leisure hours are spent. And there lay the two student examination papers; he had that weighing him down, too. And all on my own time, he thought savagely. The hell with them. Up theirs. He strode to the TV set, started to shut it off; at once a red warning light winked on, informing him that he did not have permission to shut off the set—could not in fact end its tirade and image even if he unplugged it. Mandatory speeches, he thought, will kill us all, bury us; if I could be free of the noise of speeches, free of the din of the Party baying as it hounds mankind . . .

There was no known ordinance, however, preventing him from taking snuff while he watched the Leader. So, opening the small gray packet, he shook out a mound of the black granules onto the back of his left hand. He then, professionally, raised his hand to his nostrils and deeply inhaled, drawing the snuff well up into his sinus cavities. Imagine the old superstition, he thought to himself. That the sinus cavities are connected to the brain, and hence an inhalation of snuff directly affects the cerebral cortex. He smiled, seated himself once more, fixed his gaze on the TV screen and the gesticulating individual known so utterly to them all.

The face dwindled away, disappeared. The sound ceased. He faced an emptiness, a vacuum. The screen, white and blank, confronted him and from the speaker a faint hiss sounded.

The frigging snuff, he said to himself. And inhaled greedily at the remainder of the powder on his hand, drawing it up avidly into his nose, his sinuses, and, or so it felt, into his brain; he plunged into the snuff, absorbing it elatedly.

The screen remained blank and then, by degrees, an image once more formed and established itself. It was not the Leader. Not the Absolute Benefactor of the People, in point of fact not a human figure at all.

He faced a dead mechanical construct, made of solid-state circuits, of swiveling pseudopodia, lenses and a squawk-box. And the box began, in a droning din, to harangue him.

Staring fixedly, he thought, *What is this?* Reality? Hallucination, he thought. The peddler came across some of the psychedelic drugs used during the War of Liberation—he's selling the stuff and I've taken some, taken a whole lot!

Making his way unsteadily to the vidphone, he dialed the Secpol station nearest his building. 'I wish to report a pusher of hallucinogenic drugs,' he said into the receiver.

'Your name, sir, and conapt location?' Efficient, brisk and impersonal bureaucrat of the police.

He gave them the information, then haltingly made it back to his simulated-leather easy chair, once again to witness the apparition on the TV screen. This is lethal, he said to himself. It must be some preparation developed in Washington, DC, or London— stronger and stranger than the LSD-25 which they dumped so effectively into our reservoirs. And I thought it was going to relieve me of the burden of the Leader's speeches . . . this is far worse, this electronic, sputtering, swiveling, metal and plastic monstrosity yammering away—this is terrifying.

To have to face *this* the remainder of my life—

It took ten minutes for the Secpol two-man team to come rapping at his door. And by then, in a deteriorating set of stages, the familiar image of the Leader had seeped back into focus on the screen, had supplanted the horrible artificial construct which waved its podia and squalled on and on. He let the two cops in shakily, led them to the table on which he had left the remains of the snuff in its packet.

'Psychedelic toxin,' he said thickly. 'Of short duration. Absorbed into the bloodstream directly, through nasal capillaries. I'll give you details as to where I got it, from whom, all that.' He took a deep shaky breath; the presence of the police was comforting.

Ballpoint pens ready, the two officers waited. And all the time, in the background, the Leader rattled out his endless speech. As he had done a thousand evenings before in the life of Tung Chien. But, he thought, it'll never be the same again, at least not for me. Not after inhaling that near-toxic snuff.

He wondered, Is that what they intended?

It seemed odd to him, thinking of a *they*. Peculiar—but somehow correct. For an instant he hesitated, not giving out the details, not telling the police enough to find the man. A peddler, he started to say. I don't know where; can't remember. But he did; he remembered the exact street intersection. So, with unexplainable reluctance, he told them.

'Thank you, comrade Chien.' The boss of the team of police carefully gathered up the remaining snuff—most of it remained—and placed it in his uniform—smart, sharp uniform—pocket. 'We'll have it analyzed at the first available moment,' the cop said, 'and inform you immediately in case counter-medical measures are indicated for you. Some of the old wartime psychedelics were eventually fatal, as you have no doubt read.'

'I've read,' he agreed. That had been specifically what he had been thinking.

'Good luck and thanks for notifying us,' both cops said, and departed. The affair, for all their efficiency, did not seem to shake them; obviously such a complaint was routine.

The lab report came swiftly—surprisingly so, in view of the vast state bureaucracy. It reached him by vidphone before the Leader had finished his TV speech.

'It's not a hallucinogen,' the Secpol lab technician informed him.

'No?' he said, puzzled and, strangely, not relieved. Not at all.

'On the contrary. It's a phenothiazine, which as you doubtless know is anti-hallucinogenic. A strong dose per gram of admixture, but harmless. Might lower your blood pressure or make you sleepy. Probably stolen from a wartime cache of medical supplies. Left by the retreating barbarians. I wouldn't worry.'

Pondering, Chien hung up the vidphone in slow motion. And then walked to the window of his conapt—the window with the fine view of other Hanoi high-rise conapts—to think.

The doorbell rang. Feeling as if he were in a trance, he crossed the carpeted living room to answer it.

The girl standing there, in a tan raincoat with a babushka over her dark, shiny, and very long hair, said in a timid little voice, 'Um, Comrade Chien? Tung Chien? Of the Ministry of—'

He let her in, reflexively, and shut the door after her. 'You've been monitoring my vidphone,' he told her; it was a shot in darkness, but something in him, an unvoiced certitude, told him that she had.

'Did—they take the rest of the snuff?' She glanced about. 'Oh, I hope not; it's so hard to get these days.'

'Snuff,' he said, 'is easy to get. Phenothiazine isn't. Is that what you mean?'

The girl raised her head, studied him with large, moon-darkened eyes. 'Yes. Mr Chien—' She hesitated, obviously as uncertain as the Secpol cops had been assured. 'Tell me what you saw; it's of great importance for us to be certain.'

'I had a choice?' he said acutely.

'Y-yes, very much so. That's what confuses us; that's what is not as we planned. We don't understand it; it fits nobody's theory.' Her eyes even darker and deeper, she said, 'Was it the aquatic horror shape? The thing with slime and teeth, the extraterrestrial life form? Please tell me; we have to know.' She breathed irregularly, with effort, the tan raincoat rising and falling; he found himself watching its rhythm.

'A machine,' he said.

'Oh!' She ducked her head, nodding vigorously. 'Yes, I understand; a mechanical organism in no way resembling a human. Not a simulacrum, or something constructed to resemble a man.'

He said, 'This did not look like a man.' He added to himself, And it failed—did not try—to talk like a man.

'You understand that it was not a hallucination.'

'I've been officially told that what I took was a phenothiazine. That's all I know.' He said as little as possible; he did not want to talk but to hear. Hear what the girl had to say.

'Well, Mr Chien—' She took a deep, unstable breath. 'If it was not a hallucination, then what was it? What does that leave? What is called "extraconsciousness"—could that be it?'

He did not answer; turning his back, he leisurely picked up the two student test papers, glanced over them, ignoring her. Waiting for her next attempt.

At his shoulder, she appeared, smelling of spring rain, smelling of sweetness and agitation, beautiful in the way she smelled, and looked, and, he thought, speaks. So different from the harsh plateau speech patterns we hear on the TV—have heard since I was a baby.

'Some of them,' she said huskily, 'who take the stelazine—it was stelazine you got, Mr Chien—see one apparition, some another. But distinct categories have emerged; there is not an infinite variety. Some see what you saw; we call it the Clanker. Some the aquatic horror; that's the Gulper. And then there's the Bird, and the Climbing Tube, and—' She broke off. 'But other reactions tell you very little. Tell *us* very little.' She hesitated, then plunged on. 'Now that this has happened to you, Mr Chien, we would like you to join our gathering. Join your particular group, those who see what you see. Group Red. We want to know what it *really* is, and—' She gestured with tapered, wax smooth fingers. 'It can't be *all* those manifestations.' Her tone was poignant, naively so. He felt his caution relax—a trifle.

He said, 'What do you see? You in particular?'

'I'm a part of Group Yellow. I see—a storm. A whining, vicious whirlwind. That roots everything up, crushes condominium apartments built to last a century.' She smiled wanly. 'The Crusher. Twelve groups in all, Mr Chien. Twelve absolutely different experiences, all from the same phenothiazines, all of the Leader as he speaks over TV. As *it* speaks, rather.' She smiled up at him, lashes long—probably protracted artificially—and gaze engaging, even trusting. As if she thought he knew something or could do something.

'I should make a citizen's arrest of you,' he said presently.

'There is no law, not about this. We studied Soviet judicial writings before we—found people to distribute the stelazine. We don't have much of it; we have to be very careful whom we give it to. It seemed to us that you constituted a likely choice . . . a well-known, postwar, dedicated young career man on his way up.' From his fingers she took the examination papers. 'They're having you pol-read?' she asked.

'"Pol-read"?' He did not know the term.

'Study something said or written to see if it fits the Party's current world view. You in the hierarchy merely call it "read," don't you?' Again she smiled. 'When you rise one step higher, up with Mr Tso-pin, you will know that expression.' She added somberly, 'And with Mr Pethel. He's very far up. Mr Chien, there is no ideological school in San Fernando; these are forged exam papers, designed to read back to them a thorough analysis of *your* political ideology. And have you been able to distinguish which paper is orthodox and which is heretical?' Her voice was pixielike, taunting with amused malice. 'Choose the wrong one and your budding career stops dead, cold, in its tracks. Choose the proper one—'

'Do you know which is which?' he demanded.

'Yes.' She nodded soberly. 'We have listening devices in Mr Tso-pin's inner offices; we monitored his conversation with Mr Pethel—who is not Mr Pethel but the Higher Secpol Inspector Judd Craine. You have probably heard mention of him; he acted as chief assistant to Judge Vorlawsky at the '98 war-crimes trial in Zurich.'

With difficulty he said, 'I—see.' Well, that explained that.

The girl said, 'My name is Tanya Lee.'

He said nothing; he merely nodded, too stunned for any cerebration.

'Technically, I am a minor clerk,' Miss Lee said, 'at your Ministry. You have never run into me, however, that I can at least recall. We try to hold posts wherever we can. As far up as possible. My own boss–'

'Should you be telling me this?' He gestured at the TV set, which remained on. 'Aren't they picking this up?'

Tanya Lee said, 'We introduced a noise factor in the reception of both vid and aud material from this apartment building; it will take them almost an hour to locate the sheathing. So we have'–she examined the tiny wristwatch on her slender wrist–'fifteen more minutes. And still be safe.'

'Tell me,' he said, 'which paper is orthodox.'

'Is that what you care about? Really?'

'What,' he said, 'should I care about?'

'Don't you see, Mr Chien? You've learned something. The Leader is not the Leader; he is something else, but we can't tell what. Not yet. Mr Chien, with all due respect, have you ever had your drinking water analyzed? I know it sounds paranoiac, but have you?'

'No,' he said. 'Of course not.' Knowing what she was going to say.

Miss Lee said briskly, 'Our tests show that it's saturated with hallucinogens. It is, has been, will continue to be. Not the ones used during the war; not the disorientating ones, but a synthetic quasi-ergot derivative called Datrox-3. You drink it here in the building from the time you get up; you drink it in restaurants and other apartments that you visit. You drink it at the Ministry; it's all piped from a central, common source.' Her tone was bleak and ferocious. 'We solved that problem; we knew, as soon as we discovered it, that any good phenothiazine would counter it. What we did not know, of course, was this–a *variety* of authentic experiences; that makes no sense, rationally. It's the hallucination which should differ from person to person, and the reality experience which should be ubiquitous–it's all turned around. We can't even construct an ad hoc theory which accounts for that, and God knows we've tried. Twelve mutually exclusive hallucinations–that would be easily understood. But not one hallucination and twelve realities.' She ceased talking then, and studied the two test papers, her forehead wrinkling. 'The one with the Arabic poem is ortho-dox,' she stated. 'If you tell them that they'll trust you and give you a higher post. You'll be another notch up in the hierarchy of Party officialdom.' Smiling—her teeth were perfect and lovely—she fin-ished, 'Look what you received back for your investment this morning. Your career is underwritten for a time. And by us.'

He said, 'I don't believe you.' Instinctively, his caution operated within him, always, the caution of a lifetime lived among the hatchet men of the Hanoi branch of the CP East. They knew an infinitude of ways by which to ax a rival out of contention—some of which he himself had employed; some of which he had seen done to himself and to others. This could be a novel way, one unfamiliar to him. It could always be.

'Tonight,' Miss Lee said, 'in the speech the Leader singled you out. Didn't this strike you as strange? You, of all people? A minor officeholder in a meager ministry—'

'Admitted,' he said. 'It struck me that way; yes.'

'That was legitimate. His Greatness is grooming an elite cadre of younger men, postwar men, he hopes will infuse new life into the hidebound, moribund hierarchy of old fogies and Party hacks. His Greatness singled you out for the same reason that we singled you out; if pursued properly, your career could lead you all the way to the top. At least for a time . . . as we know. That's how it goes.'

He thought: So virtually everyone has faith in me. Except myself; and certainly not after this, the experience with the anti-hallucinatory snuff. It had shaken years of confidence, and no doubt rightly so. However, he was beginning to regain his poise; he felt it seeping back, a little at first, then with a rush.

Going to the vidphone, he lifted the receiver and began, for the second time that night, to dial the number of the Hanoi Security Police.

'Turning me in,' Miss Lee said, 'would be the second most regressive decision you could make. I'll tell them that you brought me here to bribe me; you thought, because of my job at the Ministry, I would know which examination paper to select.'

He said, 'And what would be my first most regressive decision?'

'Not taking a further dose of phenothiazine,' Miss Lee said evenly.

Hanging up the phone, Tung Chien thought to himself, I don't understand what's happening to me. Two forces, the Party and His Greatness on one hand—this girl with her alleged group on the other. One wants me to rise as far as possible in the Party hierarchy; the other—*What did Tanya Lee want?* Underneath the words, inside the membrane of an almost trivial contempt for the Party, the Leader, the ethical standards of the People's Democratic United Front—what was she after in regard to him?

He said curiously, 'Are you anti-Party?'

'No.'

'But—' He gestured. 'That's all there is: Party and anti-Party. You must be Party, then.' Bewildered, he stared at her; with composure she returned the stare. 'You have an organization,' he said, 'and you meet. What do you intend to destroy? The regular function of government? Are you like the treasonable college students of the United States during the Vietnam War who stopped troop trains, demonstrated—'

Wearily Miss Lee said, 'It wasn't like that. But forget it; that's not the issue. What we want to know is this: who or what is leading us? We must penetrate far enough to enlist someone, some rising young Party theoretician, who could conceivably be invited to a tête-à-tête with the Leader—you see?' Her voice lifted; she consulted her watch, obviously anxious to get away: the fifteen minutes were almost up. 'Very few persons actually see the Leader, as you know. I mean really see him.'

'Seclusion,' he said. 'Due to his advanced age.'

'We have hope,' Miss Lee said, 'that if you pass the phony test which they have arranged for you—and with my help you have—you will be invited to one of the stag parties which the Leader has from time to time, which of course the papers don't report. Now do you see?' Her voice rose shrilly, in a frenzy of despair. 'Then we would know; if you could go in there under the influence of the anti-hallucinogenic drug, could see him face to face as he actually is—'

Thinking aloud, he said, 'And end my career of public service. If not my life.'

'You owe us something,' Tanya Lee snapped, her cheeks white. 'If I hadn't told you which exam paper to choose you would have picked the wrong one and your dedicated public-service career would be over anyhow; you would have failed—failed at a test you didn't even realize you were taking!'

He said mildly, 'I had a fifty-fifty chance.'

'No.' She shook her head fiercely. 'The heretical one is faked up with a lot of Party jargon; they deliberately constructed the two texts to trap you. They *wanted* you to fail!'

Once more he examined the two papers, feeling confused. Was she right? Possibly. Probably. It rang true, knowing the Party functionaries as he did, and Tso-pin, his superior, in particular. He felt weary then. Defeated. After a time he said to the girl, 'What you're trying to get out of me is a quid pro quo. You did something for me—you got, or claim you got, the answer to this Party inquiry. But you've already done your part. What's to keep me from tossing you out of here on your head? I don't have to do a goddamn thing.' He heard his voice, toneless, sounding the poverty of empathic emotionality so usual in Party circles.

Miss Lee said, 'There will be other tests, as you continue to ascend. And we will monitor for you with them too.' She was calm, at ease; obviously she had foreseen his reaction.

'How long do I have to think it over?' he said.

'I'm leaving now. We're in no rush; you're not about to receive an invitation to the Leader's Yangtze River villa in the next week or even month.' Going to the door, opening it, she paused. 'As you're given covert rating tests we'll be in contact, supplying the answers—so you'll see one or more of us on those occasions. Probably it won't be me; it'll be that disabled war veteran who'll sell you the correct response sheets as you leave the Ministry building.' She smiled a brief, snuffed-out-candle smile. 'But one of these days, no doubt unexpectedly, you'll get an ornate, official, very formal invitation to the villa, and when you go you'll be heavily sedated with stelazine . . . possibly our last dose of our dwindling supply. Good night.' The door shut after her; she had gone.

My God, he thought. They can blackmail me. For what I've done. And she didn't even bother to mention it; in view of what they're involved with it was not worth mentioning.

But blackmail for what? He had already told the Secpol squad that he had been given a drug which had proved to be a phenothiazine. *Then they know*, he realized. They'll watch me; they're alert. Technically, I haven't broken a law, but—they'll be watching, all right.

However, they always watched anyhow. He relaxed slightly, thinking that. He had, over the years, become virtually accustomed to it, as had everyone.

I will see the Absolute Benefactor of the People as he is, he said to himself. Which possibly no one else had done. What will it be? Which of the subclasses of non-hallucination? Classes which I do not even know about . . . a view which may totally overthrow me. How am I going to be able to get through the evening, to keep my poise, if it's like the shape I saw on the TV screen? The Crusher, the Clanker, the Bird, the Climbing Tube, the Gulper—or worse.

He wondered what some of the other views consisted of . . . and then gave up that line of speculation; it was unprofitable. And too anxiety-inducing.

The next morning Mr Tso-pin and Mr Darius Pethel met him in his office, both of them calm but expectant. Wordlessly, he handed them one of the two 'exam papers.' The orthodox one, with its short and heart-smothering Arabian poem.

'This one,' Chien said tightly, 'is the product of a dedicated Party member or candidate for membership. The other—' He slapped the remaining sheets. 'Reactionary garbage.' He felt anger. 'In spite of a superficial—'

'All right, Mr Chien,' Pethel said, nodding. 'We don't have to explore each and every ramification; your analysis is correct. You heard the mention regarding you in the Leader's speech last night on TV?'

'I certainly did,' Chien said.

'So you have undoubtedly inferred,' Pethel said, 'that there is a good deal involved in what we are attempting, here. The Leader has his eye on you; that's clear. As a matter of fact, he has communicated to myself regarding you.' He opened his bulging briefcase and rummaged. 'Lost the goddamn thing. Anyhow—' He glanced at Tso-pin, who nodded slightly. 'His Greatness would like to have you appear for dinner at the Yangtze River Ranch next Thursday night. Mrs Fletcher in particular appreciates—'

Chien said, '"Mrs Fletcher"? Who is "Mrs Fletcher"?'

After a pause Tso-pin said dryly, 'The Absolute Benefactor's wife. His name—which you of course have never heard—is Thomas Fletcher.'

'He's a Caucasian,' Pethel explained. 'Originally from the New Zealand Communist Party; he participated in the difficult take-over there. This news is not in the strict sense secret, but on the other hand it hasn't been noised about.' He hesitated, toying with his watch chain. 'Probably it would be better if you forgot about that. Of course, as soon as you meet him, see him face to face, you'll realize that, realize that he's a Cauc. As I am. As many of us are.'

'Race,' Tso-pin pointed out, 'has nothing to do with loyalty to the Leader and the Party. As witness Mr Pethel, here.'

But His Greatness, Chien thought, jolted. He did not appear, on the TV screen, to be Occidental. 'On TV—' he began.

'The image,' Tso-pin interrupted, 'is subjected to a variegated assortment of skillful refinements. For ideological purposes. Most persons holding higher offices are aware of this.' He eyed Chien with hard criticism.

So everyone agrees, Chien thought. What we see every night is not real. The question is, How unreal? Partially? Or—completely?

'I will be prepared,' he said tautly. And he thought, There has been a slip-up. They weren't prepared for me—the people that

Tanya Lee represents—to gain entry so soon. Where's the anti-hallucinogen? Can they get it to me or not? Probably not on such short notice.

He felt, strangely, relief. He would be going into the presence of His Greatness in a position to see him as a human being, see him as he—and everybody else—saw him on TV. It would be a most stimulating and cheerful dinner party, with some of the most influential Party members in Asia. I think we can do without the phenothiazine, he said to himself. And his sense of relief grew.

'Here it is, finally,' Pethel said suddenly, producing a white envelope from his briefcase. 'Your card of admission. You will be flown by Sino-rocket to the Leader's villa Thursday morning; there the protocol officer will brief you on your expected behavior. It will be formal dress, white tie and tails, but the atmosphere will be cordial. There are always a great number of toasts.' He added, 'I have attended two such stag get-togethers. Mr Tso-pin'—he smiled creakily—'has not been honored in such a fashion. But, as they say, all things come to him who waits. Ben Franklin said that.'

Tso-pin said, 'It has come for Mr Chien rather prematurely, I would say.' He shrugged philosophically. 'But my opinion has never at any time been asked.'

'One thing,' Pethel said to Chien. 'It is possible that when you see His Greatness in person you will be in some regards disappointed. Be alert that you do not let this make itself apparent, if you should so feel. We have, always, tended—been trained—to regard him as more than a man. But at table he is'—he gestured—'a forked radish. In certain respects like ourselves. He may for instance indulge in moderately human oral-aggressive and -passive activity; he possibly may tell an off-color joke or drink too much ... To be candid, no one ever knows in advance how these things will work out, but they do generally hold forth until late the following morning. So it would be wise to accept the dosage of amphetamines which the protocol officer will offer you.'

'Oh?' Chien said. This was news to him, and interesting.

'For stamina. And to balance the liquor. His Greatness has

amazing staying power; he often is still on his feet and raring to go after everyone else has collapsed.'

'A remarkable man,' Tso-pin chimed in. 'I think his—indulgences only show that he is a fine fellow. And fully in the round; he is like the ideal Renaissance man; as, for example, Lorenzo de' Medici.'

'That does come to mind,' Pethel said; he studied Chien with such intensity that some of last night's chill returned. Am I being led into one trap after another? Chien wondered. That girl—was she in fact an agent of the Secpol probing me, trying to ferret out a disloyal, anti-Party streak in me?

I think, he decided, I will make sure that the legless peddler of herbal remedies does not snare me when I leave work; I'll take a totally different route back to my conapt.

He was successful. That day he avoided the peddler, and the same the next, and so on until Thursday.

On Thursday morning the peddler scooted from beneath a parked truck and blocked his way, confronting him.

'My medication?' the peddler demanded. 'It helped? I know it did; the formula goes back to the Sung Dynasty—I can tell it did. Right?'

Chien said, 'Let me go.'

'Would you be kind enough to answer?' The tone was not the expected, customary whining of a street peddler operating in a marginal fashion, and that tone came across to Chien; he heard loud and clear . . . as the Imperialist puppet troops of long ago phrased it.

'I know what you gave me,' Chien said. 'And I don't want any more. If I change my mind I can pick it up at a pharmacy. Thanks.' He started on, but the cart, with the legless occupant, pursued him.

'Miss Lee was talking to me,' the peddler said loudly.

'Hmmm,' Chien said, and automatically increased his pace; he spotted a hovercab and began signaling for it.

'It's tonight you're going to the stag dinner at the Yangtze River villa,' the peddler said, panting for breath in his effort to keep up. 'Take the medication—now!' He held out a flat packet, imploringly. 'Please, Party Member Chien; for your own sake, for all of us. So we can tell what it is we're up against. Good Lord, it may be non-Terran; that's our most basic fear. Don't you understand, Chien? What's your goddamn career compared with that? If we can't find out—'

The cab bumped to a halt on the pavement; its doors slid open. Chien started to board it.

The packet sailed past him, landed on the entrance sill of the cab, then slid onto the floor, damp from earlier rain.

'Please,' the peddler said. 'And it won't cost you anything; today it's free. Just take it, use it before the stag dinner. And don't use the amphetamines; they're a thalamic stimulant, contraindicated whenever an adrenal suppressant such as a phenothiazine is—'

The door of the cab closed after Chien. He seated himself.

'Where to, comrade?' the robot drive-mechanism inquired.

He gave the ident tag number of his conapt.

'That halfwit of a peddler managed to infiltrate his seedy wares into my clean interior,' the cab said. 'Notice; it reposes by your foot.'

He saw the packet—no more than an ordinary-looking envelope. I guess, he thought, this is how drugs come to you; all of a sudden they're there. For a moment he sat, and then he picked it up.

As before, there was a written enclosure above and beyond the medication, but this time, he saw, it was hand-written. A feminine script—from Miss Lee:

We were surprised at the suddenness. But thank heaven we were ready. Where were you Tuesday and Wednesday? Anyhow, here it is, and good luck. I will approach you later in the week; I don't want you to try to find me.

He ignited the note, burned it up in the cab's disposal ashtray. And kept the dark granules.

All this time, he thought. Hallucinogens in our water supply. Year after year. Decades. And not in wartime but in peacetime. And not to the enemy camp but here in our own. The evil bastards, he said to himself. Maybe I ought to take this; maybe I ought to find out what he or it is and let Tanya's group know.

I will, he decided. And—he was curious.

A bad emotion, he knew. Curiosity was, especially in Party activities, often a terminal state careerwise.

A state which, at the moment, gripped him thoroughly. He wondered if it would last through the evening, if, when it came right down to it, he would actually take the inhalant.

Time would tell. Tell that and everything else. We are blooming flowers, he thought, on the plain, which he picks. As the Arabic poem had put it. He tried to remember the rest of the poem but could not.

That probably was just as well.

The villa protocol officer, a Japanese named Kimo Okubara, tall and husky, obviously a quondam wrestler, surveyed him with innate hostility, even after he presented his engraved invitation and had successfully managed to prove his identity.

'Surprise you bother to come,' Okubara muttered. 'Why not stay home and watch on TV? Nobody miss you. We got along fine without you up to right now.'

Chien said tightly, 'I've already watched on TV.' And anyhow the stag dinners were rarely televised; they were too bawdy.

Okubara's crew double-checked him for weapons, including the possibility of an anal suppository, and then gave him his clothes back. They did not find the phenothiazine, however. Because he had already taken it. The effects of such a drug, he knew, lasted approximately four hours; that would be more than enough. And, as Tanya had said, it was a major dose; he felt sluggish and inept and dizzy, and his tongue moved in spasms of pseudo-Parkinsonism—an unpleasant side effect which he had failed to anticipate.

A girl, nude from the waist up, with long coppery hair down her shoulders and back, walked by. Interesting.

Coming the other way, a girl nude from the bottom up made her appearance. Interesting, too. Both girls looked vacant and bored, and totally self-possessed.

'You go in like that too,' Okubara informed Chien.

Startled, Chien said, 'I understood white tie and tails.'

'Joke,' Okubara said. 'At your expense. Only girls wear nude; you even get so you enjoy, unless you homosexual.'

Well, Chien thought, I guess I had better like it. He wandered on with the other guests—they, like him, wore white tie and tails, or, if women, floor-length gowns—and felt ill at ease, despite the tranquilizing effect of the stelazine. Why am I here? he asked himself. The ambiguity of his situation did not escape him. He was here to advance his career in the Party apparatus, to obtain the intimate and personal nod of approval from His Greatness . . . and in addition he was here to decipher His Greatness as a fraud; he did not know what variety of fraud, but there it was: fraud against the Party, against all the peace-loving democratic peoples of Terra. Ironic, he thought. And continued to mingle.

A girl with small, bright, illuminated breasts approached him for a match; he absent-mindedly got out his lighter. 'What makes your breasts glow?' he asked her. 'Radioactive injections?'

She shrugged, said nothing, passed on, leaving him alone. Evidently he had responded in the incorrect way.

Maybe it's a wartime mutation, he pondered.

'Drink, sir.' A servant graciously held out a tray; he accepted a martini—which was the current fad among the higher Party classes in People's China—and sipped the ice-cold dry flavor. Good English gin, he said to himself. Or possibly the original Holland compound; juniper or whatever they added. Not bad. He strolled on, feeling better; in actuality he found the atmosphere here a pleasant one. The people here were self-assured; they had been successful and now they could relax. It evidently was a myth that proximity to His Greatness produced neurotic anxiety: he saw no evidence here, at least, and felt little himself.

A heavy-set elderly man, bald, halted him by the simple means of holding his drink glass against Chien's chest. 'That frably little one who asked you for a match,' the elderly man said, and sniggered. 'The quig with the Christmas-tree breasts—that was a boy, in drag.' He giggled. 'You have to be cautious around here.'

'Where, if anywhere,' Chien said, 'do I find authentic women? In white ties and tails?'

'Darn near,' the elderly man said, and departed with a throng of hyperactive guests, leaving Chien alone with his martini.

A handsome, tall woman, well dressed, standing near Chien, suddenly put her hand on his arm; he felt her fingers tense and she said, 'Here he comes. His Greatness. This is the first time for me; I'm a little scared. Does my hair look all right?'

'Fine,' Chien said reflexively, and followed her gaze, seeking a glimpse—his first—of the Absolute Benefactor.

What crossed the room toward the table in the center was not a man.

And it was not, Chien realized, a mechanical construct either; it was not what he had seen on TV. That evidently was simply a device for speechmaking, as Mussolini had once used an artificial arm to salute long and tedious processions.

God, he thought, and felt ill. Was this what Tanya Lee had called the 'aquatic horror' shape? It had no shape. Nor pseudopodia, either flesh or metal. It was, in a sense, not there at all; when he managed to look directly at it, the shape vanished; he saw through it, saw the people on the far side—but not it. Yet if he turned his head, caught it out of a sidelong glance, he could determine its boundaries.

It was terrible; it blasted him with its awareness. As it moved it drained the life from each person in turn; it ate the people who had assembled, passed on, ate again, ate more with an endless appetite. It hated; he felt its hate. It loathed; he felt its loathing for everyone present—in fact he shared its loathing. All at once he and everyone else in the big villa were each a twisted slug, and over the fallen slug carcasses the creature savored, lingered, but all the time coming directly toward him—or was that an illusion? If this is a hallucination, Chien thought, it is the worst I have ever had; if it is not, then it is evil reality; it's an evil thing that kills and injures. He saw the trail of stepped-on, mashed men and women remnants behind it; he saw them trying to reassemble, to operate their crippled bodies; he heard them attempting speech.

I know who you are, Tung Chien thought to himself. You, the supreme head of the worldwide Party structure. You, who destroy whatever living object you touch; I see that Arabic poem, the searching for the flowers of life to eat them—I see you astride the plain which to you is Earth, plain without hills, without valleys. You go anywhere, appear any time, devour anything; you engineer life and then guzzle it, and you enjoy that.

He thought, You are God.

'Mr Chien,' the voice said, but it came from inside his head, not from the mouthless spirit that fashioned itself directly before him. 'It is good to meet you again. You know nothing. Go away. I have no interest in you. Why should I care about slime? Slime; I am mired in it, I must excrete it, and I choose to. I could break you; I can break even myself. Sharp stones are under me; I spread sharp pointed things upon the mire. I make the hiding places, the deep places, boil like a pot; to me the sea is like a lot of ointment. The flakes of my flesh are joined to everything. You are me. I am you. It makes no difference, just as it makes no difference whether the creature with ignited breasts is a girl or boy; you could learn to enjoy either.' It laughed.

He could not believe it was speaking to him; he could not imagine—it was too terrible—that it had picked him out.

'I have picked everybody out,' it said. 'No one is too small, each falls and dies and I am there to watch. I don't need to do anything but watch; it is automatic; it was arranged that way.' And then it ceased talking to him; it disjoined itself. But he still saw it; he felt its manifold presence. It was a globe which hung in the room, with fifty thousand eyes, a million eyes—billions: an eye for each living thing as it waited for each thing to fall, and then stepped on the living thing as it lay in a broken state. Because of this it had created the things, and he knew; he understood. What had seemed in the Arabic poem to be death was not death but God; or rather God was death, it was one force, one hunter, one cannibal thing, and it missed again and again but, having all eternity, it could afford to miss. Both poems, he realized; the Dryden one too. The crumbling; that is our world and you are doing it. Warping it to come out that way; bending us.

But at least, he thought, I still have my dignity. With dignity he set down his drink glass, turned, walked toward the doors of the room. He passed through the doors. He walked down a long carpeted hall. A villa servant dressed in purple opened a door for him; he found himself standing out in the night darkness, on a veranda, alone.

Not alone.

It had followed after him. Or it had already been here before him; yes, it had been expecting. It was not really through with him.

'Here I go,' he said, and made a dive for the railing; it was six stories down, and there below gleamed the river and death, not what the Arabic poem had seen.

As he tumbled over, it put an extension of itself on his shoulder.

'Why?' he said. But, in fact, he paused. Wondering. Not understanding, not at all.

'Don't fall on my account,' it said. He could not see it because it had moved behind him. But the piece of it on his shoulder—it had begun to look like a human hand.

And then it laughed.

'What's funny?' he demanded, as he teetered on the railing, held back by its pseudo-hand.

'You're doing my task for me,' it said. 'You aren't waiting; don't have time to wait? I'll select you out from among the others; you don't need to speed the process up.'

'What if I do?' he said. 'Out of revulsion for you?'

It laughed. And didn't answer.

'You won't even say,' he said.

Again no answer. He started to slide back, onto the veranda. And at once the pressure of its pseudo-hand lifted.

'You founded the Party?' he asked.

'I founded everything. I founded the anti-Party and the Party that isn't a Party, and those who are for it and those who are against, those that you call Yankee Imperialists, those in the camp of reaction, and so on endlessly. I founded it all. As if they were blades of grass.'

'And you're here to enjoy it?' he said.

'What I want,' it said, 'is for you to see me, as I am, as you have seen me, and then trust me.'

'What?' he said, quavering. 'Trust you to what?'

It said, 'Do you believe in me?'

'Yes,' he said. 'I can see you.'

'Then go back to your job at the Ministry. Tell Tanya Lee that you saw an overworked, overweight, elderly man who drinks too much and likes to pinch girls' rear ends.'

'Oh, Christ,' he said.

'As you live on, unable to stop, I will torment you,' it said. 'I will deprive you, item by item, of everything you possess or want. And then when you are crushed to death I will unfold a mystery.'

'What's the mystery?'

'The dead shall live, the living die. I kill what lives; I save what has died. And I will tell you this: *there are things worse than I*. But you won't meet them because by then I will have killed you. Now walk back into the dining room and prepare for dinner. Don't question what I'm doing; I did it long before there was a Tung Chien and I will do it long after.'

He hit it as hard as he could.

And experienced violent pain in his head.

And darkness, with the sense of falling.

After that, darkness again. He thought, I will get you. I will see that you die too. That you suffer; you're going to suffer, just like us, exactly in every way we do. I'll nail you; I swear to God I'll nail you up somewhere. And it will hurt. As much as I hurt now.

He shut his eyes.

Roughly, he was shaken. And heard Mr Kimo Okubara's voice. 'Get to your feet, common drunk. Come on!'

Without opening his eyes he said, 'Get me a cab.'

'Cab already waiting. You go home. Disgrace. Make a violent scene out of yourself.'

Getting shakily to his feet, he opened his eyes and examined himself. Our Leader whom we follow, he thought, is the One True God. And the enemy whom we fight and have fought is God too. They are right; he is everywhere. But I didn't understand what that meant. Staring at the protocol officer, he thought, You are God too. So there is no getting away, probably not even by jumping. As I started, instinctively, to do. He shuddered.

'Mix drinks with drugs,' Okubara said witheringly. 'Ruin career. I see it happen many times. Get lost.'

Unsteadily, he walked toward the great central door of the Yangtze River villa; two servants, dressed like medieval knights, with crested plumes, ceremoniously opened the door for him and one of them said, 'Good night, sir.'

'Up yours,' Chien said, and passed out into the night.

At a quarter to three in the morning, as he sat sleepless in the living room of his conapt, smoking one Cuesta Rey Astoria after another, a knock sounded at the door.

When he opened it he found himself facing Tanya Lee in her trenchcoat, her face pinched with cold. Her eyes blazed, questioningly.

'Don't look at me like that,' he said roughly. His cigar had gone out; he relit it. 'I've been looked at enough,' he said.

'You saw it,' she said.

He nodded.

She seated herself on the arm of the couch and after a time she said, 'Want to tell me about it?'

'Go as far from here as possible,' he said. 'Go a long way.' And then he remembered: no way was long enough. He remembered reading that too. 'Forget it,' he said; rising to his feet, he walked clumsily into the kitchen to start up the coffee.

Following after him, Tanya said, 'Was—it that bad?'

'We can't win,' he said. 'You can't win; I don't mean me. I'm not in this; I just wanted to do my job at the Ministry and forget it. Forget the whole damned thing.'

'Is it non-terrestrial?'

'Yes.' He nodded.

'Is it hostile to us?'

'Yes,' he said. 'No. Both. Mostly hostile.'

'Then we have to—'

'Go home,' he said, 'and go to bed.' He looked her over carefully; he had sat a long time and he had done a great deal of thinking. About a lot of things. 'Are you married?' he said.

'No. Not now. I used to be.'

He said, 'Stay with me tonight. The rest of tonight, anyhow. Until the sun comes up.' He added, 'The night part is awful.'

'I'll stay,' Tanya said, unbuckling the belt of her raincoat, 'but I have to have some answers.'

'What did Dryden mean,' Chien said, 'about music untuning the sky? I don't get that. What does music do to the sky?'

'All the celestial order of the universe ends,' she said as she hung her raincoat up in the closet of the bedroom; under it she wore an orange striped sweater and stretch-pants.

He said, 'And that's bad?'

Pausing, she reflected. 'I don't know. I guess so.'

'It's a lot of power,' he said, 'to assign to music.'

'Well, you know that old Pythagorean business about the "music of the spheres."' Matter-of-factly she seated herself on the bed and removed her slipperlike shoes.

'Do you believe in that?' he said. 'Or do you believe in God?'

'"God"!' She laughed. 'That went out with the donkey steam engine. What are you talking about? God, or god?' She came over close beside him, peering into his face.

'Don't look at me so closely,' he said sharply drawing back. 'I don't ever want to be looked at again.' He moved away, irritably.

'I think,' Tanya said, 'that if there is a God He has very little interest in human affairs. That's my theory, anyhow. I mean, He doesn't seem to care if evil triumphs or people or animals get hurt and die. I frankly don't see Him anywhere around. And the Party has always denied any form of—'

'Did you ever see Him?' he asked. 'When you were a child?'

'Oh, sure, as a child. But I also believed—'

'Did it ever occur to you,' Chien said, 'that good and evil are names for the same thing? That God could be both good and evil at the same time?'

'I'll fix you a drink,' Tanya said, and padded barefoot into the kitchen.

Chien said, 'The Crusher. The Clanker. The Gulper and the Bird and the Climbing Tube—plus other names, forms, I don't know. I had a hallucination. At the stag dinner. A big one. A terrible one.'

'But the stelazine—'

'It brought on a worse one,' he said.

'Is there any way,' Tanya said somberly, 'that we can fight this thing you saw? This apparition you call a hallucination but which very obviously was not?'

He said, 'Believe in it.'

'What will that do?'

'Nothing,' he said wearily. 'Nothing at all. I'm tired; I don't want a drink—let's just go to bed.'

'Okay.' She padded back into the bedroom, began pulling her striped sweater over her head. 'We'll discuss it more thoroughly later.'

'A hallucination,' Chien said, 'is merciful. I wish I had it; I want mine back. I want to be before your peddler got me with that phenothiazine.'

'Just come to bed. It'll be toasty. All warm and nice.'

He removed his tie, his shirt—and saw, on his right shoulder, the mark, the stigma, which it had left when it stopped him from jumping. Livid marks which looked as if they would never go away. He put his pajama top on then; it hid the marks.

'Anyhow,' Tanya said as he got into the bed beside her, 'your career is immeasurably advanced. Aren't you glad about that?'

'Sure,' he said, nodding sightlessly in the darkness. 'Very glad.'

'Come over against me,' Tanya said, putting her arms around him. 'And forget everything else. At least for now.'

He tugged her against him then, doing what she asked and what he wanted to do. She was neat; she was swiftly active; she was successful and she did her part. They did not bother to speak until at last she said, 'Oh!' And then she relaxed.

'I wish,' he said, 'that we could go on forever.'

'We did,' Tanya said. 'It's outside of time; it's boundless, like an ocean. It's the way we were in Cambrian times, before we migrated up onto the land; it's the ancient primary waters. This is the only time we get to go back, when this is done. That's why it means so much. And in those days we weren't separate; it was like a big jelly, like those blobs that float up on the beach.'

'Float up,' he said, 'and are left there to die.'

'Could you get me a towel?' Tanya asked. 'Or a washcloth? I need it.'

He padded into the bathroom for a towel. There—he was naked now—he once more saw his shoulder, saw where it had seized hold of him and held on, dragged him back, possibly to toy with him a little more.

The marks, unaccountably, were bleeding.

He sponged the blood away. More oozed forth at once and, seeing that, he wondered how much time he had left. Probably only hours.

Returning to bed, he said, 'Could you continue?'

'Sure. If you have any energy left; it's up to you.' She lay gazing up at him unwinkingly, barely visible in the dim nocturnal light.

'I have,' he said. And hugged her to him.

THE STORY TO END ALL STORIES FOR HARLAN ELLISON'S ANTHOLOGY *DANGEROUS VISIONS*

In a hydrogen war-ravaged society the nubile young women go down to a futuristic zoo and have sexual intercourse with various deformed and non-human life forms in the cages. In this particular account a woman who has been patched together out of the damaged bodies of several women has intercourse with an alien female, there in the cage, and later on the woman, by means of futuristic science, conceives. The infant is born, and she and the female in the cage fight over it to see who gets it. The human young woman wins, and promptly eats the offspring, hair, teeth, toes and all. Just after she has finished she discovers that the offspring is God.

THE ELECTRIC ANT

At four-fifteen in the afternoon, TST, Garson Poole woke up in his hospital bed, knew that he lay in a hospital bed in a three-bed ward and realized in addition two things: that he no longer had a right hand and that he felt no pain.

They have given me a strong analgesic, he said to himself as he stared at the far wall with its window showing downtown New York. Webs in which vehicles and peds darted and wheeled glimmered in the late afternoon sun, and the brilliance of the aging light pleased him. It's not yet out, he thought. And neither am I.

A fone lay on the table beside his bed; he hesitated, then picked it up and dialed for an outside line. A moment later he was faced by Louis Danceman, in charge of Tri-Plan's activities while he, Garson Poole, was elsewhere.

'Thank God you're alive,' Danceman said, seeing him; his big, fleshy face with its moon's surface of pock marks flattened with relief. 'I've been calling all—'

'I just don't have a right hand,' Poole said.

'But you'll be okay. I mean, they can graft another one on.'

'How long have I been here?' Poole said. He wondered where the nurses and doctors had gone to; why weren't they clucking and fussing about him making a call?

'Four days,' Danceman said. 'Everything here at the plant is going splunkishly. In fact we've splunked orders from three separate police systems, all here on Terra. Two in Ohio, one in Wyoming. Good solid orders, with one third in advance and the usual three-year lease-option.'

'Come get me out of here,' Poole said.

'I can't get you out until the new hand–'

'I'll have it done later.' He wanted desperately to get back to familiar surroundings; memory of the mercantile squib looming grotesquely on the pilot screen careened at the back of his mind; if he shut his eyes he felt himself back in his damaged craft as it plunged from one vehicle to another, piling up enormous damage as it went. The kinetic sensations . . . he winced, recalling them. I guess I'm lucky, he said to himself.

'Is Sarah Benton there with you?' Danceman asked.

'No.' Of course; his personal secretary–if only for job considerations–would be hovering close by, mothering him in her jejune, infantile way. All heavy-set women like to mother people, he thought. And they're dangerous; if they fall on you they can kill you. 'Maybe that's what happened to me,' he said aloud. 'Maybe Sarah fell on my squib.'

'No, no; a tie rod in the steering fin of your squib split apart during the heavy rush-hour traffic and you–'

'I remember.' He turned in his bed as the door of the ward opened; a white-clad doctor and two blue-clad nurses appeared, making their way toward his bed. 'I'll talk to you later,' Poole said and hung up the fone. He took a deep, expectant breath.

'You shouldn't be foning quite so soon,' the doctor said as he studied his chart. 'Mr Garson Poole, owner of Tri-Plan Electronics. Maker of random ident darts that track their prey for a circle-radius of a thousand miles, responding to unique enceph wave patterns. You're a successful man, Mr Poole. But, Mr Poole, you're not a man. You're an electric ant.'

'Christ,' Poole said, stunned.

'So we can't really treat you here, now that we've found out. We knew, of course, as soon as we examined your injured right hand; we saw the electronic components and then we made torso x-rays and of course they bore out our hypothesis.'

'What,' Poole said, 'is an "electric ant"?' But he knew; he could decipher the term.

A nurse said, 'An organic robot.'

'I see,' Poole said. Frigid perspiration rose to the surface of his skin, across all his body.

'You didn't know,' the doctor said.

'No.' Poole shook his head.

The doctor said, 'We get an electric ant every week or so. Either brought in here from a squib accident—like yourself—or one seeking voluntary admission . . . one who, like yourself, has never been told, who has functioned alongside humans, believing himself—itself—human. As to your hand—' He paused.

'Forget my hand,' Poole said savagely.

'Be calm.' The doctor leaned over him, peered acutely down into Poole's face. 'We'll have a hospital boat convey you over to a service facility where repairs, or replacement, on your hand can be made at a reasonable expense, either to yourself, if you're self-owned, or to your owners, if such there are. In any case you'll be back at your desk at Tri-Plan functioning just as before.'

'Except,' Poole said, 'now I know.' He wondered if Danceman or Sarah or any of the others at the office knew. Had they—or one of them—purchased him? Designed him? A figurehead, he said to himself; that's all I've been. I must never really have run the company; it was a delusion implanted in me when I was made . . . along with the delusion that I am human and alive.

'Before you leave for the repair facility,' the doctor said, 'could you kindly settle your bill at the front desk?'

Poole said acidly, 'How can there be a bill if you don't treat ants here?'

'For our services,' the nurse said. 'Up until the point we knew.'

'Bill me,' Poole said, with furious, impotent anger. 'Bill my firm.' With massive effort he managed to sit up; his head swimming, he stepped haltingly from the bed and onto the floor. 'I'll be glad to leave here,' he said as he rose to a standing position. 'And thank you for your humane attention.'

'Thank you, too, Mr Poole,' the doctor said. 'Or rather I should say just Poole.'

*

THE ELECTRIC ANT

At the repair facility he had his missing hand replaced.

It proved fascinating, the hand; he examined it for a long time before he let the technicians install it. On the surface it appeared organic—in fact on the surface, it was. Natural skin covered natural flesh, and true blood filled the veins and capillaries. But, beneath that, wires and circuits, miniaturized components, gleamed ... looking deep into the wrist he saw surge gates, motors, multi-stage valves, all very small. Intricate. And—the hand cost forty frogs. A week's salary, insofar as he drew it from the company payroll.

'Is this guaranteed?' he asked the technicians as they fused the 'bone' section of the hand to the balance of his body.

'Ninety days, parts and labor,' one of the technicians said. 'Unless subjected to unusual or intentional abuse.'

'That sounds vaguely suggestive,' Poole said.

The technician, a man—all of them were men—said, regarding him keenly, 'You've been posing?'

'Unintentionally,' Poole said.

'And now it's intentional?'

Poole said, 'Exactly.'

'Do you know why you never guessed? There must have been signs ... clickings and whirrings from inside you, now and then. You never guessed because you were programmed not to notice. You'll now have the same difficulty finding out why you were built and for whom you've been operating.'

'A slave,' Poole said. 'A mechanical slave.'

'You've had fun.'

'I've lived a good life,' Poole said. 'I've worked hard.'

He paid the facility its forty frogs, flexed his new fingers, tested them out by picking up various objects such as coins, then departed. Ten minutes later he was aboard a public carrier, on his way home. It had been quite a day.

At home, in his one-room apartment, he poured himself a shot of Jack Daniel's Purple Label—sixty years old—and sat sipping it, meanwhile gazing through his sole window at the building on the opposite side of the street. Shall I go to the office? he asked himself. If so, why? If not, why? Choose one. Christ, he thought, it undermines you, knowing this. I'm a freak, he realized. An inanimate object mimicking an animate one. But—he felt alive. Yet . . . he felt differently, now. About himself. Hence about everyone, especially Danceman and Sarah, everyone at Tri-Plan.

I think I'll kill myself, he said to himself. But I'm probably programmed not to do that; it would be a costly waste which my owner would have to absorb. And he wouldn't want to.

Programmed. In me somewhere, he thought, there is a matrix fitted in place, a grid screen that cuts me off from certain thoughts, certain actions. And forces me into others. I am not free. I never was, but now I know it; that makes it different.

Turning his window to opaque, he snapped on the overhead light, carefully set about removing his clothing, piece by piece. He had watched carefully as the technicians at the repair facility had attached his new hand: he had a rather clear idea, now, of how his body had been assembled. Two major panels, one in each thigh; the technicians had removed the panels to check the circuit complexes beneath. If I'm programmed, he decided, the matrix probably can be found there.

The maze of circuitry baffled him. I need help, he said to himself. Let's see . . . what's the fone code for the class BBB computer we hire at the office?

He picked up the fone, dialed the computer at its permanent location in Boise, Idaho.

'Use of this computer is prorated at a five frogs per minute basis,' a mechanical voice from the fone said. 'Please hold your mastercreditchargeplate before the screen.'

He did so.

'At the sound of the buzzer you will be connected with the computer,' the voice continued. 'Please query it as rapidly as possible, taking into account the fact that its answer will be given in terms of a microsecond, while your query will–' He turned the sound down, then. But quickly turned it up as the blank audio input of the computer appeared on the screen. At this moment the computer had become a giant ear, listening to him—as well as fifty thousand other queriers throughout Terra.

'Scan me visually,' he instructed the computer. 'And tell me where I will find the programming mechanism which controls my thoughts and behavior.' He waited. On the fone's screen a great active eye, multi-lensed, peered at him; he displayed himself for it, there in his one-room apartment.

The computer said, 'Remove your chest panel. Apply pressure at your breastbone and then ease outward.'

He did so. A section of his chest came off; dizzily, he set it down on the floor.

'I can distinguish control modules,' the computer said, 'but I can't tell which—' It paused as its eye roved about on the fone screen. 'I distinguish a roll of punched tape mounted above your heart mechanism. Do you see it?' Poole craned his neck, peered. He saw it, too. 'I will have to sign off,' the computer said. 'After I have examined the data available to me I will contact you and give you an answer. Good day.' The screen died out.

I'll yank the tape out of me, Poole said to himself. Tiny . . . no larger than two spools of thread, with a scanner mounted between the delivery drum and the take-up drum. He could not see any sign of motion; the spools seemed inert. They must cut in as override, he reflected, when specific situations occur. Override to my encephalic processes. And they've been doing it all my life.

He reached down, touched the delivery drum. All I have to do is tear this out, he thought, and—

The fone screen relit. 'Mastercreditchargeplate number 3-BNX-882-HQR446-T,' the computer's voice came. 'This is BBB-307DR recontacting you in response to your query of sixteen seconds lapse, November 4, 1992. The punched tape roll above your heart mechanism is not a programming turret but is in fact a reality-supply construct. All sense stimuli received by your central neurological system emanate from that unit and tampering with it would be risky if not terminal.' It added, 'You appear to have no programming circuit. Query answered. Good day.' It flicked off.

Poole, standing naked before the fone screen, touched the tape drum once again, with calculated, enormous caution. I see, he thought wildly. Or do I see? This unit—

If I cut the tape, he realized, my world will disappear. Reality will continue for others, but not for me. Because my reality, my universe, is coming to me from this minuscule unit. Fed into the scanner and then into my central nervous system as it snailishly unwinds.

It has been unwinding for years, he decided.

Getting his clothes, he redressed, seated himself in his big armchair—a luxury imported into his apartment from Tri-Plan's main offices—and lit a tobacco cigarette. His hands shook as he laid down his initialed lighter; leaning back, he blew smoke before himself, creating a nimbus of gray.

I have to go slowly, he said to himself. What am I trying to do? Bypass my programming? But the computer found no programming circuit. Do I want to interfere with the reality tape? And if so, *why*?

Because, he thought, if I control that, I control reality. At least so far as I'm concerned. My subjective reality . . . but that's all there is. Objective reality is a synthetic construct, dealing with a hypothetical universalization of a multitude of subjective realities.

My universe is lying within my fingers, he realized. If I can just figure out how the damn thing works. All I set out to do originally was to search for and locate my programming circuit so I could gain true homeostatic functioning: control of myself. But with this—

With this he did not merely gain control of himself; he gained control over everything.

And this sets me apart from every human who ever lived and died, he thought somberly.

Going over to the fone he dialed his office. When he had Danceman on the screen he said briskly, 'I want you to send a complete set of microtools and enlarging screen over to my apartment. I have some microcircuitry to work on.' Then he broke the connection, not wanting to discuss it.

A half hour later a knock sounded on his door. When he opened up he found himself facing one of the shop foremen, loaded down with microtools of every sort. 'You didn't say exactly what you wanted,' the foreman said, entering the apartment. 'So Mr Danceman had me bring everything.'

'And the enlarging-lens system?'

'In the truck, up on the roof.'

Maybe what I want to do, Poole thought, is die. He lit a cigarette, stood smoking and waiting as the shop foreman lugged the heavy enlarging screen, with its power-supply and control panel, into the apartment. This is suicide, what I'm doing here. He shuddered.

'Anything wrong, Mr Poole?' the shop foreman said as he rose to his feet, relieved of the burden of the enlarging-lens system. 'You must still be rickety on your pins from your accident.'

'Yes,' Poole said quietly. He stood tautly waiting until the foreman left.

Under the enlarging-lens system the plastic tape assumed a new shape: a wide track along which hundreds of thousands of punch-holes worked their way. I thought so, Poole thought. Not recorded as charges on a ferrous oxide layer but actually punched-free slots.

Under the lens the strip of tape visibly oozed forward. Very slowly, but it did, at uniform velocity, move in the direction of the scanner.

The way I figure it, he thought, is that the punched holes are *on* gates. It functions like a player piano; solid is no, punch-hole is yes. How can I test this?

Obviously by filling in a number of holes.

He measured the amount of tape left on the delivery spool, cal-culated—at great effort—the velocity of the tape's movement, and then came up with a figure. If he altered the tape visible at the in-going edge of the scanner, five to seven hours would pass before that particular time period arrived. He would in effect be painting out stimuli due a few hours from now.

With a microbrush he swabbed a large—relatively large—sec-tion of tape with opaque varnish . . . obtained from the supply kit accompanying the microtools. I have smeared out stimuli for about half an hour, he pondered. Have covered at least a thousand punches.

It would be interesting to see what change, if any, overcame his environment, six hours from now.

Five and a half hours later he sat at Krackter's, a superb bar in Manhattan, having a drink with Danceman.

'You look bad,' Danceman said.

'I am bad,' Poole said. He finished his drink, a Scotch sour, and ordered another.

'From the accident?'

'In a sense, yes.'

Danceman said, 'Is it—something you found out about yourself?'

Raising his head, Poole eyed him in the murky light of the bar. 'Then you know.'

'I know,' Danceman said, 'that I should call you "Poole" instead of "Mr Poole." But I prefer the latter, and will continue to do so.'

'How long have you known?' Poole said.

'Since you took over the firm. I was told that the actual owners of Tri-Plan, who are located in the Prox System, wanted Tri-Plan run by an electric ant whom they could control. They wanted a brilliant and forceful—'

'The real owners?' This was the first he had heard about that. 'We have two thousand stockholders. Scattered everywhere.'

'Marvis Bey and her husband Ernan, on Prox 4, control fifty-one percent of the voting stock. This has been true from the start.'

'Why didn't I know?'

'I was told not to tell you. You were to think that you yourself made all company policy. With my help. But actually I was feeding you what the Beys fed to me.'

'I'm a figurehead,' Poole said.

'In a sense, yes.' Danceman nodded. 'But you'll always be "Mr Poole" to me.'

A section of the far wall vanished. And with it, several people at tables nearby. And—

Through the big glass side of the bar, the skyline of New York City flickered out of existence.

Seeing his face, Danceman said, 'What is it?'

Poole said hoarsely, 'Look around. Do you see any changes?'

After looking around the room, Danceman said, 'No. What like?'

'You still see the skyline?'

'Sure. Smoggy as it is. The lights wink—'

'Now I know,' Poole said. He had been right; every punch-hole covered up meant the disappearance of some object in his reality world. Standing, he said, 'I'll see you later, Danceman. I have to get back to my apartment; there's some work I'm doing. Goodnight.' He strode from the bar and out onto the street, searching for a cab.

No cabs.

Those, too, he thought. I wonder what else I painted over. Prostitutes? Flowers? Prisons?

There, in the bar's parking lot, Danceman's squib. I'll take that, he decided. There are still cabs in Danceman's world; he can get one later. Anyhow it's a company car, and I hold a copy of the key.

Presently he was in the air, turning toward his apartment.

New York City had not returned. To the left and right vehicles and buildings, streets, ped-runners, signs . . . and in the center nothing. How can I fly into that? he asked himself. I'd disappear.

Or would I? He flew toward the nothingness.

Smoking one cigarette after another he flew in a circle for fifteen minutes . . . and then, soundlessly, New York reappeared. He could finish his trip. He stubbed out his cigarette (a waste of something so valuable) and shot off in the direction of his apartment.

If I insert a narrow opaque strip, he pondered as he unlocked his apartment door, I can—

His thoughts ceased. Someone sat in his living room chair, watching a captain kirk on the TV. 'Sarah,' he said, nettled.

She rose, well-padded but graceful. 'You weren't at the hospital, so I came here. I still have that key you gave me back in March after we had that awful argument. Oh . . . you look so depressed.'

She came up to him, peeped into his face anxiously. 'Does your injury hurt that badly?'

'It's not that.' He removed his coat, tie, shirt, and then his chest panel; kneeling down he began inserting his hands into the microtool gloves. Pausing, he looked up at her and said, 'I found out I'm an electric ant. Which from one standpoint opens up certain possibilities, which I am exploring now.' He flexed his fingers and, at the far end of the left waldo, a micro screwdriver moved, magnified into visibility by the enlarging-lens system. 'You can watch,' he informed her. 'If you so desire.'

She had begun to cry.

'What's the matter?' he demanded savagely, without looking up from his work.

'I—it's just so sad. You've been such a good employer to all of us at Tri-Plan. We respect you so. And now it's all changed.'

The plastic tape had an unpunched margin at top and bottom; he cut a horizontal strip, very narrow, then, after a moment of great concentration, cut the tape itself four hours away from the scanning head. He then rotated the cut strip into a right-angle piece in relation to the scanner, fused it in place with a micro heat element, then reattached the tape reel to its left and right sides. He had, in effect, inserted a dead twenty minutes into the unfolding flow of his reality. It would take effect—according to his calculations—a few minutes after midnight.

'Are you fixing yourself?' Sarah asked timidly.

Poole said, 'I'm freeing myself.' Beyond this he had several alterations in mind. But first he had to test his theory; blank, unpunched tape meant no stimuli, in which case the *lack* of tape . . .

'That look on your face,' Sarah said. She began gathering up her purse, coat, rolled-up aud-vid magazine. 'I'll go; I can see how you feel about finding me here.'

'Stay,' he said. 'I'll watch the captain kirk with you.' He got into his shirt. 'Remember years ago when there were—what was it?— twenty or twenty-two TV channels? Before the government shut down the independents?'

She nodded.

'What would it have looked like,' he said, 'if this TV set projected all channels onto the cathode ray screen *at the same time?* Could we have distinguished anything, in the mixture?'

'I don't think so.'

'Maybe we could learn to. Learn to be selective; do our own job of perceiving what we wanted to and what we didn't. Think of the possibilities, if our brain could handle twenty images at once; think of the amount of knowledge which could be stored during a given period. I wonder if the brain, the human brain–' He broke off. 'The human brain couldn't do it,' he said, presently, reflecting to himself. 'But in theory a quasi-organic brain might.'

'Is that what you have?' Sarah asked.

'Yes,' Poole said.

They watched the captain kirk to its end, and then they went to bed. But Poole sat up against his pillows, smoking and brooding. Beside him, Sarah stirred restlessly, wondering why he did not turn off the light.

Eleven-fifty. It would happen anytime, now.

'Sarah,' he said. 'I want your help. In a very few minutes something strange will happen to me. It won't last long, but I want you to watch me carefully. See if I–' He gestured. 'Show any changes. If I seem to go to sleep, or if I talk nonsense, or–' He wanted to say, if I disappear. But he did not. 'I won't do you any harm, but I think it might be a good idea if you armed yourself. Do you have your anti-mugging gun with you?'

'In my purse.' She had become fully awake now; sitting up in bed, she gazed at him with wild fright, her ample shoulders tanned and freckled in the light of the room.

He got her gun for her.

The room stiffened into paralyzed immobility. Then the colors began to drain away. Objects diminished until, smoke-like, they flitted away into shadows. Darkness filmed everything as the objects in the room became weaker and weaker.

The last stimuli are dying out, Poole realized. He squinted, trying to see. He made out Sarah Benton, sitting in the bed: a two-dimensional figure that doll-like had been propped up, there to fade and dwindle. Random gusts of dematerialized substance eddied about in unstable clouds; the elements collected, fell apart, then collected once again. And then the last heat, energy and light dissipated; the room closed over and fell into itself, as if sealed off from reality. And at that point absolute blackness replaced everything, space without depth, not nocturnal but rather stiff and unyielding. And in addition he heard nothing.

Reaching, he tried to touch something. But he had nothing to reach with. Awareness of his own body had departed along with everything else in the universe. He had no hands, and even if he had, there would be nothing for them to feel.

I am still right about the way the damn tape works, he said to himself, using a nonexistent mouth to communicate an invisible message.

Will this pass in ten minutes? he asked himself. Am I right about that, too? He waited . . . but knew intuitively that his time sense had departed with everything else. I can only wait, he realized. And hope it won't be long.

To pace himself, he thought, I'll make up an encyclopedia; I'll try to list everything that begins with an 'a.' Let's see. He pondered. Apple, automobile, acksetron, atmosphere, Atlantic, tomato aspic, advertising—he thought on and on, categories slithering through his fright-haunted mind.

All at once light flickered on.

He lay on the couch in the living room, and mild sunlight spilled in through the single window. Two men bent over him, their hands full of tools. Maintenance men, he realized. They've been working on me.

'He's conscious,' one of the technicians said. He rose, stood back; Sarah Benton, dithering with anxiety, replaced him.

'Thank God!' she said, breathing wetly in Poole's ear. 'I was so afraid; I called Mr Danceman finally about—'

'What happened?' Poole broke in harshly. 'Start from the beginning and for God's sake speak slowly. So I can assimilate it all.'

Sarah composed herself, paused to rub her nose, and then plunged on nervously, 'You passed out. You just lay there, as if you were dead. I waited until two-thirty and you did nothing. I called Mr Danceman, waking him up unfortunately, and he called the electric-ant maintenance—I mean, the organic-roby maintenance people, and these two men came about four-forty-five, and they've been working on you ever since. It's now six-fifteen in the morning. And I'm very cold and I want to go to bed; I can't make it in to the office today; I really can't.' She turned away, sniffling. The sound annoyed him.

One of the uniformed maintenance men said, 'You've been playing around with your reality tape.'

'Yes,' Poole said. Why deny it? Obviously they had found the inserted solid strip. 'I shouldn't have been out that long,' he said. 'I inserted a ten-minute strip only.'

'It shut off the tape transport,' the technician explained. 'The tape stopped moving forward; your insertion jammed it, and it automatically shut down to avoid tearing the tape. Why would you want to fiddle around with that? Don't you know what you could do?'

'I'm not sure,' Poole said.

'But you have a good idea.'

Poole said acridly, 'That's why I'm doing it.'

'Your bill,' the maintenance man said, 'is going to be ninety-five frogs. Payable in installments, if you so desire.'

'Okay,' he said; he sat up groggily, rubbed his eyes and grimaced. His head ached and his stomach felt totally empty.

'Shave the tape next time,' the primary technician told him. 'That way it won't jam. Didn't it occur to you that it had a safety factor built into it? So it would stop rather than—'

'What happens,' Poole interrupted, his voice low and intently careful, 'if no tape passed under the scanner? No tape—nothing at all. The photocell shining upward without impedance?'

The technicians glanced at each other. One said, 'All the neuro circuits jump their gaps and short out.'

'Meaning what?' Poole said.

'Meaning it's the end of the mechanism.'

Poole said, 'I've examined the circuit. It doesn't carry enough voltage to do that. Metal won't fuse under such slight loads of current, even if the terminals are touching. We're talking about a millionth of a watt along a cesium channel perhaps a sixteenth of an inch in length. Let's assume there are a billion possible combinations at one instant arising from the punch-outs on the tape. The total output isn't cumulative; the amount of current depends on what the battery details for that module, and it's not much. With all gates open and going.'

'Would we lie?' one of the technicians asked wearily.

'Why not?' Poole said. 'Here I have an opportunity to experience everything. Simultaneously. To know the universe and its entirety, to be momentarily in contact with all reality. Something that no human can do. A symphonic score entering my brain outside of time, all notes, all instruments sounding at once. And all symphonies. Do you see?'

'It'll burn you out,' both technicians said, together.

'I don't think so,' Poole said.

Sarah said, 'Would you like a cup of coffee, Mr Poole?'

'Yes,' he said; he lowered his legs, pressed his cold feet against the floor, shuddered. He then stood up. His body ached. They had me lying all night on the couch, he realized. All things considered, they could have done better than that.

At the kitchen table in the far corner of the room, Garson Poole sat sipping coffee across from Sarah. The technicians had long since gone.

'You're not going to try any more experiments on yourself, are you?' Sarah asked wistfully.

Poole grated, 'I would like to control time. To reverse it.' I will cut a segment of tape out, he thought, and fuse it in upside down. The

412   THE ELECTRIC ANT

causal sequences will then flow the other way. Thereupon I will walk backward down the steps from the roof field, back up to my door, push a locked door open, walk backward to the sink, where I will get out a stack of dirty dishes. I will seat myself at this table before the stack, fill each dish with food produced from my stomach . . . I will then transfer the food to the refrigerator. The next day I will take the food out of the refrigerator, pack it in bags, carry the bags to a supermarket, distribute the food here and there in the store. And at last, at the front counter, they will pay me money for this, from their cash register. The food will be packed with other food in big plastic boxes, shipped out of the city into the hydroponic plants on the Atlantic, there to be joined back to trees and bushes or the bodies of dead animals or pushed deep into the ground. But what would all that prove? A video tape running backward . . . I would know no more than I know now, which is not enough.

What I want, he realized, is ultimate and absolute reality, for one microsecond. After that it doesn't matter, because all will be known; nothing will be left to understand or see.

I might try one other change, he said to himself. Before I try cutting the tape. I will prick new punch-holes in the tape and see what presently emerges. It will be interesting because I will not know what the holes I make mean.

Using the tip of a microtool, he punched several holes, at random, on the tape. As close to the scanner as he could manage . . . he did not want to wait.

'I wonder if you'll see it,' he said to Sarah. Apparently not, insofar as he could extrapolate. 'Something may show up,' he said to her. 'I just want to warn you; I don't want you to be afraid.'

'Oh dear,' Sarah said tinnily.

He examined his wristwatch. One minute passed, then a second, a third. And then–

In the center of the room appeared a flock of green and black ducks. They quacked excitedly, rose from the floor, fluttered against the ceiling in a dithering mass of feathers and wings and frantic in their vast urge, their instinct, to get away.

'Ducks,' Poole said, marveling. 'I punched a hole for a flight of wild ducks.'

Now something else appeared. A park bench with an elderly, tattered man seated on it, reading a torn, bent newspaper. He looked up, dimly made out Poole, smiled briefly at him with badly made dentures, and then returned to his folded-back newspaper. He read on.

'Do you see him?' Poole asked Sarah. 'And the ducks.' At that moment the ducks and the park bum disappeared. Nothing remained of them. The interval of their punch-holes had quickly passed.

'They weren't real,' Sarah said. 'Were they? So how—'

'You're not real,' he told Sarah. 'You're a stimulus-factor on my reality tape. A punch-hole that can be glazed over. Do you also have an existence in another reality tape, or one in an objective reality?' He did not know; he couldn't tell. Perhaps Sarah did not know, either. Perhaps she existed in a thousand reality tapes; perhaps on every reality tape ever manufactured. 'If I cut the tape,' he said, 'you will be everywhere and nowhere. Like everything else in the universe. At least as far as I am aware of it.'

Sarah faltered, 'I am real.'

'I want to know you completely,' Poole said. 'To do that I must cut the tape. If I don't do it now, I'll do it some other time; it's inevitable that eventually I'll do it.' So why wait? he asked himself. And there is always the possibility that Danceman has reported back to my maker, that they will be making moves to head me off. Because, perhaps, I'm endangering their property—myself.

'You make me wish I had gone to the office after all,' Sarah said, her mouth turned down with dimpled gloom.

'Go,' Poole said.

'I don't want to leave you alone.'

'I'll be fine,' Poole said.

'No, you're not going to be fine. You're going to unplug yourself or something, kill yourself because you've found out you're just an electric ant and not a human being.'

He said, presently, 'Maybe so.' Maybe it boiled down to that.

'And I can't stop you,' she said.

'No.' He nodded in agreement.

'But I'm going to stay,' Sarah said. 'Even if I can't stop you. Because if I do leave and you do kill yourself, I'll always ask myself for the rest of my life what would have happened if I had stayed. You see?'

Again he nodded.

'Go ahead,' Sarah said.

He rose to his feet. 'It's not pain I'm going to feel,' he told her. 'Although it may look like that to you. Keep in mind the fact that organic robots have minimal pain-circuits in them. I will be experiencing the most intense—'

'Don't tell me any more,' she broke in. 'Just do it if you're going to, or don't do it if you're not.'

Clumsily—because he was frightened—he wriggled his hands into the microglove assembly, reached to pick up a tiny tool: a sharp cutting blade. 'I am going to cut a tape mounted inside my chest panel,' he said, as he gazed through the enlarging-lens system. 'That's all.' His hand shook as it lifted the cutting blade. In a second it can be done, he realized. All over. And—I will have time to fuse the cut ends of the tape back together, he realized. A half hour at least. If I change my mind.

He cut the tape.

Staring at him, cowering, Sarah whispered, 'Nothing happened.'

'I have thirty or forty minutes.' He reseated himself at the table, having drawn his hands from the gloves. His voice, he noticed, shook; undoubtedly Sarah was aware of it, and he felt anger at himself, knowing that he had alarmed her. 'I'm sorry,' he said, irrationally; he wanted to apologize to her. 'Maybe you ought to leave,' he said in panic; again he stood up. So did she, reflexively, as if imitating him; bloated and nervous she stood there palpitating. 'Go away,' he said thickly. 'Back to the office where you ought to be. Where we both ought to be.' I'm going to fuse the tape-ends together, he told himself; the tension is too great for me to stand.

Reaching his hands toward the gloves he groped to pull them over his straining fingers. Peering into the enlarging screen, he saw the beam from the photoelectric gleam upward, pointed directly into the scanner; at the same time he saw the end of the tape disappearing under the scanner . . . he saw this, understood it; I'm too late, he realized. It has passed through. God, he thought, help me. It has begun winding at a rate greater than I calculated. So it's *now* that—

He saw apples, and cobblestones and zebras. He felt warmth, the silky texture of cloth; he felt the ocean lapping at him and a great wind, from the north, plucking at him as if to lead him somewhere. Sarah was all around him, so was Danceman. New York glowed in the night, and the squibs about him scuttled and bounced through night skies and daytime and flooding and drought. Butter relaxed into liquid on his tongue, and at the same time hideous odors and tastes assailed him: the bitter presence of poisons and lemons and blades of summer grass. He drowned; he fell; he lay in the arms of a woman in a vast white bed which at the same time dinned shrilly in his ear: the warning noise of a defective elevator in one of the ancient, ruined downtown hotels. I am living, I have lived, I will never live, he said to himself, and with his thoughts came every word, every sound; insects squeaked and raced, and he half sank into a complex body of homeostatic machinery located somewhere in Tri-Plan's labs.

He wanted to say something to Sarah. Opening his mouth he tried to bring forth words—a specific string of them out of the enormous mass of them brilliantly lighting his mind, scorching him with their utter meaning.

His mouth burned. He wondered why.

Frozen against the wall, Sarah Benton opened her eyes and saw the curl of smoke ascending from Poole's half-opened mouth. Then the roby sank down, knelt on elbows and knees, then slowly spread out in a broken, crumpled heap. She knew without examining it that it had 'died.'

Poole did it to itself, she realized. And it couldn't feel pain; it said so itself. Or at least not very much pain; maybe a little. Anyhow, now it is over.

I had better call Mr Danceman and tell him what's happened, she decided. Still shaky, she made her way across the room to the fone; picking it up, she dialed from memory.

It thought I was a stimulus-factor on its reality tape, she said to herself. So it thought I would die when it 'died.' How strange, she thought. Why did it imagine that? It had never been plugged into the real world; it had 'lived' in an electronic world of its own. How bizarre.

'Mr Danceman,' she said when the circuit to his office had been put through. 'Poole is gone. It destroyed itself right in front of my eyes. You'd better come over.'

'So we're finally free of it.'

'Yes, won't it be nice?'

Danceman said, 'I'll send a couple of men over from the shop.' He saw past her, made out the sight of Poole lying by the kitchen table. 'You go home and rest,' he instructed Sarah. 'You must be worn out by all this.'

'Yes,' she said. 'Thank you, Mr Danceman.' She hung up and stood, aimlessly.

And then she noticed something.

My hands, she thought. She held them up. Why is it I can see through them?

The walls of the room, too, had become ill-defined.

Trembling, she walked back to the inert roby, stood by it, not knowing what to do. Through her legs the carpet showed, and then the carpet became dim, and she saw, through it, farther layers of disintegrating matter beyond.

Maybe if I can fuse the tape-ends back together, she thought. But she did not know how. And already Poole had become vague.

The wind of early morning blew about her. She did not feel it; she had begun, now, to cease to feel.

The winds blew on.

CADBURY, THE BEAVER WHO LACKED

Once, long ago, before money had been invented, a certain male beaver named Cadbury lived within a meager dam which he had constructed with his own teeth and feet, earning his living by gnawing down shrubs, trees and other growth in exchange for poker chips of several colors. The blue chips he liked best, but they came rarely, generally only due in payment for some uniquely huge gnawing-assignment. In all the passing years of work he had owned only three such chips, but he knew by inference that more must exist, and every now and then during the day's gnawing he paused a moment, fixed a cup of instant coffee, and meditated on chips of all hues, the blues included.

His wife Hilda offered unasked-for advice whenever the opportunity presented itself. 'Look at you,' she customarily would declare. 'You really ought to see a psychiatrist. Your stack of white chips is only approximately half that of Ralf, Peter, Tom, Bob, Jack and Earl, all who live and gnaw around here, because you're so busy woolgathering about your goddam blue chips which you'll never get anyhow because frankly if the blunt truth were known you lack the talent, energy and drive.'

'Energy and drive,' Cadbury would moodily retort, 'mean the same thing.' But nevertheless he perceived how right she was. This constituted his wife's main fault: she invariably had truth on her side, whereas he had nothing but hot air. And truth, when pitted against hot air in the arena of life, generally carries the day.

Since Hilda was right, Cadbury dug up eight white chips from his secret chip-concealing place—a shallow depression under a minor rock—and walked two and three-quarters miles to the nearest psychiatrist, a mellow, do-nothing rabbit shaped like a bowling pin who, according to *his* wife, made fifteen thousand a year and so what about it.

'Clever sort of day,' Dr Drat said amiably, unrolling two Tums for his tummy and leaning back in his extra-heavily padded swivel chair.

'Not so very darn clever,' Cadbury answered, 'when you know you don't have it in you ever to catch sight of a blue chip again, even though you work your ass off day in and day out, and what for? She spends it faster than I make it. Even if I did get my teeth in a blue chip it'd be gone overnight for something expensive and useless on the installment plan, such as for instance a twelve million candle-power self-recharging flashlight. With a lifetime guarantee.'

'Those are darn clever,' Dr Drat said, 'those what you said there, those self-recharging flashlights.'

'The only reason I came to you,' Cadbury said, 'is because my wife made me. She can get me to do anything. If she said, "Swim out into the middle of the creek and drown," do you know what I'd do?'

'You'd rebel,' Dr Drat said in his amiable voice, his hoppers up on the surface of his burled walnut desk.

'I'd kick in her fucking face,' Cadbury said. 'I'd gnaw her to bits; I'd gnaw her right in half, right through the middle. You're damn right. I mean, I'm not kidding; it's a fact. I hate her.'

'How much,' Dr Drat asked, 'is your wife like your mother?'

'I never had a mother,' Cadbury said in a grumpy way—a way which he adopted from time to time: a regular characteristic with him, as Hilda had pointed out. 'I was found floating in the Napa Slough in a shoebox with a handwritten note reading "FINDERS KEEPERS."'

'What was your last dream?' Dr Drat inquired.

'My last dream,' Cadbury said, 'is—was—the same as all the others. I always dream I buy a two-cent mint at the drugstore, one of the flat chocolate-covered mints wrapped in green foil, and when I remove the foil it isn't a mint. You know what it is?'

'Suppose you tell me what it is,' Dr Drat said, in a voice suggesting that he really knew but no one was paying him to say it.

Cadbury said fiercely, 'It's a blue chip. Or rather it *looks* like a blue chip. It's blue and it's flat and round and the same size. But in the dream I always say "Maybe it's just a blue mint." I mean, there must be such a thing as blue mints. I'd hate like hell to store it in my secret chip-concealing place—a shallow depression under an ordinary-looking rock—and then there'd be this hot day, see, and afterwards when I went to get my blue chip—or rather *supposed* blue chip—I found it all melted because it really was a mint after all and not a blue chip. And who'd I sue? The manufacturer? Christ; he never claimed it was a blue chip; it clearly said, in my dream, on the green foil wrapper—'

'I think,' Dr Drat broke in mildly, 'that our time is up for today. We might well do some exploring of this aspect of your inner psyche next week because it appears to be leading us somewhere.'

Rising to his feet, Cadbury said, 'What's the matter with me, Dr Drat? I want an answer; be frank—I can take it. Am I psychotic?'

'Well, you have illusions,' Dr Drat said, after a meditative pause. 'No, you're not psychotic; you don't hear the voice of Christ or anything like that telling you to go out and rape people. No, it's illusions. About yourself, your work, your wife. There may be more. Goodbye.' He rose, too, hippity-hopped to the door of his office and politely but firmly opened it, exposing the tunnel out.

For some reason Cadbury felt cheated; he felt that he had only just begun to talk, and here it was, time to go. 'I bet,' he said, 'you headshrinkers make a hell of a lot of blue chips. I should have gone to college and become a psychiatrist and then I wouldn't have any problems any more. Except for Hilda; I guess I'd still have her.'

Since Dr Drat had nothing by way of comment to that, Cadbury moodily walked the four miles back north to his current gnawing-assignment, a large poplar growing at the edge of Papermill Creek, and sank his teeth furiously into the base of the poplar, imagining to himself that the tree was a syzygy of Dr Drat and Hilda both together.

At almost precisely that moment a nattily-attired fowl came soaring through the grove of cypress trees nearby and alit on a branch of the swaying, being-gnawed-on poplar. 'Your mail for today,' the fowl informed him, and dropped a letter which sailed to the ground at Cadbury's rear feet. 'Air mail, too. Looks interesting. I held it up to the light and it's handwritten, not typed. Looks like a woman's hand.'

With his gnawing tooth, Cadbury ripped the envelope open. Sure enough, the mail bird had perceived accurately: here was a handwritten letter clearly the product of the mind of some unknown woman. The letter, very short, consisted of this:

> Dear Mr Cadbury,
>   I love you.
>   Cordially, and hoping for a reply,
>   JANE FECKLESS FOUNDFULLY.

Never in his life had Cadbury heard of such a person. He turned the letter over, saw no more writing, sniffed, smelling—or imagined that he smelled—a faint, subtle, smoky perfume. However, on the back of the envelope he located further words in Jane Feckless Foundfully's (was she Miss or Mrs?) hand: her return address.

This excited his senses no end.

'Was I right?' the mail bird asked, from its branch above him.

'No, it's a bill,' Cadbury lied. 'Made to look like a personal letter.' He then pretended to return to his work of gnawing, and after a pause the mail bird, deceived, flapped off and disappeared.

At once Cadbury ceased gnawing, seated himself on a rise of turf, got out his turtle-shell snuff box, took a deep, thoughtful pinch of his preferred mixture, Mrs Siddon's No. 3 & 4, and contemplated in the most profound and keen manner possible whether (a) he ought to reply to Jane Feckless Foundfully's letter at all or simply forget that he had ever received it, or (b) answer it, and if (b) then answer it (b sub one) in a bantering fashion or (b sub two) with possibly a meaningful poem from his Untermeyer's anthology of World Poetry plus several suggestive-of-a-sensitive-nature added notations of his own invention, or possibly even (b sub three) come right out and say something such as:

Dear Miss (Mrs?) Foundfully,

In answer to your letter, the fact is that I love you, too, and am unhappy in my marital relationship with a woman I do not now and actually never really did love, and also am quite dispirited and pessimistic and dissatisfied by my employment and am consulting Dr Drat, who in all honesty doesn't seem able to help me a bit, although in all probability it's not his fault but rather due to the severity of my emotional disturbance. Perhaps you and I could get together in the near future and discuss both your situation and mine, and make some progress.

Cordially,

BOB CADBURY (call me Bob, okay? And I'll call you Jane, if that's okay).

The problem, however, he realized, consisted in the obvious fact that Hilda would get wind of this and do something dreadful–he had no idea what, only a recognition, melancholy indeed, of its severity. And in addition–but second in order as a problem–how did he know he would like or love, whichever, Miss (or Mrs) Foundfully in return? Obviously she either knew him directly in some manner which he could not account for or had perhaps heard about him through a mutual friend; in any case she seemed certain of her own emotions and intentions toward him, and that mainly was what mattered.

The situation depressed him. Because how could he tell if this was a way out of his misery or on the contrary a worsening of that same misery in a new direction?

Still seated and taking pinch after pinch of snuff, he pondered many alternatives, including doing away with himself, which seemed in accord with the dramatic nature of Miss Foundfully's letter.

That night, after he arrived home weary and discouraged from his gnawing, had eaten dinner and then retired into his locked study away from Hilda where she probably did not know what he was up to, he got out his Hermes portable typewriter, inserted a page, reflected long and soul-searchingly, and then wrote an answer to Miss Foundfully.

While he lay supine, engrossed in this task, his wife Hilda burst into his locked study. Bits of lock, door and hinges, as well as several screws, flew in all directions.

'What are you doing?' Hilda demanded. 'All hunched over your Hermes typewriter like some sort of bug. You look like a horrid little dried-up spider, the way you always do this time of evening.'

'I'm writing to the main branch of the library,' Cadbury said, in icy dignity, 'about a book I returned which they claim I didn't.'

'You liar,' his wife Hilda said in a frenzy of rage, having now looked over his shoulder and seen the beginning part of his letter. 'Who is this Miss Foundfully? Why are you writing her?'

'Miss Foundfully,' Cadbury said artfully, 'is the librarian who has been assigned to my case.'

'Well, I happen to know you're lying,' his wife said. 'Because I wrote that perfumed fake letter to you to test you. And I was right. You *are* answering it; I knew it the minute I heard you begin peck-pecking away at the disgusting cheap common typewriter you love so dearly.' She then snatched up the typewriter, letter and all, and hurled it through the window of Cadbury's study, into the night darkness.

'My assumption, then,' Cadbury managed to say after a time, 'is that there is no Miss Foundfully, so there is no point in my getting the flashlight and looking around outside for my Hermes—if it still exists—to finish the letter. Am I correct?'

With a jeering expression, but without lowering herself by

answering, his wife stalked from his study, leaving him alone with his assumptions and his tin of Boswell's Best, a snuff mixture far too mild for such an occasion.

Well, Cadbury thought to himself, I guess then I'll never be able to get away from Hilda. And he thought, I wonder what Miss Foundfully would have been like had she really existed. And then he thought, Maybe even though my wife made her up there might be somewhere in the world a real person who would be like I imagine Miss Foundfully—or rather like I imagined before I found out—to be. If you follow me, he thought to himself broodingly. I mean, my wife Hilda can't be *all* the Miss Foundfullys in the entire world.

The next day at work, alone with the half-gnawed poplar tree, he produced a small note-pad and short pencil, envelope and stamp which he had managed to smuggle out of the house without Hilda noticing. Seated on a slight rise of earth, snuffing meditatively small pinches of Bezoar Fine Grind, he wrote a short note, printed so as to be easily read.

TO WHOMEVER READS THIS!

My name is Bob Cadbury and I am a young, fairly healthy beaver with a broad background in political science and theology, although largely self-taught, and I would like to talk with you about God and The Purpose of Existence and other topics of like ilk. Or we could play chess.

Cordially,

And he thereupon signed his name. For a time he pondered, sniffed an extra large pinch of Bezoar Fine Grind, and then he added:

PS Are you a girl? If you are I'll bet you're pretty.

Folding the note up he placed it in a nearly-empty snuff tin, sealed the tin painstakingly with Scotch Tape, and then floated it

off down the creek in a direction which he calculated to be somewhat northwest.

Several days passed before he saw, with excitement and glee,
a second snuff tin—not the one which he had launched—slowly
floating up the creek in a direction which he calculated as
southeast.

Dear Mr Cadbury (the folded-up note within the snuff tin
began). My sister and brother are the only non-fud friends I
have, and if you're not a fud, the way everyone has been since I
got back from Madrid, I'd sure like to meet you.

There was also a PS

PS You sound real keen and neat and I'll bet you know a lot
about Zen Buddhism.

The letter was signed in a way difficult to read, but at last he
made it out as Carol Stickyfoot.

He at once dispatched this note in answer:

Dear Miss (Mrs?) Stickyfoot,
Are you real or are you somebody made up by my wife? It is
essential that I know at once, as I have in the past been tricked
and now have to be constantly wary.

Off went the note, floating within its snuff tin in a northwest
direction.

The answer, when it arrived the following day floating in a
southeast direction in a Camelopard No. 5 snuff tin, read briefly:

Mr Cadbury, if you think I am a figment of your wife's distorted
mind, then you are going to miss out on life.

Very truly yours,

CAROL

Well, that's certainly sound advice, Cadbury said to himself as he read and reread the letter. On the other hand, he said to himself, this is almost precisely what I would expect a figment of my wife Hilda's distorted mind to come up with. So what is proved?

Dear Miss Stickyfoot (he wrote back),

I love you and believe in you. But just to be on the safe side—from my point of view, I mean—could you remit under separate cover—COD if you wish—some item or object or artifact which would prove beyond a reasonable doubt who and what you are, if that's not asking too much. Try and understand my position. I dare not make a second mistake such as in the Foundfully disaster. This time I would go out the window along with the Hermes.

With adoration, etc.

This he floated off in a northwest direction, and at once set about waiting for a reply. Meanwhile, however, he had to visit Dr Drat once more. Hilda insisted on it.

'And how's it been going, down by the creek?' Dr Drat said in a jovial manner, his big fuzzy hoppers up on his desk.

The decision to be frank and honest with the psychiatrist stole over Cadbury. Surely there lay no harm in telling Drat everything; this was what he was being paid for: to hear the truth with all its details, both horrid and sublime.

'I've fallen in love with Carol Stickyfoot,' he began. 'But at the same time, although my love is absolute and eternal, I have this nagging angst that she's a figment of my wife's deranged imagination, concocted as was Miss Foundfully to lead me into revealing my true self to Hilda, which at all costs I need to conceal. Because if my true self came out I'd knock the frigging crap out of her and leave her flat.'

'Hmm,' Dr Drat said.

'And out of you, too,' Cadbury said, releasing all his hostilities in one grand basketful.

Dr Drat said, 'You trust no one, then? You're alienated from all mankind? You've led a life-pattern that's drawn you insidiously into total isolation? Think before you answer; the answer may be yes, and this you may have trouble facing.'

'I'm not isolated from Carol Stickyfoot,' Cadbury said hotly. 'In fact that's the whole point; I'm trying to terminate my isolation. When I was preoccupied with blue chips *then* I was isolated. Meeting and getting to know Miss Stickyfoot may mean the end of all that's wrong in my life, and if you have any insight into me you'd be damn glad I floated off that snuff tin that day. Damn glad.' He glowered moodily at the long-eared doctor.

'It may interest you to know,' Dr Drat said, 'that Miss Stickyfoot is a former patient of mine. She cracked up in Madrid and had to be flown back here in a suitcase. I'll admit she's quite attractive, but she's got a lot of emotional problems. And her left breast is larger than her right.'

'But you admit she's real!' Cadbury shouted in excited discovery.

'Oh, she's *real* enough; I'll grant that. But you may find you have your hands full. After a while you may wish you were back with Hilda again. God only knows where Carol Stickyfoot may lead the two of you. I doubt if Carol herself knows.'

It sounded pretty damn good to Cadbury, and he returned to his virtually gnawed-through poplar tree at the creek bank in high spirits. The time, according to his waterproof Rolex watch, came to only ten-thirty, and so he had more or less the entire day to plan out what he should do, now that he knew that Carol Stickyfoot really existed and was not merely another snare and delusion manufactured by his wife.

Several regions of the creek remained unmapped, and, because of the nature of his employment, he knew these places intimately. Six or seven hours lay ahead before he had to report home to Hilda; why not abandon the poplar project temporarily and begin hasty construction of an adequate little concealed shelter for himself and Carol, beyond the ability of the world at large to identify, locate or recognize? It had become action time; thinking time had passed.

Toward the latter part of the day, while he labored deeply engrossed in erecting the adequate little concealed shelter, a tin of Dean's Own came floating southeast down the creek. In a boiling wake of paddled water he rushed out to seize the snuff tin before it drifted by.

When he had removed the Scotch Tape and opened it he found a small package wrapped in tissue paper and a derisive note.

Here's your proof (the note read).

The package contained three blue chips.

For over an hour Cadbury could scarcely trust his teeth to gnaw properly, so great was the shock of Carol's token of authenticity, her pledge to him and all that he represented. In near madness he bit through branch after branch of an old oak tree, scattering boughs in every direction. A strange frenzy overcame him. He had actually found someone, had managed to escape Hilda—the road lay ahead and he had only to travel it . . . or rather swim it.

Tying several empty snuff tins together with a length of twine he pushed off into the creek; the tins floated more or less northwest and Cadbury paddled after them, breathing heavily with anticipation. As he paddled, keeping the snuff tins perpetually in view, he composed a rhymed quatrain for the occasion of meeting Carol face to face.

> There's few who say I love you.
> But this, I swear, is truth:
> The deed which I have sought to
> Is sure and sound and sooth.

He did not know exactly what 'sooth' meant, but how many words rhymed with 'truth'?

Meanwhile, the tied-together snuff tins led him nearer and nearer—or so he hoped and believed—to Miss Carol Stickyfoot. Bliss. But then, as he paddled along, he got to recalling the sly, carefully-casual remarks of Dr Drat, the seeds of uncertainty planted in Drat's professional fashion. Did he (meaning himself, not Drat) have the courage, the power and integrity, the dedication of purpose, to cope with Carol if she had, as Drat declared, severe emotional problems? Suppose Drat turned out to be correct? Suppose Carol proved to be more difficult and destructive than even Hilda—who threw his Hermes portable typewriter through the window and suchlike manifestations of psychopathic rage?

Busy ruminating, he failed to notice that the several tied-together snuff tins had coasted silently to shore. Reflexively, he paddled after them and up out of the creek onto land.

Ahead—a modest apartment with handpainted window shades and a nonobjective mobile swinging lazily above the door. And there, on the front porch, sat Carol Stickyfoot, drying her hair with a large white fluffy towel.

'I love you,' Cadbury said. He shook the creek-water from his pelt and fidgeted about in a dither of suppressed affect.

Glancing up, Carol Stickyfoot appraised him. She had lovely huge dark eyes and long heavy hair which shone in the fading sun. 'I hope you brought the three blue chips back,' she said. 'Because, see, I borrowed them from the place I work and I have to return them.' She added, 'It was a gesture because you seemed to need assurance. The fuds have been getting to you, like that head-shrinker Drat. He's a real fud of the worst sort. Would you like a cup of instant Yuban coffee?'

As he followed her into her modest apartment Cadbury said, 'I guess you heard my opening remark. I have never been more serious in my whole life. I really do love you, and in the most serious manner. I'm not looking for something trivial or casual or temporary; I'm looking for the most durable and serious kind of relationship there is. I hope in God's name you're not just playing, because I never felt more serious and tense about anything in my life, even including blue chips. If this is just a way of amusing yourself or some such thing it would be merciful for you to end it now by plainly speaking out. Because the torture of leaving my wife and beginning a new life and then finding out–'

'Did Dr Fud tell you I paint?' Carol Stickyfoot asked as she put a pan of water on the stove in her modest kitchen and lit the burner under it with an old-fashioned large wooden match.

'He told me only that you flipped your cork in Madrid,' Cadbury said. He seated himself at the small wooden unpainted pine table opposite the stove and watched with love in his heart Miss Stickyfoot spooning instant coffee into two ceramic mugs which had pataphysical spirals baked into their glaze.

'*Do* you know anything about Zen?' Miss Stickyfoot asked.

'Only that you ask koans which are sort of riddles,' he said. 'And you give a sort of nonsense answer because the question is really idiotic in the first place, such as Why are we here on earth? and so forth.' He hoped he had put it properly and she would think that he really did know something about Zen, as mentioned in her letter. And then he thought of a very good Zen answer to her question. 'Zen,' he said, 'is a complete philosophic system which contains questions for every answer that exists in the universe. For instance, if you have the answer "Yes," then Zen is capable of propounding the exact query which is linked to it, such as "Must we die in order to please the Creator, who likes his creations to perish?" Although actually, now that I think about it more deeply, the question which Zen would say goes with that answer is "Are we here in this kitchen about to drink instant Yuban coffee?" Would you agree?' When she did not answer immediately, Cadbury said hurriedly, 'In fact Zen would say that the answer "Yes" is the answer to that question: "Would you agree?" There you have one of the great values of Zen; it can propound a variety of exact questions for almost any given answer.'

'You're full of shit,' Miss Stickyfoot said disdainfully.

Cadbury said, 'That proves I understand Zen. Do you see? Or perhaps the fact is that you don't actually understand Zen yourself.' He felt a trifle nettled.

'Maybe you're right,' Miss Stickyfoot said. 'I mean about my not understanding Zen. The fact is I don't understand it at all.'

'That's very Zen,' Cadbury pointed out. 'And I do. Which is also Zen. Do you see?'

'Here's your coffee,' Miss Stickyfoot said; she placed the two full, steaming cups of coffee on the table and seated herself across from him. Then she smiled. It seemed to him a nice smile, full of light and gentleness, a funny little wrinkled shy smile, with a puzzled, questioning glow of wonder and concern in her eyes. They really were beautiful large dark eyes, just about the most beautiful he had ever seen in his entire life, and he in all truthfulness was in love with her; he had not merely been saying that.

'You realize I'm married,' he said as he sipped his coffee. 'But I'm separated from her. I've been constructing this hovel down along a part of the creek where no one ever goes. I say "hovel" so as not to give you a false impression that it's a mansion or anything; actually it's very well put-together. I'm an expert artisan in my field. I'm not trying to impress you; this is simply God's truth. I know I can take care of both our needs. Or we can live here.' He looked around Miss Stickyfoot's modest apartment. How ascetically and tastefully she had arranged it. He liked it here; he felt peace come to him, a dwindling away of his tensions. For the first time in years.

'You have an odd aura,' Miss Stickyfoot said. 'Sort of soft and woolly and purple. I approve of it. But I've never seen one like it before. Do you build model trains? It sort of looks like the kind of aura that someone who builds model trains would have.'

'I can build almost anything,' Cadbury said. 'With my teeth, my hands, my words. Listen; this is for you.' He then recited his four-line poem. Miss Stickyfoot listened intently.

'That poem,' she decided, when he had finished, 'has wu. "Wu" is a Japanese term—or is it Chinese?—meaning you know what.' She gestured irritably. 'Simplicity. Like some of Paul Klee's drawings.' But then she added, 'It's not very good, though. Otherwise.'

'I composed it,' he explained testily, 'while paddling down the creek after my tied-together snuff tins. It was strictly spur-of-the-moment stuff; I can do better seated in isolation in my locked study at my Hermes. If Hilda isn't banging at the door. You can discern why I hate her. Because of her sadistic intrusions the only time I have for creative work is while paddling or eating my lunch. That one aspect alone of my marital life explains why I had to break away from it and seek you out. In relationship to a person of your sort I could create on a totally new level entirely. I'd have blue chips coming out my ears. In addition, I wouldn't have to spend myself into oblivion seeing Dr Drat whom you correctly call a number one fud.'

'"Blue chips,"' Miss Stickyfoot echoed, screwing up her face with distaste. 'Is that the level you mean? It seems to me you have the aspirations of a wholesale dried fruit dealer. Forget blue chips; don't leave your wife because of that: you're only carrying your old value-system with you. You've internalized what she's taught you, except that you're carrying it one step farther. Pursue a different course entirely and all will go well with you.'

'Like Zen?' he asked.

'You only play with Zen. If you really understood it you never would have answered my note by coming here. There is no perfect person in the world, for you or anybody else. I can't make you feel any better than you do with your wife; you carry your troubles inside you.'

'I agree with that up to a point,' Cadbury agreed, up to a point. 'But my wife makes them worse. Maybe with you they wouldn't entirely go away, but they wouldn't be so bad. *Nothing* could be so bad as it is now. At least you wouldn't throw my Hermes typewriter out the window whenever you got mad at me, and in addition maybe you wouldn't get mad at me every goddam minute of the day and night, as she does. Had you thought about that? Put that in your pipe and smoke it, as the expression goes.'

His reasoning did not seem to go unnoticed by Miss Stickyfoot; she nodded in what appeared to be at least partial agreement. 'All right,' she said after a pause, and her large dark attractive eyes gleamed with sudden light. 'Let's make the effort. If you can abandon your obsessive chatter for a moment—for perhaps the first time in your life—I'll do with you and for you, which you could never have done by yourself, what needs to be done. All right? Shall I lay it on you?'

'You have begun to articulate oddly,' Cadbury said, with a mixture of alarm, surprise—and a growing awe. Miss Stickyfoot, before his eyes, had begun to change in a palpable fashion. What had, up to now, appeared to him the ultimate in beauty evolved as he gazed fixedly; beauty, as he had known it, anticipated it, imagined it, dissolved and was carried away into the rivers of oblivion, of the past, of the limitations of his own mind: it was replaced, now, by something further, something that surpassed it, which he could never have conjured up from his own imagination. It far exceeded that.

Miss Stickyfoot had become several persons, each of them bound to the nature of reality, pretty but not illusive, attractive but within the confines of actuality. And these people, he saw, meant much more, were much more, because they were not manifestations fulfilling his wishes, products of his own mind. One, a semi-Oriental girl with long, shiny, dark hair, gazed at him with impassive, bright, intelligent eyes that sparkled with calm awareness; the perception of him, within them, lucid and correct, unimpaired by sentiment or even kindness, mercy or compassion—yet her eyes held one kind of love: justice, without aversion or repudiation of him, as conscious as she was of his imperfections. It was a comradely love, a sharing of her cerebral, analytical evaluation of himself and of her own self, and the bonded-togetherness of the two of them by their mutual failings.

The next girl, smiling with forgiveness and tolerance, unaware of him as falling short in any way—nothing he was or was not or could do or fail to do would disappoint her or lower her esteem for him—glowed and smoldered darkly, with a kind of warm, sad, and at the same time eternally cheerful happiness: this, his mother, his eternal, never-disappearing, never-going-away or leaving or forgetting mother who would never withdraw her protection of him, her sheltering cloak that concealed him, warmed him, breathed hope and the flicker of new life into him when pain and defeat and loneliness chilled him into near-ashes . . . the first girl, his equal: his sister, perhaps; this girl his gentle, strong mother who was at the same time frail and afraid but not showing either.

And, with them, a peevish, pouting, irritable girl, immature, pretty in a marred way, with certain skin blemishes, wearing a too-frilly, too-satinish blouse, too-short skirt, with legs too thin; yet still attractive in an undeveloped way. She gazed at him with disappointment, as if he had let her down, had failed her, always would; and still she glared at him demandingly, still wanting more, still trying to call forth from him everything she needed and yearned for: the whole world, the sky, everything, but despising him because he could not give it to her. This, he realized, his future daughter, who would turn from him finally, as the two others would not, would desert him in resentful disappointment to seek fulfillment in another, younger man. He would have her only a short time. And he would never fully please her.

But all three loved him, and all three were his girls, his women, his wistful, hopeful, sad, frightened, trusting, suffering, laughing, sensual, protecting, warming, demanding female realities, his trinity of the objective world standing in opposition to him and at the same time completing him, adding to him what he was not and never would be, what he cherished and prized and respected and loved and needed more than anything else in existence. Miss Stickyfoot, as such, was gone. These three girls stood in her place. And they did not communicate to him remotely, across a break, by floating messages down Papermill Creek in empty snuff tins; they spoke directly, their intense eyes fixed on him unrelentingly, ceaselessly aware of him.

'I will live with you,' the calm-eyed Asianish girl said. 'As a neutral companion, off and on, as long as I'm alive and you're alive, which may not be forever. Life is transitory and often not worth being fucked over by. Sometimes I think the dead are better off. Maybe I'll join them today, maybe tomorrow. Maybe I'll kill you, send you to join them, or take you with me. Want to come? You can pay the travel-expenses, at least if you want me to accompany you. Otherwise I'll go by myself and travel free on a military transport 707; I get a regular government rebate the rest of my life, which I put in a secret bank account for semi-legal investment purposes of an undisclosed nature for purposes you better goddam never find out if you know what's best for you.' She paused, still eyeing him impassively. 'Well?'

'What was the question?' Cadbury said, lost.

'I said,' she said fiercely, with impatient dismissal of his low mental powers, 'I'll live with you for an unspecified period, with uncertain ultimate outcome, if you'll pay enough, and especially—and this is mandatory—if you keep the house functioning effi-ciently—you know, pay bills, clean up, shop, fix meals—in such a way that I'm not bothered. So I can do my own things, which matter.'

'Okay,' he said eagerly.

'I'll never live with you,' the sad-eyed, warm, smoky-haired girl said, plump and pliant in her cuddly leather jacket with its tassels, and her brown cord slacks and boots, carrying her rabbit-skin purse. 'But I'll look in on you now and then on my way to work in the morning and see if you've got a joint you can lay on me, and if you don't, and you're down, I'll supercharge you—but not right now. Okay?' She smiled even more intensely, her lovely eyes rich with wisdom and the unstated complexity of herself and her love.

'Sure,' he said. He wished for more, but knew that was all; she did not belong to him, did not exist for him: she was herself, and a product of and piece of the world.

'Rape,' the third girl said, her over-red, too-lush lips twisting with malice, but at the same time twitching with amusement. 'I'll never leave you, you dirty old man, because when I do, how the hell are you ever going to find anyone else willing to live with a child molester who's going to die of a coronary embolism or mas-sive infarct any day now? After I'm gone it's all over for you, you dirty old man.' Suddenly, briefly, her eyes moisted over with grief and compassion—but only briefly and then it was over. 'That will be the only happiness you'll ever have. So I can't go; I have to stay with you and delay my own life, even if it's forever.' She lost, then, by degrees, her animation; a kind of resigned, mechanical, inert blackness settled over her garish, immature, attractive features. 'If I get a better offer, though,' she said stonily, 'I'll take it. I'll have to shop around and see. Check out the action downtown.'

'The hell you say,' Cadbury said, hotly, with resentment. And experienced already a dreadful sense of loss, as if she had gone away even now, even this soon; it had already happened—this, the worst thing possible in all his life.

'Now,' all three girls said at once, briskly, 'let's get down to the nitty-gritty. How many blue token chips do you have?'

'W-what?' Cadbury stammered, startled.

'That's the name of the game,' the three girls chimed in unison, with bright-eyed asperity. All their combined faculties had been roused to existence by the topic; they were individually and collectively fully alert. 'Let's see your checkbook. What's your balance?'

'What's your Gross Annual Product?' the Asian girl said.

'I would never rip you off,' the warm sentimental, patient, cherishing girl said, 'but could you lend me two blue chips? I know you've got hundreds, an important and famous beaver like you.'

'Go get some and buy me two quarts of chocolate milk and a carton of various assorted donuts and a Coke at the Speedy Mart,' the peevish girl said.

'Can I borrow your Porsche?' the cherishing girl asked. 'If I put gas in it?'

'But you can't drive mine,' the Asian girl said. 'It'd increase the cost of my insurance, which my mother pays.'

'Teach me how to drive,' the peevish girl said, 'so I can get one of my boyfriends to take me to the motor movies tomorrow night; it's only two bucks a carload. They're showing five skinflicks, and we can get a couple of dudes and a chick into the trunk.'

'Better entrust your blue chips to my keeping,' the cherishing girl said. 'These other chicks'll rip you off.'

'Fuck you,' the peevish girl said roughly.

CADBURY, THE BEAVER WHO LACKED

'If you listen to her or give her one single blue chip,' the Asian girl said fiercely, 'I'll tear out your fucking heart and eat it alive. And that low-class one, she's got the clap; if you sleep with her you'll be sterile the rest of your life.'

'I don't have any blue chips,' Cadbury said anxiously, fearing that, knowing this, all three girls would depart. 'But I—'

'Sell your Hermes Rocket typewriter,' the Asian girl said.

'I'll sell it for you,' the cherishing, protective girl said in her gentle voice. 'And give you—' She calculated, painstakingly, slowly, with effort. 'I'll split it with you. Fairly. I'd never burn you.' She smiled at him, and he knew it was true.

'My mother owns an electric IBM space-expander, ball-type office model,' the peevish girl said haughtily, with near-contempt. 'I'd get myself one and learn to type and get a good job, except that I get more by staying on welfare.'

'Later in the year—' Cadbury began desperately.

'We'll see you later,' the three girls who had formerly been Miss Stickyfoot said. 'Or you can mail the blue chips to us. Okay?' They began to recede, collectively; they wavered and became insubstantial. Or—

Was it Cadbury himself, the Beaver Who Lacked, who was becoming insubstantial? He had a sudden, despairing intuition that it was the latter. *He* was fading out; they remained.

And yet that was good.

He could survive that. He could survive his own disappearance. But not theirs.

Already, in the short time he had known them, they meant more to him than he did to himself. And that was a relief.

Whether he had any blue chips for them or not—and that seemed to be what mattered to them—they would survive. If they could not coax, rip off, borrow, or anyhow in one fashion or another get blue chips from him, they'd get them from somebody else. Or else go along happily anyhow without them. They did not really need them; they *liked* them. They could survive with or without them. But they, frankly, were not really interested in survival. They wanted to be, intended to be, and knew how to be, genuinely happy. They would not settle for mere survival; they wanted to live.

'I hope I see you again,' Cadbury said. 'Or rather, I hope you see me again. I mean, I hope I reappear, at least briefly, from time to time, in your lives. Just so I can see how you're doing.'

'Stop scheming on us,' all three said in unison, as Cadbury became virtually nonexistent; all that remained of him, now, was a wisp of gray smoke, lingering plaintively in the half-exhausted air that had once offered to sustain him.

'You'll be back,' the cherishing, plump, leather-clad, warm-eyed girl said, with certitude, as if she knew instinctively that there could be no doubt. 'We'll see you.'

'I hope so,' Cadbury said, but now even the sound of his gone-off voice had become faint; it flickered like a fading audio signal from some distant star that had, long ago, cooled into ash and darkness and inertness and silence.

'Let's go to the beach,' the Asian girl said as the three of them strolled away, confident and assured and substantial and alive to the activity of the day. And off they went.

Cadbury—or at least the ions that remained of him as a sort of vapor trail marking his one-time passage through life and out—wondered if there were, at their beach, any nice trees to gnaw. And where their beach was. And if it was nice. And if it had a name.

Pausing briefly, glancing back, the compassionate, cherishing plump girl in leather and soft tassels said, 'Would you like to come along? We could take you for a little while, maybe this one time. But not again. You know how it is.'

There was no answer.

'I love you,' she said softly, to herself. And smiled her moist-eyed, happy, sorrowful, understanding, remembering smile.

And went on. A little behind the other two. Lingering slightly, as if, without showing it, looking back.

A LITTLE SOMETHING FOR US TEMPUNAUTS

Wearily, Addison Doug plodded up the long path of synthetic red-wood rounds, step by step, his head down a little, moving as if he were in actual physical pain. The girl watched him, wanting to help him, hurt within her to see how worn and unhappy he was, but at the same time she rejoiced that he was there at all. On and on, toward her, without glancing up, going by feel . . . like he's done this many times, she thought suddenly. Knows the way too well. Why?

'Addi,' she called, and ran toward him. 'They said on the TV you were dead. All of you were killed!'

He paused, wiping back his dark hair, which was no longer long; just before the launch they had cropped it. But he had evidently forgotten. 'You believe everything you see on TV?' he said, and came on again, haltingly, but smiling now. And reaching up for her.

God, it felt good to hold him, and to have him clutch at her again, with more strength than she had expected. 'I was going to find somebody else,' she gasped. 'To replace you.'

'I'll knock your head off if you do,' he said. 'Anyhow, that isn't possible; nobody could replace me.'

'But what about the implosion?' she said. 'On reentry; they said—'

'I forget,' Addison said, in the tone he used when he meant, I'm not going to discuss it. The tone had always angered her before, but not now. This time she sensed how awful the memory was. 'I'm going to stay at your place a couple of days,' he said, as together they moved up the path toward the open front door of the tilted

A-frame house. 'If that's okay. And Benz and Crayne will be joining me, later on; maybe even as soon as tonight. We've got a lot to talk over and figure out.'

'Then all three of you survived.' She gazed up into his careworn face. 'Everything they said on TV . . .' She understood, then. Or believed she did. 'It was a cover story. For–political purposes, to fool the Russians. Right? I mean, the Soviet Union'll think the launch was a failure because on reentry–'

'No,' he said. 'A chrononaut will be joining us, most likely. To help figure out what happened. General Toad said one of them is already on his way here; they got clearance already. Because of the gravity of the situation.'

'Jesus,' the girl said, stricken. 'Then who's the cover story for?'

'Let's have something to drink,' Addison said. 'And then I'll outline it all for you.'

'Only thing I've got at the moment is California brandy.'

Addison Doug said, 'I'd drink anything right now, the way I feel.' He dropped to the couch, leaned back, and sighed a ragged, distressed sigh, as the girl hurriedly began fixing both of them a drink.

The FM radio in the car yammered, '. . . grieves at the stricken turn of events precipitating out of an unheralded . . .'

'Official nonsense babble,' Crayne said, shutting off the radio. He and Benz were having trouble finding the house, having been there only once before. It struck Crayne that this was somewhat informal a way of convening a conference of this importance, meeting at Addison's chick's pad out here in the boondocks of Ojai. On the other hand, they wouldn't be pestered by the curious. And they probably didn't have much time. But that was hard to say; about that no one knew for sure.

The hills on both sides of the road had once been forests, Crayne observed. Now housing tracts and their melted, irregular, plastic roads marred every rise in sight. 'I'll bet this was nice once,' he said to Benz, who was driving.

'The Los Padres National Forest is near here,' Benz said. 'I got lost in there when I was eight. For hours I was sure a rattler would get me. Every stick was a snake.'

'The rattler's got you now,' Crayne said.

'All of us,' Benz said.

'You know,' Crayne said, 'it's a hell of an experience to be dead.'

'Speak for yourself.'

'But technically–'

'If you listen to the radio and TV.' Benz turned toward him, his big gnome face bleak with admonishing sternness. 'We're no more dead than anyone else on the planet. The difference for us is that our death date is in the past, whereas everyone else's is set somewhere at an uncertain time in the future. Actually, some people have it pretty damn well set, like people in cancer wards; they're as certain as we are. More so. For example, how long can we stay here before we go back? We have a margin, a latitude that a terminal cancer victim doesn't have.'

Crayne said cheerfully, 'The next thing you'll be telling us to cheer us up is that we're in no pain.'

'Addi is. I watched him lurch off earlier today. He's got it psychosomatically–made it into a physical complaint. Like God's kneeling on his neck; you know, carrying a much-too-great burden that's unfair, only he won't complain out loud . . . just points now and then at the nail hole in his hand.' He grinned.

'Addi has got more to live for than we do.'

'Every man has more to live for than any other man. I don't have a cute chick to sleep with, but I'd like to see the semis rolling along Riverside Freeway at sunset a few more times. It's not what you have to live for; it's that you want to live to see it, to be there–that's what is so damn sad.'

They rode on in silence.

In the quiet living room of the girl's house the three tempunauts sat around smoking, taking it easy; Addison Doug thought to himself that the girl looked unusually foxy and desirable in her stretched-tight white sweater and micro-skirt and he wished, wistfully, that she looked a little less interesting. He could not really afford to get embroiled in such stuff, at this point. He was too tired.

'Does she know,' Benz said, indicating the girl, 'what this is all about? I mean, can we talk openly? It won't wipe her out?'

'I haven't explained it to her yet,' Addison said.

'You goddam well better,' Crayne said.

'What is it?' the girl said, stricken, sitting upright with one hand directly between her breasts. As if clutching at a religious artifact that isn't there, Addison thought.

'We got snuffed on reentry,' Benz said. He was, really, the cruelest of the three. Or at least the most blunt. 'You see, Miss . . .'

'Hawkins,' the girl whispered.

'Glad to meet you, Miss Hawkins.' Benz surveyed her in his cold, lazy fashion. 'You have a first name?'

'Merry Lou.'

'Okay, Merry Lou,' Benz said. To the other two men he observed, 'Sounds like the name a waitress has stitched on her blouse. Merry Lou's my name and I'll be serving you dinner and breakfast and lunch and dinner and breakfast for the next few days or however long it is before you all give up and go back to your own time; that'll be fifty-three dollars and eight cents, please, not including tip. And I hope y'all never come back, y'hear?' His voice had begun to shake; his cigarette, too. 'Sorry, Miss Hawkins,' he said then. 'We're all screwed up by the implosion at reentry. As soon as we got here in ETA we learned about it. We've known longer than anyone else; we knew as soon as we hit Emergence Time.'

'But there's nothing we could do,' Crayne said.

'There's nothing anyone can do,' Addison said to her, and put his arm around her. It felt like a déjà vu thing but then it hit him. We're in a closed time loop, he thought, we keep going through this again and again, trying to solve the reentry problem, each time imagining it's the first time, the only time . . . and never succeeding. Which attempt is this? Maybe the millionth; we have sat here a million times, raking the same facts over and over again and getting nowhere. He felt bone-weary, thinking that. And he felt a sort of vast philosophical hate toward all other men, who did not have this enigma to deal with. We all go to one place, he thought, as the Bible says. But . . . for the three of us, we have been there already. Are lying there now. So it's wrong to ask us to stand around on the surface of Earth afterward and argue and worry about it and try to figure out what malfunctioned. That should be, rightly, for our heirs to do. We've had enough already.

He did not say this aloud, though—for their sake.

'Maybe you bumped into something,' the girl said.

Glancing at the others, Benz said sardonically, 'Maybe we "bumped into something."'

'The TV commentators kept saying that,' Merry Lou said, 'about the hazard in reentry of being out of phase spatially and colliding right down to the molecular level with tangent objects, any one of which—' She gestured. 'You know. "No two objects can occupy the same space at the same time." So everything blew up, for that reason.' She glanced around questioningly.

'That is the major risk factor,' Crayne acknowledged. 'At least theoretically, as Dr Fein at Planning calculated when they got into the hazard question. But we had a variety of safety locking devices provided that functioned automatically. Reentry couldn't occur unless these assists had stabilized us spatially so we would not overlap. Of course, all those devices, in sequence, might have failed. One after the other. I was watching my feedback metric scopes on launch, and they agreed, every one of them, that we were phased properly at that time. And I heard no warning tones. Saw none, neither.' He grimaced. 'At least it didn't happen then.'

Suddenly Benz said, 'Do you realize that our next of kin are now rich? All our Federal and commercial life-insurance payoff. Our "next of kin"—God forbid, that's us, I guess. We can apply for tens of thousands of dollars, cash on the line. Walk into our brokers' offices and say, "I'm dead; lay the heavy bread on me."'

Addison Doug was thinking, The public memorial services. That they have planned, after the autopsies. That long line of black-draped Cads going down Pennsylvania Avenue, with all the government dignitaries and double-domed scientist types—*and we'll be there*. Not once but twice. Once in the oak hand-rubbed brass-fitted flag-draped caskets, but also . . . maybe riding in open limos, waving at the crowds of mourners.

'The ceremonies,' he said aloud.

The others stared at him, angrily, not comprehending. And then, one by one, they understood; he saw it on their faces.

'No,' Benz grated. 'That's—impossible.'

Crayne shook his head emphatically. 'They'll order us to be there, and we will be. Obeying orders.'

'Will we have to *smile*?' Addison said. 'To fucking *smile*?'

'No,' General Toad said slowly, his great wattled head shivering about on his broomstick neck, the color of his skin dirty and mottled, as if the mass of decorations on his stiff-board collar had started part of him decaying away. 'You are not to smile, but on the contrary are to adopt a properly grief-stricken manner. In keeping with the national mood of sorrow at this time.'

'That'll be hard to do,' Crayne said.

The Russian chrononaut showed no response; his thin beaked face, narrow within his translating earphones, remained strained with concern.

'The nation,' General Toad said, 'will become aware of your presence among us once more for this brief interval; cameras of all major TV networks will pan up to you without warning, and at the same time, the various commentators have been instructed to tell their audiences something like the following.' He got out a piece of typed material, put on his glasses, cleared his throat and said, '"We seem to be focusing on three figures riding together. Can't quite make them out. Can you?"' General Toad lowered the paper. 'At this point they'll interrogate their colleagues extempore. Finally they'll exclaim, "Why, Roger," or Walter or Ned, as the case may be, according to the individual network—'

'Or Bill,' Crayne said. 'In case it's the Bufonidae network, down there in the swamp.'

General Toad ignored him. 'They will severally exclaim, "Why Roger I believe we're seeing the three tempunauts themselves! Does this indeed mean that somehow the difficulty–?" And then the colleague commentator says in his somewhat more somber voice, "What we're seeing at this time, I think, David," or Henry or Pete or Ralph, whichever it is, "consists of mankind's first verified glimpse of what the technical people refer to as Emergence Time Activity or ETA. Contrary to what might seem to be the case at first sight, these are *not*–repeat, not–our three valiant tempunauts as such, as we would ordinarily experience them, but more likely picked up by our cameras as the three of them are temporarily suspended in their voyage to the future, which we initially had reason to hope would take place in a time continuum roughly a hundred years from now ... but it would seem that they somehow undershot and are here now, at this moment, which of course is, as we know, our present."'

Addison Doug closed his eyes and thought, Crayne will ask him if he can be panned up on by the TV cameras holding a balloon and eating cotton candy. I think we're all going nuts from this, all of us. And then he wondered, How many times have we gone through this idiotic exchange?

I can't prove it, he thought wearily. But I know it's true. We've sat here, done this minuscule scrabbling, listened to and said all this crap, many times. He shuddered. Each rinky-dink word ...

'What's the matter?' Benz said acutely.

The Soviet chrononaut spoke up for the first time. 'What is the maximum interval of ETA possible to your three-man team? And how large a per cent has been exhausted by now?'

After a pause Crayne said, 'They briefed us on that before we came in here today. We've consumed approximately one-half of our maximum total ETA interval.'

'However,' General Toad rumbled, 'we have scheduled the Day of National Mourning to fall within the expected period remaining to them of ETA time. This required us to speed up the autopsy and other forensic findings, but in view of public sentiment, it was felt ...'

The autopsy, Addison Doug thought, and again he shuddered; this time he could not keep his thoughts within himself and he said, 'Why don't we adjourn this nonsense meeting and drop down to pathology and view a few tissue sections enlarged and in color, and maybe we'll brainstorm a couple of vital concepts that'll aid medical science in its quest for explanations? Explanations— that's what we need. Explanations for problems that don't exist yet; we can develop the problems later.' He paused. 'Who agrees?'

'I'm not looking at my spleen up there on the screen,' Benz said. 'I'll ride in the parade but I won't participate in my own autopsy.'

'You could distribute microscopic purple-stained slices of your own gut to the mourners along the way,' Crayne said. 'They could provide each of us with a doggy bag; right, General? We can strew tissue sections like confetti. I still think we should smile.'

'I have researched all the memoranda about smiling,' General Toad said, riffling the pages stacked before him, 'and the consensus at policy is that smiling is not in accord with national sentiment. So that issue must be ruled closed. As far as your participating in the autopsical procedures which are now in progress—'

'We're missing out as we sit here,' Crayne said to Addison Doug. 'I always miss out.'

Ignoring him, Addison addressed the Soviet chrononaut. 'Officer N. Gauki,' he said into his microphone, dangling on his chest, 'what in your mind is the greatest terror facing a time traveler? That there will be an implosion due to coincidence on reentry, such as has occurred in our launch? Or did other traumatic obsessions bother you and your comrade during your own brief but highly successful time flight?'

N. Gauki, after a pause, answered, 'R. Plenya and I exchanged views at several informal times. I believe I can speak for us both when I respond to your question by emphasizing our perpetual fear that we had inadvertently entered a closed time loop and would never break out.'

'You'd repeat it forever?' Addison Doug asked.

'Yes, Mr A. Doug,' the chrononaut said, nodding somberly.

A fear that he had never experienced before overcame Addison Doug. He turned helplessly to Benz and muttered, 'Shit.' They gazed at each other.

'I really don't believe this is what happened,' Benz said to him in a low voice, putting his hand on Doug's shoulder; he gripped hard, the grip of friendship. 'We just imploded on reentry, that's all. Take it easy.'

'Could we adjourn soon?' Addison Doug said in a hoarse, strangling voice, half rising from his chair. He felt the room and the people in it rushing in at him, suffocating him. Claustrophobia, he realized. Like when I was in grade school, when they flashed a surprise test on our teaching machines, and I saw I couldn't pass it. 'Please,' he said simply, standing. They were all looking at him, with different expressions. The Russian's face was especially sympathetic, and deeply lined with care. Addison wished—'I want to go home,' he said to them all, and felt stupid.

He was drunk. It was late at night, at a bar on Hollywood Boulevard; fortunately, Merry Lou was with him, and he was having a good time. Everyone was telling him so, anyhow. He clung to Merry Lou and said, 'The great unity in life, the supreme unity and meaning, is man and woman. Their absolute unity; right?'

'I know,' Merry Lou said. 'We studied that in class.' Tonight, at his request, Merry Lou was a small blonde girl, wearing purple bellbottoms and high heels and an open midriff blouse. Earlier she had had a lapis lazuli in her navel, but during dinner at Ting Ho's it had popped out and been lost. The owner of the restaurant had promised to keep on searching for it, but Merry Lou had been gloomy ever since. It was, she said, symbolic. But of what she did not say. Or anyhow he could not remember; maybe that was it. She had told him what it meant, and he had forgotten.

An elegant young black at a nearby table, with an Afro and striped vest and overstuffed red tie, had been staring at Addison for some time. He obviously wanted to come over to their table but was afraid to; meanwhile, he kept on staring.

'Did you ever get the sensation,' Addison said to Merry Lou, 'that you knew exactly what was about to happen? What someone was going to say? Word for word? Down to the slightest detail. As if you had already lived through it once before?'

'Everybody gets into that space,' Merry Lou said. She sipped a Bloody Mary.

The black rose and walked toward them. He stood by Addison. 'I'm sorry to bother you, sir.'

Addison said to Merry Lou, 'He's going to say, "Don't I know you from somewhere? Didn't I see you on TV?"'

'That was precisely what I intended to say,' the black said.

Addison said, 'You undoubtedly saw my picture on page forty-six of the current issue of *Time*, the section on new medical discoveries. I'm the GP from a small town in Iowa catapulted to fame by my invention of a widespread, easily available cure for eternal life. Several of the big pharmaceutical houses are already bidding on my vaccine.'

'That might have been where I saw your picture,' the black said, but he did not appear convinced. Nor did he appear drunk; he eyed Addison Doug intensely. 'May I seat myself with you and the lady?'

'Sure,' Addison Doug said. He now saw, in the man's hand, the ID of the US security agency that had ridden herd on the project from the start.

'Mr Doug,' the security agent said as he seated himself beside Addison, 'you really shouldn't be here shooting off your mouth like this. If I recognized you some other dude might and freak out. It's all classified until the Day of Mourning. Technically, you're in violation of a Federal Statute by being here; did you realize that? I should haul you in. But this is a difficult situation; we don't want to do something uncool and make a scene. Where are your two colleagues?'

'At my place,' Merry Lou said. She had obviously not seen the ID. 'Listen,' she said sharply to the agent, 'why don't you get lost? My husband here has been through a grueling ordeal, and this is his only chance to unwind.'

A LITTLE SOMETHING FOR US TEMPUNAUTS

Addison looked at the man. 'I knew what you were going to say before you came over here.' Word for word, he thought. I am right, and Benz is wrong and this will keep happening, this replay.

'Maybe,' the security agent said, 'I can induce you to go back to Miss Hawkins' place voluntarily. Some info arrived'—he tapped the tiny earphone in his right ear—'just a few minutes ago, to all of us, to deliver to you, marked urgent, if we located you. At the launch site ruins . . . they've been combing through the rubble, you know?'

'I know,' Addison said.

'They think they have their first clue. Something was brought back by one of you. From ETA, over and above what you took, in violation of all your pre-launch training.'

'Let me ask you this,' Addison Doug said. 'Suppose somebody does see me? Suppose somebody does recognize me? So what?'

'The public believes that even though reentry failed, the flight into time, the first American time-travel launch, was successful. Three US tempunauts were thrust a hundred years into the future—roughly twice as far as the Soviet launch of last year. That you only went a *week* will be less of a shock if it's believed that you three chose deliberately to remanifest at this continuum because you wished to attend, in fact felt compelled to attend—'

'We wanted to be in the parade,' Addison interrupted. 'Twice.'

'You were drawn to the dramatic and somber spectacle of your own funeral procession, and will be glimpsed there by the alert camera crews of all major networks. Mr Doug, really, an awful lot of high-level planning and expense have gone into this to help correct a dreadful situation; trust us, believe me. It'll be easier on the public, and that's vital, if there's ever to be another US time shot. And that is, after all, what we all want.'

Addison Doug stared at him. 'We want what?'

Uneasily, the security agent said, 'To take further trips into time. As you have done. Unfortunately, you yourself cannot ever do so again, because of the tragic implosion and death of the three of you. But other tempunauts—'

'We want what? Is that what we want?' Addison's voice rose; people at nearby tables were watching now. Nervously.

'Certainly,' the agent said. 'And keep your voice down.'

'I don't want that,' Addison said. 'I want to stop. To stop forever. To just lie in the ground, in the dust, with everyone else. To see no more summers—the *same* summer.'

'Seen one, you've seen them all,' Merry Lou said hysterically. 'I think he's right, Addi; we should get out of here. You've had too many drinks, and it's late, and this news about the—'

Addison broke in, 'What was brought back? How much extra mass?'

The security agent said, 'Preliminary analysis shows that machinery weighing about one hundred pounds was lugged back into the time-field of the module and picked up along with you. This much mass—' The agent gestured. 'That blew up the pad right on the spot. It couldn't begin to compensate for that much more than had occupied its open area at launch time.'

'Wow!' Merry Lou said, eyes wide. 'Maybe somebody sold one of you a quadraphonic phono for a dollar ninety-eight including fifteen-inch air-suspension speakers and a lifetime supply of Neil Diamond records.' She tried to laugh, but failed; her eyes dimmed over. 'Addi,' she whispered, 'I'm sorry. But it's sort of—weird. I mean, it's absurd; you all were briefed, weren't you, about your return weight? You weren't even to add so much as a piece of paper to what you took. I even saw Dr Fein demonstrating the reasons on TV. And one of you hoisted a hundred pounds of machinery into that field? You must have been trying to self-destruct, to do that!' Tears slid from her eyes; one tear rolled out onto her nose and hung there. He reached reflexively to wipe it away, as if helping a little girl rather than a grown one.

'I'll fly you to the analysis site,' the security agent said, standing up. He and Addison helped Merry Lou to her feet; she trembled as she stood a moment, finishing her Bloody Mary. Addison felt acute sorrow for her, but then, almost at once, it passed. He wondered why. One can weary even of that, he conjectured. Of caring for someone. If it goes on too long—on and on. Forever. And, at last, even after that, into something no one before, not God Himself, maybe, had ever had to suffer and in the end, for all His great heart, succumb to.

As they walked through the crowded bar toward the street, Addison Doug said to the security agent, 'Which one of us—'

'They know which one,' the agent said as he held the door to the street open for Merry Lou. The agent stood, now, behind Addison, signaling for a gray Federal car to land at the red parking area. Two other security agents, in uniform, hurried toward them.

'Was it me?' Addison Doug asked.

'You better believe it,' the security agent said.

The funeral procession moved with aching solemnity down Pennsylvania Avenue, three flag-draped caskets and dozens of black limousines passing between rows of heavily coated, shivering mourners. A low haze hung over the day, gray outlines of buildings faded into the rain-drenched murk of the Washington March day.

Scrutinizing the lead Cadillac through prismatic binoculars, TV's top news and public-events commentator, Henry Cassidy, droned on at his vast unseen audience, '. . . sad recollections of that earlier train among the wheatfields carrying the coffin of Abraham Lincoln back to burial and the nation's capital. And what a sad day this is, and what appropriate weather, with its dour overcast and sprinkles!' In his monitor he saw the Zoomar lens pan up on the fourth Cadillac, as it followed those with the caskets of the dead tempunauts.

His engineer tapped him on the arm.

'We appear to be focusing on three unfamiliar figures so far not identified, riding together,' Henry Cassidy said into his neck mike, nodding agreement. 'So far I'm unable to quite make them out. Are your location and vision any better from where you're placed, Everett?' he inquired of his colleague and pressed the button that notified Everett Branton to replace him on the air.

'Why, Henry,' Branton said in a voice of growing excitement,

'I believe we're actually eyewitness to the three American tempunauts as they remanifest themselves on their historic journey into the future!'

'Does this signify,' Cassidy said, 'that somehow they have managed to solve and overcome the–'

'Afraid not, Henry,' Branton said in his slow, regretful voice. 'What we're eyewitnessing to our complete surprise consists of the Western world's first verified glimpse of what the technical people refer to as Emergence Time Activity.'

'Ah, yes, ETA,' Cassidy said brightly, reading it off the official script the Federal authorities had handed to him before air time.

'Right, Henry. Contrary to what *might* seem to be the case at first sight, these are not–repeat *not*–our three brave tempunauts as such, as we would ordinarily experience them–'

'I grasp it now, Everett,' Cassidy broke in excitedly, since his authorized script read CASS BREAKS IN EXCITEDLY. 'Our three tempunauts have momentarily suspended in their historic voyage to the future, which we believe will span across a time continuum roughly a century from now . . . It would seem that the overwhelming grief and drama of this unanticipated day of mourning has caused them to–'

'Sorry to interrupt, Henry,' Everett Branton said, 'but I think, since the procession has momentarily halted on its slow march forward, that we might be able to–'

'No!' Cassidy said, as a note was handed him in a swift scribble, reading: *Do not interview nauts. Urgent. Dis. previous inst.* 'I don't think we're going to be able to . . .' he continued, '. . . to speak briefly with tempunauts Benz, Crayne, and Doug, as you had hoped, Everett. As we had all briefly hoped to.' He wildly waved the boom-mike back; it had already begun to swing out expectantly toward the stopped Cadillac. Cassidy shook his head violently at the mike technician and his engineer.

Perceiving the boom-mike swinging at them Addison Doug stood up in the back of the open Cadillac. Cassidy groaned. He wants to speak, he realized. Didn't they reinstruct *him*? Why am

I the only one they get across to? Other boom-mikes representing other networks plus radio station interviewers on foot now were rushing out to thrust up their microphones into the faces of the three tempunauts, especially Addison Doug's. Doug was already beginning to speak, in response to a question shouted up to him by a reporter. With his boom-mike off, Cassidy couldn't hear the question, nor Doug's answer. With reluctance, he signaled for his own boom-mike to trigger on.

'. . . before,' Doug was saying loudly.

'In what manner, "All this has happened before"?' the radio reporter, standing close to the car, was saying.

'I mean,' US tempunaut Addison Doug declared, his face red and strained, 'that I have stood here in this spot and said again and again, and all of you have viewed this parade and our deaths at reentry endless times, a closed cycle of trapped time which must be broken.'

'Are you seeking,' another reporter jabbered up at Addison Doug, 'for a solution to the reentry implosion disaster which can be applied in retrospect so that when you do return to the past you will be able to correct the malfunction and avoid the tragedy which cost—or for you three, will cost—your lives?'

Tempunaut Benz said, 'We are doing that, yes.'

'Trying to ascertain the cause of the violent implosion and elim-inate the cause before we return,' tempunaut Crayne added, nodding. 'We have learned already that, for reasons unknown, a mass of nearly one hundred pounds of miscellaneous Volkswagen motor parts, including cylinders, the head . . .'

This is awful, Cassidy thought. 'This is amazing!' he said aloud, into his neck mike. 'The already tragically deceased US tempu-nauts, with a determination that could emerge only from the rigorous training and discipline to which they were subjected— and we wondered why at the time but can clearly see why now—have already analyzed the mechanical slip-up responsible, evidently, for their own deaths, and have begun the laborious process of sifting through and eliminating causes of that slip-up so that they can return to their original launch site and reenter without mishap.'

'One wonders,' Branton mumbled onto the air and into his feedback earphone, 'what the consequences of this alteration of the near past will be. If in reentry they do *not* implode and are *not* killed, then they will not—well, it's too complex for me, Henry, these time paradoxes that Dr Fein at the Time Extrusion Labs in Pasadena has so frequently and eloquently brought to our attention.'

Into all the microphones available, of all sorts, tempunaut Addison Doug was saying, more quietly now, 'We must not eliminate the cause of reentry implosion. The only way out of this trip is for us to die. Death is the only solution for this. For the three of us.' He was interrupted as the procession of Cadillacs began to move forward.

Shutting off his mike momentarily, Henry Cassidy said to his engineer, 'Is he nuts?'

'Only time will tell,' his engineer said in a hard-to-hear voice.

'An extraordinary moment in the history of the United States' involvement in time travel,' Cassidy said, then, into his now live mike. 'Only time will tell—if you will pardon the inadvertent pun—whether tempunaut Doug's cryptic remarks, uttered impromptu at this moment of supreme suffering for him, as in a sense to a lesser degree it is for all of us, are the words of a man deranged by grief or an accurate insight into the macabre dilemma that in theoretical terms we knew all along might eventually confront—confront and strike down with its lethal blow—a time-travel launch, either ours or the Russians'.'

He segued, then, to a commercial.

'You know,' Branton's voice muttered in his ear, not on the air but just to the control room and to him, 'if he's right they ought to let the poor bastards die.'

'They ought to release them,' Cassidy agreed. 'My God, the way Doug looked and talked, you'd imagine he'd gone through this for a thousand years and then some! I wouldn't be in his shoes for anything.'

'I'll bet you fifty bucks,' Branton said, 'they have gone through this before. Many times.'

'Then we have, too,' Cassidy said.

Rain fell now, making all the lined-up mourners shiny. Their faces, their eyes, even their clothes—everything glistened in wet reflections of broken, fractured light, bent and sparkling, as, from gathering gray formless layers above them, the day darkened.

'Are we on the air?' Branton asked.

Who knows? Cassidy thought. He wished the day would end.

The Soviet chrononaut N. Gauki lifted both hands impassionedly and spoke to the Americans across the table from him in a voice of extreme urgency. 'It is the opinion of myself and my colleague R. Plenya, who for his pioneering achievements in time travel has been certified a Hero of the Soviet People, and rightly so, that based on our own experience and on theoretical material developed both in your own academic circles and in the Soviet Academy of Sciences of the USSR, we believe that tempunaut A. Doug's fears may be justified. And his deliberate destruction of himself and his teammates at reentry, by hauling a huge mass of auto back with him from ETA, in violation of his orders, should be regarded as the act of a desperate man with no other means of escape. Of course, the decision is up to you. We have only advisory position in this matter.'

Addison Doug played with his cigarette lighter on the table and did not look up. His ears hummed, and he wondered what that meant. It had an electronic quality. Maybe we're within the module again, he thought. But he didn't perceive it; he felt the reality of the people around him, the table, the blue plastic lighter between his fingers. No smoking in the module during reentry, he thought. He put the lighter carefully away in his pocket.

'We've developed no concrete evidence whatsoever,' General Toad said, 'that a closed time loop has been set up. There's only the subjective feelings of fatigue on the part of Mr Doug. Just his belief that he's done all this repeatedly. As he says, it is very probably psychological in nature.' He rooted, piglike, among the papers before him. 'I have a report, not disclosed to the media, from four psychiatrists at Yale on his psychological makeup. Although unusually stable, there is a tendency toward cyclothymia on his part, culminating in acute depression. This naturally was taken into account long before the launch, but it was calculated that the joyful qualities of the two others in the team would offset this functionally. Anyhow, that depressive tendency in him is exceptionally high, now.' He held the paper out, but no one at the table accepted it. 'Isn't it true, Dr Fein,' he said, 'that an acutely depressed person experiences time in a peculiar way, that is, circular time, time repeating itself, getting nowhere, around and around? The person gets so psychotic that he refuses to let go of the past. Reruns it in his head constantly.'

'But you see,' Dr Fein said, 'this subjective sensation of being trapped is perhaps all we would have.' This was the research physicist whose basic work had laid the theoretical foundation for the project. 'If a closed loop did unfortunately lock into being.'

'The general,' Addison Doug said, 'is using words he doesn't understand.'

'I researched the one I was unfamiliar with,' General Toad said. 'The technical psychiatric terms . . . I know what they mean.'

To Addison Doug, Benz said, 'Where'd you get all those VW parts, Addi?'

'I don't have them yet,' Addison Doug said.

'Probably picked up the first junk he could lay his hands on,' Crayne said. 'Whatever was available, just before we started back.'

'Will start back,' Addison Doug corrected.

'Here are my instructions to the three of you,' General Toad said. 'You are not in any way to attempt to cause damage or implosion or malfunction during reentry, either by lugging back extra mass or by any other method that enters your mind. You are to return as scheduled and in replica of the prior simulations. This especially applies to you, Mr Doug.' The phone by his right arm buzzed. He frowned, picked up the receiver. An interval passed, and then he scowled deeply and set the receiver back down, loudly.

'You've been overruled,' Dr Fein said.

'Yes, I have,' General Toad said. 'And I must say at this time that I am personally glad because my decision was an unpleasant one.'

'Then we can arrange for implosion at reentry,' Benz said after a pause.

'The three of you are to make the decision,' General Toad said. 'Since it involves your lives. It's been entirely left up to you. Whichever way you want it. If you're convinced you're in a closed time loop, and you believe a massive implosion at reentry will abolish it—' He ceased talking, as tempunaut Doug rose to his feet. 'Are you going to make another speech, Doug?' he said.

'I just want to thank everyone involved,' Addison Doug said. 'For letting us decide.' He gazed haggard-faced and wearily around at all the individuals seated at the table. 'I really appreciate it.'

'You know,' Benz said slowly, 'blowing us up at reentry could add nothing to the chances of abolishing a closed loop. In fact that could do it, Doug.'

'Not if it kills us all,' Crayne said.

'You agree with Addi?' Benz said.

'Dead is dead,' Crayne said. 'I've been pondering it. What other way is more likely to get us out of this? Than if we're dead? What possible other way?'

'You may be in no loop,' Dr Fein pointed out.

'But we may be,' Crayne said.

Doug, still on his feet, said to Crayne and Benz, 'Could we include Merry Lou in our decision-making?'

'Why?' Benz said.

'I can't think too clearly any more,' Doug said. 'Merry Lou can help me; I depend on her.'

'Sure,' Crayne said. Benz, too, nodded.

General Toad examined his wristwatch stoically and said, 'Gentlemen, this concludes our discussion.'

Soviet chrononaut Gauki removed his headphones and neck

mike and hurried toward the three US tempunauts, his hand extended; he was apparently saying something in Russian, but none of them could understand it. They moved away somberly, clustering close.

'In my opinion you're nuts, Addi,' Benz said. 'But it would appear that I'm the minority now.'

'If he *is* right,' Crayne said, 'if—one chance in a billion—if we are going back again and again forever, that would justify it.'

'Could we go see Merry Lou?' Addison Doug said. 'Drive over to her place now?'

'She's waiting outside,' Crayne said.

Striding up to stand beside the three tempunauts, General Toad said, 'You know, what made the determination go the way it did was the public reaction to how you, Doug, looked and behaved during the funeral procession. The NSC advisors came to the conclusion that the public would, like you, rather be certain it's over for all of you. That it's more of a relief to them to know you're free of your mission than to save the project and obtain a perfect reentry. I guess you really made a lasting impression on them, Doug. That whining you did.' He walked away, then, leaving the three of them standing there alone.

'Forget him,' Crayne said to Addison Doug. 'Forget everyone like him. We've got to do what we have to.'

'Merry Lou will explain it to me,' Doug said. She would know what to do, what would be right.

'I'll go get her,' Crayne said, 'and after that the four of us can drive somewhere, maybe to her place, and decide what to do. Okay?'

'Thank you,' Addison Doug said, nodding; he glanced around for her hopefully, wondering where she was. In the next room, perhaps, somewhere close. 'I appreciate that,' he said.

Benz and Crayne eyed each other. He saw that, but did not know what it meant. He knew only that he needed someone, Merry Lou most of all, to help him understand what the situation was. And what to finalize on to get them out of it.

*

A LITTLE SOMETHING FOR US TEMPUNAUTS

Merry Lou drove them north from Los Angeles in the superfast lane of the freeway toward Ventura, and after that inland to Ojai. The four of them said very little. Merry Lou drove well, as always; leaning against her, Addison Doug felt himself relax into a temporary sort of peace.

'There's nothing like having a chick drive you,' Crayne said, after many miles had passed in silence.

'It's an aristocratic sensation,' Benz murmured. 'To have a woman do the driving. Like you're nobility being chauffeured.'

Merry Lou said, 'Until she runs into something. Some big slow object.'

Addison Doug said, 'When you saw me trudging up to your place . . . up the redwood round path the other day. What did you think? Tell me honestly.'

'You looked,' the girl said, 'as if you'd done it many times. You looked worn and tired and—ready to die. At the end.' She hesitated. 'I'm sorry, but that's how you looked, Addi. I thought to myself, he knows the way too well.'

'Like I'd done it too many times.'

'Yes,' she said.

'Then you vote for implosion,' Addison Doug said.

'Well—'

'Be honest with me,' he said.

Merry Lou said, 'Look in the back seat. The box on the floor.'

With a flashlight from the glove compartment the three men examined the box. Addison Doug, with fear, saw its contents. VW motor parts, rusty and worn. Still oily.

'I got them from behind a foreign-car garage near my place,' Merry Lou said. 'On the way to Pasadena. The first junk I saw that seemed as if it'd be heavy enough. I had heard them say on TV at launch time that anything over fifty pounds up to—'

'It'll do it,' Addison Doug said. 'It did do it.'

'So there's no point in going to your place,' Crayne said. 'It's decided. We might as well head south toward the module. And initiate the procedure for getting out of ETA. And back to reentry.'

His voice was heavy but evenly pitched. 'Thanks for your vote, Miss Hawkins.'

She said, 'You are all so tired.'

'I'm not,' Benz said. 'I'm mad. Mad as hell.'

'At me?' Addison Doug said.

'I don't know,' Benz said. 'It's just—Hell.' He lapsed into brooding silence then. Hunched over, baffled and inert. Withdrawn as far as possible from the others in the car.

At the next freeway junction she turned the car south. A sense of freedom seemed now to fill her, and Addison Doug felt some of the weight, the fatigue, ebbing already.

On the wrist of each of the three men the emergency alert receiver buzzed its warning tone; they all started.

'What's that mean?' Merry Lou said, slowing the car.

'We're to contact General Toad by phone as soon as possible,' Crayne said. He pointed. 'There's a Standard Station over there; take the next exit, Miss Hawkins. We can phone in from there.'

A few minutes later Merry Lou brought her car to a halt beside the outdoor phone booth. 'I hope it's not bad news,' she said.

'I'll talk first,' Doug said, getting out. Bad news, he thought with labored amusement. Like what? He crunched stiffly across to the phone booth, entered, shut the door behind him, dropped in a dime and dialed the toll-free number.

'Well, do I have news!' General Toad said when the operator had put him on the line. 'It's a good thing we got hold of you. Just a minute—I'm going to let Dr Fein tell you this himself. You're more apt to believe him than me.' Several clicks, and then Dr Fein's reedy, precise, scholarly voice, but intensified by urgency.

'What's the bad news?' Addison Doug said.

'Not bad, necessarily,' Dr Fein said. 'I've had computations run since our discussion, and it would appear—by that I mean it is statistically probable but still unverified for a certainty—that you are right, Addison. You are in a closed time loop.'

Addison Doug exhaled raggedly. You nowhere autocratic mother, he thought. You probably knew all along.

'However,' Dr Fein said excitedly, stammering a little, 'I also calculate—we jointly do, largely through Cal Tech—that the greatest likelihood of maintaining the loop is to implode on reentry. Do you understand, Addison? If you lug all those rusty VW parts back and implode, then your statistical chance of closing the loop forever is greater than if you simply reenter and all goes well.'

Addison Doug said nothing.

'In fact, Addi—and this is the severe part that I have to stress—implosion at reentry, especially a massive, calculated one of the sort we seem to see shaping up—do you grasp all this, Addi? Am I getting through to you? For Chrissake, Addi? Virtually *guarantees* the locking in of an absolutely unyielding loop such as you've got in mind. Such as we've all been worried about from the start.' A pause. 'Addi? Are you there?'

Addison Doug said, 'I want to die.'

'That's your exhaustion from the loop. God knows how many repetitions there've been already of the three of you—'

'No,' he said and started to hang up.

'Let me speak with Benz and Crayne,' Dr Fein said rapidly. 'Please, before you go ahead with reentry. Especially Benz; I'd like to speak with him in particular. Please, Addison. For their sake; your almost total exhaustion has—'

He hung up. Left the phone booth, step by step.

As he climbed back into the car, he heard their two alert receivers still buzzing. 'General Toad said the automatic call for us would keep your two receivers doing that for a while,' he said. And shut the car door after him. 'Let's take off.'

'Doesn't he want to talk to us?' Benz said.

Addison Doug said, 'General Toad wanted to inform us that they have a little something for us. We've been voted a special Congressional Citation for valor or some damn thing like that. A special medal they never voted anyone before. To be awarded posthumously.'

'Well, hell—that's about the only way it can be awarded,' Crayne said.

Merry Lou, as she started up the engine, began to cry.

'It'll be a relief,' Crayne said presently, as they returned bumpily to the freeway, 'when it's over.'

It won't be long now, Addison Doug's mind declared.

On their wrists the emergency alert receivers continued to put out their combined buzzing.

'They will nibble you to death,' Addison Doug said. 'The endless wearing down by various bureaucratic voices.'

The others in the car turned to gaze at him inquiringly, with uneasiness mixed with perplexity.

'Yeah,' Crayne said. 'These automatic alerts are really a nuisance.' He sounded tired. As tired as I am, Addison Doug thought. And, realizing this, he felt better. It showed how right he was.

Great drops of water struck the windshield; it had now begun to rain. That pleased him too. It reminded him of that most exalted of all experiences within the shortness of his life: the funeral procession moving slowly down Pennsylvania Avenue, the flag-draped caskets. Closing his eyes he leaned back and felt good at last. And heard, all around him once again, the sorrow-bent people. And, in his head, dreamed of the special Congressional Medal. For weariness, he thought. A medal for being tired.

He saw, in his head, himself in other parades too, and in the deaths of many. But really it was one death and one parade. Slow cars moving along the street in Dallas and with Dr King as well ... He saw himself return again and again, in his closed cycle of life, to the national mourning that he could not and they could not forget. He would be there; they would always be there; it would always be, and every one of them would return together again and again forever. To the place, the moment, they wanted to be. The event which meant the most to all of them.

This was his gift to them, the people, his country. He had bestowed upon the world a wonderful burden. The dreadful and weary miracle of eternal life.

THE PRE-PERSONS

Past the grove of cypress trees Walter—he had been playing king of the mountain—saw the white truck, and he knew it for what it was. He thought, That's the abortion truck. Come to take some kid in for a postpartum down at the abortion place.

And he thought, Maybe my folks called it. For me.

He ran and hid among the blackberries, feeling the scratching of the thorns but thinking, It's better than having the air sucked out of your lungs. That's how they do it; they perform all the PPs on all the kids there at the same time. They have a big room for it. For the kids nobody wants.

Burrowing deeper into the blackberries, he listened to hear if the truck stopped; he heard its motor.

'I am invisible,' he said to himself, a line he had learned at the fifth-grade play of *Midsummer Night's Dream*, a line Oberon, whom he had played, had said. And after that no one could see him. Maybe that was true now. Maybe the magic saying worked in real life; so he said it again to himself, 'I am invisible.' But he knew he was not. He could still see his arms and legs and shoes, and he knew they—everyone, the abortion truck man especially, and his mom and dad—they could see him too. If they looked.

If it was him they were after this time.

He wished he was a king; he wished he had magic dust all over him and a shining crown that glistened, and ruled fairyland and had Puck to confide to. To ask for advice from, even. Advice even if he himself was a king and bickered with Titania, his wife.

I guess, he thought, saying something doesn't make it true.

Sun burned down on him and he squinted, but mostly he listened to the abortion truck motor; it kept making its sound, and his heart gathered hope as the sound went on and on. Some other kid, turned over to the abortion clinic, not him; someone up the road.

He made his difficult exit from the berry brambles shaking and in many places scratched and moved step by step in the direction of his house. And as he trudged he began to cry, mostly from the pain of the scratches but also from fear and relief.

'Oh, good Lord,' his mother exclaimed, on seeing him. 'What in the name of God have you been doing?'

He said stammeringly, 'I—saw—the abortion—truck.'

'And you thought it was for you?'

Mutely, he nodded.

'Listen, Walter,' Cynthia Best said, kneeling down and taking hold of his trembling hands, 'I promise, your dad and I both promise, you'll never be sent to the County Facility. Anyhow you're too old. They only take children up to twelve.'

'But Jeff Vogel—'

'His parents got him in just before the new law went into effect. They couldn't take him now, legally. They couldn't take you now. Look—you have a soul; the law says a twelve-year-old boy has a soul. So he can't go to the County Facility. See? You're safe. Whenever you see the abortion truck, it's for someone else, not you. Never for you. Is that clear? It's come for another younger child who doesn't have a soul yet, a pre-person.'

Staring down, not meeting his mother's gaze, he said, 'I don't feel like I got a soul; I feel like I always did.'

'It's a legal matter,' his mother said briskly. 'Strictly according to age. And you're past the age. The Church of Watchers got Congress to pass the law—actually they, those church people, wanted a lower age; they claimed the soul entered the body at three years old, but a compromise bill was put through. The important thing for you is that you are legally safe, however you feel inside; do you see?'

'Okay,' he said, nodding.

'You knew that.'

He burst out with anger and grief, 'What do you think it's like, maybe waiting every day for someone to come and put you in a wire cage in a truck and—'

'Your fear is irrational,' his mother said.

'I saw them take Jeff Vogel that day. He was crying, and the man just opened the back of the truck and put him in and shut the back of the truck.'

'That was two years ago. You're weak.' His mother glared at him. 'Your grandfather would whip you if he saw you now and heard you talk this way. Not your father. He'd just grin and say something stupid. Two years later, and intellectually you know you're past the legal maximum age! How—' She struggled for the word. 'You are being *depraved*.'

'And he never came back.'

'Perhaps someone who wanted a child went inside the County Facility and found him and adopted him. Maybe he's got a better set of parents who really care for him. They keep them thirty days before they destroy them.' She corrected herself. 'Put them to sleep, I mean.'

He was not reassured. Because he knew 'put him to sleep' or 'put them to sleep' was a Mafia term. He drew away from his mother, no longer wanting her comfort. She had blown it, as far as he was concerned; she had shown something about herself or, anyhow, the source of what she believed and thought and perhaps did. What all of them did. I know I'm no different, he thought, than two years ago when I was just a little kid; if I have a soul now like the law says, then I had a soul then, or else we have no souls— the only real thing is just a horrible metallic-painted truck with wire over its windows carrying off kids their parents no longer want, parents using an extension of the old abortion law that let them kill an unwanted child before it came out: because it had no 'soul' or 'identity,' it could be sucked out by a vacuum system in less than two minutes. A doctor could do a hundred a day, and it was legal because the unborn child wasn't 'human.' He was a pre-person. Just like this truck now; they merely set the date forward as to when the soul entered.

Congress had inaugurated a simple test to determine the approximate age at which the soul entered the body: the ability to formulate higher math like algebra. Up to then, it was only body, animal instincts and body, animal reflexes and responses to stimuli. Like Pavlov's dogs when they saw a little water seep in under the door of the Leningrad laboratory; they 'knew' but were not human.

I guess I'm human, Walter thought, and looked up into the gray, severe face of his mother, with her hard eyes and rational grimness. I guess I'm like you, he thought. Hey, it's neat to be a human, he thought; then you don't have to be afraid of the truck coming.

'You feel better,' his mother observed. 'I've lowered your threshold of anxiety.'

'I'm not so freaked,' Walter said. It was over; the truck had gone and not taken him.

But it would be back in a few days. It cruised perpetually.

Anyhow he had a few days. And then the sight of it–if only I didn't know they suck the air out of the lungs of the kids they have there, he thought. Destroy them that way. Why? Cheaper, his dad had said. Saves the taxpayers money.

He thought then about taxpayers and what they would look like. Something that scowled at all children, he thought. That did not answer if the child asked them a question. A thin face, lined with watch-worry grooves, eyes always moving. Or maybe fat; one or the other. It was the thin one that scared him; it didn't enjoy life nor want life to be. It flashed the message, 'Die, go away, sicken, don't exist.' And the abortion truck was proof–or the instrument–of it.

'Mom,' he said, 'how do you shut a County Facility? You know, the abortion clinic where they take the babies and little kids.'

'You go and petition the county legislature,' his mother said.

'You know what I'd do?' he said. 'I'd wait until there were no kids in there, only county employees, and I'd firebomb it.'

'Don't talk like that!' his mother said severely, and he saw on

THE PRE-PERSONS

her face the stiff lines of the thin taxpayer. And it frightened him; his own mother frightened him. The cold and opaque eyes mirrored nothing, no soul inside, and he thought, *It's you who don't have a soul*, you and your skinny messages not-to-be. Not us.

And then he ran outside to play again.

A bunch more kids had seen the truck; he and they stood around together, talking now and then, but mostly kicking at rocks and dirt, and occasionally stepping on a bad bug.

'Who'd the truck come for?' Walter said.

'Fleischhacker. Earl Fleischhacker.'

'Did they get him?'

'Sure, didn't you hear the yelling?'

'Was his folks home at the time?'

'Naw, they split earlier on some shuck about "taking the car in to be greased."'

'*They* called the truck?' Walter said.

'Sure, it's the law; it's gotta be the parents. But they were too chickenshit to be there when the truck drove up. Shit, he really yelled; I guess you're too far away to hear, but he really yelled.'

Walter said, 'You know what we ought to do? Firebomb the truck and snuff the driver.'

All the other kids looked at him contemptuously. 'They put you in the mental hospital for life if you act out like that.'

'Sometimes for life,' Pete Bride corrected. 'Other times they "build up a new personality that is socially viable."'

'Then what should we do?' Walter said.

'You're twelve; you're safe.'

'But suppose they change the law.' Anyhow it did not assuage his anxiety to know that he was technically safe; the truck still came for others and still frightened him. He thought of the younger kids down at the Facility now, looking through the Cyclone fence hour by hour, day after day, waiting and marking the passage of time and hoping someone would come in and adopt them.

'You ever been down there?' he said to Pete Bride. 'At the County

Facility? All those really little kids, like babies some of them, just maybe a year old. And they don't even know what's in store.'

'The babies get adopted,' Zack Yablonski said. 'It's the old ones that don't stand a chance. They're the ones that get you; like, they talk to people who come in and put on a good show, like they're desirable. But people know they wouldn't be there if they weren't— you know, undesirable.'

'Let the air out of the tires,' Walter said, his mind working.

'Of the truck? Hey, and you know if you drop a mothball in the gas tank, about a week later the motor wears out. We could do that.'

Ben Blaire said, 'But then they'd be after us.'

'They're after us now,' Walter said.

'I think we ought to firebomb the truck,' Harry Gottlieb said, 'but suppose there're kids in it. It'll burn them up. The truck picks up maybe—shit, I don't know. Five kids a day from different parts of the county.'

'You know they even take dogs too?' Walter said. 'And cats; you see the truck for that only about once a month. The pound truck it's called. Otherwise it's the same; they put them in a big chamber and suck the air out of their lungs and they die. They'd do that even to animals! Little animals!'

'I'll believe that when I see it,' Harry Gottlieb said, derision on his face, and disbelief. 'A truck that carries off dogs.'

He knew it was true, though. Walter had seen the pound truck two different times. Cats, dogs, and mainly us, he thought glumly. I mean, if they'd start with us, it's natural they'd wind up taking people's pets, too; we're not that different. But what kind of a person would do that, even if it is the law? 'Some laws are made to be kept, and some to be broken,' he remembered from a book he had read. We ought to firebomb the pound truck first, he thought; that's the worst, that truck.

Why is it, he wondered, that the more helpless a creature, the easier it was for some people to snuff it? Like a baby in the womb; the original abortions, 'pre-partums,' or 'pre-persons' they were called now. How could they defend themselves? Who would speak for them? All those lives, a hundred by each doctor a day . . . and all helpless and silent and then just dead. The fuckers, he thought. That's why they do it; they know they can do it; they get off on their macho power. And so a little thing that wanted to see the light of day is vacuumed out in less than two minutes. And the doctor goes on to the next chick.

There ought to be an organization, he thought, similar to the Mafia. Snuff the snuffers, or something. A contract man walks up to one of those doctors, pulls out a tube, and sucks the doctor into it, where he shrinks down like an unborn baby. An unborn baby doctor, with a stethoscope the size of a pinhead . . . he laughed, thinking of that.

Children don't know. But children know everything, knew too much. The abortion truck, as it drove along, played a Good Humor Man's jingle:

> Jack and Jill
> Went up the hill
> To fetch a pail of water.

A tape loop in the sound system of the truck, built especially by Ampex for GM, blared that out when it wasn't actively nearing a seize. Then the driver shut off the sound system and glided along until he found the proper house. However, once he had the unwanted child in the back of the truck, and was either starting back to the County Facility or beginning another pre-person pickup, he turned back on

> Jack and Jill
> Went up the hill
> To fetch a pail of water.

Thinking to himself, Oscar Ferris, the driver of truck three, finished, 'Jack fell down and broke his crown and Jill came tumbling after.' What the hell's a crown? Ferris wondered. Probably a private part. He grinned. Probably Jack had been playing with it, or Jill, both of them together. Water, my ass, he thought. I know what they went off into the bushes for. Only, Jack fell down, and his thing broke right off. 'Tough luck, Jill,' he said aloud as he expertly drove the four-year-old truck along the winding curves of California Highway One.

Kids are like that, Ferris thought. Dirty and playing with dirty things, like themselves.

This was still wild and open country, and many stray children scratched about in the canyons and fields; he kept his eye open, and sure enough—off to his right scampered a small one, about six, trying to get out of sight. Ferris at once pressed the button that activated the siren of the truck. The boy froze, stood in fright, waited as the truck, still playing 'Jack and Jill,' coasted up beside him and came to a halt.

'Show me your D papers,' Ferris said, without getting out of the truck; he leaned one arm out the window, showing his brown uniform and patch; his symbols of authority.

The boy had a scrawny look, like many strays, but, on the other hand, he wore glasses. Tow-headed, in jeans and T-shirt, he stared up in fright at Ferris, making no move to get out his identification.

'You got a D card or not?' Ferris said.

'W-w-w-what's a "D card"?'

In his official voice, Ferris explained to the boy his rights under the law. 'Your parent, either one, or legal guardian, fills out form 36-W, which is a formal statement of desirability. That they or him or her regard you as desirable. You don't have one? Legally, that makes you a stray, even if you have parents who want to keep you; they are subject to a fine of $500.'

'Oh,' the boy said. 'Well, I lost it.'

'Then a copy would be on file. They microdot all those documents and records. I'll take you in—'

'To the County Facility?' Pipe-cleaner legs wobbled in fear.

'They have thirty days to claim you by filling out the 36-W form. If they haven't done it by then—'

'My mom and dad never agree. Right now I'm staying with my dad.'

'He didn't give you a D card to identify yourself with.' Mounted transversely across the cab of the truck was a shotgun. There was always the possibility that trouble might break out when he picked up a stray. Reflexively, Ferris glanced up at it. It was there, all right, a pump shotgun. He had used it only five times in his law-enforcement career. It could blow a man into molecules. 'I have to take you in,' he said, opening the truck door and bringing out his keys. 'There's another kid back there; you can keep each other company.'

'No,' the boy said. 'I won't go.' Blinking, he confronted Ferris, stubborn and rigid as stone.

'Oh, you probably heard a lot of stories about the County Facility. It's only the warpies, the creepies, that get put to sleep; any nice normal-looking kid'll be adopted—we'll cut your hair and fix you up so you look professionally groomed. We want to find you a home. That's the whole idea. It's just a few, those who are—you know—ailing mentally or physically that no one wants. Some well-to-do individual will snap you up in a minute; you'll see. Then you won't be running around out here alone with no parents to guide you. You'll have new parents, and listen—they'll be paying heavy bread for you; hell, they'll *register* you. Do you see? It's more a temporary lodging place where we're taking you right now, to make you available to prospective new parents.'

'But if nobody adopts me in a month—'

'Hell, you could fall off a cliff here at Big Sur and kill yourself. Don't worry. The desk at the Facility will contact your blood parents, and most likely they'll come forth with the Desirability Form (15A) sometime today even. And meanwhile you'll get a nice ride and meet a lot of new kids. And how often—'

'No,' the boy said.

'This is to inform you,' Ferris said, in a different tone, 'that I am a County Official.' He opened his truck door, jumped down, showed his gleaming metal badge to the boy. 'I am Peace Officer Ferris and I now order you to enter by the rear of the truck.'

THE PRE-PERSONS

A tall man approached them, walking with wariness; he, like the boy, wore jeans and a T-shirt, but no glasses.

'You the boy's father?' Ferris said.

The man, hoarsely, said, 'Are you taking him to the pound?'

'We consider it a child protection shelter,' Ferris said. 'The use of the term "pound" is a radical hippie slur, and distorts—deliberately—the overall picture of what we do.'

Gesturing toward the truck, the man said, 'You've got kids locked in there in those cages, have you?'

'I'd like to see your ID,' Ferris said. 'And I'd like to know if you've ever been arrested before.'

'Arrested and found innocent? Or arrested and found guilty?'

'Answer my question, sir,' Ferris said, showing his black flat-pack that he used with adults to identify him as a County Peace Officer. 'Who are you? Come on, let's see your ID.'

The man said, 'Ed Gantro is my name and I have a record. When I was eighteen, I stole four crates of Coca-Cola from a parked truck.'

'You were apprehended at the scene?'

'No,' the man said. 'When I took the empties back to cash in on the refunds. That's when they seized me. I served six months.'

'Have you a Desirability Card for your boy here?' Ferris asked.

'We couldn't afford the $90 it cost.'

'Well, now it'll cost you five hundred. You should have gotten it in the first place. My suggestion is that you consult an attorney.' Ferris moved toward the boy, declaring officially, 'I'd like you to join the other juveniles in the rear section of the vehicle.' To the man he said, 'Tell him to do as instructed.'

The man hesitated and then said, 'Tim, get in the goddamn truck. And we'll get a lawyer; we'll get the D card for you. It's futile to make trouble—technically you're a stray.'

'"A stray,"' the boy said, regarding his father.

Ferris said, 'Exactly right. You have thirty days, you know, to raise the—'

'Do you also take cats?' the boy said. 'Are there any cats in there? I really like cats; they're all right.'

'I handle only PP cases,' Ferris said. 'Such as yourself.' With a key he unlocked the back of the truck. 'Try not to relieve yourself while you're in the truck; it's hard as hell to get the odor and stains out.'

The boy did not seem to understand the word; he gazed from Ferris to his father in perplexity.

'Just don't go to the bathroom while you're in the truck,' his father explained. 'They want to keep it sanitary, because that cuts down their maintenance costs.' His voice was savage and grim.

'With stray dogs or cats,' Ferris said, 'they just shoot them on sight, or put out poison bait.'

'Oh, yeah, I know that Warfarin,' the boy's father said. 'The animal eats it over a period of a week, and then he bleeds to death internally.'

'With no pain,' Ferris pointed out.

'Isn't that better than sucking the air from their lungs?' Ed Gantro said. 'Suffocating them on a mass basis?'

'Well, with animals the county authorities—'

'I mean the children. Like Tim.' His father stood beside him, and they both looked into the rear of the truck. Two dark shapes could be dimly discerned, crouching as far back as possible, in the starkest form of despair.

'Fleischhacker!' the boy Tim said. 'Didn't you have a D card?'

'Because of energy and fuel shortages,' Ferris was saying, 'population must be radically cut. Or in ten years there'll be no food for anyone. This is one phase of—'

'I had a D card,' Earl Fleischhacker said, 'but my folks took it away from me. They didn't want me any more; so they took it back, and then they called for the abortion truck.' His voice croaked; obviously he had been secretly crying.

'And what's the difference between a five-month-old fetus and what we have here?' Ferris was saying. 'In both cases what you have is an unwanted child. They simply liberalized the laws.'

Tim's father, staring at him, said, 'Do you agree with these laws?'

'Well, it's really all up to Washington and what they decide will solve our needs in these days of crisis,' Ferris said. 'I only enforce their edicts. If this law changed—hell. I'd be trucking empty milk cartons for recycling or something and be just as happy.'

'*Just* as happy? You enjoy your work?'

Ferris said, mechanically, 'It gives me the opportunity to move around a lot and to meet people.'

Tim's father Ed Gantro said, 'You are insane. This postpartum abortion scheme and the abortion laws before it where the unborn child had no legal rights—it was removed like a tumor. Look what it's come to. If an unborn child can be killed without due process, why not a born one? What I see in common in both cases is their helplessness; the organism that is killed had no chance, no ability, to protect itself. You know what? I want you to take me in, too. In back of the truck with the three children.'

'But the President and Congress have declared that when you're past twelve you have a soul,' Ferris said. 'I can't take you. It wouldn't be right.'

'I have no soul,' Tim's father said. 'I got to be twelve and nothing happened. Take me along, too. Unless you can find my soul.'

'Jeez,' Ferris said.

'Unless you can show me my soul,' Tim's father said, 'unless you can specifically locate it, then I insist you take me in as no different from these kids.'

Ferris said, 'I'll have to use the radio to get in touch with the County Facility, see what they say.'

'You do that,' Tim's father said, and laboriously clambered up into the rear of the truck, helping Tim along with him. With the other two boys they waited while Peace Officer Ferris, with all his official identification as to who he was, talked on his radio.

'I have here a Caucasian male, approximately thirty, who insists that he be transported to the County Facility with his infant son,' Ferris was saying into his mike. 'He claims to have no soul, which he maintains puts him in the class of subtwelve-year-olds. I don't have with me or know any test to detect the presence of a soul, at least any I can give out here in the boondocks that'll later on satisfy a court. I mean, he probably can do algebra and higher math; he seems to possess an intelligent mind. But–'

'Affirmative as to bringing him in,' his superior's voice on the two-way radio came back to him. 'We'll deal with him here.'

'We're going to deal with you downtown,' Ferris said to Tim's father, who, with the three smaller figures, was crouched down in the dark recesses of the rear of the truck. Ferris slammed the door, locked it–an extra precaution, since the boys were already netted by electronic bands–and then started up the truck.

> Jack and Jill went up the hill
> To fetch a pail of water.
> Jack fell down
> And broke his crown

Somebody's sure going to get their crown broke, Ferris thought as he drove along the winding road, and it isn't going to be me.

'I can't do algebra,' he heard Tim's father saying to the three boys. 'So I can't have a soul.'

The Fleischhacker boy said, snidely, 'I can, but I'm only nine. So what good does it do me?'

'That's what I'm going to use as my plea at the Facility,' Tim's father continued. 'Even long division was hard for me. I don't have a soul. I belong with you three little guys.'

Ferris, in a loud voice, called back, 'I don't want you soiling the truck, you understand? It costs us–'

'Don't tell me,' Tim's father said, 'because I wouldn't understand. It would be too complex, the proration and accrual and fiscal terms like that.'

I've got a weirdo back there, Ferris thought, and was glad he had the pump shotgun mounted within easy reach. 'You know the world is running out of everything,' Ferris called back to them, 'energy and apple juice and fuel and bread; we've got to keep the population down, and the embolisms from the Pill make it impossible–'

'None of us knows those big words,' Tim's father broke in.

Angrily, and feeling baffled, Ferris said. 'Zero population growth; that's the answer to the energy and food crisis. It's like—shit, it's like when they introduced the rabbit in Australia, and it had no natural enemies, and so it multiplied until, like people—'

'I do understand multiplication,' Tim's father said. 'And adding and subtraction. But that's all.'

Four crazy rabbits flopping across the road, Ferris thought. People pollute the natural environment, he thought. What must this part of the country have been like before man? Well, he thought, with the postpartum abortions taking place in every county in the US of A we may see that day; we may stand and look once again upon a virgin land.

We, he thought. I guess there won't be any we. I mean, he thought, giant sentient computers will sweep out the landscape with their slotted video receptors and find it pleasing.

The thought cheered him up.

'Let's have an abortion!' Cynthia declared excitedly as she entered the house with an armload of synthogroceries. 'Wouldn't that be neat? Doesn't that turn you on?'

Her husband Ian Best said dryly, 'But first you have to get pregnant. So make an appointment with Dr Guido—that should cost me only fifty or sixty dollars—and have your IUD removed.'

'I think it's slipping down anyhow. Maybe, if—' Her pert dark shag-haired head tossed in glee. 'It probably hasn't worked properly since last year. So I could be pregnant now.'

Ian said caustically, 'You could put an ad in the *Free Press*; "Man wanted to fish out IUD with coathanger."'

'But you see,' Cynthia said, following him as he made his way to the master closet to hang up his status-tie and class-coat, 'it's the in thing now, to have an abortion. Look, what do we have? A kid. We have Walter. Every time someone comes over to visit and sees him, I know they're wondering. "Where did you screw up?" It's embarrassing.' She added, 'And the kind of abortions they give now, for women in early stages—it only costs one hundred dollars . . . the price of ten gallons of gas! And you can talk about it with practically everybody who drops by for hours.'

Ian turned to face her and said in a level voice, 'Do you get to keep the embryo? Bring it home in a bottle or sprayed with special luminous paint so it glows in the dark like a night light?'

'In any color you want!'

'The *embryo?*'

'No, the bottle. And the color of the fluid. It's in a preservative solution, so really it's a lifetime acquisition. It even has a written guarantee, I think.'

Ian folded his arms to keep himself calm: alpha state condition. 'Do you know that there are people who would want to have a child? Even an ordinary dumb one? That go to the County Facility week after week looking for a little newborn baby? These ideas—there's been this world panic about overpopulation. Nine trillion humans stacked like kindling in every block of every city. Okay, if that were going on—' He gestured. 'But what we have now is not *enough* children. Or don't you watch TV or read the *Times?*'

'It's a drag,' Cynthia said. 'For instance, today Walter came into the house freaked out because the abortion truck cruised by. It's a drag taking care of him. *You* have it easy; you're at work. But *me*—'

'You know what I'd like to do to the Gestapo abortion wagon? Have two ex-drinking buddies of mine armed with BARs, one on each side of the road. And when the wagon passes by—'

'It's a ventilated air-conditioned truck, not a wagon.'

He glared at her and then went to the bar in the kitchen to fix himself a drink. Scotch will do, he decided. Scotch and milk, a good before-'dinner' drink.

As he mixed his drink, his son Walter came in. He had, on his face, an unnatural pallor.

'The 'bort truck went by today, didn't it?' Ian said.

'I thought maybe—'

'No way. Even if your mother and I saw a lawyer and had a legal document drawn up, an un-D Form, you're too old. So relax.'

'I know intellectually,' Walter said, 'but—'

' "Do not seek to know for whom the bell tolls; it tolls for thee," ' Ian quoted (inaccurately). 'Listen, Walt, let me lay something on you.' He took a big, long drink of Scotch and milk. 'The name of all this is, *kill me*. Kill them when they're the size of a fingernail, or a baseball, or later on, if you haven't done it already, suck the air out of the lungs of a ten-year-old boy and let him die. It's a certain kind of woman advocating this all. They used to call them "castrating females." Maybe that was once the right term, except that these women, these hard cold women, didn't just want to—well, they want to do in the *whole* boy or man, make all of them dead, not just the part that makes him a man. Do you see?'

'No,' Walter said, but in a dim sense, very frightening, he did.

After another hit of his drink, Ian said, 'And we've got one living right here, Walter. Here in our very house.'

'What do we have living here?'

'What the Swiss psychiatrists call a *Kindermörder*,' Ian said, deliberately choosing a term he knew his boy wouldn't understand. 'You know what,' he said, 'you and I could get onto an Amtrak coach and head north and just keep on going until we reached Vancouver, British Columbia, and we could take a ferry to Vancouver Island and never be seen by anybody down here again.'

'But what about Mom?'

'I would send her a cashier's check,' Ian said. 'Each month. And she would be quite happy with that.'

'It's cold up there, isn't it?' Walter said. 'I mean, they have hardly any fuel and they wear—'

'About like San Francisco. Why? Are you afraid of wearing a lot of sweaters and sitting close to the fireplace? What did you see today that frightened you a hell of a lot more?'

'Oh, yeah.' He nodded somberly.

'We could live on a little island off Vancouver Island and raise our own food. You can plant stuff up there and it grows. And the truck won't come there; you'll never see it again. They have different laws. The women up there are different. There was this one girl

I knew when I was up there for a while, a long time ago; she had long black hair and smoked Players cigarettes all the time and never ate anything or ever stopped talking. Down here we're seeing a civilization in which the desire by women to destroy their own–' Ian broke off; his wife had walked into the kitchen.

'If you drink any more of that stuff,' she said to him, 'you'll barf it up.'

'Okay,' Ian said irritably. 'Okay!'

'And don't yell,' Cynthia said. 'I thought for dinner tonight it'd be nice if you took us out. Dal Rey's said on TV they have steak for early comers.'

Wrinkling his nose, Walter said, 'They have raw oysters.'

'Blue points,' Cynthia said. 'In the half shell, on ice. I love them. All right, Ian? Is it decided?'

To his son Walter, Ian said, 'A raw blue point oyster looks like nothing more on earth than what the surgeon–' He became silent, then. Cynthia glared at him, and his son was puzzled. 'Okay,' he said, 'but I get to order steak.'

'Me too,' Walter said.

Finishing his drink, Ian said more quietly, 'When was the last time you fixed dinner here in the house? For the three of us?'

'I fixed you that pigs' ears and rice dish on Friday,' Cynthia said. 'Most of which went to waste because it was something new and on the nonmandatory list. Remember, *dear*?'

Ignoring her, Ian said to his son, 'Of course, that type of woman will sometimes, even often, be found up there, too. She has existed throughout time and all cultures. But since Canada has no law permitting postpartum–' He broke off. 'It's the carton of milk talking,' he explained to Cynthia. 'They adulterate it these days with sulfur. Pay no attention or sue somebody; the choice is yours.'

Cynthia, eyeing him, said, 'Are you running a fantasy number in your head again about splitting?'

'Both of us,' Walter broke in. 'Dad's taking me with him.'

'Where?' Cynthia said, casually.

Ian said, 'Wherever the Amtrak track leads us.'

'We're going to Vancouver Island in Canada,' Walter said.

'Oh, really?' Cynthia said.

After a pause Ian said, 'Really.'

'And what the shit am I supposed to do when you're gone? Peddle my ass down at the local bar? How'll I meet the payments on the various—'

'I will continually mail you checks,' Ian said. 'Bonded by giant banks.'

'Sure. You bet. Yep. Right.'

'You could come along,' Ian said, 'and catch fish by leaping into English Bay and grinding them to death with your sharp teeth. You could rid British Columbia of its fish population overnight. All those ground-up fish, wondering vaguely what happened . . . swimming along one minute and then this—ogre, this fish-destroying monster with a single luminous eye in the center of its forehead, falls on them and grinds them into grit. There would soon be a legend. News like that spreads. At least among the last surviving fish.'

'Yeah, but Dad,' Walter said, 'suppose there are no surviving fish.'

'Then it will have been all in vain,' Ian said, 'except for your mother's own personal pleasure at having bitten to death an entire species in British Columbia, where fishing is the largest industry anyhow, and so many other species depend on it for survival.'

'But then everyone in British Columbia will be out of work,' Walter said.

'No,' Ian said, 'they will be cramming the dead fish into cans to sell to Americans. You see, Walter, in the olden days, before your mother multi-toothedly bit to death all the fish in British Columbia, the simple rustics stood with stick in hand, and when a fish swam past, they whacked the fish over the head. This will *create* jobs, not eliminate them. Millions of cans of suitably marked—'

'You know,' Cynthia said quickly, 'he believes what you tell him.'

Ian said, 'What I tell him is true.' Although not, he realized, in a literal sense. To his wife he said, 'I'll take you out to dinner. Get our ration stamps, put on that blue knit blouse that shows off your boobs; that way you'll get a lot of attention and maybe they won't remember to collect the stamps.'

'What's a "boob"?' Walter asked.

'Something fast becoming obsolete,' Ian said, 'like the Pontiac GTO. Except as an ornament to be admired and squeezed. Its function is dying away.' As is our race, he thought, once we gave full rein to those who would destroy the unborn–in other words, the most helpless creatures alive.

'A boob,' Cynthia said severely to her son, 'is a mammary gland that ladies possess which provides milk to their young.'

'Generally there are two of them,' Ian said. 'Your operational boob and then your backup boob, in case there is power failure in the operational one. I suggest the elimination of a step in all this pre-person abortion mania,' he said. 'We will send all the boobs in the world to the County Facilities. The milk, if any, will be sucked out of them, by mechanical means of course; they will become useless and empty, and then the young will die naturally, deprived of many and all sources of nourishment.'

'There's formula,' Cynthia said, witheringly. 'Similac and those. I'm going to change so we can go out.' She turned and strode toward their bedroom.

'You know,' Ian said after her, 'if there was any way you could get me classified as a pre-person, you'd send me there. To the Facility with the greatest facility.' And, he thought, I'll bet I wouldn't be the only husband in California who went. There'd be plenty others. In the same bag as me, then as now.

'Sounds like a plan,' Cynthia's voice came to him dimly; she had heard.

'It's not just a hatred for the helpless,' Ian Best said. 'More is involved. Hatred of what? Of everything that grows?' You blight them, he thought, before they grow big enough to have muscle and the tactics and skill for fight–big like I am in relation to you, with my fully developed musculature and weight. So much easier when the other person–I should say pre-person–is floating and dreaming in the amniotic fluid and knows nothing about how to nor the need to hit back.

Where did the motherly virtues go to? he asked himself. When mothers *especially* protected what was small and weak and defenseless?

Our competitive society, he decided. The survival of the strong. Not the fit, he thought; just those who hold the *power*. And are not going to surrender it to the next generation: it is the powerful and evil old against the helpless and gentle new.

'Dad,' Walter said, 'are we really going to Vancouver Island in Canada and raise real food and not have anything to be afraid of any more?'

Half to himself, Ian said, 'Soon as I have the money.'

'I know what that means. It's a "we'll see" number you say. We aren't going, are we?' He watched his father's face intently. 'She won't let us, like taking me out of school and like that; she always brings up that . . . right?'

'It lies ahead for us someday,' Ian said doggedly. 'Maybe not this month but someday, sometime. I promise.'

'And there's no abortion trucks there.'

'No. None. Canadian law is different.'

'Make it soon, Dad. Please.'

His father fixed himself a second Scotch and milk and did not answer; his face was somber and unhappy, almost as if he was about to cry.

In the rear of the abortion truck three children and one adult huddled, jostled by the turning of the truck. They fell against the restraining wire that separated them, and Tim Gantro's father felt keen despair at being cut off mechanically from his own boy. A nightmare during day, he thought. Caged like animals; his noble gesture had brought only more suffering to him.

'Why'd you say you don't know algebra?' Tim asked, once. 'I know you know even calculus and trig-something; you went to Stanford University.'

'I want to show,' he said, 'that either they ought to kill all of us or none of us. But not divide along these bureaucratic arbitrary lines. "When does the soul enter the body?" What kind of rational question is that in this day and age? It's Medieval.' In fact, he thought, it's a pretext—a pretext to prey on the helpless. And he was not helpless. The abortion truck had picked up a fully grown man, with all his knowledge, all his cunning. How are they going to handle me? he asked himself. Obviously I have what all men have; if they have souls, then so do I. If not, then I don't, but on what real basis can they 'put me to sleep'? I am not weak and small, not an ignorant child cowering defenselessly. I can argue the sophistries with the best of the county lawyers; with the DA himself, if necessary.

If they snuff me, he thought, they will have to snuff everyone, including themselves. And that is not what this is all about. This is a con game by which the established, those who already hold all the key economic and political posts, keep the youngsters out of it—murder them if necessary. There is, he thought, in the land, a hatred by the old of the young, a hatred and a fear. So what will they do with me? I am in their age group, and I am caged up in the back of this abortion truck. I pose, he thought, a different kind of threat; I am one of them but on the other side, with stray dogs and cats and babies and infants. Let them figure it out; let a new St Thomas Aquinas arise who can unravel this.

'All I know,' he said aloud, 'is dividing and multiplying and subtracting. I'm even hazy on my fractions.'

'But you used to know that!' Tim said.

'Funny how you forget it after you leave school,' Ed Gantro said. 'You kids are probably better at it than I am.'

'Dad, they're going to *snuff* you,' his son Tim said, wildly. 'Nobody'll adopt you. Not at your age. You're too *old*.'

'Let's see,' Ed Gantro said. 'The binomial theorem. How does that go? I can't get it all together: something about a and b.' And as it leaked out of his head, as had his immortal soul . . . he chuckled to himself. I cannot pass the soul test, he thought. At least not talking like that. I am a dog in the gutter, an animal in a ditch.

The whole mistake of the pro-abortion people from the start, he said to himself, was the *arbitrary* line they drew. An embryo is not entitled to American Constitutional rights and can be killed, legally, by a doctor. But a fetus was a 'person,' with rights, at least for a while; and then the pro-abortion crowd decided that even a seven-month fetus was not 'human' and could be killed, legally, by a licensed doctor. And, one day, a newborn baby—it is a vegetable; it can't focus its eyes, it understands nothing, nor talks . . . the pro-abortion lobby argued in court, and won, with their contention that a newborn baby was only a fetus expelled by accident or organic processes from the womb. But, even then, where was the line to be drawn finally? When the baby smiled its first smile? When it spoke its first word or reached for its initial time for a toy it enjoyed? The legal line was relentlessly pushed back and back. And now the most savage and arbitrary definition of all: when it could perform 'higher math.'

That made the ancient Greeks, of Plato's time, nonhumans, since arithmetic was unknown to them, only geometry; and algebra was an Arab invention, much later in history. *Arbitrary*. It was not a theological arbitrariness either; it was a mere legal one. The Church had long since—from the start, in fact—maintained that even the zygote, and the embryo that followed, was as sacred a life form as any that walked the earth. They had seen what would come of arbitrary definitions of 'Now the soul enters the body,' or in modern terms, 'Now it is a person entitled to the full protection of the law like everyone else.' What was so sad was the sight now of the small child playing bravely in his yard day by day, trying to hope, trying to pretend a security he did not have.

Well, he thought, we'll see what they do with me; I am thirty-five years old, with a Master's Degree from Stanford. Will they put me in a cage for thirty days, with a plastic food dish and a water source and a place—in plain sight—to relieve myself, and if no one adopts me will they consign me to automatic death along with the others?

I am risking a lot, he thought. But they picked up my son today, and the risk began then, when they had him, not when I stepped forward and became a victim myself.

He looked about at the three frightened boys and tried to think of something to tell them—not just his own son but all three.

'"Look,"' he said, quoting. '"I tell you a sacred secret. We shall not all sleep in death. We shall—"' But then he could not remember the rest. Bummer, he thought dismally. '"We shall wake up,"' he said, doing the best he could. '"In a flash. In the twinkling of an eye."'

'Cut the noise,' the driver of the truck, from beyond his wire mesh, growled. 'I can't concentrate on this fucking road.' He added, 'You know, I can squirt gas back there where you are, and you'll pass out; it's for obstreperous pre-persons we pick up. So you want to knock it off, or have me punch the gas button?'

'We won't say anything,' Tim said quickly, with a look of mute terrified appeal at his father. Urging him silently to conform.

His father said nothing. The glance of urgent pleading was too much for him, and he capitulated. Anyhow, he reasoned, what happened in the truck was not crucial. It was when they reached the County Facility—where there would be, at the first sign of trouble, newspaper and TV reporters.

So they rode in silence, each with his own fears, his own schemes. Ed Gantro brooded to himself, perfecting in his head what he would do—what he *had* to do. And not just for Tim but all the PP abortion candidates; he thought through the ramifications as the truck lurched and rattled on.

As soon as the truck parked in the restricted lot of the County Facility and its rear doors had been swung open, Sam B. Carpenter, who ran the whole goddamn operation, walked over, stared, said, 'You've got a grown man in there, Ferris. In fact, you comprehend what you've got? A protester, that's what you've latched onto.'

'But he insisted he doesn't know any math higher than adding,' Ferris said.

To Ed Gantro, Carpenter said, 'Hand me your wallet. I want your actual name. Social Security number, police region stability ident—come on, I want to know who you really are.'

'He's just a rural type,' Ferris said, as he watched Gantro pass over his lumpy wallet.

'And I want confirm prints offa his feet,' Carpenter said. 'The full set. Right away—priority A.' He liked to talk that way.

An hour later he had the reports back from the jungle of interlocking security-data computers from the fake-pastoral restricted area in Virginia. 'This individual graduated from Stanford College with a degree in math. And then got a master's in psychology, which he has, no doubt about it, been subjecting us to. We've got to get him out of here.'

'I did have a soul,' Gantro said, 'but I lost it.'

'How?' Carpenter demanded, seeing nothing about that on Gantro's official records.

'An embolism. The portion of my cerebral cortex, where my soul was, got destroyed when I accidentally inhaled the vapors of insect spray. That's why I've been living out in the country eating roots and grubs, with my boy here, Tim.'

'We'll run an EEG on you,' Carpenter said.

'What's that?' Gantro said. 'One of those brain tests?'

To Ferris, Carpenter said, 'The law says the soul enters at twelve years. And you bring this individual male adult well over thirty. We could be charged with murder. We've got to get rid of him. You drive him back to exactly where you found him and dump him off. If he won't voluntarily exit from the truck, gas the shit out of him and then throw him out. That's a national security order. Your job depends on it, also your status with the penal code of this state.'

'I belong here,' Ed Gantro said. 'I'm a dummy.'

'And his kid,' Carpenter said. 'He's probably a mathematical mental mutant like you see on TV. They set you up; they've probably already alerted the media. Take them all back and gas them and dump them wherever you found them or, barring that, anyhow out of sight.'

'You're getting hysterical,' Ferris said, with anger. 'Run the EEG and the brain scan on Gantro, and probably we'll have to release him, but these three juveniles—'

'All geniuses,' Carpenter said. 'All part of the setup, only you're too stupid to know. Kick them out of the truck and off our premises, and deny—you get this?—deny you ever picked any of the four of them up. Stick to that story.'

'Out of the vehicle,' Ferris ordered, pressing the button that lifted the wire mesh gates.

The three boys scrambled out. But Ed Gantro remained.

'He's not going to exit voluntarily,' Carpenter said. 'Okay, Gantro, we'll physically expel you.' He nodded to Ferris, and the two of them entered the back of the truck. A moment later they had deposited Ed Gantro on the pavement of the parking lot.

'Now you're just a plain citizen,' Carpenter said, with relief. 'You can claim all you want, but you have no proof.'

'Dad,' Tim said, 'how are we going to get home?' All three boys clustered around Ed Gantro.

'You could call somebody from up there,' the Fleischhacker boy said. 'I bet if Walter Best's dad has enough gas he'd come and get us. He takes a lot of long drives; he has a special coupon.'

'Him and his wife, Mrs Best, quarrel a lot,' Tim said. 'So he likes to go driving at night alone; I mean, without her.'

Ed Gantro said, 'I'm staying here. I want to be locked up in a cage.'

'But we can *go*,' Tim protested. Urgently, he plucked at his dad's sleeve. 'That's the whole point, isn't it? They let us go when they saw you. We did it!'

Ed Gantro said to Carpenter, 'I insist on being locked up with the other pre-persons you have in there.' He pointed at the gaily imposing, esthetic solid-green-painted Facility Building.

To Mr Sam B. Carpenter, Tim said, 'Call Mr Best, out where we were, on the peninsula. It's a 669 prefix number. Tell him to come and get us, and he will. I promise. Please.'

The Fleischhacker boy added, 'There's only one Mr Best listed in the phone book with a 669 number. Please, mister.'

Carpenter went indoors, to one of the Facility's many official phones, looked up the number. Ian Best. He punched the number.

'You have reached a semiworking, semiloafing number,' a man's voice, obviously that of someone half-drunk, responded. In the background Carpenter could hear the cutting tones of a furious woman, excoriating Ian Best.

'Mr Best,' Carpenter said, 'several persons whom you know are stranded down at Fourth and A Streets in Verde Gabriel, an Ed Gantro and his son, Tim, a boy identified as Ronald or Donald Fleischhacker, and another unidentified minor boy. The Gantro boy suggested you would not object to driving down here to pick them up and take them home.'

'Fourth and A Streets,' Ian Best said. A pause. 'Is that the pound?'

'The County Facility,' Carpenter said.

'You son of a bitch,' Best said. 'Sure I'll come get them; expect me in twenty minutes. You have Ed Gantro there as a pre-person? Do you know he graduated from Stanford University?'

'We are aware of this,' Carpenter said stonily. 'But they are not being detained; they are merely—here. Not—I repeat not—in custody.'

Ian Best, the drunken slur gone from his voice, said, 'There'll be reporters from all the media there before I get there.' Click. He had hung up.

Walking back outside, Carpenter said to the boy Tim, 'Well, it seems you mickey-moused me into notifying a rabid anti-abortionist activist of your presence here. How neat, how really neat.'

A few moments passed, and then a bright-red Mazda sped up to the entrance of the Facility. A tall man with a light beard got out, unwound camera and audio gear, walked leisurely over to Carpenter. 'I understand you may have a Stanford MA in math here at the Facility,' he said in a neutral, casual voice. 'Could I interview him for a possible story?'

Carpenter said, 'We have booked no such person. You can inspect our records.' But the reporter was already gazing at the three boys clustered around Ed Gantro.

In a loud voice the reporter called, 'Mr Gantro?'

'Yes, sir,' Ed Gantro replied.

Christ, Carpenter thought. We did lock him in one of our official vehicles and transport him here; it'll hit all the papers. Already a blue van with the markings of a TV station had rolled onto the lot. And, behind it, two more cars.

ABORTION FACILITY SNUFFS
STANFORD GRAD

That was how it read in Carpenter's mind. Or

COUNTY ABORTION FACILITY
FOILED IN ILLEGAL ATTEMPT TO ...

And so forth. A spot on the 6:00 evening TV news. Gantro, and when he showed up, Ian Best who was probably an attorney, surrounded by tape recorders and mikes and video cameras.

We have mortally fucked up, he thought. Mortally fucked up. They at Sacramento will cut our appropriation; we'll be reduced to hunting down stray dogs and cats again, like before. Bummer.

When Ian Best arrived in his coal-burning Mercedes-Benz, he was still a little stoned. To Ed Gantro he said, 'You mind if we take a scenic roundabout route back?'

'By way of what?' Ed Gantro said. He wearily wanted to leave now. The little flow of media people had interviewed him and gone. He had made his point, and now he felt drained, and he wanted to go home.

Ian Best said, 'By way of Vancouver Island, British Columbia.'

With a smile, Ed Gantro said, 'These kids should go right to bed. My kid and the other two. Hell, they haven't even had any dinner.'

'We'll stop at a McDonald's stand,' Ian Best said. 'And then we can take off for Canada, where the fish are, and lots of mountains that still have snow on them, even this time of year.'

'Sure,' Gantro said, grinning. 'We can go there.'

'You want to?' Ian Best scrutinized him. 'You really want to?'

'I'll settle a few things, and then, sure, you and I can take off together.'

'Son of a bitch,' Best breathed. 'You mean it.'

'Yes,' he said. 'I do. Of course, I have to get my wife's agreement. You can't go to Canada unless your wife signs a document in writing where she won't follow you. You become what's called a "landed Immigrant."'

'Then I've got to get Cynthia's written permission.'

'She'll give it to you. Just agree to send support money.'

'You think she will? She'll let me go?'

'Of course,' Gantro said.

'You actually think our wives will let us go,' Ian Best said as he and Gantro herded the children into the Mercedes-Benz. 'I'll bet you're right; Cynthia'd love to get rid of me. You know what she calls me, right in front of Walter? "An aggressive coward," and stuff like that. She has no respect for me.'

'Our wives,' Gantro said, 'will let us go.' But he knew better.

He looked back at the Facility manager, Mr Sam B. Carpenter, and at the truck driver, Ferris, who, Carpenter had told the press and TV, was as of this date fired and was a new and inexperienced employee anyhow.

'No,' he said. 'They won't let us go. None of them will.'

Clumsily, Ian Best fiddled with the complex mechanism that controlled the funky coal-burning engine. 'Sure they'll let us go; look, they're just standing there. What can they do, after what you said on TV and what that one reporter wrote up for a feature story?'

'I don't mean them,' Gantro said tonelessly.

'We could just run.'

'We are caught,' Gantro said. 'Caught and can't get out. You ask Cynthia, though. It's worth a try.'

'We'll never see Vancouver Island and the great ocean-going ferries steaming in and out of the fog, will we?' Ian Best said.

'Sure we will, eventually.' But he knew it was a lie, an absolute lie, just like you know sometimes when you say something that for no rational reason you know is absolutely true.

They drove from the lot, out onto the public street.

'It feels good,' Ian Best said, 'to be free . . . right?' The three boys nodded, but Ed Gantro said nothing. Free, he thought. Free to go home. To be caught in a larger net, shoved into a greater truck than the metal mechanical one the County Facility uses.

'This is a great day,' Ian Best said.

'Yes,' Ed Gantro agreed. 'A great day in which a noble and effective blow has been struck for all helpless things, anything of which you could say, "It is alive."'

Regarding him intently in the narrow trickly light, Ian Best said, 'I don't want to go home; I want to take off for Canada now.'

'We *have* to go home,' Ed Gantro reminded him. 'Temporarily, I mean. To wind things up. Legal matters, pick up what we need.'

Ian Best, as he drove, said, 'We'll never get there, to British Columbia and Vancouver Island and Stanley Park and English Bay and where they grow food and keep horses and where they have the ocean-going ferries.'

'No, we won't,' Ed Gantro said.

'Not now, not even later?'

'Not ever,' Ed Gantro said.

'That's what I was afraid of,' Best said and his voice broke and his driving got funny. 'That's what I thought from the beginning.'

They drove in silence, then, with nothing to say to each other. There was nothing left to say.

THE EYE OF THE SIBYL

How is it that our ancient Roman Republic guards itself against those who would destroy it? We Romans, although only mortals like other mortals, draw on the help of beings enormously superior to ourselves. These wise and kind entities, who originate from worlds unknown to us, are ready to assist the Republic when it is in peril. When it is not in peril, they sink back out of sight—to return when we need them.

Take the case of the assassination of Julius Caesar: a case which apparently was closed when those who conspired to murder him were themselves murdered. But how did we Romans determine who had done this foul deed? And, more important, how did we bring these conspirators to justice? We had outside help; we had the assistance of the Cumaean Sibyl who knows a thousand years ahead what will happen, and who gives us, in written form, her advice. All Romans are aware of the existence of the Sibylline Books. We open them whenever the need arises.

I myself, Philos Diktos of Tyana, have seen the Sibylline Books. Many leading Roman citizens, members of the Senate especially, have consulted them. But I have seen the Sibyl herself, and I of my own experience know something about her which few men know. Now that I am old—regretfully, but of the necessity which binds all mortal men—I am willing to confess that once, quite by accident I suppose, I in the course of my priestly duties saw how the Sibyl is capable of seeing down the corridors of time; I know what permits her to do this, as she developed out of the prior Greek Sibyl at Delphi, in that so highly venerated land, Greece.

Few men know this, and perhaps the Sibyl, reaching out through time to strike at me for speaking aloud, will silence me forever. It is quite possible, therefore, that before I can finish this scroll I will be found dead, my head split like one of those overripe melons from the Levant which we Romans prize so. In any case, being old, I will boldly say.

I had been quarreling with my wife that morning—I was not old then, and the dreadful murder of Julius Caesar had just taken place. At that time no one was sure who had done it. Treason against the State! Murder most ugly—a thousand knife wounds in the body of the man who had come to stabilize our quaking society . . . with the approval of the Sibyl, in her temple; we had seen the texts she had written to that effect. We knew that she had expected Caesar to bring his army across the river and into Rome, and to accept the crown of Caesar.

'You witless fool,' my wife was saying to me that morning. 'If the Sibyl were so wise as you think, she would have anticipated this assassination.'

'Maybe she did,' I answered.

'I think she's a fake,' my wife Xantippe said to me, grimacing in that way she has, which is so repulsive. She is—I should say was—of a higher social class than I, and always made me conscious of it. 'You priests make up those texts; you write them yourselves—you say what you think in such a vague way that any interpretation can be made of it. You're bilking the citizens, especially the well-to-do.' By that she meant her own family.

I said hotly, leaping up from the breakfast table, 'She is inspired; she is a prophetess—she knows the future. Evidently there was no way the assassination of our great leader, whom the people loved so, could be averted.'

'The Sibyl is a hoax,' my wife said, and started buttering yet another roll, in her usual greedy fashion.

'I have seen the great books—'

'*How* does she know the future?' my wife demanded.

At that I had to admit I didn't know; I was crestfallen—I,

a priest at Cumae, an employee of the Roman State. I felt humiliated.

'It's a money game,' my wife was saying as I strode out the door.

Even though it was only dawn—fair Aurora, the goddess of dawn, was showing that white light over the world, the light we regard as sacred, from which many of our inspired visions come—I made my way, on foot, to the lovely temple where I work.

No one else had arrived yet, except the armed guards loitering outside; they glanced at me in surprise to see me so early, then nodded as they recognized me. No one but a recognized priest of the temple at Cumae is allowed in; even Caesar himself must depend on us.

Entering, I passed by the great gas-filled vault in which the Sibyl's huge stone throne shone wetly in the half-gloom; only a few meager torches had been lit . . .

I halted and froze into silence, as I saw something never disclosed to me before. The Sibyl, her long black hair tied up in a tight knot, her arms covered, sat on her throne, leaning forward—and I saw, then, that she was not alone.

Two creatures stood before her, inside a round bubble. They resembled men but each of them had an additional—I am not sure even now what they had, but they were not mortals. They were gods. They had slits for eyes, without pupils. Instead of hands, they had claws like a crab has. Their mouths were only holes, and I realized that they, gods forbid, were mute. They seemed to be talking to the Sibyl but over a long string, at each end of which was a box. One of the creatures held the box to the side of his head, and the Sibyl listened to the box at her end. The box had numbers on it and buttons, and the string was in rolls and heaps, so that it could be extended.

These were the Immortals. But we Romans, we mortals, had believed that all the Immortals had left the world, a long time ago. That was what we had been told. Evidently they had returned—at least for a short while, and to give information to the Sibyl.

The Sibyl turned toward me, and, incredibly, her head came across that whole gas-filled chamber until it was close to mine. She was smiling, but she had found me out. Now I could hear the conversation between her and the Immortals; she graciously made it audible to me.

'. . . only one of many,' the larger of the two Immortals was saying. 'More will follow, but not for some time. The darkness of ignorance is coming, after a golden period.'

'There is no way it can be averted?' the Sibyl asked, in that melodious voice of hers which we treasure so.

'Augustus will reign well,' the larger Immortal said, 'but following him evil and deranged men will come.'

The other Immortal said, 'You must understand that a new cult will arise around a Light Creature. The cult will grow, but their true texts will be encoded, and the actual messages lost. We foresee failure for the mission of the Light Creature; he will be tortured and murdered, as was Julius. And after that—'

'Long after that,' the larger Immortal said, 'civilization will draw itself up out of the ignorance once more, after two thousand years, and then—'

The Sibyl gasped and said, 'That long, Fathers?'

'That long. And then as they begin to question and to seek to learn their true origins, their divinity, the murders will begin again, the repression and cruelty, and another dark age will begin.'

'It might be averted,' the other Immortal said.

'Can I assist?' the Sibyl asked.

Gently, both Immortals said, 'You will be dead by then.'

'There will be no Sibyl to take my place?'

'None. No one will guard the Republic two thousand years from now. And filthy men with small ideas will scamper and scrabble about like rats; their footprints will criss-cross the world as they seek power and vie with one another for false honors.' To the Sibyl both Immortals said, 'You will not be able to help the people, then.'

Abruptly both Immortals vanished, along with their rolls of string and the boxes with numbers which talked and were talked into, as if by mind alone. The Sibyl sat for a moment, and then lifted her hands so that by means of the mechanism which the Egyptians taught us, one of the blank pages lifted toward her, that she might write. But then she did a curious thing, and it is this which I tell you with fear, more fear than what I have told already.

Reaching into the folds of her robe she brought out an Eye. She placed the Eye in the center of her forehead, and it was not an eye at all such as ours, with a pupil, but like that, the slit-like eye of the Immortals, and yet not. It had sideways bands which moved toward one another, like rows ... I have no words for this, being only a priest by formal training and class, but the Sibyl did turn toward me and look *past* me with that Eye, and she did then cry out so loud that it shook the walls of the temple; stones fell and the snakes far down in the slots of rock hissed. She cried in dismay and horror at what she saw, past me, and yet her strange third Eye remained; she continued to look.

And then she fell, as if faint. I ran forward to lend a hand; I touched the Sibyl, my friend, that great lovely friend of the Republic as she fell faint and forward in dismay at what she saw ahead, down the tunnels and corridors of time. For it was this Eye by which the Sibyl saw what she needed to see, to instruct and warn us. And it was evident to me that sometimes she saw things too dreadful for her to bear, and for us to handle, try as we might.

As I held the Sibyl, a strange thing happened. I saw, amid the swirling gases, forms take shape.

'You must not take them as real,' the Sibyl said; I heard her voice, and yet although I understood her words I knew that the shapes were indeed real. I saw a giant ship, without sails or oars ... I saw a city of thin, high buildings, crowded with vehicles unlike anything I had ever seen. And still I moved toward them and they toward me, until at last the shapes swirled behind me, cutting me off from the Sibyl. 'I see this with the Gorgon's Eye,' the Sibyl called after me. 'It is the Eye which Medusa passed back and forth, the Eye of the fates—you have fallen into—' And then her words were gone.

*

I played in the grass with a puppy, wondering about a broken Coca-Cola bottle which had been left in our backyard; I didn't know by whom.

'Philip, you come in for dinner!' my grandmother called from the back porch. I saw that the sun was setting.

'Okay!' I called back. But I continued to play. I had found a great spider web, and in it was a bee wrapped up in web, stung by the spider. I began to unwrap it, and it stung me.

My next memory was reading the comic pages in the *Berkeley Daily Gazette*. I read about Brick Bradford and how he found a lost civilization from thousands of years ago.

'Hey, Mom,' I said to my mother. 'Look at this; it's swell. Brick walks down this ledge, see, and at the bottom–' I kept staring at the olden-times helmets the people wore, and a strange feeling filled me; I didn't know why.

'He certainly gets a lot out of the funnies,' my grandmother said in a disgusted voice. 'He should read something worthwhile. Those comics are garbage.'

The next I remember I was in school, sitting watching a girl dance. Her name was Jill and she was from the grade above ours, the sixth; she wore a belly dancer's costume and her veil covered the bottom part of her face. But I could see lovely kind eyes, eyes filled with wisdom. They reminded me of someone else's eyes I had once known, but who has a kid ever known? Later Mrs Redman had us write a composition, and I wrote about Jill. I wrote about strange lands where Jill lived where she danced with nothing on above her waist. Later, Mrs Redman talked to my mother on the phone and I was bawled out, but in obscure terms that had to do with a bra or something. I never understood it then; there was a lot I didn't understand. I seemed to have memories, and yet they had nothing to do with growing up in Berkeley at the Hillside Grammar School, or my family, or the house we lived in . . . they had to do with snakes. I know now why I dreamed of snakes: wise snakes, not evil snakes but those which whisper wisdom.

Anyhow, my composition was considered very good by the principal of the school, Mr Bill Gaines, *after* I wrote in that Jill wore something above her waist at all times, and later I decided to be a writer.

One night I had an odd dream. I was maybe in junior high school, getting ready to go to Berkeley High next year. I dreamed that in the deep of night—and it was like a regular dream, it was really real—I saw this person from outer space behind glass in a satellite of some kind they'd come here in. And he couldn't talk; he just looked at me, with funny eyes.

Two weeks or so later I had to fill out what I wanted to be when I grew up and I thought of my dream about the man from another universe, so I wrote: I AM GOING TO BE A SCIENCE FICTION WRITER.

That made my family mad, but then, see, when they got mad I got stubborn, and anyhow my girlfriend, Ysabel Lomax, told me I'd never be any good at it and it didn't earn any money anyhow and science fiction was dumb and only people with pimples read it. So I decided for sure to write it, because people with pimples should have someone writing for them; it's unfair otherwise, just to write for people with clear complexions. America is built on fairness; that is what Mr Gaines taught us at Hillside Grammar School, and since he was able to fix my wristwatch that time when no one else could, I tend to admire him.

In high school I was a failure because I just sat writing and writing all day, and all my teachers screamed at me that I was a Communist because I didn't do what I was told.

'Oh yeah?' I used to say. That got me sent up before the Dean of Boys. He told me off worse than my grandfather had, and warned me that if I didn't get better grades I'd be expelled.

That night I had another one of those vivid dreams. This time a woman was driving me in her car, only it was like an old-time Roman-style chariot, and she was singing.

The next day when I had to go see Mr Erlaud, the Dean of Boys, I wrote on his blackboard, in Latin:

　　　　　　　　　　　　　　　THE EYE OF THE SIBYL

When he came in he turned red in the face, since he teaches Latin and knows that means, 'Where money rules.'

'This is what a left-wing complainer would write,' he said to me.

So I wrote something else as he sat looking over my papers; I wrote:

UBI CUNNUS REGNET

That seemed to perplex him. 'Where—did you learn that particular Latin word?' he asked.

'I don't know,' I said. I wasn't sure, but it seemed to me that in my dreams they were talking to me in Latin. Maybe it was just my own brain doing reruns of my Latin 1-A beginners class, where I was really very good, surprisingly, because I didn't study.

The next vivid dream like that came two nights before that freak or those freaks killed President Kennedy. I saw the whole thing happening in my dream, *two nights before*, but more than anything else, even more vivid, I saw my girlfriend Ysabel Lomax watching the conspirators doing their evil deed, and Ysabel had a third eye.

My folks sent me to a psychologist later on, because after President Kennedy was assassinated I got really weird. I just sat and brooded and withdrew.

It was a neat lady they sent me to, a Carol Heims. She was very pretty and she didn't say I was nuts; she said I should get away from my family, drop out of school—she said that the school system insulates you from reality and keeps you from learning techniques to handle actual situations—and for me to write science fiction.

I did so. I worked at a TV sales shop sweeping up and uncrating and setting up the new TV sets. I kept thinking that each set was like a huge eye, though; it bothered me. I told Carol Heims my dreams that I had been having all my life, about the space people, and being in Latin, and that I thought I'd had a lot more I'd never remembered when I woke up.

'Dreams aren't fully understood,' Ms Heims told me. I was sitting there wondering how she would look in a belly dancer costume, nude above the waist; I found that made the therapy hour go faster. 'There's a new theory that it's part of your collective unconscious, reaching back perhaps thousands of years . . . and in dreams you get in touch with it. So, if that's true, dreams are valid and very valuable.'

I was busy imagining her hips moving suggestively from side to side, but I did listen to what she said; it was something about the wise kindness of her eyes. Always I thought of those wise snakes, for some reason.

'I've been dreaming about books,' I told her. 'Open books, held up before me. Huge books, very valuable. Even holy, like the Bible.'

'That has to do with your career as a writer,' Ms Heims said.

'These are old. Thousands of years old. And they're warning us about something. A dreadful murder, a lot of murders. And cops putting people into prison for their ideas, but doing it secretly—framing people. And I keep seeing this woman who looks like you but seated on a vast stone throne.'

Later on Ms Heims was transferred to another part of the county and I couldn't see her any more. I felt really bad, and I buried myself in my writing. I sold a story to a magazine called *Envigorating Science Fact*, which told about superior races who had landed on Earth and were directing our affairs secretly. They never paid me.

I am old now, and I risk telling this, because what do I have to lose? One day I got a request to write a small article for *Love-Planet Adventure Yarns*, and they gave me a plot they wanted written up, and a black-and-white photo of the cover. I kept staring at the photo; it showed a Roman or Greek—anyhow he wore a toga—and he had on his wrist a caduceus, which is the medical sign: two coiled snakes, only actually it was olive branches originally.

'How do you know that's called a "caduceus"?' Ysabel asked me (we were living together now, and she was always telling me to make more money and to be like her family, which was well-to-do and classy).

'I don't know,' I said, and I felt funny. And then I began to see violently agitated colored phosphene activity in both my eyes, like those modern abstract graphics which Paul Klee and others draw—in vivid color, and flash-cut in duration: very fast. 'What's the date?' I yelled at Ysabel, who was sitting drying her hair and reading the *Harvard Lampoon*.

'The date? It's March 16,' she said.

'The *year*!' I yelled. 'Pulchra puella, tempus—' And then I broke off, because she was staring at me. And, worse, I couldn't recall her name or who she was.

'It is 1974,' she answered.

'The tyranny is in power, then, if it is only 1974,' I said.

'What?' she answered, astonished, staring at me.

At once two beings appeared on each side of her, encapsulated in their inter-system vessels, two globes which hovered and maintained their atmosphere and temperature. 'Don't say a further statement to her,' one of them warned me. 'We will erase her memory; she will think she fell asleep and had a dream.'

'I remember,' I said, pressing my hands to my head. Anamnesis had taken place; I remember that I was from ancient times, and, before that, from the star Albemuth, as were these two Immortals. 'Why are you back?' I said. 'To—'

'We shall work entirely through ordinary mortals,' J'Annis said. He was the wiser of the two Immortals. 'There is no Sibyl now to help, to give advice to the Republic. In dreams we are inspiring people here and there to *wake up*; they are beginning to understand that the Price of Release is being paid by us to free them from the Liar, who rules them.'

'They're not aware of you?' I said.

'They suspect. They see holograms of us projected in the sky, which we employ to divert them; they imagine that we are floating about there.'

I knew that these Immortals were in the minds of men, not in the skies of Earth, that by diverting attention outward, they were free once more to help inward, as they had always helped: the inner World.

'We will bring the springtime to this winter world,' F'fr'am said, smiling. 'We will raise the gates which imprison these people, who groan under a tyranny they dimly see. Did you see? Did you know of the comings-and-goings of the secret police, the quasi-military teams which destroyed all freedom of speech, all those who dissented?'

Now, in my old age, I set forth this account for you, my Roman friends, here at Cumae, where the Sibyl lives. I passed either by chance or by design into the far future, into a world of tyranny, of winter, which you cannot imagine. And I saw the Immortals which assist us also assist those, two thousand years from now! Although those mortals in the future are—listen to me—*blind*. Their sight has been taken away by a thousand years of repression; they have been tormented and limited, the way we limit animals. But the Immortals are waking them up—*will* wake them up, I should say, in time to save them. And then the two thousand years of winter will end; they will open their eyes, because of dreams and secret inspirations; they will know—but I have told you all this, in my ancient, rambling fashion.

Let me finish with this verse by our great poet Virgil, a good friend of the Sibyl, and you will know from it what lies ahead, for the Sibyl has said that although it will not apply to our time here in Rome, it will apply to those two thousand years from us, ahead in time, bringing them promise of relief:

> *Ultima Cumaei venit iam carminis aetas;*
> *magnus ab integro saeclorum nascitur ordo.*
> *Iam redit et Virgo, redeunt Saturnia regna;*
> *Iam nova progenies, caelo demittitur alto.*
> *Tu modo nascenti puero, quo ferrea primum*
> *desinet, ac toto surget gens aurea mundo,*
> *casta fave Lucina; tuus iam regnat Apollo.*

I will set this in the strange English language which I learned to speak during my time in the future, before the Immortals and the Sibyl drew me back here, my work there at that time done:

> At last the Final Time announced by the Sibyl will arrive:
> The procession of ages turns to its origin.
> The Virgin returns and Saturn reigns as before;
> A new race from heaven on high descends.
> Goddess of Birth, smile on the new-born baby,
> In whose time the Iron Prison will fall to ruin
> And a golden race arises everywhere.
> Apollo, the rightful king, is restored!

Alas, you my dear Roman friends will not live to see this. But far along the corridors of time, in the United States (I use here words foreign to you) evil will fall, and this little prophecy of Virgil, which the Sibyl inspired in him, will come true. The Springtime is reborn!

THE DAY MR COMPUTER
FELL OUT OF ITS TREE

He awoke, and sensed at once that something dreadful was wrong. Oh God, he thought as he realized that Mr Bed had deposited him in a muddled heap against the wall. It's beginning again, he realized. And the Directorate West promised us infinite perfection. This is what we get, he realized, for believing in what mere humans say.

As best he could he struggled out of his bedclothes, got shakily to his feet and made his way across the room to Mr Closet.

'I'd like a natty sharkskin gray double-breasted suit,' he informed it, speaking crisply into the microphone on Mr Closet's door. 'A red shirt, blue socks, and—' But it was no use. Already the slot was vibrating as a huge pair of women's silk bloomers came sliding out.

'You get what you see,' Mr Closet's metallic voice came to him, echoing hollowly.

Glumly, Joe Contemptible put on the bloomers. At least it was better than nothing—like the day in Dreadful August when the vast polyencephalic computer in Queens had served up everyone in Greater America nothing but a handkerchief to wear.

Going to the bathroom, Joe Contemptible washed his face—and found the liquid which he was splashing on himself to be warm root beer. Christ, he thought. Mr Computer is even zanier this time than ever before. It's been reading old Phil Dick science fiction stories, he decided. That's what we get for providing Mr Computer with every kind of archaic trash in the world to read and store in its memory banks.

He finished combing his hair—without making use of the root beer—and then, having dried himself, entered the kitchen to see if Mr Coffeepot was at least a sane fragment in a reality deteriorating all around him.

No luck. Mr Coffeepot obligingly presented him with a dixie cup of soap. Well, so much for that.

The real problem, however, came when he tried to open Mr Door. Mr Door would not open; instead it complained tinnily: 'The paths of glory lead but to the grave.'

'Meaning what?' Joe demanded, angry, now. This weird business was no longer fun. Not that it had ever been the times before—except, perhaps, when Mr Computer had served him with roast pheasant for breakfast.

'Meaning,' Mr Door said, 'that you're wasting your time, fucker. You're not getting to the office today nohow.'

This proved to be true. The door would not open; despite his efforts the mechanism, controlled miles away from the polyencephalic master matrix, refused to budge.

Breakfast, then? Joe Contemptible punched buttons on the control module of Mr Food—and found himself staring at a plate of fertilizer.

He thereupon picked up the phone and savagely attacked the numbers which would put him in touch with the local police.

'Loony Tunes Incorporated,' the face on the vidscreen said. 'An animated cartoon version of your sexual practices produced in one week, including GLORIOUS SOUND EFFECTS!'

Fuck it, Joe Contemptible said to himself and rang off.

It had been a bad idea from the start, back in 1982, to operate every mechanism from a central source. Of course, the basic idea had sounded good: with the ozone layer burned off, too many people were behaving irrationally, and it had become necessary to solve the problem by some electronic means immune from the mind-slushing ultra violet radiation now flooding earth. Mr Computer had, at the time, seemed to be the answer. But, sad to say, Mr Computer had absorbed too much freaked-out input from its human builders and therefore, like them, Mr Computer had its own psychotic episodes.

There was of course an answer. It had hurriedly been slapped together—pasted into place, as it were, once the difficulty was discovered. The head of World Mental Health, a formidable old battleax named Joan Simpson, had been granted a form of immortality so as to be always available to treat Mr Computer during its crazy periods. Ms Simpson was stored at the center of the earth in a special lead-lined chamber, safe from the harmful radiation at the surface, in a quasi-suspended animation called Dismal Pak, in which Ms Simpson (it was said) lay aslumber while being entertained by an endless procession of priceless 1940 radio soap operas, fed to her on a closed loop. Ms Simpson, it was said, was the only truly sane person on—or rather in—earth; this, plus her superb skill, as well as infinite training in the art of healing psychotic constructs, was earth's sole hope for survival.

Realizing this, Joe Contemptible felt a little better, but not a lot—for he had just picked up Mr Newspaper where it lay on the floor beside the slot of his front door. The headline read:

ADOLF HITLER CROWNED POPE. CROWDS
CHEER IN RECORD NUMBERS.

So much for Mr Newspaper, Joe realized glumly, and tossed it into Mr Garbage-slot. The mechanism churned, and then, instead of ingesting or cubing the newspaper, spat it back out again. Joe glanced briefly at the headline again, saw a photo of a human skeleton—complete with Nazi uniform and mustache, wearing the great crown of the pope—and seated himself on the couch in his living room to wait for the moment (sure to come soon) when Ms Simpson was startled out of Dismal Pak to minister to Mr Computer, and, in so doing, restore the world to sanity.

*

Half to himself, Fred Doubledome said, 'It's psychotic, all right. I asked it if it knew where it was and it said it was floating on a raft in the Mississippi. Now get a confirm for me; ask it who it is.'

Dr Pacemaker touched command-request buttons on the console of the vast computer, asking it: WHO ARE YOU?

The answer appeared on the vidscreen at once.

TOM SAWYER

'You see?' Doubledome said. 'It is totally out of touch with the reality situation. Has reactivation of Ms Simpson begun?'

'That's affirmative, Doubledome,' Pacemaker said. And, as if proving him correct, doors slid aside to reveal the lead-lined container in which Ms Simpson slept, listening to her favorite daytime soap opera, *Ma Perkins*.

'Ms Simpson,' Pacemaker said, bending over her. 'We are having a problem with Mr Computer again. It has totally spaced out. An hour ago it routed all the whipples in New York across the same intersection. Loss of life was heavy. And instead of responding to the disaster with fire and police rescue teams it dispatched a circus troupe of clowns.'

'I see,' Ms Simpson's voice came through the transduction and boosting system by which they communicated with her. 'But first, I must attend to a fire at Ma's lumber yard. You see, her friend Shuffle–'

'Ms Simpson,' Pacemaker said, 'our situation is grave. We need you. Come out of your customary fog and get to work restoring Mr Computer to sanity. Than you may return to your radio serials.'

Gazing down at Ms Simpson he was, as always, startled by her virtually unnatural beauty. Great dark eyes with long lashes, the husky, sensuous voice, the intensely black short-cropped hair (so fashionable in a world of dreck!), the firm and supple body, the warm mouth suggesting love and comfort–amazing, he thought, that the one really sane human left on earth (and the only one capable of saving same) could at the same time be startlingly lovely.

But no matter; this was not the time to think such thoughts. NBC TV news had already reported that Mr Computer had closed down all the airports in the world and turned them into baseball stadiums.

Shortly, Ms Simpson was studying a composite abstract delineating Mr Computer's erratic commands.

'It is clearly regressive,' she informed them, sipping absently at a cup of coffee.

'Ms Simpson,' Doubledome said, 'I'm afraid that's soapy water you're drinking.'

'You're right,' Ms Simpson said, putting the cup down. 'I see here that Mr Computer is playing childish pranks on the mass of mankind. It fits with my hypostatized hypothesis.'

'How will you render a return of normalcy to the vast construct?' Pacemaker asked.

'Evidently it encountered a traumatic situation which caused it to regress,' Ms Simpson said. 'I shall locate the trauma and then proceed by desensitizing Mr Computer vis-à-vis that trauma. My MO in that regard will be to present Mr Computer with each letter of the alphabet in turn, gauging its reactions until I perceive what we in the mental health movement call a flinch reaction.'

She did so. Mr Computer, upon the letter J, emitted a faint whine; smoke billowed up. Ms Simpson then repeated the sequence of letters. This time the faint whine and billows of smoke came at the letter C.

'J.C.,' Ms Simpson said. 'Perhaps Jesus Christ. Perhaps the Second Coming has taken place, and Mr Computer fears that it will be pre-empted. I will start on that assumption. Have Mr Computer placed in a semi-comatose state so that it can free associate.'

Technicians hurried to the task assigned.

The virtually unconscious mumbling of the great computer issued forth from the aud channels mounted through the control chamber.

'... programming himself to die,' the computer rambled on. 'Fine person like that. DNA command analysis. Going to ask not for a reprieve but for an acceleration of the death process. Salmon swimming upstream to die . . . appeals to him . . . after all I've done for him. Rejection of life. Conscious of it. Wants to die. I cannot endure the voluntary death, the reprogramming 180 degrees from the matrix purpose of DNA command programming . . .' On and on it rambled.

Ms Simpson said sharply, 'What name comes to you, Mr Computer? A name!'

'Clerk in a record store,' the computer mumbled. 'An authority on German Lieder and bubblegum rock of the '60s. What a waste. My but the water is warm. Think I'll fish. Let down my line and catch a big catfish. Won't Huck be surprised, and Jim, too! Jim's a man even though–'

'What name?' Ms Simpson repeated.

The vague mumble continued.

Swiftly, Ms Simpson said to Doubledome and Pacemaker, who stood rigid and attentive, 'Find a record clerk whose initials are J.C. and who is an authority on German Lieder and bubblegum rock of the '60s. And hurry! *We don't have much time!*'

Having left his conapt by a window, Joe Contemptible made his way among wrecked whipples and shouting, angry drivers in the direction of Artistic Music Company, the record store at which he had worked most of his life. At least he had gotten out of–

Suddenly two gray-clad police materialized before him, faces grim; both held punch-guns aimed at Joe's chest. 'You're coming with us,' they said, virtually in unison.

The urge to run overcame Joe; turning, he started away. But then furious pain settled over him; the police had punched him out, and now, falling, he realized that it was too late to flee. He was a captive of the authorities. But why? he wondered. Is it merely a random sweep? Or are they putting down an abortive coup against the government? Or–his fading thoughts raced–have ETIs come at last to help us in our fight for freedom? And then darkness closed over him, merciful darkness.

The next he knew, he was being served a cup of soapy water by two members of the technocrat class; an armed policeman lounged in the background, punch-gun ready were the situation to require it.

Seated in the corner of the chamber was an extraordinarily beautiful dark-haired woman; she wore a miniskirt and boots—old-fashioned but enticingly foxy—and, he saw, she had the most enormous and warm eyes he had ever seen in his life. Who was she? And—what did she want with him? Why had he been brought before her?

'Your name,' one of the white-clad technocrats said.

'Contemptible,' he managed to say, unable to take his eyes off the extraordinarily beautiful young woman.

'You have an appointment with DNA Reappraisal,' the other of the white-clad technocrats said crisply. 'What is your purpose? What ukase emanating from the gene pool do you intend—did you intend, I should say—to alter?'

Joe said lamely, 'I—wanted to be reprogrammed for . . . you know. Longer life. The encoding for death was about to come up for me, and I—'

'We know that isn't true,' the lovely dark-haired woman said in a husky, sexy voice, but a voice nonetheless filled with intelligence and authority. 'You were attempting suicide, were you not, Mr Contemptible, by having your DNA coding tinkered with, not to postpone your death, *but to bring it on?*'

He said nothing. Obviously, they knew.

'WHY?' the woman said sharply.

'I—' He hesitated. Then, slumping in defeat he managed to say, 'I'm not married. I've got no wife. Nothing. Just my damn job at the record store. All those damn German songs and those bubblegum rock lyrics; they go through my head night and day, constantly, mixtures of Goethe and Heine and Neil Diamond.' Lifting his head he said with furious defiance, 'So why should I live on? Call that living? It's existence, not living.'

There was silence.

Three frogs hopped across the floor. Mr Computer was now turning out frogs from all the airducts on earth. Half an hour before, it had been dead cats.

'Do you know what it is like,' Joe said quietly, 'to have such lyrics as "The song I sang to you / The love I brang to you" keep floating through your head?'

The dark-haired lovely woman said, suddenly, 'I think I do know, Contemptible. You see, I am Joan Simpson.'

'Then–' Joe understood in an instant. 'You're down there at the center of the earth watching endless daytime soap operas! On a closed loop!'

'Not watching,' Joan Simpson said. 'Hearing. They're from radio, not TV.'

Joe said nothing. There was nothing to say.

One of the white-clad technocrats said, 'Ms Simpson, work must begin restoring Mr Computer to sanity. It is presently turning out hundreds of thousands of Pollys.'

'"Pollys"?' Joan Simpson said, puzzled; then understanding flooded her warm features. 'Oh yes. His childhood sweetheart.'

'Mr Contemptible,' one of the white-clad technocrats said to Joe, 'it is because of your lack of love for life that Mr Computer has gone crackers. To bring Mr Computer back to sanity we must first bring you back to sanity.' To Joan Simpson, he said, 'Am I correct?'

She nodded, lit a cigarette, leaned back thoughtfully. 'Well?' she said presently. 'What would it take to reprogram you, Joe? So you'd want to live instead of die? Mr Computer's abreactive syndrome is directly related to your own. Mr Computer feels it has failed the world because, in examining a cross index of humans whom it cares for, it has found that you–'

'"Cares for"?' Joe Contemptible said. 'You mean Mr Computer likes me?'

'Takes care of,' one of the white-clad technocrats explained.

'Wait.' Joan Simpson scrutinized Joe Contemptible. 'You reacted to that phrase "cares for." What did you think it meant?'

He said, with difficulty, 'Likes me. Cares for in that sense.'

'Let me ask you this,' Joan Simpson said, presently, stubbing out her cigarette and lighting another. 'Do you feel that no one cares for you, Joe?'

'That's what my mother said,' Joe Contemptible said.

'And you believed her?' Joan Simpson said.

'Yes.' He nodded.

Suddenly Joan Simpson put out her cigarette. 'Well, Doubledome,' she said in a quiet, brisk voice. 'There aren't going to be any more radio soap operas nattering at me any more. I'm not going back down to the center of the earth. It's over, gentlemen. I'm sorry, but that's the way it is.'

'You're going to leave Mr Computer insane as–'

'I will heal Mr Computer,' Joan Simpson said in an even voice, 'by healing Joe. And–' A slight smile played about her lips. 'And myself, gentlemen.'

There was silence.

'All right,' one of the two white-clad technicians said presently. 'We will send you both down to the center of the earth. And you can rattle on at each other throughout eternity. Except when it is necessary to lift you out of Dismal Pak to heal Mr Computer. Is that a fair trade-off?'

'Wait,' Joe Contemptible said feebly, but already Ms Simpson was nodding.

'It is,' she said.

'What about my conapt?' Joe protested. 'My job? My wretched little pointless life as I am normally accustomed to living it?'

Joan Simpson said, 'That is already changing, Joe. You have already encountered me.'

'But I thought you would be old and ugly!' Joe said. 'I had no idea–'

'The universe is full of surprises,' Joan Simpson said, and held out her waiting arms for him.

THE EXIT DOOR LEADS IN

Bob Bibleman had the impression that robots wouldn't look you in the eye. And when one had been in the vicinity small valuable objects disappeared. A robot's idea of order was to stack everything into one pile. Nonetheless, Bibleman had to order lunch from robots, since vending ranked too low on the wage scale to attract humans.

'A hamburger, fries, strawberry shake, and—' Bibleman paused, reading the printout. 'Make that a supreme double cheeseburger, fries, a chocolate malt—'

'Wait a minute,' the robot said. 'I'm already working on the burger. You want to buy into this week's contest while you're waiting?'

'I don't get the royal cheeseburger,' Bibleman said.

'That's right.'

It was hell living in the twenty-first century. Information transfer had reached the velocity of light. Bibleman's older brother had once fed a ten-word plot outline into a robot fiction machine, changed his mind as to the outcome, and found that the novel was already in print. He had had to program a sequel in order to make his correction.

'What's the prize structure in the contest?' Bibleman asked.

At once the printout posted all the odds, from first prize down to last. Naturally, the robot blanked out the display before Bibleman could read it.

'What is first prize?' Bibleman said.

'I can't tell you that,' the robot said. From its slot came a hamburger, french fries, and a strawberry shake. 'That'll be one thousand dollars in cash.'

'Give me a hint,' Bibleman said as he paid.

'It's everywhere and nowhere. It's existed since the seventeenth century. Originally it was invisible. Then it became royal. You can't get it unless you're smart, although cheating helps and so does being rich. What does the word "heavy" suggest to you?'

'Profound.'

'No, the literal meaning.'

'Mass.' Bibleman pondered. 'What is this, a contest to see who can figure out what the prize is? I give up.'

'Pay the six dollars,' the robot said, 'to cover our costs, and you'll receive an–'

'Gravity,' Bibleman broke in. 'Sir Isaac Newton. The Royal College of England. Am I right?'

'Right,' the robot said. 'Six dollars entitles you to a chance to go to college—a statistical chance, at the posted odds. What's six dollars? Prat-fare.'

Bibleman handed over a six-dollar coin.

'You win,' the robot said. 'You get to go to college. You beat the odds, which were two trillion to one against. Let me be the first to congratulate you. If I had a hand, I'd shake hands with you. This will change your life. This has been your lucky day.'

'It's a setup,' Bibleman said, feeling a rush of anxiety.

'You're right,' the robot said, and it looked Bibleman right in the eye. 'It's also mandatory that you accept your prize. The college is a military college located in Buttfuck, Egypt, so to speak. But that's no problem; you'll be taken there. Go home and start packing.'

'Can't I eat my hamburger and drink–'

'I'd suggest you start packing right away.'

Behind Bibleman a man and woman had lined up; reflexively he got out of their way, trying to hold on to his tray of food, feeling dizzy.

'A charbroiled steak sandwich,' the man said, 'onion rings, root beer, and that's it.'

The robot said, 'Care to buy into the contest? Terrific prizes.' It flashed the odds on its display panel.

*

When Bob Bibleman unlocked the door of his one-room apartment, his telephone was on. It was looking for him.

'There you are,' the telephone said.

'I'm not going to do it,' Bibleman said.

'Sure you are,' the phone said. 'Do you know who this is? Read over your certificate, your first-prize legal form. You hold the rank of shavetail. I'm Major Casals. You're under my jurisdiction. If I tell you to piss purple, you'll piss purple. How soon can you be on a transplan rocket? Do you have friends you want to say goodbye to? A sweetheart, perhaps? Your mother?'

'Am I coming back?' Bibleman said with anger. 'I mean, who are we fighting, this college? For that matter, what college is it? Who is on the faculty? Is it a liberal arts college or does it specialize in the hard sciences? Is it government-sponsored? Does it offer—'

'Just calm down,' Major Casals said quietly.

Bibleman seated himself. He discovered that his hands were shaking. To himself he thought, I was born in the wrong century. A hundred years ago this wouldn't have happened and a hundred years from now it will be illegal. What I need is a lawyer.

His life had been a quiet one. He had, over the years, advanced to the modest position of floating-salesman. For a man twenty-two years old, that wasn't bad. He almost owned his one-room apartment; that is, he rented with an option to buy. It was a small life, as lives went; he did not ask too much and he did not complain—normally—at what he received. Although he did not understand the tax structure that cut through his income, he accepted it; he accepted a modified state of penury the same way he accepted it when a girl would not go to bed with him. In a sense this defined him; this was his measure. He submitted to what he did not like, and he regarded this attitude as a virtue. Most people in authority over him considered him a good person. As to those over whom *he* had authority, that was a class with zero members. His boss at Cloud Nine Homes told him what to do and his customers, really, told him what to do. The government told everyone what to do, or so he assumed. He had very few dealings with the government. That was neither a virtue nor a vice; it was simply good luck.

Once he had experienced vague dreams. They had to do with giving to the poor. In high school he had read Charles Dickens and a vivid idea of the oppressed had fixed itself in his mind to the point where he could see them: all those who did not have a one-room apartment and a job and a high school education. Certain vague place names had floated through his head, gleaned from TV, places like India, where heavy-duty machinery swept up the dying. Once a teaching machine had told him, *You have a good heart*. That amazed him—not that a machine would say so, but that it would say it to him. A girl had told him the same thing. He marveled at this. Vast forces colluding to tell him that he was not a bad person! It was a mystery and a delight.

But those days had passed. He no longer read novels, and the girl had been transferred to Frankfurt. Now he had been set up by a robot, a cheap machine, to shovel shit in the boonies, dragooned by a mechanical scam that was probably pulling citizens off the streets in record numbers. This was not a college he was going to; he had won nothing. He had won a stint at some kind of forced-labor camp, most likely. The exit door leads in, he thought to himself. Which is to say, when they want you they already have you; all they need is the paperwork. And a computer can process the forms at the touch of a key. The H key for hell and the S key for slave, he thought. And the Y key for you.

Don't forget your toothbrush, he thought. You may need it.

On the phone screen Major Casals regarded him, as if silently estimating the chances that Bob Bibleman might bolt. Two trillion to one I will, Bibleman thought. But the one will win, as in the contest; I'll do what I'm told.

'Please,' Bibleman said, 'let me ask you one thing, and give me an honest answer.'

'Of course,' Major Casals said.

'If I hadn't gone up to that Earl's Senior robot and—'

'We'd have gotten you anyhow,' Major Casals said.

'Okay,' Bibleman said, nodding. 'Thanks. It makes me feel better. I don't have to tell myself stupid stuff like, If only I hadn't felt like a hamburger and fries. If only–' He broke off. 'I'd better pack.'

Major Casals said, 'We've been running an evaluation on you for several months. You're overly endowed for the kind of work you do. And undereducated. You need more education. You're *entitled* to more education.'

Astonished, Bibleman said, 'You're talking about it as if it's a genuine college!'

'It is. It's the finest in the system. It isn't advertised; something like this can't be. No one selects it; the college selects you. Those were not joke odds that you saw posted. You can't really imagine being admitted to the finest college in the system by this method, can you, Mr Bibleman? You have a lot to learn.'

'How long will I be at the college?' Bibleman said.

Major Casals said, 'Until you have learned.'

They gave him a physical, a haircut, a uniform, and a place to bunk down, and many psychological tests. Bibleman suspected that the true purpose of the tests was to determine if he were a latent homosexual, and then he suspected that his suspicions indicated that he *was* a latent homosexual, so he abandoned the suspicions and supposed instead that they were sly intelligence and aptitude tests, and he informed himself that he was showing both: intelligence and aptitude. He also informed himself that he looked great in his uniform, even though it was the same uniform that everyone else wore. That is why they call it a uniform, he reminded himself as he sat on the edge of his bunk reading his orientation pamphlets.

The first pamphlet pointed out that it was a great honor to be admitted to the College. That was its name–the one word. How strange, he thought, puzzled. It's like naming your cat Cat and your dog Dog. This is my mother, Mrs Mother, and my father, Mr Father. Are these people working right? he wondered. It had been a phobia of his for years that someday he would fall into the hands of madmen—in particular, madmen who seemed sane up until the last moment. To Bibleman this was the essence of horror.

As he sat scrutinizing the pamphlets, a red-haired girl, wearing the College uniform, came over and seated herself beside him. She seemed perplexed.

'Maybe you can help me,' she said. 'What is a syllabus? It says here that we'll be given a syllabus. This place is screwing up my head.'

Bibleman said, 'We've been dragooned off the streets to shovel shit.'

'You think so?'

'I know so.'

'Can't we just leave?'

'You leave first,' Bibleman said. 'And I'll wait and see what happens to you.'

The girl laughed. 'I guess you don't know what a syllabus is.'

'Sure I do. It's an abstract of courses or topics.'

'Yes, and pigs can whistle.'

He regarded her. The girl regarded him.

'We're going to be here forever,' the girl said.

Her name, she told him, was Mary Lorne. She was, he decided, pretty, wistful, afraid, and putting up a good front. Together they joined the other new students for a showing of a recent Herbie the Hyena cartoon which Bibleman had seen; it was the episode in which Herbie attempted to assassinate the Russian monk Rasputin. In his usual fashion, Herbie the Hyena poisoned his victim, shot him, blew him up six times, stabbed him, tied him up with chains and sank him in the Volga, tore him apart with wild horses, and finally shot him to the moon strapped to a rocket. The cartoon bored Bibleman. He did not give a damn about Herbie the Hyena or Russian history and he wondered if this was a sample of the College's level of pedagogy. He could imagine Herbie the Hyena illustrating Heisenberg's indeterminacy principle. Herbie—in Bibleman's mind—chased after by a subatomic particle fruitlessly, the particle bobbing up at random here and there . . . Herbie making wild swings at it with a hammer; then a whole flock of subatomic particles jeering at Herbie, who was doomed as always to fuck up.

'What are you thinking about?' Mary whispered to him.

The cartoon ended; the hall lights came on. There stood Major Casals on the stage, larger than on the phone. The fun is over, Bibleman said to himself. He could not imagine Major Casals chasing subatomic particles fruitlessly with wild swings of a sledgehammer. He felt himself grow cold and grim and a little afraid.

The lecture had to do with classified information. Behind Major Casals a giant hologram lit up with a schematic diagram of a homeostatic drilling rig. Within the hologram the rig rotated so that they could see it from all angles. Different stages of the rig's interior glowed in various colors.

'I asked what you were thinking,' Mary whispered.

'We have to listen,' Bibleman said quietly.

Mary said, equally quietly, 'It finds titanium ore on its own. Big deal. Titanium is the ninth most abundant element in the crust of the planet. I'd be impressed if it could seek out and mine pure wurtzite, which is found only at Potosi, Bolivia; Butte, Montana; and Goldfield, Nevada.'

'Why is that?' Bibleman said.

'Because,' Mary said, 'wurtzite is unstable at temperatures below one thousand degrees centigrade. And further–' She broke off. Major Casals had ceased talking and was looking at her.

'Would you repeat that for all of us, young woman?' Major Casals said.

Standing, Mary said, 'Wurtzite is unstable at temperatures below one thousand degrees centigrade.' Her voice was steady.

Immediately the hologram behind Major Casals switched to a readout of data on zinc-sulfide minerals.

'I don't see "wurtzite" listed,' Major Casals said.

'It's given on the chart in its inverted form,' Mary said, her arms folded. 'Which is sphalerite. Correctly, it is ZnS, of the sulfide group of the AX type. It's related to greenockite.'

'Sit down,' Major Casals said. The readout within the hologram now showed the characteristics of greenockite.

As she seated herself, Mary said, 'I'm right. They don't have a homeostatic drilling rig for wurtzite because there is no—'

'Your name is?' Major Casals said, pen and pad poised.

'Mary Wurtz.' Her voice was totally without emotion. 'My father was Charles-Adolphe Wurtz.'

'The discoverer of wurtzite?' Major Casals said uncertainly; his pen wavered.

'That's right,' Mary said. Turning toward Bibleman, she winked.

'Thank you for the information,' Major Casals said. He made a motion and the hologram now showed a flying buttress and, in comparison to it, a normal buttress.

'My point,' Major Casals said, 'is simply that certain information such as architectural principles of long-standing—'

'Most architectural principles are long-standing,' Mary said.

Major Casals paused.

'Otherwise they'd serve no purpose,' Mary said.

'Why not?' Major Casals said, and then he colored.

Several uniformed students laughed.

'Information of that type,' Major Casals continued, 'is not classified. But a good deal of what you will be learning is classified. This is why the College is under military charter. To reveal or transmit or make public classified information given you during your schooling here falls under the jurisdiction of the military. For a breach of these statutes you would be tried by a military tribunal.'

The students murmured. To himself Bibleman thought, Banged, ganged, and then some. No one spoke. Even the girl beside him was silent. A complicated expression had crossed her face, however; a deeply introverted look, somber and—he thought—unusually mature. It made her seem older, no longer a girl. It made him wonder just how old she really was. It was as if in her features a thousand years had surfaced before him as he scrutinized her and pondered the officer on the stage and the great information hologram behind him. What is she thinking? he wondered. Is she going to say something more? How can she be not afraid to speak up? We've been told we are under military law.

Major Casals said, 'I am going to give you an instance of a strictly classified cluster of data. It deals with the Panther Engine.' Behind him the hologram, surprisingly, became blank.

'Sir,' one of the students said, 'the hologram isn't showing anything.'

'This is not an area that will be dealt with in your studies here,' Major Casals said. 'The Panther Engine is a two-rotor system, opposed rotors serving a common main shaft. Its main advantage is a total lack of centrifugal torque in the housing. A cam chain is thrown between the opposed rotors, which permits the main shaft to reverse itself without hysteresis.'

Behind him the big hologram remained blank. Strange, Bibleman thought. An eerie sensation: information without information, as if the computer had gone blind.

Major Casals said, 'The College is forbidden to release any information about the Panther Engine. It cannot be programmed to do otherwise. In fact, it knows nothing about the Panther Engine; it is programmed to destroy any information it receives in that sector.'

Raising his hand, a student said, 'So even if someone fed information into the College about the Panther–'

'It would eject the data,' Major Casals said.

'Is this a unique situation?' another student asked.

'No,' Major Casals said.

'Then there're a number of areas we can't get printouts for,' a student murmured.

'Nothing of importance,' Major Casals said. 'At least as far as your studies are concerned.'

The students were silent.

'The subjects which you will study,' Major Casals said, 'will be assigned to you, based on your aptitude and personality profiles. I'll call off your names and you will come forward for your allocation of topic assignment. The College itself has made the final decision for each of you, so you can be sure no error has been made.'

What if I get proctology? Bibleman asked himself. In panic he thought, Or podiatry. Or herpetology. Or suppose the College in its infinite computeroid wisdom decides to ram into me all the information in the universe pertaining to or resembling herpes labialis . . . or things even worse. If there is anything worse.

'What you want,' Mary said, as the names were read alphabetically, 'is a program that'll earn you a living. You have to be practical. I know what I'll get; I know where my strong point lies. It'll be chemistry.'

His name was called; rising, he walked up the aisle to Major Casals. They looked at each other, and then Casals handed him an unsealed envelope.

Stiffly, Bibleman returned to his seat.

'You want me to open it?' Mary said.

Wordlessly, Bibleman passed the envelope to her. She opened it and studied the printout.

'Can I earn a living with it?' he said.

She smiled. 'Yes, it's a high-paying field. Almost as good as— well, let's just say that the colony planets are really in need of this. You could go to work anywhere.'

Looking over her shoulder, he saw the words on the page.

COSMOLOGY COSMOGONY PRE-SOCRATICS

'Pre-Socratic philosophy,' Mary said. 'Almost as good as structural engineering.' She passed him the paper. 'I shouldn't kid you. No, it's not really something you can make a living at, unless you teach . . . but maybe it interests you. Does it interest you?'

'No,' he said shortly.

'I wonder why the College picked it, then,' Mary said.

'What the hell,' he said, 'is cosmogony?'

'How the universe came into being. Aren't you interested in how the universe—' She paused, eyeing him. 'You certainly won't

THE EXIT DOOR LEADS IN

be asking for printouts of any classified material,' she said meditatively. 'Maybe that's it,' she murmured, to herself. 'They won't have to watchdog you.'

'I can be trusted with classified material,' he said.

'Can you? Do you know yourself? But you'll be getting into that when the College bombards you with early Greek thought. "Know thyself." Apollo's motto at Delphi. It sums up half of Greek philosophy.'

Bibleman said, 'I'm not going up before a military tribunal for making public classified military material.' He thought, then, about the Panther Engine and he realized, fully realized, that a really grim message had been spelled out in that little lecture by Major Casals. 'I wonder what Herbie the Hyena's motto is,' he said.

'"I am determined to prove a villain,"' Mary said. '"And hate the idle pleasures of these days. Plots have I laid."' She reached out to touch him on the arm. 'Remember? The Herbie the Hyena cartoon version of *Richard the Third*.'

'Mary Lorne,' Major Casals said, reading off the list.

'Excuse me.' She went up, returned with her envelope, smiling. 'Leprology,' she said to Bibleman. 'The study and treatment of leprosy. I'm kidding; it's chemistry.'

'You'll be studying classified material,' Bibleman said.

'Yes,' she said. 'I know.'

On the first day of his study program, Bob Bibleman set his College input-output terminal on AUDIO and punched the proper key for his coded course.

'Thales of Miletus,' the terminal said. 'The founder of the Ionian school of natural philosophy.'

'What did he teach?' Bibleman said.

'That the world floated on water, was sustained by water, and originated in water.'

'That's really stupid,' Bibleman said.

The College terminal said, 'Thales based this on the discovery of fossil fish far inland, even at high altitudes. So it is not as stupid as it sounds.' It showed on its holoscreen a great deal of written information, no part of which struck Bibleman as very interesting. Anyhow, he had requested AUDIO. 'It is generally considered that Thales was the first rational man in history,' the terminal said.

'What about Ikhnaton?' Bibleman said.

'He was strange.'

'Moses?'

'Likewise strange.'

'Hammurabi?'

'How do you spell that?'

'I'm not sure. I've just heard the name.'

'Then we will discuss Anaximander,' the College terminal said. 'And, in a cursory initial survey, Anaximenes, Xenophanes, Paramenides, Melissus—wait a minute; I forgot Heraclitus and Cratylus. And we will study Empedocles, Anaxagoras, Zeno—'

'Christ,' Bibleman said.

'That's another program,' the College terminal said.

'Just continue,' Bibleman said.

'Are you taking notes?'

'That's none of your business.'

'You seem to be in a state of conflict.'

Bibleman said, 'What happens to me if I flunk out of the College?'

'You go to jail.'

'I'll take notes.'

'Since you are so driven—'

'What?'

'Since you are so full of conflict, you should find Empedocles interesting. He was the first dialectical philosopher. Empedocles believed that the basis of reality was an antithetical conflict between the forces of Love and Strife. Under Love the whole cosmos is a duly proportioned mixture, called a *krasis*. This *krasis* is a spherical deity, a single perfect mind which spends all its time—'

'Is there any practical application to any of this?' Bibleman interrupted.

'The two antithetical forces of Love and Strife resemble the Taoist elements of Yang and Yin with their perpetual interaction from which all change takes place.'

'Practical application.'

'Twin mutually opposed constituents.' On the holoscreen a schematic diagram, very complex, formed. 'The two-rotor Panther Engine.'

'What?' Bibleman said, sitting upright in his seat. He made out the large words PANTHER HYDRODRIVE SYSTEM TOP SECRET above the schematic comprising the readout. Instantly he pressed the PRINT key; the machinery of the terminal whirred and three sheets of paper slid down into the RETRIEVE slot.

They overlooked it, Bibleman realized, this entry in the College's memory banks relating to the Panther Engine. Somehow the cross-referencing got lost. No one thought of pre-Socratic philosophy—who would expect an entry on an engine, a modern-day top-secret engine, under the category PHILOSOPHY, PRE-SOCRATIC, subheading EMPEDOCLES?

I've got it in my hands, he said to himself as he swiftly lifted out the three sheets of paper. He folded them up and stuck them into the notebook the College had provided.

I've hit it, he thought. Right off the bat. Where the hell am I going to put these schematics? Can't hide them in my locker. And then he thought, Have I committed a crime already, by asking for a written printout?

'Empedocles,' the terminal was saying, 'believed in four elements as being perpetually rearranged: earth, water, air, and fire. These elements eternally—'

Click. Bibleman had shut the terminal down. The holoscreen faded to opaque gray.

Too much learning doth make a man slow, he thought as he got to his feet and started from the cubicle. Fast of wit but slow of foot. Where the hell am I going to hide the schematics? he asked himself again as he walked rapidly down the hall toward the ascent tube. Well, he realized, they don't know I have them; I can take my

THE EXIT DOOR LEADS IN

time. The thing to do is hide them at a random place, he decided, as the tube carried him to the surface. And even if they find them they won't be able to trace them back to me, not unless they go to the trouble of dusting for fingerprints.

This could be worth billions of dollars, he said to himself. A great joy filled him and then came the fear. He discovered that he was trembling. Will they ever be pissed, he said to himself. When they find out, *I* won't be pissing purple, *they'll* be pissing purple. The College itself will, when it discovers its error.

And the error, he thought, is on its part, not mine. The College fucked up and that's too bad.

In the dorm where his bunk was located, he found a laundry room maintained by a silent robot staff, and when no robot was watching he hid the three pages of schematics near the bottom of a huge pile of bed sheets. As high as the ceiling, this pile. They won't get down to the schematics this year. I have plenty of time to decide what to do.

Looking at his watch, he saw that the afternoon had almost come to an end. At five o'clock he would be seated in the cafeteria, eating dinner with Mary.

She met him a little after five o'clock; her face showed signs of fatigue.

'How'd it go?' she asked him as they stood in line with their trays.

'Fine,' Bibleman said.

'Did you get to Zeno? I always like Zeno; he proved that motion is impossible. So I guess I'm still in my mother's womb. You look strange.' She eyed him.

'Just sick of listening to how the earth rests on the back of a giant turtle.'

'Or is suspended on a long string,' Mary said. Together they made their way among the other students to an empty table. 'You're not eating much.'

'Feeling like eating,' Bibleman said as he drank his cup of coffee, 'is what got me here in the first place.'

'You could flunk out.'

'And go to jail.'

Mary said, 'The College is programmed to say that. Much of it is probably just threats. Talk loudly and carry a small stick, so to speak.'

'I have it,' Bibleman said.

'You have what?' She ceased eating and regarded him.

He said, 'The Panther Engine.'

Gazing at him, the girl was silent.

'The schematics,' he said.

'Lower your goddam voice.'

'They missed a citation in the memory storage. Now that I have them I don't know what to do. Just start walking, probably. And hope no one stops me.'

'They don't know? The College didn't self-monitor?'

'I have no reason to think it's aware of what it did.'

'Jesus Christ,' Mary said softly. 'On your first day. You had better do a lot of slow, careful thinking.'

'I can destroy them,' he said.

'Or sell them.'

He said, 'I looked them over. There's an analysis on the final page. The Panther—'

'Just say it,' Mary said.

'It can be used as a hydroelectric turbine and cut costs in half. I couldn't understand the technical language, but I did figure out that. Cheap power source. Very cheap.'

'So everyone would benefit.'

He nodded.

'They really screwed up,' Mary said. 'What was it Casals told us? "Even if someone fed data into the College about the—about it, the College would eject the data."' She began eating slowly, meditatively. 'And they're withholding it from the public. It must be industry pressure. Nice.'

'What should I do?' Bibleman said.

'I can't tell you that.'

'What I was thinking is that I could take the schematics to one of the colony planets where the authorities have less control. I could find an independent firm and make a deal with them. The government wouldn't know how–'

'They'd figure out where the schematics came from,' Mary said. 'They'd trace it back to you.'

'Then I better burn them.'

Mary said, 'You have a very difficult decision to make. On the one hand, you have classified information in your possession which you obtained illegally. On the other–'

'I didn't obtain it illegally. The College screwed up.'

Calmly, she continued, 'You broke the law, military law, when you asked for a written transcript. You should have reported the breach of security as soon as you discovered it. They would have rewarded you. Major Casals would have said nice things to you.'

'I'm scared,' Bibleman said, and he felt the fear moving around inside him, shifting about and growing; as he held his plastic coffee cup it shook, and some of the coffee spilled onto his uniform.

Mary, with a paper napkin, dabbed at the coffee stain.

'It won't come off,' she said.

'Symbolism,' Bibleman said. 'Lady Macbeth. I always wanted to have a dog named Spot so I could say, "Out, out, damned Spot."'

'I am not going to tell you what to do,' Mary said. 'This is a decision that you will make alone. It isn't ethical for you even to discuss it with me; that could be considered conspiracy and put us both in prison.'

'Prison,' he echoed.

'You have it within your–Christ, I was going to say, "You have it within your power to provide a cheap power source to human civilization."' She laughed and shook her head. 'I guess this scares me, too. Do what you think is right. If you think it's right to publish the schematics–'

'I never thought of that. Just publish them. Some magazine or newspaper. A slave printing construct could print it and distribute it all over the solar system in fifteen minutes.' All I have to do, he realized, is pay the fee and then feed in the three pages of schematics. As simple as that. And then spend the rest of my life in jail or anyhow in court. Maybe the adjudication would go in my favor. There are precedents in history where vital classified material—military classified material—was stolen and published, and not only was the person found innocent but we now realize that he was a hero; he served the welfare of the human race itself, and risked his life.

Approaching their table, two armed military security guards closed in on Bob Bibleman; he stared at them, not believing what he saw but thinking, *Believe it.*

'Student Bibleman?' one of them said.

'It's on my uniform,' Bibleman said.

'Hold out your hands, Student Bibleman.' The larger of the two security guards snapped handcuffs on him.

Mary said nothing; she continued slowly eating.

In Major Casals' office Bibleman waited, grasping the fact that he was being—as the technical term had it—'detained.' He felt glum. He wondered what they would do. He wondered if he had been set up. He wondered what he would do if he were charged. He wondered why it was taking so long. And then he wondered what it was all about really and he wondered whether he would understand the grand issues if he continued with his courses in COSMOLOGY COSMOGONY PRE-SOCRATICS.

Entering the office, Major Casals said briskly, 'Sorry to keep you waiting.'

'Can these handcuffs be removed?' Bibleman said. They hurt his wrists; they had been clapped onto him as tightly as possible. His bone structure ached.

'We couldn't find the schematics,' Casals said, seating himself behind his desk.

'What schematics?'

'For the Panther Engine.'

'There aren't supposed to be any schematics for the Panther Engine. You told us that in orientation.'

'Did you program your terminal for that deliberately? Or did it just happen to come up?'

'My terminal programmed itself to talk about water,' Bibleman said. 'The universe is composed of water.'

'It automatically notified security when you asked for a written transcript. All written transcripts are monitored.'

'Fuck you,' Bibleman said.

Major Casals said, 'I tell you what. We're only interested in getting the schematics back; we're not interested in putting you in the slam. Return them and you won't be tried.'

'Return what?' Bibleman said, but he knew it was a waste of time. 'Can I think it over?'

'Yes.'

'Can I go? I feel like going to sleep. I'm tired. I feel like having these cuffs off.'

Removing the cuffs, Major Casals said, 'We made an agreement, with all of you, an agreement between the College and the students, about classified material. You entered into that agreement.'

'Freely?' Bibleman said.

'Well, no. But the agreement was known to you. When you discovered the schematics for the Panther Engine encoded in the College's memory and available to anyone who happened for any reason, any reason whatsoever, to ask for a practical application of pre-Socratic—'

'I was as surprised as hell,' Bibleman said. 'I still am.'

'Loyalty is an ethical principle. I'll tell you what; I'll waive the punishment factor and put it on the basis of loyalty to the College. A responsible person obeys laws and agreements entered into. Return the schematics and you can continue your courses here at the College. In fact, we'll give you permission to select what subjects you want; they won't be assigned to you. I think you're good College material. Think it over and report back to me tomorrow morning, between eight and nine, here in my office. Don't talk to anyone; don't try to discuss it. You'll be watched. Don't try to leave the grounds. Okay?'

'Okay,' Bibleman said woodenly.

He dreamed that night that he had died. In his dream vast spaces stretched out, and his father was coming toward him, very slowly, out of a dark glade and into the sunlight. His father seemed glad to see him, and Bibleman felt his father's love.

When he awoke, the feeling of being loved by his father remained. As he put on his uniform, he thought about his father and how rarely, in actual life, he had gotten that love. It made him feel lonely, now, his father being dead and his mother as well. Killed in a nuclear-power accident, along with a whole lot of other people.

They say someone important to you waits for you on the other side, he thought. Maybe by the time I die Major Casals will be dead and he will be waiting for me, to greet me gladly. Major Casals and my father combined as one.

What am I going to do? he asked himself. They have waived the punitive aspects; it's reduced to essentials, a matter of loyalty. Am I a loyal person? Do I qualify?

The hell with it, he said to himself. He looked at his watch. Eight-thirty. My father would be proud of me, he thought. For what I am going to do.

Going into the laundry room, he scoped out the situation. No robots in sight. He dug down in the pile of bed sheets, found the pages of schematics, took them out, looked them over, and headed for the tube that would take him to Major Casals' office.

'You have them,' Casals said as Bibleman entered. Bibleman handed the three sheets of paper over to him.

'And you made no other copies?' Casals asked.

'No.'

'You give me your word of honor?'

'Yes,' Bibleman said.

'You are herewith expelled from the College,' Major Casals said.

'What?' Bibleman said.

Casals pressed a button on his desk. 'Come in.'

The door opened and Mary Lorne stood there.

'I do not represent the College,' Major Casals said to Bibleman. 'You were set up.'

'I am the College,' Mary said.

Major Casals said, 'Sit down, Bibleman. She will explain it to you before you leave.'

'I failed?' Bibleman said.

'You failed me,' Mary said. 'The purpose of the test was to teach you to stand on your own feet, even if it meant challenging authority. The covert message of institutions is: "Submit to that which you psychologically construe as an authority." A good school trains the whole person; it isn't a matter of data and information; I was trying to make you morally and psychologically complete. But a person can't be commanded to disobey. You can't order someone to rebel. All I could do was give you a model, an example.'

Bibleman thought, When she talked back to Casals at the initial orientation. He felt numb.

'The Panther Engine is worthless,' Mary said, 'as a technological artifact. This is a standard test we use on each student, no matter what study course he is assigned.'

'They *all* got a readout on the Panther Engine?' Bibleman said with disbelief. He stared at the girl.

'They will, one by one. Yours came very quickly. First you are told that it is classified; you are told the penalty for releasing classified information; then you are leaked the information. It is hoped that you will make it public or at least try to make it public.'

Major Casals said, 'You saw on the third page of the printout that the engine supplied an economical source of hydroelectric power. That was important. You knew that the public would benefit if the engine design was released.'

'And legal penalties were waived,' Mary said. 'So what you did was not done out of fear.'

'Loyalty,' Bibleman said. 'I did it out of loyalty.'

'To what?' Mary said.

He was silent; he could not think.

'To a holoscreen?' Major Casals said.

'To you,' Bibleman said.

Major Casals said, 'I am someone who insulted you and derided you. Someone who treated you like dirt. I told you that if I ordered you to piss purple, you—'

'Okay,' Bibleman said. 'Enough.'

'Goodbye,' Mary said.

'What?' Bibleman said, startled.

'You're leaving. You're going back to your life and job, what you had before we picked you.'

Bibleman said, 'I'd like another chance.'

'But,' Mary said, 'you know how the test works now. So it can never be given to you again. You know what is really wanted from you by the College. I'm sorry.'

'I'm sorry, too,' Major Casals said.

Bibleman said nothing.

Holding out her hand, Mary said, 'Shake?'

Blindly, Bibleman shook hands with her. Major Casals only stared at him blankly; he did not offer his hand. He seemed to be engrossed in some other topic, perhaps some other person. Another student was on his mind, perhaps. Bibleman could not tell.

Three nights later, as he wandered aimlessly through the mixture of lights and darkness of the city, Bob Bibleman saw ahead of him a robot food vendor at its eternal post. A teenage boy was in the process of buying a taco and an apple turnover. Bob Bibleman lined up behind the boy and stood waiting, his hands in his pockets, no thoughts coming to him, only a dull feeling, a sense of emptiness. As if the inattention which he had seen on Casals' face had taken him over, he thought to himself. He felt like an object, an object among objects, like the robot vendor. Something which, as he well knew, did not look you directly in the eye.

'What'll it be, sir?' the robot asked.

Bibleman said, 'Fries, a cheeseburger, and a strawberry shake. Are there any contests?'

After a pause the robot said, 'Not for you, Mr Bibleman.'

'Okay,' he said, and stood waiting.

The food came, on its little throwaway plastic tray, in its little throwaway cartons.

'I'm not paying,' Bibleman said, and walked away.

The robot called after him, 'Eleven hundred dollars. Mr Bibleman. You're breaking the law!'

He turned, got out his wallet.

'Thank you, Mr Bibleman,' the robot said. 'I am very proud of you.'

CHAINS OF AIR,
WEB OF AETHER

The planet on which he was living underwent each day two mornings. First CY30 appeared and then its minor twin put in a feeble appearance, as if God had not been able to make up His mind as to which sun He preferred and had finally settled on both. The domers liked to compare it to sequential settings of an old-fashioned multifilament incandescent bulb. CY30 gave the impression of getting up to about 150 watts and then came little CY30B, which added 50 more watts of light. The aggregate lumina made the methane crystals of the planet's surface sparkle pleasantly, assuming you were indoors.

At the table of his dome, Leo McVane drank fake coffee and read the newspaper. He felt anxiety-free and warm because he had long ago illegally redesigned his dome's thermostat. He felt safe as well because he had added an extra metal brace to the dome's hatch. And he felt expectant because today the food man would be by, so there would be someone to talk to. It was a good day.

All his communications gear fumbled along on autostasis, at the moment, monitoring whatever the hell they monitored. Originally, upon being stationed at CY30 II, McVane had thoroughly studied the function and purpose of the complexes of electronic marvels for which he was the caretaker—or rather, as his job coding put it, the 'master homonoid overseer.' Now he had allowed himself to forget most of the transactions which his charges engaged in. Communications equipment led a monotonous life until an emergency popped up, at which point he ceased suddenly to be the 'master homonoid overseer' and became the living brain of his station.

There had not been an emergency yet.

The newspaper contained a funny item from the United States Federal Income Tax booklet for 1978, the year McVane had been born. These entries appeared in the index in this order:

> Who Should File
> Widows and Widowers, Qualifying
> Winnings—Prizes, Gambling, and Lotteries
> Withholding—Federal Tax

And then the final entry in the index, which McVane found amusing and even interesting as a commentary on an archaic way of life:

> Zero Bracket Amount

To himself, McVane grinned. That was how the United States Federal Income Tax booklet's 1978 index had ended, very appropriately, and that was how the United States, a few years later, had ended. It had fiscally fucked itself over and died of the trauma.

'Food ration comtrix,' the audio transducer of his radio announced. 'Start unbolting procedure.'

'Unbolting under way,' McVane said, laying aside his newspaper.

The speaker said, 'Put helmet on.'

'Helmet on.' McVane made no move to pick up his helmet; his atmosphere flow rate would compensate for the loss; he had redesigned it, too.

The hatch unscrewed, and there stood the food man, head-bubble and all. An alarm bell in the dome's ceiling shrilled that atmospheric pressure had sharply declined.

'Put your helmet on!' the food man ordered angrily.

The alarm bell ceased complaining; the pressure had restabilized. At that, the food man grimaced. He popped his helmet and then began to unload cartons from his comtrix.

'We are a hardy race,' McVane said, helping him.

'You have amped up everything,' the food man observed; like all the rovers who serviced domes, he was sturdily built and he moved rapidly. It was not a safe job operating a comtrix shuttle between mother ships and the domes of CY30 II. He knew it, and McVane knew it. Anybody could sit in a dome; few people could function outside.

'Stick around for a while,' McVane said after he and the food man had unloaded and the food man was marking the invoice.

'If you have coffee.'

They sat facing each other across the table, drinking coffee. Outside the dome the methane messed around, but here neither man felt it. The food man perspired; he apparently found McVane's temperature level too high.

'You know the woman in the next dome?' the food man asked.

'Somewhat,' McVane said. 'My rig transfers data to her input circuitry every three or four weeks. She stores it, boosts it, and transmits it. I suppose. Or for all I know–'

'She's sick,' the food man said.

McVane said, 'She looked all right the last time I talked to her. We used video. She did say something about having trouble reading her terminal's displays.'

'She's dying,' the food man said, and sipped his coffee.

In his mind, McVane tried to picture the woman. Small and dark, and what was her name? He punched a couple of keys on the board beside him, her name came up on its display, retrieved by the code they used. Rybus Rommey. 'Dying of what?' he said.

'Multiple sclerosis.'

'How far advanced is it?'

'Not far at all,' the food man said. 'A couple of months ago, she told me that when she was in her late teens she suffered an–what is it called? Aneurysm. In her left eye, which wiped out her central vision in that eye. They suspected at the time that it might be the onset of multiple sclerosis. And then today when I talked to her she said she's been experiencing optic neuritis, which–'

McVane said, 'Both symptoms were fed to MED?'

'A correlation of an aneurysm and then a period of remission and then double vision, blurring . . . you ought to call her up and talk to her. When I was delivering to her, she was crying.'

Turning to his keyboard, McVane punched out and punched out and then read the display. 'There's a thirty to forty percent cure rate for multiple sclerosis.'

'Not out here. MED can't get to her out here.'

'Shit,' McVane said.

'I told her to demand a transfer back home. That's what I'd do. She won't do it.'

'She's crazy,' McVane said.

'You're right. She's crazy. Everybody out here is crazy. You want proof of it? She's proof of it. Would you go back home if you knew you were very sick?'

'We're never supposed to surrender our domes.'

'What you monitor is so important.' The food man set down his cup. 'I have to go.' As he got to his feet, he said, 'Call her and talk to her. She needs someone to talk to and you're the closest dome. I'm surprised she didn't tell you.'

McVane thought, I didn't ask.

After the food man had departed, McVane got the code for Rybus Rommey's dome, and started to run it into his transmitter, and then hesitated. His wall clock showed 18:30 hours. At this point in his forty-two-hour cycle, he was supposed to accept a sequence of high-speed entertainment audio- and videotaped signals emanating from a slave satellite at CY30 III; upon storing them, he was to run them back at normal and select the material suitable for the overall dome system on his own planet.

He took a look at the log. Fox was doing a concert that ran two hours. Linda Fox, he thought. You and your synthesis of old-time rock and modern-day strong. Jesus, he thought. If I don't transcribe the relay of your live concert, every domer on the planet will come storming in here and kill me. Outside of emergencies—which don't occur—this is what I'm paid to handle: information traffic between planets, information that connects us with home and keeps us human. The tape drums have got to turn.

He started the tape transport at its high-speed mode, set the module's controls for receive, locked it in at the satellite's operating frequency, checked the wave-form on the visual scope to be sure that the carrier was coming in undistorted, and then patched into an audio transduction of what he was getting.

The voice of Linda Fox emerged from the strip of drivers mounted above him. As the scope showed, there was no distortion. No noise. No clipping. All channels, in fact, were balanced; his meters indicated that.

Sometimes I could cry myself when I hear her, he thought. Speaking of crying.

> 'Wandering all across this land,
> My band.
> In the worlds that pass above,
> I love.
> Play for me, you spirits who are weightless.
> I believe in drinking to your greatness.
> My band.'

And behind Linda Fox's vocal, the syntholutes which were her trademark. Until Fox, no one had ever thought of bringing back that sixteenth-century instrument for which Dowland had written so beautifully and so effectively.

> 'Shall I sue? shall I seek for grace?
> Shall I pray? shall I prove?
> Shall I strive to a heavenly joy
> With an earthly love?
> Are there worlds? are there moons
> Where the lost shall endure?
> Shall I find for a heart that is pure?'

What Linda Fox had done was take the lute books of John Dow-land, written at the end of the sixteenth century, and remastered both the melodies and the lyrics into something of today. Some new thing, he thought, for scattered people as flung as if they had been dropped in haste: here and there, disarranged, in domes, on the backs of miserable worlds and in satellites–victimized by the power of migration, and with no end in sight.

> *'Silly wretch, let me rail*
> *At a trip that is blind.*
> *Holy hopes do require'*

He could not remember the rest. Well, he had it taped, of course.

> *'. . . no human may find.'*

Or something like that. The beauty of the universe lay not in the stars figured into it but in the music generated by human minds, human voices, human hands. Syntholutes mixed on an intricate board by experts, and the voice of Fox. He thought, I know what I must have to keep on going. My job is delight: I transcribe this and I broadcast it and they pay me.

'This is the Fox,' Linda Fox said.

McVane switched the video to holo, and a cube formed in which Linda Fox smiled at him. Meanwhile, the drums spun at furious speed, getting hour upon hour into his permanent possession.

'You are with the Fox,' she said, 'and the Fox is with *you*.' She pinned him with her gaze, the hard, bright eyes. The diamond face, feral and wise, feral and true; this is the Fox speaking to you. He smiled back.

'Hi, Fox,' he said.

Sometime later he called the sick girl in the next dome. It took her an amazingly long time to respond to his signal, and as he sat noting the signal register on his own board he thought, Is she fin-ished? Or did they come and forcibly evacuate her?

His microscreen showed vague colors. Visual static, nothing more. And then there she was.

'Did I wake you up?' he asked. She seemed so slowed down, so torpid. Perhaps, he thought, she's sedated.

'No. I was shooting myself in the ass.'

'What?' he said, startled.

'Chemotherapy,' Rybus said. 'I'm not doing too well.'

'I just now taped a terrific Linda Fox concert; I'll be broadcasting it in the next few days. It'll cheer you up.'

'It's too bad we're stuck in these domes. I wish we could visit one another. The food man was just here. In fact, he brought me my medication. It's effective, but it makes me throw up.'

McVane thought, I wish I hadn't called.

'Is there any way you could visit me?' Rybus asked.

'I have no portable air, none at all.'

'I have,' Rybus said.

In panic, he said, 'But if you're sick—'

'I can make it over to your dome.'

'What about your station? What if data come in that—'

'I've got a beeper I can bring with me.'

Presently he said, 'Okay.'

'It would mean a lot to me, someone to sit with for a little while. The food man stays like half an hour, but that's as long as he can. You know what he told me? There's been an outbreak of a form of amyotrophic lateral sclerosis on CY30 VI. It must be a virus. This whole condition is a virus. Christ, I'd hate to have amyotrophic lateral sclerosis. This is like the Mariana form.'

'Is it contagious?'

She did not directly answer. Instead she said, 'What I have can be cured.' Obviously she wanted to reassure him. 'If the virus is around . . . I won't come over; it's okay.' She nodded and reached to shut off her transmitter. 'I'm going to lie down,' she said, 'and get more sleep. With this you're supposed to sleep as much as you can. I'll talk to you tomorrow. Goodbye.'

'Come over,' he said.

Brightening, she said, 'Thank you.'

'But be sure you bring your beeper. I have a hunch a lot of tele-metric confirms are going to—'

'Oh, fuck the telemetric confirms!' Rybus said, with venom. 'I'm so sick of being stuck in this goddam dome! Aren't you going buggy sitting around watching tape drums turn and little meters and gauges and shit?'

'I think you should go back home,' he said.

'No,' she said, more calmly. 'I'm going to follow exactly the MED instructions for my chemotherapy and beat this fucking MS. I'm not going home. I'll come over and fix your dinner. I'm a good cook. My mother was Italian and my father is Chicano so I spice everything I fix, except you can't get spices out here. But I figured out how to beat that with different synthetics. I've been experimenting.'

'In this concert I'm going to be broadcasting,' McVane said, 'the Fox does a version of Dowland's "Shall I Sue."'

'A song about litigation?'

'No. "Sue" in the sense of to pay court to or woo. In matters of love.' And then he realized that she was putting him on.

'Do you want to know what I think of the Fox?' Rybus asked. 'Recycled sentimentality, which is the worst kind of sentimental-ity; it isn't even original. And she looks like her face is on upside down. She has a mean mouth.'

'I like her,' he said stiffly; he felt himself becoming mad, really mad. I'm supposed to help you? he asked himself. Run the risk of catching what you have so you can insult the Fox?

'I'll fix you beef stroganoff with parsley noodles,' Rybus said.

'I'm doing fine,' he said.

Hesitating, she said in a low, faltering voice, 'Then you don't want me to come over?'

'I—' he said.

'I'm very frightened, Mr McVane,' Rybus said. 'Fifteen minutes from now, I'm going to be throwing up from the IV Neurotoxite. But I don't want to be alone. I don't want to give up my dome and

I don't want to be by myself. I'm sorry if I offended you. It's just that to me the Fox is a joke. I won't say anything more; I promise.'

'Do you have the–' He amended what he intended to say. 'Are you sure it won't be too much for you, fixing dinner?'

'I'm stronger now than I will be,' she said. 'I'll be getting weaker for a long time.'

'How long?'

'There's no way to tell.'

He thought, You are going to die. He knew it and she knew it. They did not have to talk about it. The complicity of silence was there, the agreement. A dying girl wants to cook me a dinner, he thought. A dinner I don't want to eat. *I've got to say no to her. I've got to keep her out of my dome.* The insistence of the weak, he thought. Their dreadful power. It is so much easier to throw a body block against the strong!

'Thank you,' he said. 'I'd like it very much if we had dinner together. But make sure you keep radio contact with me on your way over here–so I'll know you're okay. Promise?'

'Well, sure,' she said. 'Otherwise'–she smiled–'they'd find me a century from now, frozen with pots, pans, and food, as well as synthetic spices. You do have portable air, don't you?

'No, I really don't,' he said.

And knew that his lie was palpable to her.

The meal smelled good and tasted good, but halfway through Rybus excused herself and made her way unsteadily from the matrix of the dome–his dome–into the bathroom. He tried not to listen; he arranged it with his percept system not to hear and with his cognition not to know. In the bathroom the girl, violently sick, cried out and he gritted his teeth and pushed his plate away and then all at once he got up and set in motion his in-dome audio system; he played an early album of the Fox.

> 'Come again!
> Sweet love doth now invite

> *Thy graces, that refrain*
> *To do me due delight . . .'*

'Do you by any chance have some milk?' Rybus asked, standing at the bathroom door, her face pale.

Silently, he got her a glass of milk, or what passed for milk on their planet.

'I have antiemetics,' Rybus said as she held the glass of milk, 'but I didn't remember to bring any with me. They're back at my dome.'

'I could get them for you,' he said.

'You know what MED told me?' Her voice was heavy with indignation. 'They said that this chemotherapy won't make my hair fall out, but already it's coming out in–'

'Okay,' he interrupted.

'*Okay?*'

'I'm sorry,' he said.

'This is upsetting you,' Rybus said. 'The meal is spoiled and you're–I don't know what. If I'd remembered to bring my anti-emetics, I'd be able to keep from–' She became silent. 'Next time I'll bring them. I promise. This is one of the few albums of Fox that I like. She was really good then, don't you think?'

'Yes,' he said tightly.

'Linda Box,' Rybus said.

'What?' he said.

'Linda the box. That's what my sister and I used to call her.' She tried to smile.

'Please go back to your dome.'

'Oh,' she said. 'Well–' She smoothed her hair, her hand shaking. 'Will you come with me? I don't think I can make it by myself right now. I'm really weak. I really am sick.'

He thought, You are taking me with you. That's what this is. That is what is happening. You will not go alone; you will take my spirit with you. And you know. You know it as well as you know the name of the medication you are taking, and you hate me as you hate the medication, as you hate MED and your illness; it is all hate, for each and every thing under these two suns. I know you. I understand you. I see what is coming. In fact, it has begun.

And, he thought, I don't blame you. But I will hang onto the Fox; the Fox will outlast you. And so will I. You are not going to shoot down the luminiferous aether which animates our souls.

I will hang onto the Fox and the Fox will hold me in her arms and hang onto me. The two of us—we can't be pried apart. I have dozens of hours of the Fox on audio- and videotape, and the tapes are not just for me but for everybody. You think you can kill that? he said to himself. It's been tried before. The power of the weak, he thought, is an imperfect power; it loses in the end. Hence its name. We call it weak for a reason.

'Sentimentality,' Rybus said.

'Right,' he said sardonically.

'Recycled at that.'

'And mixed metaphors.'

'Her lyrics?'

'What I'm thinking. When I get really angry, I mix—'

'Let me tell you something. One thing. If I am going to survive, I can't be sentimental. I have to be very harsh. If I've made you angry, I'm sorry, but that is how it is. It is my life. Someday you may be in the spot I am in and then you'll know. Wait for that and then judge me. If it ever happens. Meanwhile this stuff you're playing on your in-dome audio system is crap. It has to be crap, for me. Do you see? You can forget about me; you can send me back to my dome, where I probably really belong, but if you have anything to do with me—'

'Okay,' he said, 'I understand.'

'Thank you. May I have some more milk? Turn down the audio and we'll finish eating. Okay?'

Amazed, he said, 'You're going to keep on trying to—'

'All those creatures—and species—who gave up trying to eat aren't with us anymore.' She seated herself unsteadily, holding onto the table.

'I admire you.'

'No,' she said. 'I admire *you*. It's harder on you. I know.'

'Death—' he began.

'This isn't death. You know what this is? In contrast to what's coming out of your audio system? This is life. The milk, please; I really need it.'

As he got her more milk, he said, 'I guess you can't shoot down aether. Luminiferous or otherwise.'

'No,' she agreed, 'since it doesn't exist.'

Commodity Central provided Rybus with two wigs, since, due to the chemo, her hair had been systematically killed. He preferred the light-colored one.

When she wore her wig, she did not look too bad, but she had become weakened and a certain querulousness had crept into her discourse. Because she was not physically strong any longer—due more, he suspected, to the chemotherapy than to her illness—she could no longer manage to maintain her dome adequately. Making his way over there one day, he was shocked at what he found. Dishes, pots and pans and even glasses of spoiled food, dirty clothes strewn everywhere, litter and debris . . . troubled, he cleaned up for her and, to his vast dismay, realized that there was an odor pervading her dome, a sweet mixture of the smell of illness, of complex medications, the soiled clothing, and, worst of all, the rotting food itself.

Until he cleaned an area, there was not even a place for him to sit. Rybus lay in bed, wearing a plastic robe open at the back. Apparently, however, she still managed to operate her electronic equipment; he noted that the meters indicated full activity. But she used the remote programmer normally reserved for emergency conditions; she lay propped up in bed with the programmer beside her, along with a magazine and a bowl of cereal and several bottles of medication.

As before, he discussed the possibility of getting her transferred. She refused to be taken off her job; she had not budged.

'I'm not going into a hospital,' she told him, and that, for her, ended the conversation.

Later, back at his own dome, gratefully back, he put a plan into operation. The large AI System—Artificial Intelligence Plasma—which handled the major problem-solving for star systems in their area of the galaxy had some available time which could be bought for private use. Accordingly, he punched in an application and posted the total sum of financial credits he had saved up during the last few months.

From Fomalhaut, where the Plasma drifted, he received back a positive response. The team which handled traffic for the Plasma was agreeing to sell him fifteen minutes of the Plasma's time.

At the rate at which he was being metered, he was motivated to feed the Plasma his data very skillfully and very rapidly. He told the Plasma who Rybus was—which gave the AI System access to her complete files, including her psychological profile—and he told it that his dome was the closest dome to her, and he told it of her fierce determination to live and her refusal to accept a medical discharge or even transfer from her station. He cupped his head into the shell for psychotronic output so that the Plasma at Fomalhaut could draw directly from his thoughts, thus making available to it all his unconscious, marginal impressions, realizations, doubts, ideas, anxieties, needs.

'There will be a five-day delay in response,' the team signaled him. 'Because of the distance involved. Your payment has been received and recorded. Over.'

'Over,' he said, feeling glum. He had spent everything he had. A vacuum had consumed his worth. But the Plasma was the court of last appeal in matters of problem-solving. WHAT SHOULD I DO? he had asked the Plasma. In five days he would have the answer.

During the next five days, Rybus became considerably weaker. She still fixed her own meals, however, although she seemed to eat the same thing over and over again: a dish of high-protein macaroni with grated cheese sprinkled over it. One day he found her wearing dark glasses. She did not want him to see her eyes.

'My bad eye has gone berserk,' she said dispassionately. 'Rolled up in my head like a window shade.' Spilled capsules and tablets lay everywhere around her on her bed. He picked up one of the half-empty bottles and saw that she was taking one of the most powerful analgesics available.

'MED is prescribing this for you?' he said, wondering, Is she in that much pain?

'I know somebody,' Rybus said. 'At a dome on IV. The food man brought it over to me.'

'This stuff is addictive.'

'I'm lucky to get it. I shouldn't really have it.'

'I know you shouldn't.'

'That goddam MED.' The vindictiveness of her tone was surprising. 'It's like dealing with a lower life-form. By the time they get around to prescribing, and then getting the medication to you, Christ, you're an urn of ashes. I see no point in them prescribing for an urn of ashes.' She put her hand up to her skull. 'I'm sorry; I should keep my wig on when you're here.'

'It doesn't matter,' he said.

'Could you bring me some Coke? Coke settles my stomach.'

From her refrigerator he took a liter bottle of cola and poured her a glass. He had to wash the glass first; there wasn't a clean one in the dome.

Propped up before her at the foot of her bed, she had her standard-issue TV set going. It gabbled away mindlessly, but no one was listening or watching. He realized that every time he came over she had it on, even in the middle of the night.

When he returned to his own dome, he felt a tremendous sense of relief, of an odious burden being lifted from him. Just to put physical distance between himself and her—that was a joy which raised his spirits. It's as if, he thought, when I'm with her I have what she has. We share the illness.

He did not feel like playing any Fox recordings so instead he put on the Mahler Second Symphony, the 'Resurrection.' The only symphony scored for many pieces of rattan, he mused. A Ruthe, which looks like a small broom; they use it to play the bass drum.

CHAINS OF AIR, WEB OF AETHER

Too bad Mahler never saw a Morley wah-wah pedal, he thought, or he would have scored it into one of his longer symphonies.

Just as the chorus came in, his in-dome audio system shut down; an extrinsic override had silenced it.

'Transmission from Fomalhaut.'

'Standing by.'

'Use video, please. Ten seconds till start.'

'Thank you,' he said.

A readout appeared on his larger screen. It was the AI System, the Plasma, replying a day early.

SUBJECT: RYBUS ROMMEY

ANALYSIS: THANATOUS

PROGRAM ADVICE: TOTAL AVOIDANCE ON YOUR PART

ETHICAL FACTOR: OBVIATED

THANK YOU

Blinking, McVane said reflexively, 'Thank you.' He had dealt with the Plasma only once before and he had forgotten how terse its responses were. The screen cleared; the transmission had ended.

He was not sure what 'thanatous' meant, but he felt certain that it had something to do with death. It means she is dying, he pondered as he punched into the planet's reference bank and asked for a definition. It means that she is dying or may die or is close to death, all of which I know.

However, he was wrong. It meant *producing death*.

Producing, he thought. There is a great difference between *death* and *producing death*. No wonder the AI System had notified him that the ethical factor was obviated on his part.

She is a killer thing, he realized. Well, this is why it costs so much to consult the Plasma. You get—not a phony answer based on speculation—but an absolute response.

While he was thinking about it and trying to calm himself down, his telephone rang. Before he picked it up he knew who it was.

'Hi,' Rybus said in a trembling voice.

'Hi,' he said.

'Do you by any chance have any Celestial Seasonings Morning Thunder tea bags?'

'What?' he said.

'When I was over at your dome that time I fixed beef stroganoff for us, I thought I saw a canister of Celestial Seasonings–'

'No,' he said. 'I don't. I used them up.'

'Are you all right?'

'I'm just tired,' he said, and he thought, She said 'us.' She and I are an 'us.' When did that happen? he asked himself. I guess that's what the Plasma meant; it understood.

'Do you have any kind of tea?'

'No,' he said. His in-dome audio system suddenly came back on, released from its pause mode now that the Fomalhaut transmission had ended. The choir was singing.

On the phone, Rybus giggled. 'Fox is doing sound on sound? A whole chorus of a thousand–'

'This is Mahler,' he said roughly.

'Do you think you could come over and keep me company?' Rybus asked. 'I'm sort of at loose ends.'

After a moment, he said, 'Okay. There's something I want to talk to you about.'

'I was reading this article in–'

'When I get there,' he broke in, 'we can talk. I'll see you in half an hour.' He hung up the phone.

When he reached her dome, he found her propped up in bed, wearing her dark glasses and watching a soap opera on her TV. Nothing had changed since he had last visited her, except that the decaying food in the dishes and the fluids in the cups and glasses had become more dismaying.

'You should watch this,' Rybus said, not looking up. 'Okay; I'll fill you in. Becky is pregnant, but her boyfriend doesn't–'

'I brought you some tea.' He set down four tea bags.

'Could you get me some crackers? There's a box on the shelf

over the stove. I need to take a pill. It's easier for me to take medication with food than with water because when I was about three years old ... you're not going to believe this. My father was teaching me to swim. We had a lot of money in those days; my father was a—well, he still is, although I don't hear from him very often. He hurt his back opening one of those sliding security gates at a condo cluster where ...' Her voice trailed off; she had again become engrossed in her TV.

McVane cleared off a chair and seated himself.

'I was very depressed last night,' Rybus said. 'I almost called you. I was thinking about this friend of mine who's now—well, she's my age, but she's got a class 4-C rating in time-motion studies involving prism fluctuation rate or some damn thing. I hate her. At my age! Can you feature that?' She laughed.

'Have you weighed yourself lately?' he asked.

'What? Oh no. But my weight's okay. I can tell. You take a pinch of skin between your fingers, up near your shoulder, and I did that. I still have a fat layer.'

'You look thin,' he said. He put his hand on her forehead.

'Am I running a fever?'

'No,' he said. He continued to hold his hand there, against her smooth damp skin, above her dark glasses. Above, he thought, the myelin sheath of nerve fibers which had developed the sclerotic patches which were killing her.

You will be better off, he said to himself, when she is dead.

Sympathetically, Rybus said, 'Don't feel bad. I'll be okay. MED has cut my dosage of Vasculine. I only take it *t.i.d.* now—three times a day instead of four.'

'You know all the medical terms,' he said.

'I have to. They issued me a PDR. Want to look at it? It's around here somewhere. Look under those papers over there. I was writing letters to several old friends because while I was looking for something else I came across their addresses. I've been throwing things away. See?' She pointed and he saw sacks, paper sacks, of crumpled papers. 'I wrote for five hours yesterday and then I started in today. That's why I wanted the tea; maybe you could fix me a cup. Put a whole lot of sugar in it and just a little milk.'

As he fixed her the tea, fragments of a Linda Fox adaptation of a Dowland song moved through his mind.

> *Thou mighty God*
> *That rightest every wrong ...*
> *Listen to Patience*
> *In a dying song.*

'This program is really good,' Rybus said, when a series of commercials interrupted her TV soap opera. 'Can I tell you about it?'

Rather than answering, he asked, 'Does the reduced dosage of Vasculine indicate that you're improving?'

'I'm probably going into another period of remission.'

'How long can you expect it to last?'

'Probably quite a while.'

'I admire your courage,' he said. 'I'm bailing out. This is the last time I'm coming over here.'

'My courage?' she said. 'Thank you.'

'I'm not coming back.'

'Not coming back when? You mean today?'

'You are a death-dealing organism,' he said. 'A pathogen.'

'If we're going to talk seriously,' she said, 'I want to put my wig on. Could you bring me my blonde wig? It's around somewhere, maybe under those clothes in the corner there. Where that red top is, the one with the white buttons. I have to sew a button back on it, *if* I can find the button.'

He found her her wig.

'Hold the hand mirror for me,' she said as she placed the wig on her skull. 'Do you think I'm contagious? Because MED says that at this stage the virus is inactive. I talked to MED for over an hour yesterday; they gave me a special line.'

'Who's maintaining your gear?' he asked.

'*Gear?*' She gazed at him from behind dark glasses.

'Your job. Monitoring incoming traffic. Storing it and then transferring it. The reason you're here.'

'It's on auto.'

'You have seven warning lights on right now, all red and all blinking,' he said. 'You should have an audio analog so you can hear it and not ignore it. You're receiving but not recording and they're trying to tell you.'

'Well, they're out of luck,' she responded in a low voice.

'They have to take into account the fact that you're sick,' he said.

'Yes, they do. Of course they do. They can bypass me; don't you receive roughly what I receive? Aren't I essentially a backup station to your own?'

'No,' he said. 'I'm a backup station to yours.'

'It's all the same.' She sipped the mug of tea which he had fixed for her. 'It's too hot. I'll let it cool.' Tremblingly, she reached to set down the mug on a table beside her bed; the mug fell, and hot tea poured out over the plastic floor. 'Christ,' she said with fury. 'Well, that does it; that really does it. *Nothing* has gone right today. Son of a bitch.'

McVane turned on the dome's vacuum circuit and it sucked up the spilled tea. He said nothing. He felt amorphous anger all through him, directed at nothing, fury without object, and he sensed that this was the quality of her own hate: it was a passion which went both nowhere and everywhere. Hate, he thought, like a flock of flies. God, he thought, how I want out of here. How I hate to hate like this, hating spilled tea with the same venom as I hate terminal illness. A one-dimensional universe. It has dwindled to that.

In the weeks that followed, he made fewer and fewer trips from his dome to hers. He did not listen to what she said; he did not watch what she did; he averted his gaze from the chaos around her, the ruins of her dome. I am seeing a projection of her brain, he thought once as he momentarily surveyed the garbage which had piled up everywhere; she was even putting sacks outside the dome, to freeze for eternity. She is senile.

Back in his own dome, he tried to listen to Linda Fox, but the magic had departed. He saw and heard a synthetic image. It was not real. Rybus Rommey had sucked the life out of the Fox the way her dome's vacuum circuit had sucked up the spilled tea.

> *'And when his sorrows came as fast as floods,*
> *Hope kept his heart till comfort came again.'*

McVane heard the words, but they didn't matter. What had Rybus called it? Recycled sentimentality and crap. He put on a Vivaldi concerto for bassoon. There is only one Vivaldi concerto, he thought. A computer could do better. And be more diverse.

'You're picking up Fox waves,' Linda Fox said, and on his video transducer her face appeared, star-lit and wild. 'And when those Fox waves hit you,' she said, 'you have been *hit!*'

In a momentary spasm of fury, he deliberately erased four hours of Fox, both video and audio. And then regretted it. He put in a call to one of the relay satellites for replacement tapes and was told that they were back-ordered.

Fine, he said to himself. What the hell does it matter?

That night, while he was sound asleep, his telephone rang. He let it ring; he did not answer it, and when it rang again ten minutes later he again ignored it.

The third time it rang he picked it up and said hello.

'Hi,' Rybus said.

'What is it?' he said.

'I'm cured.'

'You're in remission?'

'No, I'm cured. MED just contacted me; their computer analyzed all my charts and tests and everything and there's no sign of hard patches. Except, of course, I'll never get central vision back in my bad eye. But other than that I'm okay.' She paused. 'How have you been? I haven't heard from you for so long—it seems like forever. I've been wondering about you.'

He said, 'I'm okay.'

'We should celebrate.'

'Yes,' he said.

'I'll fix dinner for us, like I used to. What would you like? I feel like Mexican food. I make a really good taco; I have the ground meat in my freezer, unless it's gone bad. I'll thaw it out and see. Do you want me to come over there or do you–'

'Let me talk to you tomorrow,' he said.

'I'm sorry to wake you up, but I just now heard from MED.' She was silent a moment. 'You're the only friend I have,' she said. And then, incredibly, she began to cry.

'It's okay,' he said. 'You're well.'

'I was so fucked up,' she said brokenly. 'I'll ring off and talk to you tomorrow. But you're right; I can't believe it, but I made it.'

'It is due to your courage,' he said.

'It's due to you,' Rybus said. 'I would have given up without you. I never told you this, but–well, I squirreled away enough sleeping pills to kill myself, and–'

'I'll talk to you tomorrow,' he said, 'about getting together.' He hung up and lay back down.

He thought, When Job had lost his children, lands, and goods, Patience assuaged his excessive pain. And when his sorrows came as fast as floods, Hope kept his heart till comfort came again. As the Fox would put it.

Recycled sentimentality, he thought. I got her through her ordeal and she paid me back by deriding into rubbish that which I cherished the most. But she is alive, he realized; she did make it. It's like when someone tries to kill a rat. You can kill it six ways and it still survives. You can't fault that.

He thought, That is the name of what we are doing here in this star system on these frozen planets in these little domes. Rybus Rommey understood the game and played it right and won. To hell with Linda Fox. And then he thought, But also to hell with what I love.

It is a good trade-off, he thought: a human life won and a synthetic media image wrecked. The law of the universe.

Shivering, he pulled his covers over him and tried to get back to sleep.

*

The food man showed up before Rybus did; he awoke McVane early in the morning with a full shipment.

'Still got your temp and air illegally boosted,' the food man said as he unscrewed his helmet.

'I just use the equipment,' McVane said. 'I don't build it.'

'Well, I won't report you. Got any coffee?'

They sat facing each other across the table drinking fake coffee.

'I just came from the Rommey girl's dome,' the food man said. 'She says she's cured.'

'Yeah, she phoned me late last night,' McVane said.

'She says you did it.'

To that, McVane said nothing.

'You saved a human life.'

'Okay,' McVane said.

'What's wrong?'

'I'm just tired.'

'I guess it took a lot out of you. Christ, it's a mess over there. Can't you clean it up for her? Destroy the garbage, at least, and sterilize the place; the whole goddam dome is septic. She let her garbage disposal get plugged and it backed up raw sewage all over her cupboards and shelves, where her food is stored. I've never seen anything like it. Of course, she's been so weak—'

McVane interrupted, 'I'll look into it.'

Awkwardly, the food man said, 'The main thing is, she's cured. She was giving herself the shots, you know.'

'I know,' McVane said. 'I watched her.' Many times, he said to himself.

'And her hair's growing back. Boy, she looks awful without her wig. Don't you agree?'

Rising, McVane said, 'I have to broadcast some weather reports. Sorry I can't talk to you any longer.'

Toward dinnertime Rybus Rommey appeared at the hatch of his dome, loaded down with pots and dishes and carefully wrapped packages. He let her in, and she made her way silently to the kitchen area, where she dumped everything down at once; two packages slid off onto the floor and she stooped to retrieve them.

After she had taken off her helmet, she said, 'It's good to see you again.'

'Likewise,' he said.

'It'll take about an hour to fix the tacos. Do you think you can wait until then?'

'Sure,' he said.

'I've been thinking,' Rybus said as she started a pan of grease heating on the stove. 'We ought to take a vacation. Do you have any leave coming? I have two weeks owed me, although my situation is complicated by my illness, I mean, I used up a lot of my leave in the form of sick leave. Christ's sake, they docked me one half-day a month, just because I couldn't operate my transmitter. Can you believe it?'

He said, 'It's nice to see you stronger.'

'I'm fine,' she said. 'Shit, I forgot the hamburger. Goddam it!' She stared at him.

'I'll go to your dome and get it,' he said presently.

She seated herself. 'It's not thawed. I forgot to thaw it out. I just remembered now. I was going to take it out of the freezer this morning, but I had to finish some letters . . . maybe we could have something else and have the tacos tomorrow night.'

'Okay,' he said.

'And I meant to bring your tea back.'

'I only gave you four bags,' he said.

Eyeing him uncertainly, she said, 'I thought you brought me that whole box of Celestial Seasonings Morning Thunder Tea. Then where did I get it? Maybe the food man brought it. I'm just going to sit here for a while. Could you turn on the TV?'

He turned on the TV.

'There's a show I watch,' Rybus said. 'I never miss it. I like shows about—well, I'll have to fill you in on what's happened so far if we're going to watch.'

'Could we not watch?' he said.

'Her husband—'

He thought, She's completely crazy. She is dead. Her body has been healed, but it killed her mind.

'I have to tell you something,' he said.

'What is it?'

'You're—' He ceased.

'I'm very lucky,' she said. 'I beat the odds. You didn't see me when I was at my worst. I didn't want you to. From the chemo I was blind and paralyzed and deaf and then I started having seizures; I'll be on a maintenance dose for years. But it's okay? Don't you think? To be on just a maintenance dose? I mean, it could be so much worse. Anyhow, her husband lost his job because he—'

'Whose husband?' McVane said.

'On the TV.' Reaching up she took hold of his hand. 'Where do you want to go on our vacation? We so goddam well deserve some sort of reward. Both of us.'

'Our reward,' he said, 'is that you're well.'

She did not seem to be listening; her gaze was fastened on the TV. He saw, then, that she still wore her dark glasses. It made him think, then, of the song the Fox had sung on Christmas Day, for all the planets, the most tender, the most haunting song which she had adapted from John Dowland's lute books.

> When the poor cripple by the pool did lie
> Full many years in misery and pain,
> No sooner he on Christ had set his eye,
> But he was well, and comfort came again.

Rybus Rommey was saying, '—it was a high-paying job but everyone was conspiring against him; you know how it is in an office. I worked in an office once where—' Pausing, she said, 'Could you heat some water. I'd like to try a little coffee.'

'Okay,' he said, and turned on the burner.

STRANGE MEMORIES
OF DEATH

I woke up this morning and felt the chill of October in the apartment, as if the seasons understood the calendar. What had I dreamed? Vain thoughts of a woman I had loved. Something depressed me. I took a mental audit. Everything was, in fact, fine; this would be a good month. But I felt the chill.

Oh Christ, I thought. Today is the day they evict the Lysol Lady.

Nobody likes the Lysol Lady. She is insane. No one has ever heard her say a word and she won't look at you. Sometimes when you are descending the stairs she is coming up and she turns wordlessly around and retreats and uses the elevator instead. Everybody can smell the Lysol she uses. Magical horrors contaminate her apartment, apparently, so she uses Lysol. God damn! As I fix coffee I think, Maybe the owners have already evicted her, at dawn, while I still slept. While I was having vain dreams about a woman I loved who dumped me. Of course. I was dreaming about the hateful Lysol Lady and the authorities coming to her door at five A.M. The new owners are a huge firm of real estate developers. They'd do it at dawn.

The Lysol Lady hides in her apartment and knows that October is here, October first is here, and they are going to bust in and throw her and her stuff out in the street. Now is she going to speak? I imagine her pressed against the wall in silence. However, it is not as simple as that. Al Newcum, the sales representative of South Orange Investments, has told me that the Lysol Lady went to Legal Aid. This is bad news because it screws up our doing anything for her. She is crazy but not crazy enough. If it could be proved that she did not understand the situation, a team from Orange County Mental Health could come in as her advocates and explain to South Orange Investments that you cannot legally evict a person with diminished capacity. Why the hell did she get it together to go to Legal Aid?

The time is nine A.M. I can go downstairs to the sales office and ask Al Newcum if they've evicted the Lysol Lady yet, or if she is in her apartment, hiding in silence, waiting. They are evicting her because the building, made up of fifty-six units, has been converted to condominiums. Virtually everyone has moved since we were all legally notified four months ago. You have one hundred and twenty days to leave or buy your apartment and South Orange Investments will pay two hundred dollars of your moving costs. This is the law. You also have first-refusal rights on your rental unit. I am buying mine. I am staying. For fifty-two thousand dollars, I get to be around when they evict the Lysol Lady who is crazy and doesn't have fifty-two thousand dollars. Now I wish I had moved.

Going downstairs to the newspaper vending machine, I buy today's Los Angeles *Times*. A girl who shot up a schoolyard of children 'because she didn't like Mondays' is pleading guilty. She will soon get probation. She took a gun and shot schoolchildren because, in effect, she had nothing else to do. Well, today is Monday; she is in court on a Monday, the day she hates. Is there no limit to madness? I wonder about myself. First of all, I doubt if my apartment is worth fifty-two thousand dollars. I am staying because I am both afraid to move—afraid of something new, of change—and because I am lazy. No, that isn't it. I like this building and I live near friends and near stores that mean something to me. I've been here three and a half years. It is a good, solid building, with security gates and dead-bolt locks. I have two cats and they like the enclosed patio; they can go outside and be safe from dogs. Probably I am thought of as the Cat Man. So everyone has moved out, but the Lysol Lady and the Cat Man stay on.

What bothers me is that I know the only thing separating me from the Lysol Lady, who is crazy, is the money in my savings account. Money is the official seal of sanity. The Lysol Lady, perhaps, is afraid to move. She is like me. She just wants to stay where she has stayed for several years, doing what she's been doing. She uses the laundry machines a lot, washing and spin-drying her clothes again and again. This is where I encounter her: I am coming into the laundry room and she is there at the machines to be sure no one steals her laundry. Why won't she look at you? Keeping her face turned away . . . what purpose is served? I sense hate. She hates every other human being. But now consider her situation; those she hates are going to close in on her. What fear she must feel! She gazes about in her apartment, waiting for the knock on the door; she watches the clock and understands!

To the north of us, in Los Angeles, the conversion of rental units to condominiums has been effectively blocked by the city council. Those who rent won out. This is a great victory, but it does not help the Lysol Lady. This is Orange County. Money rules. The very poor live to the east of me: the Mexicans in their Barrio. Sometimes when our security gates open to admit cars, the Chicano women run in with baskets of dirty laundry; they want to use our machines, having none of their own. The people who lived here in the building resented this. When you have even a little money—money enough to live in a modern, full-security, all-electric building—you resent a great deal.

Well, I have to find out if the Lysol Lady has been evicted yet. There is no way to tell by looking at her window; the drapes are always shut. So I go downstairs to the sales office to see Al. However, Al is not there; the office is locked. Then I remember that Al flew to Sacramento on the weekend to get some crucial legal papers that the state lost. He hasn't returned. If the Lysol Lady wasn't crazy, I could knock on her door and talk to her; I could find out that way. But this is precisely the locus of the tragedy; any knock will frighten her. This is her condition. This is the illness itself. So I stand by the fountain that the developers have constructed, and I admire the planter boxes of flowers which they have had brought in . . . they have really made the building look good. It formerly looked like a prison. Now it has become a garden. The developers put a great deal of money into painting and landscaping and, in fact, rebuilding the whole entrance. Water and flowers and french doors . . . and the Lysol Lady silent in her apartment, waiting for the knock.

Perhaps I could tape a note to the Lysol Lady's door. It could read:

> Madam, I am sympathetic to your position and would like to assist you. If you wish me to assist you, I live upstairs in apartment C-1.

How would I sign it? Fellow loony, maybe. Fellow loony with fifty-two thousand dollars who is here legally whereas you are, in the eyes of the law, a squatter. As of midnight last night. Although the day before, it was as much your apartment as mine is mine.

I go back upstairs to my apartment with the idea of writing a letter to the woman I once loved and last night dreamed about. All sorts of phrases pass through my mind. I will recreate the vanished relationship with one letter. Such is the power of my words.

What crap. She is gone forever. I don't even have her current address. Laboriously, I could track her down through mutual friends, and then say what?

> My darling, I have finally come to my senses. I realize the full extent of my indebtedness to you. Considering the short time we were together, you did more for me than anyone else in my life. It is evident to me that I have made a disastrous error. Could we have dinner together?

As I repeat this hyperbole in my mind, the thought comes to me that it would be horrible but funny if I wrote that letter and then by mistake or design taped it to the Lysol Lady's door. How would she react! Jesus Christ! It would kill her or cure her! Meanwhile, I could write my departed loved one, *die ferne Geliebte*, as follows:

STRANGE MEMORIES OF DEATH

Madam, you are totally nuts. Everyone within miles is aware of it. Your problem is of your own making. Ship up, shape out, get your act together, borrow some money, hire a better lawyer, buy a gun, shoot up a schoolyard. If I can assist you, I live in apartment C-1.

Maybe the plight of the Lysol Lady is funny and I am too depressed by the coming of autumn to realize it. Maybe there will be some good mail today; after all, yesterday was a mail holiday. I will get two days of mail today. That will cheer me up. What, in fact, is going on is that I am feeling sorry for myself; today is Monday and, like the girl in court pleading guilty, I hate Mondays.

Brenda Spenser pleaded guilty to the charge of shooting eleven people, two of whom died. She is seventeen years old, small and very pretty, with red hair; she wears glasses and looks like a child, like one of those she shot. The thought enters my mind that perhaps the Lysol Lady has a gun in her apartment, a thought that should have come to me a long time ago. Perhaps South Orange Investments thought of it. Perhaps this is why Al Newcum's office is locked up today; he is not in Sacramento but in hiding. Although of course he could be in hiding in Sacramento, accomplishing two things at once.

An excellent therapist I once knew made the point that in almost all cases of a criminal psychotic acting-out there was an easier alternative that the disturbed person overlooked. Brenda Spenser, for instance, could have walked to the local supermarket and bought a carton of chocolate milk instead of shooting eleven people, most of them children. The psychotic person actually chooses the more difficult path; he forces his will uphill. It is not true that he takes the line of least resistance, but he *thinks* he does. There, precisely, lies his error. The basis of psychosis, in a nutshell, is the chronic inability to see the easy way out. All the behavior, all that constitutes psychotic activity and the psychotic lifestyle, stems from this perceptual flaw.

Sitting in isolation and silence in her antiseptic apartment, waiting for the inexorable knock on the door, the Lysol Lady has contrived to put herself in the most difficult circumstances possible. What was easy was made hard. What was hard was transmuted, finally, into the impossible, and there the psychotic lifestyle ends: when the impossible closes in and there are no options at all, even difficult ones. That is the rest of the definition of psychosis: At the end there lies a dead end. And, at that point, the psychotic person freezes. If you have ever seen it happen—well, it is an amazing sight. The person congeals like a motor that has seized. It occurs suddenly. One moment the person is in motion—the pistons are going up and down frantically—and then it's an inert block. That is because the path has run out for that person, the path he probably got onto years before. It is kinetic death. 'Place there is none,' St Augustine wrote. 'We go backward and forward, and there is no place.' And then the cessation comes and there is only place.

The spot where the Lysol Lady had trapped herself was her own apartment, but it was no longer her own apartment. She had found a place at which to psychologically die and then South Orange Investments had taken it away from her. They had robbed her of her own grave.

What I can't get out of my mind is the notion that my fate is tied to that of the Lysol Lady. A fiscal entry in the computer at Mutual Savings divides us and it is a mythical division; it is real only so long as people such as South Orange Investments—specifically South Orange Investments—are willing to agree that it is real. It seems to me to be nothing more than a social convention, such as wearing matching socks. In another way it's like the value of gold. The value of gold is what people agree on, which is like a game played by children: 'Let's agree that that tree is third base.' Suppose my television set worked because my friends and I agreed that it worked. We could sit before a blank screen forever that way. In that case, it could be said that the Lysol Lady's failure lay in not having entered into a compact with the rest of us, a consensus. Underlying everything else there is this unwritten contract to

STRANGE MEMORIES OF DEATH

which the Lysol Lady is not a party. But I am amazed to think that the failure to enter into an agreement palpably childish and irrational leads inevitably to kinetic death, total stoppage of the organism.

Argued this way, one could say that the Lysol Lady had failed to be a child. She was too adult. She couldn't or wouldn't play a game. The element which had taken over her life was the element of the grim. She never smiled. None had ever seen her do anything but glower in a vague, undirected way.

Perhaps, then, she played a grimmer game rather than no game; perhaps her game was one of combat, in which case she now had what she wanted, even though she was losing. It was at least a situation she understood. South Orange Investments had entered the Lysol Lady's world. Perhaps being a squatter rather than a tenant was satisfying to her. Maybe we all secretly will everything that happens to us. In that case, does the psychotic person will his own ultimate kinetic death, his own dead end path? Does he play to lose?

I didn't see Al Newcum that day, but I did see him the next day; he had returned from Sacramento and opened up his office.

'Is the woman in B-15 still there?' I asked him. 'Or did you evict her?'

'Mrs Archer?' Newcum said. 'Oh, the other morning she moved out; she's gone. The Santa Ana Housing Authority found her a place over on Bristol.' He leaned back in his swivel chair and crossed his legs; his slacks, as always, were sharply creased. 'She went to them a couple of weeks ago.'

'An apartment she can afford?' I said.

'They picked up the bill. They're paying her rent; she talked them into it. She's a hardship case.'

'Christ,' I said, 'I wish someone would pay my rent.'

'You're not paying rent,' Newcum said. 'You're buying your apartment.'

I HOPE I SHALL ARRIVE SOON

After takeoff the ship routinely monitored the condition of the sixty people sleeping in its cryonic tanks. One malfunction showed, that of person nine. His EEG revealed brain activity.

Shit, the ship said to itself.

Complex homeostatic devices locked into circuit feed, and the ship contacted person nine.

'You are slightly awake,' the ship said, utilizing the psychotronic route; there was no point in rousing person nine to full conscious-ness–after all, the flight would last a decade.

Virtually unconscious, but unfortunately still able to think, person nine thought, Someone is addressing me. He said, 'Where am I located? I don't see anything.'

'You're in faulty cryonic suspension.'

He said, 'Then I shouldn't be able to hear you.'

'"Faulty," I said. That's the point; you can hear me. Do you know your name?'

'Victor Kemmings. Bring me out of this.'

'We are in flight.'

'Then put me under.'

'Just a moment.' The ship examined the cryonic mechanisms; it scanned and surveyed and then it said, 'I will try.'

Time passed. Victor Kemmings, unable to see anything, un-aware of his body, found himself still conscious. 'Lower my tem-perature,' he said. He could not hear his voice; perhaps he only imagined he spoke. Colors floated toward him and then rushed at him. He liked the colors; they reminded him of a child's paint box, the semianimated kind, an artificial life-form. He had used them in school, two hundred years ago.

'I can't put you under,' the voice of the ship sounded inside Kemmings' head. 'The malfunction is too elaborate; I can't correct it and I can't repair it. You will be conscious for ten years.'

The semianimated colors rushed toward him, but now they possessed a sinister quality, supplied to them by his own fear. 'Oh my God,' he said. Ten years! The colors darkened.

As Victor Kemmings lay paralyzed, surrounded by dismal flickerings of light, the ship explained to him its strategy. This strategy did not represent a decision on its part; the ship had been programmed to seek this solution in case of a malfunction of this sort.

'What I will do,' the voice of the ship came to him, 'is feed you sensory stimulation. The peril to you is sensory deprivation. If you are conscious for ten years without sensory data, your mind will deteriorate. When we reach the LR4 System, you will be a vegetable.'

'Well, what do you intend to feed me?' Kemmings said in panic. 'What do you have in your information storage banks? All the video soap operas of the last century? Wake me up and I'll walk around.'

'There is no air in me,' the ship said. 'Nothing for you to eat. No one to talk to, since everyone else is under.'

Kemmings said, 'I can talk to you. We can play chess.'

'Not for ten years. Listen to me; I say, I have no food and no air. You must remain as you are ... a bad compromise, but one forced on us. You are talking to me now. I have no particular information stored. Here is policy in these situations: I will feed you your own buried memories, emphasizing the pleasant ones. You possess two hundred and six years of memories and most of them have sunk down into your unconscious. This is a splendid source of sensory data for you to receive. Be of good cheer. This situation, which you are in, is not unique. It has never happened within my domain before, but I am programmed to deal with it. Relax and trust me. I will see that you are provided with a world.'

'They should have warned me,' Kemmings said, 'before I agreed to emigrate.'

'Relax,' the ship said.

He relaxed, but he was terribly frightened. Theoretically, he should have gone under, into the successful cryonic suspension, then awakened a moment later at his star of destination; or rather the planet, the colony planet, of that star. Everyone else aboard the ship lay in an unknowing state—he was the exception, as if bad karma had attacked him for obscure reasons. Worst of all, he had to depend totally on the goodwill of the ship. Suppose it elected to feed him monsters? The ship could terrorize him for ten years—ten objective years and undoubtedly more from a subjective standpoint. He was, in effect, totally in the ship's power. Did interstellar ships enjoy such a situation? He knew little about interstellar ships; his field was microbiology. Let me think, he said to himself. My first wife, Martine; the lovely little French girl who wore jeans and a red shirt open at the waist and cooked delicious crepes.

'I hear,' the ship said. 'So be it.'

The rushing colors resolved themselves into coherent, stable shapes. A building: a little old yellow wooden house that he had owned when he was nineteen years old, in Wyoming. 'Wait,' he said in panic. 'The foundation was bad; it was on a mud sill. And the roof leaked.' But he saw the kitchen, with the table that he had built himself. And he felt glad.

'You will not know, after a little while,' the ship said, 'that I am feeding you your own buried memories.'

'I haven't thought of that house in a century,' he said wonderingly; entranced, he made out his old electric drip coffee pot with the box of paper filters beside it. This is the house where Martine and I lived, he realized. 'Martine!' he said aloud.

'I'm on the phone,' Martine said from the living room.

The ship said, 'I will cut in only when there is an emergency. I will be monitoring you, however, to be sure you are in a satisfactory state. Don't be afraid.'

I HOPE I SHALL ARRIVE SOON

'Turn down the rear right burner on the stove,' Martine called. He could hear her and yet not see her. He made his way from the kitchen through the dining room and into the living room. At the VF, Martine stood in rapt conversation with her brother; she wore shorts and she was barefoot. Through the front windows of the living room he could see the street; a commercial vehicle was trying to park, without success.

It's a warm day, he thought. I should turn on the air conditioner.

He seated himself on the old sofa as Martine continued her VF conversation, and he found himself gazing at his most cherished possession, a framed poster on the wall above Martine: Gilbert Shelton's *Fat Freddy Says* drawing in which Freddy Freak sits with his cat on his lap, and Fat Freddy is trying to say 'Speed kills,' but he is so wired on speed—he holds in his hand every kind of amphetamine tablet, pill, spansule, and capsule that exists—that he can't say it, and the cat is gritting his teeth and wincing in a mixture of dismay and disgust. The poster is signed by Gilbert Shelton himself; Kemmings' best friend Ray Torrance gave it to him and Martine as a wedding present. It is worth thousands. It was signed by the artist back in the 1980s. Long before either Victor Kemmings or Martine lived.

If we ever run out of money, Kemmings thought to himself, we could sell the poster. It was not *a* poster; it was *the* poster. Martine adored it. The Fabulous Furry Freak Brothers—from the golden age of a long-ago society. No wonder he loved Martine so; she herself loved back, loved the beauties of the world, and treasured and cherished them as she treasured and cherished him; it was a protective love that nourished but did not stifle. It had been her idea to frame the poster; he would have tacked it up on the wall, so stupid was he.

'Hi,' Martine said, off the VF now. 'What are you thinking?'

'Just that you keep alive what you love,' he said.

'I think that's what you're supposed to do,' Martine said. 'Are you ready for dinner? Open some red wine, a cabernet.'

'Will an '07 do?' he said, standing up; he felt, then, like taking hold of his wife and hugging her.

'Either an '07 or a '12.' She trotted past him, through the dining room and into the kitchen.

Going down into the cellar, he began to search among the bottles, which, of course, lay flat. Musty air and dampness; he liked the smell of the cellar, but then he noticed the redwood planks lying half-buried in the dirt and he thought, I know I've got to get a concrete slab poured. He forgot about the wine and went over to the far corner, where the dirt was piled highest; bending down, he poked at a board ... he poked with a trowel and then he thought, Where did I get this trowel? I didn't have it a minute ago. The board crumbled against the trowel. This whole house is collapsing, he realized. Christ sake. I better tell Martine.

Going back upstairs, the wine forgotten, he started to say to her that the foundations of the house were dangerously decayed, but Martine was nowhere in sight. And nothing cooked on the stove— no pots, no pans. Amazed, he put his hands on the stove and found it cold. Wasn't she just cooking? he asked himself.

'Martine!' he said loudly.

No response. Except for himself, the house was empty. Empty, he thought, and collapsing. Oh my God. He seated himself at the kitchen table and felt the chair give slightly under him; it did not give much, but he felt it; he felt the sagging.

I'm afraid, he thought. Where did she go?

He returned to the living room. Maybe she went next door to borrow some spices or butter or something, he reasoned. Nonetheless, panic now filled him.

He looked at the poster. It was unframed. And the edges had been torn.

I know she framed it, he thought; he ran across the room to it, to examine it closely. Faded ... the artist's signature had faded; he could scarcely make it out. She insisted on framing it and under glare-free, reflection-free glass. But it isn't framed and it's torn! The most precious thing we own!

I HOPE I SHALL ARRIVE SOON

Suddenly he found himself crying. It amazed him, his tears. Martine is gone; the poster is deteriorated; the house is crumbling away; nothing is cooking on the stove. This is terrible, he thought. And I don't understand it.

The ship understood it. The ship had been carefully monitoring Victor Kemmings' brain wave patterns, and the ship knew that something had gone wrong. The wave-forms showed agitation and pain. I must get him out of this feed-circuit or I will kill him, the ship decided. Where does the flaw lie? it asked itself. Worry dormant in the man; underlying anxieties. Perhaps if I intensify the signal. I will use the same source, but amp up the charge. What has happened is that massive subliminal insecurities have taken possession of him; the fault is not mine, but lies, instead, in his psychological makeup.

I will try an earlier period in his life, the ship decided. Before the neurotic anxieties got laid down.

In the backyard, Victor scrutinized a bee that had gotten itself trapped in a spider's web. The spider wound up the bee with great care. That's wrong, Victor thought. I'll let the bee loose. Reaching up, he took hold of the encapsulated bee, drew it from the web, and, scrutinizing it carefully, began to unwrap it.

The bee stung him; it felt like a little patch of flame.

Why did it sting me? he wondered. I was letting it go.

He went indoors to his mother and told her, but she did not listen; she was watching television. His finger hurt where the bee had stung it, but, more important, he did not understand why the bee would attack its rescuer. I won't do that again, he said to himself.

'Put some Bactine on it,' his mother said at last, roused from watching the TV.

He had begun to cry. It was unfair. It made no sense. He was perplexed and dismayed and he felt a hatred toward small living things, because they were dumb. They didn't have any sense.

He left the house, played for a time on his swings, his slide, in his sandbox, and then he went into the garage because he heard a strange flapping, whirring sound, like a kind of fan. Inside the gloomy garage, he found that a bird was fluttering against the cob-webbed rear window, trying to get out. Below it, the cat, Dorky, leaped and leaped, trying to reach the bird.

He picked up the cat; the cat extended its body and its front legs, it extended its jaws and bit into the bird. At once the cat scrambled down and ran off with the still-fluttering bird.

Victor ran into the house. 'Dorky caught a bird!' he told his mother.

'That goddam cat.' His mother took the broom from the closet in the kitchen and ran outside, trying to find Dorky. The cat had concealed itself under the bramble bushes; she could not reach it with the broom. 'I'm going to get rid of that cat,' his mother said.

Victor did not tell her that he had arranged for the cat to catch the bird; he watched in silence as his mother tried and tried to pry Dorky out from her hiding place; Dorky was crunching up the bird; he could hear the sound of breaking bones, small bones. He felt a strange feeling, as if he should tell his mother what he had done, and yet if he told her she would punish him. I won't do that again, he said to himself. His face, he realized, had turned red. What if his mother figured it out? What if she had some secret way of knowing? Dorky couldn't tell her and the bird was dead. No one would ever know. He was safe.

But he felt bad. That night he could not eat his dinner. Both his parents noticed. They thought he was sick; they took his tempera-ture. He said nothing about what he had done. His mother told his father about Dorky and they decided to get rid of Dorky. Seated at the table, listening, Victor began to cry.

'All right,' his father said gently. 'We won't get rid of her. It's nat-ural for a cat to catch a bird.'

The next day he sat playing in his sandbox. Some plants grew up through the sand. He broke them off. Later his mother told him that had been a wrong thing to do.

Alone in the backyard, in his sandbox, he sat with a pail of water, forming a small mound of wet sand. The sky, which had been blue and clear, became by degrees overcast. A shadow passed over him and he looked up. He sensed a presence around him, something vast that could think.

You are responsible for the death of the bird, the presence thought; he could understand its thoughts.

'I know,' he said. He wished, then, that he could die. That he could replace the bird and die for it, leaving it as it had been, fluttering against the cobwebbed window of the garage.

The bird wanted to fly and eat and live, the presence thought.

'Yes,' he said miserably.

'You must never do that again,' the presence told him.

'I'm sorry,' he said, and wept.

This is a very neurotic person, the ship realized. I am having an awful lot of trouble finding happy memories. There is too much fear in him and too much guilt. He has buried it all, and yet it is still there, worrying him like a dog worrying a rag. Where can I go in his memories to find him solace? I must come up with ten years of memories, or his mind will be lost.

Perhaps, the ship thought, the error that I am making is in the area of choice on my part; I should allow him to select his own memories. However, the ship realized, this will allow an element of fantasy to enter. And that is not usually good. Still—

I will try the segment dealing with his first marriage once again, the ship decided. He really loved Martine. Perhaps this time if I keep the intensity of the memories at a greater level the entropic factor can be abolished. What happened was a subtle vitiation of the remembered world, a decay of structure. I will try to compensate for that. So be it.

'Do you suppose Gilbert Shelton really signed this?' Martine said pensively; she stood before the poster, her arms folded; she rocked back and forth slightly, as if seeking a better perspective on the brightly colored drawing hanging on their living room wall. 'I mean, it could have been forged. By a dealer somewhere along the line. During Shelton's lifetime or after.'

'The letter of authentication,' Victor Kemmings reminded her.

'Oh, that's right!' She smiled her warm smile. 'Ray gave us the letter that goes with it. But suppose the letter is a forgery? What we need is another letter certifying that the first letter is authentic.' Laughing, she walked away from the poster.

'Ultimately,' Kemmings said, 'we would have to have Gilbert Shelton here to personally testify that he signed it.'

'Maybe he wouldn't know. There's that story about the man bringing the Picasso picture to Picasso and asking him if it was authentic, and Picasso immediately signed it and said, "Now it's authentic."' She put her arm around Kemmings and, standing on tiptoe, kissed him on the cheek. 'It's genuine. Ray wouldn't have given us a forgery. He's the leading expert on counterculture art of the twentieth century. Do you know that he owns an actual lid of dope? It's preserved under—'

'Ray is dead,' Victor said.

'What?' She gazed at him in astonishment. 'Do you mean something happened to him since we last—'

'He's been dead two years,' Kemmings said. 'I was responsible. I was driving the buzzcar. I wasn't cited by the police, but it was my fault.'

'Ray is living on Mars!' She stared at him.

'I know I was responsible. I never told you. I never told anyone. I'm sorry. I didn't mean to do it. I saw it flapping against the window, and Dorky was trying to reach it, and I lifted Dorky up, and I don't know why but Dorky grabbed it—'

'Sit down, Victor.' Martine led him to the overstuffed chair and made him seat himself. 'Something's wrong,' she said.

'I know,' he said. 'Something terrible is wrong. I'm responsible for the taking of a life, a precious life that can never be replaced. I'm sorry. I wish I could make it okay, but I can't.'

After a pause, Martine said, 'Call Ray.'

'The cat–' he said.

'What cat?'

'There.' He pointed. 'In the poster. On Fat Freddy's lap. That's Dorky. Dorky killed Ray.'

Silence.

'The presence told me,' Kemmings said. 'It was God. I didn't realize it at the time, but God saw me commit the crime. The murder. And he will never forgive me.'

His wife stared at him numbly.

'God sees everything you do,' Kemmings said. 'He sees even the falling sparrow. Only in this case it didn't fall; it was grabbed. Grabbed out of the air and torn down. God is tearing this house down which is my body, to pay me back for what I've done. We should have had a building contractor look this house over before we bought it. It's just falling goddam to pieces. In a year there won't be anything left of it. Don't you believe me?'

Martine faltered, 'I–'

'Watch.' Kemmings reached up his arms toward the ceiling; he stood; he reached; he could not touch the ceiling. He walked to the wall and then, after a pause, put his hand through the wall.

Martine screamed.

The ship aborted the memory retrieval instantly. But the harm had been done.

He has integrated his early fears and guilts into one interwoven grid, the ship said to itself. There is no way I can serve up a pleasant memory to him because he instantly contaminates it. However pleasant the original experience in itself was. This is a serious situation, the ship decided. The man is already showing signs of psychosis. And we are hardly into the trip; years lie ahead of him.

After allowing itself time to think the situation through, the ship decided to contact Victor Kemmings once more.

'Mr Kemmings,' the ship said.

'I'm sorry,' Kemmings said. 'I didn't mean to foul up those retrievals. You did a good job, but I–'

'Just a moment,' the ship said. 'I'm not equipped to do psychiatric reconstruction of you; I am a simple mechanism, that's all. What is it you want? Where do you want to be and what do you want to be doing?'

'I want to arrive at our destination,' Kemmings said. 'I want this trip to be over.'

Ah, the ship thought. That is the solution.

One by one the cryonic systems shut down. One by one the people returned to life, among them Victor Kemmings. What amazed him was the lack of a sense of the passage of time. He had entered the chamber, lain down, had felt the membrane cover him and the temperature begin to drop—

And now he stood on the ship's external platform, the unloading platform, gazing down at a verdant planetary landscape. This, he realized, is LR4-6, the colony world to which I have come in order to begin a new life.

'Looks good,' a heavyset woman beside him said.

'Yes,' he said, and felt the newness of the landscape rush up at him, its promise of a beginning. Something better than he had known the past two hundred years. I am a fresh person in a fresh world, he thought. And he felt glad.

Colors raced at him, like those of a child's semianimate kit. Saint Elmo's fire, he realized. That's right; there is a great deal of ionization in this planet's atmosphere. A free light show, such as they had back in the twentieth century.

'Mr Kemmings,' a voice said. An elderly man had come up beside him, to speak to him. 'Did you dream?'

'During the suspension?' Kemmings said. 'No, not that I can remember.'

'I think I dreamed,' the elderly man said. 'Would you take my arm on the descent ramp? I feel unsteady. The air seems thin. Do you find it thin?'

'Don't be afraid,' Kemmings said to him. He took the elderly man's arm. 'I'll help you down the ramp. Look; there's a guide coming this way. He'll arrange our processing for us; it's part of the package. We'll be taken to a resort hotel and given first-class accommodations. Read your brochure.' He smiled at the uneasy older man to reassure him.

'You'd think our muscles would be nothing but flab after ten years in suspension,' the elderly man said.

'It's just like freezing peas,' Kemmings said. Holding onto the timid older man, he descended the ramp to the ground. 'You can store them forever if you get them cold enough.'

'My name's Shelton,' the elderly man said.

'What?' Kemmings said, halting. A strange feeling moved through him.

'Don Shelton.' The elderly man extended his hand; reflexively, Kemmings accepted it and they shook. 'What's the matter, Mr Kemmings? Are you all right?'

'Sure,' he said. 'I'm fine. But hungry. I'd like to get something to eat. I'd like to get to our hotel, where I can take a shower and change my clothes.' He wondered where their baggage could be found. Probably it would take the ship an hour to unload it. The ship was not particularly intelligent.

In an intimate, confidential tone, elderly Mr Shelton said, 'You know what I brought with me? A bottle of Wild Turkey bourbon. The finest bourbon on Earth. I'll bring it over to your hotel room and we'll share it.' He nudged Kemmings.

'I don't drink,' Kemmings said. 'Only wine.' He wondered if there were any good wines here on this distant colony world. Not distant now, he reflected. It is Earth that's distant. I should have done like Mr Shelton and brought a few bottles with me.

Shelton. What did the name remind him of? Something in his far past, in his early years. Something precious, along with good wine and a pretty, gentle young woman making crepes in an old-fashioned kitchen. Aching memories; memories that hurt.

Presently he stood by the bed in his hotel room, his suitcase open; he had begun to hang up his clothes. In the corner of the room, a TV hologram showed a newscaster; he ignored it, but, liking the sound of a human voice, he kept it on.

Did I have any dreams? he asked himself. During these past ten years?

His hand hurt. Gazing down, he saw a red welt, as if he had been stung. A bee stung me, he realized. But when? How? While I lay in cryonic suspension? Impossible. Yet he could see the welt and he could feel the pain. I better get something to put on it, he realized. There's undoubtedly a robot doctor in the hotel; it's a first-rate hotel.

When the robot doctor had arrived and was treating the bee sting, Kemmings said, 'I got this as punishment for killing the bird.'

'Really?' the robot doctor said.

'Everything that ever meant anything to me has been taken away from me,' Kemmings said. 'Martine, the poster—my little old house with the wine cellar. We had everything and now it's gone. Martine left me because of the bird.'

'The bird you killed,' the robot doctor said.

'God punished me. He took away all that was precious to me because of my sin. It wasn't Dorky's sin; it was my sin.'

'But you were just a little boy,' the robot doctor said.

'How did you know that?' Kemmings said. He pulled his hand away from the robot doctor's grasp. 'Something's wrong. You shouldn't have known that.'

'Your mother told me,' the robot doctor said.

'My mother didn't know!'

The robot doctor said, 'She figured it out. There was no way the cat could have reached the bird without your help.'

'So all the time that I was growing up she knew. But she never said anything.'

'You can forget about it,' the robot doctor said.

Kemmings said, 'I don't think you exist. There is no possible way that you could know these things. I'm still in cryonic suspension and the ship is still feeding me my own buried memories. So I won't become psychotic from sensory deprivation.'

'You could hardly have a memory of completing the trip.'

'Wish fulfillment, then. It's the same thing. I'll prove it to you. Do you have a screwdriver?'

'Why?'

Kemmings said, 'I'll remove the back of the TV set and you'll see; there's nothing inside it; no components, no parts, no chassis—nothing.'

'I don't have a screwdriver.'

'A small knife, then. I can see one in your surgical supply bag.' Bending, Kemmings lifted up a small scalpel. 'This will do. If I show you, will you believe me?'

'If there's nothing inside the TV cabinet—'

Squatting down, Kemmings removed the screws holding the back panel of the TV set in place. The panel came loose and he set it down on the floor.

There was nothing inside the TV cabinet. And yet the color hologram continued to fill a quarter of the hotel room, and the voice of the newscaster issued forth from his three-dimensional image.

'Admit you're the ship,' Kemmings said to the robot doctor.

'Oh dear,' the robot doctor said.

Oh dear, the ship said to itself. And I've got almost ten years of this lying ahead of me. He is hopelessly contaminating his experiences with childhood guilt; he imagines that his wife left him because, when he was four years old, he helped a cat catch a bird. The only solution would be for Martine to return to him, but how am I going to arrange that? She may not still be alive. On the other hand, the ship reflected, maybe she is alive. Maybe she could be induced to do something to save her former husband's sanity. People by and large have very positive traits. And ten years from now it will take a lot to save—or rather restore—his sanity; it will take something drastic, something I myself cannot do alone.

Meanwhile, there was nothing to be done but recycle the wish fulfillment arrival of the ship at its destination. I will run him through the arrival, the ship decided, then wipe his conscious memory clean and run him through it again. The only positive aspect of this, it reflected, is that it will give me something to do, which may help preserve *my* sanity.

Lying in cryonic suspension–faulty cryonic suspension–Victor Kemmings imagined, once again, that the ship was touching down and he was being brought back to consciousness.

'Did you dream?' a heavyset woman asked him as the group of passengers gathered on the outer platform. 'I have the impression that I dreamed. Early scenes from my life . . . over a century ago.'

'None that I can remember,' Kemmings said. He was eager to reach his hotel; a shower and a change of clothes would do wonders for his morale. He felt slightly depressed and wondered why.

'There's our guide,' an elderly lady said. 'They're going to escort us to our accommodations.'

'It's in the package,' Kemmings said. His depression remained. The others seemed so spirited, so full of life, but over him only a weariness lay, a weighing-down sensation, as if the gravity of this colony planet were too much for him. Maybe that's it, he said to himself. But, according to the brochure, the gravity here matched Earth's; that was one of the attractions.

Puzzled, he made his way slowly down the ramp, step by step, holding onto the rail. I don't really deserve a new chance at life anyhow, he realized. I'm just going through the motions . . . I am not like these other people. There is something wrong with me; I cannot remember what it is, but nonetheless it is there. In me. A bitter sense of pain. Of lack of worth.

An insect landed on the back of Kemmings' right hand, an old insect, weary with flight. He halted, watched it crawl across his knuckles. I could crush it, he thought. It's so obviously infirm; it won't live much longer anyhow.

He crushed it–and felt great inner horror. What have I done? he asked himself. My first moment here and I have wiped out a little life. Is this my new beginning?

Turning, he gazed back up at the ship. Maybe I ought to go back, he thought. Have them freeze me forever. I am a man of guilt, a man who destroys. Tears filled his eyes.

And, within its sentient works, the interstellar ship moaned.

*

During the ten long years remaining in the trip to the LR4 System, the ship had plenty of time to track down Martine Kemmings. It explained the situation to her. She had emigrated to a vast orbiting dome in the Sirius System, found her situation unsatisfactory, and was en route back to Earth. Roused from her own cryonic suspension, she listened intently and then agreed to be at the colony world LR4-6 when her ex-husband arrived—if it was at all possible.

Fortunately, it was possible.

'I don't think he'll recognize me,' Martine said to the ship. 'I've allowed myself to age. I don't really approve of entirely halting the aging process.'

He'll be lucky if he recognizes anything, the ship thought.

At the intersystem spaceport on the colony world of LR4-6, Martine stood waiting for the people aboard the ship to appear on the outer platform. She wondered if she would recognize her former husband. She was a little afraid, but she was glad that she had gotten to LR4-6 in time. It had been close. Another week and his ship would have arrived before hers. Luck is on my side, she said to herself, and scrutinized the newly landed interstellar ship.

People appeared on the platform. She saw him. Victor had changed very little.

As he came down the ramp, holding onto the railing as if weary and hesitant, she came up to him, her hands thrust deep in the pockets of her coat; she felt shy and when she spoke she could hardly hear her own voice.

'Hi, Victor,' she managed to say.

He halted, gazed at her. 'I know you,' he said.

'It's Martine,' she said.

Holding out his hand, he said, smiling, 'You heard about the trouble on the ship?'

'The ship contacted me.' She took his hand and held it. 'What an ordeal.'

'Yeah,' he said. 'Recirculating memories forever. Did I ever tell you about a bee that I was trying to extricate from a spider's web when I was four years old? The idiotic bee stung me.' He bent down and kissed her. 'It's good to see you,' he said.

'Did the ship–'

'It said it would try to have you here. But it wasn't sure if you could make it.'

As they walked toward the terminal building, Martine said, 'I was lucky; I managed to get a transfer to a military vehicle, a high-velocity-drive ship that just shot along like a mad thing. A new propulsion system entirely.'

Victor Kemmings said, 'I have spent more time in my own unconscious mind than any other human in history. Worse than early-twentieth-century psychoanalysis. And the same material over and over again. Did you know I was scared of my mother?'

'I was scared of your mother,' Martine said. They stood at the baggage depot, waiting for his luggage to appear. 'This looks like a really nice little planet. Much better than where I was . . . I haven't been happy at all.'

'So maybe there's a cosmic plan,' he said, grinning. 'You look great.'

'I'm old.'

'Medical science–'

'It was my decision. I like older people.' She surveyed him. He has been hurt a lot by the cryonic malfunction, she said to herself. I can see it in his eyes. They look broken. Broken eyes. Torn down into pieces by fatigue and–defeat. As if his buried early memories swam up and destroyed him. But it's over, she thought. And I did get here in time.

At the bar in the terminal building, they sat having a drink.

'This old man got me to try Wild Turkey bourbon,' Victor said. 'It's amazing bourbon. He says it's the best on Earth. He brought a bottle with him from . . .' His voice died into silence.

'One of your fellow passengers,' Martine finished.

'I guess so,' he said.

'Well, you can stop thinking of the birds and the bees,' Martine said.

'Sex?' he said, and laughed.

'Being stung by a bee, helping a cat catch a bird. That's all past.'

'That cat,' Victor said, 'has been dead one hundred and eighty-two years. I figured it out while they were bringing us out of suspension. Probably just as well. Dorky. Dorky, the killer cat. Nothing like Fat Freddy's cat.'

'I had to sell the poster,' Martine said. 'Finally.'

He frowned.

'Remember?' she said. 'You let me have it when we split up. Which I always thought was really good of you.'

'How much did you get for it?'

'A lot. I should pay you something like—' She calculated. 'Taking inflation into account, I should pay you about two million dollars.'

'Would you consider,' he said, 'instead, in place of the money, my share of the sale of the poster, spending some time with me? Until I get used to this planet?'

'Yes,' she said. And she meant it. Very much.

They finished their drinks and then, with his luggage transported by robot spacecap, made their way to his hotel room.

'This is a nice room,' Martine said, perched on the edge of the bed. 'And it has a hologram TV. Turn it on.'

'There's no use turning it on,' Victor Kemmings said. He stood by the open closet, hanging up his shirts.

'Why not?'

Kemmings said, 'There's nothing on it.'

Going over to the TV set, Martine turned it on. A hockey game materialized, projected out into the room, in full color, and the sound of the game assailed her ears.

'It works fine,' she said.

'I know,' he said. 'I can prove it to you. If you have a nail file or something, I'll unscrew the back plate and show you.'

'But I can—'

'Look at this.' He paused in his work of hanging up his clothes. 'Watch me put my hand through the wall.' He placed the palm of his right hand against the wall. 'See?'

His hand did not go through the wall because hands do not go through walls; his hand remained pressed against the wall, unmoving.

'And the foundation,' he said, 'is rotting away.'

'Come and sit down by me,' Martine said.

'I've lived this often enough now,' he said. 'I've lived this over and over again. I come out of suspension; I walk down the ramp; I get my luggage; sometimes I have a drink at the bar and sometimes I come directly to my room. Usually I turn on the TV and then—' He came over and held his hand toward her. 'See where the bee stung me?'

She saw no mark on his hand; she took his hand and held it.

'There is no bee sting,' she said.

'And when the robot doctor comes, I borrow a tool from him and take off the back plate of the TV set. To prove to him that it has no chassis, no components in it. And then the ship starts me over again.'

'Victor,' she said. 'Look at your hand.'

'This is the first time you've been here, though,' he said.

'Sit down,' she said.

'Okay.' He seated himself on the bed, beside her, but not too close to her.

'Won't you sit closer to me?' she said.

'It makes me too sad,' he said. 'Remembering you. I really loved you. I wish this was real.'

Martine said, 'I will sit with you until it is real for you.'

'I'm going to try reliving the part with the cat,' he said, 'and this time *not* pick up the cat and *not* let it get the bird. If I do that, maybe my life will change so that it turns into something happy. Something that is real. My real mistake was separating from you. Here; I'll put my hand through you.' He placed his hand against her arm. The pressure of his muscles was vigorous; she felt the weight, the physical presence of him, against her. 'See?' he said. 'It goes right through you.'

'And all this,' she said, 'because you killed a bird when you were a little boy.'

'No,' he said. 'All this because of a failure in the temperature-regulating assembly aboard the ship. I'm not down to the proper temperature. There's just enough warmth left in my brain cells to permit cerebral activity.' He stood up then, stretched, smiled at her. 'Shall we go get some dinner?' he asked.

She said, 'I'm sorry. I'm not hungry.'

'I am. I'm going to have some of the local seafood. The brochure says it's terrific. Come along anyhow; maybe when you see the food and smell it you'll change your mind.'

Gathering up her coat and purse, she came with him.

'This is a beautiful little planet,' he said. 'I've explored it dozens of times. I know it thoroughly. We should stop downstairs at the pharmacy for some Bactine, though. For my hand. It's beginning to swell and it hurts like hell.' He showed her his hand. 'It hurts more this time than ever before.'

'Do you want me to come back to you?' Martine said.

'Are you serious?'

'Yes,' she said. 'I'll stay with you as long as you want. I agree; we should never have been separated.'

Victor Kemmings said, 'The poster is torn.'

'What?' she said.

'We should have framed it,' he said. 'We didn't have sense enough to take care of it. Now it's torn. And the artist is dead.'

RAUTAVAARA'S CASE

The three technicians of the floating globe monitored fluctuations in interstellar magnetic fields, and they did a good job up until the moment they died.

Basalt fragments, traveling at enormous velocity in relation to their globe, ruptured their barrier and abolished their air supply. The two males were slow to react and did nothing. The young female technician from Finland, Agneta Rautavaara, managed to get her emergency helmet on in time, but the hoses tangled; she aspirated and died: a melancholy death, strangling on her own vomit. Herewith ended the survey task of EX208, their floating globe. In another month, the technicians would have been relieved and returned to Earth.

We could not get there in time to save the three Earth persons, but we did dispatch a robot to see if any of them could be regenerated from death. Earth persons do not like us, but in this case their survey globe was operating in our vicinity. There are rules governing such emergencies that are binding on all races in the galaxy. We had no desire to help Earth persons, but we obey the rules.

The rules called for an attempt on our part to restore life to the three dead technicians, but we allowed a robot to take on the responsibility, and perhaps there we erred. Also, the rules required us to notify the closest Earthship of the calamity and we chose not to. I will not defend this omission nor analyze our reasoning at the time.

The robot signaled that it had found no brain function in the two males and that their neural tissue had degenerated. Regarding

Agneta Rautavaara, a slight brain wave could be detected. So in Rautavaara's case the robot would begin a restoration attempt. However, since it could not make a judgment decision on its own, it contacted us. We told it to make the attempt. The fault—the guilt, so to speak—therefore lies with us. Had we been on the scene, we would have known better. We accept the blame.

An hour later the robot signaled that it had restored significant brain function in Rautavaara by supplying her brain with oxygen-rich blood from her dead body. The oxygen, but not the nutriments, came from the robot. We instructed it to begin synthesis of nutriments by processing Rautavaara's body, by using it as raw material. This is the point at which the Earth authorities later made their most profound objection. But we did not have any other source of nutriments. Since we ourselves are a plasma we could not offer our own bodies.

The objection that we could have used the bodies of Rautavaara's dead companions was not phrased properly when we introduced it as evidence. Briefly, we felt that, based on the robot's reports, the other bodies were too contaminated by radioactivity and hence were toxic to Rautavaara; nutriments derived from that source would soon poison her brain. If you do not accept our logic, it does not matter to us; this was the situation as we construed it from our remote point. This is why I say our real error lay in sending a robot in rather than going ourselves. If you wish to indict us, indict us for that.

We asked the robot to patch into Rautavaara's brain and transmit her thoughts to us, so that we could assess the physical condition of her neural cells.

The impression that we received was sanguine. It was at this point that we notified the Earth authorities. We informed them of the accident that had destroyed EX208; we informed them that two of the technicians, the males, were irretrievably dead; we informed them that through swift efforts on our part we had the one female showing stable cephalic activity, which is to say, we had her brain alive.

'Her *what*?' the Earth person radio operator said, in response to our call.

'We are supplying her nutriments derived from her body—'

'Oh Christ,' the Earth person radio operator said. 'You can't feed her brain that way. What good is a brain? Qua brain?'

'It can think,' we said.

'All right; we'll take over now,' the Earth person radio operator said. 'But there will be an inquiry.'

'Was it not right to save her brain?' we asked. 'After all, the psyche is located in the brain, the personality. The physical body is a device by which the brain relates to—'

'Give me the location of EX208,' the Earth person radio operator said. 'We'll send a ship there at once. You should have notified us at once before trying your own rescue efforts. You Approximations simply do not understand somatic life forms.'

It is offensive to us to hear the term 'Approximations.' It is an Earth slur regarding our origin in the Proxima Centaurus System. What it implies is that we are not authentic, that we merely simulate life.

This was our reward in the Rautavaara Case. To be derided. And, indeed, there was an inquiry.

Within the depths of her damaged brain, Agneta Rautavaara tasted acid vomit and recoiled in fear and aversion. All around her, EX208 lay in splinters. She could see Travis and Elms; they had been torn to bloody bits and the blood had frozen. Ice covered the interior of the globe. Air gone, temperature gone ... what's keeping me alive? she wondered. She put her hands up and touched her face—or rather tried to touch her face. My helmet, she thought. I got it on in time.

The ice, which covered everything, began to melt. The severed arms and legs of her two companions rejoined their bodies. Basalt fragments, embedded in the hull of the globe, withdrew and flew away.

Time, Agneta realized, is running backward. How strange!

Air returned; she heard the dull tone of the indicator horn. And then, slowly, temperature. Travis and Elms, groggily, got to their feet. They stared around them, bewildered. She felt like laughing, but it was too grim for that. Apparently the force of the impact had caused a local time perturbation.

'Both of you sit down,' she said.

Travis said thickly, 'I—okay; you're right.' He seated himself at his console and pressed the button that strapped him securely in place. Elms, however, just stood.

'We were hit by rather large particles,' Agneta said.

'Yes,' Elms said.

'Large enough and with enough impact to perturb time,' Agneta said. 'So we've gone back to before the event.'

'Well, the magnetic fields are partly responsible,' Travis said. He rubbed his eyes; his hands shook. 'Get your helmet off, Agneta. You don't need it.'

'But the impact is coming,' she said.

Both men glanced at her.

'We'll repeat the accident,' she said.

'Shit,' Travis said, 'I'll take the EX out of here.' He pushed many keys on his console. 'It'll miss us.'

Agneta removed her helmet. She stepped out of her boots, picked them up . . . and then saw the Figure.

The Figure stood behind the three of them. It was Christ.

'Look,' she said to Travis and Elms.

Both men looked.

The Figure wore a traditional white robe, sandals; his hair was long and pale with what looked like moonlight. Bearded, his face was gentle and wise. Just like in the halo-ads the churches back home put out, Agneta thought. Robed, bearded, wise and gentle and his arms slightly raised. Even the nimbus is there. How odd that our preconceptions were so accurate.

'Oh my God,' Travis said. Both men stared and she stared, too. 'He's come for us.'

'Well, it's fine with me,' Elms said.

'Sure, it would be fine with you,' Travis said bitterly. 'You have no wife and children. And what about Agneta? She's only three hundred years old; she's a baby.'

Christ said, 'I am the vine, you are the branches. Whoever remains in me, with me in him, bears fruit in plenty; for cut off from me, you can do nothing.'

'I'm getting the EX out of this vector,' Travis said.

'My little children,' Christ said, 'I shall not be with you much longer.'

'Good,' Travis said. The EX was now moving at peak velocity in the direction of the Sirius axis; their star chart showed massive flux.

'Damn you, Travis,' Elms said savagely. 'This is a great opportunity. I mean, how many people have seen Christ? I mean, it *is* Christ. You are Christ, aren't you?' he asked the Figure.

Christ said, 'I am the Way, the Truth, and the Life. No one can come to the Father except through me. If you know me, you know my Father too. From this moment, you know him and have seen him.'

'There,' Elms said, his face showing happiness. 'See? I want it known that I am very glad of this occasion, Mr—' He broke off. 'I was going to say, "Mr Christ." That's stupid; that is really stupid. Christ, Mr Christ, will you sit down? You can sit at my console or at Ms Rautavaara's. Isn't that right, Agneta? This here is Walter Travis; he's not a Christian, but I am; I've been a Christian all my life. Well, most of my life. I'm not sure about Ms Rautavaara. What do you say, Agneta?'

'Stop the babbling, Elms,' Travis said.

To him, Elms said, 'He's going to judge us.'

Christ said, 'If anyone hears my words and does not keep them faithfully, it is not I who shall condemn him, since I have come not to condemn the world but to save the world; he who rejects me and refuses my words has his judge already.'

'There,' Elms said, nodding.

Frightened, Agneta said to the Figure, 'Go easy on us. The three of us have been through a major trauma.' She wondered, suddenly, if Travis and Elms remembered that they had been killed, that their bodies had been destroyed.

The Figure smiled at her, as if to reassure her.

'Travis,' Agneta said, bending down over him as he sat at his console, 'I want you to listen to me. Neither you nor Elms survived the accident, survived the basalt particles. That's why he's here. I'm the only one who wasn't–' She hesitated.

'Killed,' Elms said. 'We're dead and he has come for us.' To the Figure, he said, 'I'm ready, Lord. Take me.'

'Take both of them,' Travis said. 'I'm sending out a radio HELP call. And I'm telling them what's taking place here. I'm going to report it before he takes me or tries to take me.'

'You're *dead*,' Elms told him.

'I can still file a radio report,' Travis said, but his face showed his dismay. And his resignation.

To the Figure, Agneta said, 'Give Travis a little time. He doesn't fully understand. But I guess you know that; you know everything.'

The Figure nodded.

We and the Earth Board of Inquiry listened to and watched this activity in Rautavaara's brain, and we realized jointly what had happened. But we did not agree on our evaluation of it. Whereas the six Earth persons saw it as pernicious, we saw it as grand–both for Agneta Rautavaara and for us. By means of her damaged brain, restored by an ill-advised robot, we were in touch with the next world and the powers that ruled it.

The Earth persons' view distressed us.

'She's hallucinating,' the spokesperson of the Earth people said. 'Since she has no sensory data coming. Since her body is dead. Look what you've done to her.'

We made the point that Agneta Rautavaara was happy.

'What we must do,' the human spokesperson said, 'is shut down her brain.'

'And cut us off from the next world?' we objected. 'This is a splendid opportunity to view the afterlife. Agneta Rautavaara's brain is our lens. This is a matter of gravity. The scientific merit outweighs the humanitarian.'

This was the position we took at the inquiry. It was a position of sincerity, not of expedience.

The Earth persons decided to keep Rautavaara's brain at full function, with both video and audio transduction, which of course was recorded; meanwhile the matter of censuring us was put in suspension.

I personally found myself fascinated by the Earth idea of the Savior. It was, for us, an antique and quaint conception; not because it was anthropomorphic but because it involved a schoolroom adjudication of the departed soul. Some kind of tote board was involved listing good and bad acts: a transcendent report card, such as one finds employed in the teaching and grading of children.

This, to us, was a primitive conception of the Savior, and as I watched and listened—as we watched and listened as a polyencephalic entity—I wondered what Agneta Rautavaara's reaction would have been to a Savior, a Guide of the Soul, based on *our* expectations. Her brain, after all, was maintained by our equipment, by the original mechanism that our rescue robot had brought to the scene of the accident. It would have been too risky to disconnect it; too much brain damage had occurred already. The total apparatus, involving her brain, had been transferred to the site of the judicial inquiry, a neutral ark located between the Proxima System and the Sol System.

Later, in discreet discussion with my companions, I suggested that we attempt to infuse our own conception of the Afterlife Guide of the Soul into Rautavaara's artificially sustained brain. My point: it would be interesting to see how she reacted.

At once my companions pointed out to me the contradiction in my logic. I had argued at the inquiry that Rautavaara's brain was a window on the next world and hence justified—which exculpated us. Now I argued that what she experienced was a projection of her own mental presuppositions, nothing more.

'Both propositions are true,' I said. 'It is a genuine window on the next world and it is a presentation of Rautavaara's own cultural racial propensities.'

What we had, in essence, was a model into which we could introduce carefully selected variables. We could introduce into Rautavaara's brain our own conception of the Guide of the Soul, and thereby see how our rendition differed practically from the puerile one of the Earth persons'.

This was a novel opportunity to test our own theology. In our opinion, the Earth persons' had been tested sufficiently and been found wanting.

We decided to perform the act, since we maintained the gear supporting Rautavaara's brain. To us, this was a much more interesting issue than the outcome of the inquiry. Blame is a mere cultural matter; it does not travel across species boundaries.

I suppose the Earth persons could regard our intentions as malign. I deny that; *we* deny that. Call it, instead, a game. It would provide us aesthetic enjoyment to witness Rautavaara confronted by *our* Savior, rather than hers.

To Travis, Elms, and Agneta, the Figure, raising its arms, said, 'I am the Resurrection. If anyone believes in me, even though he dies he will live, and whoever lives and believes in me will never die. Do you believe this?'

'I sure do,' Elms said heartily.

Travis said, 'It's bilge.'

To herself, Agneta Rautavaara thought, I'm not sure. I just don't know.

'We're supposed to decide,' Elms said. 'We have to decide if we're going to go with him. Travis, you're done for; you're out. Sit there and rot—that's your fate.' To Agneta, he said, 'I hope you find for Christ, Agneta. I want you to have eternal life like I'm going to have. Isn't that right, Lord?' he asked the Figure.

The Figure nodded.

Agneta said, 'Travis, I think—well, I feel you should go along with this. I—' She did not want to press the point that Travis was dead. But he had to understand the situation; otherwise, as Elms said, he was doomed. 'Go with us,' she said.

'You're going, then?' Travis said, bitterly.

'Yes,' she said.

Elms, gazing at the Figure, said in a low voice, 'Quite possibly I'm mistaken, but it seems to be changing.'

She looked, but saw no change. Yet Elms seemed frightened.

The Figure, in its white robe, walked slowly toward the seated Travis. The Figure halted close by Travis, stood for a time, and then, bending, bit Travis's face.

Agneta screamed. Elms stared, and Travis, locked into his seat, thrashed. The Figure, calmly, ate him.

'Now you see,' the spokesperson for the Board of Inquiry said, 'this brain must be shut down. The deterioration is severe; the experience is terrible for her; it must end now.'

I said, 'No. We from the Proxima System find this turn of events highly interesting.'

'But the Savior is eating Travis!' another of the Earth persons exclaimed.

'In your religion,' I said, 'is it not the case that you eat the flesh of your God and drink his blood? All that has happened here is a mirror image of that Eucharist.'

'I order her brain shut down!' the spokesperson for the Board said. His face was pale; drops of sweat stood out on his forehead.

'We should see more before we shut down,' I said. I found it highly exciting, this enactment of our own sacrament, our highest sacrament, in which our Savior consumes us, his worshippers.

'Agneta,' Elms whispered, 'did you see that? Christ ate Travis. There's nothing left but his gloves and boots.'

Oh God, Agneta Rautavaara thought. What is happening?

She moved away from the Figure, over to Elms. Instinctively.

'He is my blood,' the Figure said as it licked its lips. 'I drink of this blood, the blood of eternal life. When I have drunk it, I will live forever. He is my body. I have no body of my own; I am only a plasma. By eating his body, I obtain everlasting life. This is the new truth that I proclaim, that I am eternal.'

'He's going to eat us, too,' Elms said.

Yes, Agneta Rautavaara thought. He is. She could see now that the Figure was an Approximation. It is a Proxima life form, she realized. He's right; he has no body of his own. The only way he can get a body is—

'I'm going to kill him,' Elms said. He popped the emergency laser rifle from its rack and pointed it at the figure.

The Figure said, 'Father, the hour has come.'

'Stay away from me,' Elms said.

'In a short time, you will no longer see me,' the Figure said, 'unless I drink of your blood and eat of your body. Glorify yourself that I may live.' The Figure moved toward Elms.

Elms fired the laser rifle. The Figure staggered and bled. It was Travis's blood, Agneta realized. In him. Not his own blood. This is terrible; she put her hands to her face, terrified.

'Quick,' she said to Elms. 'Say "I am innocent of this man's blood." Say it before it's too late.'

'"I am innocent of this man's blood,"' Elms said.

The Figure fell. Bleeding, it lay dying. It was no longer a bearded man. It was something else, but Agneta Rautavaara could not tell what it was. It said, *'Eli, Eli, lama sabachthani?'*

As she and Elms gazed down at it, the Figure died.

'I killed it,' Elms said. 'I killed Christ.' He held the laser rifle pointed at himself, groping for the trigger.

'That wasn't Christ,' Agneta said. 'It was something else. The opposite of Christ.' She took the gun from Elms.

Elms was weeping.

The Earth persons on the Board of Inquiry possessed the majority vote and they voted to abolish all activity in Rautavaara's artificially sustained brain. This disappointed us, but there was no remedy for us.

We had seen the beginning of an absolutely stunning scientific experiment: the theology of one race grafted onto that of another. Shutting down the Earth person's brain was a scientific tragedy. For example, in terms of the basic relationship to God, the Earth race held a diametrically opposite view from us. This of course must be attributed to the fact that they are a somatic race and we are a plasma. They drink the blood of their God; they eat his flesh; that way they become immortal. To them, there is no scandal in this. They find it perfectly natural. Yet, to us it is dreadful. That the worshipper should eat and drink its God? Awful to us; awful indeed. A disgrace and a shame—an abomination. The higher should always prey on the lower; the God should consume the worshipper.

We watched as the Rautavaara Case was closed—closed by the shutting down of her brain so that all EEG activity ceased and the monitors indicated nothing. We felt disappointment, and in addition the Earth persons voted out a verdict of censure of us for our handling of the rescue mission in the first place.

It is striking, the gulf which separates races developing in different star systems. We have tried to understand the Earth persons and we have failed. We are aware, too, that they do not understand us and are appalled in turn by some of our customs. This was demonstrated in the Rautavaara Case. But were we not serving the purposes of detached scientific study? I myself was amazed at Rautavaara's reaction when the Savior ate Mr Travis. I would have wished to see this most holy of the sacraments fulfilled with the others, with Rautavaara and Elms as well.

But we were deprived of this. And the experiment, from our standpoint, failed.

And we live now, too, under the ban of unnecessary moral blame.

THE ALIEN MIND

Inert within the depths of his theta chamber, he heard the faint tone and then the synthovoice. 'Five minutes.'

'Okay,' he said, and struggled out of his deep sleep. He had five minutes to adjust the course of his ship; something had gone wrong with the auto-control system. An error on his part? Not likely; he never made errors. Jason Bedford make errors? Hardly.

As he made his way unsteadily to the control module, he saw that Norman, who had been sent with him to amuse him, was also awake. The cat floated slowly in circles, batting at a pen that somehow had gotten loose. Strange, Bedford thought.

'I thought you were unconscious with me.' He examined the readout of the ship's course. Impossible! A fifth-parsec off in the direction of Sirius. It would add a week to his journey. With grim precision he reset the controls, then sent out an alert signal to Meknos III, his destination.

'Troubles?' the Meknosian operator answered. The voice was dry and cold, the calculating monotone of something that always made Bedford think of snakes.

He explained his situation.

'We need the vaccine,' the Meknosian said. 'Try to stay on course.'

Norman the cat floated majestically by the control module, reached out a paw, and jabbed at random; two activated buttons sounded faint *bleeps* and the ship altered course.

'So you did it,' Bedford said. 'You humiliated me in the eyes of

an alien. You have reduced me to idiocy vis-à-vis the alien mind.'
He grabbed the cat. And squeezed.

'What was that strange sound?' the Meknosian operator asked.
'A kind of lament.'

Bedford said quietly, 'There's nothing left to lament. Forget you
heard it.' He shut off the radio, carried the cat's body to the trash
sphincter, and ejected it.

A moment later he had returned to his theta chamber and,
once more, dozed. This time there would be no tampering with his
controls. He dozed in peace.

When his ship docked at Meknos III, the senior member of the
alien medical team greeted him with an odd request. 'We would
like to see your pet.'

'I have no pet,' Bedford said. Certainly it was true.

'According to the manifest filed with us in advance—'

'It is really none of your business,' Bedford said. 'You have your
vaccine; I'll be taking off.'

The Meknosian said, 'The safety of any life-form is our business.
We will inspect your ship.'

'For a cat that doesn't exist,' Bedford said.

Their search proved futile. Impatiently, Bedford watched the alien
creatures scrutinize every storage locker and passageway of his ship.
Unfortunately, the Meknosians found ten sacks of dry cat kibble. A
lengthy discussion ensued among them, in their own language.

'Do I have permission,' Bedford said harshly, 'to return to Earth
now? I'm on a tight schedule.' What the aliens were thinking and
saying was of no importance to him; he wished only to return to his
silent theta chamber and profound sleep.

'You'll have to go through decontamination procedure A,' the
senior Meknosian medical officer said. 'So that no spore or virus
from—'

'I realize that,' Bedford said. 'Let's get it done.'

Later, when decontamination had been completed and he was
back in his ship starting up the drive, his radio came on. It was one

THE ALIEN MIND

or another of the Meknosians; to Bedford they all looked alike. 'What was the cat's name?' the Meknosian asked.

'Norman,' Bedford said, and jabbed the ignite switch. His ship shot upward and he smiled.

He did not smile, however, when he found the power supply to his theta chamber missing. Nor did he smile when the backup unit could also not be located. Did I forget to bring it? he asked himself. No, he decided; I wouldn't do that. They took it.

Two years before he reached Terra. Two years of full consciousness on his part, deprived of theta sleep; two years of sitting or floating or—as he had seen in military-preparedness training holofilms—curled up in a corner, totally psychotic.

He punched out a radio request to return to Meknos III. No response. Well, so much for that.

Seated at his control module, he snapped on the little inboard computer and said, 'My theta chamber won't function; it's been sabotaged. What do you suggest I do for two years?'

THERE ARE EMERGENCY ENTERTAINING TAPES

'Right,' he said. He would have remembered. 'Thank you.' Pressing the proper button, he caused the door of the tape compartment to slide open.

No tapes. Only a cat toy—a miniature punching bag—that had been included for Norman; he had never gotten around to giving it to him. Otherwise . . . bare shelves.

The alien mind, Bedford thought. Mysterious and cruel.

Setting the ship's audio recorder going, he said calmly and with as much conviction as possible, 'What I will do is build my next two years around the daily routine. First, there are meals. I will spend as much time as possible planning, fixing, eating, and enjoying delicious repasts. During the time ahead of me, I will try out every combination of victuals possible.' Unsteadily, he rose and made his way to the massive food storage locker.

As he stood gazing into the tightly packed locker—tightly packed with row upon row of identical snacks—he thought, On the other hand, there's not much you can do with a two-year supply of cat kibble. In the way of variety. Are they all the same flavor?

They were all the same flavor.

AFTERTHOUGHT BY THE AUTHOR

The basic premise dominating my stories is that if I ever met an extraterrestrial intelligence (more commonly called a 'creature from outer space') I would find I had more to say to it than to my next-door neighbor. What the people on my block do is bring in their newspaper and mail and drive off in their cars. They have no other outdoor habits except mowing their lawns. I went next door one time to check into the indoor habits. They were watching TV. Could you, in writing an sf novel, postulate a culture on these premises? Surely such a society doesn't exist, except maybe in my imagination. And there isn't much imagination involved.

The way out of living in the middle of an under-imaginative figment is to make contact, in your own mind, with other civilizations as yet unborn. You're doing the same thing when you read sf that I'm doing when I write it; your neighbor probably is as alien a life form to you as mine is to me. The stories in this collection are attempts at reception—at listening to voices from another place, very far off, sounds quite faint but important. They only come late at night, when the background din and gabble of our world have faded out. When the newspapers have been read, the TV sets shut off, the cars parked in their various garages. Then, faintly, I hear voices from another star. (I clocked it once, and reception is best between 3:00 a.m. and 4:45 a.m.) Of course, I don't usually tell people this when they ask, 'Say, where do you get your ideas?' I just say I don't know. It's safer.

Let's take these stories, then, and assume them to be (one) garbled receptions mixed with pure inventiveness, and (two) an alternative to dog food commercials in living color on TV. Both bypass what is immediately available. Both assumptions reach out as far as possible. Both sweep the void and return with something to report: that the universe is full of scheming, living, busy entities intent on their own pursuits, oblivious to the interests of others, alienated from their next-door neighbors, and, most of all, wondering who they can contact when all else fails. Wondering who lives as they do; wondering, maybe, about us.

The majority of these stories were written when my life was simpler and made sense. I could tell the difference between the real world and the world I wrote about. I used to dig in the garden, and there is nothing fantastic or ultradimensional about crab grass … unless you are an sf writer, in which case pretty soon you are viewing crab grass with suspicion. What are its real motives? And who sent it in the first place?

The question I always found myself asking was, What is it really? It only looks like crab grass. That's what they want us to think it is. One day the crab grass suits will fall off and their true identity will be revealed. By then the Pentagon will be full of crab grass and it'll be too late. The crab grass, or what we took to be crab grass, will dictate terms. My earlier stories had such premises. Later, when my personal life became complicated and full of unfortunate convolutions, worries about crab grass got lost somewhere. I became educated to the fact that the greatest pain does not come zooming down from a distant planet, but up from the depths of the heart. Of course, both could happen; your wife and child could leave you, and you could be sitting alone in your empty house with nothing to live for, and in addition the Martians could bore through the roof and get you.

As to what the stories in this collection mean, I will not cite the usual copout that the story must speak for itself, but rather the copout that I don't really know. I mean, know above and beyond what it says, which is what any reader can extract from them. One time a whole class of kids wrote me about my story 'The Father-Thing', and every kid wanted to know where I got my idea. That was easy, because it was based on childhood memories of my father; but later on, in rereading my answers, I noticed that I never said the same thing twice. With all intent at honesty, I gave each kid a different answer. I guess this is what makes a fiction writer. Give him six facts and he'll link them together first one way and then another, on and on until you forcibly stop him.

Literary criticism, probably, should be left to the critics, since that's their job. One time I read in a distinguished book of criticism on sf that in my novel *The Man in the High Castle* the pin which the character Juliana used to hold her blouse together symbolized all that which held together the themes, ideas, and subplots of the novel itself—which I hadn't known when I wrote that section. But what if Juliana, also not knowing it, had removed the pin? Would the novel have fallen apart? Or at least come open in the middle and exposed a whole lot of cleavage (which was why her boyfriend insisted she put on the pin in the first place)? I will do my best, though, to unpin these stories.

The advantage of the story over the novel is that in the story you catch the protagonist at the climax of his life, but in the novel you've got to follow him from the day he was born to the day he dies (or nearly so). Open any novel at random and usually what is happening is either dull or unimportant. The only way to redeem this is through style. It is not what happened but how it is told. Pretty soon the professional novelist acquires the skill of describing everything with style, and content vanishes. In a story, though, you can't get away with this. Something important has to happen. I think this is why gifted professional fiction writers wind up writing novels. Once their style is perfected, they have it made. Virginia Woolf, for instance, wound up writing about nothing at all.

In these stories, though, I remember that in every case before I sat down to write, I had to have an idea. There had to be some real concept: an actual thing from which the story was built. It must always be possible to say, 'Did you read the story about—' and then capsulize what it was about. If the essence of sf is the idea (as Dr Willis McNelly maintains), if indeed the idea is the true 'hero,' then the sf story probably remains the sf form par excellence, with the sf novel a fanning out, an expansion into all ramifications. Most of my own novels are expansions of earlier stories, or fusions of several stories—superimpositions. The germ lay in the story; in a very real sense, that was its true distillate. And some of my best ideas, which meant the most to me, I could never manage to expand into novel form. They exist only as stories, despite all my efforts.

from *The Best of Philip K. Dick* (1976)

NOTES

All notes in italics are by Philip K. Dick. The year when the note was written appears in parentheses following the note. Most of these notes were written as story notes for the collections *The Best of Philip K. Dick* (published 1977) and *The Golden Man* (published 1980). A few were written at the request of editors publishing or reprinting a PKD story in a book or magazine.

When there is a date following the name of a story, it is the date the manuscript of that story was first received by Dick's agent, per the records of the Scott Meredith Literary Agency. Absence of a date means no record is available. The name of a magazine followed by a month and year indicates the first published appearance of a story. An alternate name following a story indicates Dick's original name for the story, as shown in the agency records.

These four volumes include all of Philip K. Dick's short fiction, with the exception of short novels later published as or included in novels, childhood writings, and unpublished writings for which manuscripts have not been found. The stories are arranged as closely as possible in chronological order of composition; research for this chronology was done by Gregg Rickman and Paul Williams.

ORPHEUS WITH CLAY FEET
Apr. 16, 1963 [published in *Escapade* circa 1964 under the pseudonym Jack Dowland].

THE DAYS OF PERKY PAT ('IN THE DAYS OF PERKY PAT')
Apr. 18, 1963. *Amazing*, Dec. 1963.
'The Days of Perky Pat' came to me in one lightning-swift flash when I saw my children playing with Barbie dolls. Obviously these anatomically super-developed dolls were not intended for the use of children, or, more accurately, should not have been. Barbie and Ken consisted of two adults in miniature. The idea was

that the purchase of countless new clothes for these dolls was necessary if Barbie and Ken were to live in the style to which they were accustomed. I had visions of Barbie coming into my bedroom at night and saying, 'I need a mink coat.' Or, even worse, 'Hey, big fellow . . . want to take a drive to Vegas in my Jaguar XKE?' I was afraid my wife would find me and Barbie together and my wife would shoot me.

The sale of 'The Days of Perky Pat' to Amazing was a good one because in those days Cele Goldsmith edited Amazing and she was one of the best editors in the field. Avram Davidson at Fantasy & Science Fiction had turned it down, but later he told me that had he known about Barbie dolls he probably would have bought it. I could not imagine anyone not knowing about Barbie. I had to deal with her and her expensive purchases constantly. It was as bad as keeping my TV set working; the TV set always needed something and so did Barbie. I always felt that Ken should buy his own clothes.

In those days—the early Sixties—I wrote a great deal, and some of my best stories and novels emanated from that period. My wife wouldn't let me work in the house, so I rented a little shack for $25 a month and walked over to it each morning. This was out in the country. All I saw on my walk to my shack were a few cows in their pastures and my own flock of sheep who never did anything but trudge along after the bell-sheep. I was terribly lonely, shut up by myself in my shack all day. Maybe I missed Barbie, who was back at the big house with the children. So perhaps 'The Days of Perky Pat' is a wishful fantasy on my part; I would have loved to see Barbie—or Perky Pat or Connie Companion—show up at the door of my shack.

What did show up was something awful: my vision of the face of Palmer Eldritch which became the basis of the novel The Three Stigmata of Palmer Eldritch which the Perky Pat story generated.

There I went, one day, walking down the country road to my shack, looking forward to eight hours of writing, in total isolation from all other humans, and I looked up at the sky and saw a face. I didn't really see it, but the face was there, and it was not a human face; it was a vast visage of perfect evil. I realize now (and I think I dimly realized at the time) what caused me to see it: the months of isolation, of deprivation of human contact, in fact sensory deprivation as such . . . anyhow the visage could not be denied. It was immense; it filled a quarter of the sky. It had empty slots for eyes—it was metal and cruel and, worst of all, it was God.

I drove over to my church, Saint Columba's Episcopal Church, and talked to my priest. He came to the conclusion that I had had a glimpse of Satan and gave me unction—not supreme unction; just healing unction. It didn't do any good; the metal face in the sky remained. I had to walk along every day as it gazed down at me.

Years later—after I had long since written The Three Stigmata of Palmer Eldritch and sold it to Doubleday, my first sale to Doubleday—I came across a picture of the face in an issue of Life magazine. It was, very simply, a World War One observation cupola on the Marne, built by the French. My father had fought in the Second Battle of the Marne; he had been with the Fifth Marines, about the first group of American soldiers to go over to Europe and fight in that ghastly war. When I was a very small child he had showed me his uniform and gasmask, the entire gas-filtration equipment, and told me how the soldiers became panic-stricken during gas attacks as the charcoal in their filtration systems became saturated, and how sometimes a soldier would freak and tear off his mask and run. As a child I felt a lot of anxiety listening to my father's war stories and looking at and playing with the gasmask and helmet; but what scared me the most was when my father would put on the gasmask. His face would disappear. This was not my father any longer. This was not a human being at all. I was only four years old. After that my mother and father got divorced and I did not see my father for years. But the sight of him wearing his gasmask, blending as it did with his accounts of men with their guts hanging from them, men destroyed by shrapnel—decades later, in 1963, as I walked alone day after day along that country road with no one to talk to, no one to be with, that metal, blind, inhuman visage appeared to me again, but now transcendent and vast, and absolutely evil.

I decided to exorcise it by writing about it, and I did write about it, and it did go away. But I had seen the evil one himself, and I said then and say now, 'The evil one wears a metal face.' If you want to see this yourself, look at a picture of the war masks of the Attic Greeks. When men wish to inspire terror and kill they put on such metal faces. The invading Christian knights that Alexander Nevsky fought wore such masks; if you saw Eisenstein's film you know what I am talking about. They all looked alike. I had not seen Nevsky when I wrote The Three Stigmata, but I saw it later and saw again the thing that had hung in the sky back in 1963, the thing into which my own father had been transformed when I was a child.

So The Three Stigmata is a novel that came out of powerful atavistic fears in me, fears dating back to my early childhood and no doubt connected with my grief and loneliness when my father left my mother and me. In the novel my father appears as both Palmer Eldritch (the evil father, the diabolic mask-father) and as Leo Bulero, the tender, gruff, warm, human, loving man. The novel which emerged came out of the most intense anguish possible; in 1963 I was reliving the original isolation I had experienced upon the loss of my father, and the horror and fear expressed in the novel are not fictional sentiments ground out to interest the reader; they come from the deepest part of me: yearning for the good father and fear of the evil father, the father who left me.

I found in the story 'The Days of Perky Pat' a vehicle that I could translate into a thematic basis for the novel I wanted to write. Now, you see, Perky Pat is the eternally beckoning fair one, das ewige Weiblichkeit—'the eternally feminine,' *as Goethe put it. Isolation generated the novel and yearning generated the story; so the novel is a mixture of the fear of being abandoned and the fantasy of the beautiful woman who waits for you—somewhere, but God only knows where; I have still to figure it out. But if you are sitting alone day after day at your type-writer, turning out one story after another and having no one to talk to, no one to be with, and yet pro forma having a wife and four daughters from whose house you have been expelled, banished to a little single-walled shack that is so cold in winter that, literally, the ink would freeze in my typewriter ribbon, well, you are going to write about iron slot-eyed faces and warm young women. And thus I did. And thus I still do.*

Reaction to The Three Stigmata *was mixed. In England some reviewers described it as blasphemy. Terry Carr, who was my agent at Scott Meredith at the time, told me later, 'That novel is crazy,' although subsequent to that he reversed his opinion. Some reviewers found it a profound novel. I only find it frightening. I was unable to proofread the galleys because the novel frightened me so. It is a dark journey into the mystical and the supernatural and the absolutely evil as I understood it at the time. Let us say, I would like Perky Pat to show up at my door, but I dread the possibility that, when I hear the knock, it will be Palmer Eldritch waiting outside and not Perky Pat. Actually, to be honest, neither has shown up in the seventeen or so years since I wrote the novel. I guess that is the story of life: what you most fear never happens, but what you most yearn for never happens either. This is the difference between life and fiction. I suppose it's a good trade-off. But I'm not sure.* (1979)

STAND-BY ('TOP STAND-BY JOB')
Apr. 18, 1963. *Amazing*, Oct. 1963.

WHAT'LL WE DO WITH RAGLAND PARK? ('NO ORDINARY GUY')
Apr. 29, 1963. *Amazing*, Nov. 1963.

OH, TO BE A BLOBEL! ('WELL, SEE, THERE WERE THESE BLOBELS . . .')
May 6, 1963. *Galaxy*, Feb. 1964.

At the beginning of my writing career in the early Fifties, Galaxy was my eco-nomic mainstay. Horace Gold at Galaxy liked my writing whereas John W. Campbell, Jr at Astounding considered my writing not only worthless but as he put it, 'Nuts.' By and large I liked reading Galaxy because it had the broadest range of ideas, venturing into the soft sciences such as sociology and psychology, at a time when Campbell (as he once wrote me!) considered psionics a neces-sary premise for science fiction. Also, Campbell said, the psionic character in the story had to be in charge of what was going on. So Galaxy provided a latitude which Astounding did not. However, I was to get into an awful quarrel with Horace Gold; he had the habit of changing your stories without telling you: adding scenes, adding characters, removing downbeat endings in favor of upbeat endings. Many writers resented this. I did more than resent this; despite the fact that Galaxy was my main source of income I told Gold that I would not sell to him unless he stopped altering my stories—after which he bought nothing from me at all.

It was not, then, until Fred Pohl became editor of Galaxy that I began to appear there again. 'Oh, To Be a Blobel!' is a story which Fred Pohl bought. In this story my enormous anti-war bias is evident, a bias which had, ironically, pleased Gold. I wasn't thinking of the Viet Nam War but war in general; in particular, how a war forces you to become like your enemy. Hitler had once said that the true victory of the Nazis would be to force its enemies, the United States in particular, to become like the Third Reich—i.e. a totalitarian society—in order to win. Hitler, then, expected to win even in losing. As I watched the American military-industrial complex grow after World War Two I kept remembering Hitler's analysis, and I kept thinking how right the son of a bitch was. We had beaten Germany, but both the US and the USSR were getting more and more like the Nazis with their huge police systems every day. Well, it seemed to me there was a little wry humor in this (but not much). Maybe I could write about it without getting too deep into polemics. But the issue presented in this story is real. Look what we had to become in Viet Nam just to lose, let alone to win; can you imagine what we'd have had to become to win? Hitler would have gotten a lot of laughs out of it, and the laughs would have been on us . . . and to a very great extent in fact were. And they were hollow and grim laughs, without humor of any kind. (1979)

Here I nailed down the ultimate meaningless irony of war; the human turns into a Blobel, and the Blobel, his enemy, turns into a human, and there it all is, the futility, the black humor, the stupidity. And in the story they all wind up happy. (1976)

THE LITTLE BLACK BOX ('FROM ORDINARY HOUSEHOLD OBJECTS')
May 6, 1963. Worlds of Tomorrow, Aug. 1964.

I made use of this story when I wrote my novel Do Androids Dream of Electric Sheep? Actually, the idea is better put forth in the story. Here, a religion is regarded as a menace to all political systems; therefore it, too, is a kind of political system, perhaps even an ultimate one. The concept of caritas (or agape) shows up in my writing as the key to the authentic human. The android, which is the *unauthentic human, the mere reflex machine, is unable to experience empathy. In this story it is never clear whether Mercer is an invader from some other world. But he must be; in a sense all religious leaders are . . . but not from another planet as such. (1978)*

THE WAR WITH THE FNOOLS
Galactic Outpost, Spring 1964.

Well, once again we are invaded. And, humiliatingly, by a life form which is absurd. My colleague Tim Powers once said that Martians could invade us simply by putting on funny hats, and we'd never notice. It's a sort of low-budget invasion. I guess we're at the point where we can be amused by the idea of Earth being invaded. (And this is when they really zap you.) (1978)

A GAME OF UNCHANCE
Dec. 9, 1963. Amazing, July 1964.

A carnival is feral; another carnival shows up and is pitted against the first one; and the antithetical interaction is preplanned in such a way that the first carnival wins. It's as if the two opposing forces that underlie all change in the universe are rigged; in favor of thanatos, the dark force, yin or strife, which is to say, the force of destruction. (1978)

PRECIOUS ARTIFACT
Dec. 9, 1963. Galaxy, Oct. 1964.

This story utilized a peculiar logic which I generally employ, which Professor Patricia Warrick pointed out to me. First you have Y. Then you do a cybernetics flipflop and you have null-Y. Okay, now you reverse it again and have null-null-Y. Okay, the question is: Does null-null Y equal Y^3? Or is it a deepening of null-Y? In this story, what appears to be the case is Y but we find out the opposite is true (null-Y). But then that turns out not to be true, so are we back to Y? Professor Warrick says that my logic winds up with Y equals null-Y. I don't agree, but I'm not sure what I do wind up with. Whatever it is, in terms of logic, it is contained in this particular story. Either I've invented a whole new logic or, ahem, I'm not playing with a full deck. (1978)

RETREAT SYNDROME
Dec. 23, 1963. Worlds of Tomorrow, Jan. 1965.

A TERRAN ODYSSEY
Mar. 17, 1964 [previously unpublished; put together by PKD from sections of Dr Bloodmoney].

YOUR APPOINTMENT WILL BE YESTERDAY

Aug. 27, 1965. *Amazing*, Aug 1966. [Included in adapted form in PKD's novel *Counter-Clock World*.]

HOLY QUARREL

Sept. 13, 1965. *Worlds of Tomorrow*, May 1966.

WE CAN REMEMBER IT FOR YOU WHOLESALE

Sept. 13, 1965. *Fantasy & Science Fiction*, Apr. 1966. [Nebula Award nominee]

NOT BY ITS COVER

Sept. 21, 1965. *Famous Science Fiction*, Summer 1968.

Here I presented what used to be a wish on my part: that the Bible was true. Obviously, I was at a sort of halfway point between doubt and faith. Years later I'm still in that position; I'd like the Bible to be true, but—well, maybe if it isn't we can make it so. But, alas, it's going to take plenty of work to do it. (1978)

RETURN MATCH

Oct. 14, 1965. *Galaxy*, Feb. 1967.

The theme of dangerous toys runs like a tattered thread throughout my writing. The dangerous disguised as the innocent . . . and what could be more innocent than a toy? This story makes me think of a set of huge speakers I looked at last week; they cost six thousand dollars and were larger than refrigerators. Our joke about them was that if you didn't go to the audio store to see them, they'd come to see you. (1978)

FAITH OF OUR FATHERS

Jan. 17, 1966. *Dangerous Visions*, edited by Harlan Ellison, Garden City, 1967. [Hugo Award nominee]

The title is that of an old hymn. I think, with this story, I managed to offend everybody, which seemed at the time to be a good idea, but which I've regretted since. Communism, drugs, sex, God—I put it all together, and it's been my impression since that when the roof fell in on me years later, this story was in some eerie way involved. (1976)

I don't advocate any of the ideas in 'Faith of Our Fathers'; I don't, for example, claim that the Iron Curtain countries will win the cold war—or morally ought to. One theme in the story, however, seems compelling to me, in view of recent experiments with hallucinogenic drugs: the theological experience, which so many who have taken LSD have reported. This appears to me to be a true new frontier; to a certain extent the religious experience can now be scientifically studied ... and, what is more, may be viewed as part hallucination but containing other, real components. God, as a topic in science fiction, when it appeared at all, used to be treated polemically, as in Out of the Silent Planet. But I prefer to treat it as intellectually exciting. What if, through psychedelic drugs, the religious experience becomes commonplace in the life of intellectuals? The old atheism, which seemed to many of us—including me—valid in terms of our experiences, or rather lack of experiences, would have to step momentarily aside. Science fiction, always probing what is about to be thought, become, must eventually tackle without preconceptions a future neo-mystical society in which theology constitutes as major a force as in the medieval period. This is not necessarily a backward step, because now these beliefs can be tested—forced to put up or shut up. I, myself, have no real beliefs about God; only my experience that He is present ... subjectively, of course; but the inner realm is real too. And in a science fiction story one projects what has been a personal inner experience into a milieu; it becomes socially shared, hence discussable. The last word, however, on the subject of God may have already been said: in AD 840 by John Scotus Erigena at the court of the Frankish king Charles the Bald. 'We do not know what God is. God Himself does not know what He is because He is not anything. Literally God is not, because He transcends being.' Such a penetrating—and Zen—mystical view, arrived at so long ago, will be hard to top; in my own experiences with psychedelic drugs I have had precious tiny illumination compared with Erigena. (1966)

THE STORY TO END ALL STORIES FOR HARLAN ELLISON'S
ANTHOLOGY 'DANGEROUS VISIONS'
Niekas, Fall 1968.

THE ELECTRIC ANT
Dec. 4, 1968. Fantasy & Science Fiction, Oct. 1969.

Again the theme: how much of what we call 'reality' is actually out there or rather within our own head? The ending of this story has always frightened me ... image of the rushing wind, the sound of emptiness. As if the character hears the final fate of the world itself. (1976)

CADBURY, THE BEAVER WHO LACKED
Written Dec. 1971 [previously unpublished].

A LITTLE SOMETHING FOR US TEMPUNAUTS
Feb. 13, 1973. Final Stage, edited by Edward L. Ferman and Barry N. Malzberg, New York, 1974.

In this story I felt a vast weariness over the space program, which had thrilled us so at the start–especially the first lunar landing–and then had been forgotten and virtually shut down, a relic of history. I wondered, if time-travel became a 'program' would it suffer the same fate? Or was there an even worse possibility latent in it, within the very nature of the paradoxes of time-travel? (1976)

The essence of the time-travel story is a confrontation of some sort, best of all by the person with himself. Really, this is the drama of much good fiction anyhow, except that in such a story as 'A Little Something for Us Tempunauts' the moment in which the man meets himself face-to-face permits an alienation that could not occur in any other variety of writing . . . alienation and not understanding, as one might expect. Addison Doug-One rides alive on the casket containing the corpse of Addison Doug-Two and knows it, knows he is now two persons–he is split as in a physical schizophrenia. And his mind also is divided rather than united; he gains no insight from this event, neither of himself nor of that other Addison Doug who can no longer reason or problem-solve, but can only lie there inert and in darkness. This irony is just one of the enormous number of ironies possible in time-travel stories; naively, one would think that to travel into the future and return would lead to an increase in knowledge rather than to a loss of it. The three tempunauts go ahead in time, return, and are trapped, perhaps forever, by ironies and within ironies, the greatest one of which, I think, is their own bewilderment at their own actions. It is as if the increase in information brought about by such a technological achievement–information as to exactly what is going to happen–decreases true understanding. Perhaps Addison Doug knows too much.

In writing this story I felt a weary sadness of my own, and fell into the space (I should say time) that the characters are in, more so than usual. I felt a futility about futility–there is nothing more defeating than a strong awareness of defeat, and as I wrote I realized that what for us remains merely a psychological problem–over-awareness of the likelihood of failing and the lethal feedback from this–would for a time-traveler be instantly converted into an existential, physical horror-chamber. We, when we're depressed, are fortunately imprisoned within our heads; once time-travel becomes a reality, however, this self-defeating psychological attitude could spell doom on a scale beyond calculation. Here again, science fiction allows a writer to transfer what usually is an internal problem into an external environment; he projects it in the form of a society, a planet, with everyone stuck, so to speak, in what formerly was one unique brain. I don't blame some readers for resenting this, because the brains of some of us are unpleasant places to be in . . . but on the other hand, what a valuable tool this is for us: to grasp that we do not all really see the universe in the same way, or, in a sense, the same universe at all. Addison Doug's dismal world suddenly spreads out and becomes the world of many people. But unlike a person reading a story, who can and will finish it and abolish his inclusion in the author's world, the people in this story are stuck fast forever. This is a tyranny not yet possible so readily ... but, when you consider the power of the coercive propaganda apparatus of the modern-day state (when it's the enemy state we call it 'brainwashing') you might wonder if it isn't a question of degree. Our glorious leaders of right now cannot trap us in extensions of their heads merely by lugging some old VW motor parts around, but the alarm of the characters in this story as to what is befalling them might rightly be our own alarm in a lesser way.

Addison Doug expresses the desire 'to see no more summers.' We should all object; no one should drag us, however subtly or for whatever evidently benign reasons, into that view or that desire: we should individually and collectively yearn to see as many summers as we can, even in the imperfect world we are living in now. (1973)

THE PRE-PERSONS
Dec. 20, 1973. *Fantasy & Science Fiction*, Oct. 1974.

In this I incurred the absolute hate of Joanna Russ who wrote me the nastiest letter I've ever received; at one point she said she usually offered to beat up people (she didn't use the word 'people') who expressed opinions such as this. I admit that this story amounts to special pleading, and I am sorry to offend those who disagree with me about abortion on demand. I also got some unsigned hate mail, some of it not from individuals but from organizations promoting abortion on demand. Well, I have always managed to get myself into hot water. Sorry, people. But for the pre-person's sake I am not sorry. I stand where I stand: 'Hier steh' ich; ich kann nicht anders,' as Martin Luther is supposed to have said. (1978)

THE EYE OF THE SIBYL
May 15, 1975 [previously unpublished].

THE DAY MR COMPUTER FELL OUT OF ITS TREE
Written summer 1977 [previously unpublished].

THE EXIT DOOR LEADS IN
June 21, 1979. *Rolling Stone College Papers*, Fall 1979.

CHAINS OF AIR, WEB OF AETHER ('THE MAN WHO KNEW HOW TO LOSE')
July 9, 1979. *Stellar #5*, edited by Judy-Lynn del Rey, New York, 1980. [Included in PKD's novel *The Divine Invasion*.]

STRANGE MEMORIES OF DEATH
Mar. 27, 1980. *Interzone*, Summer 1984.

I HOPE I SHALL ARRIVE SOON
(Titled 'Frozen Journey' in its magazine appearance; 'I Hope I Shall
Arrive Soon' is PKD's title)
Apr. 24, 1980. *Playboy*, Dec. 1980. [*Playboy* Award winner]

RAUTAVAARA'S CASE
May 13, 1980. *Omni*, Oct. 1980.

THE ALIEN MIND
The Yuba City High Times, Feb. 20, 1981.